A CROWN OF IVY AND GLASS

THE MIDDLEMIST TRILOGY • BOOK ONE

CLAIRE LEGRAND

sourcebooks
casablanca

to Ken,
for loving me even when—especially
when—my light dims

Copyright © 2023, 2024 by Claire Legrand
Cover and internal design © 2023, 2024 Sourcebooks
Cover illustration © Nekro
Internal design by Ashley Holstrom/Sourcebooks
Map illustration by Travis Hasenour

Sourcebooks and the colophon are registered trademarks of Sourcebooks.

Published by Sourcebooks Casablanca, an imprint of Sourcebooks
P.O. Box 4410, Naperville, Illinois 60567-4410
(630) 961-3900
sourcebooks.com

Cataloging-in-Publication Data is on file with the Library of Congress.

Printed and bound in the Canada.
MBP 10 9 8 7 6 5 4 3 2 1

ALSO BY
CLAIRE LEGRAND

The Empirium Trilogy
Furyborn
Kingsbane
Lightbringer

AUTHOR'S NOTE

Though this is a fantasy novel, its characters face very real challenges. Please note that this story contains discussions of self-harm and suicidal ideation.

THE CONTINENT OF GALLINOR

THE NORTHERN ISLES

THE FALKERON CLOISTERS

THE SPINE OF

CAWDER

MARROWGATE

N
W E
S

THE SEA OF THE DAWN

BIG DEEP

BLIGHDON

CAIATHOS

THE TORDELL CLOISTERS

BATHYN

EAST TO AIDURRA

Brightrun River

BEROGES

CHAPTER 1

I never liked visiting my sister Mara, though I loved her so desperately that sometimes I found myself convinced the feeling was not love at all, but something much fouler: guilt, bone-crushing shame, a confused, defensive revulsion.

We visited her on the third Wednesday of every month—Farrin, Father, and me. By conventional means, it would have been an excruciatingly boring four-day journey to the center of the continent, where the Mist stretched from coast to coast like a seething silver river.

Fortunately—or unfortunately, according to Farrin—no one in the Ashbourne family could be described as conventional. Centuries ago, at the time of the Unmaking, hundreds of families were chosen by the gods to receive kernels of their power and serve as guardians of Edyn, the human realm. Our family was among them—one of the great Anointed clans. Yet even among our Anointed peers, we stood apart. Generations of eminent magicians, shrewd investments, and even shrewder political maneuvering will do that—a reality that Farrin despised.

I didn't, though I'd never admit that to her. To admit that I actually liked being not only an Anointed family but one of the most respected in the world would mean acknowledging the horrible truth to Farrin: Yes, when the Warden came to our home twelve years past, it was me she was meant to take away. Yes, I was the one originally meant to serve at the Middlemist—Farrin, the heir; Mara, the spare; and me, Imogen, the youngest, the superfluous. And yes, Mara took my place because at the last moment, Father fretted that I, fragile kitten that I am, was ill suited for such a life.

And yes, Farrin, I know, of course, that it was not long after Mara was taken to the Mist that Mother left us, because grief is deadlier than poison, Father says, and will bring anyone crashing helplessly to their knees, no matter their beauty or cunning or how passionately they are loved.

The whispers flew across the country like storms. No one could believe it; little Mara Ashbourne had actually persuaded the Warden of the Middlemist, for the first time in recorded history, to break with the tradition of recruiting a family's youngest daughter to serve in the Order of the Rose. Mara Ashbourne had insisted on taking the place of her younger sister, and the Warden had *acquiesced*. And wasn't it remarkable that the Ashbournes even had three daughters in the first place, when most Anointed families were blessed with only one or two?

This was what I could never tell Farrin—that I *liked* all the gossip, even when our neighbors chewed over the shreds of our grief as though they were bonbons, lighter than air and easily forgotten. Even then, I liked how people whispered and bowed and watched us with dreamy admiration wherever we went. I liked the gowns our wealth and status afforded us. I could enter any restaurant in the capital and immediately be seated at the best table. At our lavish parties, I could hold my beaded fan a certain way, cast my gaze just so about the ballroom, and in less than two minutes have twenty of the room's most exquisite people crowded around me with their sweeping brocaded coats and plunging necklines, each of them desperate for my favor.

I liked this about my life. I reveled in it. What girl wouldn't? I was breathtaking and wealthy and beloved, and I wouldn't have given up any of that, not even if it meant bringing Mother and Mara back. Even if some diamond-eyed artificer from the Old Country came to Ivyhill and offered me a new strong body, free of ailment, fear, or strangeness, and in exchange I need only live a humble but peaceful life out on a country farm somewhere—even then I'd laugh in their face and have Father expel them from the grounds.

Unbidden, the family story of my pet name flashed through my mind. Three-year-old Mara, insistent on speaking as often and impressively as possible, had one night struggled with my name so spectacularly that Imogen quickly became Immie, then Genna, then Gemma, which was the one to stick. Triumphant once she had settled upon the word, little Mara had pounded her fist on the table, catapulting a spoonful of mashed vegetables onto Father's vest, and shouted joyfully, "Gemma!"

Imagining this, my heart broke into a thousand pieces—and yet, if given the opportunity, I would not have exchanged my pretty life for Mara's freedom.

That selfish cowardice was my deepest, most terrible secret. I shared it with no one, not even my dearest friend, Illaria. Farrin would have despised me for such thoughts. She probably suspected the truth and despised me anyway.

She despised most things, Farrin, but she wasn't always that way.

This spring morning, as the three of us strode through the dew-sprinkled hedge maze just before sunup, I looked at Farrin sidelong, trying to find in her pale face the echo of the laughing girl she had once been. Sharp chin and cheekbones, a coy little mouth most often held in a grim line of displeasure. Honey-gold hair, unglamoured and a bit darker than mine, tied back from her face in a ruthless braid. Brown eyes, just like Father and Mara. A serious brow that never seemed to relax into contentedness, not anymore. She would have wrinkles in a year if she wasn't careful, and if she kept refusing to be fitted for a glamour. As a child, Farrin was always serious, but she was never bitter, and she was never cruel. Now, at twenty-four years old, Farrin was made of thorns.

Just before we passed through the greenway, she caught me watching her. Her mouth thinned.

"Have I not groomed myself well enough this morning to satisfy your standards?" she snapped.

In reply I showed her the sweetest smile I could muster, though my chest pulled tight with anger. On an ordinary morning, I wouldn't have so much as flinched at a lash from Farrin's sharp tongue, but visiting Mara always left me feeling brittle as old glass.

When a girl has condemned her sister to a life of servitude, that girl does not much relish the times when she must look said doomed sister in the eye.

"You look stunning, as always, dear sister of mine," I said, cupping Farrin's cheek. "A paragon of fashionable taste and refined manners."

Then I looked pointedly at her rather severe gown—slate gray and high necked, tiny buttons at her wrists and throat, unadorned with lace or ribbon. No one had worn dresses like that in a decade. I remembered it well: the entire continent of Gallinor had suddenly become fascinated with the Order of the Rose and had begun imitating the reclusive, demure Roses. I'd hated those few months. At ten years old, I'd been without my sister for two years, and my breath had caught painfully in my throat every time I glimpsed some giggling debutante garbed in austere Middlemist gray. Kerrish, my stylist—an ancient old viper with eyes and hands of steel—had informed me back then that such obsessions with the Order swept through Gallinor quite regularly. The collective fixation would surface in every art, from the sartorial to the culinary.

Farrin had long ago stopped caring about such things. *Frippery and fashion is your specialty, Gemma,* she would say, wearing a smile as false as my own.

But before she could draw breath to reply, before Father could scold me for goading her, I turned away with a breezy little laugh and closed my eyes. Ignoring the pain buffeting up my spine with a force I knew from experience would bruise me, I reached out for a nearby hedge, thick and glossy with tangled ivy.

At my touch, the greenery gave way to a cold, snapping mouth of air that enveloped my hand. As I stepped into its hungry pull, I hoped this time would be different. Surely this time, I prayed desperately to the gods, something inside me would shift. I would no longer grow ill at the touch of this magic. I would emerge from the greenway just as sure-footed and unbothered as Farrin and Father, both of them right on my heels.

Father's stern reprimand chased me into the darkness. The greenway's magic twisted his voice, first deepening it, then muddying it, then turning it shrill and sharp as an angry jay's. Even without understanding his words, I knew what they would be.

Gemma, you know you must never enter the greenway first. You must always follow me or Farrin.

Gemma, how could you be so foolish as to risk becoming ill and upsetting Mara?

Gemma, you know these rules exist for a reason—to protect you.

The greenway released me with a vicious little shove, and I fell forward onto the ground, into a patch of thick green clover at the back of Rosewarren's garden. It was hidden from the house by a stone wall and an iron gate, the latter of which was draped with heavy vines of snow-blossoms.

Years ago, when the Warden took Mara, Father had hired an elemental to magick that thick tangle of blooms to forever chime and jingle like tiny winter bells to mask our arrivals. Here, my family could emerge from the greenway unseen and unheard. People would think we had simply strolled up the long winding dirt road that led up the mountain from the main thoroughfare below. They would never know of the greening magic—rare and staggeringly expensive—that allowed us to travel instantaneously from our family estate of Ivyhill to the priory of Rosewarren. They wouldn't know, but they would suspect, and wonder, and whisper to their friends with sparkling eyes.

We were Ashbournes, after all.

I curled my fingers around cool clumps of clover, swallowing hard against the urge to be sick. I would not allow it, not this time. I would stand up, cheerful and smiling, and Father and Farrin would have to admit that the rules were ridiculous. I no longer needed protection. My body had healed itself. I would now be able to be near magic, to work magic, to *be* magic—as everyone else in my family had always been and done—without issue.

I pushed myself up. With a smile, I turned to watch Farrin and Father emerge. I was determined to plow through the pain, though my stomach was roiling and my chest was on fire.

But then Father and Farrin emerged from the greenway's mouth, and their magic rippled toward me like the wake of a boat pushing fast through the water. The wave of it smacked me in the gut, hard as fists—one for Father, two for Farrin.

Stars of pain burst at my knees and shoulders, my ribs, behind my eyes. My legs buckled, and I fell back into the clover, shaking all over, and was promptly sick at Father's feet.

He stood there until I was finished. Then, after only a slight hesitation, he stepped over me, silent, the tug of his disappointment like a hook in my mouth. The hands that helped me sit up, cleaned my face, rubbed my back until I calmed—those hands were Farrin's. Always, no matter how angry she was, no matter how completely I tried her patience, they were Farrin's.

I allowed myself to lean against her shoulder, blinking back tears. Each breath I drew stirred up the sick feeling inside me. Even the flutter of my lashes sent pain booming through my bones.

"I don't think you'll try that again for a long while, will you, Gemma?" said Father from near the iron gate, not a scrap of triumph in his voice. He was tired, I knew that. He loved me, and I made him tired.

Farrin glared at him over my shoulder. I could feel her tensing, drawing upon her seemingly endless stores of fury, and knew that whatever she said would only make things worse.

I squeezed her hand once, then drew a deep breath and rose to my feet, smoothing the silken folds of my gown. I will admit it cheered me to know that even though I'd just been sick in the dirt, I looked resplendent in that dress—robin's-egg blue with tiny embroidered flowers across the bodice; a neckline that displayed my flawless, creamy décolletage; a wide lace sash that accentuated my tiny waist. My golden curls were tied back in a loose chignon with satin ribbons of palest pink.

I was the very picture of spring in full bloom, and I knew it. Not even the sickness that raged inside my traitorous body could take that from me.

"Thank you for waiting, dearest Father," I said lightly. I glided past him through the gate and up the path toward Rosewarren, trying to ignore the frigid, angry pull of the greenway hidden behind me in the thicket. I could feel it gnawing on whatever it had taken from me—not malicious, just beastly. Until the pain of this day had faded and I once again broke my father's rules, that tangle of green would be content to wait, patient and slumbering, for another taste.

Because Mara was still out in the Mist on patrol, we were forced to lunch with the Warden in her private parlor—a pretty enough space, as was everything in Rosewarren. The Warden was notoriously strict, the Roses under her command permitted only certain foods, dress, recreation. But the priory itself was disgustingly opulent, designed to impress and humble.

The Warden's private parlor boasted arched wooden rafters stained a rich red brown, each plank elaborately carved with vines, birds, and roses. Stained glass windows depicted notable shield-maidens of past generations, some in battle, others in prayer. The furniture was heavy and antiquated, monstrous in size and gaudy in ornamentation, piled high with tasseled velvet cushions in shades of emerald, crimson, amber, violet. Floor-to-ceiling shelves packed with thousands of books covered every wall. The sight should have appealed to my love of stories but instead always made me feel slightly queasy. My imagination summoned forth images of the walls growing taller and taller, wider and wider, the books multiplying, thousands becoming millions, and then tumbling down the halls in a torrent of paper and ink. Eventually they would consume the priory and the strange ancient woodlands surrounding it, pushing down into the dark earth everyone unlucky enough to live here—including Mara.

I forced down a buttery shortbread biscuit softened with fragrant herbal tea. Only the Roses were deprived of such little niceties; for her guests, for the visiting families of her shieldmaidens, the Warden spared no expense.

Now she stood over the table with Farrin on one side and Father on the other, all of them eagerly poring over newly drawn maps of the Mist, held flat by the remains of our lunch.

"As you can see," the Warden was saying in her cool, clipped voice, "these new patrol routes here and here will strengthen the Mist along its southeastern expanse."

Father pointed at said expanse. "And how many Roses are stationed there at any given moment?"

"A dozen. More than our usual contingent, but as you know, there have been more sightings of intruders from Marrowgate to Cawder over the past six weeks."

"Intruders?" Farrin asked, looking up. "What sort of intruders, exactly?"

The Warden seemed unbothered by the edge in Farrin's voice. "Most recently we have heard repeated reports of a band of monstrous women who roam the countryside abducting civilians. But you know how hysterical people can be." The Warden raised a single eyebrow of disdain. "Any shadow within fifty miles of the Middlemist must mean the presence of some Olden monster. Never mind that people disappear all the time for less sinister reasons."

Farrin clutched the table, her knuckles white. "And this is where Mara will go with the next deployment?"

"Of course. Mara is one of my best girls. She goes where the need is greatest."

Father crossed his arms, shaking his head in wonder. "Who would have thought it? Our little Mara, queen of the Roses."

His smug smile sickened me, even though it brought some life to his haggard face. A distracted thought flitted through my mind: the next time Kerrish visited Ivyhill, I would commission a glamour to smooth Father's face and brighten his skin. Lord Gideon Ashbourne, master of Ivyhill and a formidable Anointed sentinel, really should not be seen looking so rough around the edges.

Disgust came swiftly on the heels of my musings. In that moment I hated myself even more than the Warden, even more than Father, who looked immensely satisfied to hear that his imprisoned daughter was fulfilling her bounden duties so very well. I was no better than him, distracted as I was by thoughts of glamours when I should have been thinking of Mara. Only there, near the Mist, did I allow myself to doubt the substance of who I was, the value of the things I loved.

I hated the Mist. I hated the Warden.

Sometimes I even hated Mara.

If she hadn't been so strong, so lithe and quick and irresistible to the Warden all those years ago, when she was ten years old and I only eight, *I* would be in the Order instead. But Mara had always been such an athlete, so beguilingly gentle in affect, and I so pathetically ailing. Not even the Warden could argue against tradition when faced with the two of us. She had practically salivated watching little Mara spar with our father, holding her own against a sentinel thirty years her senior.

And now, twelve years later, I was the sister with the sparkling life, coddled and cosseted, quietly dying of guilt, while poor unlucky Mara could rest easy at Rosewarren, safe in the knowledge of her own nobility.

On the nights I let those thoughts consume me, my body teeming with resentment Mara didn't deserve, sleep eluded me.

The Warden gave Father the tiniest of smiles, her taut pale face hardly moving. I didn't think I'd even once seen the woman look genuinely happy, not that I blamed her. The only person in the world I pitied more than myself and Mara was the Warden of the Mist, cursed to spend her life searching the churning silver fog for monsters and sending good, strong Gallinoran girls to their deaths.

Self-pity and hatred and the bitter bite of shame—these were the feelings I knew most intimately. What a pathetic creature I was.

"Mara is hardly a queen, Lord Ashbourne," said the Warden, "but she is indeed an impressive warrior."

Father's smile widened. Farrin and I exchanged a sharp glance. We knew what he was thinking.

That was one thing the Bask family could not boast—that they had a high-ranking daughter in the Order of the Rose.

Suddenly I couldn't bear being in that room any longer. There we all were, perusing maps in a plush parlor over tea and cookies, Father with that satisfied air as he doubtless thought not of his daughters but of the godsdamned *Basks*—all while Mara roamed the Mist, hunting for Old Country trespassers, each one more dangerous than the last.

My throat tight and hot, I rose from the table and sank into a curtsy. "If you'll excuse me," I murmured. Especially in that particular dress, such a combination of my prim voice and the excellent view down my bodice would have utterly charmed anyone else, regardless of gender or station.

But the Warden didn't even glance up. She leaned over the table with her back to me, her body tall and rail thin in that stiff black gown, her dark hair gathered into a severe bun at her nape. She said something to Farrin and Father, but the blood roaring in my ears distorted her voice just as the greenway would have. My skin was beginning to tingle and warm, the room's still, perfumed air drawing far too close. My gauzy spring dress suddenly felt snug enough to choke me.

I hurried out of the room, not even bothering to keep the door from slamming, and stormed down the hallway and around a corner, desperate for some quiet nook where I could collect myself—and ran straight into a blur of color and scent that I knew at once to be Mara. Mother's pale skin and brown hair, eyes huge and dark like a watchful doe's, the rich tang of earth and old books.

Mara caught me before I could fall, her hands callused and warm. Her strong, steady touch was like a pin to the bubble of my rising agitation. My breath burst and my knees wobbled, and before I knew it, I was in her arms—I, the spoiled youngest child who enjoyed the sort of cushioned life that had left my skin smooth and soft as the day I was born. I wept in the arms of my quiet, uncomplaining sister who for twelve years had been hardly more than a prisoner.

It was unfair of me, even revolting. But Mara never scolded me, even though she had more right to than anyone. She simply ushered me out of the house, across the grounds, and into an ivy-choked stone chapel devoted to Kerezen, goddess of the senses—our goddess, the one who had Anointed our ancestors with power. The air was cool here, the humble circular building surrounded by fat oak trees. Mara led me to a stone bench, where she sat beside me in easy silence until I found my breath.

"Thank you," I whispered at last.

"Tell me what happened," she said. "Was it the panic?"

I could have cried anew upon hearing her voice—sweet and low, gentle as a kitten. How I had missed that voice. I nodded helplessly, smiling a little at our old name for my frequent bouts of inexplicable, breathless dread. *The panic.* I rubbed my face clean with my fluttery chiffon sleeve. Jessyl, my lady's maid, would kill me for smearing rouge across the fabric, but I hardly cared just then.

"I should be asking you how you are," I said, "not blubbering all over you. Gods, I can't believe it's been an entire month since we saw you last."

Mara shrugged. "I'm the same as ever. I'd much rather hear what's bothering you. Did Farrin say something cruel? Has Father's mind skipped right out of his head again?"

This time my laugh was a little stronger. I looked up, ready to spin my distress into some clever story, something that would make Mara let loose the throaty laugh I so adored—but when I raised my eyes to hers, what I saw shocked me into silence.

Now that some steadiness had returned to me, I saw that angry red slashes marred my sister's alabaster cheek and snaked down her neck, below the collar of her drab, dirt-colored tunic. She shook her hair over the worst of it, but not even Mara's thick brown waves could hide what I had seen.

"Mara…" I whispered.

She would not look at me. She stared at the chapel floor with an eerie calm. "It's not as bad as it looks."

I let out a sharp laugh. "Oh, no. You can't dissuade me, not this time. Come, we're speaking to the Warden about this."

I grabbed her hand, tried to pull her up from the bench. But long years of service had left Mara strong and lean and with a will like iron. I might as well have tried to move a mountain.

"It will heal quickly," she said, watching me steadily. "You know it will. It always does."

"But this is worse than I've ever seen!"

"Well, you've seen very little of my life here."

She didn't say it unkindly, and yet the words cut me to my marrow. I drew myself up and tried to look imperious. "Isn't there a clause in your contract requiring the Warden to provide adequate protection to the women under her care? Clearly she has been negligent and is in breach. We're taking you home. Come, we'll go tell Father at once."

Mara smiled fondly at me. "You sounded like Farrin just then."

I began to see that this would go nowhere. I could command a ballroom of admirers but neither of my sisters.

I knelt before her, clasped her hands. A different, sweeter tack. "Mara, please tell me what's happened. What did this to you? Is this sort of injury common? How often does it happen? Have you gone to see the healers?"

Mara freed one of her hands to cup my cheek, still wearing that maddening soft smile. "So many questions you have for me. Where to even begin?"

"Does it...does it hurt?"

That surprised her. I saw it on her face—a tiny flit of some great sadness that escaped before she could catch it.

"Yes," she whispered. "Very much."

The words blew something out of her. She sagged a little, and I noticed faint lines around her eyes and mouth that I hadn't seen before. They frightened me even more than her wounds, aging her in an instant. Right before my eyes, I could see my twenty-two-year-old sister turning brittle and old, all the life pummeled out of her by this wretched place.

Then she began to speak, and her voice changed—careful, hushed. Her brown eyes fixed on mine, holding me rapt.

"I have to tell you something," she began slowly. "Something you can't tell Father. Not yet. But do tell Farrin. Ask her to summon Gareth from the university and tell them both at the same time—I don't trust the post, nor even a wilder's messenger, not with this. Make certain that no one is around to hear. Maybe the three of you together can do something before it's too late."

Mara laughed a little, quietly, like a hitched breath. "At the very least, the secrets I keep will weigh less on me once you and Farrin share the burden." Then she frowned, her gaze drifting away. "All the weapons at my fingertips, and yet my hands have long been tied…"

Her expression was so distant and strange, shifting from fear to sadness to anger, that my blood turned cold with dread.

"I don't understand," I said. "Before it's too late? Too late for what?"

She fell silent, staring at the floor.

I touched her chin and made her look at me. "Mara, tell me right this instant what you need to say."

But before she could, a clangor of bells exploded from the priory, so sudden and cacophonous that I nearly jumped out of my skin.

Mara was on her feet at once, her tiredness gone. She loomed over me, tense and coiled, palm hovering over the dagger at her waist. A falcon's cry pierced the air, and Mara whispered, "*Freyda.*" Then, without looking at me, she barked, "Get inside the priory, Gemma. *Now.*"

With that, she ran out of the temple and down the mountain, her strides liquid and long, her footfalls nearly silent. I should have obeyed—oh, I should have obeyed—but I couldn't forget that awful look on her face or the haunted quality of her voice. And I knew what those bells meant.

An intruder, as the Warden called them. A creature or being from the Old Country had slipped through the Middlemist somewhere along its thousand-mile length, breaching the rift between that realm and ours by accident or design.

To the Order of the Rose, the reason mattered not. Intruders were wrangled back to where they belonged or killed. No exceptions. No delays. When the bells rang, the Roses attacked.

And if I didn't act immediately, I might never hear what Mara had to say. The moment would be lost—she would feign ignorance and never speak of it again, or something terrible would happen to her and she would lose the opportunity altogether.

Before it's too late, she had said. Words I knew I must take seriously no matter what it cost me.

I ran down the mountain after my sister, clumsy in my boots and gown, pumping my thin legs as fast as I could. "Mara! Wait! What did you need to tell me?"

Mara whipped her head around and roared, "Go inside, Gemma!"

Other women were flooding out of the priory—some younger than Mara, some older, all of them impossibly graceful as they bounded through the trees toward the thick silver river that abutted the grounds.

The Middlemist.

My blood chilled as I watched them—faces flinty, hands clutching quivers of arrows, sabers, crossbows. I knew I should stop, that I wasn't meant to see what would happen next, but I had to know what Mara needed to tell me. I couldn't go back to that day twelve years ago and stop the Warden from taking her, but I could do this.

The Mist was not far now. My body seized up with fear as I approached its shimmering veil, but I pushed onward, ignoring the shouts of Farrin and Father some ways behind me. Their frantic voices ordered me to stop, begged me to stop.

Dozens of Roses launched themselves into the air or leapt through the trees, their bodies changing as I watched them—elongating, sharpening, swelling. Bare feet hardened into scaly claws. The hands clutching weapons sprouted wicked talons. Great wings of black, gray, and speckled brown erupted from each woman's shoulder blades. Their transforming bodies shredded whatever garments they wore, the scraps of fabric fluttering to the ground like molted feathers, and it occurred to me then, startling a gasping laugh out of me, why all the Roses wore such plain, threadbare garments. What was the point of wearing fine clothes if they would be destroyed every time the bells rang?

Foolish girl that I was, I had never considered the practicality of their garb, only the dreariness of it.

Just before I plunged into the Mist, I drew in my breath and held it, bracing myself.

I was not disappointed.

As the Mist hit me, washing over me with a strange supple coolness, agony ripped through me like nothing I had ever felt before. Our greenway's hungry pull was nothing in comparison. The Mist had a thousand relentless teeth, and all of them were digging into my skin, my muscle, my bone.

I staggered, dizzy and sick, and caught myself against a tree. Fighting through the shock of pain, I frantically searched for Mara, desperate to find her before the tingling blackness encroaching on my vision swallowed me whole.

But as I stood there, a horrible chorus of shrieks assailed my ears—first only a few, then dozens, vicious and clearly not of our world. The sound made my pain worse. I blacked out for an instant and came to in the dirt on my hand and knees. I gasped for breath, not understanding what I was hearing. I had thought Mara and the others would travel through one of the priory's greenways to whatever distant expanse of the Mist had been breached, but these bestial cries were close and growing closer. Intruders so close to Rosewarren? Impossible. Unheard of. When the gods created the Middlemist just before their deaths on the day of the Unmaking, they had ensured that the expanse of Mist nearest the priory was doubly strong. A final pitying gift for those doomed to serve there.

Intruders had never managed to reach the grounds of Rosewarren, nor even the nearby town or any settlement within ten square miles. But they were here now, and that could mean only one thing:

The Middlemist, crafted and fortified by the gods themselves, was weakening.

But was it losing strength only here, near the priory? I hoped so, despite the danger to Mara. The alternative was too horrific to imagine.

All around me, the Roses called to each other in their strange language, a hybrid of the common tongue and whatever coded words the Warden had taught them. I recognized only a few: *They want the girl! Get her out of here!*

My stomach plummeted to my toes, and my instincts screamed at me to run. I knew without doubt that the girl they spoke of was me.

I tried to rise but couldn't, my legs useless. I scrambled for something, anything—a tree or rock to hide behind, some dropped weapon I could pretend I knew how to fire—but I was lost in the Mist, the world around me opaque with slithering gray.

And then I heard a cry of fury, both human and not, shattering in its despair and distorted, multiplied, as if the sound had been run through with claws and each bleeding strip had its own voice.

Even so, I knew to whom the cry belonged, and my chest seized hard around my heart.

A huge figure crashed out of the trees and threw itself before me, protecting me from whatever approaching enemy was issuing those piercing shrieks.

My breath caught in my throat.

Mara.

I had never seen her transform; none of us had. She had made sure of it. But now I was in the Mist, a trespasser, and she could not hide herself from me—her lambent golden eyes, the wild fall of dark hair and feathers cascading down her back, the enormous brown wings sprouting from naked, knotted muscles she had not possessed only moments earlier in the temple. Her skin was no longer entirely human, a mosaic of pale flesh, scales, and sleek feathers. Her face was her own, but sharper, feral, wreathed in gleaming velvet fur.

"Leave, now!" She roared the words, her changed voice breaking with sorrow and shame, and I wanted to—gods help me, I wanted to flee as I would a monster in a nightmare—but I no longer had control over my limbs. The pain was too great, my sickness too complete. I tried to apologize, but my voice croaked in vain.

A strong hand gripped my arm, pulled me up, helped me run. I let it guide me, trusting it, glad for it, because it was leading me away from this creature that was both my sister and not. The air cleared; the hand was taking me out of the Mist, thank all the gods, and as my vision righted itself, I saw that the hand belonged to my father. His countenance was utterly changed—no longer a proud preening father but instead a ferocious hunter, a sentinel. His Anointed power gave him heightened strength and agility, unfailing precision with any weapon he might grab.

But there was no need for weapons. Father's speed was enough to save us. We burst through the iron gate and into the thicket where Farrin waited, looking pale and small—the cheery chiming of the snow-blossom vines around us suddenly sounded comically absurd—and then plunged into the greenway's mouth. Its magic swirled around me, eager to scent the Mist on my skin, but in that moment, I didn't care about the greenway's hunger, nor the tingling fresh pain spreading fast through my body.

I could think only of Mara, the howl of her despair, the tears streaking her face—female and avian, both stunning and repugnant.

It was only the second time I could remember seeing my sister cry. The first was the day the Warden took her from us, and in both instances, Mara's tears—her fear and sorrow, the horrible loss radiating from her like churning waves—were all because of me.

CHAPTER 2

T he moment we stepped out of the greenway and into the elaborate green bowels of our hedge maze, Father shoved me away from him. I lost my footing and fell to the ground, and this time, Farrin didn't help me.

She stood at the greenway's mouth, framed by the shimmering vines, her arms rigid at her sides and her hands in angry fists. One glance at those flashing brown eyes was more than enough. I searched instead for Father, whose temper was fierce but short-lived.

That day, though, was different. In stormy silence, he strode a few paces away. The ivy-draped iron arbor that capped this stretch of the maze drew ropes of sun and shadow across the fluttering tails of his coat.

I watched him through the mussed golden coils of my hair, which had fallen loose from its ribbons. With every breath, my ribs seemed to catch fire.

"I'm sorry—" I began, but Father whirled around and pointed furiously at me.

"Don't you dare apologize," he snapped. "Anything you could

offer as an excuse for that unforgivable display would only serve to make me angrier. Foolish, selfish girl!" He turned away, raking a hand through his hair—light golden-brown waves, very like Farrin's—and then spun back around. "The *Mist*, Imogen? In your condition?"

That spurred me to my feet, unsteady as they were. "I'm not hurt, Papa. What about whatever was attacking the priory? What about *Mara*?"

"Mara, the Mist, the priory—none of these things are your concern. *Not hurt*, you say? And how would you know? None of us do!" He waved his arm to encompass himself, Farrin, me, our sprawling estate. "No healer has been able to treat you. No scholar has been able to find a case similar to yours. We don't know what magic will pass over you, harmless, and what could kill you. And even knowing this, you ran heedlessly into the Middlemist, the single most powerful magical site on the continent."

He looked in disbelief to Farrin as if to confirm that he was right in his contempt. But my eldest sister stayed silent.

"Thank you, I am well aware of what a burden I am to all of you," I said, hating how my voice caught on every other word. "And I wasn't *heedless*. Mara needed to tell me something important, but she didn't get the chance before the bells started ringing, and..."

I trailed off, realizing too late how childish I sounded, how rash I had been.

Father nodded grimly. "Yes. Now you understand, now that it's too late. I hope whatever foul spirits live in the Mist didn't burrow into you just now, Imogen. I hope you don't wake screaming in the night from some Olden curse eating your insides, because I have to tell you, at this moment I'm not at all certain that I would come running to help you! *Gods*." He looked bitterly up at the arbor. "Sometimes I think your mother had the right idea, leaving before she could see how senseless you would grow up to be."

Farrin drew in a sharp breath and whispered, "*Papa.*"

He blinked at us both, at first not understanding. The sentinel fever was on him still, stoked high by the danger we had all just been in. He couldn't help his temper, not entirely, and I knew that. Once it awakened, the Anointed magic in his blood that gave him his sentinel abilities overtook everything else that he was.

But he was also a grown man, nearly sixty years old, and had lived with his power long enough to have learned how to hold his tongue, even with fierce warrior magic lashing through his body.

Staring at him, I could hardly breathe. My skin flushed hot-cold, and there was a faint ringing in my ears, as if I'd been struck hard on the temple. Not that I'd ever been struck hard on the temple, but I'd read hundreds of novels in which someone was, and I imagined that no fist could have dealt a worse blow than my father's words.

His face fell, the awful haggard quality returning. He looked suddenly pathetic, despite his fine vest and coat and his perfectly tailored trousers. Even his mustache seemed to droop.

"Gemma, I didn't mean that," he began, holding out his hands.

But I refused to hear it. "You did," I said tightly. "It was the worst thing you could have possibly said to me, and I'll never forget it."

Then I fled, hurrying out of the maze and across the grounds to the stables. Neither Farrin nor Father tried to stop me, and I was glad. I wished to be neither mollified nor groveled to.

As I neared the stables, I saw Byrn, our oldest groomer, leaning against a paddock fence as one of his apprentices worked with a yearling colt. Byrn was a low-magic tamer and the favorite of all our horses—and of my dog, Una, a white fleethound who lay at his feet, her tufted ears pricked as she watched my approach. Byrn noticed me not long after. Quite a sight I must have looked—hair tumbling haphazardly, dress rumpled and stained, face red from crying.

Byrn's bushy white eyebrows shot up, but he said nothing. We had an understanding, he and I. Farrin was forever occupied with managing the estate, and Father was obsessed with his little war. I actually listened to Byrn's stories when I visited, and I was the same age as the beloved granddaughter he'd left back home in Lumyra, and any time our kitchen staff baked pastries, I brought him a steaming fresh batch. I avoided most of the servants; they had seen me sick from magic too many times for me to particularly enjoy meeting their eyes unless necessary.

But Byrn I liked. He was fresh air and easy silence and the smell of horses, and he never once looked at me differently from anyone else. On that day, then, he said nothing, asked no questions. He simply prepared my horse, a beautiful dapple-gray mare named Zephyr, and then stepped back to let me pass, his worried expression so sweet and sad that I felt like crying all over again.

Before I could, I looked away and urged Zephyr into a trot, then a smooth canter. Una followed us, her long fleethound legs easily keeping pace. With my father's words ringing in my ears, I fled across the grounds and escaped into the blessed cool sanctuary of our wooded game park. Deer scattered at our thundering approach.

Senseless. Heedless. Foolish girl.

I blinked hard against the wind, saying the words to myself over and over. Better to relive Father's temper than to remember the look on Mara's face when I had recoiled from her, agape with horror I could not disguise.

When Illaria answered my knock at the door of her workshop later that afternoon, she took one wide-eyed look at me and whisked me into her house without a word.

Within ten minutes, my dearest friend had me settled in her

reading room with a cup of fresh herbal tea, a plate of my favorite chocolate wafers dusted with icing sugar, and a soft old quilt tucked around my shoulders. Una chewed happily on a bone by the fire, and I knew Zephyr would be tended to in Illaria's stables nearly as well as at home—which I would never admit to Byrn.

The chair I huddled in was enormous and upholstered with blue velvet. I had long ago claimed it as "mine." As children, and then in all the years after, Illaria and I had devoured novel after novel in that room. Illaria's parents were low-magic savants with keen talents for designing scents and a thriving business empire to run. Before they deemed Illaria old enough to begin her official apprenticeship, she and I were often left to our own devices—to read, gossip, practice dancing, practice kissing. This room, this house, had sometimes felt more like a home than my own. I settled into the soft cushions and nearly cried with relief.

Illaria reclined in the chair opposite mine, kicked off her work boots, and rested her bare feet on the tasseled stool at her feet. Even at the end of a long day of overseeing her workshop, her face bare and her clothes reeking with too many heady aromas to count— coffee, sandalwood, vanilla, rose—she was enviably gorgeous. Smooth honey-brown skin, a profusion of soft dark-brown ringlets, and sharp green eyes framed in thick lashes. She made even her plain work trousers and heavy leather apron seem the height of fashion.

"Well?" she said at last. "Out with it."

I hid my face in my cup, reveling in the fragrant floral steam of my tea. "This blend is divine. Is it yours?"

"Of course. All the good teas are mine. All the good perfumes are mine." Illaria waved her hand. "You won't distract me with flattery. Tell me what's happened. It's not every day you appear on my doorstep looking as if you've just fought your way to the surface of some reeking bog."

I took a long sip and stared at my bare toes. "Can we just sit here in silence for a while instead? I'm tired."

Illaria arched one elegant eyebrow. "I can't imagine why."

"Please, Lari. Just for a while."

"Very well." For a moment she was quiet. Then she said briskly, "All right, that was a while."

"Hardly."

"By my reckoning, it was a while."

"Well, your reckoning is wrong."

"That is very seldom true." Illaria set her cup on the table beside her and regarded me, her smile softening. "I'm only worried about my friend, is all."

I drew in a breath, then let it out slowly. "We visited Mara today."

Illaria nodded. "Never a good start."

"And we were waiting for her to come back from patrol, lunching with the Warden—"

"Madam Insufferable," Illaria interjected smoothly. "Continue."

That made me smile a little. "I couldn't bear it, sitting there in that ridiculous stuffy parlor while Mara was off in whatever gods-awful place they'd sent her to. I couldn't stop thinking about it, and the thoughts kept climbing and climbing, and…"

I looked away, waves of shame washing over me, shrinking me. I hated the feeling. I wasn't some cowering worrywart. I was Lady Imogen Ashbourne.

But when the panic came, it reduced me to something else, something that felt utterly unfamiliar, as if a foreign force were taking possession of me, reshaping me.

"And then the panic came," Illaria said, her voice gentle.

I nodded. "And then the panic came."

I told her the rest—talking with Mara in the temple, the ringing bells. The Middlemist, the shrieks.

Mara, transformed.

Father yelling at me in the hedge maze.

After I finished, the silence seemed to stretch on forever. Then Illaria rose to her feet, shrugged off her apron, and climbed into my chair, tucking herself against me. I closed my eyes, letting the warmth of Illaria's body soak into mine and listening to the popping fire. Una, now asleep on her back with her legs in the air, was in the thrall of a dream, whuffing quietly.

Mara sometimes held me like this during our visits, when her schedule allowed it. She and Illaria were the only ones who understood that often it was what I needed most of all—to sit in silence, to feel their touch, to breathe in tandem with them until I found myself again. No talking, no concerned questions, no looks of pity. I had endured more than enough of that in my life.

Finally Illaria cleared her throat and shifted against me. The aromas of her perfumery wafted up from her skin.

"Your father," she declared, "is an ass."

I laughed. Her indignation warmed me all the way through. "He isn't always."

"He was today."

"I'll concede that."

"He should know better than to let loose his temper at you. He's a grown man, for gods' sake."

Content, I snuggled against her. "My thoughts precisely."

She fumed in silence for another few moments before I felt her slowly begin to relax. "What will you do about Mara? She said nothing else to indicate what she needed to tell you?"

I shook my head. "Part of me thinks she might have been glad that the bells rang just then. It was as though even beginning to speak about her secret was agony for her."

"Well, it seems to me that the first thing you should do is pay her another visit as soon as possible. Write to the Warden, request a dispensation."

A nauseating fist clenched in my stomach. I couldn't imagine looking Mara in the eye ever again, much less *as soon as possible.*

Then inspiration struck.

"A party," I murmured.

"What party?"

I sat up, shaking off the day's grief like an out-of-fashion cloak. I could see it all unfurling before my eyes—the strings of golden lights, the gauzy window hangings, the gleaming silver platters piled high with iced cakes, the string orchestra playing a waltz by the wall of windows in the Blue Ballroom.

"*My* party," I announced. "Soon everyone will hear about the attack so near Rosewarren—nearer than I've ever heard of, certainly. They'll be afraid, and they'll have questions. Mist hysteria will sweep the countryside."

"*Mist*-eria," Illaria interjected, amused.

"And what better thing to take everyone's minds off the danger than a grand, opulent, raging-through-the-night party?"

"And what better way for the Ashbournes to flaunt their wealth and status in front of the Basks?" Illaria added wryly.

I dismissed her with a wave. My father's war with the Bask family was his problem, not mine. If my party happened to please him and give us some advantage in that fight, so be it. He and Farrin could cackle and gloat and scheme as much as they wanted. I would be sure to invite the Basks, but that's all I would contribute. They had never asked me to help them with our family's pointless grudge war, and I wasn't about to start.

"Oh, hang the Basks," I muttered. "This party will be for *me.*"

Illaria's voice was all innocence. "And for the good people of

Gallinor, whom you're so intent upon comforting in these uncertain times."

I absently waved at her again. "Of course, of course."

It was as if I had been stuck in a dismal winter and suddenly all of spring had rushed into me at once. My vision sharpened; my limbs felt strong and reborn. I rose from the chair and began to pace. Una awoke and watched my progress eagerly, her tail thumping the rug.

"I'll tell Mrs. Rathmont to begin preparing a menu first thing tomorrow," I said, ticking off items on my fingers. "The orchestra—no, something smaller, simpler...the Ogwood Octet, I think—they'll need to be booked at once. Oh, I hope they're available. We're right in the middle of the spring party season."

I whirled around, clapped my hands, and looked at Una, whose tail began wagging even more fiercely once my eyes locked with hers.

"My dress," I proclaimed, "will require serious thought. It must strike just the right balance of reassurance and solemnity and grateful jubilation. *No, we needn't worry about that attack at Rosewarren. A mere aberration. Yes, we must pay all due respect to the Order of the Rose, which fought so bravely. And yes, we must also celebrate with unbridled merriment the fact that we are alive and safe and protected by the grace of the gods.*"

I crouched by Una and took her long white snout in my hands. "For sight and sound and taste and touch, for the scent of the wind and the strength of my limbs, thanks be to Kerezen, goddess of my body, maker of bone and blood. And so it shall ever be." I crooned the prayer, scratching behind Una's tufted ears all the while. "Yes, Una, my girl, we must give proper thanks to her and all the rest of those lovely old gods, mustn't we?"

Behind me, Illaria snorted. "I don't believe I've ever heard you pray with quite so much conviction."

"Well, that's what happens when one comes face-to-face with

death," I said cheerfully. "One experiences a renewed appreciation for the gods and life and all its trimmings."

Una was in a state of pure bliss, her white belly exposed for a rub, but one grave word from Illaria made me turn.

"Gemma."

She was intent upon me, leaning forward with her elbows on her knees, her hands clasped. "A party is all well and good. I cannot argue with your reasoning, much as I would like to. Word of the attack will travel, and an Ashbourne party will be something ordinary and familiar. A reassurance. And a distraction, giving time for the Warden and her Roses to do their work."

Triumphant, I opened my mouth to agree, but she cut me off.

"But before you go running off to raid your closet and rally your staff, I need to say two things. One is a question. One is not."

The giddy feelings racing inside me slowed and shrank, making room once more for the memories of my awful day—Mara's despair, Mara's wings, Father's fury.

Refusing to give them my attention, I flashed Illaria a coy smile. "How very mysterious you are all of a sudden. Do go on."

Illaria blew out a sharp breath. "You know I love you. You know I'm happy to sit with you and listen to you and hold your hand through a thousand panics, if it comes to that. But someday you must actually talk to someone besides me about what you're dealing with. A healer, a midwife, a scholar—anyone who might have some knowledge of what it means when the panic comes for you so hard and fast that you can't breathe or eat or sleep."

Her expression softened. "I've never seen you like you were today, Gemma. You were frantic, fragmented. When I opened my door, you weren't speaking sense. You were crying and gasping for air. Do you even remember that? Do you remember riding away from Ivyhill on Zephyr?"

I stared at her. Tears of humiliation built behind my eyes, but my smile held them back. I shrugged. I could not tell her the real answer, that I remembered very little of what had happened between mounting Zephyr and inhaling the steam of my tea. That stretch of time was a confused chasm of sharp colors and roiling, unstoppable fear.

Illaria came to me and took my hand. "Promise me you'll at least think about it. I refuse to believe you're the only one in the world who loses herself to panic she can't control. Someone out there understands what you're feeling. Someone out there can help much better than I can."

I turned away, gazing at the fire until my vision cleared. I couldn't bear to look upon her gentle, earnest face for another moment.

"I promise," I said at last, the lie hardly more than a whisper. There was a deep wrongness in me, and I would never let the true scope of it be known outside of this room, no matter what I promised my friend.

Once I had collected myself, I looked back at her, dry-eyed. "And the second thing? The question?"

Illaria studied me for a long moment. Then she took hold of my shoulders and said with the utmost seriousness, "Will you, Imogen Ashbourne, do me the honor of adorning your wrists and throat with my newest formulation on the night of this sure-to-be-legendary party?"

I was so relieved that I burst out laughing. "You're giving me the chance to introduce all of Gallinor society to the newest scent from master perfumier Illaria Farrow? How could I possibly refuse?"

She melted, smiling with the satisfaction of a spoiled cat. "You'll love it. Notes of white lily and pine, a bit of pink sea salt, a fresh bite of apple. It's fresh and sultry and surprising." She lifted her chin, fluffing her curls. "Much like myself."

Then she bowed, and I applauded her with such gusto that Una jumped to her feet and started barking, exuberant as a puppy. Illaria rang for fresh tea, and we drank and talked, laughing well into the night as Illaria regaled me with the latest gossip from the dramatic lives of her apprentices.

Even then, in the back of my mind, I fiercely gripped the steel cords of my resolve.

Promise or no, I was an Ashbourne. A sick Ashbourne, yes— breakable and exhausting and a liability and a disappointment and my middle sister's unwitting executioner. The only one in my prestigious Anointed line to be born without magic since my ancestors were chosen centuries ago by the goddess Kerezen to receive a piece of her power.

But I was an Ashbourne nonetheless, rich and privileged, the great beauty of my generation. My party would be the talk of the continent, as my parties always were—and the shameful dread that lived inside me would remain no one's burden but my own.

CHAPTER 3

E ven on an ordinary day, my family's estate of Ivyhill was a splendid place—twelve square miles of parks and gardens, farms and fields worked by our tenants, cottages for the groundskeepers, and temples built centuries ago to glorify the gods.

Then, of course, there was the house itself. Two hundred and fifty rooms and a staff of fifty; housing for all our servants, visiting nobility and diplomats and merchants, and our extended family—a passel of cousins, aunts, and uncles who came and went without much ceremony. Few of them, even those with reasonably diverting magical talents, interested me beyond whatever gossip they brought from elsewhere.

I hungered for gossip more than anything. Due to my debilitating sensitivity to magic, I was often confined to Ivyhill under my father's watchful eye. During those periods, it felt as if the rest of the world no longer existed and I was alone, trapped inside the fraying web of my own frantic, frustrated thoughts. I had long ago resigned myself to eventually withering away in my lofty tower suite once I became too infirm to leave it.

There were, of course, worse places to be confined forever. I was not so oblivious to the rest of the world as to be unaware of that. But a breathtaking prison to which one has been relegated for one's own benefit is still a prison.

Therefore, two weeks after the day I witnessed Mara transform, on the day of my party—a spring night, mild and sweet, the air scented with tender flowering trees, the entire country gathered with excitement at our doors—I made certain that Ivyhill shone as it never had before.

I took stock of it all as our guests arrived, breezing through the proper greetings and introductions despite most of my attention being focused on the silk window hangings, the octet's song choices, the candles flickering in every sconce, the ornate chandeliers dripping with magicked light, the servants gliding expertly from ballroom to sitting room to receiving hall with platters of refreshments.

In each room—ornamenting every doorway, spilling down every banister, hanging from every rafter—were the glossy, lush ivy vines my mother had designed shortly after she married my father.

An elemental from a perfectly respectable low-magic family, young Philippa Wren was lovely and witty and could manipulate botanicals, as could many in her family. The Wrens had been fortunate enough to receive magic from Caiathos, god of the earth, just after the Unmaking. It was but a stray bit of magic flung across the world upon his death, bestowed by accident rather than by design, and so they were a low-magic family instead of an Anointed one, their power limited but dependable. Philippa, though, could only work her magic with great effort and with the help of others.

A poor match, everyone had thought of my parents, skeptical

and amused; Gideon Ashbourne had, like many men before him, fallen prey to a pretty face and forgotten what really mattered. But then the new Lady Ashbourne had begun her work, starting with one sprig of ivy and growing it over a series of weeks into our house's second skin. She had hired an alchemist and a spellcrafter to help ensure the vines' longevity, and one could not argue with the results, nor with the flurry of awed visitors who'd streamed through the house for months afterward to admire Mother's work and marvel at her savvy. Why, the sheer brazen artistry of the vines enhanced the already-impressive estate and added to the family's mystique! How cunning, how shrewd. Philippa Wren— who ever would have guessed? And then she brought Farrin into the world, a perfect little songbird of a girl and as much a child of Kerezen as her sentinel father. No one dared doubt Philippa Ashbourne's worth after that.

I ducked underneath a stone archway draped with said vines and skillfully maneuvered Lady Grattery away from her nemesis, Lady Keighline, by gushing over the stunning emerald earrings she wore. I steered her toward the Rose Room, where Colonel Mettalin of the Lower Army had begun a raucous game of cards, and only then did I allow myself a moment to catch my breath in one of the curtained sitting rooms along the Blue Ballroom's perimeter.

I already felt battered head to toe by the proximity of so many guests with magic in their blood. I was always in some discomfort at Ivyhill; my Anointed father and sister made that inevitable, as did the presence of my mother's vines, the removal of which I wouldn't dare request, for they were all I had left of her. But my party had brought to Ivyhill not only several members of Anointed families, but also dozens who possessed low magic. I always made a point of inviting a vast number of low-magic citizens. After all, it wasn't their fault that their ancestors had not been chosen by the gods. At the moment the gods died—an event known as the Unmaking—magic had scattered across the world in thousands of random shards, and those who had been fortunate enough to ingest, inhale, or simply lay eyes upon one of these shards had unwittingly claimed a piece of true, if diluted, magic. And now their descendants could claim such power as well, along with the quite useful abilities that came with it—animal taming, minor spellcrafting and elemental magic, a keen memory.

Ivyhill teemed with it tonight—the high magic of the Anointed and the lower magic of the lucky. To me the sound of it was like that of an apian swarm, and the odor of so many individual magicks left me feeling as though I were trapped in a steaming hothouse, the warring fragrances of a hundred different flowers weaving a rank tapestry. But I was not so green a hostess that I would allow myself to be conquered by such an onslaught.

I put two fingers to my left temple, willing my pounding head to calm, and slowly sipped my sparkling wine, a delicious fruity blend that brought a rush of warmth to my aching limbs. Once the glass was half drained, I began looking over my dance card for the evening. I had hardly paid attention to the flock of admirers requesting dances, merely scribbling each name down with a flirtatious laugh before continuing on my rounds.

The first name on the docket was Rasia Reest, which delighted me. A skilled low-magic artisan from the continent of Aidurra, renowned for her stunning oil paintings, Rasia would be sure to have the latest cultural news from across the Sea of the Dawn.

After her was Lieutenant Arkin Martel, a notorious rake who served in the Lower Army in Beroges, on Gallinor's southern coast. By all accounts, it was a rather dull assignment; the boundary between worlds in Beroges was known to grow somewhat thin during high tide, but only somewhat, and only five times a year. Arkin was one of those unfortunate people whose family had neither received nor happened upon magic during the Unmaking, but what Arkin lacked in magic, he made up for with finesse of hands and tongue. I shivered in delight, remembering our first brief liaison when I was eighteen, during which the good lieutenant showed me how delicious it could feel when a girl's lover kissed her between her legs.

Perhaps, I thought, I could tempt him upstairs after our dance. I laughed a little, lifting my glass for another long sip. As I well knew, there would be no tempting required. Every time the lieutenant came through the area, he made sure to pay me a visit, one that required no declarations of love or promises neither of us would keep. Just a quick tumble in whatever dark corner we could find, a fond kiss farewell, and yet another distracting memory to turn to for comfort the next time I lay sick in bed.

I sighed in contentment, continuing down the dance card. Varidien Nighy, Erya Remkin, the delectable Lieutenant Martel once more, Arden Odair, Talan d'Astier.

Frowning, I paused. I had no memory of meeting a Talan d'Astier. Indeed, I didn't even recognize the name, and yet I had curated the evening's guest list. That could mean only one thing: if I of all people did not know a Talan d'Astier, there was only one other person in attendance who would.

I knocked back the rest of my wine, desperate for the bubbling warmth it would bring, and stepped out of my hiding spot to find my father—but before I got very far, a hand seized my arm and hurried me into another curtained alcove.

During the twenty years of my life, I had been grabbed quite often by my eldest sister, usually to keep me from getting too near someone with especially volatile magic. I knew the vise of her grip quite well. Thankfully the wine's warmth softened the pinch of her iron fingers.

"The *Basks* are here," Farrin hissed, peeking out from behind the curtain.

I followed her gaze to the far side of the ballroom, where a small chattering crowd had gathered. At its heart stood two unmistakable figures—Alastrina Bask, tall and slender and pale as winter, draped in a gown of sparkling midnight blue, her shoulder-length black hair glamoured with gold and silver strands; and her brother, Ciaran, in a dramatic brocade coat, a midnight-blue vest to match his sister's, and his own dark hair tied back from his face with a braided leather cord. *Ryder*, he preferred to be called, which annoyed Farrin to no end and therefore delighted me. I allowed myself a moment to admire the rugged slash of his beard and how deliciously his impeccably tailored trousers hugged his hips.

Then I shook myself free of Farrin. "Of course they're here," I said. "I invited them. Everyone who's anyone attends my parties, and they are without a doubt *anyone*, no matter how much you and Father might wish otherwise." Then I looked down at her gown, unsuccessfully trying to hide my dismay as I beheld the garment—plain and gray as the dead of winter, the collar stiff, high, and buttoned. Its only adornments were embroidered lines of tiny silver leaves at the hems of the sleeves and skirts. "Farrin, that is decidedly not the gown I selected for you."

"The gown you selected was itchier than my legs in winter. And you told me you wouldn't invite them!"

"I lied."

Farrin whirled on me, spots of angry color on her cheeks. "You exhausting little *ass*. I wanted a night, just one night, of neither thinking nor talking about the godsdamned Bask family."

"Farrin, good gods." I withdrew a tin from the clever pocket sewn into my bodice—one of Illaria's concoctions, a silky rose-scented tint. "You're only twenty-four years old, and yet you look like a dour old spinster."

Farrin glared at me as I dabbed the tint on her lips. "You say *dour old spinster* as if it's a bad thing rather than an aspiration I hold quite close to my heart."

I rolled my eyes. "You are an Ashbourne, are you not? You could at least try to look the part. People look to you as an example."

She snorted. "Of what? Lip color?" Then she glanced into the tiny gilded mirror hung beside the curtain and made a face. "Fine, I'll admit it does look nice. And smell nice."

"*You* look nice, even in that horrid dress. It flatters your figure impeccably, but even so, I'm trying not to shrivel away to a dried-out husk of embarrassment at the thought of you standing next to Alastrina Bask in something so drab."

"No need to worry about Alastrina. As soon as I can work out a way to get her and her dreadful brother out of here, they'll be gone." She pinched her nose, rubbed the bridge. "Father has been itching for a fight these past few weeks, and the last thing we need tonight is him deciding he'd like to cross swords with Ciaran Bask in the midst of all these people."

"Ryder."

"What?"

"Ciaran prefers to be called that. It's a nickname. He's quite the skilled equestrian, apparently, even more so than the typical Anointed wilder."

Farrin rolled her eyes. "How wonderful for him." Then she paused, looking even more annoyed. "That second violinist needs to calm himself down before I do it for him. Every piece they've played tonight he's rushed half to death."

I fiddled with her hair, pulling loose some golden wisps to soften her face. Not for the first time, I wished passionately for the ability to craft a glamour for my sister—or to craft glamours at all. To craft *anything* magical, even a tiny fetching spell. How diverting it would be to have something like that to occupy my mind when I felt ill, or when the pain crept up on me after being too long around someone more powerful than my body could tolerate.

After all, if magic was poison to my body, it seemed only right that I should be able to *enjoy* some of that poison every once in a while.

"There were whole years when you didn't have to think about the Basks, you know," I told Farrin quietly, pushing away my dark thoughts.

"That hardly matters," Farrin replied. "They're here now."

"How happy you were back then. You actually smiled. You *laughed.*"

"I still laugh."

"You smirk sometimes."

Farrin batted away my hands. "I don't know why I came to you for comfort. I don't know why I came to this party at all."

"Because Gareth's here," I said, "and you'd be a horrible friend if you abandoned him to suffer through a party alone. And because you don't have it in you to disappoint Father."

"Maybe you can give me lessons on how best to achieve that."

The blow glanced off me. I was used to evading them. "Maybe *you* should tell Father to make peace with the Basks, put an end to all of this."

Her expression flickered. "I can't. *He* can't, and you know it."

I pounced on that. "And will you tell me why? The truth, not just wild legends?"

"No."

"Because Father said not to? Or because you don't *know* the truth?"

Farrin's jaw clenched. "Yes."

"Yes to which?"

She said nothing, just shot me a scornful glare.

I expected as much. When it came to the matter of our family's feud with the Basks, Father and Farrin had never once taken me into their confidence—for my own good, they assured me. Most of the time I was content to leave them to their own devices and live my life, such as it was.

But tonight I could not contain my irritation.

"I've asked you this many times," I said, "but perhaps this will be the night the question knocks some sense into you at last. Do you even know the reason why our families hate each other?"

A slight beat. "No."

I didn't believe her, but I pressed on anyway. "Is it due to some ancient grudge stemming from a stupid fight no one can remember?"

"Possibly."

"Has it cost everyone time and money and injuries over the years and very nearly killed us all on more than one occasion?"

"Yes."

"And is it the very thing that drove our mother away?"

"Many things drove Mother away."

I took a glass of fresh wine from a passing servant's tray. "For which she's now thanking the gods, I'm sure."

Farrin leaned out after the servant, a middle-aged man with ruddy skin and neat auburn curls. He was new to our staff, and his name was…something I couldn't remember. I flushed to realize I couldn't remember when he'd been hired or if I'd spoken to him even once during all the preparations for tonight.

A familiar sour feeling turned in the crook of my throat as I remembered Father's words.

Foolish, selfish girl!

"You did a wonderful job with those floral arrangements, Carver," Farrin called out after the servant, and he turned back and beamed, gushing thanks with such earnestness that it embarrassed me.

Once he'd gone, Farrin was quiet for a moment. Then she touched my arm lightly. "Papa shouldn't have said those things to you that day. I'm sorry he did."

"Don't be," I said, tossing back the rest of my drink with a bright, bitter smile. "I'm not. He was right. I *am* a fool, and selfish too. Heedless, I think he said? Anyway, you're right not to tell me about the Basks and all that nonsense. Undoubtedly I would ruin everything."

"Gemma—"

"Oh, don't give me that *poor Gemma* look. That day wasn't the first time Father wounded me with his words, and I'm certain it won't be the last."

"What did I wound?" came a sudden voice.

Farrin jumped; I did not. I'd seen him coming.

I handed Farrin my empty glass, glided out of the alcove, and took Father's arm. I held up my dance card. "Talan d'Astier. Someone put his name on my dance card, and it wasn't me. Do you know him?"

Father glanced at me, a brief moment when our eyes locked and each of us knew what the other was thinking about—that day in the hedge maze, the air acrid with Father's furious magic, the scythe of his words. I thought I saw something like sorrow in his expression, and my foolish heart jumped at the sight.

Then his gaze dropped to the dance card, and I knew that

was the end of it. We would never speak of what had happened that day. It had become the way of things between us—I disobeyed him, he erupted with anger. I regretted my rashness, he regretted his temper. I forgave him, knowing that Mother leaving had changed him forever, knowing that he loved me and that sometimes his fear for me, his genuine desperation for my safety, turned into something ugly. And he forgave me, knowing it was unfair for a beautiful young woman to be so often stuck in her father's house, racked with unending pain and sickness through no fault of her own, knowing that it was unfair of him to direct his frustrated grief at me.

At least that was what I imagined he felt. That was the tug of conflict I hoped made his heart ache just as profoundly as it did mine.

I swallowed hard against that ache and pressed it flat, as I always did, and leaned closer, conspiratorial, as we took a promenade around the room.

"Talan d'Astier," Father said, nodding. "One of my personal guests for the weekend. Didn't I tell you about him?"

That distant look on his face—distracted and bored, as if he longed to be anywhere else. "I suppose not," I said brightly, forcing a smile. "I think I would have remembered such a name. Is he from Vauzanne?"

"Indeed. The sole heir of a once-great low-magic family, mostly artisans and scholars, that fell out of favor with the high queen at the turn of the century."

Despite my best efforts, I felt a twinge of intrigue. Few things interested me more than other people's misfortunes, if only because they reminded me that mine was not the only family riddled with angst.

"What did they do to deserve the queen's displeasure?"

Father nodded at Madam Lisabetta of Blighdon, a low-magic elemental who owned foundries that supplied the Lower Army on two continents, as well as quite possibly more clothes than even I had. She reclined on a velvet chaise in the corner, smoking a scented water pipe and holding court amongst her many ardent admirers. As we passed, her gaze traveled down the length of my gown and back up to my face, and she gave me a slow nod of approval before returning her attention to the starry-eyed young man beside her.

I fought back a triumphant smile, my body's pain momentarily forgotten. I knew I'd been right to choose this dress: a shimmering mosaic of iridescent colors and swirling ivy designs, impeccably draped to accentuate the slight curves of my slender physique. Tasteful yet tantalizing. One of Kerrish's creations, of course. I made a mental note to send her a bouquet of camellias from our gardens.

"My understanding," Father was saying, "is that instead of cultivating the magic their ancestors were lucky enough to stumble upon, the d'Astier family turned to growing *grapes*, of all things, even though it was Jaetris's magic they possessed, and not that of Caiathos. Why they chose to shun their ancestral magic and turn to the practices of another god is a mystery yet unsolved. Talan was a child at the time and has no insight on the matter."

"Much of Vauzanne's climate *is* perfect for growing grapes," I pointed out.

Father continued, ignoring me. "They acquired countless vineyards, some magically enhanced by elementals—which cost a pretty bit of coin, as you can imagine. Soon they were out of money and out of the queen's favor, both their nascent business and their reputation in tatters. The patriarch, I believe, took his own life out of sheer mortification. Poor fellow. May the gods find him and keep him."

As we passed one of the refreshment tables, Father took a fresh glass of the same wine I'd consumed and took a long sip. "It is a true pity," he continued with an appreciative glance at his glass. "There was something there, you know, power of Jaetris notwithstanding. This is from the d'Astier stores, in fact—some of their finest remaining vintage. A gift from Talan. You'd think they *had* been blessed by Caiathos after all."

Ah. I was starting to see the why of everything. "And Talan d'Astier thinks that by befriending us, he might be able to restore his family's name in the eyes of the queen."

Father finally looked right at me, genuinely pleased. "Right you are, my sweet one. We shall see what we think of him, hmm? He has an interesting business proposal that would get this wine of his into every fine establishment in Gallinor—and earn our family a pretty penny. But is he deserving of the Ashbourne mark of approval?" Father patted my arm fondly. "I'll depend upon your keen sense of character to help me decide."

The two glasses of wine I'd downed in rapid succession were beginning to take hold of me. Instead of feeling rankled by Father's endearment—he certainly had not found me *sweet* in the hedge maze—I took pride in it, devoured it. *My sweet one.* When I was a child, he had showered me with such words. I had been his treasure, his joy. *My dearest heart*, he'd called me. *My radiant little dove.* But the older I became, the less frequent were his kindnesses. Whenever I found the courage to confide in Farrin about it, she briskly dismissed my concerns and blamed the Basks for any strangeness in Father's behavior. Sometimes I even believed her; it wasn't until the Basks had reappeared a little over a year ago that Father had closed himself off so completely.

Other times, though, I was convinced that whatever meanness was sprouting in Father somehow came back to me—some ignorant thing I had done, whatever happened to frighten Mother away, the times I grew impatient and broke the house rules. Something was driving my father away from me, but tonight things felt different. Familiar, and as they once were. Between Father's words and the wine, I was beginning to float.

That was when Father stopped walking, his smile broadening at something beyond me. "Ah, Talan! There you are. Come, my Gemma is eager to meet you."

A rush of excitement coursed through me. Here was the man himself, a chance to prove to Father that his trust in me was not unfounded. Ignoring my niggling suspicion that Father was going to pull this oblivious new guest into some sort of scheme to humiliate the Basks, I turned to greet Talan d'Astier with a smile of polite interest on my face—and was struck silent with shock.

CHAPTER 4

I had long considered myself an expert in the realm of beauty, both in terms of my own appearance and my assessment of others. But in all my study of garments and jewels, flora and design, hair and eyes and bodies, not once had I seen a creature as beautiful as Talan d'Astier.

He was even paler than Mara, with loose dark brown curls that were nearly black—neatly groomed, but with a sort of careless ease, as if he had woken up that morning looking just as he did in that moment. A lock of it, a shining dark wave, kissed his brow, and I was caught up in the senseless urge to run my fingers through it and test its softness. His face had a sort of delicacy to it, with fine cheekbones, a clean defined jaw, and a mouth that turned up slightly at the corners, practically begging to be kissed. Beneath a serious, striking brow were eyes dark as black coffee and tinged with a quiet, patient sort of sadness that seemed to me a remnant of his family's misfortune. Broad shoulders, a slim waist, a brocaded black vest beneath a long red velvet coat. He was slender, but there was nevertheless a power to him, a solid, steady presence that hinted at quiet strength.

I called upon all my restraint to keep from leaning into his body and feeling that strength for myself.

"Lady Gemma," said Talan, his voice soft and rich as a spill of honey, lilting with a slight Vauzanian accent. He bowed, then offered me a bashful smile that brought a sparkling warmth to those sad eyes. "It is truly a pleasure. Everyone I've met here in Gallinor speaks so highly of you."

I tried not to imagine how foolish I no doubt looked, gaping up at him with naked admiration, and quickly schooled my features into a coquettish smile. No beautiful foreigner with a tragic past would best me at my own game.

"Flattery will not get you far with me, I'm afraid," I said, offering him my hand. "But dancing might, if you can keep up."

His eyebrows lifted. How charmingly flummoxed he looked. "But Lady Gemma, I thought there were several others before me on your dance card. I wouldn't want to offend—"

"This is my party, Mr. d'Astier. I can dance with whomever I please whenever it pleases me."

With a small smile and a nervous little glance around the crowded ballroom, he took gentle hold of my hand. "Well, then, I would be honored to dance with you as often as you desire it. And please, call me Talan."

"Actually, I don't think I will. Not yet." I flashed him a grin, and as we moved onto the dance floor, I looked back over my shoulder at Father—but he was no longer watching us, already engaged in conversation with a group of uniformed officers from the Upper Army.

I set my jaw, pushing back against the rising familiar feeling of sick disappointment. No matter. Whether or not Father cared to notice, I would do my duty.

The octet was playing a rather languorous little waltz I

recognized, one of the more popular recent pieces written by the high queen's court composers. Hoping to catch Talan off guard and reassert my authority, I spun him without warning into the tight swirl of dancers, ignoring the twinge of pain at the small of my back. The magic I'd felt all night was most powerful on the dance floor, concentrated into a small space and whipped into hot, sweaty eagerness by dozens of twirling bodies. I gritted my teeth against the prickling sensation that swept over me. The feeling made me imagine a hundred tiny claws carving little crescent moons out of my flesh. I took desperate comfort in the knowledge that this sad-eyed man was no doubt terrified of me.

However, much to my dismay, Talan slipped gracefully into the rhythm of the dance without pause, his hand firm on my waist.

"Is it not customary to wait until the beginning of the next song to start dancing," he said somewhere above my head, "so as not to disturb the other dancers and throw them off their steps?"

"Mr. d'Astier," I returned cheerfully, "I must say I find it odd that you would attend a party in a foreign land and proceed to educate the hostess on her own customs."

I looked up at him—he quite towered over me, a tall lean figure, striking in his whirling red coat. But even so, he looked abashed, his eyes huge with mortification.

"Forgive me, Lady Gemma," he murmured, ducking his head a little, which allowed a few soft waves to fall forward and kiss his brow in a frustratingly appealing fashion. "I did not mean to offend. It has been…difficult to find my footing since I arrived on your continent. I am not used to gatherings such as these."

"Parties, you mean?"

He nodded. "With all their rules, the unsaid protocols that must be obeyed lest you find yourself shunned by the very people you wish to impress." He gave me a rueful smile that warmed my cheeks. "I fear I've never been very good at understanding such things. I've no instinct for it. My parents didn't either."

"That surprises me, Mr. d'Astier," I said coolly, hoping to catch him in a lie. "For someone who claims to be ignorant of such things, you seem to know your way quite well around a dance floor, and a conversation."

"Sure feet and a keen wit are quite different from understanding the intricacies of high society."

A fair point I could not argue with. I pivoted quickly. "Father tells me you intend to restore your family's reputation with the High Queen Yvaine by insinuating yourself into our good graces."

Talan stumbled a little, and I swallowed a smug smile as I corrected our misstep, steering us back on course. A few more triumphs like that, and I would entirely forget the pain blooming throughout my body.

"You are quite direct, Lady Gemma," he said after a pause. Then he laughed shyly, a low, soft sound that was altogether too enticing for my comfort. "I find myself uncertain what to say."

"The truth would be my preference."

He cleared his throat, his cheeks attractively flushed. "Well, then I must admit that what you say is true. Everyone I've spoken to says your family is a favorite of the queen."

"Mostly it's Farrin who's her favorite," I confessed. "The rest of us are beloved by association and because, well, the queen has always liked the Ashbournes. It's simply the way things are done."

"Lady Farrin is your eldest sister? The musician?"

"Yes, though she hardly plays anymore, which, as you might imagine, horrifies our peers. An Anointed savant ignoring the high magic gifted to her ancestors by Kerezen herself? If she weren't such a dear friend of the queen, I'm not sure she could get away with it."

"I've heard there was a recital she gave as a child that caused something of a riot."

"You did your research, didn't you? It was less of a riot and more of...an expression of spiritual ecstasy, shall we say." I laughed breezily to shake off some of the delicious but distracting delight I felt at being the object of this beautiful man's earnest dark gaze. "Anyway, Farrin's too busy managing the estate now, and I think she's glad of it, really. She didn't know what to do with all the acclaim, the scores of admirers. Seeing to our tenants' needs, managing the staff, keeping all the accounts straight—she's far more comfortable doing that than she was on a stage before hundreds of people."

"Is she more comfortable," Talan mused quietly, "or does she simply feel safer?"

I drew back a little, surprised. It was a topic I often discussed with Farrin's dearest friend Gareth when we got it into our heads to encourage my sister back to her music, but it was certainly not something I ever discussed with anyone else in the world.

Talan winced delicately. "I should not have said that. Forgive me. It's only that I know quite well how easy it is to convince yourself that you are fine and comfortable in the life you lead when in fact you are desperately unhappy, and remain where you are only because doing otherwise feels too frightening to imagine."

I considered him in stony silence until he looked away, embarrassed, and bit his delectable lower lip. Satisfied that I had regained the upper hand, I said smoothly, "Well, Talan d'Astier of Vauzanne, you're bold, perhaps even brazen, but you're not wrong. Maybe after our dance, you and Farrin can exchange sad stories by the fire."

Talan laughed, then shook his head a little and cleared his throat. "Well, now that I've made a thorough fool of myself, perhaps I can attempt to right our conversation. You spoke of Farrin managing the estate, the accounts, the tenants. I'm curious, are those not your father's duties?"

"They were once," I answered, "but these days Father is far too busy planning the downfall of the Basks to bother with mundane things like bookkeeping."

The words spilled out of me before I could stop them. Cursing Talan for so disarmingly unbalancing me, and the wine for loosening my tongue, I nevertheless glanced longingly at a tray of fresh glasses as we glided past them.

"The Basks?" A slight pause, then Talan clicked his tongue. "Ah, yes. That northern family who vanished, yes? And only recently reappeared?"

"Mmm, it wasn't that they *vanished*," I corrected him, "but rather that they were *trapped*."

"Trapped? By what?"

I looked up at him in surprise, but there was no guile on his face, only pure, adorable puzzlement. "You mean to tell me that you've been on this continent for more than an hour and haven't heard the story?"

He shook his head in apology. "Should I have?"

Suddenly I realized that we had come to a stop in the middle of the ballroom, earning curious glances from the dancers whirling by. Irritated with myself for too many reasons to count, I pushed Talan rather forcefully back into our waltz.

"The story of the Basks has been the talk of the continent for the past year," I explained, "much to my father's dismay. It's no wonder he invited you to stay for the weekend. He's desperate for the company of someone who isn't enraptured by the tale of the poor piteous Bask family." I leaned closer to Talan, relishing the heat of his tall, lean body so near the heat of my own much smaller one. "They were trapped by a curse, you see, their estate hidden from the world for years by an impenetrable forest."

Trapped indeed. A thought arose unbidden: what it might feel like to be trapped between a wall and Talan's body, tugging on his vest as his thigh wedged itself between my legs and I claimed his lips with my own.

I shook myself, nearly stumbling over my own feet. That wine's potency was not to be underestimated.

Oblivious Talan's gorgeous dark eyes widened. "Trapped? The whole family? Who would do such a thing to them?"

I giggled, shaky with nerves. Even drunk as I was, a distant part of me understood that I was treading on dangerous ground. That our family and the Bask family had long been enemies was common knowledge, but very few people knew the true extent of it, not even me.

"*We* would do such a thing," I answered. "We Ashbournes. There was a fire, you see, some years ago, when my sisters and I were younger. It burned down much of Ivyhill. None of our wards could stop it. Even our head groundskeeper, a formidable elemental, was helpless against it. We had to rebuild almost everything. Mother had to regrow all her ivy from seedlings."

"A fire that could overpower the wards of an Anointed family?" Talan was rapt, my story holding him in thrall just as the wine held me. "I wouldn't think such a thing was possible."

"Normally it wouldn't be. But the Basks are special, and so are we. You see…"

I trailed off, looking around to ensure no one could hear us, and discovered that Talan and I were no longer dancing at all. Somehow, we had wandered to one of the curtained alcoves on the ballroom's perimeter, huddled close together like lovers sharing secrets.

Incensed, I tried to push him away, but the effort nearly sent me crashing to the floor. Talan caught me and helped me settle on the alcove's cushioned bench. I looked around, fogged with confusion, all my artifice stripped away.

"Would you be so kind as to remind me how we got here?" I mumbled, gripping the cushion's velvet piping to remain upright.

Talan looked deeply embarrassed for me. "Well, you rather veered off from the dance floor and stumbled over here. Shall I bring you some water? Or perhaps a cool cloth for your head?"

"Or perhaps," I said slowly, pressing one finger into his chest, "another glass of wine."

He made a doubtful sound, his brow furrowed with earnest worry that melted my heart. "I don't think that would be wise. In fact, perhaps I should find someone on your staff to help you upstairs to your rooms?"

"Before I finish my story?" I said, indignant. "I think not, sir! You must listen and listen hard, for it's important, and you need to know, if you're going to be here at Ivyhill. Father doesn't invite visitors without an agenda. He'll want to use you somehow in one of his little schemes. His business ventures, whatever he's told you about your family's wine stores, that's only the surface of things. So, you see, you need to listen. You need to *understand*."

"All right," said Talan with admirable patience. "What do I need to understand?"

"The Basks and the Ashbournes, we're special," I repeated. "You'll hear all kinds of stories explaining why. Farrin and Father won't tell me the *real* truth—they're probably afraid I'd spill it to someone like you, which I can't say I blame them for—but here's the most popular story people like to tell. It's absurd, and something of a legend in this country. It's part of why people like us. We're *mysterious*."

I waggled my fingers at Talan, then leaned close and whispered, "There's a demon, you see. A demon who's promised us eternal power and life and unending favor with Queen Yvaine if only we destroy the Basks, whether that's quite literally, or spiritually, or simply by tarnishing their good name so thoroughly that they can't come back from it. And we can't stop fighting each other, not ever, or else the demon will wreak unthinkable havoc upon us and everyone we've ever known. So they say. The details vary depending on who's telling the story, as happens with all good legends. The Man with the Three-Eyed Crown—that's the demon's name, so they say, or at least one of them. His true name, of course, being a creature from the Old Country as he is, can't be uttered by a human tongue. So Farrin's best friend, Gareth, tells me. He's a student of the arcana—an Anointed sage, a librarian with a mind like a trap. He teaches at the university in the capital."

It was as if some spellcrafter had enchanted me, tugging each word out of me on a knotted string I simply had to expel from my body. I could not stop telling the story, and I did not want to. It felt *good* to say it aloud, the whole ridiculous tale. I even found it rather funny, sitting there in the curtained shadows with Talan staring at me, aghast, though nothing about my family's situation had ever seemed funny to me before that night.

"And the demon, he offered the same prize to the Basks," I continued breathlessly, "which is why they burned down Ivyhill when I was seven years old. That did actually happen," I added, gratified by Talan's horrified expression. "That fire nearly killed Farrin because she got stuck inside the house. And then, as revenge, Mother and Father commissioned a beguiler to set a curse on Ravenswood—that's the Basks' ancestral home—and their curse wrapped Ravenswood in a forest no one could pass through. No one could get in, no one could get out. For *years*. Twelve years, in fact. And we all thought that was the end of it. We'd won. And Farrin was happy, and Father was happy—well, as happy as people can be when their mother and wife has run off, for Mother left us not long after Mara was taken to the Mist."

Mother. Mara. Mist. As the words left my mouth, none of them sounded quite real. I giggled, swooned a little, then braced myself against the bench. Talan's strong warm hands helped me remain upright—one hand at my waist, the other gentle around my left wrist. His touch was tender, deferent. The sensation made me ache.

"But even powerful curses can only hold for so long," I continued, "and when this one fell, the forest shriveling up like dead crops, the Basks were alive and well, not starved or gone mad, not in the slightest. They were resplendent, even, hale in that hardy northern way. The garments they'd made for themselves while shut away were so absurdly out of fashion that they seemed to everyone quite daring and sophisticated indeed. It was as though the curse had never existed, for all that it had hurt the Basks in the eyes of Gallinor. And so the war goes on. A war started by a *demon*, if you believe the legend, which I absolutely do not. Demons and promises of eternal life—absolute nonsense. No, this war was started by stupid prideful men ages ago, and it lives on thanks to their stupid prideful descendants who can't bear to do the sensible thing and call a truce. Anyway, the Basks returned a little over a year ago, and Father's been a right bastard ever since. And that's the most important thing to remember from all this: Gideon Ashbourne's a bastard, and I wish I could bring myself to hate him."

I sagged back against the wall, utterly spent, and looked at Talan with a dumb, soppy grin on my face.

But Talan looked changed, his expression gone rigid with something too dark for me to name. Hatred, perhaps, or fear. A desolation so complete that for a moment I was stunned out of my buzzing, wine-soaked stupor.

"What is it?" I asked, the words slightly slurred.

"Do you know the story of my family's disgrace?"

His voice was deadly soft, fraught with emotion. A quiet chill raced down my spine.

"Father said you fell out of the queen's favor," I managed to say. "You were Anointed by Jaetris, and you rejected your ancestral magic, choosing instead to cultivate vineyards."

He laughed bitterly, looking away. "No, there was no *choosing*. My parents were forced to do what they did—compelled, coerced—all the while knowing in the back of their minds that it would doom them, undo everything their ancestors had built, and insult both the high queen and the gods." Another dark laugh, soft and full of wonder. "How strange, how utterly fitting, that both our families have been ruined by a demon's touch. Yours has trapped your family in an endless, senseless, violent feud. Mine wormed into my parents' minds, changed them, seduced them, tormented them, deluded them. And by the time she grew bored of watching us destroy ourselves and left to hunt some other family, the damage was done. We were finished. My mother withered away. My father killed himself. Our estate fell into ruin. The d'Astier name was like poison. No one wanted to acknowledge that we'd ever existed."

His voice broke, and I touched his arm gently. "Talan..."

He turned to me, grasped my hands, and brought them to his lips. He pressed a fierce kiss against my fingers, his eyes shut tight as if in agony. Unsettled and bewildered as I was, shaken by the grim hopelessness of his story, I could not look away from him. In fact, I suddenly longed to hold him, to cradle his dark head against me, and barely restrained myself from doing so.

"We can help each other, Gemma," he whispered, his voice like silk against my skin. "I have to believe we can help each other."

Then he looked up, and our eyes locked, and a warm liquid feeling spilled through my body—an anchored feeling, as if I stood with my feet firm on the summer-warmed ground, all the great heat of the world pressing up against my toes. It was a feeling of absolute rightness, and it terrified me, for it came without warning and seemed to have a will of its own.

"How can we do that?" I whispered. Beyond the shadowed world of our alcove, the octet began a new waltz—merry and quick, breathless.

"I have spent the long years since my father's death learning all I could of demons," Talan said. "I have been taught by scholars of the arcana, like your sister's friend Gareth, and I have collected countless stories of others who have been preyed upon by these foul creatures.

"If you help me restore my family's name and honor," he said very low, his eyes fixed on me, his breath hot and wine-sweet on my mouth, "I will help you hunt your family's demon, and I will not rest until he is destroyed and you and yours are free. I could not save my own family. But maybe if we work together, I can save yours."

I stared at him, my heart pounding so hard I could feel it in my cheeks. The story of his family's ruin had unearthed too many unwelcome memories of my own—Farrin covered with ash and barely breathing, my mother's wail of grief the day the Warden took Mara. The first time my father warned me against embracing him or Farrin, for if they were tired or ill or distracted, their magic might lash out and hurt me. And if it someday became impossible for me to be near my own family, what would I do? Where would I go? It was best, Father had said, to exercise caution.

My thoughts began to race, and my stomach dropped as I felt the familiar, ferocious downward spin take hold of me. The panic was coming. The shock of this conversation, the pain of my magic-battered body, and Talan's own distress combined to flay me, leaving me vulnerable, like a soldier with all her armor stripped away. I felt helpless before it, too drunk and ragged to face it, too weak in body and mind to fight it.

"But the legend of our family's demon is just that—a legend," I said weakly. I was beginning to regret saying anything. I was beginning to regret taking Talan's hand, drinking that wine, even dreaming up the party in the first place. "It's a story people made up to turn a boring, stupid feud between rich families into something more interesting, something to gossip about. There hasn't been a demon in Gallinor since the Unmaking."

Talan shook his head. "And yet one was on my continent, in Vauzanne, and was the ruin of my family. Not even the gods in all their glory were perfect, and with a sister serving at the Middlemist, you should know better than most that no seal between worlds is impenetrable."

The memory stabbed me, quick but lethal—Mara's transformation, the shrieks of whatever monsters she was duty bound to fight. The silver fog of the Mist slithering all around me.

"In every legend," Talan said quietly, urgently, pulling me back to him, "there is a kernel of truth, and when the word *demon* is uttered, you cannot be too careful. If one of those creatures is indeed behind the conflict between your families, there may be something even deeper and darker at work. I can help you find out. I can help you hunt him—a fair exchange for your good word with the high queen on my behalf. Even more than that, though,

Gemma, it would be a chance for me to kill your demon as I was never able to kill my own."

He laughed in disbelief, scrubbed a beautiful white hand through his hair. "The gods work in unknowable ways indeed. That my path has brought me here, to this night, and to you…"

I stood and moved away from him too quickly, my knees wobbling. My head spun, and I leaned hard against the wall to steady myself. Whatever comfort the wine had brought to my aching body was beginning to fade, and quickly, as if Talan's words had fallen upon me like fists. The frenzied magic in the ballroom swarmed and swirled just beyond my reach, crowding closer with each unsteady breath I drew.

Talan was there at once, a strong arm around my waist and his other hand smoothing back the damp hair from my cheek. I was sweating and shivering as if seized in the grip of a fever.

"Gemma, what is it?" His voice came from somewhere distant, tense with concern. "Are you ill? I'll fetch one of your staff. Just wait here a moment, try to breathe slowly."

I grabbed his arm to keep him near me, shook my head, struggled to catch my breath. "I'm fine," I said faintly, my tongue fat and slow. "Too much wine. My body doesn't like rooms like this, so full of people and their shimmer."

He said something else, something I couldn't hear for the pulsing roar in my head—the pain of my body and the panic of my mind joining in terrible chorus—but I dug deep for whatever shreds of strength I could find, and gripped his arm hard, and looked up at him.

"Meet me tomorrow at midday," I said quickly. "Near the hothouses by the footbridge, there's a fountain, a statue of Kerezen, and beside it an old oak. We'll speak further then. I can't…" I gritted my teeth and looked away so he wouldn't see how utterly the sudden revolt of my body devastated me. "Please leave me. Find a servant, have them send for Jessyl. My lady's maid. She'll come for me."

I turned away from him, pressed my burning cheek against the heavy velvet curtain. I felt movement, and then the bench beneath me, and the floor throbbing under my feet, or perhaps my feet were the throbbing things, all the bones inside them at war with one another. Something soft brushed against my damp forehead. Then Talan's fingers sweetly pressed mine, and then he hurried past me and was gone, and so was I.

CHAPTER 5

I awoke to the familiar smells of lavender and bergamot and knew at once, before I had quite recovered my other senses, that I was safe.

I shifted in the softness around me, realizing slowly that I was in my room, in my bed, nestled among fat floral-print pillows and the twin quilts I had slept with since I was a child—one of soft gold, cornflower blue, and pale rose, the other a green patchwork of embroidered ivy scattered with tiny white blooms. Both had been made by my mother long ago, during the months when I was still inside her and she was confined to her bed. It had been a difficult pregnancy and an even more difficult birth.

My eyes burned at the thought, and I groped through the dim candlelight with aching arms.

"Jessyl?" I croaked, my throat raw and sick-tasting. A horrible fear came over me that this was a dream, some trick of my mind, and that in fact I had died there in that curtained alcove, eaten alive by my endless frightened thoughts while Talan futilely went to find help.

"Here I am, Lady Gemma, I'm right here, it's all right," came the familiar voice of my lady's maid, followed by the comforting rustle of her prim skirt. I cried with relief to see her familiar freckled face and auburn hair, the stern little frown she always wore when focused on her work. She was Farrin's age, only four years older than me, brisk in manner but tender in heart, and the most competent person I knew.

She hurried over, holding a tray of tea and toast. "I'm terribly sorry, my lady. I thought you were fast asleep, and I went to gather a few things—your oils, a comb, a novel for when you're feeling up to it."

She sat in the chair beside my bed, retrieved a damp cloth from my night table, and patted my temples and brow. Her own brow was knotted, her lips pursed grimly. I clung to her arm even as she worked, desperate with gratitude that she was there, that I was safe in my room, that no words were needed between us to explain what had happened to me, and that neither Father nor Farrin would find out any of it. Jessyl was a master of discretion; caring for me had necessitated cultivation of that particular skill. No doubt my father and sister were still down at the party, ignorant of what had happened—one making the rounds, the other brooding in the shadows and scowling at Ryder Bask.

"Didn't I urge you not to drink tonight?" said Jessyl, gently enough that the admonishment didn't feel like one. "With so many people around, and you having worked yourself nearly to death since that day to get everything ready?"

That day. The day I saw Mara transform; the day I ran away from Father's fury to the safety of Illaria's arms and decided I must throw a party.

"You did," I admitted, "for you are wise and good from head to toe, and I do not deserve you."

Jessyl gave me a cheeky little smile. "Too right you are, my lady."

"Is everyone still here?"

"Oh, yes. Four in the morning, and the house still full of dancing and drinking and guests sneaking off to the upper floors to do gods know what. Poor Gilroy is quite beside himself."

I laughed faintly at the thought of our long-suffering head butler trying in vain to keep a house of hundreds in order. "We shall have to give him a nice long holiday after this."

"I think that is a must, my lady, or else he might very well revolt."

Jessyl rose and began bustling about the room, tidying and lighting fresh candles, all while providing me an account of how the staff had fared throughout the night. Lilianne, one of our newer maids, had been caught kissing young Lady Porsha in the scullery, for which our housekeeper, Mrs. Seffwyck, would have fired her had it not been for Jessyl's intervention. Ellys and Bradeny, two of the underbutlers, had dropped a giant tray of bacon-wrapped dates plated meticulously on swirling beds of mint and thyme, which had sent our head cook, Mrs. Rathmont, into a howling frenzy.

I watched Jessyl work and let the comforting wry lilt of her voice wash over me. Soon my burning eyes fell shut and tears slipped down my cheeks, but Jessyl let them fall without remark. She knew how utterly it tired me—the attacks of panic that came over me, the constant mutiny of my body—and she knew that speaking of it only tired me further. Not that this would stop her from bluntly rebuking me for my recklessness once I'd adequately recovered.

But until then she would spare me. Instead she simply worked and gossiped, her voice lulling me. At one point, I thought I heard her say Talan's name and tried to ask her how he was, what he had thought of my collapse, if she would send him a message of thanks on my behalf. But exhaustion claimed me before I could do so, and I drifted off to sleep with his name on my lips.

—◆—

It was near dawn when I next woke. A soft gray light peeked in through the lace curtains, for Jessyl had tied back the heavier embroidered drapes with thick velvet ribbons. She knew how I adored mornings.

I sat up, taking stock of the room. Jessyl was sleeping in her favorite chair near the hearth, her feet propped up on a stool and an open book lying facedown on her belly. The candles had all burned out save the one on my night table, a mere flickering stub.

Something was different. Something had changed as I slept those last hours, though I couldn't say what. I noticed the feeling immediately, the skin on the back of my neck prickling as though I were being watched—but the sensation did not frighten me. It awakened me. I felt sharp and supple all over, like a coiled beast ready to pounce.

I remained in my nest of pillows for a moment, examining the feeling, considering my body and the quiet air around it. Carefully I flexed my arms and legs, turned my wrists around and around to stretch out their usual stiffness—but there *was* no stiffness, no ache or pop. I felt only a fierce pit of hunger in my belly and a brimming restlessness that made me want to shout the whole house awake. I trapped the sound in my throat, slowly swung my legs over the side of the bed, and then stood, hardly breathing. Too sudden a movement might burst the spell of what was surely a dream, for never could I recall feeling so strong, so vigorous. The constant scream of pain in my body was a distant echo, easily ignored. My thoughts were quiet, free of cruelty. I felt only need and eagerness, a desire to *move*.

I padded softly through my rooms—bedroom, sitting room, receiving room, small tidy atrium bursting with greenery. I peeked around every corner without fear, calmly searched my closet, quietly pulled aside every curtain. But there was no intruder in my rooms, no lurking villain.

And yet I knew Jessyl and I were not alone. Another presence was very near, as if I could reach out and touch it with ease, though there was nothing to touch. For a moment I wondered if something from the Old Country had found its way here to watch me as I slept, but I dismissed the thought immediately. A battalion of wards protected Ivyhill from invasion; nothing had penetrated that boundary since the fire all those years past. And the Basks weren't stupid; surely they wouldn't dare risk their new popularity by staging some act of outright villainy, not at a lively party full of happy guests.

And yet...

I entered my bathing room, the white tiles like a sheet of ice under my feet. I lit a fresh candle and sat at my dressing table, placed my hands flat on the polished wood, and examined the trays of creams, jewelry, and hairpins that glittered before me, a sea of finery. I saw, but I did not see. I was there, and yet I was not. The presence I felt was tugging me somewhere, and though I hadn't yet followed it, I wanted to desperately. I knew it would take me somewhere radiant. Somewhere fresh and luminous, a place of pine and earth and dew. A black sky spangled with a million stars, purple blooms pulsing with light. I had only to look up, and there I would be, in that faraway world of unrivaled beauty. I had only to look up, and I would have everything I wanted.

I looked up.

Staring back at me was my own reflection, surrounded by my mirror's ornate gilded frame. My blue eyes—my mother's eyes—shone in the dim candlelight as I beheld myself. Lightly I touched my cheeks, my chin, the downy silk of the fine hair at my temples. I looked down, hungry for the sight of my pale collarbones, laid bare by the wide neck of my nightgown, and the swell of my breasts beneath the sheer white fabric, and the slim lines of my torso.

"Beautiful," I whispered, for I was, and I traced the lines of my body with trembling hands because I knew that as beautiful as I was, I could be even more so. I could be ravishing. I could have the entire world of Edyn at my feet, and every one of my fellow humans, whether blessed or overlooked by the gods, would beg for a simple touch, a mere glance.

If only I had the courage to try.

As I imagined it, my heart raced. A slight heat tingled at my fingertips; a tightness in my belly tugged me closer to the mirror. All I needed to do was craft a single small glamour—perhaps a bit more of a pout to my full lower lip, or a slightly longer neck to evoke the image of the dancer savants who performed ballets in Fairhaven, the queen's city. I wouldn't require more than a slight nudge in the right direction in order to truly shine.

I had read about the art of glamouring for years. The memoirs of the most famous magical stylists throughout Edyn's history were the only books for which I would ever set aside my beloved novels. And whenever I sat through an appointment with Kerrish—my own Anointed stylist, one of the most prestigious in the country; Father would have settled for nothing less—I peppered her with a thousand questions and requested that she try all the latest spells on me. Change my eye color, thread my hair with silver and gold, tint my skin with a pale blue shimmer. She never gave in to my demands. Father was the one to pay her fees, after all, and he forbade such things. Anything Kerrish did to me was done with brush and powder and needle and thread—divine in design but not in substance.

Nevertheless, I always asked my questions, and I watched her every movement with the eyes of a hawk. I begged her for descriptions of the glamours she crafted for her other clients, and when she occasionally relented and indulged me, I devoured every word, ravenous for magic I would never see.

It was past time for me to put all my years of fervent study to the test, and with my body so sure and steady, I had never felt more capable of it. There must have been *some* scrap of magic in me, even if only a scrap, buried deep. I was an Ashbourne, chosen by the goddess Kerezen. Everyone else in my Anointed family had been blessed with the gift of her power. Father and Mara had the nimble warrior strength of sentinels; Farrin had her devastating crystalline voice and deft pianist fingers that made even the queen's court musicians weep with envy. I had long hungered to join their ranks, but this morning my hunger felt ravenous, irresistible.

Closing my eyes, I took a long, slow breath. Some used words to work their magic, but I found that inelegant, even vulgar. Kerrish had told me long ago that she worked in silence, and I decided I would do the same. The trick, I'd read, was to imagine what I wanted to create—not just a fleeting vision, but something specific, intentional, and small. A broad picture of my desires would result only in chaos. I needed to think through every color, every singular stroke of my mind's brush.

I lifted my hands, imagined dipping my fingers in thick pools of color—aquamarine, violet, sunny gold—and then drew them through my hair. That one movement cracked me open, like the surface of a frozen lake that had finally warmed enough to shatter.

I worked quickly, a series of images I hardly understood running through my mind, as if someone had grabbed hold of me and was steering me down a rushing waterfall. The world was blurred by the roaring water, but I could still see vague shapes, strange and warped beyond the foam—my jawline sharpening; my unimpressive muscles growing lithe and taut.

When at last I opened my eyes, my reflection knocked the wind out of me.

I was still myself, yes, but I was also different, *more*. My hair was a shimmering cascade, luminescent strands of amber, lilac, and turquoise shining among my ordinary fair curls. My cheekbones were sharp as knives; when I blinked, my eyes flashed from blue to gold in the candlelight; and my alabaster skin shimmered, an undulating luminescence. I was fearsome, magnificent, as if some otherworldly creature had slipped under my skin and my body had changed to accommodate her.

Gingerly I touched my face. My fingertips tingled from the work I had done, and I truly began to realize what had happened— that somehow, though I had never before felt even a twinge of magic within me, I had accomplished a glamour of which even Kerrish would approve. I laughed, breathless and afraid. I should have been *more* afraid, but my beauty had left me too awestruck to feel much else.

I traced the delicate line of my jaw. This transcended the work of a mere stylist. This was something closer to legend, to the work artificers of the Old Country could do, according to the tales. Theirs were not glamours that faded with time. They were true changes to the body—permanent, reversible only by the magic's original worker. Bones broken and reshaped; innards poisoned by disease discarded and fresh ones fashioned from the dregs. An artificer's work was not about healing what was hurt, nor was it a craft of mere disguise; it was, the stories said, about true transformation. An alchemy of flesh, blood, and meat.

A noise behind me caught my attention, and I turned on my stool to see Jessyl standing at the door, her face slack with mesmerized wonder, her cheeks flushed.

"My lady?" she breathed, and then she rushed toward me, too quickly for me to move or even utter her name. She pulled me from my seat and pressed me against the wall, her hands gripping my face as she frantically surveyed my appearance, and then she sobbed once and kissed me.

At first I was too shocked to do anything but submit to her fevered kisses. But then she began fumbling with the buttons of my nightgown, and the ecstasy that had come over me as I crafted my glamour vanished at once. I heard Jessyl's sobs at my neck and pushed her away long enough to see the terror in her eyes, the tears streaking her cheeks.

Something was very wrong. Whoever this was—*what*ever this was—it was not my Jessyl.

A horrible cold flooded my body, and in its wake all my old hurts began to return. I caught sight of myself in the mirror; the new colors in my hair remained, as did the new shape of my face and my flashing eyes, but already I could see the glamour beginning to fade, as if it and my illness could not exist at the same time.

Jessyl gasped out my name—a bewildered, breathless plea—before pulling me hard into her arms. The terrified look on her face shocked me into strength. Saying a silent prayer to the gods that Jessyl would forgive me, I shoved her away hard, then grabbed a heavy vase from my dressing table, flung the water and flowers to the floor, and brought the vase slamming down onto her shoulder.

Jessyl collapsed with a groan and fell to the rug, still as death. I dropped the vase. My knees gave out, and I sank to the floor. I crawled to her, gently lifted her head into my lap. A few long moments passed, during which I swear to the gods I did not breathe, I did not exist, and then Jessyl's hazel eyes fluttered open. I laughed and kissed her brow over and over, for it was her own true self looking back at me. Whatever had seized her was gone, and I realized as I glanced across the room, where an enormous mirror leaned against the wall, that whatever had seized *me*—the glamour I had made—had also vanished. My hair was an ordinary human gold, my eyes blue. The formidable sharp lines of my face were once again round and youthful.

I pressed my lips tight to hold back a sob of fear and frustration. I wanted it back, that secret thing I had made for myself— how exquisite I had been, ferocious and vital, lit up as if kissed all over by the sun and stars. And yet I sensed that if I tried it again, it could undo me as it had nearly undone Jessyl. No glamour I had ever seen had affected someone nearby in such a way, turning them mad with desire. Perhaps an artificer in the Old Country could do such things, but that was only a supposition and not something I had ever heard of happening in Edyn.

I resolved to shut away the incident in a drawer deep inside my mind, to never think of it or touch it again.

A lie, and I knew it even then. But I tried with everything in me to believe it.

"What happened, my lady?" Jessyl whispered, groaning as she tried to sit up. "Did I fall?" Then she noticed my torn sleeping gown, and her eyes widened. "Lady Gemma! Are you hurt?"

A quiet horror closed my throat. She remembered nothing, and yet my lips still stung from the force of her wild kisses.

My voice trembled when I answered her. "There was a brawl," I said. "Some drunken fools wandered upstairs from the party, and we tried to stop them from killing each other, but they knocked us both out."

Jessyl tried again to sit up, her face going hard with fury, but I hushed her at once. "Don't worry, my dear," I said gently. "I'm quite well, and Father has seen to everything. Those brutes won't step foot in Ivyhill ever again. Now let me take care of you for once."

As I helped Jessyl back to her chair, crooning soothing words I hardly remembered forming, I fought to keep from glancing over my shoulder at the mirror above my dressing table. Its presence pulled at the aching hot place between my shoulder blades, as if my flashing glamoured eyes were buried in that pane of glass, watching me walk away.

CHAPTER 6

O nly a few hours later, at midday, I hid behind one of our hothouses and peered around the corner to spy upon Talan d'Astier.

He waited near Kerezen's fountain just as I'd instructed, hands clasped behind his back, looking up at the statue of the goddess: a woman draped in queenly robes, her long hair flowing down to her knees. In her hand she held a horn, out of which water trickled merrily. She had no face, for it was considered blasphemous to attempt to capture the gods' true splendor in any form of art—but even without eyes, nose, or mouth, she was exquisite.

I pressed my fingertips against the hothouse's smooth glass wall, searching for courage. I tried not to think about the awful night I had just endured—Jessyl's frantic kisses, the sight of my radiant altered visage in the mirror—and instead focus on the long, lean lines of Talan's body. Emotional distress be damned; I could not in good conscience ignore such beauty.

That morning he wore a light gray vest over a soft white tunic and snug trousers embellished with a faint swirling pattern. He had rolled up his sleeves to his elbows and held his jacket over his shoulder with a masculine, insouciant air that did unspeakable things to my insides. And as for his lustrous dark hair, ruffling prettily in the breeze, I thought even Kerezen herself would have approved.

He wandered around the fountain, then found a spot under the nearby oak, the heavy branches of which touched the ground. He smiled up at the ancient thing and patted its broad trunk in appreciation, an oddly endearing gesture that softened the hard knots of tension in my shoulders.

I could do this. I could shed the night's horrid memories and be only myself: Lady Gemma Ashbourne, who feared no guest of her father's, no matter how unnervingly gorgeous he might be, no matter what sad stories he had to tell.

Lifting my chin, I smiled and strode across the lawn to greet Talan. He saw me coming and ducked out from under the oak, shrugging on his jacket. Then he squinted up at the bright midday sky, removed the jacket, and retrieved from its perch atop the fountain's low wall an ebony walking stick capped with a topaz stone. Juggling the jacket and stick awkwardly, a nervous little smile on his face, he looked like a dashing but harried university student on his first day of classes.

It was not, I must acknowledge, a bad look.

"Lady Gemma," he said, with something of an ungainly bow.

I swallowed my teasing comments. "Mr. d'Astier, thank you for meeting with me. I'm certain the night's festivities have left you wishing you were still abed."

"On the contrary, Lady Gemma, I could hardly sleep, I was so eager to see you and assure myself that you were well." He ducked his head a little, searching my face, then looked away and sheepishly ruffled his hair. "Forgive me for being so bold, so intrusive. I...Lady Gemma, I was so worried about you. When I found your lady's maid, she ushered you upstairs so quickly that I had no chance to say goodbye."

I waved him off, sauntering past to allow him a full view of my gown—pastel pink like a tender spring blossom, the sleeves spilling lace at my elbows, a snug bodice, a neckline designed to tantalize.

"Poor Mr. d'Astier." I looked back at him over my shoulder, gave an airy little laugh. "You needn't have troubled yourself on my account. I simply let your family's sparkling wine get the best of me. It's delicious, by the way, not to mention effective. Truly, my head is still a bit fuzzed from the bubbles."

Talan looked chagrined. "Though I wish I could set all our stores ablaze, they are unfortunately the only thing I have to offer as thanks to anyone who will receive me."

I began circling the fountain, wrapping my scattered thoughts around our conversation the night previous—demons and dead parents, the Bask family's forest prison.

"If you'll forgive me for my candor," Talan said, joining me, his voice grave, "you seemed far more distressed last night than any drunk person I've ever encountered."

"Ah, but you've never met me before, have you, Mr. d'Astier?" I turned to regard him, idly spinning my silk parasol. "Didn't my father tell you? I'm *sensitive*."

Talan frowned. "I'm afraid I don't understand."

"Magic makes me sick," I said bluntly. "It hurts me. Sometimes the agony is so overwhelming it knocks me unconscious."

Talan stared. "But you're an Ashbourne, an Anointed. Your ancestors were chosen by Kerezen—"

"Yes, and every Ashbourne since has been blessed with magic. But not me." I turned away, continuing my leisurely stroll. "Something went wrong. All the magic in my blood turned inside out and upside down, forgot how to be itself, perhaps. And now here we are—not a whit of power to be found, and in its place a bounty of ailments."

My throat tightened around the words. I swallowed hard.

Not a whit of power indeed. Unless the glamour I had crafted during the night had come from somewhere else—some*one* else—some kind of magic did in fact live in me after all. A terrifying kind.

I hoped for the former explanation. Much more frightening than the notion of some nighttime intruder pushing their magic on me was that of myself working magic all on my own, and not knowing how I'd done it, or if I'd be able to do it again—or, if I *did* manage it again, if the magic would overwhelm someone else as it had poor Jessyl.

"I am truly sorry, Lady Gemma," Talan said at last, his voice grave. "I didn't know you had this affliction. Living at Ivyhill must mean you are in constant discomfort."

Despite my determination to remain as sunny as the day itself, a dark laugh burst out of me. "Discomfort—yes, that's a word for it. Being here, though, is safer than anywhere else. Everyone—Father, Farrin, the staff—they restrain their magic around me whenever possible. An imperfect solution, but it's the best we can do."

I expected him to utter another apology, but instead there was silence. Turning, I found him staring at the fountain's gently rippling water as if deep in thought.

"Have I bored you, Mr. d'Astier?"

He looked up at me gravely. "Quite the contrary, Lady Gemma. In fact, I wonder…the demon you spoke of last night, the Man with the Three-Eyed Crown?"

My smile fell. I had hoped to broach the subject on my own terms. "As I told you, he belongs to a story dreamt up by a bored populace. Father and Farrin are only too happy to entertain their vulgar Olden obsessions. It keeps us at the forefront of people's minds."

"Very well," Talan conceded. "But *if* this demon exists—just humor me for a moment—could it be that part of his design on your family is your illness? It could be a curse he set upon you. One more way to hurt your parents and weaken them, make them vulnerable."

"My, you are a fanciful one. When I tell you that my parents brought every healer in the world to Ivyhill to treat me, I do not exaggerate. And not one of them found signs of a curse on me."

"But demons are cunning, the true reach of their power unknowable. And not even the most skilled healer or the most learned academic can understand everything of the Old Country. It isn't possible. It's too vast, too strange."

I turned away with a bored sigh, though I felt more than a little queasy. "You should meet my sister's friend, Gareth."

"The librarian?" Talan asked.

With a twinge, I recalled that I had told Talan about Gareth during my appalling verbal deluge the night before. "Indeed. He's visiting Ivyhill right now but normally travels between the university in Fairhaven, where he teaches, and his family's estate in Big Deep. Are you familiar with that canyon? Or have your studies of our continent not been as thorough as you'd like me to think?"

I blinked at him innocently, and he opened his mouth, then closed it again.

Refusing to be seduced by that charming little crease between his eyebrows, I turned away. "You and Gareth would get along splendidly, with all your talk of lore and legend."

"Lady Gemma—"

"The Old Country is real and dangerous; I'll agree with you

on that point. But at least on this continent, we have the Lower Army and the Upper, and the Order of the Rose, including my own sister, who could knock you on your ass if I asked her to."

"But *Gemma*—"

I rounded on him. "Why persist? What have you to gain from trying to convince me that my pain is due to some demon who's got his claws in me? I'm *ill*, Talan. I'm not cursed. And if that's distasteful to you, if it strips me of my allure, then I'll ask you to leave us at once and take all that dreadful wine with you."

Talan stepped back, looking thoroughly abashed. "You are far from distasteful to me, Lady Gemma. Quite the opposite. From the moment I first saw you across the ballroom last night, I was entranced."

I scoffed, but he kept on, spots of embarrassed color blooming on his cheeks. "Not just by your beauty, Gemma, but by the *light* of you. Your wit, the keen radiance in your eyes, the calculation beneath that dazzling smile. I wonder how many of your admirers see that fire in you."

Gaping at him, I felt the wind quite knocked out of me. That deep voice of his had gone a little hoarse, those impassioned eyes lit up as if with distant storms. No one in all of my days, during even my most diverting liaisons, had ever looked at me quite like that.

Despite my determination to remain unaffected by him, my body flushed all over with a slow, tingling heat.

"And now," Talan said, a little softer, "I think I understand that part of what I felt last night was the pull of fate woven by the ghosts of the gods."

He hesitated, then reached for me and held out his hand, his gaze hopeful as a pup's.

I did not wish to accept the invitation, and yet I did anyway, placing my hand softly in his own. A traitorous part of me hoped for another passionate speech about my eyes. But even more than that, I craved a kind touch from someone, a reassurance after everything that had transpired overnight. His words had shattered the defenses I'd tried so hard to reinforce over the past few hours.

I drew in a trembling breath. Talan's eyes were locked on mine with a singular focus that made my knees wobble—*my* knees, which were not new to this particular dance—and I realized that I did not crave a kind touch from just anyone. I craved it from *him*. Suddenly I felt that if I were to tell him everything that had happened, if I were to cry as I really wanted to and confess to him how frightened and entranced I had been by my changed reflection, how I had wanted to howl with grief when that feeling of eager strength had left me—he would neither judge nor ridicule me but would instead only listen and hold me until I steadied.

As if he knew the shape of my thoughts, Talan bent his head low, as he had done the night before, and softly pressed his mouth to my fingers. The kiss spilled over my skin in a soft rush of warmth. I marveled at how gently he touched me, how tenderly his hand held mine, and despite the fresh memory of Jessyl's mad-eyed assault, I did not flinch away. With the press of Talan's lips came an easy, luxurious calm, a blanket of serenity, one I was too glad of to question.

A pang of regret twisted in my chest when he straightened and let my hand fall.

"I do not wish to frighten you," he said, proclaiming it with the solemnity of a prayer. "But I do wish to work with you. An alliance, Lady Gemma, as I proposed last night."

"I help you restore your family name, and you help me hunt a demon that can't possibly exist," I said flatly, once I had regained the power of speech. "I hope you'll forgive me when I say that this seems an uneven bargain."

"I could sweeten it, if that would help sway you."

His voice lowered on the words, drawing a tiny shiver out of me. "How so?"

"Demon hunting is no small task. It will take time, patience, and effort. In the meantime, I can offer my services to your family, help you chip away at the Basks' popularity."

I smiled at him, genuinely surprised. "Why, Mr. d'Astier, how positively fiendish. What have the poor Basks ever done to you?" I waved off his protestation of the word *fiendish* and began walking away. "Besides, Father would never allow that. This little war is not for outsiders to fight. Surely you don't think you're the first social climber to offer us aid?"

Then I stopped dead in my tracks, my back to him, for the precise feeling of calm that had touched me when Talan had kissed my hand had suddenly returned, perfectly duplicated though we were several strides apart. I could not mistake it; the sensation of contentment rippled through me like a swell of soft summer rain. In the wake of it, I felt only utter peace. Sultry, sleepy, feline. I searched for the pain in my bones, the constant ache in my stomach, and instead found an easy warmth coaxing me to calm. When I tried to push away the feeling, it resisted.

And I knew all at once what that meant. Father had taught my sisters and me very well how to recognize such sensations.

I turned slowly, gratified even in my astonishment to see Talan's discomfiture written so plainly on his face. The feeling of calm retreated in an instant, and I nearly cried out with despair to feel it leave.

"Father told me your ancestors found a remnant of Jaetris's magic after the Unmaking," I said slowly.

He nodded. "God of the mind."

"Scholars. Librarians. Writers. Your family possesses *low* magic."

"I'm one of the few in my family lucky enough to possess a higher magic."

Such misalignments were not unheard of. In a low-magic family, magic powerful enough to masquerade as Anointed *could* emerge, though it was uncommon. Or in an Anointed family, some unfortunate soul might boast none of the impressive magic befitting his station and instead possess only a lowly one—a stylist whose fragile glamours lasted just long enough for the painting of a portrait, or a savant musician who, unlike my sister, could play the piano only well enough to entertain a drunken audience at a pub. Effectual, but lacking in both inspiration and genius.

Rarer still, of course, was my special circumstance—a dud of a girl with no magical talents whatsoever, surrounded by her Anointed kin.

In short, magic was unpredictable.

But that was no excuse for what Talan had done.

"You're an empath," I said tightly.

He squared his shoulders and looked me right in the eye. "I am, Gemma."

Fury exploded in me at the sound of his gentle voice. "I know nothing of the customs in Vauzanne, but here in Gallinor, it is considered rude, even unforgivable, for a guest to conceal such a fact from one's host."

With that I stormed off, intending to go straight to Father with this information, but Talan hurried around me and stood in my path, reaching for me with an earnest, pleading expression. I recoiled, and he stopped at once, raising his hands in deference.

"I'm sorry, Gemma, truly," he said quickly. "Of course I should have told you, but there wasn't time. We met, we danced, we talked—you talked quite a lot, in fact—you grew ill, you went to bed."

I glared at him, unimpressed. "'Lady Gemma, I am an empath.'" I paused, considering the words, then nodded sharply. "Yes, you're right, that *did* take a long time to say."

I stalked away again. He easily kept pace. "I deserved that," he said after a moment. "But consider this: as the sole survivor of a ruined family, I was already uncertain of my reception at Ivyhill. If I had disclosed the truth about my magic, I might have been turned away."

"As would have been our right!"

"Empaths are not required by Gallinoran law to disclose their identity—"

"Of course not," I said, appalled at the thought, and stopped short. We had reached the largest of our four hothouses, which would soon be crawling with guests taking a stroll before luncheon. I ducked underneath a golden willow beside a wall of green glass, the world beyond it flush with riotous color. Once Talan had joined me inside the private shell of the willow's slender branches, each of them heavy with shimmering honey-colored flowers, I whirled on him.

"When visiting someone else's home," I said angrily, "where people believe themselves to be safe and therefore let down their guard—"

"I know." Talan's shoulders sagged. He ran a hand through his hair, stared hard at the ground for a time, and then looked up at me with a resigned sort of resolve. "I have wronged you, my lady. I cannot change that. But I can make it up to you—I can prove my good intentions a thousand times over—if you agree to my proposal."

I fixed him with a piercing glare I modeled after Farrin's. "You help me destroy the Basks in the eyes of Gallinor and the high queen so that the war ends and my family can finally live in peace—"

"And help you hunt the demon holding both your families in thrall."

"Yes, fine, and help me"—I infused my voice with scorn—"*hunt my family's demon*, and in exchange, I help you restore your family's honor."

"And I can offer you something else in payment as well," Talan added quickly, taking an urgent step toward me before retreating and clenching his fists at his sides. "I mentioned sweetening our bargain."

Wary, I raised an expectant eyebrow at him and said nothing.

"My power, my empathic magic—the feeling of calm I gave you only moments ago. I can...Gemma, I can do that again. And again, and again. I can give that peace to you for as long as we work together."

My shock was complete. I had been too angry at his intrusion into my feelings to even fathom making such a request, but now that *he* had suggested it, the idea seemed perfectly sensible. Sensible, and intriguing, and wholly tempting, and such a relief to consider that I felt stunned, unbalanced, as if I'd been knocked clean off my feet. I could not even bring myself to be embarrassed by the small sound of want that escaped me.

"I cannot cure what ails you," Talan said gently, his eyes so soft and sad that I simultaneously wished to strike him and kiss him—a not unenjoyable sensation. "But I can offer you a reprieve. I cannot erase the pain, but I can disguise it, divert your attention from it. And my power does not require touch to function," he added. "It requires only a meeting of minds. A nearness and an intent." His smile turned carefully wry. "I would not have to constantly hold your hand, in other words."

Sudden tears slid down my cheeks as I stood there, silent and still, and when Talan at last moved slowly toward me and cupped my face in his palm, I could not help but lean into his touch, close my eyes, and nod my consent against his fingers.

"Please," I whispered, too eager to hate myself for begging.

An immediate peace once again rushed over me, leaving me feeling light as air, pliable and limpid and *happy*. For once I could breathe the magic-soaked air of my family home and not feel sick. I could shift my body without a distant dull ache throbbing in my joints. I could *think* without a fog of pain as my companion, coloring my every waking moment.

Parting my lips as if to sip a sweet drink, I opened my giddy thoughts to Talan's nearness, imagining his voice in my head, recalling his lips against my skin, anything to enhance this feeling. How dreadful it was to understand in that moment, more than I ever had before, how starkly pain and illness had defined my existence, and what it would feel like to live without it.

Eyes still closed, I stepped back from him and shook my head, my hands in fists. This gift was too exquisite, too dear, no matter that it was a form of payment in a fair transaction, and yet I could not resist it.

I could not resist him.

When I opened my eyes, I thought of Farrin and her flinty courage, her voice of steel, but my own came out choked.

"I hate you," I whispered, "and I always will, for offering me this thing I cannot possibly refuse."

Talan looked away, his jaw working. "For the chance to avenge my family and help yours as well," he said quietly, "earning your hatred is a price I will pay. Not happily, but willingly."

"And as soon as we have finished what we set out to do," I pressed on, a lump building in my throat, "as soon as the terms of our bargain have been met, you will take your leave of me and never set eyes on me or speak to me again. Because as long as you are near, I will accept your offer. I will ask you to do this thing for me, to disguise my pain again and again, always and forever, and I do not wish to be beholden to you for the rest of my life. And while you *are* here, and we are allies, you will offer this relief only when I ask it of you." I drew in a ragged breath. "I will not exchange the prison of my illness for the prison of craving someone else's power."

Talan nodded once, his face pale and taut. "I understand what you ask and will do as you command."

"Then remove your magic this instant." I forced out the words. "Take this feeling away from me."

I stepped back from him, gritting my teeth as the sensation of peace slowly faded, leaving my body hollowed out and aching, the familiar cloud of illness seeping back into my thoughts like ink into water.

"We will begin our work at once," I said briskly, shutting my parasol with a snap before I pushed through the willow's branches and started marching back toward the house. "If there is indeed some truth to this idea of a demon, Father might know it, or he might not. Either way, he won't tell me, and asking him will only make him suspicious."

Talan caught up with me in a few long strides. "Your sister's friend Gareth—is he well versed in demonic lore in particular, or is his knowledge of Old Country arcana merely general?"

I shook my head, grateful for the change in subject. It distracted me from Talan's nearness, the knowledge of what that beautiful body and the mind it contained could do for me. "We'll approach Gareth in due time. But first I'd like to discover what we can without telling another soul. You underestimate how quickly and ferociously everyone in my life will come down on both of us if we're found out."

"A fair point." After a moment of frowning in thought—which I was beginning to realize he did rather frequently—Talan said, "I propose we visit the Basks, see what we can glean from a meeting with them. What is their estate called? Ravenswood?"

"Yes, but we can't simply pay them a visit, at least not a formal one. Attending a party is one thing, but asking pointed questions about feuds and demons is quite another. We would need a suitable excuse, or..."

A thrill raced down my arms as I realized what we would have to do. The gooseflesh it raised prickled painfully, my body left raw and sensitive in the wake of Talan's power.

"Father visits Ravenswood once a month since the forest fell," I said quietly. "Farrin let it slip once. I pretended I hadn't heard. I don't know when he goes there, and I don't know why. To spy on them, I suppose, or plant traps. I wonder how he gets there and back. A greenway, I assume, though not one I'm aware of. It must be hidden, warded well."

"Greenway?" Talan asked, frowning. Then he relaxed. "Ah, the magic of wayfarers. Paths of power, rooted in the earth magic of Caiathos."

"My ancestors commissioned several of them during Ivyhill's construction." I nodded, thinking quickly. "We'll do as Father does and visit Ravenswood in secret. There must be a map of the greenways in Father's office, or at the very least a clue as to their whereabouts. Some code, perhaps. He and Farrin are always speaking in code. Meet me in the north atrium at eight o'clock tonight. I'll claim a lingering headache from the party, and we'll sneak into his office while he's downstairs at dinner."

Talan nodded, listening carefully. "North atrium. Visit Ravenswood, spy and eavesdrop. Study their movements, learn their habits. There are tricks to tracking a demon's presence that

I can use—changes to the natural surroundings if a demon has recently killed, certain scents they leave behind, items of protection the Basks may have in place."

"Excellent. Meanwhile I'll arrange a circuit of parties for you to attend, full of people you'll need to meet if you eventually want to enjoy an audience with the queen."

At his expression of dismay, I laughed, slowed my pace, and hooked my arm through his. As we stepped onto one of the pebbled garden paths that meandered around the main house, it was as if our conversation beneath the willow had never happened. If anyone peered into the gardens, they would see only Lady Gemma Ashbourne flirting with her father's handsome foreign guest. I leaned gratefully into the familiar role.

"Don't worry, I'll accompany you to most of them, my health permitting," I reassured Talan. "Just not anything hosted by Dayne Towland. I can't stand the woman. She refuses to wear Illaria's perfume and instead douses herself in cheap elixirs from the Northern Isles, all of which smell like scented candles lit to mask the stink of a seedy tavern."

Talan shook his head, looking genuinely puzzled. "After everything that's just happened, this is what you wish to talk about?"

I patted his arm and offered up a beaming smile. He had seen a fire in me, he'd said. I hoped in that moment that he could see how fiercely it burned.

"Don't think for one moment that I trust you, Talan d'Astier," I said. "I may know how to ensure that you're invited to all the season's most important parties, and what to wear to each of them, and which perfumes are worth the money, but believe me when I say this: you would be wise not to underestimate me. At the first sign of trouble, the first hint of deceit from you, I'll end this and go to my father. A sentinel, I'm sure you've heard, with the high magic of an Anointed warrior. I'll tell him that you used your empathic power to coerce me into hunting a demon for your own selfish mission of vengeance, even knowing how magic adversely affects me. You'll be ruined, and so will any chance for your family's redemption."

Then I leaned close, offering him a view of my corseted breasts—at which, I was gratified to notice, he could not resist stealing a glance.

"And then," I said softly, as if to entice him into my bed, "Father will hunt you, no matter where you run, and he will not stop until he's snapped your neck in two with his bare hands."

With that, I sashayed up the broad stone steps to the terrace, where Mrs. Rathmont's apprentices were setting out a luncheon of cucumber sandwiches, spinach quiches, and lemon ices. Once inside the house, safely in the shadows, I hurried up to my rooms without a backward glance, slammed the door shut behind me, ripped off my gloves, and slid to the floor, hands clapped over my mouth to stifle my sudden wrenching sobs.

The unbearable loss of Talan's power had felled me. Every scrap of peace he'd given me had vanished, and what remained was only me—my despised body, my lack of magic, my incurable illness. I hated him for showing me a life I so desperately wanted and could never truly have. I hated myself for allowing him to do such a thing to me.

And I hated my body with such sudden, violent loathing that I began punching it. I struck my arms and my face. I pinched my skin until I drew blood. I hid my face in my skirts and screamed until my throat hurt.

The familiar, tired thought ran its weary path through my mind, a thought that only showed itself in these most desolate moments: *what a relief it would be to die.* No more pain; no more *anything.* No more popping out of ballrooms to discreetly be sick in the nearest closet. No more days spent abed and in agony after an encounter on the road with some hapless traveler peddling her low-magic card tricks to children. No little voice in my head telling me how futile it all was—the dresses, the sex, the parties, Illaria, Farrin. In the end, after all of that, I was still me, and I still hurt, and I was still a sick aberration in an otherwise superlative family.

I wept until I couldn't, until my stomach ached and my head pounded. I rang for Jessyl so she could help me undress and sat there in a heap of pink silk, waiting. As I did, sniffling and bleary-eyed, I stared dully at a distant sunlit blur on the wall. By the time my cheeks had dried, I understood that the blur was in fact my mirror, the one that only hours before had held my changed reflection—ferally, devastatingly, preternaturally beautiful—and I crafted a plan.

I'd never wanted to believe the stories about the demon binding my family and the Basks in our stupid little war. But I had also never believed that I could perform magic—not once in my life had I managed it, and gods know I had tried—and yet, in front of that mirror, I *had.* I had changed my face, and its beauty had driven Jessyl to madness.

Slowly I stood and walked to the mirror, my heart racing. I touched my fingers to the cool glass and examined my puffy, splotchy reflection. Something had been inside this mirror last night, something that had pulled me toward it as surely as a fish to a lure. Or had the lure been my own self, finally realizing my power? Was it my own magic that had changed me, or was it magic belonging to someone else, someone hidden?

I could not answer these questions, but I knew this: Talan had remarked that the Old Country could never be fully understood.

It was too vast and strange. He wasn't wrong. As Gareth was so fond of saying, *Edyn is undeniable. The Old Country is indefinable.* Perhaps demons did now live in Gallinor. Perhaps one of them owned my family, and the Basks too.

Maybe a woman born without magic could *earn* it.

Maybe, once attained, that magic could change her for good.

If this demon from the stories, this Man With the Three-Eyed Crown, did in fact exist, and if Talan and I found him, I would not fight him or beg him to end my family's war.

No, I would tell him that I wanted magic of my own, that I wished to be remade down to my bones—and then I would ask what price I must pay him to help me do it.

CHAPTER 7

T hat evening at precisely eight o'clock, I watched from the
shadows as Talan entered the north atrium outside Father's
office. Determined to claim whatever advantages I could, I had
arrived five minutes prior and hidden behind a white marble
statue of a prancing griffin. *Talan* would be the vulnerable one,
standing there like a fool in the moonlight, anxiously awaiting *my*
arrival, and I would approach him when I was good and ready.

He did look mightily gorgeous in moonlight though, I had to
admit, even after stopping in his tracks to stare up at the ceiling
in naked astonishment. Clothed in dirty riding boots and trousers, fur-trimmed gloves, and a dark night coat with a high collar,
he looked ready for a late-evening ride. Clever. He could easily
have happened upon me in the halls and stopped to make conversation, unable to resist the sight of me in my long lace nightgown and midnight-blue velvet robe—faint with a headache,
wandering the house in search of solace. Golden curls tumbling,
feet bare.

It was a good lie, something straight out of one of my most
delicious novels, and I smiled as I watched Talan stare around

wonderingly, satisfaction warming my chest. The thoughts that had swarmed through my head all afternoon on dark wings flew away.

Wherever my mother was—dead, alive but in hiding, or maybe living a happy life with a new name, content with a far more ordinary, more lovable family—I sent her a silent prayer of gratitude.

When young Philippa Wren had married my father six years before I was born and become Lady Ashbourne of Ivyhill, she had at once set to work modifying the great house to suit her tastes—elaborate statuary of the gods and various Old Country beasts; the countless vines of ivy that rambled through the house like green veins; atria like this one, designed to safely admit the outside elements.

And not even the beautiful Talan d'Astier, it seemed, was impervious to the effects of her handiwork.

"Oh, you're here," I said airily, approaching Talan at last. "I was half convinced you would think twice and flee back home to Vauzanne. I'm glad to see you appreciate the atrium. You should see it in winter. The snowfall drifts down from the ceiling and then vanishes just above the lower windows, allowing one to enjoy the wintry atmosphere while keeping dry and tidy."

Talan drew his fingers through the lower reaches of moonlight as if it were a tangible thing he could pull down to eye level.

"That must have been an expensive piece of spellcraft," he murmured.

Pleased, I gave a careless shrug. "Frightfully so, but Mother wouldn't rest until it was done."

He turned to face me, his dark hair moon-silvered. "Also, as I've said, I have no home left in Vauzanne. Not really. If I were to leave here, I'd have nowhere else to go. It would take rather a lot to frighten me away."

I opened my mouth to respond, but he beat me to it.

"And I should tell you now that I don't scare easily," he continued, almost cheerfully. "Just to assuage any concerns you may have about me pulling my weight in this partnership." He clasped his hands behind his back and fixed me with a searching look. "Where is your mother now?" he asked easily, as if we were conversing over afternoon tea. "I haven't been fortunate enough to meet her yet."

That was more than enough to wrest me from my stupefied admiration of his handsome moonlit visage.

"I haven't the faintest idea," I said, sweeping past him. "If you ever find out, do let me know."

He nodded earnestly, his brow furrowing as if he'd immediately begun sifting through his memories for sightings of my mother.

Irritated, I stabbed the lock on Father's door with my copy of his key. I couldn't read this man. Was he sincere or full of guile? Was that remark about not scaring easily meant to reassure or frighten me? One moment I felt quite in control of the situation; the next, Talan would say something to unnerve me, or the simple fact of his beauty would do it.

"Get hold of yourself," I muttered, my temper making me clumsy with the lock.

Talan came up beside me in velveteen silence. "Your father allows you a key to his office?"

"Both Farrin and I have them. It's one of the—" I swallowed the rest of that sentence, horrified by how close I'd come to informing Talan that Father's office was one of our family's safe rooms, connected to a network of passages and tunnels that would allow us to flee the estate if need be. My parents had commissioned the work thirteen years prior, spooked by how close the Basks' fire had come to killing us all.

Flustered, I finally managed to unlock the door and peer inside, my heart suddenly pounding with a giddy sort of fear. "We have perhaps a half hour before anyone gets up from the dinner table," I said, "so I suggest we search quickly."

When Talan didn't respond, I shot him a look over my shoulder. "Is there a problem?"

The expression he wore—sad, a little shocked, a little angry, all swiftly stifled—sent a chill of dread rolling down my back. I quickly took stock of my body but sensed nothing of his power's presence on me.

Even so, though I'd checked the mirror ten times before leaving my room, it suddenly felt as if all the places on my arms and face that I'd struck earlier that day had bloomed into vivid life. Talan quickly looked me over head to toe, his gaze lingering on the lace trim of my nightgown's wide collar—and then found my eyes once more.

I stared at him, dry-mouthed. It wasn't possible for him to know what I had done in my rooms. There was no physical sign of it. He was not currently using his power; I would have known. My body ached as it normally did. My stomach sat in its perpetually queasy knots. Talan's power had brought comfort, and a strange, reassuring nearness, and at the moment I felt nothing of the sort.

"What is it?" I laughed a little, as if he were a preposterous creature. "Examining me? Do I satisfy?" I paused, flashed him a smile. "Maybe you see something you like?"

"Gemma..." he said quietly, his voice achingly tender. But then, after another moment of searching my face, whatever had come over him was gone. He returned my smile—a small quirk of his lips that made my heart flutter.

"The moonlight suits you," he said simply. He opened his mouth again, shifted a little. I held my breath. Would he say something else? What did I *want* him to say?

But he simply moved past me into the office, his hand brushing my sleeve as he glided by. "Remind me why we can't just follow your father around until he leads us to Ravenswood himself?"

I shook myself and hurried in after him, leaving the door ajar. If someone found us, we would tell them I'd been giving the curious Mr. d'Astier a tour of the house, hoping it would distract me from my headache.

"That would be too great a risk," I replied. "Father's an Anointed sentinel. He'd either move too quickly for us to follow or hear us creeping along behind him, and then..." I swallowed hard, spooked by my own imaginings. "Well, he'd no doubt lock me in my rooms forever and put guards at the door night and day. You he'd probably just murder."

"Ah. A fine reason indeed." Talan looked around at the enormous office, scratching the back of his head with a grim smile. "Searching his office without his permission it is, then. Where does one even begin with such a crime?"

"I doubt Father would leave a map of the estate's greenways just lying about," I said, "but he and Farrin speak in code, play games together. What if something happened to him and she needed access to his private affairs? He might have left clues for her around the office, telling her where to find things."

"A map of objects and secret jokes," Talan said, nodding as he perused the bookshelves. "An interesting idea."

A pang of longing arrowed through my chest. I ignored it, beginning a careful search of the papers scattered atop Father's desk. "Yes, well, they've always had their little secret language. I think Farrin started it after Mother left to entertain Father, distract him from himself."

I stopped, clamping my mouth shut. My family's stories—not

the rumors or legends but the true, painful ones—were not any-one's business but our own.

"He must have grieved terribly in her absence," Talan said, his back to me. "And that was your sister's way of helping."

"Indeed," I said lightly, "and it seemed to work. They've been the best of friends ever since."

"Does that bother you?"

I riffled through a stack of papers with such haste that I nearly ripped one. "I'm glad they have each other. Farrin has few friends, and Father even fewer. Not real ones anyway. They need each other." I flung down the papers in disgust. "These are nothing interesting, just financial accounts. I suppose there could be some code embedded in them, but gods, I'm no scholar. We'd need Gareth for help with that."

"Are there books they mention often?" Talan asked. He pulled a book down from one of the shelves lining the room and blew a light coating of dust off its woven brown cover. "Or charac-ters, places, historical figures? Maybe the things they talk about in casual conversation, things no one would bother listening too closely to, hold clues."

"Perhaps," I said, only half hearing him. I stood near the desk, gazing distractedly at the floor. Saying Gareth's name had reminded me of seeing Mara at Rosewarren, her cryptic words, her transformation into a creature more at home in the Old Country than here in Edyn.

Too much time had passed since that day, during which I'd stubbornly shoved Mara's frightening strangeness to the back of my mind. I needed to speak to Gareth, and Farrin too, and I needed to see Mara again. I needed to find the greenway that led to the Basks' estate, engineer a scheme that would tear them down and earn me Father's praise, and insinuate Talan into the next few weeks of high society parties, maybe even the queen's masque the following month, and find this demon and pay him to *fix* me, and—

I needed—

I whirled away from Talan to hide my face, nearly screaming with frustration. The panic had come—stupid me, I had *let* it come, I hadn't slept well enough, and I'd spent all afternoon crying in my rooms, and then I'd let myself fall into a spiral of frantic thoughts—and now it was here, and it was too late to stop it. In its sudden violent wake, I was helpless, swept along by its frantic currents and the booming ache of my joints. The room of heavy upholstered furniture, glossy wood-paneled walls, and books upon books upon books reminded me of the Warden's parlor at the priory. A sea of dark colors, each blurring into the next. Walls that grew and arched overhead like the gnarled boughs of a great forest. I longed to throw open the window and gulp down fresh air, but instead I bit my tongue hard and tried to force a sense of calm.

I moved to a stack of papers sitting on a small table across the room, hardly seeing what I was doing, not noticing the hot prickle of tears I was holding back until Talan's gloved hand gently touched mine, steadying me. Then he tilted up my chin so I was forced to lock eyes with him, and the expression on his face was so tender, so dear and open—as if he could see right down to the core of me and did not simply pity my pain but *knew* it—that for a moment I lost my breath.

"Gemma," he said softly. "I'm here. I'm right here beside you. Breathe with me. In and out. I've got you."

I shook my head and looked away. "Don't you dare use your power on me, you awful man."

"I need no empathic powers to see you trembling, or hear

your breath catching, or to notice the grief on your face. I swore not to use my power to influence you or read you without your consent, and I will honor that pledge."

"I can't describe how much I despise having to trust the word of someone I hardly know," I managed to say, struggling to catch my breath.

"I understand. It isn't ideal. Let me remind you that we can end this bargain at any time, if you wish it."

"Yes, and then I'd have to watch you slink off like a kicked puppy and live forever with the guilt of turning you away."

He nodded sagely. "And the guilt of knowing you'd condemned my family's reputation to remain forever in tatters."

"Keep annoying me like this, and I'll manage it quite nicely." I waved him off, searching blearily for a chair. "I need to sit."

"Of course." He helped me to a worn reading chair and somehow gracefully folded his tall, beautiful body onto the tiny stool at my feet. "I'm sorry I asked about your sister. It's just that I had to talk about *something*." He smiled a little, glancing up at me through the dark curls falling over his brow. "The truth is, Lady Gemma, you make me nervous."

I laughed out a little sobbing gasp. "Oh, for the love of all the gods..."

"It's true. This is my first ever foray into political intrigue, you know. Ancient family feuds, secret codes, and with such an exquisite little wildcat as my partner. One hardly knows what to do with oneself in such a scenario."

Perhaps I should have bristled at the surprising endearment, but in fact I delighted in it for one sweet, delicious moment before the reality of who I truly was returned.

"I'm no wildcat," I said with a bitter laugh. "That's Farrin. Or Mara, even. I'm just..." Helplessly, hating myself for falling apart in front of Talan two nights in a row, I shrugged. "I'm the runt of the litter. The pitiful limping kitten who never should have been born. *Gods. Listen* to me. What a pathetic, sweaty little *weed.*" I wrenched myself up from the chair, scrubbing my face dry. "I'm so angry right now I could scream."

"Well, perhaps not just yet," Talan said pleasantly from his stool. "Everyone would come storming upstairs to your rescue, and things could very quickly become awkward."

"Stop trying to cheer me up. You don't know what it's like to live like this."

"Like what?"

"Like *this!*" I whirled around and gestured at my body. "With this awful screaming panic living inside you that anything could set off at any moment! And sickness that comes at you like a hammer if you dare to do something as simple as visit your sister, and bone-crushing pain that knocks you about if someone possessing just the right kind of potent magic gets too close to you. And—"

I froze. Talan's eyes widened. We'd both heard it, then: quick footsteps in the corridor.

There was no time to do anything else. My face was splotchy and swollen, my breath still evening out, my body wound tight. They would think Talan had hurt me or that we'd had an awful row that would require some ungainly explanation. Our plan would crash to pieces before it even got its feet set right on the ground.

So I did what I had to do. I rushed toward Talan, tugged hard on his arms, and once he was on his feet, I launched myself at him, hooked one of my legs over his, and kissed him.

CHAPTER 8

Though my build was slight compared to his, Talan stumbled back, quite caught off guard. But I held fast to his coat, pulling him closer to me. The fool wasn't catching on quickly enough. I whimpered a little in frustration, and the sound unleashed something in him. His body tightened against mine as he took over, deepening our kiss with his tongue. He slid his gloved hands under my robe to cup my waist, and I thrilled to remember how thoroughly buttoned up he was while I was wearing only thin nightclothes.

Heat bloomed inside me so ferociously that for a moment I forgot where we were, what we were doing, *why* we were doing it. I knew only his lips on my cheeks; his hands pinning me against his body; the silk of his hair under my fingers as I cupped his head, desperate for more of him, hungry for his taste—

"A-*hem.*"

The sound of a delicately annoyed voice cut through the haze of my lust like the hack of a knife. I whirled around, the abrupt force of my departure causing Talan to stagger back.

Besides Father, the person at Ivyhill whom I would least want to find us in here had, in fact, found us: our family's librarian, carrying a packet of leather-bound papers and looking entirely unsurprised to find me in such a state.

"Madam Baines!" I covered my mouth with one hand and giggled nervously while struggling for composure. My robe had slipped down my arms, and I hastily tugged it back up to cover myself. "I...I didn't realize we'd left the door open, I—oh, how utterly mortifying." I glanced at Talan and reached for his hand. "Talan d'Astier, this is Madam Adamantia Baines, our family's librarian. Madam Baines, Talan d'Astier of Vauzanne."

Talan took my hand and bowed his head. "Madam Baines, what a lovely surprise," he said, his voice slightly hoarse. He cleared his throat. "I heard your name mentioned at last night's party and was hoping to meet you soon."

Madam Baines raised one eyebrow, the sight of which left me queasy with nerves. On the surface, she was a perfectly pleasant-looking woman—slightly plump with enviously flawless pale skin, a cap of lustrous brown curls, and really rather lovely hazel eyes flanked by laugh lines. But I'd never—not once—seen the woman laugh or smile. At least not in my direction.

This might have had something to do with the number of novels I'd lost or unwittingly defaced while reading out on the grounds—or the number of times she'd caught me in the library with someone, decidedly *not* reading and instead using the shelves for, well, *leverage*.

"Mr. d'Astier," said Madam Baines, looking at Talan coolly, "I find it extremely unlikely that anyone at that party mentioned my name and am in fact quite appalled at the flimsiness of your lie. How nice it is to meet you."

"On the contrary," Talan continued, "Lord Ashbourne quite enthusiastically told me of your work translating and cataloging

Willem Ashbourne's journals." Talan shook his head in admiration. "I don't envy you that task. Third-century Gallinoran is no easy read. Are those the original entries you're carrying?"

One corner of Madam Baines's mouth quirked in what I hoped was a sign of concession. "No, these are copies. Lord Ashbourne requested them for review. And for a librarian like me, translation work, even of this degree, is hardly an onerous task." She deposited her books on the desk and began circling the room, inspecting everywhere we'd been searching. My stomach churned with apprehension. We'd not been careful enough. Papers were scattered, books were out of place—

"You are a sage, then?" Talan said pleasantly.

Madam Baines delicately picked up a piece of paper from Father's desk. "An *Anointed* sage," she said. "My ancestors were blessed by Jaetris himself."

"How well suited you must be to the work of a librarian," Talan continued. "The Ashbournes are fortunate to have you in their employ."

"Indeed they are." Madam Baines glanced up from the desk to look at me. "Were you in need of something, Lady Gemma?"

"Oh, not at all," I said, throwing a coy smile Talan's way. "I mean, not in the way of books, that is. I'd only wanted to give Mr. d'Astier a tour of the house, and Father's office was empty, so—"

"It's only that I see no fewer than twenty-three items in this office that have been displaced since I brought up the previous batch of copies a half hour ago. Clearly you were searching for something." Her mouth thinned. "Or did you have a difficult time of it, deciding which part of the room to sully with your activities?"

My cheeks stung with heat as Madam Baines stared me down—she would never have scolded Father or Farrin like they were errant children. But then an idea came to me, lighting up my mind with a different kind of fire, and I found my next words quickly, my heart pounding with sudden excitement.

Here was our family librarian, with a memory that retained everything it encountered.

And here beside me, his lips still flushed from our kisses, was an empath with the ability to make her feel happy and care-free—so foolishly lighthearted, perhaps, that she'd share whatever information we requested.

"Oh, Madam Baines, surely you yourself have sullied an office or two," I said sweetly, casting a demure look up at Talan. "When someone is as dashing and beautiful as Mr. d'Astier, one finds oneself quite overcome."

Talan's expression gentled, his eyes so dark and soft I felt that I could sink into them and be forever safe there, forever warm. He raised my hand to his lips and kissed it, his eyes still locked with mine, and the hot ache between my legs returned with a vengeance.

"Hmph." Madam Baines picked up a stray book Talan had been looking at and turned to reshelve it. "I've found that one can control one's baser desires in any situation if one simply has a strong enough will."

With her back turned, I mouthed at Talan, *Use your power*, then glanced pointedly at Madam Baines.

His eyebrows shot up. He frowned, stepping back from me, and shook his head.

I understood. Using his power to influence Madam Baines without her knowledge was a moral breach that in any other circumstance would have horrified me.

But I needed to find that demon, if he did exist—gods, for the first time in my life, I hoped that the silly stories about my family's tormentor were true—and visiting Ravenswood was the best place to start.

Please, I said silently, squeezing Talan's hand and biting my lip. As I knew it would, his gaze dropped to my mouth, and though he looked unhappy about it, he only gave a little sigh before saying, "Madam Baines, I don't suppose you'd have the time to give me a tour of your library tonight, would you?"

The change in the air was subtle—a slight warming, like the sun had peeked out from behind a cloud. My joints twinged in pain as Talan used his magic, as if protesting that he would dare to direct his power not to me but to someone else. I gritted my teeth and ignored the sting, watching Madam Baines with bated breath.

Then she turned, and I nearly gasped in shock to see her expression so changed—open and soft, utterly relaxed, as if she'd...well, as if she'd recently enjoyed a nice bit of sullying.

"Why, Mr. d'Astier," she said, beaming, her eyes shining with a dreamy glaze, "nothing would delight me more. Please follow me. You too, Lady Gemma, if you would? I can't imagine you've ever had a proper tour." She came to me and drew my arm through hers with a slight maternal pat. "This one loves her novels," she said over her shoulder to Talan, "but not much else. Recommend a historical text and you'd think she'd been presented with someone's lopped-off head."

As we made for the library, Talan just behind us, I pushed past the wall of my surprise—and the stitch of guilt in my stomach—and said carefully, "Madam Baines, while we have you, I wonder if you could help me with something."

"Anything, child." She sighed blissfully, a sound of such pure, unfettered joy that it hardly seemed possible she could have made it. "I must tell you, I've never felt so at ease in my entire life. What can I do for you, my lady?"

"Well, you see, I wanted to show Mr. d'Astier around the estate. A proper tour, as you call it. Not only of the house but also the grounds."

"That seems perfectly sensible." Madam Baines turned to smile at Talan. "Our Lady Gemma is a wonderful host. She always knows how best to entertain Lord Ashbourne's guests. Why, she's been planning his parties since she was eight years old! Ever since Lady Philippa left." She wrinkled her nose. "Awful woman. Abandoning the family like that, *vanishing* without explanation, her darling girls waking up to find their mother gone. Lord Ashbourne didn't leave his rooms for *weeks*."

"And if I'm going to show Talan around the estate, I want to make sure I don't forget anything," I said hastily, my throat tightening as I remembered that awful time—Mother gone, and Mara only just taken to the Mist, and Father shut up in his rooms, and Farrin doing her best to keep the house running, and me, sobbing constantly, clinging to her skirts like a baby.

"Oh, yes," Madam Baines said, nodding. "Mr. d'Astier must see all the gardens, the aviary and orangery, the prayer temples, the summer houses by the lake—"

"And of course, the greenways."

Madam Baines stumbled, abruptly falling silent. That had shaken her, even gripped as she was by Talan's power. I looked back at him frantically, and he shook his head a little, put a finger to his lips, and closed his eyes.

The air warmed again, a subtle ripple of force and heat that made me bite down a yelp as pain bloomed at my temples. Talan steadied me with a strong hand on my back.

"Of *course* the greenways," Madam Baines agreed after a long moment, her cheery tone returning. "They are truly impressive works of magic. The Ashbournes, going all the way back to their earliest days after the Unmaking, have spared no expense on anything here at Ivyhill, but especially not on that greening magic. Wayfarers charge a criminal fee for their work, in my opinion, but no Ashbourne has ever blinked at that. Ah, here we are!"

She swung open the doors of the library—an impressive feat, considering they were enormous and wooden, carved from top to bottom with intricate spirals of flowering vines—and led us inside. The room was massive, its walls looming four stories high. Mezzanines appointed with desks and reading chairs offered several places to sit and work; polished ladders on golden wheels stood propped against countless shelves of books. And on every surface—the walls, the tiles on floor and ceiling—painted murals depicted scenes from Edyn's history. The Upper Army's naval victory over an insurgence of Old Country sea monsters, The crowning of High Queen Yvaine Ballantere.

The gods, all five of them erupting in ecstatic rays of light on the day of their deaths—the Unmaking.

Talan grabbed my arm, holding me back. "I don't like this, Gemma," he said, his breath hot against my ear. "I don't use my power like this. It's a violation. It's wrong."

I shivered a little and pulled away from him. "I don't like it either, but we're not going to waste this opportunity to speed along our plans. We both need this, Talan. I know you agree. Think of your *family*, of everything you've suffered. This is your chance to change all of that."

It was rotten of me to use the memory of his family to my advantage, but my determination bordered on desperation.

Talan's mouth thinned. "And if I refuse to participate?"

"Then I'll take that as a sign that this arrangement of ours has run its course and have Father's guard escort you off the grounds."

He looked away, his brow furrowed in distress and his shoulders square. "We *will* talk more about this later."

"And for now?"

"For now I'll continue—*very unhappily*," he added.

I swallowed down the hot lump of shame in my throat, braced myself against the pain continuing to pulse through my body as Talan's power rippled past me, and hurried after Madam Baines. She was bustling toward one of the library's back rooms, which housed special collections—Willem Ashbourne's journals, meticulously preserved writings from the days of the Unmaking, missives from Queen Yvaine to the Ashbourne family in Gallinor's early days.

"We'll start our tour back here," Madam Baines was saying cheerily. "Lord Ashbourne prides himself on having the largest collection of Gallinoran historical documents in the country. Well, except for the royal archives, of course."

"You mentioned the greenways before," I said quickly, interrupting her. "I'm keen to show them all to Talan, you see." I paused, then whispered with a nervous little laugh, "I'm rather desperate to impress him, really. I think I might be in love."

Madam Baines stopped before a door to one of the back rooms and hummed agreeably as she searched through her ring of keys.

"It's only that, while I know where quite a few of the greenways are located," I continued, "I imagine there are several I *don't* know about."

"Oh, you're right about that, my lady." Madam Baines began opening the door's series of locks. "There are thirty-eight greenways on the estate."

I blinked in surprise. "That many?"

"Out of those, eighteen are known only to Lord Ashbourne and Lady Farrin."

That bit of information cut me to the bone. "They've kept me ignorant of *eighteen* different greenways?"

"And then there are two known only to Lord Ashbourne." Madam Baines looked back at me knowingly. "Don't take it too hard, my dear. Not even Lady Farrin knows *everything*." She finished unlocking the door and threw it open with a flourish. "You can see, perhaps, why your father pays me so well. As an Anointed sage, my power ensures that I remember everything there is to know about this estate—I dare say more than even the late Lady Ashbourne knew. My services are worth a robust salary; my silence is worth even more."

Bristling, I abandoned all attempts at delicacy. "Tell me where these secret greenways are. *Now*."

Madam Baines paused, blinking into the dimly lit room before us. She shook her head and put her hand to her temple. "The secret greenways?" she murmured.

Talan glided over with a dark look back at me and gently touched her arm. "Madam Baines—"

"The secret greenways…"

"Why don't we all sit down for a moment and ring for some tea? You can tell us about the history of—"

"Well," Madam Baines said quietly, as if entranced, "there's the greenway that connects with that haberdashery in the capital's Market District, which is a front for one of Lord Ashbourne's more unsavory business endeavors, something about smuggled poppy seeds from Aidurra—which I do *not* approve of, I must tell you. And then there's the greenway that takes Lord Ashbourne up north to Ravenswood, and then there's the hidden one, the sunken one, the one that goes straight to—"

"Ravenswood," I said quickly. "That's the one we want. Tell us where it is? Please, Madam Baines."

Absently she drifted to one of the bookshelves in the unlocked room and, humming to herself, her eyes a bit glazed, retrieved a single slim volume.

I took it from her, my heart pounding so frantically I could feel it in the back of my throat.

"It's here," she said dreamily, with a soft giggle and a girlish look at Talan. She tapped the book's cover with one finger. "I found it."

Talan frowned. "The greenway's inside a book? Can wayfaring magic do that?"

"Of course not," I said, smiling slowly, for the book's cover bore a faded illustration I recognized immediately. "It's at the lake."

"Your family has a lake?"

I shot him a look. *Of course we have a lake.*

"Thank you so very much, Madam Baines, for your help," I said, folding the book back into her hands. "Unfortunately we must be going now, so we'll have to finish our tour another day."

Nodding, Madam Baines teetered back with a chuckling sigh and somehow managed to sway herself into a reading chair without toppling anything.

"What do we do with her?" I whispered to Talan. "She'll be all right, won't she?"

Talan glared at me. "You're just considering that now?"

Flushing with shame, I jerked up my chin. "I had to think quickly, and it's not as if you were offering any brilliant alternatives."

"I need to tend to her for a few moments," he said with an irritated sigh. "It's a palliative empathic practice, to ensure she's relaxed and that she won't be frightened when the magic fades."

"Excellent. I'll keep watch at the doors. Then we'll go to the lake."

He raised his eyebrows. "Tonight?"

"Can you think of a reason to wait?"

"You mean something other than, 'This evening has quickly plunged into uncomfortable chaos'?" He paused. "No."

"Well, then, do what you need to do so we can leave," I whispered, waving at Madam Baines's slumped figure.

It was only then, as I hurried away from them toward the doors, that guilt crested in my chest like a scorching wave I could not hold back. Wrong. It was *wrong*, what we had done, and I'd known it and pushed for it anyway.

I paced fretfully at the doors until Talan reappeared, looking surprisingly pleased with himself.

"What did you do?" I whispered.

"Luckily a quick search of the good librarian's office yielded a bottle of wine stashed away in her desk," Talan said. "One of my family's, in fact. I emptied most of it and left the bottle in her lap. When she wakes, she'll blame whatever she remembers on the wine."

"Whatever she remembers?" I stepped back, horrified. "Do you mean that your power can alter people's *memories*?"

"No, nothing like that. It's not an alteration. It's more of a fogginess that will fade with time—but by then she'll have convinced herself that this was all an unfortunate lapse in judgment due to the wine, and she'll dismiss any other explanation."

The realization of how little I knew about Talan's power—and how quickly I had nonetheless aimed it at another person—sank inside me like a stone. I shoved the feeling aside. What was done had been done. Would Farrin have hesitated to do such a thing if it meant possibly ending our feud with the Basks? Would Father?

"I hope you're right," I whispered. "And…I'm sorry I asked that of you. I panicked. I didn't know what else to do, and I had this awful feeling that this was our only chance. That if we didn't act tonight, we'd never be able to again."

Talan's expression softened. He touched my hand. "I appreciate the apology. And I promise you, Madam Baines will be fine. And, eventually, we'll get better at this."

"*This?*"

"This. You know. Our carefully thought-out partnership of intrigue, plots, and subterfuge."

I smiled faintly. It was a fair attempt at lightening the mood, but my stomach still roiled with a feeling I knew intimately. Fortunately, shame had been my constant companion since the day the Warden came to bring me to Rosewarren and took Mara instead, and after so many years of living with the feeling, I'd learned very well how to ignore it. Instead I focused on what mattered: my bargain with the demon—*oh gods*, I prayed, *please let there actually be a demon*—and what it would give me. A new body, whole and hale. Strong and sharp and glinting. Reborn from a demon's touch.

The thought gave me strength. "To the lake, then?" I asked.

Talan nodded once. "To the lake."

CHAPTER 9

Three hours later, I was at my wit's end, my hems were ruined, and my feet were cold as ice.

"We've slogged through the mud around this entire lake," I said through gritted teeth, "and I've not seen or felt a single godsdamned *leaf* with greening magic on it." I glanced enviously at Talan's thick leather boots, deeply regretting my own choice of attire. My vanity had led me to select a floral dress with a pretty sweetheart neckline and soft gray boots meant for nothing more strenuous than a leisurely promenade through the gardens. They were soaked through, my stockings wet all the way up to my knees. I might as well have remained in my nightgown, robe, and bare feet instead of wasting precious time sneaking up to my rooms to change clothes, for all the good they were doing me.

"Does your magic dull people's senses?" I asked. "Could Madam Baines have been out of her head when she showed us that book?"

"Being influenced by an empath is not like being drunk," Talan said in a maddeningly patient tone.

"It certainly looked that way to me."

"To your unpracticed eyes, perhaps. I understand how you could misinterpret things."

I opened my mouth to issue a blazing retort, but before I could, Talan stopped walking and took gentle hold of my hand.

"Gemma, we really *must* return to the house. You're shivering."

"I'm not," I insisted, just as an inconveniently timed chill made me shudder.

His lips quirked in amusement. "A convincing argument."

"Who knows what will happen when Madam Baines regains her senses? This might be our only chance to explore the lake before Father...I don't know, figures out what we've done and closes the greenway entirely." I spun around, gesturing at the lake's shining black surface. "If it's even *here*. The gods must be laughing themselves to tears watching us."

"If I were a god, I certainly would be," Talan said. "Listen, we're tired, we've been walking for hours, and your party was only last night. Let's return to the house, get some sleep, and talk about this at luncheon tomorrow."

But I hardly heard him. Looking out at the still, silent lake, an idea had formed.

"It's in the lake," I whispered.

"What was that?"

I whirled around, beaming. "It's *in* the lake. It has to be. This is one of Father's secret greenways, after all. He wouldn't just leave it out in the trees for anyone to find." I laughed, elated, and clasped my hands under my chin. "Gods, of *course*. Why didn't we think of this earlier?"

Talan was staring at the lake with immense trepidation. "You cannot be serious."

"As serious as a grumpy old sage," I crowed, hiking up my

skirts and plunging into the water. "I can't imagine how much Father had to pay for this—"

Talan caught my hand and pulled me back into his arms. His body was so warm that I barely fought the urge to burrow into him.

"Gemma, have you gone mad?" He laughed in disbelief. "We can't go swimming around the lake looking for greenways. Greenways don't even *exist* in lakes. They're *green*ways, not waterways."

"Ah, but there are water-dwelling plants. And where there are plants, there's the potential for greening magic, don't you think?"

"But I've never even heard of such a thing!" Talan said, dragging a hand through his hair in exasperation. "Have you?"

"No, but it makes perfect sense to me, now that I'm thinking about it." I tapped Talan right on the tip of his indignant nose before squirming out of his arms to turn back toward the water.

"Oh, no, no, no," Talan said, his grip on my arm both firm and exceedingly gentle. "We're not going to plunge into the water and swim around for ages. If you insist on doing this, we'll search again from the shore—"

"But keep our feet in the water so as to better sense the greenway's presence."

Talan glanced down at my sodden boots, and a genuine, baffled smile lit up his face so beautifully that I lost my breath for a moment.

"You are a maddening creature," he said, shaking his head. Then he cupped my face in his hands and locked his eyes with mine. Our foreheads touched, his breath caressed my lips, and I nearly melted, remembering how sweetly that mouth had kissed mine only a few short hours ago. The air pulled taut between us, and for an instant my body ached to abandon our search altogether and press against him instead.

"If your feet freeze off," Talan said gravely, "you'd better not blame me for it."

"That's a promise," I said with a smile, and then turned away before I did something utterly foolish, like ravish him right there in the mud. I would have to do something—and soon—about the wild thoughts that entered my mind whenever I looked at him. They were *most* distracting, and so dazzlingly overwhelming that one might think I had never before done so much as kiss another person.

We circled the lake once more, wading through the shallows, which came halfway to my knees. Neither of us spoke, intent upon our search. The night was quiet, windless, interrupted only by the occasional rustling of an animal foraging for food. This time I directed my thoughts not toward the dense woods and undergrowth surrounding the lake but toward the water itself.

I reached for Talan's hand and closed my eyes, allowing him to guide me as I concentrated on the sensation of the cool water lapping against my legs, the pull of it on my skirts, the thick squelch of mud under my boots. I had traveled through greenways with my family for as long as I could remember, and I knew all too well the sharp pain that punched up and down my spine whenever I neared one. Instinctively my body tensed, bracing itself against the pain it feared would come, but I pushed forward anyway, trying to relax even as my skin began to tingle painfully with memory. The last time I'd traveled through a greenway—the day Mara had transformed—the greening magic had pummeled me without mercy, stars of pain bursting behind my eyes like firecrackers.

Suddenly something jolted me—a quick but vicious lash, as if an arrow shot from the water's depths had grazed my ankle. I stumbled, leaning hard against Talan's solid warmth.

"What is it?" His voice was tight with worry. "Are you hurt?"

My eyes fluttered open. I set my jaw against the familiar sensation of needles stabbing their way up my legs. "It's here," I whispered. "It's close. Can't you feel that?"

"Feel what?" Talan stilled, looking around. "I don't feel anything."

"It's hurting me. It must be near."

"*What's* hurting you?"

"The greenway." I pulled away from Talan, wading deeper into the water. "I told you magic hurts me. The more potent the magic, the worse the hurt." I stared out across the lake, hardly breathing, listening to the pulse of my pain and trying to read its course.

Then I saw it.

"There," I whispered, pointing. "That lagoon."

"But...that wasn't there before," Talan said slowly. "Was it? How could we have missed it?"

Shivering, I kept my eyes fixed upon the little cove at the lake's edge. "No," I agreed, "it wasn't there before."

Neither of us elaborated; we knew as well as anyone in Edyn that magic could be fickle, even coy. The more expensive the spell, the more complex it could be. A beguiler could even imbue a distinct personality into the spell they crafted for their client.

Oaks draped with heavy sheets of dark moss encircled the lagoon, and when we pushed past them into the glade, the air tightened with a small sucking sound. The world beyond the circle of trees disappeared. There was no sound but our breathing—Talan's, I noticed, quicker and shallower than mine.

"I don't understand," he whispered.

Now I was the one to take his hand, steadying him. He looked younger somehow in those trees, his eyes wider as he peered about, his brow furrowed with confusion and fear. I found myself wishing I could wrap him in my arms, perhaps near a crackling fireplace, and soothe him with a long, winding trail of kisses.

Shaking myself free of yet another distracted daydream, I looked back at the lagoon's still water. "It could be any number of things. Maybe the lagoon is spelled to recognize Ashbourne blood, or maybe it only shows itself to someone who's looking for it. Who knows what elaborate disguises Father constructed? Or maybe it was someone before him—Grandfather Darrien, or *his* father, or—"

A fist of pain drove into my belly and twisted.

I doubled over, gasping for air.

Talan caught me, held me up. "Gemma? Gemma! What is it?"

The agony ripping through my body muffled his voice. I reached for him blindly, my head spinning and roaring. It stabbed again, an awful punch to my gut. Gripping my insides, it clenched tight and pulled. My traitorous body fought the tug of nearby magic—and that magic was clearly impatient to be found by whatever strange creature was resisting its call.

Another wave of pain swept up my body, crackling and white hot. The wild thought came to me that this must be what it felt like to be struck by lightning. Then I hit something cold, the shock of it stabbing me like knives, and sank quickly into utter darkness. I tried to suck in air and choked on water instead.

A distant splash sounded from somewhere above me. I heard someone yelling, their voice distorted by the water's thick murk.

Water.

I was in the lagoon.

Something brushed my leg—a hand, I thought, until I managed to glimpse through the darkness a massive tangle of drifting weeds and ferns. Despite everything, I felt a small surge of excitement. There it was. Its tug on my limbs and the sharp, smarting throbs seizing my body were unmistakable.

Father's secret greenway, about which even Farrin was ignorant.

Remembering Talan, doubting he had ever traversed a greenway as powerful as this one surely was, I wished I could explain to him what was about to happen. But that required breathing, and returning to the surface was not an option. The greenway's magic was insistent, ravenous, as if a great maw in the center of the world had opened up and was set on devouring everything it could find, including me.

My lungs burning, I kicked as hard as I could and dove down toward the undulating greenery. Movement beside me, another weight parting the water, filled me with hope. Talan was there, swimming along with me. His arms flailed, searching for me. I grabbed his hand, held on tight, and plunged into the weeds, praying that when we emerged we would still be alive.

The greenway tossed us through a narrow dark passage. An immense pressure bore down on me, a brutal weight squeezing my shoulders, my ribs, my skull. The greening magic roared and howled around us—not bestial, but rather as if the world itself were twisting, creaking, reshaping itself—and just as I feared my bones would shatter and I would burst open like a stomped bug, everything stopped.

I gasped for air, choking and coughing, and a few burning moments later, I realized that I was lying on cold, damp ground, blinking up at a sky dusted with stars.

We were through. We had survived the greenway.

I laughed a little, still coughing, and tried in vain to push myself upright. The agony ricocheting through my body was scorching, balls of fire flung back and forth by merciless catapults.

At once Talan was there, helping me sit, soaked through and shivering just as I was, and as my pulverized senses slowly worked through their shock, I realized two things: I was going to be sick, and Talan was crying.

I turned away from him just in time. As I emptied my stomach, he rubbed the aching spot between my shoulders and held back my soaked hair. Shakily, I wiped my mouth with a wet sleeve and turned back to him.

"Are you all right?" I whispered, my voice a mere rasp.

"Am *I* all right?" Talan let out a choked little laugh. "Gemma, I thought..."

He shook his head, unable to speak, and gathered me close. He pressed cold kisses to my brow and cheeks, and I nestled against his chest, letting him tuck my head under his. Even dripping and drenched, there was somehow a heat to him, as if his body housed an inner fire that refused to be snuffed out. I closed my eyes and gripped the lapel of his coat, letting his frantic embrace warm me.

"You're crying," I whispered against his collar.

"I thought you were dying," he said thickly, his voice hoarse. "I thought you would drown. I didn't know what was happening."

"I didn't either at first. But it seemed like the only sensible thing to do."

"To dive into a great mass of weeds at the bottom of a magicked lagoon?"

"Precisely." I pulled back just enough to cup his face with my cold, trembling fingers and offered him a shaky smile. "And to think—two days ago you didn't even know me, and now we're here."

He smiled, pressed two fierce kisses to my fingers, and scrubbed his face roughly with his sleeve. "Yes, Lady Gemma, we're here." He glanced into the dark trees. "Wherever *here* is."

Huddled next to him in the dirt, I took a moment to look around for myself and saw that we were in a dense wood of black pines, the branches above us frosted with snow. Standing took tremendous effort; my knees wobbled like a newborn colt's, my dress clung to me like a clammy molted skin, and breathing through the pain still shooting up my body left me light-headed.

Nevertheless, as I leaned against a nearby pine and peered through the trees, I couldn't help but grin.

"What is it?" Talan asked, coming to stand behind me. "Did you find something?"

I pointed ahead of us and up. Past the woods, so shadowed I could barely make out its silhouette, stood a massive sprawling house cradled by the foothills of a looming mountain.

Still shivering, I nevertheless felt a fierce thrill of triumph as I whispered, "Ravenswood."

CHAPTER 10

T alan allowed what must have been half an hour of tramping through the quiet woods abutting the Bask family's estate before delicately clearing his throat beside me.

"I think you'll agree that I've been exceedingly patient," he said lightly.

"Admirably so," I replied.

"And I think you'll acknowledge that you're breathing quite hard, betraying the exhaustion you insist on denying."

I forced myself to walk faster, ignoring the stitch cramping my side. "My legs aren't as long as yours, and I'm unaccustomed to this rocky terrain, but I assure you, Talan, I can—"

"I think you'll also agree," he interrupted, blocking my path, "that it's very late and horrifically cold, and that we should return to Ivyhill at once before one or both of us drops dead."

I stepped around him and continued onward. "You know, this is not as frightful a place as I'd always imagined it to be, which is rather disappointing."

"Gemma—"

"I'd always thought these northern lands would feel desolate and boring, cut off from the more populated regions of the continent as they are. Did you know the only way to travel between the north and the south is by sea? Unless you're rich enough to have a greenway that takes you from one side of the Mist to the other, that is. Anyway, there's actually something rather invigorating about the snow and the cold, the dramatic mountains. And the stars seem so much brighter and closer than they do back home."

"*Gemma.*"

This time when he blocked my path, he took my hands in his, rubbed them, blew on them, and as warmth returned to my fingers with a hesitant prickle, I realized with some shock that I had in fact started to go numb.

Talan gave me a grim smile. Dark curls coated in a light dusting of ice framed his pale brow. "You see? They're lovely fingers, and quite useful besides. I don't think you want to lose them."

I blew out an irritated breath and looked away. "But we've made it this far—"

"And we can do it again, with proper clothing, and with less marching about in lakes, and perhaps wearing boots that aren't falling apart." Gentle fingers on my chin brought my eyes back to his. He was smiling down at me, and then he lifted my fingers to his lips—each knuckle, each finger, one by one—until I was warm all over, kissed back to life by his mouth.

"Much has happened tonight," he said quietly. "But it does not *all* need to happen tonight."

I felt perilously close to pouting. "The next time we come, we'll survey the land, draw a map."

"An excellent idea."

"You said you knew how to track demons, how to spot where they've recently been and recognize protective wards."

"That's correct."

"And you've seen no signs of demons here tonight?"

Talan sighed. "Honestly, Gemma, I haven't been as concerned with tracking demons as I've been with deciding whether or not to throw you over my shoulder and carry you back to the greenway."

"Now, there's an idea," I said slyly, the effect rather diminished by a full-body shudder followed by a slight cough.

Talan raised an eyebrow, his dark eyes sparkling. "I'll have you know that I'm resisting making about a dozen smug comments at the moment."

I glared at him, searching my sluggish, exhausted thoughts for a blisteringly witty reply—but then placed two fingers on Talan's lips and froze.

He stilled as well, a question in his eyes.

I nodded over his shoulder, in the direction of the sound I'd heard.

We waited, hardly breathing. The distant screech of an owl dropped ominously from the sky.

Then the sound came again, louder and longer. I finally recognized it as the flapping of many wings. In its wake came the high, nervous whicker of a horse followed by two voices, a man's and a woman's.

My eyes locked with Talan's. Without saying a word, we turned and followed the sounds through the woods, picking our way with excruciating slowness through the dense undergrowth of moss and ferns. At last, as a light snow began to fall, a faint orange glow seeped through the trees ahead. My body ached to run for it; surely that glow meant fire and warmth.

Instead we crouched in the thick bracken a few paces away from a clearing. Talan delicately pulled aside a large frosted frond to provide a better view, revealing a scene that made my blood run even colder than it already was.

The Basks.

Alastrina Bask and her brother Ryder, to be exact—alone within a large ring of torches and surrounded by dozens of gigantic black birds.

"Ravens," Talan whispered. "How appropriate."

I said nothing, my bile rising as my memory summoned forth that awful day from my childhood—the taste of ash and the acrid sting of smoke. Flames painting the grounds a grotesque, shuddering orange. Father and Byrn and Gilroy and three other men on our staff fighting with all their might to keep my wailing mother from running back into the burning house. Farrin was inside, trapped somewhere amid that awful forest of roaring flames—the flames the *Basks* had set loose on our home—and she was going to die. That was the singular thought filling my tiny seven-year-old body that night as I trembled in the sooty, sweat-slicked arms of one of the housemaids, watching that monstrous fire devour my home: *my sister is going to die.*

Talan touched my hand, pulling me back to myself. "Gemma?" he whispered.

I shook my head, tearing my gaze away from the flickering torches and releasing my iron grip on the branch in front of me.

"I'm fine," I muttered, shoving past the lingering echoes of my mother's keening screams. "I'm *fine.*"

Shifting forward as much as I dared, I squinted through the trees for a better look. The ravens were everywhere—a glistening black coat of them on the ground, on the branches nearest the clearing, and even on Alastrina Bask herself, as if she had sewn herself a dramatic cape of feathers.

Despite the state I was in—nearly frozen, my body still throbbing with pain from our passage through the greenway—I had to admit with grudging approval that Alastrina looked more stunning than I'd ever seen her. She wore only a simple work dress—dark, with a high collar and a column of tiny brass buttons up the back. A lovely detail, though they must have been murder for her maid to fiddle with.

But it wasn't the dress that impressed me. It was the *glow* of her, the serene confidence with which she stood there, surrounded by ravens, her shoulder-length black hair pulled back into an efficient little bun at her nape. She held out her hand, and a bird alighted on her fingers. Even from this distance, I could see the glint of her icy blue eyes. She smiled at the bird, stroked its breast, and then brought it close to her mouth and whispered to it, cupped hand and all, as if sharing with it some titillating secret. Then she released the bird, and it flapped away into the night.

A few seconds later, a second bird took its place. Again Alastrina stroked it in greeting and whispered something against its shining black head.

"What is she doing?" Talan whispered, his voice holding the same note of horrified wonder that I felt. The second bird, its secret received, flew away in the opposite direction of the first bird. A third bird landed on Alastrina's outstretched hand, and all at once the sea of gathered ravens rippled as if they had shifted forward in an orderly feathered line.

Dread coiled tight in my stomach. "She's an Anointed wilder," I said quietly. "Ryder is too, but she's always been the more talented one. She must be sending the birds out to spy for her. They'll be her eyes and ears. Once she's wilded them, wherever they are in the country, she'll be able to move in and out of their bodies as needed."

"That," Talan said, obviously impressed, "is an extremely useful bit of magic."

"I wonder where she's sending them. To Ivyhill perhaps, to spy on us, or to the tournament grounds in Bathyn. The cheater."

"What tournament?"

"The one you're accompanying me to next month."

"Ah." Talan was quiet for a moment. "I assume you'll tell me more about this later?"

"Of course. Gods, if I see *one* raven within ten miles of Ivyhill, I'll shoot down the nasty little beast myself."

"You're a skilled archer as well?" Talan said mildly. "My, my, Lady Gemma, is there anything you can't do?"

Ignoring him, I examined Ryder. He sat on the ground not far from his sister, cradling a raven in his hands. Several more perched on his legs and shoulders, and I noted bitterly—and with no small amount of appreciation—how achingly handsome he was. Such a big, burly titan of a man with a rakish beard and long dark hair tied back from his pale northern face, as if he fancied himself a sea-hardened sailor—and yet he cradled the raven in his large hands as gently as he might a newborn kitten. It was a poetic study in contrasts that, once again, my beauty-loving heart could not ignore.

The bird he held cawed quietly, and Ryder seemed to murmur something in response. Beyond them, a huge dark horse that I recognized as Ryder's stamped his hoof and whickered.

"I wonder what he's talking to them about," Talan said. "Assessing their health, perhaps?"

"After all," I said dryly, "one must carefully assess the constitutions of one's birds before enlisting them for cheating schemes and spy work."

"You can't know for sure that they're doing anything illicit."

I turned to him, incredulous. "They're *Basks*. Of course it's illicit."

Talan gave me a pitying, searching sort of look, as if he could see my memories and was deciding how best to comfort me. But before I could disabuse him of that notion, the branch just beside my left ear shifted, its leaves rustling.

I whirled around with a muted yelp and came face-to-face with an enormous raven.

The awful creature had just landed, the branch still bobbing from its arrival. It blinked its beady black eyes at me a few times in silence before cocking its head—left, then right—and then opening its beak to let out a shrill, rasping call.

Immediately the ravens gathered in the clearing launched themselves into the air. The sound of their flight was deafening. Amid the storming roar of a thousand flapping wings were hoarse calls that, to my panicked ears, sounded like angry cries of warning.

In one swift movement, Ryder surged to his feet, retrieved the bow strapped to his back, and nocked a fat arrow with black fletching. Alastrina, standing within the cyclone of her birds like some fearsome queen, pointed in my direction and called out a word I did not know. But while the language was unfamiliar, the intent was clear: *attack*.

The ravens gathered and reformed, as if they were one creature instead of many. A wheeling black cloud rose up into the air above the clearing.

Talan grabbed my hand, shattering the grip of my shock, and we raced back toward the greenway, crashing through the trees and tearing through thick tangles of ferns. I felt clumsy, hopelessly doomed. My feet were heavy as stones; several times I tripped and fell, scraping up my legs and palms, only to be yanked back to my feet by Talan. My chest burned from gulping down the chilled air, and as we came closer to the greenway, my body revolted, the familiar pain bursting open at my joints and pounding against my temples like mallets.

But I couldn't stop running. From behind us came the raucous cascade of pursuing ravens, a furor of wings and harsh avian screams, and with each pained breath I sucked down, they came closer to catching us.

My toe caught on a gnarled root, and I fell, knocking my chin hard against the cold ground.

Talan came back for me and scooped me up into his arms. I clutched his coat, buried my face against his neck, and directed him through the woods, reading the rhythm of the pain wracking my body as if it were some sinister map. My vision became a swirling sea of disjointed red shapes—there were trees, a sharp scrape of something against my cheek, then cold water and awful, skull-splitting pressure. Talan called my name. I tried to answer but choked on a thick, gritty blackness instead and allowed it to drown me.

CHAPTER 11

When I next woke, I was not alone. My companions were a raging headache, Una whining quietly by the hearth, and worst of all, Jessyl, sitting in her customary chair in the corner and looking more furious than I'd ever seen her.

The expression on her freckled face was enough to send me bolting upright in a blind panic—after which I promptly sank back into my nest of pillows, groaning and holding my head.

"Jessyl," I croaked, "what happened? What time is it?"

"*What happened*, indeed," was all she said.

The silence that followed, broken only by the sound of the quietly snapping fire, held a pointed question. I scrambled to come up with some excuse to explain away whatever Jessyl was thinking, but I didn't know what exactly had transpired between entering the greenway and waking up in my bedroom, and therefore I could only gape at her like a confused fish.

Jessyl nodded briskly, as if my silence confirmed her worst suspicions. Then she rose from her chair to perch primly on the edge of my bed. Only then did I notice that her wavy red hair, normally worn in an immaculate knot, had fallen askew, stray strands trailing limply down her neck. Una sat up, her tail thumping uncertainly against the rug.

"I will say only three things, my lady," Jessyl began, staring straight ahead at the wall instead of at me. "One, I have never been more frightened than I was last night when I discovered you were not in your bed—and indeed nowhere else in the house. Two, I have never been more *relieved* than when Mr. d'Astier burst into your rooms early this morning and brought you back to me, even half-alive and raving as you were."

My chest seized around my heart, and I sent a quick prayer to Jaetris, god of the mind, that somehow in my delirious state I had found enough sense not to give away what Talan and I had done.

"And third," Jessyl said, then paused and finally glanced at me, her bottom lip trembling and her eyes bright. "I don't know what you and Mr. d'Astier got up to last night, but the next time you feel like disappearing into the night on some secret adventure, only to come back scratched and bruised and half-frozen so that I have to use a frightening amount of my stores to treat you...at least tell *me* about it, my lady, so I can cover for you if anyone inquires as to your whereabouts. And so I can know, for the sake of my own heart, that you're well and alive and that I will in fact see you again, *hopefully* in one piece. What if you'd come back even worse for wear and I couldn't treat you? I may have had to send for Madam Moreen, and then we'd *both* have had some uncomfortable explanations to cobble together."

Thoroughly ashamed and lost for words, I stared at my fingers until Jessyl gave me a small watery smile, squeezed my hands, and bustled over to the door that led to my receiving chamber. At the threshold, she paused and looked back over her shoulder.

"I'll come check on you in an hour or so," she said gently. "I'll bring lunch and whatever sweet thing Mrs. Rathmont has baked for us today. You should rest. And don't worry, I told your father you're not feeling well. Before you have to see him, we'll get you healed up nicely. Una, take care of her while I'm gone."

Jessyl gave me one more smile and left, shutting the door quietly behind her. Una leapt up onto the bed, turned around twice, plopped down beside me in a manner endearingly at odds with her elegant long-nosed profile, and rested her head on my leg with a plaintive sigh.

For a long moment, all I could do was lie there among my pillows, clutch my mother's green quilt, and absently scratch the soft spot behind Una's left ear. It seemed impossible that I was back in my rooms, alive and safe—but there was my little atrium and its cheerful profusion of flowers, there was my bathing room and my closet stuffed full of gowns...

And there, tucked underneath a pitcher of water on my bedside table, was a small piece of paper signed with the letter *T*.

My heart racing, I grabbed the paper and unfolded it. Talan's penmanship was, unsurprisingly, exquisite, all symmetrical lines and elegant flourishes.

Lady Gemma,

Never in my life have I enjoyed such a rapturous night as the one we spent together. I will, I hope, be lucky enough to see you again as soon as tomorrow morning at eleven o'clock. I will wait for you at our fountain with bated breath, and until then I will ache to once more hear your voice, revel in your scent, and feel the velvet kiss of your touch. Rest that delicious little body of yours, wildcat, and let your heart be soothed by the day's warmth. I've never seen such a dazzling blue sky, disturbed by neither cloud nor bird. Perhaps the sun too is enamored of you and will abide no distractions as it searches longingly for your bed. I know the feeling well.

Yours,
Talan

Though I recognized the note for what it was—a clever ruse designed to dispel any suspicions as to how and where we had spent our night, not to mention a reassurance that no ravens had followed us—Talan's words nevertheless warmed me from head to toe. I squirmed a little against my pillows, allowing myself to imagine for just a brief moment this invented night we'd spent together. What *would* we have done?

The images unfurled smoothly in my mind. We would have indeed toured the house, but our tour would have been cut short, for somewhere around the art gallery on the east wing's third floor, the moonlight streaming through the windows, we would have succumbed to the irresistible delight of each other's beauty. Talan would have kissed me beneath those frowning oil portraits of Ashbournes past, his beautiful pale hands unbuttoning my nightgown until I was laid bare to him, and perhaps we wouldn't have been able to *stand* the thought of traveling all the way back to my rooms.

Instead, maybe he would have taken me right there against the wall, behind the solemn white statue of the Shepherd Who Heard the Song of the Skies. Still wearing his dark riding coat, his cheeks flushed with desire, he would have placed a gloved hand over my mouth to stifle my cries of pleasure.

Look at me, Gemma, he might have said, his voice smooth and soft, falling like a song against my skin. *Keep those eyes open as you come for me.*

Una barked, wrenching me out of my unexpected but not unwelcome daydream. My cheeks flamed with humiliation, as if she had actually caught Talan and me mid-sully.

"You," I said to myself, folding up the note decisively, "need to calm down in numerous ways."

Shaking the images of a half-naked Talan from my mind, I retrieved a pen and fresh piece of paper from the drawer of my bedside table and then kissed the soft little dip between Una's huge brown eyes. My mind was a jumble, my body felt as if it had been the victim of a stampede, and I needed to think.

Without hesitation, I began writing down everything that had happened since the evening of the party to clear it all from my head and determine what was to be done next.

Father's office
Madam Baines—what does she remember?
Talan's empathic powers—find out more
Father's secret greenway in the lake
Another secret greenway—not even Farrin knows this one?
Ryder and Alastrina—wilded ravens. Spies? Messengers?
The Bathyn tournament
The glamour that drove Jessyl mad—how did it happen? What caused it?

A twist of guilt tightened my chest. Reluctantly I added one more item to my list:

Mara—what did she want to tell me? Visit her?

I paused, chewing my lip anxiously as my mind raced through possible scenarios. I could sneak through the greenway that led to Rosewarren and visit Mara on my own, but I needed to preserve my strength for Talan's and my visits to Ravenswood. I could travel to Rosewarren by carriage, but that would take far too long, and I had no time to waste. I could appeal to Father's pity and beg him to escort me properly, but that would require an official request for dispensation from the Warden, and perhaps it would draw undue attention to me, which was the last thing I wanted at the moment. I could try to convince Farrin to be my escort instead, but that seemed unlikeliest of all. My sister was very fond of order; she abhorred the breaking of rules and would pounce on me for even suggesting such a thing.

And even if I did get to Rosewarren somehow, then what? Once Mara made her request of me or revealed whatever information had so tormented her, I would no longer be able to ignore the memory of her haunted face—and, even worse, the memory of her obvious utter humiliation when I witnessed her transformation. I would have no choice but to help her, even though I couldn't imagine what help someone like me could possibly provide. And besides, the thought of devoting my limited strength to anything but Talan's and my plans made me tense up with a terrible panic. We needed to find out whether the Man with the Three-Eyed Crown existed, and if he did, I couldn't bear the thought of anyone or anything distracting me from making my request of him:

Heal me. Remake me. Bind me if you must. I will offer whatever you require in exchange: my wealth, my loyalty, my body.

No. Nothing would divert me from this end. Not even Mara.

Una barked, wresting me from my musings. Her tail wagged as she watched me. No doubt she was eager to go for a long walk under the birdless blue sky about which Talan had waxed rhapsodic.

"Not today, my sweet girl," I crooned, appeasing Una with a series of belly scratches. I smiled a little, determined to ignore the sour taste of shame on my tongue, and resumed writing.

Farrin—can I trust her with our scheme?
Gareth—send him to Rosewarren in my stead?
Illaria—tell her about the "rapturous night" with
    Talan
Talan
Talan
Talan

I stared at my list for a long time, avoiding the words *Madam Baines* and *Mara*. It was perhaps my greatest talent: turning away from things that frightened or overwhelmed me and pretending they did not exist. Instead I focused on the word *Talan*. I'd written his name again and again, unable to form a coherent thought regarding him but hearing his name run through my mind nevertheless— almost *feeling* it, as if it were the very thrum of my blood.

Feeling a little more clearheaded, my worries successfully shut away in the darkest corners of my mind, I took one final glance at my list and rose from my bed, hobbled on tender feet to the quieting fire, tore the paper into pieces, and fed it to the flames.

◆

I remained in bed for the rest of the day with only Una for company.

After only a few hours, my feet had nearly healed, thanks to Jessyl's impressive collection of rare, and accordingly expensive, medicinal supplies—salves and tinctures, an entire wall of tiny drawers filled with meticulously labeled roots and herbs, and even some experimental elixirs concocted by the reclusive Anointed Brothers of Kerezen at the Pallas Cloisters. Many times I'd tried to dissuade Jessyl from spending her wages on such things, but she would hear none of my protests. *One can never be too prepared for catastrophe* was her unwavering rebuttal.

I knew what that meant. Jessyl had lived at Ivyhill her whole life, born to two of our tenant farmers who had worked the southeastern portion of our estate for generations. Jessyl had been eleven years old when the Basks' fire had nearly destroyed the mansion. Many on our staff had suffered burns, as had I, but Jessyl had been fortunate enough to escape the house unscathed, and ever since then, she had obsessively collected remedies, preparing for some disastrous future attack.

Of course there was another reason for this habit of hers: one of the medicines she collected could someday prove to be the very thing to cure my body of all its ailments.

I brooded on this in the late afternoon sunlight, perversely amused by imagining how Jessyl would react when I someday marched through the front doors, not only healed but *remade*, courtesy not of medicine but a demon.

If, that is, Talan and I could find him.

And if he was amenable to my proposition.

And if he didn't somehow trick me right out of my skin and proceed to wear it like a cloak around Gallinor.

Una whined, lifting her head from my pillow.

I glared at her. "What? I'll figure it out. There's time yet. We still have to *find* him, after all."

She whined again, apparently unconvinced. Then she stilled for a moment before whipping her head around to stare at my bedroom door with pricked ears and a hopeful wag of her tail.

I sat up, listening. At first I heard nothing—no approaching footsteps, no creak of hinges—but then, very faintly, a distant trill of music met my ears. Impossibly, it sounded as though someone was playing the piano. A soaring melody floated up through the house, the chords tragic but determined and without a single note out of place.

A little chill of joy raised gooseflesh on my arms, and all at once I was smiling, and everything I'd been ruminating over flew out of my mind. I scrambled out of bed, retrieved my longest dressing gown to cloak my healing wounds and a pair of soft leather boots that would cushion my feet. As fast as my still-aching body was able to carry me, I hurried down the long windowed hallway that housed my family's chambers, past the winter garden, lush ferns and southern palms sprinkled among its stately white columns, and gingerly down a flight of stairs into the central wing, which housed, among other things, the Green Ballroom.

A small rapt crowd huddled at the entrance—servants, cousins, lingering party guests. Some grinned like children, hands over their mouths as if they could hardly contain their glee. Others pressed their ears to the double doors, their faces contorted with quiet desperation. Our head butler, Gilroy—a stern and staggeringly competent man with a ruddy complexion and fearsome black eyebrows that could stop even Father in his tracks—lay flat on the gleaming parquet floor, tears streaming silently down his face.

An embarrassing display in any other context, but given what was happening in the ballroom, I couldn't blame any of them.

"I'm quite sure you all have somewhere better to be," I said briskly, fighting hard against my own emotions as I approached.

Una unhelpfully ran mad circles around me. "This is not a circus for you to gawk at. Off with you, all of you, this instant."

Most of them scattered quickly, but some lingered, including Gilroy, who'd picked himself up off the floor only to stand there and gaze with naked longing at the ballroom doors.

I placed myself directly in front of him and said, "*Gilroy.* Control yourself, would you? And direct everyone currently on this floor elsewhere—outside, to the kitchens, I don't care."

He blinked at me, helpless and dumbfounded, until I tried a different tack and gently touched his arm.

"You know what this means, don't you, Gilroy?" I said quietly. "What it means to our family. What it means to *her.*"

That seemed to shake him out of his stupor. He coughed, hastily wiped his eyes, harrumphed a few times, and then turned to the gaping stragglers.

"I believe you all heard Lady Gemma," Gilroy declared, his deep baritone voice rough with emotion. "We will all adjourn to the veranda overlooking the southern lawn, to which I will have Mrs. Rathmont send up refreshments."

I waited sternly at the ballroom doors until Gilroy had managed to usher them all away. The last of them—a second cousin of my father's, a man dry and boring as sand—clung to the frame of a foyer door, pleading for permission to stay, which forced poor Gilroy to physically pry him loose.

When the foyer was empty, I took a deep breath, briefly pressed Una's silky head against my thigh for reassurance, and entered the ballroom.

There at the room's heart, sitting at the piano, was Farrin.

For a moment I simply leaned back against the closed doors and took in the scene, my heart hammering. The piano was a glorious instrument of rich cherrywood, elaborately ornamented with finely carved vines and commissioned for Farrin by our parents when she was barely old enough to walk. It had been obvious even then what her Anointed power was, and though it had been years since that disastrous final performance that had nearly roused the audience into an ecstatic riot, Farrin had clearly lost none of her gods-given touch.

My eldest sister was never more beautiful than when she played music, whether the instrument was the piano or her beloved fiddle—which had not left its velvet-lined case in years—or simply her own voice. The severe lines of her face softened, the tension in her shoulders melted away, and her body seemed to *fit* her more easily, as if this were the one thing it was meant to do and everything else was simply marking time like a bored and embittered Lower Army soldier.

Farrin's hands danced upon the keys, striking each one with a combination of power and impossible delicacy, and her face glowed with such happiness that it made me ache to watch her. Strands of golden hair had fallen loose from her customary severe braid. She seemed like a child again, bathed in the afternoon sunlight pouring through the west-facing windows in streams of rich gold. Even the ballroom itself seemed imbued with new life. Empty save for the piano, its green walls looked velvet-soft in the warm light, each one adorned simply with long white drapes and my mother's ubiquitous ivy vines. The gilded molding sparkled, and even the painted white flowers festooning the floor seemed more vivid, as if freshly bloomed.

At last Farrin finished with a slow, tender wave of notes cascading upward from the lower registers and ending on the highest keys like a tender sprinkle of rain. She paused, her hands hovering over the keys, and then sighed and relaxed, sitting back on the cushioned bench with a small secret smile on her face.

Seeing her like that, my chest clenched painfully. I hated to disrupt such a rare moment of peace, but it would be worse if Farrin turned around to find me spying.

I cleared my throat as delicately as I could. "Farrin, I love you so much I can hardly breathe."

My sister stiffened and glared over her shoulder. Osmund, her long-haired black cat—a gorgeous creature save for the perpetually scornful expression on his face—jumped down from his perch beside Farrin and began primly cleaning his paws. An innocuous enough action for another cat, perhaps, but the warning was clear: if I were to approach, it should be slowly and with great care.

I obeyed, Una for once walking quietly beside me. Wishing desperately to pull Farrin into my arms and hug her as I hadn't in what felt like ages, I instead sat on the floor at the piano's feet and looked up at her, waiting. Hesitantly, Una curled her long body into an awkward ball on the floor a safe distance from Osmund, who had stopped cleaning himself to watch her.

Farrin stared at the keys, her body hunched over a little as if expecting a blow. The soft openness her face had worn only moments before had vanished.

After a long moment, she said quietly, "Father wishes for me to perform at the tournament."

Sudden anger flared hot in my chest and cheeks, but I stifled my outburst. "And when you say *wishes*, you mean *demands*."

Farrin let out a quiet laugh. "Shocking, is it not?"

A thousand indignant words gathered on my tongue—namely how unfair it was for Father to ask this of her when he knew very well how thoroughly terrified she'd been after that last performance—but I remained silent. Farrin had a great respect for quiet and stillness; they gave her room to think.

"I haven't played a single note since that day," she said slowly, still looking at the piano's gleaming keys. "It's been ten years."

I smiled a little. "Tell that to your fingers. They seem to think no time at all has passed."

"Playing just now..." Farrin fell silent, her mouth twisting. When she looked up at me, her eyes were bright, and I had to sit on my hands to keep from reaching for her.

"I feel as if I've been dead all these years," she whispered, "and today she brought me back to life." Reverently, light as a butterfly's kiss, Farrin touched the keys and played a soft note. Then she squeezed her eyes shut. "But I can't bear it, Gemma. I can't bear the thought of hearing them shout my name, shower me with flowers, beg me to marry them, beg me to even just *look* at them, roar and curse at me when I refuse. That's not what the gods intended. That's not what I *want*."

Farrin drew in a shaky breath, and when she opened her eyes, her face was set in grim determination. "I'll perform at the tournament. It will make Father happy, and so few things do anymore. But after that I won't do it again, not even here at home. It's too dangerous. I know they were listening outside. I could feel the sweaty huddle of them itching to throw open the doors." She laughed bitterly, wiped her nose with her arm, looked up at the ceiling, and blinked hard. "I know. Such a lie. If Father asks me to do it again, I will, of course. I'll do it every time, no matter how horrible it makes me feel. I'll die and live and die again at his command."

Gripped by the desolate tone of her voice, I hardly moved, could hardly breathe. Every reply that came to my mind seemed a laughably meager balm for such naked grief. I remembered my burned list. *Farrin—can I trust her with our scheme?*

Maybe I could someday, once the tournament was a distant memory. Until then, I knew I couldn't burden Farrin with Talan's and my secrets, and certainly not those secrets that were mine alone. Demons and greenways and the strange anomalous glamour I'd made seemed foolish, even childish, in that moment.

Finally I said the safest thing I could think of.

"Tell me what it's about," I said. "That piece you just finished. You wrote it, didn't you?"

Farrin clutched her hands in her lap and nodded. "Do you remember the shining boy?"

Of course I did—the boy Farrin swore had saved her from the Basks' fire. Father had long ago given up trying to convince her that whatever she had seen was an apparition conjured by her dying, smoke-clogged mind.

"When he came to me," Farrin said slowly, a familiar recitation, "he shone as if bathed in white light, and he wore a strange cloth mask with blacked-out eyes. He reached for me and said, *Don't be afraid. I know the way out.*" She breathed in and out slowly. "And he did."

I had never known what, if anything, to believe about that story, but I nevertheless loved the romance of it, the mystery. Real or not, the shining boy had guided my sister away from an awful, fiery death.

"The piece is about him, then?" I asked.

"Yes. About that night, and where he might be now. *Who* he might be. What it would feel like if we were to meet now that we're grown. And what it would feel like if I spent my whole life wondering about him and never found an answer."

In the silence that followed, Osmund—shocking all of us—sauntered over to Una and curled up beside her like a kitten with its mother. His sly yellow eyes narrowed contentedly, as if we were fools for ever doubting him. My darling Una dared not move. Her tail gave a single cautious wag.

Farrin and I laughed, and Farrin wiped her eyes with a wry shake of her head, and for a moment—fleeting, and all the more precious for it—we were children again, before Mara left, before Mother left, all huddled together in our playroom attic, pretending we were Old Country beasts and laughing madly at gods knew what.

I touched Farrin's hand. "Play it again for me?"

My sister's brown eyes, ordinarily so sharp and stern, softened as she looked down at me. She kissed the crown of my head and then, with a brave little sigh, began to play.

As the notes of her composition washed over me and the afternoon light warmed us, I thought only of my sisters—one near, one far—and how it would feel to be nestled between them once again, as so often happened when I was small. Mara holding open a book, Farrin reading it aloud, and me squashed happily in the middle, wide eyes glued to the inked pages, hands clutching Farrin's sleeve, silently begging the gods to make the story last forever.

CHAPTER 12

Two days later, three-quarters of an hour through my weekly styling appointment with Kerrish, she threw up her hands, stepped back from me, and glared at my reflection in the mirror.

"Out with it, whatever it is," she said sharply. "You've been acting strange ever since I walked in, and now you're so tense I'm afraid you'll snap in two with one wrong pull of my brush. And then I'll have to approach your father on bended knee, holding the shattered halves of your body in my arms, and beg for forgiveness."

A significant pause. Then Kerrish raised one perfectly manicured eyebrow. "I can't imagine that would go very well. What do you think?"

I swallowed hard and glanced down sheepishly at my hands, quickly going over in my mind everything Talan and I had talked about the day before. It wasn't the first time I'd attempted to wheedle something out of Kerrish, but it *was* the first time her cooperation truly mattered.

"I'm sorry, Kerrish," I began quietly, but she cut me off with a scornful click of her tongue, pulled my chair around until I faced her, and sat down on the stool across from me.

"Don't waste my time, Gemma," she said. "If you want something from me, ask. Either that or stop your fidgeting. You're making me nervous."

I lifted my eyes to Kerrish's face. My Anointed stylist was a formidable old woman—stout and short with sharp, beady brown eyes and the smooth golden-brown skin of a child, making it impossible to guess her true age. Her thick silver hair shone like starlight; today she wore it in an elaborate crown of braids. Her lashes were long and lush, her fingernails were painted a glossy pastel pink, and her ears glittered with jewels. She wore an outrageous periwinkle gown with a high ruffled collar, a plunging neckline, a corseted bodice that flattered her voluptuous curves, and an enormous bustle of lace and satin that swished most becomingly when she walked.

Naturally the dress was of her own design, which meant it would soon be copied hundreds of times over by anyone who paid attention to fashion—but not before the tournament in Bathyn, when I would debut my own custom version of it, which Kerrish promised would be even lovelier than the original.

Being an Ashbourne—and Kerrish's favored pet besides—had its benefits.

"Well, you see," I began, then hesitated, biting my lip and smiling coyly, "I've met someone."

"Shocking," Kerrish said, her eyes sparkling. "And who's the lucky lover this time?"

"His name is Talan d'Astier."

"A Vauzanian?"

I nodded eagerly, batting the lashes Kerrish had just curled and painted. "I met him at our party. He has such a sad story, and such a delectably talented mouth. We, er…"

I bit my lip again, then withdrew Talan's note from my pocket and handed it to Kerrish. She read it quickly and rolled her eyes.

"Gods unmade," she swore, smiling ruefully. "The 'velvet kiss of your touch'? I don't know whether to congratulate you or question your taste."

"Oh, congratulations are *definitely* in order." I leaned forward with a grin. "The man never tires. He brought me to completion no less than four times during our first night together. And…" I looked around my empty rooms as though worried we'd be overheard. "Last night he took me right in front of the window overlooking the south lawn veranda, which was *crawling* with guests enjoying their supper under the stars. If anyone had looked up… gods, maybe some of them *did*. Well, if so, they got quite a show."

I sat back on my stool with a sensual sigh, heated all over by my own fabricated story. "He's so…*fun*. And freeing. When I'm with him…" I shook my head, laughing a little, and then said earnestly, "Kerrish, when I'm with him, I don't notice my pain. Not my headaches, not my throbbing joints, not even the sting of magic in the air. I only notice how *good* he makes me feel."

Kerrish's knowing little smile softened. Gently she pressed my hands between hers, and I felt a twinge of guilt at the tapestry of lies I was weaving.

"And for how long will this god among men be staying at Ivyhill?" Kerrish asked.

"Indefinitely, as far as I know. He's a friend of Father's. They're working on a plan to sell the wine stores Talan inherited." I giggled, covering my mouth with one hand. "I'm not sure Father would have allowed him within twenty miles of the estate if he'd known how utterly Mr. d'Astier would ravish his daughter."

"Tut, tut. Naughty girl." Kerrish tapped my hand, then stood to resume combing a smoothing oil into my curls. "So what is it you want, then? Yet another new dress, perhaps designed for swift disrobement?"

Nerves fluttered in my belly on trembling wings. I managed an airy laugh. "Not exactly. You see, Talan and I want to visit Derryndell, but we don't want to go as *ourselves* in case we happen to be"—I delicately cleared my throat—"caught in a compromising position. I want to *help* Talan restore his family's name, not ruin his chances all in one go."

Kerrish's comb stilled in my hair. "You want me to craft glamours for the two of you," she said, her face stern in the mirror, "so you can go gallivanting off to the town your father practically owns—where you could encounter gods know *what* stray magicks from any number of strange travelers—and enjoy a night of wild public sex with a man you've known for only a few days?"

My cheeks felt like they were on fire, so intense was my growing guilt, but I nevertheless met Kerrish's eyes with the expression I had practiced earlier in the mirror—one of grave but determined resignation.

"No one knows what's wrong with me, Kerrish," I said quietly. "No one knows if I'll wake up tomorrow and enjoy an ordinary day or if Jessyl will bring me my breakfast only to find me dead, shocked lifeless during the night from whatever gods-forsaken illness I carry." I drew in a deep breath, surprising even myself with how easily I was able to summon forth twin wells of tears. "Can you blame me for wanting to enjoy to the fullest this tortured existence the gods have given me? For however much longer I'm alive, that is."

I paused, worried my performance had gone too far. Earlier that day, I'd rehearsed my little speech without issue, but voicing it to Kerrish made it feel more like truth than a lie. A sort of hot-cold calm settled upon me as I remembered it was indeed quite possible that I *could* go to bed and not wake up, that someday a magic I'd never before encountered could prove shockingly fatal to my fragile body.

Familiar ghastly thoughts began their slow crawl into the fore-front of my mind.

I could die, and there was nothing anyone could do about that. No one knew what was wrong with me. No one knew how to heal me.

I could die, and maybe it wouldn't be so terrible a thing.

I could die even with a demon's help—or *because* of a demon's help.

But I had to try, didn't I? And if even that failed, if not even a demon could mend me, then maybe that would be a sign from the gods that I should never have come into existence in the first place, that there was a wrongness deep inside me, that I should give up at last.

The sound of Kerrish sniffling startled me free of my morbid daze. Even more shockingly, she yanked me into a fierce hug—our first ever embrace.

"Fine," she said, her voice thick. "You awful girl, I'll do it. But this Talan fellow had better take good care of you during all this sex you're going to have, because if something should happen to you while you're with him, I swear I'll pray every morning there-after for Zelphenia's specters to torment *both* of your souls until the Remaking."

A surge of relief shook free my remaining dark thoughts. I forced out a bright, bubbling laugh.

"Oh, Kerrish, *thank you*," I gushed, grabbing her hands. "You don't know what this means to me!"

Kerrish shook me off with a grin. "Four times in one night, you said? My dear, thanks to your continuing tendency to over-share, I in fact know *quite* well what this means to you."

With that she returned to her work—dusting my face with shimmering powder, brushing dusky shadows onto my eyelids.

Last of all, pursing her lips in silent disapproval, she granted my request for a small glamour. With a light caress of her fingers and a charged shock of pain as her magic hit me, she smoothed away the last of the self-inflicted bruises on my arms.

Love marks, I'd told her slyly. *I told Talan to be as rough as he likes.*

And for a moment, with my lovely smiling reflection staring back at me, I let myself believe my own lie.

When Talan and I emerged from the greenway, sopping wet and panting, I fell to my hands and knees in the cold bracken of the Ravenswood forest.

I had been smart enough not to eat much that day in anticipation of our trip to the Bask estate, but my stomach nevertheless protested our rough passage through the greenway—the fifth in two weeks—and my head felt clasped between huge scorching hands determined to crush me.

With a jolt of equal parts frustration and excitement, I realized what I had to do. During our first four trips to Ravenswood, I'd been stubbornly determined not to ask it of Talan unless dire circumstances arose, but I decided being half out of my mind with dizzy pain while sneaking around the Basks' forest certainly counted.

"Talan," I whispered, "I need your help."

He came to me at once, opening the small bag of supplies slung around his torso—a watertight construction of Kerrish's made of treated leather. My *purse*, commissioned for my supposed evenings in town with Talan.

"What can I do?" he asked quietly, opening the bag. "Do you want a tonic for your headache?"

"No," I replied, "I need your *help*."

He ducked down to look at me. Our fifth journey to Ravenswood, and I still wasn't quite used to Talan's glamoured visage—certainly not unattractive, but rounder than his own, with soft brown eyes and a scruffy mess of brown hair. That kissable mouth, though, full and slightly turned up at the corners as if he had just thought of something deliciously naughty—that at least remained his. A gift from Kerrish, who, when she met Talan for the first time, had stood in open-mouthed shock for a long moment before turning to me and swearing with hearty approval, "*Gods remade*, my girl."

"A lovely mouth you have, husband," I murmured. My splitting headache—and Talan's mouth—made it difficult to think, but I did remember the amusing little false history we'd constructed. Our glamoured selves were a husband and wife, a cobbler and a blacksmith, happily married for years in no small part due to their exhibitionist sojourns around Gallinor.

"You must tell me in plain words, er, wife," Talan said, a little awkwardly. "Do you wish for me to ease your pain with my empathic power?"

Amused by his grave formality, I laughed, which of course made the pain worse. I hunched over, mouth open in a silent agonized cry.

"*Gemma*," Talan urged.

"Yes," I gasped out. "Use your power and make it stop, or whatever nonsense you said."

The relief was immediate—a rush of smoothing warmth that spread quickly through my entire body. The feeling of calm contentment was so swift, so comforting and complete, that I slumped into a crumpled heap on the forest floor.

Talan helped me sit up against his chest. "I'm sorry if that was overwhelming," he said quietly. "You looked so miserable, I wanted to work quickly."

Trembling, I clung to him as he gently moved dripping strands of black hair out of my glamoured face—ruddier than my own, with a square jaw and incredible hawkish eyebrows. I closed my eyes, allowing my body to revel in its new strength. A false strength, but I didn't care. It was the first time since the beginning of our arrangement that I'd asked Talan for the gift of his power, and in that moment I couldn't begin to fathom why I'd waited so long. My eyes, my head, my joints—they all felt wiped clean and reinforced, as if that sublime warmth had indeed remade my every bone rather than simply disguising their anguish.

Tears gathered treacherously in my lashes, but I blinked them back and said nothing until my eyes were safely dry.

"Thank you for that," I said quietly.

"You're welcome," Talan replied, "and gods, Gemma, I hope you ask me to help you more often from now on instead of needlessly suffering in silence. It destroys me every time I see you gritting your teeth through obvious pain."

I rose to my feet, invigorated by the sharpness of my vision, the steadiness of my limbs. "Astonishing what one can experience without constant pain gumming up the works," I said lightly, though I don't think Talan was fooled. I ignored his pitying expression and briskly took the bag from him, which held a few stoppered vials of medicines from Jessyl's stores, rags for drying ourselves, and, most importantly, a small journal and pen.

Once we'd tended to our appearances as best we could, I opened the journal, assessed where we'd left off during our previous visit, and marched westward through the trees, Talan close behind. We worked in silence; it was our fourth proper surveillance of the forested land surrounding Ravenswood, and we'd decided after our first disastrous venture to speak only when it was absolutely necessary. Crude hand signals, facial expressions, and occasional abbreviated scribblings in our journal had proven surprisingly effective, as if we'd been traipsing off on secret missions to enemy territory for years.

I smiled to myself as we worked, noting the locations of significant landmarks, dangerous slopes in the earth, low stone walls that wove through the woods like ancient serpents. The illusion of my galvanized body left me gleefully content and allowed me room to think of other things, such as how I should eventually propose to Talan that we enjoy an *actual* night in town, and then relish the expression on his face when I suggested how we ought to spend said night.

We deserve some fun after all this sneaking about, I'd tell him, perhaps whilst slowly unbuttoning whatever garment I happened to be wearing at the moment—not a complete reveal, just enough to tantalize. *Don't you want me, Talan?*

Abruptly Talan halted and put out an arm to stop me. I froze, listening. We'd been lucky to encounter no one during our previous visits, not even a single raven—but that night, with the half moon dimly lighting the undergrowth and a chill breeze ruffling the ends of my hair, something suddenly felt different. Tense and watchful. My instincts screamed out a warning: we were not alone.

"Do you smell that?" Talan whispered. "A sour tang, like blood or metal."

I sniffed. "Actually, yes. And a slight sweet scent too. It reminds me of dead flowers gone rotten in a vase." I glanced at Talan. "What does that mean?"

Talan searched the sea of pines with narrowed eyes. "I think it means a wardstone is nearby."

"Wardstone—a protection against demons. Isn't that right?"

His mouth quirked. "So you *do* listen when I tell you things."

"Mmm. Only occasionally."

"If we can find the wardstone and take it back to Ivyhill, we might be able to learn from it—if it's been designed for general demonic defense or for something specific, like the Man with the Three-Eyed Crown. And if it *has* been designed to defend against him and we're able to decipher the spellwork, we could learn what he looks like and how many times he's come within range of the wardstone."

"If he actually exists," I said flatly, a familiar refrain I insisted upon, though inwardly I was teeming with excitement. Finally we'd found something useful.

Talan sighed. "I think we've established by this point that yes, all of this will be rendered moot should this demon not in fact exist."

Then his body tensed, all amusement gone. I followed his gaze and saw it for myself—at the top of a slight rocky ridge just ahead of us, beneath a clutch of three pine trees leaning precariously out over the slope, stood a child. A girl, perhaps ten years of age, cowering behind one of the pines. Dressed in muddy rags, wide-eyed and pale, her hair a matted blond mess, she wept quietly.

"Can you help me?" the child whimpered, her voice kitten-sweet. She stepped closer, into the light. Bloody streaks marked her face. "Please help me. They're hurting me. They won't let me go."

The sight of her stumbling down the ridge broke my heart. I started toward her at once, but Talan grabbed my arm and pulled me around to face him.

"Don't go to her," he said tensely. "Don't even look at her. *She's* the smell. She's a wardwraith."

"A *what*?" I whispered.

"I've read about them. Wardstones create various tricks to distract and thwart intruders, to lure demons away from their prey. Wardwraiths are one such defense."

I felt a small tap on my arm. "Are you listening to me?" cooed a plaintive voice. "I'm so cold. They've been hurting me. Can you take me away from here?"

A chill raised all the hairs on my arms. That limping child should not have been able to reach us so quickly.

"Don't look at her," Talan warned. "Look at me. She'll hold you in thrall and you'll be helpless, trapped."

"You're not *listening*," the child said, a slight edge to her voice. "Don't you want to help me?"

An idea began to form. "But she's only a child, and she needs our help."

"She's an illusion," he hissed. "A piece of magic engineered to kill us, if it comes to it."

A small filthy hand tugged on Talan's sleeve. "Listen to me!" the child shrieked, beside me now.

"She needs our *help*." I glared pointedly at the woods. "I can help her, darling husband, if you won't."

Talan's expression cleared. He blinked twice. "Ah. I see."

My heart hammered with fear as I turned to kneel before the child and forced a kind smile onto my face. I prayed desperately to the gods that this would work, that I could distract the girl long enough for Talan to find the wardstone. We needed that stone and the information it held; *I* needed it.

"Hello, little one," I said quietly. "Slow down, now. Tell me what's happened. Tell me everything from the beginning, and then I'll know how best to help you."

The child stopped her furious crying, sniffling herself quiet. She wiped a dirty sleeve across her face and stared at me with a strange, curious expression.

"You're interesting," she said, frowning. She tilted her head to the side. "I like you. I'd like to learn more about you." She extended her left hand with a shy smile. "Would you come with me?"

I bit down against a rising swell of fear, refusing to look back at Talan, who was slowly moving away through the woods.

"Don't you want to tell me what's happened to you?" I asked gently. "We can sit down right here, beneath all these lovely trees—"

"Oh, I'll tell you. I'll tell you all about it. But first we have to fetch Willow. She's my kitten. We can't leave her."

I hesitated. "Where is Willow?"

The child pointed back up the ridge in the general direction of the distant Ravenswood mansion.

"It's not far," she said cheerfully, taking my hand. "Come, I'll show you!"

Once more I hesitated, but the girl's grip was iron, and as she stared down at me with that smiling bloody face, I realized I had not once seen her blink.

I sent up two quick prayers—one to Kerezen that she would help Talan move quickly and search keenly, and one to Zelphenia, goddess of the unknowable, that she would keep me safe from this strange being leading me through the forest. The child started humming to herself, each happy little note tightening the knot of fear in my stomach.

"What's your name, child?" I asked, desperate to hear something other than her eerie song. "You never told me."

"I don't have a name, silly. Look!" The child pointed through the thinning trees. "That's where Willow lives."

Swallowing hard, barely resisting the urge to look back over my shoulder for Talan, I let the child lead me across a tidy clearing toward a large stone building. Torches crackled merrily on brackets at each corner of the structure. Two more marked the entrance to a nearby road of smooth stone that wound up a tree-covered slope—to the Basks' mountainside mansion, I assumed.

As we neared the building, the child tugged violently on my

arm and started walking faster, and faster, until I could barely keep up with her. Fresh pain surged back through my body like hard torrents of rain. Alarmed, I realized Talan must be too far away for his power to help me. Or worse, something terrible had happened to him.

"Oh!" the child squealed with delight. "My favorite puppy!"

Panting, I struggled to right my suddenly rocking vision. I heard a horse whicker softly, smelled feed and dung, and relaxed slightly. The building was a stable, then, and presumably not some nefarious den of torture.

"I thought Willow was a kitten," I managed, just before the child dragged me around the corner of the stable and sent me stumbling straight into Ryder Bask.

For a moment we simply stared at each other, my racing heart thundering in my ears.

Ryder carried a freshly oiled saddle and wore a coil of rope slung over one shoulder. His shirt and trousers were filthy, his riding boots scuffed, and his hair sat in a messy knot on top of his head. Absurdly, my mind thought it important to notice the tiny piece of straw stuck in his dark beard.

Ryder cut his sharp gaze toward the child. "Who is this?"

The child swayed side to side, her hands behind her back and an adoring, almost swoony expression on her face. "An intruder, Lord Bask. But I like this one. Please don't kill her?"

The word *kill* plunged me into an animal panic. I spun around and ran toward the trees, the wardwraith's giggles scampering after me.

Ryder caught me easily. He whirled me around and wrenched my arm behind my back.

"Are you alone?" he growled, his mouth hot against my ear. He smelled like manure and oil, and the strength in his large callused hands assured me that he could kill me in two seconds if he chose to.

Terror rendered me mute.

He yanked my arm into an even worse position, so hard I thought my shoulder might tear free from my body. I screamed, and for an instant, the world turned black. A strange sensation like wading through water flickered over me. Briefly the world shimmered, as if I were viewing it through rippled glass, and I realized with horror that my glamour was fading.

Ryder saw it too. His eyes narrowed, and he spun me around to face him fully.

"Who are you?" he said, deadly quiet. "You have five seconds to tell me something useful before I break your arm."

"My lord Bask, please let me go!" I gasped, my thoughts wild and fumbling. "They're after my wardstone, that child and her guardian! I don't know what she is, perhaps a shapeshifter from the Old Country, but she stole my face and is pretending—"

"Pathetic," Ryder interrupted, laughing. His blue eyes glinted with a cruel light. "You're no wardwraith, girl, nor are you Olden. What is it, then? Thief? Poacher? Or are you a worthless piece of shit working for the Ashbournes?"

Before I could manage any sort of response, the air shifted around us as if the wind had suddenly changed direction. A familiar warmth touched the small of my back.

I could have cried from relief. Talan was near.

Ryder turned ashen, his face contorting into an expression of absolute horror.

"Oh, gods," he whispered. Then he abruptly released me and ran in the opposite direction, toward the road that led up to the mansion.

Baffled, I watched him flee.

"Trina!" he cried, his voice cracking open. "*Trina!*"

His sister's name, uttered with such naked grief that goose-flesh broke out on my arms.

"Ciaran Bask's greatest fear," came a soft, tired voice from behind me. "His sister in pain, his sister dead. He practically reeks of it. It wasn't hard to find, nor to exploit."

All the breath went out of me. *Talan.*

I spun around and ran into his arms, heedless of my screaming shoulder and so unspeakably glad to see his glamoured face that I let out a choked sob.

He kissed my brow, then drew back with a hiss. "You're hurt. The pain's coming off of you in waves. A muscle in your shoulder is torn."

I waved him off. I couldn't bear the tenderness of his concern, not until we were safely home. "Did you find the wardstone?"

Talan glanced down at his bag. "I did. It's...it's much more advanced than anything I've read about. An elaborate mechanism—" His voice dropped away. Suddenly tense, he stared at something behind me. "Can you run?"

In answer, I tore off into the trees toward the greenway, trying not to think of how far away it was—at least I thought it was far away. Everything before taking the wardwraith's hand was a muddled blur.

Talan ran up beside me. I glanced over at him just as he looked back over his shoulder.

"I'm sorry I can't spare the energy to ease your pain," he said.

"What is it?" I panted, ducking under a low branch. "The wardwraith?"

"I'm trying to confuse it, but it's fast and clever."

From behind us erupted an inhuman shriek in a language I did not understand—some Old Country tongue? Whatever it was, it turned my blood cold. More screams split open the night sky, like the death knells of some great bird of prey, but each one sounded more and more distant. Just before we crashed through the greenway, its eager magic pulling on my limbs, a furious shriek rang out through the forest and then abruptly fell silent.

—◆—

On the other side of the greenway, beside the black mouth of my father's secret lagoon, we found the dry clothes we'd left behind.

The pain in my shoulder was like fire. Talan eased it enough for me to dress, our backs to each other. By the time we turned around, our glamours had faded, shattered by the force of two savage journeys through the greenway.

Talan was himself again—pale and dark-eyed, wearing a simple white tunic and brown trousers, his damp black hair a tousled mess. He sat at the lagoon's edge, a cube of stone resting on his palm. Elaborate carvings marked its surface: a staring eye, a fat star with seven points, a flat hand held up as if to fend off an enemy.

"She ran too far from the wardstone," he murmured. "The distance snuffed her out."

I stood over him, shivering in a gauzy gown of shimmering gray silk, cut low to reveal a scandalous expanse of skin. If anyone were to find us sneaking about the grounds in the middle of the night, they'd think we had been up to something else entirely.

"The wardwraith?" I asked.

He hummed an affirmative. "Whatever defenses this stone provided Ravenswood, they're gone now." He raised the cube to eye level, peering closely at it. "But there is still much left to learn from this, I'd wager."

"Do you know how to do that?"

"Learn from it, you mean?" Talan shook his head. "Not

really. I'm familiar with the *theory* of dismantling wardstones, but I've never actually done it myself, and each stone boasts a unique design, both inside and out. Not to mention that the dregs of whatever spellwork remains intact inside it could have been crafted in a language neither of us knows."

"Gareth could help us."

He looked up at me. "Your sister's friend?"

"He knows more about Old Country arcana than anyone I've ever met, and he has numerous contacts at the university and in the capital. We can send it to him tomorrow—"

"No, we can't possibly trust a messenger with this."

I thought for a moment, so tired and in the grip of such pain, both from my shoulder and from the greenway's lingering teeth, that my mind felt sluggish, recalcitrant.

"Well, Gareth will be at the tournament in Bathyn," I said wearily. "We can ask him about it then."

"An excellent idea." Talan jumped to his feet with renewed energy, his eyes glinting. "Until then, you'll need to hide it."

"Me?"

"And tell no one." Talan retrieved our little bag and carefully tucked the wardstone inside. "What if the Basks—or someone worse—tries to steal it back? They wouldn't dare attack you directly, not without serious risk. But me, simply a guest at Ivyhill? I'm more vulnerable to capture, attack, interrogation. I *can't* know where it is. It'll be safer that way."

I laughed weakly, swaying a little. The pain was spreading from my shoulder like wildfire, encroaching on my vision in hot red waves.

"Interrogation?" I mumbled. "And I thought *I* was dramatic."

Talan swore quietly and rushed to my side. "Gods, Gemma, I'm sorry. Here I am babbling, and you can barely stand." He cupped my face in his hands and tenderly stroked my cheeks with his thumbs. "How can I help you? Tell me what you want."

I looked blearily up at him—those gorgeous dark eyes gone soft and warm as they searched my face, that dear brow furrowed with such earnest worry.

"I'm not sure you could handle hearing about all the things I want from you," I said, my words slightly slurred.

He grinned and shook his head. "Come, Gemma, tell me to do it. Say the words, love."

I closed my eyes and rested my brow against his cheek.

"Such a devoted husband," I whispered. "Yes, Talan. Please help me. Make the pain go away."

I felt him smile. He kissed my temples, the corners of my mouth, the curve of my chin. The world shifted as he lifted me into his arms. I hid my face against his neck, letting the warmth of his kisses—and the soothing wave of his power rushing through my body—pull me into blessed oblivion.

CHAPTER 13

O ne week later, on the morning we were all meant to caravan south to the Bathyn tournament, the sky was a brilliant
azure, not a wisp of cloud in sight. I stared up at it, my mouth
dry despite the delicious breakfast I'd just consumed. My heart
pounded as if I'd not been enjoying a picnic on the lawn but a run
from one end of Ivyhill to the other.

The state I found myself in was entirely Talan's fault. He lay
right beside me, sprawled out on his back in a gorgeous morning
suit of charcoal gray. One long leg propped up on the other, jacket
laid neatly at his side. He had rolled up the sleeves of his white
shirt, and I couldn't stop stealing glances at the slender muscles of
his forearms, the delicate turns of his wrists, his long fingers idly
braiding long stalks of grass. Deft, nimble.

As I wondered just how those fingers might perform under
very different circumstances, truly salacious images flitted through
my mind—a distraction I could not afford. Letting Talan hold me
in the aftermath of a dangerous trip to Ravenswood was one thing,
but in the clear light of day, I could not ignore the fact that our
partnership, at its root, was a scheme. Nothing more.

Glancing to my right, past the brim of my parasol and through the curtain of white-and-pink azaleas beside us, I glimpsed the guests taking their breakfast on the veranda in the morning sun— Father's friends, a few acquaintances of mine, and several cousins, all come to make the trip to Bathyn with us. The distant sounds of clinking glasses and polite conversation met my ears. The azaleas sheltered us somewhat, but any curious onlooker would be able to see us well enough.

If they did so, they would think it odd to espy me lying stiff as a corpse on my back, hands clasped tightly on my stomach. Talan and I were meant to look the picture of a flirtatious new couple enjoying a picnic breakfast before the day's travels.

I took another long, slow breath, turned on my side to face Talan, forced my body to relax, and touched his arm—a move that seemed safe enough, and yet that single soft press of my fingers to the warm skin just above his wrist made my heart flutter in my throat.

"You have the spell?" I asked quietly, trying on a coquettish smile and letting my voice slip just beyond the edge of modesty into something more suggestive.

Talan turned to look at me and propped himself up on his elbows. "I could have sworn I already told you I have it," he said, brow furrowed in mock concern. "Tucked away in my jacket"—he plucked a grape from the half-eaten bunch beside him—"in a secret inner pocket"—he popped the grape into his mouth and bit into it with a cheeky little grin—"snug and safe"—he leaned closer to me, his voice lowering to match mine—"in its little brass case."

I shivered a bit and looked away with a laugh. "Fair play, sir."

"Why, madam," he replied, all innocence as he popped another grape into his mouth, "I've no idea what you mean."

I allowed my gaze to drop to that beautiful mouth once more, noticing a little glint of juice at the corner, and then made the mistake of looking back up to meet his eyes. They twinkled merrily, and yet I thought I read something less playful in those dark depths—something hotter, a need that perhaps matched my own.

His tongue darted out to clean the corner of his mouth, his lips quirking into a mischievous little smile, and I quickly looked away, amused despite myself and flushed all over.

"We should talk through our plans for the tournament one more time," I said briskly. I was perfectly capable of controlling myself and focusing on the task at hand. "Tonight in my family's tent, we'll show Gareth the wardstone and, with his help, begin the process of dismantling it. Then tomorrow, at Alastrina Bask's wilding show—"

"Lady Gemma," Talan interrupted, that smile still lighting up his face, "we've talked through our plan at least a dozen times."

I fixed a glare on him, determined to ignore how devastatingly handsome he looked in the morning sun—his pale skin smooth and creamy, light gilding the soft dark waves of his hair. I swallowed hard, exercising every bit of self-control I possessed to resist running my fingers through that hair and drawing him toward me for a kiss.

"*Tomorrow*," I insisted, "at Alastrina Bask's wilding show..."

He sighed and stretched, the awful man, allowing me a lovely view of the long lines of his body. "We'll wait until the height of Alastrina's performance," he recited, "when the audience is most rapt, then release the spell."

I nodded, sat up, and primly arranged my skirts. "Which will ruin said performance and humiliate her in front of thousands of people." I ran my hands over the bodice of my gown, cleaned off bits of grass that did not exist.

Talan's eyes shot at once to my fingers, following them wherever they went—my neckline, the slight swell of my breasts, the dip of my waist.

I bit down on a smile. He was not the only player in this particular game.

I looked up at him coolly, arching an eyebrow. "And then?"

"The next day, at the fighting pits, I'll use my power to coax Ryder Bask into violence. Send him running into a fray of sentinels with neither caution nor sense. Force the tournament officials to disqualify him and banish him from future competitions. Again"— Talan turned on his side to look at me—"utter humiliation."

Imagining Ryder's and Alastrina's public disgrace made me smile. "They'll be furious beyond measure."

"Yes, they will." Talan grew serious, his voice grave. "Are you prepared for that, Gemma? If and when they realize it was us who did this to them—"

I dismissed him with a wave. "They won't. How would they? You were careful as you traveled, and you wore Kerrish's glamour."

Talan nodded, but he didn't look convinced. During the past week, while Jessyl grimly tended my wounds from our terrifying night at Ravenswood, and Father and Farrin bustled about in preparation for the tournament, Talan had journeyed northwest to the quaint little village of Tullacross. A low-magic beguiler named Serra Breen lived there, an erstwhile paramour of mine who possessed not only a dexterous tongue and a cunning knack for minor spellcrafting but also a marvelous sense of discretion. We had commissioned from her a spell, which she had managed easily and with no questions; the only sign of curiosity, Talan had reported, had been a slight quirk of the mouth when she'd handed him the finished spell, housed in a small velvet-lined brass case shaped like a toad.

"The spell bears no identifying marks," I continued. "I trust Serra, and I trust you." I stilled, fixed him with a glare. "Are you implying that I shouldn't?"

Talan shook his head slowly. "No, Gemma. You can trust me, and you should." He sat up and scooted closer to me. The heat of his body was suddenly so near my own that I quite literally felt faint and had to brace myself against the nearest solid thing, which happened to be his thigh.

He glanced past me, through the azaleas, and leaned into me, his mouth hovering over mine. "A table of guests is watching us and gossiping," he murmured. "I thought it best to give them a little of what they so desperately want."

I stared up at him, lost in his eyes, and forced myself to keep my hand right where it was, clutching the hard muscle of his thigh, and not move it even an inch upward no matter how much I wanted to.

But my control was far from perfect. Before I quite knew what I was doing, I wetted my lips and whispered, "What *they* want?"

Something flashed in Talan's eyes—a dark heat that made me squirm. "Gemma," he said quietly. I watched him swallow, drank in the sight of his obvious flustered preoccupation with my mouth.

Warmed from head to toe, my skin tingling, I moved closer to him and brushed my lips against his. A light kiss, chaste compared to the false kiss we'd shared in Father's office, and yet it was the most intimate one I'd ever had—my hand on his thigh, his dark head bowed over mine, the illicit thrill of our plans, the memory of sneaking through the dark Ravenswood forest. The danger of it, the gall of what we had done and would do.

Though I had been the one to start our little game, I soon found myself overcome. I let out a soft gasp against Talan's mouth, pushed up against him to deepen the kiss. My hand released his thigh, groping blindly. I found the front of his shirt and grabbed on, and his hand came around my waist, both holding me steady and pulling me hard against him. Sitting there on the blanket, half in his arms, my parasol forgotten, I dimly remembered what he had said a few moments before and pulled away just enough to whisper against the corner of his mouth, "Tell me, then, Talan d'Astier, why it is that I should trust you."

He stilled at once, and I opened my eyes to meet his. We were both a little out of breath, burning inside and out. The heat of his desire was obvious enough to make even me blush, and the air between our bodies felt pulled so taut that I half expected it to snap and catch fire.

Talan searched my face, his expression suddenly serious enough to alarm me, but then he closed his eyes, lifted my palm to his lips, and kissed it. He lingered there, holding my hand against his mouth, his breath trembling on my skin, until a bell sounded from the direction of the house's front doors. It was the carriage bell, signifying that the footmen had begun loading our bags and that the caravan would depart for Bathyn in a half hour.

Talan pulled away, gently lowering my hand. "In truth," he said at last, his voice deliciously hoarse, "there is no good reason you should trust me, Gemma. When I tell you there is nothing more important to me than what you and I are trying to do—for my family and for yours—you'll simply have to take me at my word or choose not to."

His expression had become so sad, so deadly serious, that I couldn't stop myself from reaching up and smoothing back the mussed black waves falling over his flushed forehead.

"There's no need to get so dramatic," I told him gently. Suddenly things were fraught between us for some reason I could not explain. I felt desperate to make the feeling going away, to return to our kiss and then turn that kiss into something more, something easy and joyous that would clear his face of shadows.

"I know very well that I have no reason to trust you, and yet I've chosen to anyway." I raised a playful eyebrow. "For now, that is. You should fear the day my good sense catches up with my ambition and I turn you away forever."

Talan shook his head fondly, his expression unbearably tender—more so than I thought my words deserved—and so sweet and wondering, as if he were marveling at me, seeing me for the first time, that my chest ached.

"Gods, what you do to me," he whispered. "I've never..."

Then he moved away, releasing me entirely. In his absence, the world felt cooler, lonelier. I clenched my fists in my skirts instead of reaching for him as so I longed to.

"You've never what?" I asked him once I found my voice. He'd turned away from me to look down the sloping lawn toward the fountain and its neighbor, the old oak.

"I've never felt like this," he answered, his voice carefully even. "Not ever. I never thought I could."

I reached for him again, but he flinched away as if my touch were painful. "Please go, Gemma. Gather your things and fetch the wardstone. The caravan will leave soon, and I need a few moments to make myself respectable."

His voice was gentle, and yet I heard a note of quiet despair inside it, one that seemed too immense for the simple disappointment of frustrated desire. It unnerved me and left me wondering just how deeply his tragic past had wounded him. How little I still knew about this man I'd kissed, this man whom I'd entrusted with so much.

I left quickly, feeling foolish and vulnerable in the wake of our strange conversation. I set out for my safe room and the wardstone it held, not once looking back. As I entered the great house, my pain returned swiftly, no longer muffled by Talan's presence and stoked by my discomfiture. Each step pounded fresh agony into my bones, but I refused to slow. By the time I reached the third floor of the east wing, the brisk walk had left me breathless and my stomach roiled, queasy with a potent combination of pain and nerves, doubt and lingering want.

Thus preoccupied, I was paying very little attention to my surroundings and nearly ran into Madam Baines.

"Oh, Lady Gemma, thank the gods," she said. "I've been wanting to talk to you for some time now. But I haven't had the courage, you see."

I stared at her, struck speechless by the ruthless return of my stifled guilt.

Neither Talan nor I had seen Madam Baines since the night she revealed to us the location of the Ravenswood greenway, and though sometimes it shamed me to admit it, that was the way I preferred things. Madam Baines hadn't realized the truth of what had happened that night and told Father about it, she hadn't dropped dead from an adverse reaction to Talan's magic, and we had found our greenway. In my estimation, there was no reason to think any more about Madam Baines than I ever had—or so I told myself, desperate to justify what we had done.

"Madam Baines," I managed, smiling politely. "What a lovely surprise to see you this morning. What can I do for you?"

At first she said nothing, just wrung her hands and glanced furtively about the corridor as if worried the ivy itself was listening. My body pulled tight with alarm as I noticed how much Madam Baines had changed since I'd last seen her. Her typically immaculate brown curls were a frizzy mess, boasting none of their ordinary shine. She had grown thinner in a way that suggested sleepless nights and poor eating, her cheeks drawn and her rumpled clothes ill-fitting. Her lips looked chapped and bitten, her ordinarily flawless skin was greasy and dotted with tiny pimples, and there was a brittle feeling about her, as if a gust of wind might come along and scatter her like a bundle of twigs.

"Madam Baines," I whispered. I reached for her, then hesitated, my hand hovering awkwardly in the air. "What's happened?"

"I'm mortified to speak plainly about it," she replied in a strained whisper, her gaze frantic and darting. "I'm sorry I haven't come to you before now, but I...my lady, I was so afraid. I don't wish to be dismissed. I don't know where I would go. I could find employment, mind you—of course I could, Anointed sage that I am—but I don't quite know how that would work, seeing as how I'm full to the brim with all sorts of information Lord Ashbourne doesn't want anyone to know. Which brings me to the thing I must tell you."

She began picking at her fingernails, which I noticed were cracked and dirty. "That night you and Mr. d'Astier requested a tour of the library facilities..."

She fell silent, her eyes glazing over. I waited for as long as I could bear, my heart pounding so hard I felt freshly ill.

"Yes?" I prompted.

"There's no excuse for my humiliating behavior," she said at last, "but I must apologize for it. I'm not some careless sot, I promise you, and I don't know *why* I drank an entire bottle of wine that evening, but drink it I did, and I can't exactly remember everything I did whilst I was not myself, but I do remember some things, fuzzy things. I remember..."

Madam Baines squeezed her eyes shut. "I remember telling you and Mr. d'Astier about Lord Ashbourne's greenways. I remember blabbing on and on even though you tried to stop me."

Now I truly felt sick, my shame so complete I felt I might burst. I opened my mouth to set her straight, heedless of what consequences such a confession might bring, but Madam Baines plowed on before I could speak.

"Please, I beseech you with all the strength I possess, don't tell anyone what I disclosed to you that night—about the greenways, or about anything else I may have foolishly divulged. And please ask Mr. d'Astier to do the same. Oh, I can't bear asking him myself. You I've known all your life, so although it's awful to say all this to you, I can bear it somewhat."

Then she grabbed my hands, squeezing them so hard it hurt. Her eyes were wild, bloodshot. "You haven't told anyone, have you? You haven't gone to your father? Am I too late?"

That at least I could answer truthfully, with an air of serene magnanimity that I somehow managed despite my churning insides. "No, Madam Baines, neither Talan nor I have told anyone about what happened that night, nor will we ever. I promise you. You've nothing to worry about, and if there's anything I can do to help you move past this whole unfortunate business—"

"Oh, Lady Gemma!" She released my hands and, to my horror, pulled me into a bone-crushing hug. "Thank you, thank you, thank you a thousand times. I don't know how to put into words what a relief this is. It's been a month of torment, truly, you've no idea what my mind has—"

She startled, falling abruptly silent. Her whole body was suddenly tense as if with some awful terror. She whirled about and searched the corridor, the curved rafters inlaid with colored glass, the elaborate tapestries lining the wood-paneled walls.

"Did you see that?" she muttered.

Quickly I looked around myself, worried that someone had overheard our conversation, but it seemed the entire wing was empty, what with everyone preparing to depart for Bathyn. I heard nothing except for Madam Baines's panicked breathing and the distant sounds of carriage preparations.

"I did," Madam Baines whispered. "I saw it, and I heard it. I hear it every day. Be careful. Even the shadows have eyes these days. And they never close them, and they never sleep."

My blood ran cold as I watched her leave, still muttering to no one, still glancing frantically about like a rabbit, flinching at every sound.

Once she was gone, I stood for a moment hugging myself, collecting my scattered thoughts and striving for calm. The woman had simply worked herself up into a panic similar to my own occasional fits, that's all it was. Her extremely orderly life had taken an extremely disorderly turn that night she'd caught me and Talan in Father's office, and she had been worried about her position as our head librarian ever since. The fact that she had spiraled into such a frenzy about the whole thing was no fault of mine, nor was I obligated to run after her and soothe her frazzled mind.

Those were the lies I told myself as I hurried down the corridor.

Inside a tiny empty sitting room overlooking the north lawn, a worn tapestry depicted the faceless goddess Neave in a flowering meadow, holding a newborn calf. Behind that tapestry was an unremarkable wall of solid wood—unless one knew which plank to push, in which case a little door swung open, revealing a small safe room stocked with provisions. On the far wall stood a locked door, spelled to open only when touched by my hand. Beyond that, a passage led down through the house and then underground, all the way past the game park, its other end disguised by a tangled thicket.

And in the center of the room, where the wardstone should have been, tucked away in our watertight bag, there was nothing.

For a moment I stared in shock at the bare floor, hoping I was somehow mistaken. But a frantic search of the stacked provisions confirmed the truth:

The wardstone was gone. Someone, somehow, had stolen it.

CHAPTER 14

The second our carriage arrived at the Bathyn tournament grounds, before the wheels had even come to a full stop, I leapt out the door and hurried into the colorful, bustling circle of tents reserved for my family, ignoring my father's furious shouts behind me.

Despite using all my restraint to hide my frantic fear and keep from running at full speed, I no doubt looked like a madwoman—hat ribbons flying, elbows everywhere, skirts hiked up to my knees.

I'd spent the entire eight-hour carriage ride quietly boiling in a stew of my own frayed nerves while Farrin and Father occupied themselves with one of their maddening secret conferences—no doubt about the Basks—and one of my most irritating distant cousins, Lady Delia Ashbourne, sorely tempted me to murder. An Anointed silvertongue whose linguistic talent lent her fluency in every known language, including ancient Old Country tongues in which she had absolutely no interest, twenty-six-year-old Delia was also an unstoppable chatterbox whose voice, I was convinced, would forever haunt my dreams. But we'd *finally* arrived in Bathyn, I'd escaped Delia's nattering, and now I needed to find Talan—*immediately*.

Unfortunately the tournament grounds were teeming with more magic than I'd been around since the night of my party, and the clever little chew Jessyl had given me—a chalky white blob that tasted like death—only somewhat dulled the throbbing pain in my joints. Staying upright was a challenge, my head a swirling mire.

I blinked hard against the black spots encroaching on my vision and burst into our family's main tent, a huge construction of light-green canvas adorned with flowers and, of course, ivy vines. Inside, polished oak tables sat laden with gleaming silver place settings, lace-trimmed napkins, crystal goblets. Our staff, who had arrived at the grounds several hours before us, had begun serving supper—golden roasted game hens resting on beds of thyme and sage; a light vegetable soup topped with sprigs of rosemary; hot loaves of freshly baked bread glistening with garlic sauce.

Famished, my stomach growling ferociously, I nevertheless hurried past the buttery, flaky canapés loaded with smoked salmon, dill, and lemon zest, rounded a corner in the maze of tables and servants and steaming plates, ducked under a streamer of cheerful blue-and-yellow bunting, and nearly cried out with relief. There was Talan straight ahead, coming toward me, looking far less distressed than he had when I'd left him on the lawn.

Hating what I had to tell him, I grabbed his arm and pulled him toward the tent's perimeter, where a little ivy-trimmed nook sat beside one of the tent's wooden support beams.

"What is it?" Talan's voice, gentle with worry, kissed me like a cool breeze. "I saw you from across the room. You're white as the moon, Gemma. You look wild."

I shook my head, swallowing hard against my rising nausea. "First, please help me. The pain is immense here."

He obeyed without question. The air grew warm and supple, and suddenly I felt as cozy and safe as if he stood with his arms around me, sheltering me from the world.

I swayed a little from the sudden relief, smiling dreamily, and allowed myself a moment to lean against him. He smoothed back a damp curl that clung to my cheek and lifted my chin with one gentle finger.

"You're frightened," he said softly. "What is it?"

I tried to catch my breath, my heart still pounding. "The wardstone...is gone."

Talan grew very still. "What?"

"I went to my safe room to fetch it after breakfast, and it was *gone*. Nothing disturbed, no obvious signs of trespassers, but someone stole it, Talan. Someone's on to us."

"But that's impossible. You said your safe room was unknown to anyone but you."

It was true. Each of us Ashbourne girls had been granted five safe rooms by our parents, and even they did not know the rooms' locations throughout the house.

"Only the crews who designed and warded the rooms know where they're located," I said. "And their business is elite, prestigious. They make disgusting gobs of money and pride themselves on their discretion. They can't be behind this. There have been no burglaries since the rooms' construction, not even a single instance of trespassing. Farrin would have told me." I paused, wondering if that was true, then pushed through my doubt. I could handle only so many worries at once. "And anyway, how would anyone even have known the wardstone was there?"

Talan blew out a long breath and looked away, absently

watching our guests trickle in for supper. "Someone must have followed you the day you hid it there," he muttered sharply. "This is *not* good."

"No one followed me," I insisted, bristling. "I was meticulously careful, and besides, the rooms in that wing are not in use at the moment. Not even the servants visit daily."

Then I fell silent, my heart sinking as I remembered my earlier exchange with Madam Baines.

Talan caught on immediately. "What is it? You've thought of something."

"I..." I shook my head, frustration winding my chest into a knot. "When I went to retrieve the wardstone this morning, I ran into Madam Baines. She looked awful, Talan. She's been tormented with guilt since that night we tricked her. She's not well at all. She kept looking around in utter fear, and she said..."

"Tell me," Talan said, his voice softening.

"She said, 'Be careful, Lady Gemma. Even the shadows have eyes these days. And they never close them, and they never sleep.'"

Talan stared at me, his face ashen.

"Could your magic have made her ill somehow?" I whispered. "You said she would be fine, but she certainly wasn't fine today—"

"Empathic power can't hurt people like that, not if the proper measures are taken. And I *did* take those measures when I set up the ruse with the wine bottle. I soothed her mind with a prayer chant known as the Balm of Jaetris—that's the palliative remedy I mentioned. Remember?"

"But could there be some people for whom even the most carefully worked empathic magic is harmful?" My stomach dropped as I considered it. "Have you ever used your magic on an Anointed sage like Madam Baines? Someone with a mind so complicated and dense?"

Agitated, he ran a hand through his hair, tousling his gleaming dark waves. "Never on an Anointed sage, no, but the principles are the same, no matter the mind. What I did should not have harmed her."

I bit my lip, thinking back to that night I'd tried so hard *not* to think about. "You were aggressive with it though," I said, my voice very small, "and you did that because I urged you to. I essentially threatened you."

Talan lifted an eyebrow, looking down at me with harried amusement. "You're half my size, Gemma. You were no threat to me."

"But I told you I'd send you away from Ivyhill—"

"Irrelevant. I could have refused to use my power on Madam Baines, and I didn't. It's my fault, not yours."

I didn't agree, but I felt so sick and tense with anxiety that for a moment I couldn't speak. It took all my strength to calm my racing thoughts and avoid a swift slide down into the panic.

"You said she told you something about the shadows having eyes," Talan said slowly, hands behind his back as he stared at the ground, deep in thought. "Maybe that's important and not merely a random thought from an exhausted mind."

A memory returned with blazing, sickening clarity—the night of my party, when I'd sat at my dressing table, pulled to it by some unseen presence, and performed for the first time in my life a piece of magic: the glamour that had driven Jessyl temporarily out of her mind.

"I've felt that before," I murmured. "Eyes in the shadows, I mean. The night of my party, I felt something very like that. But it wasn't frightening, like it clearly is for Madam Baines. Or rather, it wasn't *entirely* frightening. I..." I flushed, remembering my changed reflection in the mirror: sharp and breathtaking and unafraid, brimming with light. More than I truly was. *Better* than I was. The memory brought an ache to my throat.

Talan looked at me hard. "Describe the feeling. Was there a distinctive scent in the air when it happened? Did you feel changed somehow, as if a foreign influence were prompting you to do something out of the ordinary?"

The tent was hot and crowded, full of food smells and roaring bursts of laughter, and yet I still felt a little chill of unease at his question.

"I don't remember a scent," I said, "but I certainly felt changed, more clear-eyed, as if the world had sharpened and so had I. I felt strong, even...powerful. Something was calling to me, and I had to follow."

Talan gently took my hand, turning me to face him. "This is important, Gemma. There could have been demonic magic at play that night—some fiend working alone, or maybe the Man with the Three-Eyed Crown himself, come to seduce you on command of the Basks. Tell me *exactly* what happened, from the beginning."

But before I could begin to put that awful night into words, a familiar crow of laughter erupted from behind me, and a pair of sinewy tanned arms swept me up and spun me around into a ferocious hug.

"Gemmy-Gem, you flawless jewel," said the man hugging me. "Do try not to scold me for the state of my clothes. When I'm away, I quickly forget every bit of your sartorial wisdom and devolve into an absentminded scholar once again. For that I apologize and humbly beg your mercy."

"I'll consider it," I said with a laugh, my horrible mood lifting despite everything, for grinning down at me was Gareth Fontaine—brilliant librarian, adored professor, incorrigible puppy of a man, and Farrin's dearest friend.

My sister came up behind him, arms crossed. "It would be more than he deserves," she said wryly, but I wasn't fooled. I saw the little smile tugging at her mouth and how her shoulders had lost some of their usual tense squareness.

Gareth slung his arm around Farrin's shoulder and planted a kiss on her cheek. "I am rotten, aren't I?"

"As a pile of cow dung."

He clucked his tongue, his eyes sparkling. "Such a foul mouth on this one."

Only then did Gareth seem to notice Talan, who stood watching in astonishment.

Gareth thrust out his hand. "Gareth Fontaine. And you must be Talan d'Astier, the mysterious Vauzanian with devastating good looks who has so charmed our little Gemmy."

Talan clasped Gareth's hand with a small smile. "A pleasure, Professor Fontaine. I've heard much about you and your accomplishments."

"Boasting on me, eh, Gem? You darling." Gareth winked at me, then clapped one large hand onto Talan's back. "Come, my good fellow," he said loftily, "let us sit and dine and bask in our excellent fortune that tonight we have the company of these marvelous Ashbourne women."

Talan glanced at me, eyebrows raised, as if to say, *This is the supposedly brilliant dismantler of wardstones?*

He nevertheless allowed Gareth to lead him toward one of the room's central tables, Gareth already chattering away about gods knew what—anything and everything, most likely. They couldn't have been more different—Gareth, lean and tan with rumpled blond hair and sparkling green eyes behind a pair of brown-rimmed eyeglasses, every inch of him exuding good cheer. And Talan, dark-haired and pale, his body tense with worry that perhaps no one else could see...but I could. I felt it myself as I followed Farrin to our seats.

Even the shadows have eyes, Madam Baines had said. As I picked up my goblet of punch, my hand shaking, I wondered if that was true, if those eyes belonged to demon or Bask, and if they were there even now, hidden in the corners of our sparkling tent, watching me and waiting.

→◆←

Hours later, I stumbled into the sleeping tent I was meant to share with Farrin, but my sister wasn't there.

Illaria was instead, serenely sipping a nightcap of brandy from a small crystal glass. She wore a gown of deep violet chiffon and a fringed shawl embroidered with gold draped around her bare shoulders.

"Oh, thank the gods," I whispered. The evening's tension flooded out of me at once. I hurried to Illaria, drew her into a fierce embrace, and buried my face in the soft black mass of her curls. She smelled of sandalwood and orange blossom, her everyday fragrance, and the familiar scent warmed me down to my toes. "I can't tell you how wonderful it is to see you, Lari. I have so much to tell you."

"If it's about this man Talan d'Astier," she began, her voice cool, "then I already know quite enough about him, no thanks to you."

Only then did I realize that Illaria was standing stiffly in my arms, refusing to return my embrace.

I stepped back to consider her. "What's wrong? You're angry with me."

Illaria looked at me evenly for a moment and then sighed, her expression softening. She set her empty glass on the small table between my bed and Farrin's.

"I'm not angry with you," she replied. "Not really. I'm just wondering why I haven't seen you for a month, why you haven't answered my letters, and most of all I'm wondering why you haven't told me about this mysterious foreigner you've apparently fallen in love with."

"In love?" I laughed. "Lari, I would hardly call it *love*. I've only known him since the party."

"The party at which you ignored me," Illaria added, watching me carefully. "So it's not love. I'll accept that for the moment. What is it, then?"

I hesitated to answer. Talan would not want me to disclose all our secrets, but I was accustomed to telling Illaria everything— every detail of my life, every secret hope and fear—and suddenly, standing there with her watching me so closely, the weeks since the party took on a startling new clarity. A *month*. It had been an entire *month* since I'd met Talan, and during that time I had neither seen nor spoken to my dearest friend in the world.

The realization worked its way through my body in an ice-cold wave.

"Your letters," I whispered. Slowly I sank into the chair at my bedside. "I put them in a drawer and meant to write you. I did, Lari. I just…I forgot." I touched my temple, unnerved by the surfacing memories—Illaria's normal weekly letters brought up to my room by Jessyl, sealed and folded, tucked away into my nightstand by my own hands, unopened.

"I forgot they'd even arrived, in fact," I continued, flummoxed and shaky. "How strange. I suppose I've been distracted."

Illaria stood in silence for a moment and then sat on the edge of my bed and took my hands in hers.

"Gemma, listen to me. Are you listening? Look at me. Show me you hear me."

I obeyed, finding her worried brown eyes.

"This man, Talan," Illaria began. "I don't trust him, and I don't think you should either."

My astonishment was complete, my indignation immediate. I yanked my hands away from her, feeling suddenly exposed, as if she'd caught me doing something terrible. "I don't know what I expected you to say, but it certainly wasn't that."

Illaria frowned. "You see? Now you're angry at me for doubting him."

"I'm not." Except, inexplicably, I was.

"I've known you forever, Gemma. I can see it in your face."

I tried to smooth over whatever expression she saw and softened my voice. "I'm sorry I've been distant, Lari. Truly I am. It's just that..." I struggled to find the words I had said to Kerrish when I'd convinced her to craft our glamours. "I feel different when I'm around him. I feel freer, less encumbered by *this*." I waved my hands at my body in disgust. "He helps me. He...he *enlivens* me, lifts me out of my panic, my pain, my despair. When I'm with him I forget myself. Everything I hate, everything that darkens my thoughts, falls away. And," I added with a little smile, "I've never known such pleasure as when he's in my bed."

A little lie, but not an unforgivable one. After all, I'd certainly spent many a night over the past month thinking of him—what sort of lover he might be, what his lips would feel like as he kissed all the places my own touch could not satisfy.

Illaria, however, seemed wholly unimpressed. "He reeks, Gemma."

I stared at her. "Pardon me?"

"He reeks. His scent is terrible. It's fine on the surface— pine and rosewood and anise, a little bite of lemongrass. Most people would smell only that. But I'm not most people. The odor underneath, Gemma, is putrid. I've been trying to describe the scent to myself, and the best I can come up with is that it's like some deep, damp part of the woods where something has died and the air is musky with rot."

"How poetic," I said flatly. "You haven't even met him. How would you know his scent?"

Illaria's face fell just a little. "I was at your party, you know, although you and I never spoke. And I was in your tent tonight, dining at your table. You didn't see me there?"

My skin prickled. I looked back through my memories of the evening and couldn't find Illaria anywhere. "I...I suppose I was—"

"Distracted?" Illaria's expression was grim. "You've had many lovers, but you've never enjoyed them at the expense of our friendship. Not until Talan."

My rising confused panic made me feel wild. "Ah, so that's what this is about. You're jealous."

"No, Gemma, I'm *worried*. You aren't yourself."

"Why wouldn't you want me to feel better? He makes me feel better. He makes me *feel*, in all the good ways and none of the bad."

"And that doesn't strike you as unusual? There are very few things in life that are all good all of the time."

"And maybe he is one of those rare things, at least for me." I stood, blood roaring in my ears, my chest a conflicted tangle of anger and dismay. "I need to sleep," I said imperiously. "Father will be at the fighting pits in the morning, and Farrin performs in the afternoon. I must be in top form to support them. Good night, Lari."

Illaria watched me for a long moment, looking sad and small on the edge of my bed. Then she rose and embraced me, gentle but firm.

"I will always love you," she said quietly against my cheek, "even when you accuse me of jealousy, even when you're bedding a man I sincerely dislike. Remember that. I'll be there for Farrin's performance tomorrow. Once the tournament is over, come to my house for a visit. Your chair and I both miss you."

Then she squeezed my hands and left me. I watched her slip out of the tent with a hot lump in my throat and a sick niggling feeling in my gut, both of which disappeared as I slept, smoothed away by dreams of Talan moving inside me, whispering my name. Damp earth beneath us and stars above. Our bodies naked and glistening, speckled with mud. My legs hooked around him, urging him deeper inside me. His dark sad eyes fixed on my face, pleading silently, desperately, for something I could not understand.

CHAPTER 15

The next morning, I stood at the edge of the central fighting pit, watching from above as Father nearly beat the life out of his opponent. Lord Grey Runnemead was the man's name, a formidable Anointed sentinel from the village of Summer's Amble—a popular holiday destination famed for its wildflowers, rolling hills, and the supposed arousing qualities of its famous sighing winds.

But no amount of stimulating winds, it seemed, had prepared poor Lord Runnemead for this particular match.

Father darted across the pit floor with extraordinary speed, leapt up onto the wall, ran horizontally for a moment like a deft spider, and then pushed off the wall, spun through the air toward Lord Runnemead, and landed a resounding punch to his jaw with a sickening crack—all in the space of three blinks.

Lord Runnemead collapsed, the crowd roared as my barechested father threw up his arms in sweaty victory, a team of healers rushed down the pit stairs to treat Lord Runnemead's shattered jaw, and I, my hands clasped tightly on the polished wood railing, shivered. Not from the violence before me or the din of the crowd or the magic shimmering viciously through the air like summer heat, but from the heady thrum of Talan's nearness.

He had just emerged from the crowd to join me at the pit's edge, and he surveyed the scene with a low, impressed whistle.

"Brutal," he commented, "and efficient. I imagined the fight would go on for some time, and here I've already missed it."

A tournament arbiter was presenting Father with his prize for this first round of fighting—a sealed envelope of marbled gold paper, marked with the royal crest and containing a voucher for ten coveted invitations to the high queen's masquerade ball.

I turned away from the bluster of it all, though I should have been waving at Father with a dutiful smile, nodding graciously at everyone cheering his name. "When I speak of Father's might," I said, "I do not exaggerate."

"Clearly not," Talan replied lightly. "I wonder how he would go about dismembering me if he were to find out about our secret trips to the north."

"In whatever way he thought would be most painful for you."

"Naturally."

"Or using whatever method I requested."

At the sound of my strained voice, Talan glanced over at me, but I ignored him, my jaw clenched tight as we made our way across the sprawling tournament grounds toward the wilding paddocks. The crowd parted around us, murmuring their admiration. We were a striking couple, Talan in his fine black waistcoat and long jacket, both embroidered with vines in honor of his hosts, his hair's dark waves practically iridescent in the sunlight, his gait smooth and confident.

And me beside him in the gown Kerrish had made for me, which had taken my breath away when she'd presented it to me earlier that morning. It was similar to the one I'd seen her wear—a high ruffled collar, a neckline that plunged to my navel, sheer sleeves that gathered at my wrists with rows of delicate mother-of-pearl buttons, a bustle designed to draw the eye to my hips. But in contrast to the vivid periwinkle of her own gown, Kerrish had constructed mine from a creamy, lace-trimmed chiffon that perfectly matched my skin. From a distance, it looked as though I wore merely a netting of embroidered emerald vines and tiny golden flowers. Up close, the gown begged closer inspection: Where did that coy, filmy fabric end and my pale skin begin?

As we walked, my skirts fluttering about my legs, an insistent heat crawled up my bare neck that had nothing to do with the midmorning sun. My dreams were not far from my mind, nor were Illaria's disturbing words.

Some deep, dank part of the woods where something has died.

Talan kept looking at me, each step tightening the air between us. When the jostling crowd knocked us gently against each other, my body sang at the contact even as my troubled mind wanted me to recoil from him.

"Forgive my silence," Talan said after a moment. He ducked beneath the long bough of an oak tree festooned with tiny rib-boned bells, a shortcut to avoid the crowds. "It's just that I'm having trouble finding words to describe how lovely you are today, Gemma."

His soft voice so close to me brought my night of dreams rushing back in vivid waves. Feeling slightly hysterical, I made a mental note to return to my tent before Farrin's performance and change my undergarments; if I couldn't manage to control my thoughts, the poor silken things would be ruined by lunchtime.

Waves of lust crashed against the memory of Illaria's warning, and I stopped suddenly beneath the oak to stand with my hands in frustrated fists. Talan stopped too, towering over me. I could feel his concern even without looking at his face. I stared past him at the gnarled tree.

"What is it?" he asked. "Something's wrong. Your presence is charged and dark. Stormy. Did something happen?" He looked around, then leaned in and spoke more quietly. "I've been searching for any suspicious persons in the Ashbourne entourage but have found nothing—no violent thoughts, no curls of deception, not a single trace of furtive malice that could mark a thief."

I braced myself for the beauty of his face and shot a glare at him. "You used your power to determine this?"

"I'm being very subtle," he assured me. "Not invading people's emotions but simply testing the air. Like wetting a finger and holding it up to see which way the wind is blowing."

"Wetting a finger," I repeated flatly, the phrase evoking a series of most unhelpful images. For the first time in my life, I found myself wishing I was indifferent to sex or simply content with my own imagination, as Farrin seemed to be. Such an existence seemed dull to me, but it would certainly be less frustrating.

Talan frowned and gathered my hands in his. Never had I been more grateful for the invention of gloves. If my hands had been naked, I might have lost myself at the touch of his skin.

"Gemma, tell me what's going on," he said. "You don't seem well."

I blurted it out without thinking: "Illaria says I shouldn't trust you."

Talan blinked at me, looking genuinely perplexed. "Illaria. Your perfumier friend, isn't that right?"

"My *best* friend. She says you reek of something dead and rotting. Her nose is unmatched. She's a savant, you know—low magic, but peerless nevertheless. I'm convinced there's Anointed blood somewhere in her lineage. I trust her instincts on these matters."

"You...you think I...*reek?*"

"Illaria does. I've never smelled anything but your skin, the cologne you wear." I stopped myself before I could explain how delicious I found the scent of said cologne and how it figured into my dreams of late. "But then, I'm not a savant. Why would she think this about you? What does it mean?"

"Honestly I don't know. I...perhaps it's my Vauzanian blood, the scent of which she is unfamiliar with." His face lit up with sudden inspiration. "Or maybe it's an emanation tied to my empathic power. I've never heard of such a thing, but I've also never met a perfumier savant. The idea is certainly strange, but I suppose it's possible."

The tension in my body began to ease as he spoke. Examining his face, I could find nothing but earnest confusion.

"Maybe she can devise a scent to counteract my natural one," he went on. "I certainly don't want to repulse anybody. The last thing I need is to attend the masquerade ball only to have the high queen banish me for my stink."

He said this so seriously that I had to laugh. "What a picture that would be."

Talan smiled a little, but it quickly faded. "Whatever the reason for it, this is most unfortunate. Your best friend doesn't trust me."

"In fact, I think she despises you."

He raised his eyebrows. "I can't help the way I smell."

"It's not only that." I looked away, fiddling with a sprig of baby's breath that had come loose from the crown of braids into which Kerrish had woven my hair. "She's...jealous. I've been ignoring her since you arrived. I've been ignoring most things other than you. It isn't like me."

"I don't blame her for feeling jealous," Talan said softly. He tucked the flowers back into my hair. "I would feel jealous too if I thought someone was trying to steal you away from me."

I looked up at him, admiring the sharp line of his jaw. "As if I were yours in the first place."

He gave me a rueful little smile. "Of course. A poor choice of words. But you know what I mean, wildcat. Only a month I've known you, and yet I already feel as if you're a part of me." He brought my hand to his lips and kissed my fingers, his eyes locked with mine all the while. "Losing you would feel like tearing off my own skin."

"That's disgusting," I whispered, feeling quite undone by the use of his endearment for me, "and yet bizarrely romantic."

He swallowed hard; his throat, half hidden by his collar, transfixed me. I stretched up on my toes and dropped a chaste kiss onto that white stretch of skin. His pulse pounded beneath my mouth like a hot drum.

"Gemma," he whispered, his lips in my hair. "Gemma, Gemma..."

He shifted, his hands sliding up my bodice. The fabric was so fine it felt as though he were caressing my bare skin.

I stepped back, struggling for composure. "I'll invite Illaria to dinner tonight. You'll be nice to her. You'll make her like you. You'll flatter her until she agrees to concoct a scent for you."

Talan nodded, his gaze hot and dark. "I'll do anything you ask of me. Tell me what you want, and I'll obey."

His words snared me, held me rapt. *Take me.* My reply boiled inside me, fire underneath my skin that I could not ignore, Illaria's concern be damned. *Make me yours. Ravish me until I can't see straight.*

A huge rush of wings outside the oak's canopy rent the moment asunder, bringing us both back to our senses.

"Damn it," Talan muttered, dragging a hand through his hair, "we're late."

I peered past the branches toward the wilding paddocks, where a glinting black cloud of feathers spiraled into the air. Somehow I found my voice. "The spell?"

Talan, smiling grimly, withdrew from his jacket pocket the tiny brass toad. A thrill of nerves tore through me; the moment had arrived, and I was suddenly seized with doubt.

But Talan was already hurrying out from under the oak. Quickly, I followed him and slipped my arm through his, forcing him to slow his pace. He threw me a grateful glance, and by the time we arrived at the paddock, the crowd making way for us with starry eyes, our pace was languorous, assured. I was Lady Gemma Ashbourne, gorgeous and envied, and I was on the arm of a dashing foreigner with exquisite cheekbones. Illaria's suspicions and the stolen wardstone were things of the past.

A pair of gawking women relinquished to us their coveted spots in the front row, and suddenly I sat in the shadow of Alastrina Bask's ravens.

She stood in the center of the grassy paddock with her arms outstretched. Her gown was, of course, black to match her ravens, with an opaline sheen that glinted in the sun—jade, aquamarine, indigo. Feathers adorned her collar and sleeves, and she wore her short black hair in a slick bun. She should have seemed out of place in the bright midmorning sun—pale and northern and sharp-eyed, her bearing formidable and her gown more appropriate for winter. But in fact it felt perfectly natural that she was standing there, barking out commands in a harsh northern tongue as her ravens circled around her. She held her audience rapt; all Talan's and my admirers had quickly forgotten we were there and instead stared at the awesome display before them.

Fortunate, that. We couldn't be seen skulking about in the shadows; given what was about to happen, that would look suspicious. Nor did we want our arrival to seem portentous.

As the show continued, Alastrina's ravens slipping in and out of various formations as fluidly as black water, I glanced about, looking bored. No Ashbourne would be outwardly impressed by a Bask, no matter their talent. But in fact I *was* impressed, and unsettled, my stomach tight and churning. I remembered all too well that shimmering carpet of ravens in the forest clearing weeks before, as well as the beady black eyes of the bird who had found Talan and me hiding in the bracken.

Then, as I yawned behind my hand, I saw him.

Ryder Bask, dressed in feathered black to match his sister—a long coat with dramatic square shoulders, a dark cane capped with an obsidian stone, icy blue eyes rimmed with kohl and staring straight at me.

All at once I remembered everything about our last night at Ravenswood: the eerie wardwraith, the searing pain of Ryder wrenching my arm behind my back, the stink of dung and oil.

Resisting the urge to shrink into Talan's side, I finished my yawn and raised an eyebrow, holding Ryder's cold stare until it slid away, back to his sister.

Talan must have sensed my fear, or else he heard the thunder of my heartbeat, which was for a moment the only sound I knew. He reached for my hands and covered my tightly clenched fingers with his. I focused gratefully on the warmth of his skin, as if I were dangling off the edge of a cliff and his touch was my only chance for salvation. My shoulder throbbed with the remembrance of pain. My head spun; I was trapped in the shadows of that northern stable. Any moment now, Ryder would rip my arm from my body.

"Talan," I whispered, my voice thin beneath the deafening roar of raven wings. "Please."

I dared not say more, but Talan understood. A feeling of safety enveloped me, as warm and solid as if he had wrapped his arms around me and tucked me into the dark sanctuary of his coat, where no one could find me and nothing could hurt me. My heart to his heart, my softness sheltered against his hard, lean strength.

It was in that moment, as my body relaxed in the embrace of Talan's power, that the truth struck me like a gut punch. I grew very still, shock juddering quietly through me, and my entire world narrowed to this small space—Talan sitting beside me on a bench beneath a cloudless sky full of birds.

I knew that I could very easily love him.

I could love Talan—and maybe I already did.

A small click sounded to my left. I glanced over and saw the brass toad sitting half-hidden in Talan's palm, its body snapped open to reveal the emptiness within.

He had released the spell we had commissioned from Serra Breen—the spell that would ruin Alastrina Bask's impressive display.

I squeezed Talan's hand hard, my head reeling from the revelation. I could love him, *I could love him.*

"Talan, *wait*," I whispered, "I'm not ready—"

He hushed me with a feeling of calm. Silken and slow, it slid down my body as if I had stepped through a warm, gentle waterfall. I leaned against him, supple and liquid. He held me up with one firm arm around my torso and whispered my name, his voice faint even though his lips were right against my ear. Again and again he said my name, said *Don't worry*, said *We wanted this*, said *I've got you, wildcat.*

And then, from the direction of the paddock, Alastrina's voice broke off midcommand and dissolved into a horrible, guttural croak.

The strangeness of it was uncanny. At first no one knew how

to react. Alastrina stood there, stricken, her mouth a tight line and her hand clutching her throat. Beyond her, Ryder glowered and shifted tensely. I half expected to see his ears prick, lupine.

Overhead, the ravens broke their orderly formation with a few scattered harsh cries and began flapping about in confusion.

Alastrina cleared her throat, lifted her chin with a determined glare. Everything had fallen silent, the audience waiting for the joke.

She tried again, opening her mouth to utter her next command—but what came out was not her voice, and certainly not a word.

It was a series of croaks, each uglier and harsher than the last. And she didn't stop. She screamed at the sky, at her poor confused cloud of ravens, trying again and again to utter the proper commands. But it was futile. The only sound her mouth would produce was spellcrafted—the cries of a male bullfrog during mating season, as Serra Breen had promised.

The demonstration dissolved into chaos. Ravens scattered—some flying away, dipping drunkenly; some dropping to the ground; others wheeling into each other, their indignant, pained cries cascading through the air like a perverse echo of Alastrina's croaks.

Some in the audience ran, covering their heads. Others stood in horror, unable to look away. Still others guffawed, hooting as Alastrina's anger bloomed into outright fury. Red blotches marred her alabaster skin. She struck out at the healers and arbiters who rushed to help her and screamed at the ravens tottering around at her feet, as if that would prompt them to obey commands they could not understand. Ryder shoved toward her through the teeming crowd, held her face in his hands, shouted at her in a northern tongue. Her croaks transformed into something bestial and horrible. She grabbed his obsidian staff and flung it like a spear, shrieked at him.

The crowd broke, spilling away from where the staff had plunged into the ground like a bolt of black lightning. The current of bodies lifted Talan and me from our seats, and we hurried away with the rest of them, the cacophony of Alastrina's rage chasing us all through the tournament grounds. Talan hurried me through the central square of food stalls, where spits of roasting meat sizzled in the smoky air. In other arenas throughout the grounds, competitors had stopped to gape in morbid fascination at the chaos.

When at last we burst into the blessed refuge of my empty sleeping tent, Talan was laughing.

"Did you see her face?" he said, wiping his eyes. "Oh, gods, that was even better than I imagined it would be. We'll have to send Serra a bonus payment. She outdid herself."

I laughed weakly. My heart wasn't in it. I felt dizzy with everything that had happened, with the beaming, brilliant beauty of Talan's face when he laughed.

"They'll be so angry," I murmured.

He gave me a puzzled look. "Of course they will be. That's the whole point, isn't it? To humiliate them and reduce their social standing? Weaken them in the eyes of the queen? You swore you were prepared for any repercussions, that the possible retaliation was worth the risk."

"Yes, I know, but...Ryder." I hugged myself, looking over my shoulder at the tent flaps. Outside, the distant sounds of bedlam continued. "He saw me across the paddock. He was looking at me as though he knew everything—the spell, our glamours..."

"Nonsense. He knows nothing except that you're an Ashbourne and that you're the most beautiful woman in the world—which irks him, I'm sure. He'd much rather you be a hideous crone."

Talan grabbed my hands and spun me around in a little dance of triumph, singing some silly song about the most noble and devious House of Ashbourne that soon left me giddy and giggling despite myself. His hands were everywhere—around mine, cupping my face, guiding my lips to his—and I sank into his touch, eager for escape and for safety. I could have sworn I felt Ryder's eyes following me through the tournament grounds as we fled the wilding paddock. Undoubtedly he'd been wholly focused on helping his sister, and yet I could not shake away the feeling, not on my own.

I needed distraction, something to clear my mind of all worry. I didn't want to think about the Basks, or Illaria, or the stolen wardstone. I wanted sweet oblivion. I *craved* it. As I gripped Talan's head, my fingers winding into his hair and forcing him to meet my eyes, the heady rush of fear inside me broke open and turned blazing, desperate.

"Kiss me," I whispered fiercely against Talan's mouth. "Keep going, Talan, please."

His laughter faded. He pulled away only a little, his eyes full of stars. "You're afraid."

I nodded, pressed my lips together.

"Of what?"

I shook my head, too overwhelmed to explain. Talan's strange scent. Father's secret greenway. Madam Baines's cryptic warning. Alastrina's rage. Ryder's eyes stabbing me with icy-blue rage. Mara, shoved away into a guilty corner of my mind I refused to acknowledge.

My panic, my pain—ever-present, never-ending.

The salvation that could await me if we ever found the Man with the Three-Eyed Crown. The salvation, or the doom, or maybe they were one and the same. Maybe doom *was* my salvation. An escape. An ending. A peace I'd never known.

"Everything," I replied, looking up at Talan. Trembling with nerves, feeling suddenly like the virgin girl I hadn't been for years, I found one of his hands and slid it up my body to cup my breast. "Touch me, Talan. I don't want to be afraid. Just for a little while. I want to forget everything. I want to forget all of this."

His face softened. He touched his brow to mine. "I can't..." He shook his head, squeezed his eyes shut. "*Gods*, I want to, you can't possibly know how much I want to, but...not here. Not hasty and sloppy in some tent where anyone could walk in and find us."

"Then just kiss me instead," I commanded. "Kiss me, hard."

He searched my face for another moment, eyes glittering, and then backed me up slowly until I met the tent's central pole. Gently he guided my hands behind the pole, pinned them in place with his own, and then he bent low over me and showered me with kisses—my neck, my jaw, my brow, my hair. It wasn't enough; I needed more. I freed my hands, tugged on his sleeves, let out a wordless plea.

Obeying, he followed the long path of skin my gown's neckline bared, feathered his lips from throat to breasts to navel. He knelt before me and clutched my hips, pressed his face to my thighs, breathed in deeply, let out a soft moan of longing. Kissed me there between my legs, once, his breath scorching and his lips right where I wanted them.

I cried out, twisted my fingers in his hair, and shoved his face hard against me, wanton and unthinking. All the desire I'd felt for him over the past month, the tenderness, the secret delight of our wild scheme—it all broke open inside me, leaving me undone. I was a woman on fire, drunk on his nearness, dizzy with his scent. I circled my hips against him, breathless, and then he rose, captured my mouth with his, opened my lips with his tongue. He nipped lightly at my throat, gently pinched my nipples through the sheer fabric of my gown. Then he tapped his fingers lightly against my aching heat again and again, his face buried in my neck as he kissed me, his deft fingers working tirelessly between my legs, teasing me through my skirts, pressing harder, harder, up, and up.

"Talan," I sobbed, light-headed, weightless. I ground against his hand in desperation. "Please, *gods*…"

"Yes, that's it, Gemma," he whispered against my lips. My eyes fluttered open just long enough to see him watching me, his eager gaze so dark that for a wild moment I could not see any white in his eyes, only a thick, liquid blackness. "Come for me, my lovely girl," he growled. "You beautiful creature." He hiked up my skirts and slid his hand up my thigh, wedged his fingers beneath the lace-trimmed satin of my underwear.

Just before he touched me, he paused. His palm hovered over me; his breath trembled against my cheek. I keened beneath him, begging, aching.

He leaned close, pressed his lips to the soft skin beneath my ear. "In my entire life," he murmured, "I've never wanted anything more than I want to fuck your perfect, sweet little cunt."

The delicious obscenity of his words shocked me into pleasure such as I'd never known. I cried out, clutched his shoulders, and arched up against him. I felt his desire, hot and hard against my leg, and I turned incandescent, my body pulling tight with need. Dazed, I found his dark eyes, his thick lashes, the light sheen of sweat on his temples—and then he slid two fingers inside me, thrust them into me again and again, pressed his thumb against me once, twice, three times.

When my body found its completion, it happened with such sudden force that my vision dimmed. I shuddered, trapped between Talan's body and the hard pole behind me, and cried out into his mouth, curled my body around his, whimpered against his kisses. My breath hitched, catching on every shock of pleasure that rippled through my body. I mumbled Talan's name, hid my face against his chest, clenched my trembling thighs around him and rode his hand until I was too tender and exhausted to hold myself up any longer.

After that, the world was languid and dim, my mind blessedly quiet. I remember Talan holding his wet fingers to my lips, that together we sucked and kissed them clean. I remember him carrying me to my bed, murmuring something about changing for luncheon. A soft kiss beneath each of my eyes, my head full of my own sharp-sweet scent, and the world a golden haze around me as I fell gratefully into a dreamy, contented sleep.

CHAPTER 16

L ater that afternoon, the light turning fat and golden as the sun crept down the western sky, I hurried backstage at the tournament's grandest tent, a huge construction of midnight-blue canvas spangled with thousands of silver stars.

This was the stage where the artisans and savants of the tournament would perform—painters creating new masterworks before the eyes of a breathless audience; prodigious playwrights premiering their latest gut-wrenching dramas; dancers twirling effortlessly from curtain to curtain.

And musicians, of course—or, more accurately, one musician.

The shadowed backstage area was quiet, its emptiness enforced by a perimeter of Father's stolid guards. My only other companion was Gareth. He paced fretfully in the wings, his vest and tie undone and his sleeves rolled haphazardly up to his elbows.

"You're going to make her nervous," I chided him, gently catching his hand. "Worse, you're making *me* nervous."

Gareth blew out a halfhearted laugh. He squeezed my hand once, then pulled away and scrubbed his palms through his hair and across his face, then found my hand again and gripped my fingers hard.

I glanced up at his wild mop of blond hair, his eyeglasses that now sat slightly askew, and fought back a smile.

"I look like a madman, don't I?" he asked, deadpan.

"Your hair is indeed rather…well, *disheveled* doesn't seem emphatic enough a word."

Gareth smiled faintly, looking across the stage at my sister. Farrin sat at the piano in utter stillness, her eyes closed and her hands resting lightly upon the polished white-and-gold keys. She wore one of her many gray gowns, this one with long buttoned sleeves, a high collar, and a severely structured bodice that resembled an armored breastplate a Lower Army soldier might wear. She held her mouth in a grim line, and a single lock of golden-brown hair had fallen loose from her braid.

The sight of it broke my heart. I itched to hurry out there and tuck away the errant lock. It made my eldest sister seem too young, too small, dwarfed by the towering velvet curtains. Beyond the dark haven of the stage, the low murmur of the waiting audience was rising, growing teeth.

"Did you know," Gareth asked quietly, "that every other musician who had entered the tournament withdrew upon hearing she would perform?"

I nodded, my heart swelling with pride. "Father said none of them even cared about losing potential invitations to the queen's ball. All they cared about was—"

"Hearing Farrin play," Gareth finished, a little wistful, a little grim. He had of course been at that terrible, riotous performance ten years ago that had frightened fourteen-year-old Farrin away from the thing she loved most in the world—her music.

"Do you remember that awful day?" he said after a moment, his voice hushed, reverent, as if to speak too loudly of what happened would coax it back to life like some rank act of Olden necromancy. "All those people cheering her name. Drunk on her talent, demanding encore after encore. Not seeing *her* at all, only what she could make them feel."

"If Father hadn't restrained you, I'm certain you would have murdered someone."

"Or several someones."

"Gods forbid anyone look at Farrin in an admiring fashion."

Gareth scoffed. "Not a single one of those slobbering fools begging her to marry them was worthy of being within ten miles of her. Or even, if I'm being honest, on the same continent."

I looked up at him with a fond smile. "I know you tire of me saying this, but…"

He made a face. "This fixation of yours is unbecoming."

"But wouldn't it be *easier* for both of you if—"

"If we were in love with each other? If we wanted to fuck and have babies and…I don't know, what else do people in love do? Wash each other's backs?"

I barely stifled my laughter. "And scrub between each other's toes."

He shuddered. "Romantic life is truly abhorrent. But I'm sure you know all about that."

"I…what?"

"Oh, come now, Gemmy-Gem. Let's not be coy. You look all dreamy and sated, and you smell like sex."

Mortified, I backed away from him. "I most certainly do *not*."

"Oh, all right, then," he said with a shrug. "Must be someone else." He looked pointedly at the empty space around us. "Hmm. Well, now, that's awkward."

I swatted his arm. "All right, you awful man. Talan and I, just before lunch…well. It's not what you think."

"It's at least *partially* what I think, though?"

My cheeks grew hot. "Partially, yes. Perhaps."

Gareth, grinning, bent down to peer at me. "What's this? Gemma Ashbourne blushing? I've never known you to be shy about these things. He must truly have you wrapped around his... well, let's exercise some restraint and say his *finger*, shall we?"

I swallowed hard and looked away, Illaria's words once again ringing in my ears.

The underneath, Gemma, is putrid.

"If indeed I'm wrapped around anything," I said tightly, "I've done so all by myself and of my own will, thank you very much."

Something must have passed over my face before I could hide it. Gareth came around and gently took my shoulders.

"Oh, Gem. I'm sorry, I took that too far. Blame my nerves, I suppose, though that's no excuse." He leaned down to look at me, quiet now, and grave. "What is it? You look deeply unhappy."

Collecting myself, I focused not on him but on the tie hanging loose around his rumpled collar—a professor's tie from the university in Fairhaven, the queen's city, striped in librarian colors of gold, blue, and black. I would have found anyone else's insistence on wearing the tie outside of the university pretentious and obnoxious. But I knew Gareth wore it for only one reason: so that some curious amateur philosopher or humble country tutor would see it and approach him, eager for a conversation about all the things Gareth loved. His work on an exhaustive new collection of folktales gathered from every continent. Some obscure topic of Old Country arcana, like the complicated lineage of the lesser fae clans. The Middlemist.

My stomach dropped.

The Mist.

Suddenly one of the many unanswered questions I had successfully locked away and avoided thinking about returned with a vengeance. My memory took me back to Rosewarren on the day of Mara's transformation, how I'd huddled with her in that quiet temple of stone and greenery, trying in vain to decipher her strange words.

All the weapons at my fingertips, and yet my hands have long been tied...

Maybe the three of you together can do something before it's too late.

The three of us. Farrin, Gareth, me.

Shame heated my face. For weeks Mara had no doubt been waiting for a letter from us, or even a visit. And I had done nothing to help her, had told no one what she had said. Instead I'd tricked Madam Baines, snuck into Father's secret greenway, lost a wardstone, and daydreamed endlessly about Talan while breaking every one of my father's rules in order to find a demon who could, maybe, if he existed, give *me* what I'd always wanted—me, and no one else. Meanwhile Mara served the Order and hadn't been home to Ivyhill since the day the Warden took her away from us. Mara had never even *met* Gareth. He and Farrin had become friends when she was thirteen years old and he fifteen, during one of our family holidays to the queen's city—a city Mara hadn't had the chance to visit for years.

I felt sick, poisoned by my own self-loathing as I thought of the list I had burned in my fireplace: *Gareth—send him to Rosewarren in my stead?* An easy escape, and I hadn't even managed to do that much for my sister.

"Gareth," I whispered, clutching his sleeve, "I have something to tell you, and it will be difficult to explain."

But just then, an urgent hush fell. The stage's spellcrafted curtains pulled apart, revealing Farrin sitting at the piano, alone, silent, still. Beyond her, what must have been thousands of people stared at her, waiting—just as silent, just as unmoving. They crowded the rows of curved seats, stood clustered at the edge of the stage, clung to tree branches for a better view.

"*Shit*," Gareth hissed, grabbing my hand. "Come on, we're late."

We hurried toward the two empty chairs in the first row, which four of Father's guards protected from the eager masses. With a muttered word of thanks to the guards, I slipped into my seat between Illaria and Talan, not daring to look at either of them and fervently wishing I hadn't forgotten to apply perfume before leaving my tent.

Fortunately they both kept their mouths shut. What was about to happen was more important, and they knew it, and I loved them for it. I grabbed their hands and squeezed, taking comfort in the press of Illaria's rings and the smooth warmth of Talan's palm.

Then I found my sister's eyes.

Farrin was sitting at the piano, still unmoving, but her head had tilted slightly toward the audience, and she glanced over at me, her gaze obscured by that stubborn lock of hair. Such an expression on her face—fear, exhilaration, a silent, childlike plea.

My chest twisted into a tight knot. I wished that it were possible for me to sit beside her and hold her hand throughout her performance, shield her from the audience with my body, or, even better, whisk her from the stage like one of the sly Olden Winds and bring her safely back home. We could hide in her bed, brow to brow, fingers intertwined between us in an unbreakable knot, just as we'd done every night in the long, awful months after Mara was taken away from us, and then again after Mother left. I had never felt safer than I had on those nights, sheltered from the sorrow of Mara's absence by Farrin's warm embrace and the fierce light in her brown eyes. The nearness of her rich magical blood had been excruciatingly painful, and yet I had relished it all the same.

When my grief overwhelmed me, when my body shuddered with pain and strange fevers left me convinced the room's shadows were beasts snuffling for my scent, I would ask Farrin to stay awake through the night and guard us both against my imagined terrors. And she did, every time, with neither question nor ridicule. Despite her presence, I never slept soundly on those nights, and whenever I woke, I did so without moving. I kept my breath slow and sleep-steady, and every time I cracked open my eyes, I saw that Farrin's were wide open, tireless and unafraid. She stroked my hair and kept our quilts tucked securely around me, glaring at the shadows as if daring them to try something.

But that was long ago, before we grew older and then, quietly, apart; before the curse lifted and the Basks returned, reigniting our families' blood feud; before I turned my attentions to parties, gowns, lovers, anything that would help me forget the things that hurt me—my body, my vanished mother, my imprisoned sister, my distant father.

What a fool I was. Not until that moment, watching Farrin draw in a breath and close her eyes, an expression of poignant grief falling over her face as she pressed her fingers to the keys, did it cross my mind that she might be lonely.

Maybe those sleepless nights of watching over me had brought her a comfort she sorely missed. Maybe having Father's confidence was not as desirable a gift as I had always thought. I tried to recall the last time I had been alone with Farrin and talked of something other than the Basks, or Father, or some matter of the estate. The answer came to me at once: sitting at her feet in the Green Ballroom three weeks prior as she performed the piece she'd written about the shining boy.

And before that?

Shame sewed my throat up tight as I realized I could not find the answer. Before that day in the ballroom, when had Farrin and I last enjoyed a true conversation, a moment only for us? When was the last time we had thought to seek each other out and share secrets, laugh ourselves silly over some stupid piece of gossip, speak of real and true things?

Too long. Whatever the reason, whoever was to blame, it had been far too long.

You, a mean little voice hissed at me, one of the many that lived in my head. *You are to blame.*

I drew in a soft choking breath, my eyes welling up. The voice spoke a cruel truth. Farrin ran the estate, Farrin helped Father with his machinations, Farrin kept the cogs of Ivyhill oiled and in working order.

And I—I hurt inside and out, and I hid myself away. A refuge of silk and amorous liaisons and dusk-till-dawn parties was nevertheless a refuge. An escape. An excuse.

Talan stroked my palm with his thumb, bringing me back to myself. On my other side, Illaria leaned close.

"Gemma?" she whispered. "Is it the panic?"

I shook my head and redirected my attention to the stage, to Farrin, to the cautious, tender melody she wove across the keys—the opening passage of her original composition. The piece that told a story about a girl trapped in a fire and the shining boy who was her salvation.

The music quickly coaxed me out of the mire of my thoughts and into what felt like another realm entirely—some gentle green place lit softly by a rising sun, the air drawn tight and quiet with anticipation. I could see it so clearly, the story Farrin was telling—the peace of Ivyhill before everything went wrong, the slowly emerging sinister undertones of our feud with the Basks, the back-and-forth of light and dark, danger and safety, a trick played here, an ugly public argument there. Through it all, a hopeful, sweet melody came and went, fighting for air. Each time those notes returned, they sounded more harried, more desperate.

My skin prickled. That was us. That melody clawing for a foothold was Farrin, Mara, and me, careening toward a grief we could not see coming.

I held my breath, watching Farrin's fingers fly across the keys—the poise of her tireless slender arms, how her body moved as the music did, as if she and the rippling crescendo of notes and the piano itself were all one creature.

The audience around me, behind me, above me in the trees seemed as rapt as I was—unmoving, hardly breathing, all of us leaning forward in our seats like hungry birds stretching for food.

For sight and sound and taste and touch, I prayed fervently, *for the scent of the wind and the strength of my limbs, thanks be to Kerezen, god of my body, maker of bone and blood. And so it shall ever be.*

Keep my father's guards steady.

Keep these people calm and clear-eyed.

Keep my sister safe.

At first it seemed my concerns were unfounded. Farrin played on, a series of rising staccato passages signifying the discovery of the fire, and still the audience stayed in their seats. I dared to turn around once and saw them all, thousands of them, gazing at the stage, their faces soft, their eyes bright. Some wore absent little smiles; others held their hands clasped just under their chins, their mouths wobbling with stifled tears. Others wept openly. Gareth, sitting on Illaria's other side with his elbows on his knees and his hands folded in front of his mouth, beamed up at the stage, his eyes shining and his face lit up with pride.

At the sight of him, some of the tension faded from my

shoulders. I turned back to the stage and forced myself to breathe. Farrin's music continued, the rage of the inferno receding before the theme of the shining boy began—a melodic passage descending from the highest keys, mysterious and elusive at first, then stronger, ringing with hope.

The music's power ravaged my body. Waves of quiet agony pulsed through me from the tips of my toes to the crown of my head, but I didn't care. In fact, I welcomed them. This pain I could withstand, and gladly.

This pain meant that my sister, for a moment, was forgetting hers.

Then, without warning, chaos erupted.

A sharp, masculine cry behind me made me whirl around. My mouth went dry with fear.

Ryder Bask was barreling toward the stage.

He pushed through the crowd of people as if they were nothing, mere weeds before the scythe of his strength. He crawled over shoulders, launched off laps. People reached up to grab him, tried to hold him back, but Ryder broke free of them easily. He beat them away with the obsidian end of his staff. His eyes were wild, his face ruddy with excitement, and the sounds escaping him were animal—need, despair, fury at anyone who dared attempt to restrain him.

"What in the name of the gods?" Illaria whispered beside me. "He's gone mad."

Ryder's outburst lit up the crowd, igniting a frenzied hysteria. They clambered after him, some cheering him on, delighted by the chance to move closer to the stage. Others yanked at Ryder's arms, punched him, yelled at him to stop. But he was unstoppable, a wild brute force with eyes trained on my sister.

Gareth bounded toward the stage, pulled himself up onto the

edge, and threw himself in front of Farrin, blocking Ryder's path. She had stopped playing and sat stricken with fear on the piano bench, but as Ryder neared, howling northern words I could not understand, Farrin slowly stood, half hiding behind Gareth, and stared past him at the uproar. I could not read the expression on her face. Terror? Wonder?

Father roared for his guards to blockade the piano and then tore through the seething crowd like a shot arrow. I felt the impact of him crashing into Ryder in my teeth, heard the sickening crunch of bone and the shrieking whoops of the eager crowd.

A woman's voice pierced the din, formidable and choked with furious sobs, begging Father to stop: Alastrina Bask, who had somehow fought her way to her brother even with four desperate tournament arbiters trying to restrain her. Her hair had fallen loose. The feathers on her gown were splintered, flattened. An arbiter smacked her across the face, no doubt hoping it would shock her into complacency, but instead she felled him with a swift kick to his groin.

And still Ryder shouted, his anguished voice muffled by whatever my father had done to him. He had lost his coat, and his shirt hung about him in tatters, revealing stretches of straining muscle and taut, work-roughened skin. My last glimpse of him was his arm, reaching desperately toward the stage. I tried to fix his foreign words in my memory so I could search for their meaning later, but the tumult of stray magic careening through the crowd pummeled me. A hot knife of pain stabbed my skull, and I swayed, my vision clouding over.

"Come, Gemma," Talan said quietly, his voice suddenly in my ear. "There's nothing more to see here."

I thought I heard a note of glee in his words, and my heart sank as I caught sight of his face—eyes sparkling, luscious mouth quirked in a satisfied smile. I searched for Illaria, but she was occupied, helping a group of frightened old women to safety.

Digging my heels into the earth, I looked back over my shoulder for Farrin, but only Father's guards remained on the stage. Farrin and Gareth were gone.

"Don't be afraid," Talan reassured me, his arm strong around me as he guided me through the uproar. "She and Gareth are safe. He's taking her to the university tents. It's quieter there."

I nodded, dazed. That seemed entirely sensible. I let Talan shepherd me away, his long strides and fluttering dark coat cutting an efficient path through the confused throng. By the time we entered my sleeping tent at last, the sounds of mayhem were fainter, and the smothering press of magic lifted away. Shaking, I sank onto one of the tasseled floor cushions.

Talan found a cloth near the washbasin, fetched a glass of water, and joined me.

"Do you want me to help you?" he murmured, dabbing my fevered brow with the cloth so gently that it seemed comical in light of the violence we had just witnessed. The incongruity pulled a strange laugh out of me. I pushed Talan's hand away.

"No, don't help me, don't you dare," I said tightly. "You did that, didn't you? You got in Ryder's head. You turned him violent, desperate. Not himself."

A flash of guilt moved across Talan's face before he smoothed it away and lifted his chin, defiant. "As we intended to do."

"Yes, but *not* at Farrin's performance. The plan was to coax Ryder into violence *tomorrow* at the *fighting pits*. Humiliate him there, where he could easily be controlled and no one but sentinels would get hurt. And instead you did *this*."

I rose unsteadily to my feet, angry tears pricking my eyes. "You ruined Farrin's performance. You put her in danger. Nothing matters besides that. Not wardstones, not the Basks, none of it. Do you understand?" I let out a choked sob, remembering the last time I was in this tent with Talan's name on my lips, his hands stroking me to ecstasy. A gorgeous memory, now tainted. "Why did you do it, Talan? Explain it to me, please."

He watched me quietly from the floor, his expression desolate. I was gratified to see his bearing change, guilt lending an unusual haggard quality to his beautiful face.

"I'm so sorry, Gemma. I..." He squeezed his eyes shut, turned his head slightly away. Clenched his fists, unclenched them. "I understand why you're angry."

I knelt before him, tilting his face back to me. When he opened his eyes, they were bright with shame.

"Then explain it to me," I said quietly. "Help me understand." With a little frisson of cold, I remembered the mischievous sparkle in his eyes. "Did you think it would be fun? Did you want to scare me?"

His eyes widened. "No. *Never*. I didn't want to scare you, or your sister, or your friend Illaria—who should be an interesting dinner companion tonight after this," he added wryly.

I did not respond, watching him closely.

"I knew the plan," he continued. "Of course I did. Tomorrow at the fighting pits. But then I felt Ryder, Gemma. I felt...something strange. I don't know what it was or how to explain it. But he..."

Talan paused, frowning. "I suppose the best way to describe it is that something awoke in him. It shocked him. It confused him. Sitting there, listening to the music, he was tormented, the agony of it almost physical, and he didn't know why." Talan blew out a slow breath, his expression distant, haunted. "The feeling was... startling, to say the least, and intoxicating. Terrifying. I didn't understand it, and I wanted to, and I also knew it wouldn't take much to push that fear and confusion Ryder felt into outright hysterics. And the immense potential for humiliation with such a crowd of witnesses there to see him come undone..."

Seemingly lost for words, he put out his hands, a man bereft, and looked at me helplessly. "I acted without thinking. Or rather, I was thinking only about us—you and me, and our plan to disgrace the Basks. How Ryder hurt you at Ravenswood." His expression darkened. "For that, I do not regret what I did. He deserved every blow your father dealt him."

His explanation made sense, and his remorse seemed genuine, yet a lingering ill feeling nibbled at me. I looked at him for a long while, content to let him squirm, astonished at how, even sapped of color and tense with worry, he was such a sight to behold, infuriatingly lovely. His wide dark eyes were bright with sadness, and that beautiful perfect jaw of his worked as if he were fighting back a terrible sadness. The afternoon sunlight poured through the tent's netted windows to paint soft golden shapes across his shining dark hair.

My body and mind were at war. Ludicrously, even after what had just happened, I ached to hold him, but he needed to understand the seriousness of what he had done.

"I don't know what to say to you right now," I confessed at last, glad to hear my voice sound firm. "I understand why you did it, and I'm as curious as you are about whatever strange thing Ryder was feeling. And I'd be lying if I said I'm not pleased by how his unhinged outburst will be the talk of every party from now until the queen's ball." I ignored his small, sad smile and steadied myself. "However, that you would even consider disrupting Farrin's performance and endangering her life, that you would alter our plans without consulting me...that is an enormous breach of my trust, Talan."

I drew in a shaky breath and rose to my feet. "I'm not certain how you can mend that breach," I said quietly, "or if it can be mended at all."

Then I turned, stone-faced, and left him. Not until I reached Father's tent, where two sentries stepped aside silently to let me pass, did I let myself crumple. Fist pressed to my mouth, my burning eyes squeezed shut, I curled into a tight ball on my father's bed and tried to remember how to breathe.

CHAPTER 17

We left for Ivyhill the next day. Considering what had happened, the tournament arbiters allowed my family's entourage to leave early with sixty invitations to the queen's masquerade ball in hand—ten for Father's victory in the fighting pits and an additional fifty as an apology for Farrin's interrupted performance. It was the most invitations to a royal function that a single family had ever been granted.

And yet our caravan back to Ivyhill was a somber affair, one I spent in a small uncovered gig with only my blathering cousin Delia, who drove our pair of horses. I couldn't bear to be trapped inside a closed carriage with Father, Farrin, or Talan, and silvertongue Delia had something I wanted: a translation of the words Ryder Bask had shouted as he beat a path toward the tournament stage.

Unfortunately, in order to get that information, I had to endure Delia's insatiable appetite for her own voice, and by the time she turned our horses onto Ivyhill's grand stone drive, she had run through twenty additional topics of conversation and had just begun on a twenty-first—how her gorgeous new boots had sliced open her ankles, a sacrifice she was happy to have made, for she was convinced the cunning footwear had earned her the calling card of some hapless young Lower Army soldier from the southern coast.

Delia alighted from the carriage as soon as the horses stopped, a flounce of auburn curls and admittedly lovely ruffled green poplin. I quickly crept away as she found a much more interested receptacle for her thoughts—a pretty, starry-eyed young stable hand who looked astonished to be Delia's newest acquaintance.

I hurried through Ivyhill's gigantic front doors, all four of them thrown open to the afternoon, and found refuge in the small rose-colored sitting room off the main foyer. Safe within the ivy-trimmed walls, I paced, my mind racing.

Beloved one, Delia had told me. *Star of my life.*

Do not leave me.

That was what Ryder had shouted—no, howled in agony—as he ran like a desperate madman toward my sister, and I couldn't understand why. The word *beloved* sat in my stomach like a slimy stone.

His behavior had of course reminded me of that day at Ravenswood when Talan had used his power to send Ryder dashing away from me, screaming his sister's name in utter terror.

Ciaran Bask's greatest fear, Talan had said. *It wasn't hard to find, nor to exploit.*

It seemed sensible that Ryder Bask's greatest fear would be the loss of his sister. That was no great surprise.

But that he would reach for Farrin as if she were something dear and precious, that he would call her *beloved*, seemed unthinkable.

"My guess is the curse that kept the Basks trapped at their estate got inside their heads over the years and turned them a bit loony," Delia had said matter-of-factly. "Ryder probably thought

Farrin was somebody else, some girl from a dream, or a lover. Ugh, can you imagine bedding a Bask?" She had shuddered delicately before glancing at me sidelong. "Do you think that's possible? That the curse could have poisoned their minds?"

It wasn't the first time someone had plied me for information about the cursed forest that had imprisoned the Basks, and it surely would not be the last—especially not from Delia, whose curiosity was as indefatigable as her mouth.

I stared out the sitting room window, the panes of amber and rose glass punctuated with tiny splashes of green leaves. Talan stepped out of his carriage, tall and dark, lissome as a cat unfurling from a sun-warmed perch. He stretched, shrugged off his green spring jacket, and shook my father's hand; they had shared a carriage, I realized, which both alarmed and relieved me for reasons I could not articulate. Then Talan turned toward the sitting room window, his jacket draped loosely over his arm. It was as if he somehow knew I would be watching him from behind the colored glass.

A buzz of heat fluttered through me, a thrill of both fright and desire. I yanked closed the tasseled damask curtains and pressed my back against them, trying to catch my breath. My head was too full, my body exhausted from pain and want. I longed for the quiet sanctuary of my rooms, for Jessyl to soothe me with tea and household gossip, and considered how best to move through the house unseen.

But before I could, a series of inhuman shrieks pierced the air, then warnings and pleas in a ragged voice I recognized at once.

"Get away! Don't touch her! *Don't touch her!*"

My blood turned to ice.

That voice belonged to Madam Baines.

I rushed out into the foyer, joined by rivers of wide-eyed people coming from all directions—befuddled servants, travelers from our caravan. I saw Gareth and Farrin, Delia, then Talan, whom I tried not to acknowledge, though I could feel his eyes on me. Two housemaids raced down the grand staircase, both of them in hysterical tears. One of them—Marys, a trim, severely meticulous woman who had worked at Ivyhill for as long as I could remember—was too far gone to speak.

The other, young Lilianne, her cleaning cap askew, her freckles standing out starkly on her ashen cheeks, screamed, "She's killed her! Oh, gods, someone help us!"

Gilroy met them at the bottom of the stairs, clearly mortified by the commotion. His face was flushed red all the way up to his silver hairline.

"What in the world are you screaming about?" he demanded.

Father swept through the front doors in his long traveling coat, yanking off his gloves with a grimace. "Gilroy, stop your blustering and help poor Marys sit down somewhere." Father took off his hat, his golden-brown hair slightly damp from the trip. He knelt before Lilianne. "Now, tell me what happened, slowly and clearly."

The gentleness of his voice cut me in two. I couldn't remember the last time he had spoken so sweetly to me.

"Marys and I were in the third-floor hallway of the east wing, finishing our weekly cleaning," Lilianne said, her voice trembling, "and we found…"

She dissolved into fresh sobs.

The world around me grew still, my throat tightening with panic. The third floor of the east wing—the location of my safe room, where I had encountered Madam Baines only two days prior.

Frantic, I glanced at Talan, but he was looking toward the second-floor mezzanine, his expression one of utter horror.

I followed his gaze and saw why. My hands flew to my mouth, my stomach twisting.

There at the top of the stairs stood Madam Baines—brown curls a mess, eyes bloodshot and wild, a knife in her hands, and her entire front wet with blood.

"Oh," she said faintly, "you're home."

I wanted to be sick.

Madam Baines was looking straight at me.

The foyer burst into action. Father raced up the stairs, followed closely by Farrin. Gilroy and Gareth kept the others back, blocking their passage.

I slipped past them, ignoring Gareth's plea for me to stay where I was. Talan was right behind me, his silent, sure presence a balm in the midst of such madness. When we reached the landing, I saw Father crouching in the shadows down the hallway, where the light from the foyer windows dimmed. Beside him was a pile of something, a still heap. Farrin stood nearby, her body tense and square.

Madam Baines approached them slowly, the knife still in her hand. "My lord?" she asked faintly, dazed. "Is everything all right?" A wobbly smile stretched across her face. She raised the knife, then recoiled from it and let out a sharp sob.

With a curse, Talan darted ahead of me and caught Madam Baines's wrist.

"Let me have that, Adamantia," he said softly, lowering her arm and guiding her away from Father and Farrin. "You don't want that anymore."

"I don't?" Madam Baines asked, blinking at him like a lost child.

"No, it's not safe anymore. It's time to put it away."

When Talan pried her fingers loose from the knife's hilt, I felt dizzy with relief. Madam Baines lowered herself to the carpet and sat in placid, expectant silence.

I swallowed hard, hurried past Talan, and joined Farrin at Father's side. My sister seemed to be frozen in shock, but Father saw me and rose, caught my hands in his, and said with uncharacteristic gentleness, "Gemma, my darling, don't, please." But it was too late.

I smelled the body before I saw her face—Jessyl, *my* Jessyl. Eyes open, throat slit, covered with a shining curtain of her own blood.

After that I could no longer stand. I staggered back from Jessyl's body on boneless legs. Someone caught me, and beyond the whine of my shock, I heard voices—Father, Farrin. Gilroy. Mrs. Seffwyck, the head housekeeper.

Talan.

"Gods, I'm so sorry, Gemma." His voice came to me as if in a dream. "Breathe, love. I've got you. You're all right. You're safe."

I turned toward him, let him hide me in his arms. It was a warm, dark place, solid and steady, and it smelled of him. Pine and rosewood and anise, Illaria had said. A bite of lemongrass, and a putrid scent underneath.

I pressed my face into the darkness, inhaled so hard it made my head spin, but I could find nothing rotten, only more Talan. Greedy and desperate, I breathed him in. If I filled up my body with his scent until there was nothing left of me, then everything I had just seen would cease to exist—the blood, the death, Jessyl staring with her frozen glass eyes—and I would know only Talan.

Someone moved; *I* was moving, though I hadn't told my legs to carry me anywhere. I sank into a softness, felt a gentle brush of warmth across my forehead. A rustle of fabric, a smooth glide of brass rings—curtains being pulled. The light around me gently dimmed.

With immense effort, I pushed myself up onto my elbows and saw not Talan but Farrin. She was drawing closed my bedroom curtains. The grim determination on her face was the thing that drew me out of my shock. She had used that expression to guard me against shadow monsters, and now she was grown, and so was I, and the things she had to guard against were infinitely more frightening.

"Farrin?" My voice had shrunk since the last time I'd used it.

"Oh, good," she said, leaving the window to join me. "A few minutes more and I might have been forced to slap you back to life."

A joke of sorts, but her voice was gentle, her smile sad. She touched my face and I grabbed her hand, held it tight. I was teetering on the edge of a precipice, and Farrin's grip was the only thing keeping me from plummeting. My mind whirled, thinking of the chaos no doubt unspooling downstairs.

"Doesn't Father need your help with..." Bile rose, sour and hot in my throat. "With everything?"

"I'm needed here more," Farrin replied.

I nodded, my lips drawn tight, and kept nodding, pressing Farrin's hand against my cheek. If only I tried hard enough, perhaps I could somehow absorb her—her strength, her calm, her life that had not just been shattered.

Gently she shifted us both, guiding me to lie beside her on the bed. She pressed her brow to mine, tucked our clasped fingers between us. My nest of floral pillows framed her face with pink and blue petals. Her eyes were a steady expanse of deep honey brown flecked with green and gold.

Farrin's nearness, the gentle strength of her hands around mine, broke me. I made an awful heaving sound, as if someone had punched all the air out of my body, and then, clinging to my sister in desperation, wept myself to exhaustion in the safety of her arms.

When I next awoke, Farrin was gone and Talan had taken her place—not in my bed, but beside it.

He wore a white linen shirt, dark trousers with a faint iridescent brocade, gorgeous black leather boots embossed with an intricate pattern of five-pointed leaves. He sat in Jessyl's chair with one long leg crossed languidly over the other and a book open in his lap. Beyond my closed curtains, a soft rain tapped on the windows. When he heard me stirring, he looked up and gave me a gentle smile.

The sight of him rendered me breathless, a confusion of joy and revulsion blooming inside me. He said my name quietly, reached for my hand.

I slapped him away.

His smile faded.

"We killed her," I whispered hoarsely. The thought of saying her name nearly unraveled me, but I made myself do it: "We killed Jessyl."

Talan had been expecting that. "No, we did not," he answered firmly. "Madam Baines killed her."

"And since that night in the library, Madam Baines has not been herself, thanks to us." I sat up, holding my quilts tightly around me. I was glad Farrin had dressed me in one of my plainer, more modest nightgowns. "We have to confess what we did, exonerate her."

Talan's eyebrows lifted. "And reveal myself as an empath in the process? After what's happened, I'd be run off the continent by the righteous, wrathful power of all the Upper Army troops within one hundred miles. Or worse, by your father."

"Then you'll be run off the continent," I said, though even imagining it made my chest clench painfully.

"And then what? Will you abandon our search for the Man with the Three-Eyed Crown, or will you continue alone, telling no one else what we've been planning, and perhaps face this demon—who's kept your family in thrall for decades—with no one to help you? Or will you reveal everything we've done—every trip to Ravenswood, the stolen wardstone, the spell we unleashed upon Alastrina Bask—and live out the rest of your life trapped in this house as your sister is trapped at Rosewarren, deprived of freedom? What would your father think of all this, Gemma? How thoroughly would the truth destroy whatever love remains between you?"

His ferocious passion left me speechless. He was close to me now, his hands holding mine, his expression earnest and imploring.

"Talan..." I could say nothing else. His words had cut me open and filled my wriggling insides with such abject terror that I knew he was right: I would never tell anyone what we had done. Farrin would despise me, and Father...what precious little time he spent with me would disappear entirely. He would see to it that I was confined to my rooms, fed and clothed and bathed, and I would never see him again. He would do his paternal duty and then storm away from me forever, not once looking back. I knew that with a certainty as solid as the earth. I let out a shaking breath and felt the fight bleed out of me.

Talan watched me for a moment, his face unreadable, then released me, dragged a hand sharply through his hair, rose swiftly, and stalked across the room to stand at the door to my atrium, his back to me. Raindrops pinged merrily on its glass roof.

"Anyway, it doesn't matter," he said after a moment, his voice flat and tired. "Exoneration is no longer a possibility. Madam Baines is dead. She hanged herself in her room."

I was out of bed and rushing at him before I quite knew what

I was doing. "Did you do that too?" I shoved him feebly, unsteady on my feet. "Did you make her kill herself?" My head ached from crying. Talan caught me before I could fall, and I pounded ineffectually on his chest. I couldn't bear the idea of him comforting me, yet I craved his touch so desperately that my whole body ached.

He tried to lead me back to bed, murmuring sweet, soothing things, but I shoved him again, harder this time, and stumbled away from him.

He stood at the foot of my bed, watching me with such devastation on his face that I felt a fresh crawl of shame.

"You really think this is my fault," he said quietly. "*Our* fault. I feel the truth of that. You think I tricked Madam Baines into taking her own life."

"Jessyl's death," I said, my jaw clenched with disgust, "is undeniably our fault."

"You don't know that." Talan hurried back toward me, and I let him gather my hands in his with awful euphoric relief blazing through me. "You *can't* know that. Even I can't. Madam Baines's emotions were horribly confused, indecipherable. There was a great strange sickness in her mind, and it was no work of mine, and now she's dead. How can we know her mind wasn't primed to break regardless of our interference? How do we know that some other magic didn't invade her thoughts and drive her to madness?"

"We can't know that," I admitted. "But the coincidence is too extreme to ignore. We tricked her into revealing information. She unraveled, she..." I swallowed hard, fighting the rise of tears. They were a reprieve I did not deserve. "She killed Jessyl. *My* maid. *My* friend. And then she killed herself. If this chain of events did not begin with our actions, it would be truly remarkable."

"Remarkable things happen every day," Talan said, his brow

knotted with sadness. I longed to kiss it smooth, allow us both a moment of solace.

Instead I stepped back from him. He released my hands and let out a soft, shattered sound, as if I'd torn something from him.

"I didn't make her kill herself," he said dully. His gaze was flat, his face shadowed. "I swear to you, Gemma. Whatever cruel force pushed her toward that path, it didn't come from me."

An awful thought arose. "Perhaps that's true," I said slowly. "The cruel force could have come from the demon. He could have been watching us this whole time. He could have seen us with Madam Baines in the library, watched you work your empathic magic, thought, *Ah, an opportunity*, and planted the seed in Madam Baines's mind that very night. And that seed grew and grew and tore apart her mind until she no longer knew herself, or right from wrong, or even Jessyl's face."

Talan nodded eagerly. "I had the same thoughts. And it occurred to me that if we could find records of other such incidents and draw parallels between them, it could explain everything, perhaps even provide us with the answers we've been searching for. This is how we could *find* him, Gemma."

A sensible suggestion. But then I thought of Ryder Bask howling endearments at my sister, reaching for her like a dying man even as my furious father pounded him to a pulp.

"Maybe Madam Baines thought Jessyl was someone else entirely," I said, shivering a little. "Maybe Ryder looked at my sister and saw a different person looking back at him."

Talan was hardly breathing, looking down at me with anguished hope.

"Madam Baines lost her mind and killed Jessyl. Ryder Bask temporarily lost his mind, or near enough, and I refuse to think what he might have done had he gotten to Farrin. I cannot ignore those similarities, Talan. And you cannot expect me to."

"No, Gemma," Talan said, his voice cracking. "That wasn't me. I sensed that strangeness in Ryder, remember? That feeling of utter fear and bewilderment. That was there all on its own. Farrin's music awoke it in him, or something else did. *Someone* else. I took advantage of that opportunity, yes, and amplified it to accomplish our goal, but I did not—"

"The point is that you deceived him," I interrupted, "even if the lie was a small one, a mere nudge against whatever foul feelings already lived inside him. And you deceived Madam Baines that night in the library." I took a breath, let it out. "And you deceived *me* when you took it upon yourself to change our plans at the tournament."

"That was an error in judgment, not a lie."

Shaking my head, I stepped back from him and freed my hands from his desperate grip. "I cannot trust you," I said, the words foul on my tongue. I despised them. I despised Talan, and myself, and the painful longing cracking my shattered heart into even smaller pieces. "Maybe I will again someday, but not now." I paused, loath to say my next words, but I needed to say them, and he needed to hear them. In truth, he had probably already felt them.

"I'm afraid of you, Talan," I whispered. "I'm afraid of how ardently I want you. I'm afraid of what you might have done, what I become when I'm around you. My friend is dead, and if you hadn't come here, it's possible she might still be alive."

All the light went out of him, despair falling over his face like a shadow. Even his stature seemed to shrink, as if my words had lopped an inch off his height. His jaw worked as he struggled for composure, and I clenched my fists to keep from going to him. Whatever cord of coincidence and fate had hooked into our hearts, drawing us together, I wished passionately that I could sever it.

When he spoke at last, his dark eyes were bright with sadness. "I understand, Gemma, and I don't blame you. I only wish…" He swallowed hard, looked away for a moment, then straightened, his face wooden. "I'll leave you now," was all he said, and then he fetched his book and coat from Jessyl's chair and slipped out of my bedroom without another word.

◆◆

The next morning, when I was still abed, nibbling halfheartedly at my breakfast, Lilianne—blotchy-faced, her eyes swollen from crying—brought me two small sealed notes and curtsied bashfully before hurrying away.

My heart frantically drumming against my breastbone, I tore open the first note to find Gareth's wild penmanship. He had left that morning, heading back to Fairhaven several days early.

Your friend Talan has proposed a most intriguing course of research that I, dreary scholar that I am, could not resist: incidents of spontaneous derangement in otherwise sane individuals and the possibility of demonic influence. Superb! Outlandish! You can understand my fascination. Sorry not to say a proper goodbye, Gemmy, but I'll see you at the ball in two weeks, yes? I'll be a good boy and wear something shockingly suitable—WITHOUT my tie, I swear it. The gods saw me write this, and I can't possibly risk adding to my already lengthy list of offenses. I'm quite sure they were wholly unimpressed by that night last month when I—oh, never mind, I'll save that story for another time. Or you can ask your sister, who gave me a verbal lashing I very much deserved. Watch after her, will you, Gem? She's not as strong as she looks. And take heart, my dear—every time I spoke with your Jessyl over the years, she was happy, healthy, sincere. Her life was a good one, and she loved you unfalteringly.

Yours,
Gareth

My heart a gnarl of grief, I let Gareth's letter fall and opened the second note—a simple square of paper, unsigned, with two short sentences written in exquisite lettering:

I will not rest until I've earned back your trust. Be safe, my wildcat.

CHAPTER 18

F or two days I kept to my rooms, hardly eating, tormented by terrible dreams that tossed me back into the waking world covered in sweat and certain that someone was watching me. I tore my rooms apart, tossing books off their shelves, uprooting and repotting every plant in my atrium, emptying my closet until the floor was littered with glittering piles—lace, chiffon, silk, fur, velvet, beadwork.

Nothing. No staring eyes, no hidden monsters. Meticulously I reassembled it all. Lilianne interrupted my work several times with food, drink, shy offers to wash and braid my hair. Farrin had assigned her to be my new lady's maid, a decision I seriously questioned. The poor girl was barely seventeen and looked terrified of me, and I couldn't blame her for that. Each time she crept into my rooms, I dismissed her with as much kindness as I could muster and wondered if she saw the awful red smile of Jessyl's slit throat whenever she looked at me.

I saw that smile. I saw it every time I closed my eyes, and even though I hadn't seen Madam Baines hanging from the rafters, I imagined that too with stark, ruthless clarity. In my mind,

I conjured her room in the servants' wing, the white linens she had knotted together, the toppled chair, her lifeless face. I forced myself to imagine the sensation of the life being squeezed out of me by my own design. The second evening after Jessyl's death, I awoke choking from a listless, feverish nap, convinced that hands had closed around my throat.

Hours later, as Father and Farrin slept and Mrs. Rathmont started the day's cooking fires downstairs, I crept out of the house in the plainest garment I owned—a housedress of dusty blue linen that I often wore when tending to my plants—hurried across the quiet, dew-soaked grounds, slipped into the hedge maze, and headed straight for the greenway that would take me to Rosewarren.

My grief was wild, Jessyl's absence an open wound, and with Talan gone, I felt lost, as if I'd forgotten how to live inside my own house.

I needed to run away. Not forever, but for a little while.

I needed Mara—and I tried not to think of how when she had needed me, I had pushed her out of my mind, too overwhelmed to give her my attention, terrified of what she had to say and how it might throw my life out of balance.

I tried not to think of how I had failed her and what she might think when I showed up unannounced at the priory, asking for help I did not deserve.

Without Father and Farrin beside me, the gigantic doors of Rosewarren felt more like beasts—enormous wooden slabs buttressed with thick bars of iron and capped with a pair of stone falcons in flight. The birds' eyes were hooded, fierce. They stared down at me in silent judgment, noting all the throbbing lesions under my skin where the greenway's teeth had chewed me up.

When the doors opened, a young girl stood there—chestnut-brown skin, thick black hair in two braids, wide brown eyes. She wore a long gray linen tunic, dark trousers, knee-high leather boots. Strapped across her hips was a belt that carried three sheathed knives.

She looked me up and down, her expression guarded. Though she couldn't have been more than thirteen or fourteen years of age, she held herself with impressive poise.

"You're here to see Mara, aren't you?" she demanded.

"Yes, and—"

"But the others already came. Your father and your sister. That was Mara's family visit for the month."

My stomach dropped. Father and Farrin had come *without* me.

I blew out a sad puff of laughter. Of course they had; I could imagine that conversation so clearly. It would have been brief:

But Papa, what about Gemma?

Her careless behavior the last time we visited Rosewarren has cost her the privilege of further visits—unless, Farrin, you're particularly keen on bringing more unnecessary chaos and pain into Mara's life?

"I see," I said quietly. Once I would have attempted to charm my way in regardless of the rules. I was an Ashbourne, and my sister was the pride of Rosewarren.

But on that day, I'd given the last scraps of my courage to the greenway, and the news of my family's secret visit gutted me.

"I'm sorry to have bothered you," I murmured, mortified to feel myself close to crying, as though I were a scolded child too young and foolish to withstand defeat. "I didn't realize…I'm sorry."

I turned to leave, but the girl caught my wrist. Her touch was strong but gentle.

"Wait." She looked over her shoulder, then grimly back at me. "Follow me. Don't fall behind or you'll be on your own. I'm Cira."

Stunned, I obeyed, following her through the towering entrance hall, up a curving flight of stairs, and through parts of the priory that I'd never seen before—long hushed corridors lined with quiet classrooms; small orderly libraries with words like DREAMWALKERS and TITANS stamped on brass plates above their doors; inner courtyards teeming with gardens, the air fresh and green with herbal perfume; and finally, the Roses' private rooms.

Here the crimson carpet and oppressive dark-wood panels of the snaking corridors opened up into a cavernous compound. Bedrooms and bathing rooms ringed a colossal tree that sprouted up through the stone floor and nearly reached the high ceiling. Enormous skylights of rippled glass admitted rays of morning light, transforming the space into something much cheerier than the rest of the priory. The tree's lower branches had been strung with pieces of colored glass cut into various shapes—swallows, red foxes, great leaping stags—and rosebushes grew rampant along curved walls of smooth stone. It was a grand space, but plainly adorned, all the decorations simple and handmade.

Some of the tree's massive roots jutted out aboveground, creating strange misshapen passages and moss-lined alcoves. A few Roses were nestled in these little hollows reading, napping, talking quietly, mending socks, patching trousers. Some were girls, others grown women. None of them looked very old, which didn't surprise me. Most Roses didn't survive past thirty years of age, maybe thirty-five—a fate I had long ago convinced myself would not befall my sister.

They all looked up as we passed, most of them watching in wide-eyed silence. But one young woman who looked perhaps a few years older than me whistled low and shot Cira a gleeful look.

"You're mad if you think we'll keep this quiet for you," she said. "The Warden won't like this at all."

"And we all know, Danesh, how *intimately* you're aware of what the Warden likes," Cira responded coolly. The other Roses within earshot laughed and hooted; Danesh, flushing, slammed shut the book she had been reading. I was glad to round the next corner in the maze of tree roots and escape her furious glare.

But then Cira led me to the end of a corridor that branched off the main room, the walls an odd mix of stone, wood planks, and gnarled tree bark, and suddenly I couldn't have cared less about Danesh.

Cira had taken me to Mara's room. The door stood open. Cira stepped aside to let me enter, her face sharp with curiosity.

But I couldn't move. Shock nailed me to the threshold. I wanted to look everywhere at once, absorb it in one gulping breath so the pain would be over quickly, but there was too much to see, and my heart couldn't contain it all.

My sister had painted Ivyhill.

It covered every inch of her room's walls and ceiling—the rolling green grounds and farmlands, the game park, the horse trails and stables, the lake, the little footbridge that crossed the small river at the bottom of the south lawn, the hothouses bursting with color. The great house, of course, was the most breathtaking element, a meticulous depiction of every turret, every window, every sweeping veranda. Through it all, connecting house to lake to fountain, were veins of ivy painted in shades of emerald, moss, mint, pine.

"I started painting you and Farrin," came a quiet voice from behind me, "but I couldn't get your faces quite right, so I gave up. I'm much better at landscapes than people."

I whirled about and threw my arms around Mara, fighting hard against the waves of sadness threatening to crest behind my eyes. It was an awkward embrace—she was carrying a sack of laundry—but I didn't care. I relished her little *oof* as I slammed into her; I devoured the rich tones of her laugh. I would have stayed like that for an hour if she'd let me.

Instead she pulled gently away from me, bent to drop a soft kiss on Cira's head in thanks, and led me inside her room. The last thing I saw before she shut the door was Cira's face, open and soft with love as she watched Mara walk away, and I realized with a bitter taste in my throat that although I was Mara's little sister by blood, Cira had become her little sister in all the ways that truly mattered.

Perhaps it was that sour tang of jealousy that made me tell Mara everything—Talan, the demon who had destroyed his family, the bargain we had made to help each other; Father's greenway in the lagoon, our nights at Ravenswood, the wardstone. Madam Baines. Jessyl. The glamour I'd crafted weeks ago and not dared to attempt again. Farrin's performance at the tournament and how it had devolved into chaos. Talan's kisses, his beauty, his tenderness. The fire he had lit inside me, illuminating all the good secrets of my body and disguising the bad.

When at last I finished, I was utterly wrung out. We faced each other on her bed, right next to the painted trees of Ivyhill's deer park. Little round deer eyes peered out of the thick piney green. I nervously worried the seams of Mara's quilt between two fingers. My sister was quiet for a long time, her gaze distant and her expression grave. I followed the faded, jagged path of an old scar down her cheek and neck until it disappeared beneath her collar.

Desperate to break the silence, I added miserably, "All of that and I never wrote you. I didn't tell Farrin or Gareth what you said that day in the temple. You asked me for help, and I did nothing.

I've no excuse. I simply didn't want to think about it. Along with everything else, it felt like too much." I smiled weakly. "I'm very good at pretending away things that frighten me, as you know. I suppose you should ask Farrin for help next time."

The joke sounded pathetic the moment it left my lips. Mara's eyes lifted to meet mine; a shadow flickered across her face and was gone.

"I'm sorry, Mara, and I'm sorry about that day, I..." I blinked back a rush of sadness, remembering the grotesque beauty of her transformed self—scales and skin, woman and not. "I don't know how everything's become such a mess, but it has, and I don't know what to do. I couldn't bear to be at Ivyhill any longer. I had to get away and see you. But it's unfair of me to come here like this. I should have written earlier, and I should have come back to see you long before now, not just when my own troubles overwhelmed me. Mara, I'm so sorry."

Mara shook her head. "The Warden wouldn't have allowed you to visit on your own. You know the rules." She threw a worried glance at the closed door. "I'll have to speak to her on Cira's behalf. She can be so cruel, and though Cira puts on a good front, her heart's too gentle for this line of work."

"Like yours?" I asked.

She let out a soft laugh. "You wouldn't say that if you knew the way I am now. I mean, *really* knew."

That flat look on her face chilled me. "What do you—"

"Farrin and Father came without you. I'm sure Cira told you."

I flinched. "Yes, she did."

Mara watched me steadily—Father's brown eyes in Mother's pale face. Mother's long dark hair and Father's ability to punch a man flat with one swing of his fist.

"It was wrong of them," she said.

"No, it was wise. I'm no good for anyone—you, Jessyl, Farrin."

"Stop that. It's a foolish way of thinking. I'll have you know it broke my heart to enter the greeting rooms that day and see only them and not you. I gave Father a sound lashing for it. He'd never heard me curse like that before. The look on his face was a sight to behold. It's wonderful, the things I can get away with. What can he do, after all? Banish me to the Mist?"

A little sniffling laugh burst out of me. Mara cupped my face in her hands, the touch of her callused palms so gentle that I wanted to cry—*again*.

"Don't cry, Gemma darling," she said softly. "It destroys me when you cry. It reminds me of when we were small. You were so tiny for so long. I was so terrified of hurting you that I refused to hold you. I regret that now." She smiled wistfully. "Those would be nice memories to have."

"Gods, you're an ass." I collapsed onto the bed and scooted my head into her lap. "You tell me not to cry and then say something like that?"

Mara stroked my hair and laughed. "Well, you ran into the Mist and scared the shit out of me. I suppose we're even now."

I peered up at her. The way she wore her hair—the great dark mass of it gathered into a sloppy knot, tiny braids hidden throughout—reminded me of something animal and wild, and I wondered if, when Mara transformed, her feathers felt as soft as her hair. "I really am so sorry, Mara."

She shook her head. "What's important is that you're here. You've brightened a very dreary day. Though I have no idea how to respond to everything you've just told me, except to say, of course, that I'm deeply sorry about poor Jessyl. And"—she stopped stroking my hair to gently tilt up my chin and meet my eyes—"that her death was *not your fault*. Do you hear me?"

"Yes."

Her eyes narrowed. "Do you believe me?"

I couldn't lie to her. The sight of her was too dear, too rare. "No. I don't believe you. Or rather, I disagree with you." I hurried on, cutting off her protest. "Tell me what you didn't get the chance to say that day. I can't change the fact that I've been no help to you so far, but I'm here now. Your hands were tied, you said. You wanted me to tell Farrin and Gareth something before it was too late."

Mara looked at me for a long moment. "Speaking of avoidance, is this an attempt to avoid talking about your friend Talan? Because I have *many* questions about him, not the least of which is where he was when Madam Baines killed herself."

I bit the inside of my lip. It felt both absurd and shockingly intimate to hear Mara utter Talan's name, as if he were some made-up creature that had until recently lived only in my head.

"I genuinely want to know, Mara," I said. "It's been weeks since that day. You've waited long enough. We can talk about Talan later, I promise."

A beat, then two. Mara's gaze was a sharp blade. "If I tell you, how you look at the world will be forever changed. So far you've managed to evade this frightening thing by ignoring me. Are you prepared to face it now?"

Her voice was not unkind, simply matter-of-fact, but her words stung. Determined not to succumb to self-pity, I tried to look brave. It was the very least I could offer. "I'm prepared," I replied.

Mara nodded, rose, and extended her hand.

At her touch, a delicate wave of pain swept through me. Mara's magic was rising, as if she were readying it for battle. I swallowed hard against a twinge of fear.

"The best way to tell you, then," she said, "is to show you."

CHAPTER 19

Deep in the woods south of Rosewarren, in the opposite direction of the Middlemist, overgrown tangles of brush and weeds hid the mouth of a cave so small we had to enter it on our hands and knees.

Once inside, we could stand, but the darkness was smothering, Mara's lantern barely penetrating the gloom. She easily navigated the strange dips and turns of several stone passages, warning me where to tread carefully, pointing out treacherous slicks of moss. The air grew dank and cold around us. Alarmed, I realized we were descending—to where, I could not imagine.

Perhaps sensing my terror, Mara gently took my hand. "This isn't the most direct path to where we're going, and I'm sorry for it. But your unexpected arrival at Rosewarren might have been noticed, could have stirred up something. The Mistlands hold many secrets, many eyes and ears. I can't be too careful."

Even the shadows have eyes. My skin prickled. I looked back over my shoulder but could see nothing beyond the dim bobbing ring of Mara's lantern light.

"I might have been noticed?" I whispered. "By whom? The Warden?"

"The Warden is a complicated woman but not a danger," said Mara. She did not elaborate, and I was too spooked to ask again.

Finally the passage we traversed widened. We edged down a slope of smooth stone, stepped over a runnel of trickling water, and ducked under an arch of gray rock before stepping into a huge cavern. Huddles of dripping stone protruded from the ceiling. The floor was a patchwork of smooth rocks, smatterings of lichen, slim silver fingers of running water.

I stopped short, stunned into astonished silence.

The chamber was a museum of the obscure and the abominable—singed shards of strange artifacts and a vast array of paintings and sculptures, each depicting scenes of shocking violence. A man ripping out an infant's throat using his own teeth. A pack of yellow-eyed dogs tearing stringy chunks of flesh from a fleeing passel of children. A woman sitting in front of a mirror, clawing out her own eyes as her mouth contorted in agony.

And then there were the corpses, each preserved with some sort of rank bright-green substance that made my eyes sting. Men and women and children, some of them human—skin tones I recognized, limbs and eyes like mine—and others most certainly not. There was a long-limbed maiden with webbed hands and iridescent scales striping her faded blue skin. A squat human-shaped creature made entirely of stone. A horned man, furry and hooved, with long curved claws at the ends of his fingers and narrow cat-like pupils, a frozen toothy smile on his face. And beasts too—a rabbit, a fawn, a vulture. A long-armed creature with huge blunt hands, gigantic bat ears, a hairy snout. A small white horse with a thin spindled horn growing from its head.

I let out a choked, frightened laugh and turned around to find my sister watching me. "A unicorn?"

Mara nodded. "The only one we've found so far, thank the

gods. Cira was inconsolable. They're her favorite of the Olden creatures."

Looking more closely at the unicorn, my bile rose. "They're all *deformed*, every one of them."

I hadn't realized it immediately; only as I forced myself to walk among the stiff deathbound creatures did I see the twisted limbs, the shattered faces, the splintered nails. Heads caved in, legs growing out of stomachs. Jagged lines of silver outlined the maimed jowls of some vaguely bearlike beast I could not name. Shards of glittering black rock had impaled the neck of a pale knobby creature with no eyes.

I peered more closely at that one, fighting the urge to gag as I neared the creature's sagging pocked skin. The rocks jutting out from its neck were bulbous, twisted, as if they had somehow melted and reformed.

Every nerve in my body sang with dread. *Mara wouldn't have brought me to such a place if it were dangerous*, I reassured myself. *Mara doesn't play tricks. Mara loves me.*

I turned back to her, my throat dry as sand. "What happened to them?"

"We call them Mistfires," she said gravely. "One moment the Middlemist is itself. Silver. Waiting. Watching. Docile, even. The next it contracts, combusts. No warning, no time to run. If you're caught in a Mistfire…" She gestured at the corpses. "The force could blow you apart, mash you into whatever's nearby—rocks, trees, another person. Or it could crush you. It happened to a friend once. I saw it with my own eyes. A huge crash of thunder, a horrible popping sound, and she was gone. Her blood fell to the ground like rain."

Feeling a bit faint, I leaned on a nearby rock. The blessed thing kept me standing. "And this happens to people and animals here in Edyn, and—"

"And to the Olden. These are corpses we found on the Edynside. Beyond the Mist in the Old Country? We've no way of knowing how many lives the Mistfires have taken there."

"For how long has this been happening?"

"A few months. At first the fires were rare. Now one bursts open somewhere along the Mistline at least once a week."

"And the..." I glanced at a nearby painting. Splatters of garish colors and scrawled crude lines showed a beast with the torso of a man and a wild, grinning furred face. He held a woman in his arms. She slept, or maybe she was dead. The man gnawed on her foot, his tongue long and speckled.

"The art was made by people living throughout the Mistlands," Mara explained. She walked down the orderly lines of paintings, considering each one dispassionately. "They suffered visions, horrible images they had to get out of their heads. The fortunate among them managed it with art, writing, music. The art is easiest for us to steal for further study."

"Us," I repeated. "You mean the Order of the Rose?"

Mara glanced up at me. "Yes."

Something about her voice made me certain she was lying, but I didn't press. "Why do you study them?"

"We think all of this is connected—the Mistfires, the rash of visions invading people's dreams, even their waking moments. The more daring attacks on the Order's outposts."

As she spoke, I remembered what the Warden had said weeks ago, on the day I'd witnessed Mara's transformation: *Most recently we have heard repeated reports of a band of monstrous women who roam the countryside abducting civilians.*

"Have any of these attacks been carried out by...strange women?" I hesitated, the words feeling both too ridiculous and too terrifying to utter. "Monstrous women?"

"Actually, yes. We in the Order haven't had a proper sighting yet, but the stories are too numerous and consistent to dismiss. The women are swift, cunning. It seems they are able to disguise themselves in the forest as effectually as any beast." Mara looked curiously at me. "You've heard rumors of this down south?"

"The Warden mentioned it to Father, Farrin, and me when I last visited the priory."

A dark look flickered across Mara's face. "She shouldn't have said anything to you, but she is very fond of boasting. Most likely she hoped the tale would impress you."

"It didn't impress me, it frightened me," I said quietly. "It made me even more worried for you than I already was."

"That reaction would satisfy her all the more," Mara said mildly. "The point of all I'm telling you is that something fundamental about these lands is changing, and we don't know why or even exactly how. I haven't yet heard reports of visions plaguing settlements down south, but the madness is spreading further every day. It's only a matter of time."

My scrambling thoughts landed on something. "That day in the temple, you said your hands were tied. Someone's keeping you from studying all of this, which is why you do it in secret. You collect corpses and art and bring it all here, look for patterns, keep a log of it. Not you alone though."

"No. I'm not alone."

"But the Warden doesn't like this," I guessed. "She doesn't think it's safe. She doesn't want to lose *you*, especially. So you have to hide all of it."

Again, that quiet dark look. "I've tried to tell her something's wrong, but she won't listen. She thinks I'm dramatic, fanciful. Sometimes she accuses me of laziness. In truth, she's afraid. If something's happening to the Middlemist, what does that mean for her? For us?"

I wrapped my arms around myself, feeling small and sick, my head a fuzz of questions and terrible images.

Then I saw it—a fragment of familiar stone into which a fat seven-pointed star had been carved. Silver specks dusted the gray stone—remnants of a Mistfire, I assumed—but otherwise it was unchanged.

A bristle of cold washed over me.

"Ah, and this is what I wanted to show you most of all," Mara said. "Your story about your trips to Ravenswood reminded me of it. I found it near the site of a recent Mistfire. I scavenge the ruins when I can. The land bleeds after a Mistfire. Charred and raw, throbbing. It cries out for help."

I joined her at the makeshift stone table upon which the shard sat, a little wary of the strange lilt in her voice. Her eyes were dark in this cave, fervent, sharp as stars. There was a mightiness to her that I was not used to seeing, as if she were far older than her years and knew of ancient things I couldn't comprehend.

She pointed to the star-marked shard. Several other pieces surrounded it, forming the incomplete echo of a cube.

My heart pounded at the back of my throat. I reached out with trembling fingers to touch each piece of stone and convince myself that what I saw was real.

A fat seven-pointed star. A single staring eye. A flat palm held upright as if to fend off an enemy.

Each stone boasts a unique design, Talan had said that night by the lagoon, *both inside and out*.

"It's possible these fragments are from a different artifact altogether and not the one you told me about," Mara offered. "I couldn't find every piece. The others must have been obliterated by the Mistfire."

She was right; the shards laid out before me *could* have belonged to anything. Without all the pieces, I couldn't be certain.

But my gut knew the truth. The core magic that had once suffused these remnants was gone, but the faintest echo of it remained, each lick of it sending a faint shock of familiar pain rippling through the sensitive planes of my body.

I had no doubt that these were the remains of the wardstone Talan and I had taken from Ravenswood. Someone had stolen it from my safe room at Ivyhill, and somehow it had made its way to the Middlemist before being blown to pieces.

Had the thief simply been unlucky? Or had they meant for this very thing to happen, to throw Talan and me off the scent of the demon we hunted?

I suspected the latter.

"What do you think it means?" Mara asked quietly.

"Talan and I were on the right path," I whispered, "and someone knew and didn't like it." As I stared at the eye in its bed of glittering stone, dread ran cold in my bones. "They didn't like it one bit."

During the long walk back to Rosewarren, my head was a whirl of grotesque images. A knot of mangled corpses, Talan's sad smile, Jessyl's staring dead eyes, Madam Baines wearing Jessyl's blood, the giggling wardwraith at Ravenswood. The confused jumble of it all careened through my mind with dizzying speed. The longer we walked, my body screaming with fatigue, the less able I was to push the images away. A stitch in my side throbbed painfully, and the Mist's nearness gnawed at my extremities like frostbite.

At the bottom of a gentle wooded slope that led up to Rosewarren's lawn, I stopped to lean against an old hunched oak.

I blinked hard, trying to clear the dancing black spots from my vision. The beginnings of panic thrummed quietly at the back of my mind, stirred awake by the shock of what I had seen and all the alarmed questions buzzing for answers I did not have.

Mara took my arm. "Here, come sit. We'll rest for a moment."

Frustrated, I shook her off and gestured sharply at the looming priory. "We're nearly there, for gods' sake. I can manage."

"There's no point in being stubborn. That won't impress me."

Suddenly Mara went rigid with tension. "Gods unmade," she swore quietly.

I followed her gaze up the lawn. Standing at the bottom of the wide gray steps that marked the priory's front entrance was a still, pale figure, hands clasped at her waist. Tall and thin, dark hair slicked into a tight knot, she watched us impassively. Her black dress was modest and severe, the shoulders slightly square. I was reminded of an owl glaring down at the world from its perch, silent and unblinking.

The Warden.

"Head for the greenway and go home," Mara said, her voice heavy with defeat. Some essential strength had disappeared, leaving her sapped of color and life. "Talking to her will only make things worse."

Truthfully I was relieved for the chance to escape, chilled right down to my bones by the Warden's obvious motionless anger. But I hesitated, lightly touched Mara's elbow.

"Will she hurt you?" It was something I'd always wondered. The Warden's methods were a mystery, and Mara's letters home never held any clues.

"That's not her way," Mara replied simply. I thought I saw something on her face—a shadow, a memory. Then she gently squeezed my hand. "Please go. I'll write to you. Think about what I've shown you, but don't tell Farrin or Gareth. I was tired that day and foolish to ask it of you. The fewer people know about all of this, the better—at least for now. I love you, Gemma. Keep your eyes open."

As she began the long trudge up the lawn, I hurried away through the trees at a brisk walk, my posture unabashed. If the Warden was watching me leave, she would see neither shame nor fear.

But as soon as I felt I'd gone a safe distance and looked back over my shoulder to confirm I could no longer see Mara or the Warden, only the looming dark bulk of Rosewarren, my barely restrained panic exploded, and I ran. My body protested, but I ignored it, crashing clumsily through the woods. As desperately as I'd needed to leave Ivyhill that morning, I now needed to leave this awful place—the strange endless house, the trapped Roses, the dripping cavern's monstrous secrets. When I reached the familiar patch of clover and thick sheets of snow-blossom vines that marked my family's hidden greenway, I stopped for a moment and leaned against the stone wall that sheltered me from view of the priory. Breathless, I fought in vain for calm.

Birdsong rang out from above, unjustly cheerful, and I ached to think of poor Mara walking bravely up the lawn toward whatever punishment no doubt awaited her.

Then the birdsong fell abruptly silent. The air around me went still, as if all the secret hollows inside it had snapped closed.

The sudden change made my hair stand on end. I quieted my breathing and shrank back against the stone wall.

Something was near. I knew it with the certainty of cornered prey. It was the feeling that had touched me the night of my party, drawing me to my dressing table.

I was being watched. A presence had found me, though whether it was human or beast or something else, something *other*, I could not say. I felt compelled to run, but not from fear—I wanted to run simply because suddenly I felt strong enough to do it. My pain did not disappear, but it diminished. A might was building in me. My vision sharpened. I felt restless, eager; nervous excitement bubbled in my stomach. With great effort, I kept my feet planted firmly on the ground.

I waited, searching the trees, but saw nothing, heard nothing—not even the slightest rustle of wind—until a very faint sound met my ears. High and soft, crystalline. Undulating.

A song.

My first wild thought was that the music belonged to Farrin. She'd come to bring me home and had decided for some unthinkable reason to announce her arrival by singing.

But as my pounding heart slowed, I understood that the wordless, keening song did not belong to Farrin. No, this was a voice foreign to my ears, so plaintive and lonesome that I could hardly breathe. Perhaps it was a child, lost and frightened in the woods, or someone mourning the loss of a great love.

As I listened, my head emptied of all panic, all horror. My body was as sturdy and strong as a small mountain. The dreary colors of the darkening forest turned vibrant. Glowing viridian leaves, shimmering white moss, black soil that gleamed with flecks of gold when lit by the setting sun.

My purpose was clear: I had to follow the song.

Fearless, I pushed into the forest, leaving the pulsing drum of the greenway's magic behind me. The ground was velvet under my feet. Briar patches bashfully curled away at my approach. Only moments ago, this forest had been a thing of dread, an unfamiliar labyrinth reeking of the nearby Mist—but no longer. I forged an easy path through the trees, noting with delight when their trunks grew taller, bloated, as if they teemed with all manner of mysteries.

Odd that I should ever have found the Mist's scent putrid. I inhaled deeply, relishing the pleasant aromas of honeysuckle, spring rain, freshly turned soil, spiced cinnamon tea. All scents I adored. I gorged myself on them, gulping them down as if they were dishes at a feast.

The song I followed grew louder, its clarion tone bright as the full moon. I began to run, eager to find whatever mysterious singer could create such exquisite music. My muscles obeyed eagerly, my legs smooth pistons. I leapt across a ravine with the easy grace of a doe. The air was cooling, trickling past my fingers like rivulets of snowmelt. My ears roared with song.

A small bluebird appeared in the air just ahead of me, its wings shimmering with silver shapes that resembled strange shouting faces. I ran harder, caught up to it, held out my hand, and delighted when the creature flew to rest on my palm. I petted its small silken head, smiled as it closed its eyes with pleasure. Its throat trembled; perhaps it was preparing to sing, eager to expand the voice's solo to a duet. I pressed a soft kiss to its breast, awestruck by the frantic hot drum of its heart.

Then a thunderous noise erupted behind me—a raucous crash, a smashed window.

Panting, confused, I searched the forest for answers, blinking hard to clear my suddenly ringing head, and saw that the entire world had changed—no longer a vivid sunlit green but a writhing silver. The light was dim, and I couldn't find the sky. The only illumination seemed to come from the cold silver sea billowing past me in a swift, silent current.

A smarting pain drew my attention downward. No scream could contain my terror; I stared in silence at my tattered dress, my bleeding legs and arms. They'd been scratched to pieces. My feet and fingers throbbed, raw from climbing.

I had climbed up a tree.

I was *in* a tree, clinging to high branches, crouched there like some wild thing. My hair had fallen loose from its chignon. My left shoulder was bare, stained with a gelatinous green liquid; the sleeve had been torn away.

When I saw what I clutched in my right hand, I nearly fell off my perch. Blood, torn flesh, shredded feathers. A bird—I'd been following a bird. Frantically I wiped my hand on my ruined skirts. My fingernails were black crescent moons, mud and gods knew what else wedged beneath them.

At the sound of rustling nearby, somewhere in the silver gloom, I froze and clamped a hand over my mouth to stifle a frightened sob. I waited, listening, for what felt like an endless age of torment.

Then I saw her moving quietly through the trees down below—a ruddy-skinned woman with a cap of shaggy blond hair. A twig snapped under her foot, a familiar sound, and I realized that had been the sound to pull me out of my wild run—a soft snap of wood that my clearly deranged ears had amplified into a horrible crash. The woman was tall and solid, formidably muscled, and she wore a gray tunic, dark trousers, and a knife belt around her hips. A quiver of arrows hung from a leather sash slung around her torso, and in one hand she held a long polished bow.

A Rose. The woman was a Rose on patrol.

The pieces of what had happened finally settled into place in my mind. Somehow, without realizing where my feet were taking me, I'd run straight into the Middlemist.

My stomach roiled. Terror made me clumsy; I nearly slipped off my branch and yelped out a choked scream.

In one fluid movement, the Rose spun around, grabbed an arrow from her quiver, nocked it, and aimed.

I raised one shaking hand, praying to Zelphenia that the Rose would see the truth: I was not some strange Olden creature set on beguiling her. I was a foolish woman half out of her mind with fear.

"Please don't hurt me," I cried out. My voice was hoarse, as if I'd been screaming. "I'm...my name is Gemma. I'm Mara's sister. I came to see her." I glanced down at the forest floor and squeezed my eyes shut. My breathing quickened; my head began to spin. "I don't...I don't know how to get back. I don't know how far I ran. There was a voice, a beautiful song, and I couldn't...I don't know where it...please help me. Tell me where to go."

I felt no shame at the pathetic smallness of my voice. My fear was absolute; I knew nothing else.

The Rose lowered her bow, returned her arrow to its quiver. She stalked over to my tree and climbed it with such swift ease that for a moment I worried she was some Olden forest spirit in disguise.

But then she was beside me, so close I could see the faint sheen of scars on her neck and the fierce guarded light in her pale blue eyes. I smelled the musky tang of sweat, felt the heat of exertion radiating from her. She shifted a little, improving her grip on the branches. Her expression was grim. It was not easy for her to hang there.

I hoped this meant she was human. Relief left me weak.

"It's a long way down, but there are many footholds," she said. Her voice was rough, clipped. Cool but not unkind. The fine lines around her eyes made me think she was quite a bit older than the other Roses I'd seen. "Follow the path I take. Then I'll escort you to safety." She paused. "My name is Brigid. I love your sister very much. I won't let anything happen to you."

I fought the urge to burst into tears.

Brigid climbed down slowly, pausing to direct my descent. She was right—the tree's gnarled bark provided a decent ladder down—but I broke out in a cold sweat nevertheless, my hands clammy and shaking. How was it possible that I had climbed to such a height on my own?

When I reached the bottom and felt the soft earth under my feet, my knees nearly buckled. Brigid hooked a solid arm around me, helped me stand.

"Can you walk?" she asked. "Quickly?"

I looked around, frantic. "Are we in danger?"

"Not presently. That could change at any moment. Can you walk?"

"I think so."

She nodded briskly. "Tell me if you tire. I can carry you."

I bit the inside of my lip, tempted to ask that of her right away, but instead I followed her through the trees in silence. Now that my feet were firmly on the ground, my shock began to fade, making room for hot blooms of pain. The unnatural strength I'd felt earlier had vanished completely. Moving felt slow, labored, as if I were pushing my way through water. Each breath I took of the damp silvered air felt stifling. I imagined the Mist pouring down my throat, seeping into my skin, burrowing under my filthy nails. We walked for ages, or perhaps for only a few moments. The passage of time was lost to me. The Mist smothered all sound.

Brigid glanced back at me. "Keep breathing. We're nearly there."

I tried my best to obey her. In that moment, I would have done anything she asked of me. *Die, Gemma,* she might have said, and I would have lain down right there in the dirt to await whatever doom the Mist might conjure.

At last, color bled back into the world: bright-green moss, a rust-red carpet of pine needles, the black-and-gold flit of a finch. I heard the snow-blossoms first, ringing merrily like a thousand tiny bells, and then saw the white curtain of them, the stone wall and iron gate beyond, the soft piles of clover. A dense thicket of tangled vines marked the entrance to my family's private greenway and my path home.

I let out a faint sob. "Oh, gods. I'm alive, I'm alive." I flung my arms around Brigid, heedless of dignity. "Thank you, *gods*, thank you!"

With a slight flush, she detached herself from my blubbering embrace. "Yes. Well. You're very lucky. There's a reason, you know, why the Warden is so strict with visitors, only allowing them on prearranged days. This is a dangerous place, Gemma. We have enough to do without chasing after stray sisters."

I nodded, wiping my face. "Of course you do. It won't happen again, I promise."

Brigid's face was impassive except for a slight quirk of one eyebrow. "Indeed. I'll wait here for a while, ensure that nothing follows you in." She hesitated, then reached out and plucked a downy black feather from my hair. "You said you heard a song," she said slowly. "Can you describe it?"

"It was a single voice. High and clear as a bell." A chill shook me at the memory.

"Were there words?"

"No. It was simply...sad. Lonely. Its despair overwhelmed me. I had to follow it. I ran. I was happy, strong. Everything was bright and easy. The next thing I knew, I was in that tree." My heart sank. Brigid's face was blank with confusion. "Have you heard of such a thing happening before?"

"I haven't, but that means nothing. New strange things occur in the Mist every day. It likes to play tricks. It's more alive than you might think." She nodded toward the greenway. "Go on," she said, and at my obvious shocked hesitation, she added, "Mara told me some time ago about your family's secret greenway, in case of any number of dire scenarios. She told Cira too. We're her seconds. But even so, I won't tell anyone what happened today, not even Mara, unless you wish me to."

"No, please don't. She has enough to think about." I hesitated, thinking of the Warden with distaste. "Will you watch over her? Mara, I mean. You said you love her. I'm glad of that. She deserves love, and from so far away, I can't always give her that."

Brigid's implacable face softened the slightest bit. She nodded once. "Off with you now," she said gently.

Head aching, body bright with pain, I stepped into the churning mouth of the greenway and thought of Mara—brave Mara—surrounded by love. Cira, and Brigid, and surely other Roses too. She was not alone; her life was not without tenderness. I clung to that small, faint joy as the vicious storm of greening magic carried me home.

CHAPTER 20

Two weeks after my strange visit to Rosewarren came the high queen's midsummer masquerade ball—a night that in simpler times would have delighted me.

It was the hugest, most lavish party of the year, and one of the only occasions upon which the Citadel at the heart of Fairhaven opened its doors, not only to Anointed courtiers and envoys from other countries, but to any citizen who managed to pique the queen's interest. Anyone from anywhere in the world could earn an invitation, whether they were Anointed or low-magic or possessed no magic at all.

Upon entering the Pearl of the Sea Ballroom—an enormous cavern of opalescent stone, mirrored walls, and five levels of mezzanines overlooking a dance floor—I slipped away from Father and Farrin, ignoring my sister's protests, and grabbed a crystal goblet of sparkling wine from the first servant I passed. Unfortunately, downing most of the glass in one desperate gulp did nothing to quell my nerves, so I kept moving, found another servant with a tray of glasses, and quickly drank another, then grabbed a third.

Reeling slightly, I paused on the perimeter of the dance floor and tried to catch my breath. The wine fizzed up and down my body, though not as vividly as Talan's family's vintage.

I ached at the thought of him—his face, his smile, the way he had held me after we escaped Ravenswood, the way he'd touched me that day at the tournament. It had been a little more than two weeks since he'd left Ivyhill with Gareth, and his absence still felt like a wound. Much to my dismay, my disturbing visit to Rosewarren had only deepened the cut of loss. The desperate hope I held in my heart—that I would see Talan at the masque, that Gareth would convince him to come—was embarrassing, appalling. Who was I to long for him after what he had done? Ruining my sister's performance, putting her life in danger, thinking that was a fine choice as long as it furthered our plans. That rash, selfish, intoxicating, irresistible man.

Worse even than these thoughts was another darker, more frightening one: Why would a man like him want a woman like me? A woman so fragile, who lived with so much pain that she was exhausting to love and impossible to live with?

A woman who had gotten lost in the Middlemist like a foolish child. Taken by madness, blood and feathers smeared on her hand, her weak mind and even weaker body lured into danger by a song—this was not a woman deserving of anyone's affection. This was a grotesque creature. *I* was grotesque.

I tried to appear neither eager nor crazed as I stood there nursing my drink, my heart in my throat and my skin crawling with self-loathing, but I was certain anyone looking at me could see plainly that I was searching for someone. What they wouldn't be able to see was the truth—that Lady Imogen Ashbourne, already half-drunk and looking ravishing in a green silk dress, had been, over the past two weeks, slowly losing her mind. Not because of a lover's spat—though that was part of it—but because she had gone into the Middlemist and the cunning silver sea of it had reminded her what she really was.

I pushed my way through the crowd, ignoring anyone who attempted conversation. At last year's masque, I'd danced and drunk for hours, refusing to be cowed by the great mash of people and their painful careening magic. I'd sampled every dish prepared by the royal chefs, all of them Anointed savants, until I'd sworn I would never eat again. The highlight of the evening had been a most enjoyable half hour spent in a small parlor near the ballroom, where a gorgeous silver-haired captain from the Lower Army had kissed me senseless.

But on this night, every elbow that jostled me made me flinch as if I'd been struck. Every hopeful dance partner who approached me was a villain I ducked away from in unthinking panic.

There was a washroom door in the far wall. I hurried toward it, cursing the ballroom's size. The space was so gigantic that Ivyhill's largest ballroom could have fit inside it three times. A tiled mosaic that spanned the soaring ceilings depicted the gods, robed and jeweled, dancing in jubilant celebration. Garlands of huge coastal flowers with fat creamy petals hung from every rafter, spellcrafted to bob and shine like fireflies. Their perfume turned my stomach; the sounds of laughter and dancing and clinking glasses hurt my teeth. A bead of sweat rolled down my back.

I began to run, no doubt eliciting more than a few strange looks, but I couldn't breathe, and I was quite possibly going to be sick, and I needed to run, I needed *out*, or else I was going to die.

All the fear and confusion and disgust that had been brewing inside me for days boiled over at last. The panic arrived with ferocious force, as if it were a flesh-and-blood creature, ravenous and without mercy.

I burst into the washroom, which was blessedly empty,

stumbled toward the marble basin in the room's farthest corner, yanked closed the heavy brocade curtain, crashed to my knees, and heaved.

Something was inside me, a hateful squirm of fear that burned my throat with every breath. I couldn't swallow it down, couldn't dislodge it. The horrible thought occurred to me that while I ran through the Mist, insensate, I could have consumed something without knowing it, something tainted and evil that was now sprouting roots in my gut. I clawed at my tongue, dug around at the top of my throat until I gagged.

Panting, I clung to the basin. My eyes burned with exhaustion and the horrible fear that I would soon die—not from my illness, the way I had always expected, but from whatever inhuman Olden *thing* had crawled out of the Mist and wriggled inside me.

My skin itched, hot and prickling all over. I sat heavily on the floor, hiked up my skirts, and began scratching my stockinged legs with frantic animal zeal. My fingernails—painted rosy pink and bejeweled with tiny emeralds, courtesy of Kerrish—broke the skin of my thighs. Through the blur of my agitation, I saw thin lines of blood unfurl. The familiar bright red color and sting of pain choked me with relief. Whatever evil lived inside me, whatever heartbreak awaited me, for the moment I was still human, and I was alive.

"Gemma?" Illaria's voice came suddenly from beyond the curtain. "I'm coming inside."

"No, wait," I croaked, mortified that she should see me in such a state, but she was already ducking through the drapery.

For a moment she simply surveyed me in silence. Then she knelt beside me, the azure and aquamarine shades of her gown pooling beautifully on the gleaming floor. She had decided to attend the masquerade as a peacock. A gilded mask with a curved beak hung loosely from her elbow. The colors of her gown and glittering turquoise earrings perfectly complemented her honey-brown skin and the long black gloss of her hair.

"You look so beautiful," I whispered faintly.

"Tell me what's happening." Illaria's voice was soft as velvet, hard as iron. She grabbed my hands, held them still. "The *truth*, mind you, or I will quite literally drag you out of this palace, dump you into my carriage, and drive you straight home. And then I will watch you day and night. You won't be able to escape me. I'll sit on you and chain our ankles together."

I laughed, tears slipping down my cheeks. "It's only a minor attack of the panic. I just needed a moment alone."

"No, that's not it. The panic, maybe, but it's also more than that. I saw you run over here just now. Farrin tells me you've seldom left your rooms of late and that your new maid has to wheedle you into eating. Your sister is very distressed, and so am I." Illaria looked steadily at me. "Well? I'm waiting."

Distant music floated through the silence. Then the door to the washroom swung open, admitting a spill of laughter and rustling skirts.

Illaria whipped open the curtain only enough to show the new arrivals her face. They were a trio of madly giggling girls—young, maybe sixteen years old. Carefree, jubilant, glowing.

I ducked behind Illaria, feeling monstrous. My legs stung, red and raw, and my beautiful green gown seemed suddenly like a cruel joke, as if someone had caught a scraggly rat and dressed it in a diamond tiara. Hundreds of exquisitely crafted silk flowers ornamented the gown's slippery folds, my pinned golden curls, my fingers, the ribbons of my thin netted mask. Petunias, roses, honeysuckle, wisteria.

"Get out," Illaria commanded imperiously, molding her voice

into the prim accent common to residents of the capital. "Do it now, or I'll have no choice but to tell your parents of your drunken escapades in the royal gardens."

The girls fell silent, wide-eyed with horror.

"What?" Illaria smirked. "You thought no one saw you?"

Without another word, the girls hurried away, leaving us alone once again.

"Fools," Illaria muttered. "They reek of brandy and vomit and fresh earth. I wouldn't be surprised if they retched all over the queen's roses."

I stared at my hands, hardly hearing her. Delicate fronds fashioned of slim golden chains and forest-green gossamer thread encircled my bare arms, wound around my wrists and fingers instead of gloves. I was a brilliant summer garden bursting with blooms I did not deserve—a design long ago chosen by Jessyl and me.

"We sat up until the early hours of the morning," I whispered, "Jessyl and I. We pored over the sketches Kerrish had sent over. This dress was her favorite, and so it became mine."

"As terrible as losing Jessyl has been, whatever's happening to you goes beyond that," Illaria insisted. "Is it Talan? Did he do something to you?"

"No. He's been here in the capital with Gareth for more than two weeks."

"That doesn't answer my question."

Suddenly I felt too tired to lie. All the air bled out of me, the story spilling out along with it.

"It's the Mist," I said quietly. "I went to see Mara two days after Jessyl was killed. She showed me things, terrible things. Something's happening in the Mistlands. People are suffering visions of violence and monsters. A song lured me into the Mist. I chased a bird, and I think I did something terrible to it, but I can't remember what. I ran and ran and didn't realize I was running. I was so *strong*, Lari. I could have run for days. When I came back to myself, my hands were covered in blood and I found I had climbed up a tree, a huge one. In my right mind, I'd never have been able to do such a thing. A Rose on patrol found me and helped me out of the Mist, but I think I brought something back with me."

I tapped my throat. "Something's inside me. I can feel it, but I can't get it out. Maybe what I feel is only the panic, some new way it's found to torment me." I shook my head. "But I think it's something else. I think something's happening to me. I can't stop thinking about the song I heard. I wake up humming it some mornings."

Illaria looked ill. "Gods, Gemma. And you've told no one about any of this since getting home?"

"The night of the party at Ivyhill," I continued, ignoring her question, "I crafted a glamour."

"That's not possible. You have no magic."

"And yet it happened. Something pulled me from my bed. I felt a presence somewhere close, watching me. I sat down at the mirror. I felt strong, whole, clear-eyed, just as I did in the Mist when I heard the song. I glamoured colors into my hair. My eyes were blue and gold." Gingerly I traced the line of my jaw. "My cheeks sharpened. Colors glowed beneath my skin. It was as though my body had begun to transform."

Illaria stood abruptly and held out her hand. "Come with me right now. We're going home. Specifically to my house, where no one has been killed and no mysterious foreigners have bedded you."

"But the ball's only just begun," I protested automatically.

"Do you hear yourself? You worked magic when you shouldn't be able to. You changed the shape of your face. You ran through the Mist like a madwoman."

Though I'd told myself the same things, hearing someone else say them made me bristle, as if I were hearing unfair judgment passed on someone I dearly loved.

Then Illaria glanced down at my legs. She knelt once more. "You've hurt yourself, Gemma," she said gently.

I didn't know what to say to that. I stared at her, shrugged a little.

"Have you done this before?" she asked.

Still I said nothing, ashamed of the truth and more disgusted with myself than I had ever been.

Illaria was very quiet. "Why did you do it?"

Telling her would kill me, but I knew she would not accept silence. "It helps me feel better when the panic comes," I whispered. "If I don't do it, I'll die—that's what it feels like. The pain unknots me, helps me breathe again. I can withstand pain. Pain is nothing to me, and everything. Pain is my every day. But the panic…" I closed my eyes, each word reducing me to shreds. "The panic I cannot abide. When it comes, I have to do something about it or else lose my mind."

There was silence for a moment. Then Illaria said softly, "May I hug you, my darling?"

Miserably I nodded, and when Illaria's arms came around me, it was the sweetest embrace I'd ever felt. I clung to her and hid my face in her hair.

"You know that hurting yourself won't actually make the panic go away," she said.

"I'm not a fool."

"And you know that this revelation is one I won't ignore."

I closed my eyes, immediately regretting having opened my mouth. "What if I ask very nicely?"

"Sadly, I'm immune to niceness." Illaria released me. "Can you stand? It's time to go. I promise we don't have to talk about anything else until we're at my house and you're safely ensconced in your chair, but we are leaving as soon as my carriage is brought around."

"I'm not going anywhere," I muttered, wiping my face. In the wake of my confession, I felt foolish, bared against my will. The feeling made my hackles rise. I'd answered Illaria's questions, but I would do no more. "Do you know how it would look if I disappeared before Queen Yvaine arrived?"

"Yes, however will you endure such a hardship?" Illaria grabbed my hand and pulled me up. "I'll send a message to your father that you took ill."

I laughed bitterly. Thinking of Father bolstered my resolve and helped clear my aching head. "That's probably just what he expects, for me to take ill and have to leave. I won't give him the satisfaction."

"Gemma, for gods' sake—"

"I'm not leaving, Lari. Thank you for your help, but I've had enough of it for tonight. I'm feeling much better now, in fact, and I've a full dance card to get through."

I tied my mask into place and stormed away, my ravaged legs only slightly wobbly as they brought me back into the ballroom. I heard Illaria hurrying after me and fled from her as quickly as I could, dodging hailstones of stray magic. They hurtled at me from every direction as masked revelers whirled across the dance floor. I gritted my teeth against the onslaught and kept walking, ignoring the constant cheery greetings of oblivious partygoers and hoping my mask hid the worst of my distress. I didn't know where I was heading exactly, but I knew I couldn't bear to remain around Illaria and see the sadness in her eyes when she looked at me.

Unfortunately my friend was as deft at navigating crowded ballrooms as I was. She quickly caught up to me and grabbed my hand.

"Gemma, stop running away from me," she said. Her voice was furious, her eyes bright. She had neglected to tie her mask back on. "You're ill, and being here at the masque won't help."

I shook free of her grip, heedless of who might be watching. "Of course I'm ill. I'm always ill. But I refuse to allow that to cage me. I will enjoy my life, for it's the only one I have."

Past Illaria, a tall man caught my attention—dark hair, dark coat. At the sight of him, my whole body lit up, interrupting my tirade. But then he turned and I saw his face. It wasn't Talan; it was just a perfectly agreeable-looking man with ordinary features who seemed taken aback to discover Gemma Ashbourne gaping at him.

Illaria glanced behind her, saw the man, then turned back to me angrily. "Is this about enjoying your life, or is it about enjoying Talan?"

"And what if those things are the same?" I shot back, startling even myself.

Illaria stood blinking at me, astonished, but before she could say anything more, a low drone of horns sounded from across the ballroom. At first it was a simple sustained note. Then it expanded into a chord of somber majesty. The orchestra at the far end of the room ceased playing; onlookers flocked to the mezzanines, and the dancers whirled to a halt. Breathless, they turned to face the wide central staircase. Illaria and I turned with them, for a moment forgetting our anger.

Two columns of musicians lined the marble stairs, their horns gleaming. Chimes sounded somewhere above us, as if dozens of bells had been hidden in the rafters. The call of the horns grew, the movement from chord to chord bringing tears of wonder to my eyes even though I'd witnessed this a dozen times. What had Farrin called it? A harmonic progression. This one broke my heart, just as it was designed to do—a lament for the dead gods and a prayer of thanks for the woman they'd chosen to watch over us in their stead.

The pealing chimes became a joyous clamor. The air swelled with music; the floor vibrated beneath our feet. Then all at once, a ringing silence fell.

High Queen Yvaine Ballantere had arrived.

A reverent hush accompanied her slow descent down the stairs. She was a slight thing, though her bearing tricked the eye into thinking she stood taller than anyone else present. Theories of who she had been before the gods had chosen her varied, though every historical account that had survived agreed on one thing: the gods had selected Yvaine Ballantere to watch over the world they'd created because her spirit was purer and stronger than that of any other living human.

Whatever the gods had done to her in those last days before the Unmaking had given her an unnaturally long life. It had also left behind a pink star-shaped scar in the center of her forehead and eyes of two different colors—one a deep violet, the other a pale gold. Her skin and hair had been shocked a startling glacial white. She wore her hair in an elaborate net of jeweled pins, gleaming braids, clusters of iridescent feathers. Her gown's bodice of violet and lilac was rather severe in construction, with a high buttoned collar and long sleeves with a slight sheen that clung to her arms—dyed snakeskin perhaps, or gauntlets of tiny jewels. But her skirts were much more playful, even girlish—a ruffled cascade of lavender, shimmering gold, vivid turquoise, and frothy white lace.

The crowd parted as she glided through the ballroom, everyone she passed sinking silently into bows and curtsies. This was the woman the gods had chosen to serve Edyn as a protector, a great unifier, a keeper of the world's history, the highest authority on godly magic, and I knew without looking whom she was cross-ing the room to find.

When Queen Yvaine found Farrin—a plain dove in a simple beaked gray mask, feathers of white and dusky brown ornament-ing her gray skirts—my sister's head was bowed like everyone else's, but the queen did not allow that for long. Her back was to me, but I could *feel* her smile, how it rippled through the room and brightened the air like the first spill of daylight. The crowd tittered happily, awestruck and adoring, echoing Queen Yvaine's joy. She hauled my sister to her feet, kissed each of her cheeks, and wrapped her in a tender embrace.

All at once, the celebration resumed. The royal musicians filed somberly up the stairs, the orchestra's conductor wrangled her players back to their instruments, dancers found their partners and leapt gaily into a new waltz.

"There, you see?" Illaria said, tugging lightly on my arm. "The queen is here, so you can safely leave without agonizing over a social misstep that doesn't actually matter."

I ignored her. Suddenly my heart was a beating drum, and even the high queen in all her strange glory faded from my mind.

Instead my attention was halfway across the room, focused on a cluster of figures engaged in conversation: Father, resplendent in a suit of green brocade with silver piping, his mask a matching silver falcon; Gareth, wearing a grinning gold fox mask and, I was glad to see, a perfectly respectable and smartly tailored tan coat over a trim red vest and russet trousers. His shaggy blond hair was a bit wild, looking rather more tousled than was appropriate for a ball at the Citadel, but I decided to allow him that slight misstep.

And then there was Talan.

My body warmed at the sight of him. He cut a tall, striking figure beside my father, wearing a long coat of white-and-gold brocade. The sleeves ended in dramatic cuffs of light-green velvet hemmed with swirling golden thread—the colors were a nod to Ivyhill, I thought, terribly pleased. Knee-high boots in a tawny suede, cream-colored trousers that fit him with perfectly delicious snugness. A white vest, embroidered with green, blue, and light-brown botanical designs, stretched up to the ruffled white collar at his throat with a proud line of polished brass buttons. His gold mask was trimmed with sculpted flowers, capped with the antlers of a stag.

If I was a garden bursting with color, he was the lord of high summer.

I started to move toward them, but Illaria held me fast.

"You cannot be serious," she hissed. "Not ten minutes ago, you were a bleeding, sobbing mess on the washroom floor. Let's go. *Please*, Gemma."

"I only need a few minutes," I assured her. "I haven't seen him in—"

"Two weeks, yes, you mentioned that. And two *months* ago, you didn't even know him."

"Many people have fallen in love in far less time than that."

Illaria stared at me. "Love," she said quietly.

"Yes, love," I replied, realizing all at once that it was true, that being apart from him had done nothing to diminish my feelings for him and had in fact only stoked the fire. I tore my gaze from him to glare defiantly at Illaria. "I love him," I declared. I couldn't hide my growing smile. I laughed a little. The words felt wild, outlandishly wonderful. I tried them out once more. "I love him."

Illaria looked defeated. "And what of my concerns? I told you about his scent. You care nothing about what I think? You don't trust my judgment?"

"Of course I do, but even *your* nose isn't perfect. And anyway, nothing will happen to me if I simply go speak with him. The queen is here, for gods' sake. And Gareth is with him. No doubt they've been studying demonic lore ever since leaving Ivyhill. Maybe he's learned information that explains everything—Jessyl, Madam Baines, what happened to Ryder at the tournament."

As if my voice had traveled to him through the din, Talan turned and found me from across the room. I couldn't see his eyes behind his mask, but I saw his soft, fond smile and felt my whole body open up, all the tense knots inside me melting away. For a precious moment of peace, I forgot every awful thought I'd ever had about myself.

"He said he wouldn't rest until he earned back my trust," I said quietly. "Don't I owe him the chance to try?"

"Actually," Illaria said, "I'm not at all sure that you do."

I blew out an impatient breath. All of a sudden, Illaria's sour gloom felt more exhausting than the panic. "Lari, I need him. I need the joy of him, how he lights me up inside and helps me forget all the things I spend every day trying to forget. I need to believe that he and I can mend things, and I need to try. Let me have this."

Behind her feathered peacock mask, Illaria's deep brown eyes were sad but resolute.

"If you walk away from me right now," she said, "when I'm trying yet again to help you, I'm not certain I'll care to offer that help the next time you need it."

Her words stung, but that made it easier for me to step away. "I understand," I said coolly. "I love you, Lari. Nothing can change that, not ever."

She hesitated as if to say something else, then turned and left me. I watched her vivid blue gown get lost in the crowd, fighting stubbornly against a rising tide of sadness. I would not allow it to take hold of me. I would not let them win—not Illaria, not the panic, not the godsforsaken Middlemist.

As the orchestra soared toward the end of its merry waltz, I moved across the room, dodging swirling skirts and spinning coattails. Talan met me halfway just as the final notes sounded. Appreciative applause filled the air as he took my hand and raised it to his lips. Behind the sculpted gold of his mask, his dark eyes shone.

"Lady Gemma," he murmured, his mouth hot against my fingers. "I'm not sure I can adequately express what a joy it is to see you again."

The sound of his voice overwhelmed me—so grave and formal and tender, as if I myself were the queen and he a mere devoted servant. For a moment I considered turning him away. As far as I knew, nothing had changed since I'd last seen him. Nothing could undo his rash actions at the tournament. A wiser person would have forever mistrusted him after that.

And yet the idea of parting from him yet again, now that he stood so near, felt unthinkable.

"Mr. d'Astier," I said instead, smiling, feeling suddenly bashful, "I encourage you to try."

His face lit up with a broad, easy grin, so open and happy that for a moment I lost my breath. Without taking his eyes off mine, he folded my hand gently into his and placed his other hand on my waist. His touch sent a charge of lightning through me, his palm hot against my skin even through the fabric of my gown. The orchestra began a quick, pulsing waltz, the lilting melody bittersweet and passionate. Dancers spun around us, but I hardly noticed them as Talan guided me into their midst.

We danced in silence, our steps light and easy and perfectly matched. When I dared to look up at him, I saw a bashfulness on his face, a deference, as though he could hardly believe his luck and was nervous to look at me. When the music stopped, we did not release each other to clap for the orchestra. Talan's other hand fell to my waist; I placed my palms against the silky brocade of his vest and felt the drum of his heart beneath my fingers. The urge to kiss him was unbearable, but before I could, the image of Illaria walking away from me flashed before my eyes, a most unwelcome intrusion. I pressed my cheek against his chest and let out a soft sob of frustration.

"I might have just lost my dearest friend," I told him, "all because I was happy to see you."

Talan gently cupped the back of my head, stroked my nape with his thumb. "Surely there's more to it than that?"

"Of course there is," I said wearily, "but I don't want to talk about any of that. Not Illaria, not the Mist, not the panic. I just want to…" I shook my head against him, overcome.

"The panic?" He sounded confused.

I pulled away and placed my hands on his cheeks. "I've missed you," I said simply, then abandoned all pretense of dignity. I stretched up on my toes, even though doing so left my shredded thighs smarting, and slid my arms around his neck. "I've missed you," I said again, quieter, my face buried in his collar. "I shouldn't have missed you. I was so angry with you, Talan. I still am, but it hardly matters. Right now nothing matters except that you're here."

Talan held me tight against him for a moment, then gently lowered me to the ground. The orchestra started playing a new waltz; we were without doubt obstructing the dance floor. But I couldn't pry myself away from him. If I moved, he might disappear again, and I didn't think I could bear losing the anchor of his presence, the warmth of his body.

"I know that your trust in me remains shattered," Talan said, his voice low and rough, his dark eyes locked earnestly on my face, "and I know we have much to talk about. But first I must tell you this: Gemma, being apart from you has left me hardly able to think straight. You've been on my mind every night and every morning and all the moments in between. Dare I believe that the dance we just shared truly means you haven't entirely forsaken me?"

I smiled up at him. "Someone cleverer than I am might walk away from you right now, maybe forever. But I don't want to, Talan, even if that makes me a fool. I don't ever want to walk away from you."

He closed his eyes, lowered his brow to mine, held my hands to his chest. "Gemma," he whispered, as if the word hurt him, as if that single word held his whole heart. When he opened his eyes again, his gaze was so soft I could hardly bear to keep looking at him. "Can we find somewhere quiet to sit and talk?"

I gave him a mocking little pout. "Talk, and nothing else?"

He laughed and kissed my forehead. "Lady Gemma," he said, "you and that mouth of yours will be my undoing."

Elated to hear him laugh, I stepped away from him, my hand still in his. I began guiding him outside to the gardens, where we could speak freely. But as I turned back to smile at him, an impossible thing caught my eye, and I froze, jolted with a horror so cold and complete that it knocked the wind out of me.

Frowning, Talan turned to follow my gaze. When he saw what I'd seen, his whole body tensed, and he moved in front of me as if to shield me from a terrible blow. But it was too late; the blow had landed squarely on my heart.

A pale, dark-haired woman was running across the ballroom toward my father—gaunt, unmasked, her clothes threadbare, her face streaked with tears.

Philippa Ashbourne.

My *mother*.

CHAPTER 21

The next few moments unspooled quickly.

My mother tore through the crowded ballroom in a crazed panic, screaming my father's name, shoving past anyone who blocked her path. At first the crowd seemed merely confused, irritated, but enough of them recognized Mother's face that the room soon began to buzz with excited curiosity: Philippa Ashbourne, who'd vanished in the night twelve years ago, leaving her entire family behind, had returned.

Dancers spun to a stop. The musicians stopped playing, causing their conductor to throw up her hands in exasperation at yet another interruption. Revelers resting along the ballroom's perimeter abandoned their conversations to stare.

Through a haze of shock—unable to move, barely registering Talan's steady hand on my lower back—I watched my mother crash to her knees at my father's feet. He stared down at her, ashen, rigid with stupefaction.

"Gideon, you're here, you're safe, oh, thank the *gods*," she sobbed. She grabbed Father's coat, used it to pull herself up, then collapsed against his chest. "They took me, darling, they took me from our bed that night. *Specters*, my love."

The gaping crowded shifted, murmurs of alarm rippling through the room. Specters were spirits of the dead trapped in the Old Country by demons, necromancers, their own fatal curiosity, or simply awful luck. Tethered there, they could not pass on to Ryndar, Realm of the Far Light, where, according to the lore left to us by the gods, all things begin and end. Specters appeared often in Olden arcana, but a genuine encounter in Edyn had not once been confirmed by scholars.

"They smothered me so I couldn't scream," Mother continued, her voice choked, tearful. "They muffled your ears so you wouldn't hear them drag me out the door. I tried to fight them, but I wasn't strong enough."

She spun around, still clutching my father's coat, and looked wildly about the room, eyes wide, hair a matted mess. "Are they here? Oh, please, gods save me if they followed my path..."

"Philippa?" Father at last managed to speak. He brought his hands up to cradle her shoulders, her face, the back of her head. It was as though he couldn't remember how to hold her. "You're here. You're alive."

Mother clasped Father's hands and gave him a watery smile. "I am, Gideon. I'm sorry that escape took me so many long unbearable years, but I'm here now. I've come back to you and the girls. Oh, gods unmade, my poor girls." Mother straightened, still holding on to Father. She looked around, her voice frantic with hope. "Farrin? Gemma?"

I felt the crowd part around Talan and me, allowing my parents a better view. A similar thing happened near the high queen's sitting room, which stood open to the ballroom and was flanked by gold-armored guards. The crowd shifted away, revealing my sister sitting beside the queen. I couldn't quite read her face, but her body was stiff with shock. Gareth, who sat with them, rose slowly to his feet, his shoulders square and his hands in fists.

I understood his anger. Philippa Ashbourne had abandoned her children, and Gareth had long ago sworn he would never forgive her for it.

"Something's wrong," Talan muttered. "If there weren't so many people here, I could determine *what.*"

Drawing breath felt like inhaling sand. I squeezed Talan's hand so hard it must have hurt him. "What is it?" I asked him. "What do you sense?"

Queen Yvaine stepped forward, a petite but fearsome shield that completely obscured Farrin from my line of sight.

"For gods' sake, someone fetch this woman a coat and some water," she commanded, "and send for the healer on duty."

As two royal pages hurried off to obey, I stared at my father, whose stoic expression had crumpled into something soft and unrecognizable. Even from where I stood, I could feel the joy quietly unfurling from him like a butterfly from its cocoon. I was desperate to look away and implore everyone else to do the same, embarrassed to see him in such a state. It was too intimate, too awful. I knew what Farrin would say, stone-faced and brimming with barely contained anger: *Mother doesn't deserve to see him happy. Mother gave up her claim to any part of us long ago.*

Father made a noise then, an awful sob of laughter that freed him at last from his shock. He swept Mother into a crushing embrace and kissed her, she threw her arms around his neck, and the room tittered with applause—first uneasy, then reassured, hearty. What a happy scene it was, this reunion of husband and wife, and how miraculous that it should happen on the eve of the summer solstice, in the Citadel, with so many eyes upon them.

Sick with dread I did not understand, suddenly terrified to

be so far from my sister, I started to hurry toward her, but Talan caught my hand.

"Don't, not yet," he said urgently, his narrowed eyes fixed on my embracing parents. "Wait a moment, if I could just..." He grew very still. Then his jaw clenched. "Shit," he said quietly. "Gemma, please don't look—"

But of course I looked, and therefore I saw the moment when Mother's body began to change. A flicker of darkness rippled across her body like the darting shadow of a bird. Long, wild, matted hair shrank to her shoulders, turned glossy and black. Skin covered in mud and bruises paled to a flawless alabaster. She gained a bit of height, her tattered dress stretching around a taller, leaner body.

Time slowed to a crawl. Such an act shouldn't have been possible. Ancient wards maintained by a rotation of Anointed beguilers denied entry to any glamoured person when the high queen opened her doors to the populace. The glamour's magic would crumble, and the wards would lash the offender to their knees.

And yet here was a glamour smoothly melting away to reveal its wearer.

The room erupted into gasps, nervous laughter, cries of dismay.

Blood roared in my ears as the world narrowed to a singular point: Father opening his eyes to see not my mother staring back at him but Alastrina Bask, a triumphant smile on her face.

"Gideon, darling," she crooned, mocking him, mocking all of us who had dared to hope, "I've come *back* to you. Kiss me again, won't you?"

The tension in the room snapped into bursts of shocked laughter; many in the crowd were clearly of the opinion that this was grand entertainment.

A sick, icy heat crawled up my body as I watched Father's face slacken into abject despair, all the life draining out of him. He did not fight, did not move; he simply stood there, a defeated man. Alastrina fondly patted his cheek.

My shock was so complete that I didn't see Ryder Bask approach until it was too late. Dressed in a fine black-and-blue riding outfit complete with swirling velvet cape, jaunty feathered hat, and black leather riding crop, he grabbed Father's hand and flung it up as if they were actors on a stage.

"My friends," he shouted to the crowd, "please show your appreciation for the great, the noble, the brilliant, and the *impressively* canny Lord Gideon Ashbourne of Ivyhill!"

An uproar of hooting laughter and applause swept through the room—drunkards, scandal enthusiasts, people delighted to see the head of a powerful Anointed family so degraded. I was numbly gratified to see that not *every* guest of the queen reveled in my father's abasement. Many guests looked appalled or stood in bewildered silence, unsure of what to do next. But I knew that this humiliation, the cruelty of it, the insult of being duped in the high queen's palace—the gift of Mother's face, however false—would follow Father for the rest of his days and would prompt him to retaliate as he had never done before.

Numb, revolted, I watched Ryder release Father's hand, spin around, and punch him hard in the jaw. Father didn't dodge the blow, though I knew—everyone knew—that he could have easily. Ryder was a wilder like his sister, a whisperer of beastly tongues; brawny and fearsome as he looked, he was no sentinel. And yet he felled my father as if he were a mere reedy boy.

Distantly I heard Ryder roar out his fury as he kicked Father over and over; he straddled him and punched him; he struck him with his riding crop. And Father, inert, streaked with blood, let it happen. He had humiliated Ryder at the tournament, beaten him senseless; now it seemed he was content to accept his punishment.

Waves of people surged toward them—Father's personal guards; Gareth; my second cousin Finn and his tottering drunken sons; the Basks' private retainer of guards, all of them dressed as various birds. The royal guards plowed through the chaos, yanked Ryder away from my father, and restrained Alastrina, who stood unabashed and smirking in her ill-fitting rags.

"*Ariinya voshte!*" Ryder roared in a rough northern tongue. The rage in his voice made my skin prickle with dread. Even as the queen's guards hauled him away, he kept shouting it over and over—"*Ariinya voshte! Ariinya voshte!*"—and his bannermen, also seized by the royal guards, answered in kind.

Queen Yvaine stormed into the center of the ballroom, her violet and gold eyes hard as steel, and the crowd scurried out of her path. A gleaming floor mosaic depicting the joined hands of the gods marked the ballroom's heart. Queen Yvaine came to an abrupt stop upon it and flung her arm straight up into the air. A quick flick of her wrist, and all sound in the room disappeared with a sharp sucking pop.

The high queen seldom performed magic. Some scholars believed that the gods had gifted her only a finite amount, forcing her to strictly conserve it for the remainder of her perhaps endless life. Others thought it mere business savvy; restricting demonstrations of her power to rare strategic moments ensured a mystique that both engendered adoration and bolstered her authority.

Whatever the reason for its rarity, on this night Queen Yvaine's magic rippled through the room in a blaze of lightning-quick anger. Her power hit me hard, sharp as a new blade. I staggered into Talan's arms. White-hot pain sluiced down my body. My vision blurred, blackened, then righted itself. For an unbearable moment, we existed in complete silence; I couldn't even hear myself breathe.

Then the queen lowered her arm. All at once, the world came back to us—nervous murmurs, relieved laughter, spitting waves of gossip. But the furious shouts of Ryder and his soldiers had, blessedly, disappeared. At a fierce little nod from the queen, the orchestra's conductor guided her musicians into a comically cheerful waltz.

My body was a drum of horror, and my head was where the mallet struck—sharp and mean, right between my ears. My limbs throbbed with echoes of the queen's magic. I was nauseated, dizzy. Farrin—I needed Farrin. I searched for her, found her beside the queen. The royal guards had formed a protective circle around them and were leading them toward a curtained doorway—to peace and safety, a quiet room, a stiff drink. I tried to call for my sister, but my jaw was frozen shut, my voice trapped.

"This way, darling," Talan murmured, his voice achingly tender. "Come on, I've got you. Lean on me. Can I help you? Please, Gemma, let me help you."

I moved toward his voice, turned helplessly into the shelter of his arms. Somewhere in my mind's fuzzy corners, I sensed that we were being watched, an object of intense curiosity for everyone around us.

"Please, husband," I whispered, with a weak little laugh at the memory of our glamoured escapades. "Yes, please. Do it."

He pressed his lips to my forehead. "Wife, you have only to ask."

Warmth fell over me—slow, cautious, complete. I shuddered with relief and clutched Talan's hand. Dimly I sensed his nearness—his arm around me, his swift strides, how he nimbly moved us through the crowd and dodged every attempt at sympathy, every provocation.

We moved through a hazy sea of color and sound and masks. Voices crested and ebbed: *We're with you Ashbournes, Lady Gemma. The Basks are simply* foul. *An abhorrent bloodline, truly disgusting. That's what you deserve, Lady Gemma, you and all the Ashbournes. So high and mighty. You don't deserve what the gods gave you. It's tragic, Lady Gemma, what happened to you and your sisters. Where do you think your mother really is, Lady Gemma?*

"Vile wretches," Talan muttered. "Every one of them. Sycophants and machinators."

"I'm not sure that attitude will do you or your family's legacy any favors," I managed weakly. "You want these people to like you, remember?"

"At the moment I'd prefer wandering nameless and penniless for the rest of my life."

"Liar. You couldn't live without your many fine shoes. Eventually they'd wear out, you know."

"Hmm. A slight hiccup indeed. Here we are. Sit here, love."

I lifted my head to find that Talan had led us out of the ballroom and into the royal gardens. Floating spellcrafted candles and lazy paths of wilded fireflies lit the pebbled walkways. The air was sweet with floral perfume—rose, honeysuckle, gardenia. Flowering trees and stone walls laden with lush curtains of ivy formed hidden trails and quiet green alcoves. The masquerade continued merrily without us, as if nothing had happened. The distant murmur of conversation and the orchestra's lilting waltz joined the simpler, sweeter chorus of chirping crickets.

Talan had found a secluded patch of grass beneath the heavy boughs of an old oak, very like the one standing watch by Kerezen's fountain back at Ivyhill. There was a low stone wall cushioned with ivy and wisteria beside it, and he guided me to it, helped me sit, gently untied first my mask and then his own. The sight of his face—gorgeous in the moonlight, all furrowed brow and great sad eyes—gave me a scrap of courage.

"You couldn't have chosen a more romantic spot," I said, desperate for lightness, attempting a flirtatious smile—but not even Talan's power or beauty could soothe the awful fist of pain driving into my throat. I drew in a shaky breath and exhaled a single cracked sob.

"Gemma," Talan said, his hand gentle on my face. "I'm so utterly, horribly sorry."

The sound of his voice destroyed me. I could no longer contain my grief and didn't try to. I hid my face against his chest and wept, awful ugly sobs that made my stomach hurt and my head ache. I couldn't escape the horrid images: Father on the ground, stunned with grief, as Ryder pummeled him. Father embracing my mother; false as it had been, the sight of my parents reunited had cut me to the quick. It brought me perverse comfort that Talan should feel every bit of pain that I did. I pushed it at him through my shuddering sobs, hoping the waves of despair and anger slammed into him without mercy. I loved him, yet I needed him to understand. More than anyone else, he needed to understand.

"I've got you," Talan said, his head bent protectively over mine, his voice choked with sadness. "You're safe here. It's all right. I hear you, I understand, and I'm right here with you. My little wildcat, I'm here." He stroked my hair. He helped settle me more comfortably, my legs bent over his lap, my whole body cradled against his. I cried until I was worn out and my head buzzed with exhaustion. Talan gently rubbed my back. We were quiet for a long time.

"Your entire front is now a mess of tears and snot," I informed him at last, my voice hoarse from crying.

"What else are vests for?" he replied gamely. "Wipe away, my dear, and with vigor."

I laughed a little and peeked up at him, certain I was an absolute fright.

"You're not," he said, tenderly tucking a lock of hair behind my ear. "I felt that, and you're not. Your eyes are tired, your face is blotchy, you're a vision in that dress, and I've missed you." He smiled softly. "I missed you so much it made me ache. I've never felt that before, not once in my life. I didn't think I could."

I shivered a little. His gaze was so earnest, so ardent. I clung to it in greedy desperation. Looking at him gave me strength and a shred of wit.

"I find it hard to believe that a man who looks like you would have trouble in that department," I teased.

"Finding someone to share my bed is not the same as meeting someone whose spirit resonates with mine," he replied quietly, "whose mind and voice and companionship I crave as passionately as I do their body." He kissed my hand, his eyes locked with mine. "I think you know that, Gemma."

My heart pounded a wild rhythm against my breastbone, heat rising in me as the feeling between us shifted, grew urgent. This was a thing I could have—simply, easily, deliciously, and right now. A diversion, a distraction, a denial. Here in the shadows, I could claim what I wanted and revel in the singularly selfish power of ignoring every other horrible thing clamoring for my attention.

"We have much to talk about," I said slowly, repeating his earlier words.

"Yes," he agreed, "we do, but perhaps not tonight, after what's happened."

Then his hand landed gently on my thigh, and I flinched at the soft sting of pain. The shameful memory of my fit in the washroom rose up quickly before I could properly shut it away.

Talan grew very still. Silence enveloped us. I hardly breathed, as if that would somehow prevent him from feeling the truth.

But he had felt it, of course he had—the shame, the pain, the frantic fear that drove me to claw at my skin, the relief that came after. A flash of feeling, and he knew it all. I tried to turn away from him, mortified, but he took one of my hands in his, then lifted my chin and looked at me.

"Gemma," he said quietly. "Gemma, I'm so sorry."

I tried to laugh, but it sounded terribly sad. "You say my name rather frequently, Mr. d'Astier."

"Because I love it. Because saying it brings me joy, and more of it every time." He glanced down at my legs. "May I see? Will you show me?"

I had never shown anyone this awful thing I did to myself when the panic grew too great to bear. But that night, perched on that stone wall soft with ivy and flowers, I lifted my skirts and showed Talan. I showed him my tattered stockings and the fresh angry marks on my thighs. I showed him, and then I waited, sick and afraid, to see what he would do.

What he did was consider the wounds carefully, then look up at me and take my face in his hands as if it were a precious thing, a treasure he would die before breaking. He kissed me softly on my mouth and beside each of my eyes.

"I understand what that feels like," he said to me, grave and quiet. "It's different for me, and yet the same. I've done...not this, but other things. I understand what it means. I understand the horrible relief that destruction brings."

This astonished me. I could find no words except for his name. I held on to him, crying again; I couldn't seem to stop.

"Truly?" I said. Tears streamed quietly down my cheeks.

He rubbed my hands with his thumbs, and then it seemed he

could look at me no longer. He stared at our hands, his expression darkening. The shadows of memory, I thought.

"Will you tell me?" I asked. I had never felt so shy and so bold at once. "How it feels for you, I mean."

"I will," he replied, "but not tonight, if you'll forgive me. Tonight I want only to take care of you." He lifted his gaze to mine. "Will you wait here while I fetch supplies? I promise to return. This doesn't frighten me, nor does it repulse me." He kissed me, sweet and soft. "Far from it, Gemma."

I had no strength to protest or ask him what sorts of supplies he meant, and so I waited on the wall, alone and shivering, until he returned a few minutes later with ointment and cloth bandages, striding toward me like a man with a singular purpose.

"Did you raid the royal stores?" I asked with a watery laugh. "Or did you charm one of the healers?"

Talan gave me a cheeky little grin. "I'll leave that to your vivid imagination."

"I should scold you for that."

"Scold away. I'd charm a thousand healers, exhaust all my power and keep going even so, if it meant I could help you."

He said it as if it was nothing, then furrowed his brow in concentration as he set to work. First he saw to my stockings, untying the silken ribbons that attached them to my underthings, then unrolling the delicate fabric down my legs with infinite tenderness. I shivered, breathless, watching him with rapt attention as he applied an ointment to my wounds, a cooling salve that made me wince from the sting, but I couldn't have asked for a gentler nurse and soon forgot everything but his touch—unthinkably gentle, his fingers cool and quick. He unrolled the bandages, wrapped them around my thighs, neatly tied them off around each of my legs, and then, before he drew down my skirts, he knelt before me and kissed me twice on each thigh: once at the bottom edge of each bandage, near my knee, and again at the top, where the skin was tender and trembled at his touch. The crown of his head brushed against my gathered skirts, and then he was standing, settling my dress around me.

Crying still, I gestured ruefully at my tearstained face and then managed to say, "Talan, please come here," because I couldn't bear to live another minute without touching him.

He obeyed. He put his arms around me and pressed his face against my hair. He whispered, "We'll help each other. I understand, Gemma, and I'm not afraid of it. Please know that you don't deserve it, that pain. Hear me tell you that and believe it."

"I promise I'll try," I responded, and though it seemed too simple a thing to say after what he had done, I drew his face toward mine and whispered, "Thank you," against his lips, tasting the salt on my own, and then I kissed him.

He responded with the utmost care, very still above me, very gentle, until gentle was no longer what I craved, and I tugged on his vest to tell him so, hooked one leg around his to pull him closer.

He moved back to look at me, his eyes hot and dark, and shook his head. "Gemma." He touched my face, my hair. "We don't need to do this. You need rest."

"I need *you*," I insisted, "and right now I don't want to think about anything else but that." I put my hands in his hair and leaned up to kiss his throat, his jaw. "As long as you don't mind a few tears while I kiss you."

He laughed quietly, a sound that turned into a soft groan as our kisses deepened. I twisted atop the wall, desperate to move closer to him though I was already pressed tight against his body. His hands were steady and warm on my hips, grounding me, and then one of his hands moved to my hair, cupping the back of my head, and his tongue was in my mouth, and any tenuous control I had slipped away from me.

I gasped out his name, grabbed his collar, pulled myself half off the wall so I could better reach him. Swiftly his arms came around me, lifting me, and then he was the one sitting on the wall, and I was on his lap, my skirts rucked high and the hard heat of his hips beneath me.

He kissed me until my head spun, until we had to break apart for air.

"Is this hurting you?" he asked, breathing hard. "Your legs?"

I shook my head, dropped kisses into his hair and on his brow. He turned his face up to meet them, his eyes closed, and I kissed his thick dark lashes, his temples, every bit of skin I could find. Soon he was murmuring my name like a fervent prayer. I squirmed a little in his lap, felt how beautifully we would fit together, and cried out softly. It burst out of me, the wanting inside me too great to contain. The sound undid something in him. His hands found my hips, pulled me down hard against him with a sharp, short curse that made me laugh, utterly charmed, out of my head with love.

Then he did the most marvelous thing. He tugged me higher on his lap, achingly gentle even though I could feel quite clearly how desperately he wanted me, and kissed my breasts through the thin soft fabric of my gown.

My arms flew around him. I held his head against me, feverish, the edges of my vision sparkling. With Talan's mouth on me, I was free of pain; my body prickled, strong and alive and liquid and unbreakable. The sky was pulling at me; I arched up toward it, convinced that at any moment I would find I could fly.

"Gemma, you're exquisite," Talan groaned against my breasts, his voice muffled as he kissed me. "I can hardly bear it."

I bent my head over his, held him to me. He began fumbling with the fabric of my dress, tugging gently at the bodice with shaking fingers.

"Is this all right?" he whispered. "I want to see you, love. Can I?"

"If you don't," I gasped out, "I'll do it for you."

Somehow we managed it—the buttons down my back, the ribbons around my wrists. The bodice slid down my torso and pooled at my hips, and then Talan's hands were on my skin—my neck, my back—holding me to him as he lowered his mouth to my breasts with a moan, a little wondering sound of disbelief.

"*Gods*, Gemma," he rasped, and I had never known a touch like this, never known kisses like these. I didn't know whether it was his empathic power, his ability to read the book of my desire to learn just what I wanted, or something else, whatever strange whim of the dead gods had brought us together—but whatever the reason, he knew just what I wanted. Where to put his mouth, how to drag his tongue just so. He teased my right breast with his fingers and tormented the other with his mouth, and when he grazed the delicate skin with his teeth, I nearly lost my balance and had to grab his shoulders hard.

"I've got you," he whispered against my breastbone, and he did, his arms a warm cradle of strength that kept me upright, settled, safe.

I moved on top of him, dizzy with pleasure. He groaned to feel me circle against him, and I smiled at the sound, and then I looked up at the branches above us and the stars beyond. Their light dazzled me and lit a fresh fire in my belly. I was ravenous for more—more of Talan, yes, but also something else, something akin to the starlight and the branches shivering overhead and the flowers bobbing in the breeze around us. I couldn't name the hunger, and yet I chased it, pulling Talan's mouth back up to mine and claiming it as my own. The feeling of him under me, the kiss of cool evening air on my bare shoulders, the flowers' heady perfume—I felt remade by it all, as if our kisses had welded my fragile body to a stronger, steelier frame.

Somewhere in the haze of pleasure, a familiar sensation crawled across my nape: someone or something was watching us. It was the same sense of nearness I'd felt at my dressing table and then again in the Middlemist, a sense of approaching something momentous, or that momentous thing approaching *me*. A tug at my chest, a restlessness under my skin. With Talan's arms around me, the feeling didn't frighten me. In fact, I relished it.

"Even the shadows have eyes," I whispered, smiling, my lips forming words I did not tell them to say. "And they never close them, and they never sleep."

"What?" Talan whispered. He looked up at me, cheeks flushed, eyes dark with desire. "What did you say?"

I shook my head, ground shamelessly against him. I couldn't speak. I buried my face in his hair.

"Yes, that's it," he murmured. He held me tight to him, hissed out a breath against my neck. "You're going to come for me, aren't you? Right now, just like this."

I nodded, hardly believing that my body could find its release so easily, so utterly. As I moved against him, deep red thrums of pleasure pulsed within me. I gasped out Talan's name, clutched his shoulders. He held my hips with iron strength, helped me move just where I wanted to, murmured encouragement against my skin until I shattered in his arms and all the tension in my body melted away in shuddering waves of gold.

After, I clung to him, gasping, laughing a little, half sobbing. I had bedded many people, had enjoyed release countless times, but never so powerfully as this—not only the pleasure itself, but the renewal that came after. I gripped the vines beneath us as we caught our breath. The waves of my pleasure kept coming, as if the sun were painting me in endless circles of warmth. The air pulled taut against my skin; the feeling of watching eyes felt closer now, rapt with anticipation.

And then Talan tensed beneath me. Rigid, frozen, he let out a choked sound of fear.

"Gods unmade," he hissed. He lifted me off his lap and set me on the wall, then stepped hurriedly away, his face slack with fear. "What is this? What's happened to you?"

Baffled, I sat there, half-naked in the piles of ivy and flowers, my body still trembling, and glanced down.

What I saw made my blood run cold.

It had happened again, just as it had the night of my party at Ivyhill—a glamour, this time unbidden and more powerful than the last. I was *changed*. My skin glowed with faint pulses of iridescent light; my hair had fallen loose and hung about me in glimmering strands of gold, silver, copper, rose. I touched my face, noted the planes of my sharper cheekbones with sickening recognition. A dull pain in my mouth prompted me to drag my tongue across my teeth, which made my stomach lurch with fear. My teeth were sharper, longer. I had fangs, like some feral woodland creature.

I clamped my mouth shut, swallowed a cry of terror.

"Your eyes," Talan whispered, ashen. He stepped away from me. "They're...what did you do?"

When I didn't answer, he shouted it, making me flinch. "What did you *do*?"

I held up my hands to placate him, to plead with him, and quickly hid them in my skirts. My fingernails had elongated to gleaming points.

"It's all right," I said, my voice coming out strained, ragged. Familiar and yet not. "Please don't be frightened." I let out a shaky little laugh and immediately wished I hadn't, not with Talan looking so horrified. "I don't know what it means, but it won't last."

"You mean this has happened before?"

I nodded miserably. "The night of my party. I told you I felt a pull, like something was watching me, calling to me. I followed it to my dressing table and was able to craft a glamour that night, very like this one." I gestured helplessly at myself. "But I don't know why or how. I didn't try to do it this time, and yet it happened all the same."

Talan was still backing away from me. "You should have told me this," he said hoarsely. He wouldn't look at me. He looked everywhere *but* at me.

I felt sick watching him, my eyes stinging from this utter, unthinkable humiliation. "I'm sorry. I was afraid to tell you. I almost did when we arrived at the tournament, but then everything else happened, and then you left."

Talan shook his head, still refusing to meet my eyes. "No, no, no," he muttered angrily. "I didn't know. I didn't realize." He searched the trees with a fierce, terrible expression on his face before finally looking back at me. The desperate light in his eyes knocked the breath out of me. Anguish, terror, revulsion—I couldn't decipher it.

Then, without another word, he turned and ran.

I called out after him, stumbled clumsily away from the wall on wobbly legs, and fell to the ground. When I looked back up, trembling with sudden cold and a terrible, primal fear, Talan was gone.

CHAPTER 22

I stayed under the tree, damp and shivering, until my body returned to its ordinary self—pale skin, blunt teeth and nails, tangled mess of blond curls, every muscle screaming with fresh pain. My joints ached as if metal traps had been thrust into them and now their grinning silver smiles were driving my bones apart.

Was this the sort of agony Mara endured every time she transformed?

I choked out a small sob at the thought, crawled to the oak, and used its trunk to pull myself up. I straightened my gown as best I could, fumbling with the laces of my bodice. I took a few steadying breaths, scraped together two fistfuls of courage, and ducked out from under the tree without a backward glance.

The gardens were largely unoccupied, their visitors no doubt drawn back to the palace by the earlier outburst. *The earlier outburst*—that was good, that was a phrase I could think to myself with cold precision, and I did so again and again—an incantation, a prayer.

I crept through the gardens, flinching at every sound, until I emerged into the huge stone courtyard housing the guests' carriages. I hurried toward the small covered carriage I recognized as Gareth's. Generations ago, the high queen had gifted my family a beautiful villa in the nearby hills, which my ancestors named the Green House. We rarely used it, preferring instead to spend our visits to the capital in the Citadel itself, pampered with every luxury we desired—culinary delicacies from around the world, long hours of steaming in the royal baths, beds piled high with linens soft as a kitten's belly.

But I couldn't bear to remain on the grounds of the palace for another minute—not that night, perhaps not ever again. Our own carriages were parked some distance away in the royal stables, and I couldn't possibly make such a trek. Instead I headed straight for Gareth's old footman, Jerob, a kindly man who worked for the university and had been Gareth's personal attendant for years. He was lounging on the driver's bench with a book in hand, idly chewing on the end of his pipe, but he dropped both when he saw me. His stunned stare flicked down my body only briefly before he pulled himself together with an embarrassed flush and sat up straight.

Clearly my efforts to make myself presentable had been inadequate.

"Lady Gemma," he said gruffly, with a little bow. "It's been some time since I've had the pleasure."

"Hello, Jerob. It's good to see you. I regret the interruption, but I..." I drew in a shaky breath, my courage wobbling at the sight of his familiar whiskered face. "I must ask you a favor."

"Anything, my lady."

"Please send a message to Lord Ashbourne and Lady Farrin that I've retired to the Green House for the duration of our stay and that they may retrieve me there upon their departure. And then, Jerob, would you please take me there?" My voice shrank as

I spoke, every word sapping more of my strength. "Gareth won't mind. In fact, I think he would approve, considering everything."

Jerob's brow knotted in confusion. Apparently word of the night's excitement had not yet reached him.

"Of course, my lady," he agreed. He helped me into the carriage, then summoned a page to deliver my messages. Before we departed, Jerob opened the carriage door and looked up at me.

"My lady, is there anything else I might do to help you?" he asked gently. "Shall I perhaps send for a healer?"

My eyes burned as I found my voice. "I'm not hurt, Jerob. There's no need to worry. I simply wish to hide for a little while. This party has outlived its usefulness."

"That I understand, my lady," he said. "Never been a lover of parties myself. Sounds to me like what you need is a quiet house and a good book, which is my remedy for most things."

I gave him a thin smile. His kind brown eyes reminded me of Una, and my chin wobbled as I tried not to imagine the comfort of her warm, lanky body curled up beside mine.

"We are similar in that way, Jerob," I said. "And thank you."

He squeezed my hand, then quietly shut the door. As Jerob called softly to his horse and the carriage rolled out of the courtyard, I wrapped my arms around myself—my stomach aching, my chest tight with heartbreak—and wept.

Once back at Ivyhill, I stayed in my rooms for days. No one disturbed me but Lilianne, who kept me fed and coaxed me into drinking water from time to time.

I hadn't seen Farrin or Father since our awful, awkward journey back from the capital. The royal healers had forbidden traveling by greenway until Father fully recovered, forcing us to spend a dreadful week traveling home by horse and carriage. During the trip, we'd all said perhaps five words to one another. Farrin had folded into herself, her face a closed door, and I'd hardly dared to look at our father.

I couldn't see him without hearing the sickening crunch of Ryder Bask's boots against his ribs.

Stepping into my rooms at last was a shattering relief. I shut the door behind me and slid to the floor and pressed my palms hard against my temples, desperate to silence the incessant drum of terrible thoughts. Talan's face twisting in horror, the wrenching coldness of his abandonment. Alastrina Bask's glamour fading to reveal her true face. Father accepting Ryder's blows with dead-eyed resignation.

Talan beneath me, kissing me, loving me. His voice quietly breaking as he whispered my name.

My changed body—sharper and stronger and savage, aglow with an inner light I didn't understand.

When the vise of my hands proved ineffective at silencing my tumbling thoughts, I slapped my temples instead—swift, hard strikes of my palms that left me dizzy, reeling. Unable to catch my breath, I crawled to my bathing room and huddled on the floor before the basin. I tried to make myself sick and failed. The panic kept rising, booming between my ears. I clutched at my stomach, desperate to wrench out the sick feeling churning inside it. In a fit of terror, I tugged off my traveling clothes; the fabric was smothering, abrasive, and if I didn't get it off, it would kill me.

Naked on the floor, I tore the bandages from my legs, pressed my cheek to the cold tile, and scratched my itching thighs until the scabs reopened. The hot sting of pain settled my roiling insides until I looked down and saw the ravaged mess of what I had done.

I tucked my knees to my chest. Too tired to cry, I keened quietly, soft animal moans.

An hour passed. I fell in and out of ragged sleep, then dragged myself to my bathtub and filled it with scorching water. I scrubbed my skin clean, drained the tub of my filth, retrieved cloth and ointment from Jessyl's plentiful stores.

"Jessyl," I choked out. The little storeroom still smelled of her. Tears slipped down my cheeks. Miraculous—I thought surely I'd gotten rid of them all. "I'm so sorry, darling," I whispered to my empty rooms. I touched her chair. Then I clumsily wrapped up my thighs in bandages and crawled into my bed and fell asleep.

When I woke the next morning, my head felt remarkably clear. I watched the cheerful summer wind paint dapples of sunlight across my windows until Lilianne arrived with breakfast. Our whole staff of course knew that the Basks had assaulted Father at the queen's ball, which had cast a pall over the entire household, but I'd told no one about Talan and me, and I wouldn't.

Lilianne, however, was more perceptive than I would have guessed—or perhaps I was not as skilled at hiding heartbreak as I thought.

"Good morning, my lady," she said, entering with a little curtsy. She set my breakfast tray on the bedside table and then fussed about the room in obvious distress. I watched her, picking at my food. Several times she opened her mouth as if preparing to say something, paused, and then stopped herself, shook her head a little, continued tidying.

After a few minutes of that, my patience ran out.

"What is it?" I asked. "You're upset about something." Thinking of Jessyl, I paused until I could speak again. "I know it must be difficult for you to be near me after everything that's happened."

She looked mortified. "No, my lady, that's not it at all. If I may speak plainly, though I wish Jessyl were alive—may the gods find her and keep her—I'm happy to be your lady's maid. I'm better suited for it, I think, than I am for housework. I've never been thorough enough for Mrs. Seffwyck." She clutched her dust rag, stricken. "Not that I won't be thorough in my work for you, my lady. I meant only that Mrs. Seffwyck is terribly exacting. As she should be, of course."

I stopped her with a wave before she could unsettle herself further. "I understand what you mean. Think nothing of it. But that's not why you're upset, is it?"

"No, my lady."

I watched her fret and waited.

At last she spoke. "It's only that, well, something has happened. A guest has arrived this morning, my lady, and I don't want to trouble you, but I think you should know of it."

The miserable look on her face told me everything. My body grew warm all over, a horrible, mortified feeling. What must Lilianne think of me, of all this?

"It's Mr. d'Astier, isn't it?" I said quietly, an ache in my throat. "He's returned from the capital."

"Yes, my lady. He and Lord Ashbourne are taking their breakfast in the dining room just now."

I set my toast back on its plate, what little appetite I'd had suddenly gone. "Did he send a message for me?" I asked carefully. "Did you hear him say anything about me to Lord Ashbourne or to Lady Farrin?"

Lilianne hesitated. "No, my lady. He hasn't yet asked for you. But I'm sure he will."

I laughed. No, of course he hadn't, and he wouldn't. He had kissed a monster. He had come close to bedding one. He would finish conducting his business with Father, ensure his family's wine would be stocked at all the finest dining halls in the capital, and then he would leave to wash himself clean somewhere. I would never see him again. And I was glad of it.

"He won't ask for me, Lilianne," I said, "and if he does, you will tell him that I am unwell and not receiving any visitors or messages." I looked up at her coolly, remembering to gentle my voice. None of this mess was her fault. "That will be all, thank you."

Lilianne, wide-eyed, hurried out, leaving me alone once more. I lay back down in my nest of pillows, watched my breakfast grow cold, and let my thoughts solidify around a single truth: whatever had existed between me and Talan was gone. I was alone, and lying there brokenhearted in my bed, I began to feel strangely relieved.

The plans he and I had made were mine to see through or discard, and I knew what I would do, what I *must* do. I had wasted too much time simpering after him like some lovesick child, hoping for something I couldn't even put a name to. The wardstone had been stolen, but that hardly mattered. Our nights wandering about Ravenswood had been fool's errands, the result of my own cowardice. I had been too afraid of my father to risk a direct path to what I wanted. I had been too afraid of the impossible to truly acknowledge the idea of some ancient Olden creature holding my family in thrall and had chosen instead to play at subterfuge with the handsome stranger from Vauzanne.

No longer.

After what had happened to me at the ball, I found it easy to accept—with my whole heart, my whole self, without question or doubt that the demon existed. A woman with no magic had begun transforming into something else, something repulsive and unknown. In a world where such a thing could happen, a demon could, and must, exist.

I would find this demon, this Man With the Three-Eyed Crown, before Father determined his course of retaliation and plunged us all into more violent chaos. I knew no other way to move forward. This was the thing that steadied my mind and kept me from hurting myself further—a complication I could no longer afford. I would heal, recover my strength, and then find this demon and demand that he bring the Bask family—everything they owned, everything they loved—to irredeemable ruin.

And in exchange I would offer him my own wretched body. I no longer cared about what was wrong with it, how to mend it, how to understand the glamours I'd conjured. I simply wanted to be rid of it.

Weeks ago, Madam Baines had admitted the existence of two greenways known only to my father. One led to Ravenswood, and the other? *The hidden one,* she had called it. *The sunken one, the one that goes straight to—*

Thoughtlessly I'd cut her off, in that moment caring only about getting to Ravenswood. But a hidden, sunken greenway seemed to me just the kind of path one might take if one wanted to speak with a demon…if only one could find it.

Without the distraction of Talan, free of the burden of hope, such a task would be much simpler.

I sat up in my bed, calm and clear-eyed, accepting my familiar daily pain without protest. I wouldn't have to endure it for much longer. I withdrew paper and pen from my bedside table and proceeded to draw up a plan.

Every day I dutifully nibbled at the meals Lilianne brought me. Lounging in bed with my food, I asked her to tell me about everything that was happening in the house. What was Father doing?

What about Farrin? Had they resumed their ordinary routines? When did Father visit his study upstairs? Had she overheard any conversations between Lord Ashbourne and Mr. d'Astier?

At first Lilianne spoke haltingly, clearly baffled to have been chosen as my new conversation partner. But she soon warmed to the idea and chattered away as I ate, reporting the minutiae of the house in startling detail. She was quite the observant little mouse and took pride in understanding the clockwork of life at Ivyhill.

Father spent most of his days in meetings with Talan and other visitors, she reported. Guests came and went at least once a day. She gave their names to me: Willem Boyde, a lieutenant from the Upper Army whom I knew to be a skilled elemental; Lord Ossian Killipar, the Aidurran ambassador; Lady Plumeria Gelling, an Anointed beguiler from a northern family that had enjoyed unprecedented popularity while the Basks remained trapped in my parents' cursed forest.

The list of names made my stomach churn. An elemental. A diplomat. A beguiler. And Talan, a disgraced foreigner whose only fortune lay across the sea in a house full of wine.

What was Father plotting? I couldn't make sense of it or figure out Talan's place in the scheme. Wondering about it left me sleepless, wretched with worry and curiosity. It became clear to me that I could no longer hide in my rooms.

I would need to become a shadow, swift and sly, all-seeing. *Even the shadows have eyes*, Madam Baines had said. Well, now those eyes would be mine.

I told Lilianne to allow me undisturbed rest, that I would see her at mealtimes and otherwise ring for her if I required assistance. When she brought me my food, I made sure she caught me weeping piteously over Talan's old letter or gazing mournfully out the window. Then, one day during luncheon, a harried kitchen boy delivered a letter of outrage from my cousin Delia, who had been appalled to hear of the Basks' awful trick at the masque. In his hurry, the kitchen boy forgot to knock and barged into my sitting room unannounced. Lilianne rounded on him like a bear.

"Get out of here before I ring for Mrs. Seffwyck and have you dragged off the grounds," she hissed, stalking out of my rooms with the poor boy's collar gripped in one hand. He was taller than she was, and yet he shrank before her fury. "Lady Gemma has quite enough to deal with without being bothered by the likes of you. And tuck in your shirt!"

Watching the scene unfold, I smiled behind my hand. Lilianne was becoming quite the loyal soldier. With her protecting me, my solitude would be safe indeed.

During the quiet hours between meals, I began my strange new work. I crept through the secret door hidden behind a tiled wall in my bathing room and traveled the house's network of passages. They had long ago been built to provide the household with escape routes during times of crisis. I reminded myself of the paths I knew and introduced myself to those I did not. I took pen and paper with me to draw a map, which I studied at night. I made note of which doors I could not open, as they had been spellcrafted for use by other members of my family. I also marked the places where one could peek out into the main house and spy unobserved—iron grates, thin gaps in wood-paneled walls, tiny crumbling holes in those made of stone. Neglected in Mother's absence, the ivy running rampant through the estate was slowly wedging its way into the house's structure, pushing and pulling it apart. A most convenient consequence of Philippa Ashbourne's eccentric tastes.

Once I took a wrong turn, and then several more, until finally I saw a ventilation grate in the wall ahead of me, admitting into the passageway tiny stipples of light. I hurried toward it, eager to get my bearings, but when I peered through the elaborate iron-work, my stomach dropped.

Somehow I'd found my way into the wing where guests were housed, and right on the other side of the wall stood Talan, his torso bare, his belt undone at his hips. He was dressing for dinner in front of the mirror. He was a vision in the lamplight, his dark hair aglow with it. His expression was distant and grave.

Watching him, I hardly breathed. He tugged on a silk shirt that draped beautifully over his slim torso, and then he began fastening his belt, and I should have moved, I should have left right away, but something kept me rooted there, a part of me that craved the agony of watching him.

Suddenly he froze. I must have made some tiny sound. His eyes cut toward me in the mirror, and I darted away from the grate as quietly as I could, flattened my back against the wall beside it, clamped my hand over my mouth, waited.

A moment, and then he was there. I could feel him on the other side of the wall, real and solid, pulling at me through the wood and stone. I closed my eyes, imagining it: he was looking through the grate into the darkness beyond, listening, wondering. He would see nothing; he would hear nothing. He would place his hand on the wall.

I flattened my own palm against the stone, as if even through inches of rock my hand could meet his. Hating how lovesick I was, how furious and sad, I waited until Talan moved away, shrugged on his jacket, and strode out of the room. Silence fell, and after a few minutes I felt safe enough to move. He wasn't coming back. He would never come back. Soon he would leave, and that would be the end of all this, and I was glad of that ending. I was glad. I had things to do, and I wanted him nowhere near any of it.

I slid to the ground in the dusty passageway and hugged myself until the urge to cry had passed.

—◆—

I spent my days and nights scurrying through the house's walls—observing the servants, the endless flow of Father's guests, and Father and Farrin most of all. I followed them from bedroom to study to kitchens to library. I even traversed the passages that led out of the house and into the grounds, marking where each one emerged—past the game park, in a thicket; a storeroom of riding tack in the stables; the round stone temple devoted to Neave, goddess of the beasts, which stood near the farmlands on the estate's northern border.

For days this was my life, and I took to it with fervent enthusiasm. The distraction of it, the purpose, was intoxicating. I found that I enjoyed the life of a recluse, especially when Lilianne reported every day that Talan remained at the house. I tried not to care that neither Father nor Farrin came to inquire after me, telling myself that they were merely respecting my request for solitude and had not in fact abandoned my monstrous self forever. I tried not to worry about how the rooms in which Father took his meetings had been cloaked in a spell that muffled all sound, making it impossible to eavesdrop. The work of Lady Plumeria Gelling the beguiler, I assumed, one of Father's most frequent guests.

Most of all, I tried to resist the passageway that led to Talan's room. What good would it do me to torment myself by spying on him? Besides, I was many things, but I was no deviant.

A week passed, and another. Then one night, the thing I'd been waiting for finally occurred.

The night before, I'd discovered a new passage. It descended through the house via narrow twisting stairs before pushing out into the grounds and emerging in one of our hothouses. Striped with cobwebs, it had clearly not been used for some time. I visited it again the next night, moving slowly, listening to the thick stillness for signs of nearby greening magic—a rumbling hiss like boiling water, the lash of a stray bit of magic snapping loose from its tether—but I heard nothing.

I decided to rest in the hothouse for a short while before making the long trek back upstairs, and while I was there, hidden from view by piles of sleeping flowers, a flicker of movement in the inky night beyond the glass caught my eye. I stayed perfectly still, my heart pounding, and watched two distant figures hurry across the grounds toward the fountain.

The moon was new, the sky streaked with thin clouds. I had to squint to make them out—Farrin and Father, cloaked and dark. I watched them disappear beneath the branches of the old oak tree. Shadows consumed them. I stared at the tree and counted down a minute, and then another, waiting for them to emerge. When a third minute had passed, I could bear it no longer. I shoved my maps into the pocket of my own cloak and hurried across the lawn toward the oak, but when I ducked under the heavy branches, Farrin and Father were not there. I was alone with the tree and the night and the sharp jab of my frustration, and then another sudden, sharp jab, this one like a quick cut of teeth across my left palm.

I hissed and whirled around, heart in my throat. At first I saw nothing, but then, squinting, creeping closer with horrified wonder, I saw on the oak's great fat trunk an undulating blackness—thin as a blade, tall as a man. It wavered, disappeared, then reappeared. Whenever the blackness revealed itself, a quiet whip of magic cut across my body. Something deep inside the tree rumbled, then hissed quietly. Meat on a hot stove.

My stomach turned over. I knew the feel of this magic, the hot-cold grit of it on my tongue.

It was a greenway, its entrance sewn into the fabric of this tired old oak. How I had never noticed it before was a stunning mystery—unless, I thought, my mind racing, it only surfaced when summoned and otherwise remained hidden. Was this the sunken thing Madam Baines had spoken of?

Fearing the strange slip of greenway might disappear at any moment, that I would lose this precious opportunity, I braced myself, held my breath, and walked toward the magic's pull. Four quick steps, and it snatched me off the ground and swallowed me.

This greenway was thin, pinched, its passage swift and sharp, much more vicious than the greenway that led to Rosewarren but also much shorter.

I fell out on the other side into a tiny clearing surrounded by an unfamiliar woodland and for a moment could only lie there with the wind knocked out of me, my body soaked in greening magic and screaming in pain. As soon as I found the strength, I scrambled back into the trees and crouched in the shadows, breathing hard. The air was still and close and quiet, disturbed by neither wind nor creature, and the trees grew so thickly that I could not see the sky. I loathed the place at once. The unnatural silence of it made my skin crawl. There was no sign of Farrin or Father, but after a tense moment, I heard murmured voices. They rose and fell, then rose again. My father's voice and my sister's. An argument.

I crept through the woods toward the sounds and stopped once I could see them. Father, his back to me, faced a tall, narrow black door with a pointed top. Not a solid door, but an opening, an empty space framed by a thick wall of trees. The sight of it filled me with icy dread.

Farrin was standing beside him, her hands in fists.

"This is absurd," she was saying. "Why bring me here and then refuse to let me go with you?"

"I don't want you anywhere near him for even a moment before you have to be," Father said, his voice eerily calm. "But it occurred to me recently that if something should happen to me, no one left alive would know where to find this place. Now you know. You'll need to someday. Perhaps soon."

Farrin touched his arm. "What are you planning, Papa?" When he didn't answer, she continued, "Whatever it is, you don't need to do it. We can be done with this fight, we can have peace at last, if only you have the courage to make that choice. The Basks—"

"The Basks will die, and I will not rest until they do." Father shook her off with an abrupt, shocking violence. "If you come here again while I still live, I'll know it at once. His wards will tell me, and gods help you if that happens, my daughter. You've never seen me truly angry, but you would on that day."

Farrin blanched, stepping away from him. "Yes, Papa," she said quietly.

Father let out a tired breath. I ached to see the back of his head, the sag of his shoulders.

"Go home now," he said dully. "Leave me."

Farrin turned to obey, but Father gently caught her wrist. He didn't even look at her, and yet I could see the fondness in the way he held on to her, the trust that she would obey him, the familiar ease that existed between them even in such a tense moment. An awful longing pierced me. I cowered in the shadows, hand over my mouth.

Farrin stretched up to kiss Father's cheek and then left, her face stony with despair as she hurried past me toward the clearing. I shrank into the trees, rabbit-still, willing the woods to hide me.

Once I lost sight of her, I turned back to Father just in time to see him walking through that awful black door. He stepped down once, twice, perhaps using a flight of stairs set into the earth. His body flickered. A violent sheet of magic lashed through the trees, so powerful it sucked the breath out of my lungs. I fought to keep my eyes open against the sudden onslaught of pain, watching as Father disappeared, then reappeared. There was a shriek like knives against metal—brief, deafening—and then Father disappeared once more and the sound abruptly ended.

I stared at the spot where my father had been, drawing in ragged, terrified breaths. I had no sense of what to do—follow him in? Wait for him to return? Run home and never look back? Time passed at an excruciating crawl. Every nerve in my tired body screamed at me to run, but the desperate resolve of the last several days kept me right where I was. *His wards will tell me*, Father had said. *He* had to mean the demon. If I ran back home to safety, I might lose this chance to find him and never get another one.

My eyes had begun to droop by the time Father emerged, ashen and silent, from the foul black door. I couldn't read his expression, but he showed no sign of injury, and aside from the stark paleness of his face beneath his beard, he looked exactly as he had when he'd left.

I watched him walk back toward the clearing that led home, waiting until I could no longer see him. Then I sucked in a sharp breath and forced my shaking legs to carry me toward the black door. I didn't stop; if I hesitated even for an instant, I would crumble and flee. I ducked through the door, stepped down into a strange, damp warmth and onto something rank and spongy. I recoiled. A truly impressive greenway was nearby, bigger and older than any I'd encountered. The air at my fingers vibrated from the force of its hunger. Its magic flooded my nose and mouth with sour fumes.

I took another step, and when my foot squelched against whatever vile thing formed the ground beneath me, my head exploded with the sudden sound of screams. A great sucking force grabbed me by the ankles, the throat, the wrists, and swallowed me all the way down.

CHAPTER 23

I came to on my hands and knees in a damp clearing surrounded by thin white trees. The agony of my passage through the ancient greenway gripped me in a blazing cramp that twisted my insides from head to toe. I heaved in the dirt, my mouth open in a silent cry.

"Ah, the littlest Ashbourne," came a voice, whispering and velvet. "What a delightful surprise."

As the voice spoke, it split into multitudes, a horrific chord—a high, shrill pitch, a low, glottal one, and between them a tangle of muddy tones I couldn't decipher. Then the voice solidified into its singular self once more.

Movement circled me, strange and fluttering, a sucking flap of naked wings, but when I raised my eyes I saw only the trees and the darkness beyond them. Faint undulations moved in the expanse of black—another forest swaying in a wind I could not feel? A flicker of movement caught the corner of my eye. I scrambled around in the dirt and saw only a wisp of black smoke, the gleam of a boot.

My fear was crystalline, sharp as a blade, and dragged all the way down my spine. I thought I felt something touch my nape—something cold and hard—and scrambled around to look, but again, saw nothing.

Finally I caught my breath and pushed myself unsteadily to my feet. "Are you the Man with the Three-Eyed Crown?" I asked the darkness.

"I am," the voice replied.

The simplicity of his response shook me. I had expected a meandering, mischievous conversation, rife with deception. His directness left me no time to gather my thoughts. I broke out in a cold sweat, resisting the urge to wipe my palms on my cloak.

"You are the demon who bound my family and the Bask family in a blood feud?" I asked.

"I am."

That fluttering sound circled me again—fleshy, sticky. Strange footsteps jerked across a tarry ground. I spun around to look, caught a flash of furry hide, a tall, darting figure.

I clenched my jaw against a prickle of fear. "Why did you do it?"

"You are a woman of many questions," he responded, amusement curling his voice. "Do you expect me to answer all of them?"

"I ask that you do."

"And what will you give me in return?" he whispered, suddenly very close.

His breath was hot against my neck, his voice wriggling and wet. I did not dare look behind me; I stared at the tree nearest me, the familiar, comforting shape of trunk and branches. I had come this far, and I could not falter now. I thought of Farrin, how fearless and unflinching she would be in such a place.

"Answer my questions first," I managed, "and hear my request, and then we will discuss terms."

I held my breath and waited, the silence deafening.

"An unusual way to conduct business," he said at last, "but I appreciate the novelty of it. Very well. Ask me your question again, dear child."

The endearment sickened me. "I am not a child."

Something whipped past me, a quick brush of fur. "You are a sack of bones and meat just like all the others," he snapped. "You live and die, and I live on. You are all children. Flies come into the world. They buzz around, bump into windows, spawn their larvae, die with neither dignity nor meaning. Thus are you and your kind to me. Now, ask me your question again. I advise you against trying my patience."

I swallowed, my mouth dry. "Why did you bind our families together in this fight?"

"Because I can. Because I was bored. Because you taste good."

"Surely there are more interesting ways for you to spend your long life?"

His laughter slithered into my ears. "What makes you think I am confined to only one form of entertainment?"

I didn't dare ask for elaboration on that point.

"Do you know what happened at the high queen's masquerade?" I asked instead. "Do you know what the Basks did to my father?"

"I saw the gleeful, gaping crowd. I felt the Bask boy's boot connect with your father's ribs. I felt the horror of your sister and of you as well, little Ashbourne. The violence of it all, the shock of such meanness on such a glittering occasion. Delicious. I slept utterly sated that night."

"How did you see all of that from so far away?"

"Ah-ah, now. I cannot tell you *all* of my secrets. We have only just met, after all, and we must observe at least some little niceties."

"And did you also see Ivyhill burn thirteen years ago?" I demanded. "Did you watch as my sister nearly died?"

"Yes, I saw that too," he whispered.

"Did you tell the Basks to do that to us?"

"Oh, no. None of the cruel blows your families have dealt each other over the years have been commands of mine. I care not what you do; I care only that you do it. It is truly marvelous, the things a human mind can think of. Such barbarity, such an insatiable taste for blood."

A slickness striped my lips, a reptilian kiss, though I could see nothing in the blackness. I flinched, tried to move away, and backed into something invisible and unyielding—a wall where no wall stood.

I tried without success to slow my breathing. "What do you look like?"

"What do you think I look like?"

Images arose in my mind—illustrations from every book about Old Country arcana that Gareth had ever shoved at me. My throat clenched to think of him, of home, of the wondrous simplicity of something as innocuous as books.

"No one can be certain what demons look like," I answered, shaking, "but I've read many stories that claim to know. Fat serpents that breathe fire. Huge, lumbering men with the heads and hooves of bulls who trail blood wherever they walk. Faceless pillars of flesh that envelop anyone who turns their back on them."

"Such colorful tales!" the demon crowed. "And which one do you believe?"

I hesitated, afraid the question was some sort of trick. "I prefer to keep my mind open to all possibilities."

"Oh, you are a *joy*, little Ashbourne. So much more fun than your father. Gideon is old, worn out, a glove full of holes, all his ideas stale and irritating. You, though, are so new. Nubile and fresh, eager to please."

Then he paused. The air trembled with a sudden flood of heat. "Little Ashbourne," he said, his voice strained, fundamentally changed somehow. Thinner, more tired, as if it had been torn apart and sewn back together one too many times. "If only I could…"

Another silence, fraught with something terrible and urgent that made me want to run. But instead I held my breath, waiting, and soon the demon's voice returned, smooth and delighted. Whatever strangeness I'd felt had passed.

"Yes, I like you very much," he said, "and will therefore grant you the gift of sight—only for a moment though. Watch closely. If you blink, I will consider it the gravest of insults."

I obeyed, staring into the darkness for so long that my vision began clouding with pain. Just as my eyes began to flutter closed, the black emptiness between the two nearest white trees shifted fitfully. A blurry image manifested, shuddering in and out of my understanding—a flash of thick ram's horns; a long, sinuous body of dark fur with a white belly; underneath a bulbous crest of bone, an empty space where a face should have been, and three staring yellow eyes.

The world jolted, and suddenly the demon was looming over me. One clawed finger traced the line of my throat. Something lifted me; my feet swung in the air.

Then the flickering image of him disappeared, snuffed out like a candle. I dropped to the ground and huddled in the dirt, and my body seized with a heaving sob.

"There, there," came his voice from somewhere above me, perversely gentle. "The more time we spend together, the easier it will be for you to see me. And I do look forward to that. It seems unfair that I should be able to gaze so easily upon your beauty while you are denied the sight of mine."

I pushed myself up with shaking arms and glared at the space where he had been. I refused to grant him the pleasure of a response to that last remark.

"Why are you called the Man with the Three-Eyed Crown?" I asked angrily.

A slight pause. The air bristled, then calmed.

"Because it is accurate," he replied. His voice was harder now.

"Is it your true name?"

"I have many names, all of them true. Most of them, if you heard them uttered, would kill you."

The threat was plain, but the horror of seeing him even for an instant had for the moment numbed me to my own fear. I wrenched myself to my feet.

"Will you release my family from whatever binds us to you?"

"No."

I had expected that. I dried my face, trying to steady my hands. "Very well. Then I request that you help me destroy the Bask family. Not just the piddling back-and-forth that's kept us limping along all this time—a blow here, a curse there. I want utter destruction. The erasure of their existence. We can design the act in such a way that the violence of it will sustain you for years."

"Years?" A sound plopped into the clearing like the soft, wet clucking of a fat tongue. "I did not realize you were so familiar with the workings of demonic appetites."

His voice, though, betrayed him. I had intrigued him.

"I wouldn't ask you to do this thing for me all on your own," I continued. "Already you've given me one gift. I merely ask for your help, not your service. An exchange."

A sustained silence fell. Then came the sound of heavy foot-falls—an enormous creature, circling the spot where I stood.

"And what," he asked, "would you offer me as payment?"

I steeled myself. "My body, my mind, my spirit, to do with as you please for as long as you desire."

A burst of laughter puffed against my ear. "What a grand view you have of yourself. I have possessed many throughout my long years."

"But none like me," I countered. "There is something inside me that I do not understand. An illness, but also, I think, a power. For my whole life, I've been denied the magic given to my blood-line by the gods. But twice in the past three months—without study or practice—I've conjured magic, modified my body as a stylist might. Once I meant to do this; the other time it happened unbidden. My teeth became fangs. My skin shone, luminescent. Then I was myself again."

I paused, licked my dry lips. "I lack the proper knowledge of the arcana to work out what this means—but you could do it, I'd wager. You, with all your might and your mastery of the Olden." I felt a flutter of movement to my right and thrust my hand out into the darkness. A ridged, rough paw scraped against my palm. Something else—a claw, a foot—snagged the hem of my cloak. Then the footsteps circling me jerked to a halt. The strange, fraught feeling from before came again, pulling the air hot and tight.

"No," the demon said quietly into the darkness, his voice changed once again—tired shreds, thin with anger. "No, you can't."

Silence followed his cryptic words. Was he telling me I couldn't leave? That I wasn't allowed to touch him? But then, it almost sounded as though he were talking to someone else, and not to me at all. My bile rose; I swallowed hard, barely restraining myself from fleeing. The tension was unbearable, and I struggled to breathe.

Then, at last, the air shifted and cooled. The demon's slow footsteps resumed as he paced in a circle around me.

"Little Ashbourne," he said smoothly, "you tantalize me with your offer and with your brazen flattery. There is nothing a demon loves more than a mystery, not even violence. The unknown is seductive, irresistible."

He stopped behind me, the towering height of him like a mountain. Two soft weights alighted upon my shoulders, but I was too terrified to look down and determine their form—hands with fingers and thumbs? Twin clouds of roiling shadow?

"However, while I consider what you have proposed, you must do something for me," he said softly. "A pledge of good faith."

"Very well," I said, my body rigid. "Tell me what you want."

"Your sister, the eldest Ashbourne. She is a musician."

My stomach dropped. "Yes," I whispered.

"I wish to hear her play and sing. Not here. This place is ill-suited for a concert. No, I wish to hear her perform for me, a proper recital, in the comfort of her own home. She is most herself there, the power of her Anointed talent potent beyond compare." He let out a shivering breath. "I have heard her from elsewhere, but I need to be closer. I crave the immediacy of the notes against my skin."

Hysterical fear crawled up my body as I imagined Farrin in the clutches of this awful creature. "Demons enjoy music?"

"We are alive, just as you are. We enjoy pleasures as you do. Food and drink, music and sex."

His breath warmed the crown of my head. The hands on my shoulders disappeared, and a dip of darkness formed in the air just before my eyes, like the flat of a large palm with neither flesh nor definition. In the middle of it rested a dull brass eye the size of a walnut.

"Take it," he whispered. "Place it near her instrument, or in a place where she might sing for her own pleasure. Be discreet. It will provide the clearest emanation when it is engulfed happily in shadow, unknown to anyone but you. Encourage her to sing, to play. Tell her you wish her to give you a personal concert. A gift for her sister."

I hesitated, my fingers hovering over the eye. This was the most foolish thing I'd ever considered doing. Even with only my cursory knowledge of the arcana to draw upon, I knew that to trust the word of a demon was to invite certain doom. But if obeying him meant an end to the Basks, a chance at peace for my family, and an end to the torment that was my body, then the risk was one I had to take.

I glanced up at where I thought the demon might be and caught only the grotesque wet gleam of what I feared might be a tongue.

"You will not hurt her?" I asked.

"If I hurt her, she cannot play music for me," he replied, impatient. "Think before you speak, child."

"You won't hurt anyone else at Ivyhill?"

"Not if I am pleased by what I hear."

That was ominously vague. "Define what that means, to be pleased by what you hear."

An unseen force, hot and seething, struck my chest and flung me to the ground. My head slammed hard against the dirt, and I sucked in a shocked breath, the world spinning around me.

"You grow too bold, tiny Ashbourne," said the Man with the Three-Eyed Crown, his voice a spitting chorus. "Do not think that my interest in your proposal exempts you from behaving yourself."

The eye dropped into the dirt next to my face with a heavy thud that reverberated in my chest. "Do we have a bargain?" he asked silkily.

I stared at the eye for only a moment before curling my fingers around it. It was hot in my fingers, and in my mouth I tasted blood.

"Yes," I whispered. "We do."

CHAPTER 24

My journey home from the demon's lair was a frantic blur: the greenway that brought me back through the black door, the dense forest, the other greenway that lived inside the old tree by the fountain, the trek up the lawn and the wide veranda steps, the soft agony of our defensive wards rippling against my skin like fire, the confused sentries nodding at me as I hurried past them in the entrance hall.

"I couldn't sleep," I muttered. "I needed a walk."

"Of course, my lady," they replied, and then no doubt proceeded to discuss the various eccentricities of our family. During my days of scuttling through the house's passages, I had heard many such conversations between the servants. None of them had been cruel, merely wry and baffled and patiently fond, as if we were children who couldn't be blamed for the chaos we attracted.

If only they'd known where I had been that night, what I had seen and promised. I held the demon's eye tightly in my slick palm, too afraid to drop it into one of my pockets. Somehow it felt safer to keep it where I could see it, feel it, and be reminded of what I had done.

I swallowed a burst of hysterical laughter as I slipped into the Green Ballroom. The night's shadows made Farrin's piano resemble a slumbering beast. I didn't pause to deliberate; I hurried toward a slim pedestal made of green-veined marble that stood near one of the tall windows. A lush potted fern sat atop the pedestal. I dropped the eye into the fern's nest of leaves, deciding the Man with the Three-Eyed Crown didn't need a direct line of sight to my sister at the piano. He would be able to hear her; that would have to suffice.

Then I ran, feeling chased by something that wasn't there. Upstairs in my rooms, Una trotted over to greet me and then paused, sniffing, one uncertain foot in the air. She shrank back with a growl, ears flat, tail tucked between her legs. Only after I had balled up my clothes, shoved them into a corner of my closet, and scrubbed myself vigorously in the bath did she finally creep close enough for me to pet the silky spots behind her ears. She sat beside my bed, rested her head on my quilts, and whined quietly, staring at me with obvious woeful concern until I fell asleep.

That night I dreamed of fur and bone, and I woke up tasting smoke.

The days passed in fits of fear.

Terrified that Father or Farrin would smell the demon on me, I bathed constantly and asked Lilianne to comb scented oils through my hair at least once a day. She didn't mind; in fact she seemed to relish the quiet time in my bathing room, the glide of my pearl-tipped comb. I let her choose the scents—cinnamon, rosemary, mint. Desperate to assure myself that no danger was near, I listened to her chattering reports about the state of the household and picked apart every phrase for some sign of latent evil. But things at Ivyhill went on much as they had before. Father and his many visitors spent hours at a time locked up in conference. Sometimes Talan was with them; other times I looked out my window and saw him walking the grounds, stopping beside each tree to admire it. One day I noticed him taking such a walk with our head groundskeeper, Mr. Carbreigh. When they stopped to discuss a stately elm that marked the path to the orangery, I yanked my drapes shut in a fit of anger.

I could have gone to him. I could have demanded that he explain what he and Father were up to, why he remained at Ivyhill, why he had left me that night at the queen's ball.

But I was a coward. I kept to myself and began to abhor looking in the mirror.

When Una seemed her old self again, loping happily through my rooms with me and curling up beside me at night, I deemed it safe to become Farrin's shadow. I took meals with her, haunted her rooms in the evenings to read beside her. The suspense of waiting would surely kill me if it continued for much longer. I needed her to make some kind of music, and soon, before the demon burst through Ivyhill's front doors, impatient and angry.

One morning, I watched Talan leave the grounds on one of our horses and turn onto the distant road that eventually led south to the capital. To meet with Gareth, Lilianne had informed me, and continue their research into demonic possession. The sight of him galloping away, his traveling coat fluttering about him, the wind in his dark hair, twisted my heart into a knot.

To distract myself, I accompanied Farrin on her daily walk around the estate. She was unintentionally adorable in her huge leather boots, grubby trousers, and shabby coat, a kerchief tied around her hair and a walking stick in hand. Her pockets bulged with work gloves and shears and little bouquets tied with silk ribbons. We were to visit our tenant farmers after our inspection of the grounds, and Farrin liked bringing them flowers from our hothouses.

"Interesting attire you've chosen for this," she remarked, glancing at me sidelong.

My mouth thinned as I pushed myself to keep up with her brisk strides—a difficult task in my soft gray boots and ruffled summer dress of striped blue poplin, garments that were decidedly *not* intended to be worn whilst traipsing through mud and brush.

"I was distracted this morning," I muttered, which was true. Six days had passed since my conversation with the demon, and every moment that crept by felt more ominous than the last. I couldn't be sure how long he would wait for what he wanted. My only comfort came from the thought that he was no doubt enjoying watching me squirm and might be content to do so for some time.

"You're always distracted these days," Farrin said. "Lilianne tells me you hardly sleep."

I swallowed a jolt of anger. Perhaps Lilianne wasn't the loyal ally I'd thought her to be. "Lilianne is fanciful and searches for intrigue where none exists. And anyway, I'm here now, aren't I? I thought you'd be happy about that."

"I am, and I'm also curious: Will you continue to loiter about my rooms *every* single night, or will I at some point enjoy a peaceful evening to myself? You jump at every noise, which makes *me* jumpy."

"Careful, Farrin. What if I suddenly become a recluse in anticipation of the day when my illness gives me no choice in the matter? You'd regret scaring me off."

Farrin snorted. "You, a recluse? That role is mine to fill. You wouldn't last a month." She looked at me keenly; I could feel her doing it even though I kept staring straight ahead. "Is there something you'd like to talk about?" she asked gently. "I'm worried about you, Gemma. You aren't yourself."

I had to say something, *anything*, to stifle the confession burning a brand on my tongue. "Not everyone can recover from a night like the masquerade ball as quickly as you can, Farrin."

Farrin laughed sharply, all her softness gone. "I don't have time to linger in those memories. I have an estate to run, accounts to manage, servants to attend to."

"As well as schemes to concoct with Father and all his friends."

A stormy silence fell.

"Yes," Farrin said bitterly, after a moment. "And then there's that."

There was no sense in bandying about the issue any longer. I let loose a string of questions: "What sort of retaliation is he planning against the Basks? I saw Byrn preparing Father's carriage. Where is he going? What are all these meetings for? And why is Talan in any of them? He's a wine peddler from a ruined family, not an ally of any value."

"Concerning Talan, all I know is that he's become something of a pet of Father's. He likes having interesting people around him, and Talan is interesting—sad story, pretty face, sharp wit. He's meeting Father at the Pallas Cloisters tomorrow, in fact. Father's visiting some monk who specializes in remedies for sore backs, whatever *that* means."

Farrin had answered what she wished to and ignored the rest. Fighting for patience, I tried not to picture Father and Talan on the road, regaling each other with stories about what a burden I was, what a curiosity, like a specimen to be kept under glass. Maybe Talan would tell my father what had happened at the masque, which would most likely not shock him at all but instead confirm what he'd always suspected: there was a wrongness in me, and I should be locked away for everyone's protection.

"It could be that Father simply has a sore back," I pointed out, trying not to cry.

"An ailment we could treat very well here at home. I can only assume it's an excuse meant to disguise his true purpose. Anyway, I shouldn't have mentioned it. You don't want any part of this business."

The old rejoinder made me bristle. "Because I don't need to know, is that right? I'm not strong enough. My health is the important thing."

"That's exactly right," Farrin replied, marching on.

With a vicious thrill of satisfaction, I wondered what my family would think when the Basks were dead and they realized whom they had to thank for it. Poor, frail, strange Gemma with her poor, strange body. I wondered if, once I was gone, the guilt of knowing what I had sacrificed would weigh on them for the rest of their lives.

I waited until the lump in my throat had dissolved, then said airily, "You're right, I suppose. And speaking of ailments, you look rather haggard this morning. Maybe you should play your piano later today. You know it relaxes you, and it's been some time now since the tournament. What better way to defy the Basks than to enjoy the music they so cruelly interrupted that day?"

That was the thing that stopped Farrin in her tracks. "That's the eighth time this week that you've said something to me about my music. Why? You've never been so insistent before."

Her voice was angry. I turned to face her. We stood at the crest of a sloping ridge near a stone wall the height of my hips. Beyond it a field of sunflowers bobbed cheerfully in the light breeze. A small stream trickled at the bottom of the ridge, sparrows bathing in its shallows.

"I just want you to be happy," I began.

"No, you don't. You don't want Father or me to be happy. A punishment for excluding you."

I gaped at her, a flush crawling up my cheeks. "That isn't true at all," I lied, "nor is it fair."

She stared at me hard for a moment, then sighed and looked away. The sunlight threw her tired face into harsh relief.

"I'm sorry," she said wearily, "about all of it. I shouldn't have said that, and I don't think it, and I don't want to argue. I just want to finish my work and go to sleep." She squeezed my hand. "I'll consider it. The music, I mean. All right?"

A nervous flutter of fear rose in my chest. I wanted her to do it, I *needed* her to do it—we all did, though no one knew that but me. And yet I also wanted to take her by the shoulders and shake her, and scream at her never to touch her piano again, never to sing another note, and to tell me all the secrets she and Father kept to help me get out of this awful situation I'd created for myself.

Instead I put on my sweetest smile. "I'll stand guard at the door and punch anyone who stands around gawking for too long."

She let out a sharp laugh. "That would be a sight. Are you even capable of punching?"

"I think I could manage it if properly motivated."

For a moment she looked at me fondly, the breeze toying with strands of golden-brown hair that had fallen loose from her kerchief. Then she kissed me on the cheek and strode on. I hurried to keep up, the heels of my boots sinking into the damp earth with each step. A shadow flitted over my body, and the wind rustling through the sunflowers brought with it the faint whiff of something rotten and boiling. But when I searched for a tall, horned silhouette, a furry hide, a white belly, I saw nothing but a forest of yellow and green, and the next time I took a breath, the wind was once again mild and sweet, spiced with nothing but summer.

◆◇◆

That night, during the deep dark hours, I awoke to the sound of Una crying in pain.

I lurched up out of bed, or tried to, but a stifling pressure kept me flat, as though I was being smothered by a thick blanket. A white torrent of pain crashed through me. The magic pinning me down was vicious and solid, heavy as stone. I fought against it, clawing at the air. The sound of Una's distress made me wild. I pushed and kicked, bones blooming with pain, muscles screaming in agony.

Just when I thought I would crack open from the stress, a hot point of light gathered in my chest, fast and angry like a fist clenching closed, and then exploded.

The sound of a great crash spiked my ears, and when I managed to heave myself out of bed, dripping with sweat, I looked about woozily and saw that the window nearest me had shattered. I stepped carefully through the glass, tripping over the blankets I had kicked off, searching for a stone or piece of shot—something that explained what had happened to the window—but found nothing. My body clenched around a terrible sinking fear.

I went to Una, who was writhing near my bedroom door, and sank to my knees beside her. I felt her all over, searching for wounds that did not exist, but something was clearly wrong. She whined constantly, rubbing her face with her paws. She crashed to the floor, dragged one side of her body against the rug, then stood up and crashed onto her other side.

In a cold flash of understanding, I realized Una must be hearing something, or smelling it—something awful and wrong, something that didn't belong in this house.

I flung open the door and raced down the corridor. Farrin's rooms were empty, her door standing ajar. My terror choked me. I ran through the house like a woman deranged, my mind teeming with images so terrible that I could hardly breathe. I didn't think to find a weapon or wake Father; I didn't think about anything but Farrin, and speed, and the black fist of anger punching a hole in my chest.

When I tumbled down the stairs into the house's central wing, the hall was eerily silent, the air hot and fetid. I had to push through it as if it were a thick mire of mud. Trudging toward the Green Ballroom, my head dizzy with the effort of moving, I noticed Marys, one of our housemaids, huddled under the stairs. Silent tears ran down her face. Her eyes were wide, staring. She rocked slowly from side to side, and when she noticed me, she shook her head in childlike disbelief.

Osmund, Farrin's black cat, paced frantically before the closed doors of the Green Ballroom, all his hair standing on end. I saw his mouth move, knew he must be crying, but could hear no sound. The air was so thick it muffled everything. Even my own steps were silent. I strained toward the doors, pushed Osmund gently away with one foot, screamed at him to run to safety. I did hear that—my voice, distant and distorted as if underwater.

I threw my body against the doors with a crazed burst of strength. They flew open and I tumbled inside. Sound returned in a violent gust that popped my ears, and the first thing I heard was Farrin screaming.

She was on the floor in her nightgown, being dragged away from the overturned piano by a shuddering mass of shadows twice the height of my father. It flickered madly, a jagged confusion of darkness, and it howled, a furious, agonized cry so loud and terrible that my knees gave out and I collapsed against the wall. At the sound of the doors crashing open, the thing whipped around in a swirl of black, and shapes flickered in the abyss of its body—a furry black flank, a thick horn, a man's clawed, scabbed fist, three round yellow eyes.

The Man with the Three-Eyed Crown.

He let out a piercing shrink, and a teeming mass of wriggling black worms and unthinkable meaty viscera spewed out of him. I dodged the bulk of it and ran, gagging on the stench as gods knew what plopped to the floor all around me.

I ran toward him, unthinking, my mind reduced to animal fury. He had lied to me. He had said he wouldn't hurt my sister, and here she was on the floor, her hair in his fist. She was bruised and bloody; she sobbed for mercy. I knew then that the eye he had given me had enabled him to trick our wards and invade my house—and I had let him do it.

I don't know what came over me then or how it happened—perhaps I uttered a command deep inside myself without realizing it, or maybe some faint, ancient remnant of the gods took pity on me and leapt into my body. For whatever reason, as I ran toward the demon with an inferno of desperate wrath blazing in my heart, I became as incandescent as the stars.

Hands in fists, I flew at the demon with neither strategy nor finesse, a battering ram determined to smash him apart. I swung wildly at him, caught a glimpse of his three wide staring eyes—dumbfounded and yellow with black pupils thin as hairs—and then a huge eruption split the air, lightning-hot and deafening. The ballroom disappeared in a flash of white, and a shower of needles pierced my skin—thousands of them, millions.

I crashed to the floor and hit my head hard. My vision spinning, the taste of blood flooding my mouth, I kept my eyes open long enough to see Farrin crawling toward me, sobbing my name, and then gave up and let myself fade.

CHAPTER 25

T he first thing I noticed upon opening my eyes was that my skin had changed.

I was on the floor with my head in Farrin's lap, and my hand was resting on her leg, and it was glittering, a subtle iridescent patina. I rubbed my hand against Farrin's nightgown, curious if the strange sheen would come off, but it didn't budge. I turned my hand around in the air and stared at my softly gleaming fingers in utter confusion.

Then Farrin's voice floated down from above me.

"Oh, thank the gods," she said on a tearful breath. "You're alive."

I tried to sit up, but I felt shaky, newborn, and couldn't do it without Farrin holding me up. She put her arms around me, cradling me against her, and I saw the bloody scratches across her skin and remembered everything.

I wrenched away from her and whirled around, searching wildly for the Man with the Three-Eyed Crown, but I found only Farrin, and Father standing a few paces away in his nightclothes and dressing gown, and Gilroy hovering at the ballroom doors with several servants behind him.

I searched blearily for Talan's face, expecting him to burst through the doors at any moment and hurry toward me and hold me, tuck me safely away in his arms. Everything would be as it had been, and we would never speak of that awful night at the masque.

But Talan was not there, I reminded myself. He had gone to the capital to work with Gareth. A fist of disappointment closed around my throat. I tried to tell myself that his absence was nothing to me. The important thing was that Farrin was safe. I was safe. The demon was gone—and so, I noticed suddenly, were the windows.

The frames were empty and clean; every bit of glass had disappeared. It was the same with the mirrors that had once lined the ballroom. The tall gilt frames were there, but no glass remained inside them.

I thought of the shattered window in my bedroom and searched for signs of broken glass, but the floor was clean except for the ruined piano, its toppled bench, and a few streaks of Farrin's blood.

"What happened?" I whispered. I looked back at my sister, but her attention was no longer on me. It was on our father, whose face was ashen.

"I was playing the piano, and suddenly the room went dark and still," Farrin said tightly. She was glaring furiously at Father, which I thought odd. "The next thing I knew, I was being dragged across the floor by..." She made a strange noise in her throat, shook her head. "That *thing*. I screamed and fought him. He told me not to be afraid. He licked me all over. He told me I tasted too good to resist. He was a man, and a beast, and a shadow."

"The Man with the Three-Eyed Crown," I whispered.

Father's eyes cut to me. "How do you know that?"

"He had three yellow eyes, for one," I said wearily, "and he was a horrific-looking monster. An easy guess to make."

I spoke slowly. It was difficult even to think with such a pounding headache, and I didn't want them to know the truth of the deal I'd made, and I couldn't stop staring at my own skin.

"And then Gemma saved me," Farrin continued. Her arms were tight and fierce around me. My unstoppable sister, who somehow had the strength to speak. "I don't know what you did, darling, but I saw you running toward me, and then there was an enormous flash of light, a boom that shook the walls. The windows shattered, and the mirrors too. I dropped to the floor, covered my head with my arms, but I felt no pain. I waited, and when I looked up, the demon was gone, and so was every bit of glass."

Farrin hesitated. Her thumb tenderly rubbed the top of my hand. She was warm and good and soft; I could almost imagine we were children again, hugging each other to sleep.

"Does that hurt?" she asked.

"No," I answered, wonderingly, and then I raked my fingernails down my arm before she could stop me. But even that didn't dislodge the glimmer.

"All the glass in the house is gone," Father said quietly. His eyes were slates, blank and inscrutable. "Every mirror, every pane."

"It's in me, isn't it?" I looked up at Farrin, and then at Father, and held up my arm. Thousands of tiny specks glittered faintly when I moved. "This is where it went."

The pained look on Father's face chilled me. As my eyes locked with his, I knew I'd guessed right. That wasn't shock on his face. He wasn't surprised by what had happened. His expression was that of a man who had seen at last the very thing he'd been dreading.

"How is such a thing possible?" Farrin asked.

"A powerful enough act of magic can have repercussions for the person performing it," Father said thickly. "I've seen it before. What you did shattered the glass, and then the glass fused with you. A second skin."

As he spoke, his eyes grew bright, which terrified me. I hadn't seen him cry in years. I had convinced myself that he was no longer capable of it. He turned away and hid his face in his hands.

"Papa?" I asked quietly. A horrible thought was beginning to take shape in my mind. Father had seen this sort of thing happen before, he'd said. I held on to the words carefully, frightened of what they could mean.

A terrible quiet fell, which seemed to bring Gilroy back to his senses. He hurried the servants away and shut the doors behind him.

Once we were alone in the ballroom, Farrin's sharp voice hacked the silence in two. "It's interesting to me, Papa, what you said after you found us here: 'I'm sorry, Gemma.' You said it again and again. You wouldn't come closer than you are now. You looked revolted. 'I'm sorry.' What a strange thing to say to your daughter. What a strange thing indeed not to come immediately to her side after she nearly lost her life and instead stand there crying and hiding your face as if you can't bear to look at her." Farrin's arms tensed around me as if bracing us both for a blow. "What are you sorry for, Papa? What's happened here? Why are you afraid of Gemma?"

He shook his head, ran both hands through his golden-brown hair.

"I'm not afraid of her," he whispered, clearly lying.

"You look at her as if you are," Farrin said. "Come to her. Embrace her. She did something miraculous, and it saved me. Is that not worth even a scrap of your love? Why are you simply *standing* there?"

Father stared at the floor. His beard was untidy, his nightclothes rumpled. I thought, rather ungraciously, that he looked pathetic—a worn-out glove full of holes, just as the demon had said.

"It's all right, Papa," I said, suddenly unbearably tired. "I've known for some time that you don't love me, at least not like you love Farrin and Mara. I've accepted it."

Father squeezed his eyes shut, made an awful noise.

"Gemma, let's go upstairs," Farrin said tightly. "I cannot stand this. Let him gape like a coward with no sense left in his head. We'll have Madam Moreen look you over, mix a tonic to help you sleep."

"No, don't go," said Father quietly. "Please. I just need a moment more to think."

"Think about what? What is *wrong* with you? Why are you looking at her like that?" Farrin's anger boiled over. She started to rise, and I knew that if I let her, she would march over to him and do something she would later regret. I caught her wrist and kept her still.

"He knows what I did," I said, realizing the truth with perfect clarity. "And he knows how I did it. All this time I thought I had no magic, but I do, and he's never told me about it, but he knows what it is."

"No, I don't," Father burst out, "nor do I know anything about how it works, which is exactly why we—" He stalked away, tense and agitated. For an agonizing moment he stood with his back to us, shoulders high and square, as if bracing himself.

"We did it to keep you safe, Imogen," he said at last, very quietly. "You must understand that. The things you did—they were different, unpredictable. Frightening. Mara had her strength, Farrin her music. But you...your magic was not so simple."

He turned to look at me, his face haggard. "One morning

when you were quite small, too small to walk, you woke up choking. Your throat was jammed full of white flowers. We dug in your mouth to pull them out, but they kept coming. You turned blue, unable to breathe. We thought we would lose you. But when we extracted the last soggy petal, you came to and squealed with laughter, unhurt and happy. Your mother didn't sleep for months, and neither did you. She woke you and checked your mouth every five minutes. All our nightmares were full of flowers.

"When you were four years old, you were playing chase with your mother, and you glamoured her appearance into that of a tall, faceless man with long flaps of pale skin and a crown of twigs. She didn't realize what had happened, and neither did you. I came around the corner and thought some Olden creature was attacking you. I ran at your mother and threw her across the room. She crashed into the wall and her head split open. The glamour faded. You grabbed on to her as she bled and wailed, terrified. Madam Moreen saved her, but only just. I told her Phillipa had fallen down the stairs."

He spoke swiftly, as if the words were cursed and he was desperate to be rid of them. It was a grotesque story, too fantastical to be real, but my bones ached as I listened, and that told me the tale was true. My body remembered, even if I did not.

"When you were six years old," he continued, his eyes bright, "you were playing hide-and-go-seek with Farrin and Mara out on the grounds, and I suppose you thought, 'Oh, wouldn't it be clever if I were a tree and could hide in plain sight?' We ran out of the house when we heard you screaming. You were trapped inside the sprouting branches of an enormous elder tree I'd never seen before. Leaves spilling out of your mouth, tiny white flowers bursting from your fingernails, bark creeping slowly across your eyes."

Father's voice broke. He sank slowly to his knees. Farrin was crushing my fingers, her body rigid beside me.

"We didn't know how to free you," he said hoarsely. "Was the tree a separate thing, or was the tree *you*? If we hacked it apart to free you, would we kill you? But the tree was growing too fast for us to send for help. The bark had covered your face completely. You had stopped screaming. We had no choice. I found an axe in the stables and started chopping until your body tumbled out. If I'd swung once more, I would have chopped off your left foot."

Father dragged a shaking hand across his face. "Thank the gods it was a festival day. All the servants were in town save for Mrs. Seffwyck, who slept through the whole thing. And your sisters were still tramping around the grounds—they had found an abandoned fawn and forgotten all about the game. We were lucky. We managed to explain away every awful thing you ever did. But we knew that luck wouldn't last."

He looked miserably at his hands, and even before he confessed the rest of it to us, I knew what he would say. I knew it deep down in my belly, in the meaty place where fear and anger live, and I hated him for it. The feeling grew like a weed inside me; my heart broke around it. I hated him, and I would always hate him.

"What did you do?" Farrin whispered.

"We had to do it," Father said, a quiet defiance in his voice. "No one we consulted could tell us what in the name of all the gods was wrong with her."

"With *me*." I felt like I had swallowed fire. "I'm right here. No one could tell you what was wrong with *me*."

He looked up at me, his face carefully blank. "Well, then. What if the next time *you* accidentally glamoured your mother, the healers couldn't reconstruct her head? What if you choked on brambles in your sleep, or what if your sisters did? And can you imagine if the Basks had gotten their hands on you? If things continued as they had been, word would have gotten out, and either the Basks or someone else would have tried to abduct you, or kill you, or cut you open to study you, or perhaps toss you into the Old Country. Maybe the Basks would've turned you against us, convinced you we were the cause of these terrifying incidents, and you would have destroyed us."

His voice broke. He wiped his face with his sleeve and looked at me with an apology in his eyes—an apology I had no interest in hearing.

"Papa, what did you *do*?" Farrin asked again, in desperation.

Father breathed in, then out, then rose unsteadily to his feet. He said the rest flatly, quietly. A horrid ending. "Your mother and I hired an artificer, exiled from the Old Country and happy for the work. We asked him to bury whatever power you had, and he did. He wove a net of blood and bone and sinew that would keep it trapped and dormant deep inside your body. You were six years old by the time we found him. The process took several days and required you to be awake for some of it. Your mother stayed beside you the entire time but wouldn't let me in the room. She had birthed you, she said, and she was the one who had failed you, so she would make herself watch as he cut you. She said…"

He squared his jaw and tried to speak three times before he could find his voice again. "Your mother," he said, "told me every day thereafter that she heard your screams in her sleep, saw the memory of your tiny thrashing body whenever she closed her eyes. You were luckier. The artificer made sure you wouldn't remember any of it."

Blood roared in my ears. I wrenched my arm away from Farrin and slapped her away when she reached for me again.

"Is that why I'm..." I gestured at my body. My glass-dusted fingers glimmered softly, and I wanted to be sick, I wanted to throw up everything inside me, whatever disgusting Olden things that artificer had done to me, and shove it down my father's throat, let *him* feel the pain of being torn apart and sewn back together against his will.

"Is that why I'm sick?" I could barely form the words. The horror of it all was too cruel, too huge. "Is that why magic hurts me?"

Father looked at the floor once more. I hated him for that most of all. Everything he'd done, and he couldn't bring himself to look at me.

"We believe so," he answered. "The artificer warned us there could be consequences, certain sensitivities. Olden magic belongs in the Old Country, not in Edyn. And this technique was particularly old. An ancient practice, he said, seldom performed. He said your body might fight it forever. But if you survived the procedure, you would live, and you would be safe. Your power would sleep." He held his hands in fists at his sides. "Gemma, please, you have to understand—we were terrified for you, for all of us. We couldn't bear the constant fear of losing you to some horrible act of your own magic. We had to take the risk."

"And all the healers we visited, the scholars you brought here to study me?"

"He had to act like a parent who cared that you were in pain," Farrin said, her voice curling with disgust. "He couldn't let you or anyone else suspect that he knew exactly what ailed you and was in fact the cause of it."

Father glared at Farrin with red-rimmed eyes. "Would you have preferred us to let her run rampant and someday destroy us all?"

"She was only a child, her power still in its infancy! With time and care, it might have settled into itself, but you denied her the chance to find out."

I touched Farrin's leg, silencing her. "That's why Mother left, isn't it?" A sudden calm descended over me, smothering my anger, snuffing out all my angry light. "She couldn't stop dreaming about it, couldn't stop remembering how I'd suffered. Every time she looked at me…"

Father's face fell, and when he met my eyes, I wished he hadn't. This conversation had clearly cost him. He looked as though he'd been gutted.

"Every time she looked at you," he said quietly, "she saw nothing but guilt and shame. Then the Basks set their fire and Mara went to Rosewarren. She couldn't bear so many blows."

And then he said the worst thing he could have said. I didn't know what made him do it. Perhaps he was simply tired after such a confession and could no longer think clearly.

"If you hadn't been born," he said, his gaze distant, his voice thick with grief, "she would probably still be here. Your sisters would still have their mother. I would still have my wife."

The words stunned me, left me breathless. Dimly I felt Farrin move me off of her, and then I watched her hurry toward Father and strike him hard across the face. She was shouting at him, her whole body shaking with anger.

I let her have at him and decided I wouldn't stay in my house that night, that I couldn't stay in my house ever again. I left the ballroom and walked through the entrance hall in the shredded remains of my nightgown. No doubt it left little to the imagination of the staring servants, but I could not have cared less in that moment. After I'd sent for my horse, as I stood waiting on the steps outside the front doors, Lilianne hurried to me. Her tear-bright eyes were ferocious, my Lilianne. She clung to me unafraid and asked if I would take her with me, wherever I was going. I would need her, she said. It wasn't right for me to be alone at such a time. I said nothing. I gently detached myself from her and stepped away.

Some stupid part of me kept hoping Talan would suddenly come pounding down the road on his horse, called back to the estate by a protective instinct that allowed him to make the journey back from the capital in mere moments. Of course this was nonsense. He didn't come, and he wouldn't. I stared into the night, unblinking, until my eyes burned. I decided I would not cry, no matter how much I wanted to. I would cry for other things, I would grieve and rage, but not for that. Not for Talan, and not for how much I wished he would appear.

"What are you doing?" Farrin had abandoned her tirade to join me. "Come inside, come sit with me. Father's locked himself in his rooms, and good riddance. We need to make sure you're not hurt."

"I'm not." I shook her off. "Leave me alone, Farrin. Get away from me. Go to Madam Moreen. Tend to your wounds."

She sobbed a little. "Gemma, *please*—"

I whirled on her, shoved her hard. "Get away from me!" I screamed, and immediately despised myself for making her look like that—that wounded expression she quickly hid away. She didn't want me to worry about her; she didn't want me to go. Neither of us knew how to say the things that should have been said.

A stable hand brought Zephyr around. She looked as grumpy and tired as a horse could look. I swung up into the saddle, shivering in my bare feet, and urged Zephyr into a trot, then a canter, then a blazing-fast gallop. My mind was clear, my face dry. A white flash caught my eye—Una joining us, her legs long and fluid, and even then I didn't cry, not even when I stood at Illaria's door and knocked and watched my friend's eyes widen as she took in the sight of me, tousled and glittering, my skin pocked with glass.

She did not shrink from me, nor did she shut the door in my face for abandoning her at the masque, as she very easily could have. I wouldn't have blamed her for it. Instead she pulled me into a fierce embrace and kissed my cheek. Una, panting and happy, pressed her body against Illaria's leg.

That was the thing that shattered me: the sight of my oblivious dog greeting one of her oldest friends in the manner she preferred—a polite, quiet lean.

Sobbing, I hid my face in my hands and let Illaria help me inside.

CHAPTER 26

Illaria nursed me for days.

Whenever she wasn't in her workshops, ordering about her dozen apprentices and concocting her next ingenious fragrance, she was fussing over me with lavender rose tea and rich Aidurran chocolates and a stack of our favorite lighthearted comedic novels, none of which featured demons or death or anything but inconsequential low magic—and none of which made me laugh as they once had, though I tried to for Illaria's sake. I couldn't even feel guilty for guzzling all her time like some greedy leech. I didn't know what I would have done with myself if she hadn't come and found me every hour or so with some new diversion.

She never once asked me how I was feeling, nor did she mention Father or Farrin, or Mother, or my new skin of glass, or the terrible thing that had been done to me when I was a child. She never even asked about Talan, despite how she and I had left things the night of the masque. I'd told her everything when I'd come to her that first night, and it had emptied me out, left me an aching shell of myself.

"I don't want to talk about it ever again," I'd whispered to her as I sat rigidly on my favorite blue chair, shaking and cold, refusing tea or a blanket until I'd gotten every awful word out of me. Even as I made the request, I knew it was childish and wouldn't keep, but Illaria, gods bless her, had so far honored it. I loved her for it. In those first dark days, that was the only thing I *could* feel: that I loved her and that I would have died had she not opened her door to me. I would have kept running until Zephyr had collapsed from exhaustion, and then I would have done the same myself, all the while praying that the Man with the Three Eyed-Crown would leap out of the shadows, furious and vengeful, and finish me off.

My thoughts were wild, far too dramatic, and yet I couldn't stop them. The pain I felt was unpredictable; sometimes it disappeared for hours, only to return without warning in pulses of hot agony that rendered me unable to stand, even though Illaria had restricted the magic worked in my part of the house. That didn't seem to matter; whatever I'd done in the ballroom remained within me like an infection. The demon entered my dreams whenever I dared to sleep—a mass of shadows, a haunch of fur, three yellow, hate-filled eyes.

When I found the strength to move, I drifted from my rooms in Illaria's house to the library or sometimes to one of the benches outside her workshops, even though I knew the nearness of magic would worsen my pain. Sitting there, my nose and mouth tingling from the rich, heady scents spicing the air—pumpkin, cinnamon, tangy red winterberry; she was putting the finishing touches on her fall and winter fragrances—I stared at nothing and listened to the sounds of the steaming oil vats, the hissing compressor pistons, Illaria's happily chattering apprentices. Una, lying on my feet, whuffed irritably whenever someone hurrying in or out of the workshops lingered for too long near the benches, trying to sneak looks at me. I wasn't sure what Illaria had told them all and didn't much care, but I did manage to amuse myself by imagining what they must think of me—the mute Ashbourne girl with shadows under her eyes and shimmering skin, sitting there blank-eyed like some bizarre statue.

I hoped that I frightened them. I hoped at least some of them shivered when they walked past me and prayed to the goddess Zelphenia that whatever had happened to me would never happen to them.

In addition to my rooms in the main house, Illaria granted me the use of one of the private guest cottages on the grounds. Though I think it made her nervous to let me out of her sight, she recognized instinctively that I craved the seclusion and the quiet that came with it.

The cottage was small, a cozy little nest of solitude, and like everything on the Farrow estate, it was lavishly appointed—walls of vibrant cobalt, creamy linens embroidered with flowers in hues of bright marigold, gleaming brass finishings on the warm mahogany furniture. The bed was massive, a fluffy cloud of luxury with tasseled silk hangings draped across its posts.

Lovingly painted portraits of Illaria's ancestors adorned the walls. I threw blankets over each of them so they wouldn't see me when I stood naked in front of the full-length mirror to consider my new body.

Every inch of my pale skin shone with a delicate luster that glinted at the touch of light. It wasn't ugly, not at all; in fact, I suspected that once I made my next public appearance, if I ever did, painting oneself with shimmering powder—not just as an accent on cheeks and collarbones, but head to toe—would become something of a craze.

The idea made me sick. I searched desperately for *some* part of me that had been spared, but it seemed that whatever magic I'd performed in the ballroom had flung every bit of glass it could find into my skin. No bit of me had been spared—my scalp, my belly, the dip above my bottom, the backs of my knees. My skin was a map of constellations I couldn't read, and when it occurred to me one evening that my outsides now matched my insides— both scarred by acts of magic I did not consent to—I laughed myself to tears.

That night I bathed for hours in the cottage's claw-foot tub. No amount of scrubbing helped; my glass-dusted skin was immutable, glittering, smooth as a pearl. The first night I'd arrived, once Illaria had gone to bed, I'd picked and scratched at my arms until they bled, but even those scabs now had a sheen. I stared at them in the bath, shivering in the cooling water. I could cut myself to pieces, it seemed, and nothing would change. The glass had become a part of me, deeply rooted.

I sat in the bath until the water turned cold, staring at nothing, then staggered into the bedroom, naked and dripping, tugged on a nightgown to cover at least some of my skin, and crawled misera- bly into bed. My head hurt from crying; I scratched and punched at my stomach until it hurt too. Whatever that artificer had done, whatever abominable Olden thing lived inside me, I would tear it out someday. Whether with magic or my own hands, I would see that it happened, and surely I wouldn't be able to keep on living after that, eviscerated and unmade.

What a relief that would be: the spill of my guts as my insides emptied out, all the specks of glass that had become part of me dropping to the ground like scattered jewels. As I imagined it, I felt no horror, only gladness. There would be no more pain after that, no more secrets, and what a blessing it would be to my father, whose life I had ruined, and to Farrin, for she would no longer have to worry about at least this one thing. And maybe Mother, if she still lived, would someday hear what had happened and be comforted to know that the daughter she had mutilated no longer had to suffer.

This imagined sequence of events lulled me into a strange calm. A soft rain began to fall. I watched it slide down the window until my eyes drifted shut and I slept.

I awoke to the sound of someone pounding on the cottage door.

Jolted out of sleep, I lay in bed for a moment with my eyes wide open and listened. The gentle rain had become a storm that lashed at the windows, and the wind howled, whistling down the chimney to rattle the closed flue.

Strangely, I was afraid of neither the storm nor the insistent knocking. In fact, a calm came over me. Perhaps this was the beginning of the end I'd imagined; maybe the demon loomed on the steps, steaming with outrage, itching to gut me. If so, I would welcome him. There was no need to be frightened.

I slipped out of bed, numbly retrieved a fringed shawl from the footboard, and draped it around my shoulders. It was cold in the cottage, and I saw no reason to live my last moments in unnecessary discomfort. As I walked across the bedroom, I caught a glimpse of my strange new self in the mirror and let out a sob that surprised me. I wanted this, did I not? And yet my body didn't care that it was an atrocity; it was simple and animal and wanted only to survive.

My body shaking with a sudden chill, I opened the front door and promptly froze with shock.

Talan stood there on the cottage steps, every bit of him

drenched with rain—thick traveling coat, sodden boots, dark hair plastered to his pale brow. The desperate sadness on his face stunned me. He took a step toward me, raised his hands as if to touch my face, and then stopped, lowered his arms, clenched his hands into fists at his sides.

"Farrin wrote to Gareth to tell him what happened," he said hoarsely, "and we came to Ivyhill as fast as we could. Farrin said you'd run off that night, that Illaria had sent her a note saying only that you were being taken care of quite well and that we should stay away, but I...Gemma, I had to see you. I had to see you with my own eyes and know that you were safe."

I blinked back a fresh rush of tears, my traitorous body aching to lean into him, soaked clothes and all, but I did not allow it. I stepped back into the cottage, shawl clutched tightly at my throat.

"You left me," I whispered.

Talan shut his eyes as if in pain. "I know. I know, and I'm so sorry."

"You left me there under that tree. You looked at me as though I were a monster." I laughed bitterly. "I suppose you weren't wrong."

"You're not a monster, Gemma."

"Then why did you run from me?"

"I panicked. You changed in my arms, right before my eyes. In my shock, I thought you might be some Olden creature in disguise, having taken on Gemma Ashbourne's appearance to seduce me. That was a childish thought, and I was wrong to think it."

"Oh, but I am some Olden creature in disguise," I whispered, "or at least near enough. I assume Farrin told you what my parents did to me?"

"She told Gareth everything, and he told me. Perhaps he shouldn't have."

"I don't care who he tells. Soon everyone will know. The minute they see me, they'll know I'm something *else*." I gestured at my body, hardly able to speak. "Leave me, please. I don't want to see anyone. I want to be alone."

He took a step toward me, then backed away once more and wiped the wet hair from his face, agitated and miserable. "Please, before I go, I must tell you something. And then I'll walk away forever if you tell me to, though doing so will destroy me. Gemma," he said, lifting his tired eyes to mine, "I've been aching for you since that night. I've been in agony trying to work out if and when and how to approach you and what to say, though really it's a simple thing: I'm immeasurably sorry for that night at the Citadel. I left you right when you needed me most. It was unforgivable, and yet here I am, a fool and a coward, asking you nevertheless— *begging* you—to forgive me.

"My wildcat," he whispered, and then took my face gently in his hands, his soaked gloves cold against my skin, his eyes searching my face with agonized hope. "I want you, Gemma— all of you, everything that you are, even the parts of you that we don't yet understand. Horrible things have been done to you, and I want to help you live with that truth and move through it so you can someday feel safe again. I want to protect you from everything I can and fight at your side against everything I can't. I want to spend my nights in your bed, spoiling you with all the pleasure you deserve, helping you forget everything that hurts you."

His face softened as he smiled down at me. His eyes shone, and a single tiny raindrop hovered on the tip of his nose, such a sweet thing to see that I had to touch him, had to lean up and kiss his cold nose and claim that droplet for myself. He closed his eyes at the touch of my lips.

"I've been alone for so long," he said quietly, "that I haven't ever learned how to be a person in love. Love, to me, has been a foul thing, nothing but lies and false hopes. The demon that destroyed my family promised love, gave love, and then took it away. I long ago decided it wasn't safe to be vulnerable, to allow someone to truly *see* me."

He took a deep breath and opened his eyes, and the passion I saw blazing in those dark depths left me breathless.

"But you let me see you that night," he said, "*all* of you, even the secret parts, the things that terrify you. It might not have been your choice to reveal to me whatever power you carry, but it was nonetheless a gift, one I was too foolish to appreciate at the time. I want to earn the chance to try again and return that gift however I can. To let you see *me* as no one else ever has. I have very little to offer you, but I offer it anyway—my devotion and protection, my body, mind, and heart."

He stepped closer, carefully, as if afraid I would turn him away at any moment. "Will you have me, Gemma? Will you give me the chance to redeem myself and try to earn back your love?" He swallowed hard, a silent plea burning in his eyes. "You did love me, Gemma, didn't you? Until I ruined everything, that is. Please tell me I wasn't wrong to think you might love me."

His words left me undone. I looked up at him as steadily as I could manage. "You never came to me after the masque. You've been at Ivyhill, and you never once came to see me."

"I didn't imagine you would want me to. But I had to stay all the same—not for your father's business contacts or my family's godsforsaken wine, but for *you*. I decided I would say and do whatever I must to earn a room in your father's house on the slim chance that I would see you, that you would come to me and allow me to apologize—or that I would find the courage to go to you myself, no matter that you could have turned me away. I wouldn't have blamed you if you had."

"One might consider you a coward for staying away from me," I said, "or even worse, deem you heartless. I knew you were in the house and that you chose to stay away from me even so. I was the one who'd been hurt, yet you expected me to make the first overture? You could have come to me. You could have tried." Tears slipped down my cheeks as I spoke. "I should have told Father to send you away. Instead I chose to torment myself."

Talan's expression was utterly devastated. "Gemma, I feel the awful wrenching truth of what you say. I feel what you've suffered, and I'm so sorry for it. You're right—all I've done is bring you misery." He looked away, dashed his sleeve across his face. "I'm a fool for thinking I could bring you anything else. I'll leave you now. I'm sorry. I'll be sorry for the rest of my life."

Then he started to turn away, and I could no longer bear to stand there and hold myself away from him. It was foolish and rash of me; I should have slammed the door in his face. Instead I grabbed his coat and pulled him back to me, whispered his name, and leaned up to kiss him—the corners of his mouth, his chin, his cheeks, his lips. My mind scolded me unhappily, but my body sang to be near him again, as if a part of me had been lost and now was found. With the solid strength of him under my hands, I felt once more like the Gemma of old—ignorant of what I now knew, my skin wholly human.

Talan was frozen, soaked to the bone, but soon he melted under my desperate touch, and our kisses deepened. I wrapped my arms around his neck, determined to warm him. My shawl slipped to the ground, and I shivered as his cold hands glided down my back.

"I shouldn't love you," I murmured between kisses, a hot lump in my throat. Despair, fear, anger—I didn't know, and I didn't care. "I should tell you to leave me and never come back."

His hands fisted the thin billowing fabric of my nightgown. "Tell me to leave and I will," he murmured against my mouth. "Tell me to fall to my knees before you and I'll do it. Anything, darling. I'll do anything you ask, even if it kills me."

I nuzzled his neck, tasting the rain on his skin. "Then come inside," I told him, "and show me this love you claim to feel." I opened my eyes to meet his. "Help me forget what's happened, just for a while. Help me forget everything, Talan. When I'm with you, everything feels a little bit easier, even when it hurts. What kind of sense does that make?"

He shivered a little at my words and bent his head low, searching my face. "You must be clear, Gemma. Tell me plainly what you want of me. Tell me in words."

I stretched up to press my cheek against his. "Make love to me, Talan," I whispered. "Show me I'm not wrong to think I might still love you."

He held me to him, let out a choked laugh of relief against my hair, and then we stumbled inside, clumsy and eager as virgins. I helped him unbutton his coat and shirt, and he touched me all over with trembling hands. He lifted a few curls of my hair and pressed his face to them, and then his mouth was on mine. His kisses were long and slow, drawing thick golden spools of light up from my belly, leaving me limp and liquid in his arms. I flicked my tongue against his lips, and he parted his mouth for me with a groan.

Together we tugged off his sodden shirt and tossed it to the floor. I ran my hands over the smooth muscles of his back, the flat planes of his stomach, the line of dark hair that led my wandering fingers down to his belt.

"Not so fast, wildcat," he gasped, catching my hands. "Let me take my time with you. Let me unravel you inch by inch."

I tugged at his waistband with an impatient whimper, torn between delight at the idea of a long, slow night of lovemaking and a desperation to feel him inside me at once.

Then I glanced over his shoulder and caught sight of us in the mirror that stood against the wall—him, with his beautiful creamy skin, the lean muscles of his back, and me, newly gaunt after everything that had happened, my body glinting and strange.

My stomach lurched. I stepped back from him and turned away.

"What is it? Gemma," he said, breathing hard, touching my shoulder, "talk to me, please."

Though my body still thrummed from his kisses, I jerked away from the warmth of his hand.

"Look at me," I said, fighting the urge to rake my nails up and down my body until there was nothing left to see. "Just *look* at me. I can't do this. I can't do this ever again, with anyone."

"I am looking at you," he said gently, "and I see before me the most fascinating, most intoxicating, most beautiful woman I've ever laid eyes on. I see the woman I love."

My eyes burned with fresh sadness. "You don't love me. You can't. It's impossible." I turned away from him and forced myself to stare at my shining, bleary-eyed reflection. "Unless I can find the artificer who cut me open and sewed me back together and made me into this...this *creature* you see before you, I'll never know what I was or what I truly am now. Who knows what else may happen to me someday? No one does—no one *can*. I fought a demon and broke all the glass in my house. I played a game with my mother and changed her appearance into something so frightening that my father nearly killed her."

Talan slowly walked toward me. The storming wind outside and the dim lamp in the corner conspired to cast alluring shapes across his bare chest. I looked up at him helplessly, terrified for him to touch me and longing for it all at the same time—the safety of his body against mine, the calm he might give me if only I would let him. But how could I?

"What if I hurt you someday?" I whispered. "I could hurt you even now, here, tonight. I can't stand the thought." I fumbled for his hand when he reached for me, pressed his palm against my mouth in a fierce kiss. "I don't want to hurt you, not now, not *ever*."

"Come here," he said, pulling gently on my hand. "Come see this."

He guided me toward the mirror, his touch so exhilarating that I couldn't tear myself away. I let him position us before the mirror and lower my arms to my sides. He towered behind me, the top of my head just meeting his shoulder. He leaned down to kiss my cheek, and his eyes met mine in the mirror.

"The first time I saw you at your party," he said, "I thought you were lovely, yes, and certainly the most glamourous person in attendance, but it wasn't until I saw your eyes that I found myself entranced."

He lifted his hands to caress my face, just the slightest feather of a touch across my cheekbones, then the arches of my eyebrows. "Your eyes were full of such light, such *life*," he continued. "You have an indomitable strength in you. I don't think you know that. You see yourself as less than your sisters. You fear that all you have to offer is your looks, your social savvy, and that this isn't enough, not nearly enough, to make up for the burden you are to your family. But you're no burden, Gemma. Not to me, and not to your family, and even though your father may speak rashly in moments of anger or fear, he loves you fiercely. I've felt it. I feel it every time he looks at you."

His thumb brushed against my lips, and I shivered, crying quietly, aching more with his every word.

"You're *strong*, Gemma," he murmured into my hair. "Your spirit is an ocean, vast and relentless and hungry."

His hands drifted down, hovering over the ties of my nightgown. "Can I, love?" he whispered. "I want to show you what I see."

I nodded, breathless, speechless. I tore my eyes from his to watch his deft fingers untie the ribbons at my neckline, then undo the column of five tiny buttons below that. So loosened, the fabric fell off my shoulders, slipped down my body, and pooled at my feet.

Appalled at the sight of myself, I tried to turn away, but Talan wouldn't let me. He caught my hand and kissed my fingers, his eyes still on mine in the mirror, and with his other hand he drew tender lines down my shoulder, my arm, the dip of my waist, the slight swell of my hips. I was so transfixed by the sight of his hand on me that I forgot to notice the soft glimmer of glass on my skin.

"Gods, look at you," he said, his voice low and rough. "You're a vision, Gemma. You were before, and you are now. Your body might have changed, but you have not, not to me. I want to make love to you under a full moon and watch the light play on your skin." Both his hands were on me now. One cupped my breast, his thumb softly caressing my nipple; the other slid down my belly toward my thighs. "I want to take you on the floor before a roaring hearth so the firelight paints you gold as embers."

"But Talan," I sobbed, arching up into his touch. "What if... what *if*..."

"We could spend our lives worrying about *what if*," he said, "or we could begin each day loving each other, ready to face whatever comes together."

He turned my face toward his, held it gently in place so he could kiss me—at first softly, reverently, and then with a rising passion that left me panting against him, near tears, desperate for more. His hand slipped between my legs, and when he found me, hot and wet and aching for him, he groaned against my mouth and began circling his thumb around me, slow and teasing.

"You're beautiful, Gemma," he whispered into my hair, then turned his glittering dark eyes toward the mirror. "Look at you, writhing against my hand."

I did, dazed, and for a blazing, diamond moment, I saw what he did—his arms around me, one hand gently cradling my throat, the other moving between my thighs. Naked and pale, gleaming with glass and a faint sheen of sweat. My legs trembling as he slipped a finger inside me, my unbound golden hair falling to my hips. He lowered his dark head to my neck and kissed me, sucked lightly on my nape.

"You're glorious," he rasped. "You're perfect. And I will not run away from you ever again. I swear it. No matter what the future may hold, I'm yours, now and always, if you'll have me." Then he glanced up at the mirror and said my name, his voice breaking around the word. "Gemma, look at us. *Look* at us. Watch yourself while I make you come. See how beautiful you are."

Though keeping my eyes open was almost impossible, I obeyed, feverishly noting every exquisite detail: his hands on me, his fingers in me, my body trembling, his flushed cheeks, his mouth pressed against my temple, his ardent gaze meeting mine in the mirror. I arched back against his chest, and he moved us quickly back toward the bed, sat on the edge of it, pulled me up into his lap. The hard heat of his desire pressed against my bare bottom, and I gasped, whimpered with delight, twisted back against him. He hiked up my left leg and let it drape over his arm, then hooked his own leg around my right, opening my thighs, locking me against him. The position allowed him more room, more control, and he used that advantage deliciously, his fingers curling deeper inside me. Watching our reflection made my head spin—my legs open wide, my body trapped in his arms, his dark eyes roving hungrily over my skin. His hand curled around my chin; his thumb pushed between my lips. I grabbed on and sucked; he swore against my ear, murmured how beautiful I was, how divine.

A hot wave of pleasure climbed up my body, pulling me tighter and tighter. My toes curled in the air, and I began to shake.

"*Yes*, Gemma, that's it," he hissed, and though I wanted to keep watching the sensual tableau of my body twisting against him, I couldn't, not there at the end as I cried out and fell apart in his arms. My eyes squeezed shut, and I curled my body around his hand, still moving on him, riding the waves of my release for as long as I could. His arms tightened around me, and he whispered encouragements as my body jerked against his.

When I had finished, I clung to him, murmuring nonsense and tingling all over, and he kissed my forehead, lifted me into his arms, and walked around the bed to lay me tenderly against the pillows. I caught his wrist before he could move away and looked up at him.

"More," I whispered, tugging him back to me, then on top of me. I ran my fingers through his damp black hair, then clasped his hand and moved it down his naked torso until I found the hard length of him through his trousers. I moved his palm, guiding him to caress himself, and he hissed out a breath, squeezed his eyes shut, bit his lip. I started to undo his belt, and he laughed, caught my mouth in a kiss.

"Wait, Gemma," he murmured. "We have time to do this slowly, properly."

I smiled, my eyes fixed on his.

"We've waited long enough," I whispered. "I want you now. Slow can come later." I slipped my hand into his trousers and thrilled to find him hard and hot, aching for me. "You said you've never wanted anything more than to fuck my perfect, sweet little cunt, so *fuck* me."

My words shattered his control. He groaned and tugged down his trousers just enough to free himself, then lowered his hips to mine and rubbed against me. My eyes fluttered shut with pleasure as I relished the sensation of him teasing me—hard against soft, the easy glide of him against my soaked curls. When he entered me at last, achingly slow, he let out a hoarse cry that nearly sent me over the edge once more.

"Later tonight though," he said, holding himself over me, breathing hard, "later tonight I'll take you as slowly as I wish."

I grabbed his hips and pulled him farther into me. With a sharp thrust, he filled me completely, and I hooked my legs around him to keep him there. He stayed there for a moment, murmured my name, his voice thick, and then started to move, deep steady thrusts that pushed me gently back into the pillows.

"Promise?" I said, closing my eyes and smiling. "We'll do this again tonight? And again and again?"

He buried his face against my neck and sucked on my skin. "Yes," he murmured, "as many times as you want me."

"You'll wrap me in your arms so I can feel you, *all* of you?" I shivered, arched up against him, all my imaginings from the past months roaring through my body. "You'll take me from behind if that's what I want? You'll make me come using only your tongue?"

"*Yes*," he growled, with a hard thrust. "All of that and more, my beauty."

I cried out, wound my fingers in his hair, and tugged. "Do that again."

He obeyed, sucking on my throat. The sound of his hips slapping against mine made me swoon.

"Again, Talan," I whispered, and then I could no longer speak. I let go of his hair to wrap my arms around his shoulders, and I clung to him as he drove into me again and again, so hard and deep that my mouth fell open in a silent cry of pleasure. Another tight pull of ecstasy built inside me, sharper and faster this time, and when Talan finished inside me with a rough gasping cry, his face buried in my hair, I followed him and held on to him, both of us soaked and trembling, and whispered his name into the stormy night.

"Talan, I love you," I told him. I kissed his shoulder, pressed my face against his. As I said the words, my eyes burned. Relief overwhelmed me, and rightness, and the hope that what he said was true: that he would protect me against what he could and fight with me against what he couldn't. He would be mine, body, mind, and heart. These thoughts drowned out all others. In that moment, my body golden and buzzing, I was a hopeless romantic, devoted to him and us and nothing else. My thoughts were clear as a sunny sky, all my worries gone.

"My wildcat," Talan said, his hands shaking as he pushed my hair back from my cheeks. His face was tired, soft, happy. "I love you, I love you, I love you." He kissed me with a reverence that made my chest hurt, and as he drew up the blankets around us, he mumbled my name over and over, a soft litany. His arms came around me in a sleepy, possessive embrace. He stroked my hair, soothing my eyes closed. The storm was subsiding, the thunder gone quiet; I was warm and safe, held by a man who loved me, whom I loved in return. It was a miracle, a blessing from the gods.

My body hummed with satisfaction, heavy and spent and free of all pain. In that moment, I was a woman and nothing more. I fell asleep content.

CHAPTER 27

L ater in the night, I woke Talan by sliding down his body and taking him into my mouth. Not long after, he did the same for me, coaxing me gently out of sleep with soft kisses on my thighs. I held his head against me as he pinned my hips to the bed, buried his face between my legs, and used his tongue to unravel me completely. Slick and writhing, I wound my fingers in his hair and arched up against his clever, hungry mouth again and again. He moaned against my soaked skin, his voice muffled and deep, and the sound of his ravenous satisfaction was the thing that sent me over the edge with a hoarse scream.

After, the bed linens hopelessly mussed around us and my trembling body curled up against his, he roused me once more with soft kisses against my neck, under my hair. We kissed until my lips tingled, and then I whispered a suggestion against his ear, and he obeyed, his dark gaze hot with desire. He turned me onto my stomach and tugged up my hips to enter me from behind.

The rain still fell against the windows, an endless cascade of it, as if we had taken up residence inside a gentle waterfall. I closed my eyes, gripping the sheets as Talan moved in me, and listened through a drunken, blissful haze to the soft whisper of rain, Talan's low groans, the slap of our hips as his pace increased. I begged him for more, and he gave it to me. He put one forearm across my shoulders and pinned me to the mattress, held my hips with his other hand and drove into me with such feverish passion that when my pleasure at last crested and shattered, I saw spots, little floating whorls of gold, and let out a shaky laugh. When Talan drew me into his arms after that, I ·cried against his chest.

"It's a release," I explained. It was important that he knew my tears were not a sign of pain or distress but rather staggering, overwhelming pleasure. "It's just that I've never felt it like this before, never so completely. I'm...I feel..." My ability to form words disappeared. I pressed my face to Talan's neck and kissed him, weary and happy.

"I understand," he said quietly. "At least I think I do. I feel much the same. I..." He paused. His arms tightened around me. "There is still much you don't know about my life before I came to Ivyhill. How lonely it's been, how desolate. I've told you some of it, but not all, and when I do, you'll understand how astonishing this is to me—the gift of being with you." He drew in a shuddering breath. "A precious thing, wholly undeserved."

I lay quietly in the nest of his arms. My eyelids were growing heavy; I would sleep again, and when next I woke it would be dawn, and I would kiss Talan in the golden wash of morning sunlight. I smiled tiredly at the thought.

"What a pair we are," I said. "You think yourself unworthy of my love, and I look in the mirror and see an exhausting, broken creature who shouldn't be touched. We're both fools, I suppose, and therefore extremely well matched."

Talan laughed into my hair. The sound was strangely sad.

"Perhaps we can help each other learn to abandon such thoughts and together achieve true wisdom."

"Mmm, perhaps," I agreed, draping my leg over his and scooting closer to him. "But it will take immense amounts of study, I think, to accomplish such a thing."

He laughed again, this time a soft burst of genuine delight. "Oh, to be sure. Innumerable hours of practice, creative experimentation…"

I grinned as his hands slid down my back. He cupped my bottom and pulled me close to him, and as exhausted as I was, I thrilled to feel him hard against my stomach.

"Do you never tire?" I said, grinning. I couldn't resist circling my hips against him. "There's something called sleep, you know, during which one rests and *doesn't* have sex. A shocking idea to you, perhaps."

"Just once more?" he whispered with a playful little pout. "I'm curious if I can make you come yet again."

I let out a contented moan and stretched my body against him. The movement brought my breasts closer to his mouth, and he lowered his head to them at once.

"You are insatiable," I said, giggling, but then he took my nipple lightly between his teeth and flicked his tongue against it, and my laughter broke off into a sharp, wanton cry.

"Say yes, Gemma," he murmured against my breasts, one hand cradling my head and the other drawing slow circles between my legs. "Do you want me, or shall I stop?"

I clutched his shoulders. I was already wet for him all over again, my legs shaking with anticipation. Sleep would come later, or perhaps never. In that moment I didn't care.

"Don't stop," I whispered.

"Tell me when," he said, his voice soft, strained. He pressed

just slightly inside me, and I cried out, lit up with wanting him—
to be filled by him, to feel the strength of him driving inside me,
claiming me as his own.

"*Yes*, gods, yes, please, *now*, Talan," I gasped out, desperate,
and then he entered me with one smooth thrust and kissed me. I
slid my fingers into his hair, returned his kisses hungrily, and we
said nothing more.

◆

It couldn't have been long after that when I awoke again; the room
was full of the same gentle shadows. Dawn had not yet come.

Talan slept behind me, my back to his front, one of his arms
draped over me—a warm weight, heavy with sleep. He snored
ever so slightly, little puffs of air against my neck. Otherwise
everything was quiet, and yet my skin prickled with a warning
I didn't at first understand. Without moving, I glanced out the
window nearest the bed and saw that the rain had stopped and
a thick fog had taken its place. For a long moment nothing happened; my eyes began to fall shut as I watched the window. I
dismissed the strange prickle of alarm as the lingering remnant of
a dream.

Then I saw it—quick and dark, a darting movement through
the fog like a fish through water.

Immediately I was fully awake, my stomach flooding with a
sick rush of dread. I knew for certain that it was the Man with
the Three-Eyed Crown come to exact his revenge. But then more
quick darting shadows cut through the fog, at least half a dozen
of them, their paths swift and jagged, fox-like. They raced for the
cottage with such speed that before I'd managed to break free of
my shock and wake Talan, the shadows had come near enough for
me to understand that they were neither shadows nor the demon,

but rather women—a whole pack of them slinking fast across the ground like spiders, their bellies low, their naked limbs knobby and scrabbling.

I knew them at once for what they were, what they had to be: the monstrous women both the Warden and Mara had said were roaming the Mistlands, attacking settlements and abducting civilians.

And now they were here in Gallinor's heartlands, far from the Mist, and they were heading straight for us.

My sudden blinding fear must have reached Talan even as he slept. Immediately he was awake and out of bed. He glanced out the window at the crawling women closing in on us, and if he was afraid, I couldn't see it. His face was hard, furious. He strode across the room to his discarded coat and pulled a fine pearl-handled revolver out of one pocket. He grabbed an iron poker from the hearth, and it should have been absurd, him standing there naked and sleep-mussed with weapons in hand, but instead he looked fearsome, primal, like some ancient creature who knew only that he must protect his mate. I had never seen him look so ferocious. He had always seemed strong, yes, and capable, but never like a warrior. Clearly that perception had been wrong. He moved with fluid grace, his expression murderous.

"Hide, Gemma, *now*," he said sharply over his shoulder, "and when you hear me shout 'wildcat,' run for the house and don't look back. Tell Illaria to bolt all the doors and windows, and gather weapons and anyone who can fight."

Then he strode out the cottage's front door and slammed it shut behind him.

I scrambled out of bed, clumsy with panic, and hurried toward the little closet in the bathing room, which was full of stacked linens and a selection of garments appropriate for the season. If I had to run for my life, I'd prefer not to do so without a stitch of clothing on. I grabbed a light linen shift from its hanger and tugged it on with shaking fingers. It seemed that Talan knew who those women were, or *what* they were, and that brought me a small flare of hope even as horrible sounds from outside met my ears: shots from the revolver, and then hard, bone-crunching crashes. The fireplace poker, I hoped, right on the heads of those awful women. Talan roared random words as he fought—*elder*, *apple*, *stallion*—which baffled me until I realized that, buried in the stream of words, *wildcat* would be disguised, meaningless to all but me.

I crouched on the floor, preparing myself to run, but then a silence fell, abrupt and terrifying. Talan stopped shouting; the gunshots ceased.

The cottage's front door creaked open, interrupting my frantic prayer. I held my breath and listened for footsteps but heard none. The stillness in the air was heavy, a presence all on its own. Something was in the house with me. I put my hand over my mouth, told myself not to scream. Suddenly the closet door trembled; something was on the other side, sniffing like a hound. I heard the soft slide of a foot against the tiled floor.

A beat of silence, horrible and portentous, and then the door flew open, revealing not Talan but a woman—tall and willowy, skin alarmingly pale and cracked all over, huge black eyes and a mouth stained purple and fingernails dark with rot. Her long hair was a tangled mass of weeds, brambles, and matted brown locks, and a dozen ropy scars lined with bright wildflowers marked the skin I could see, as if old wounds had been stitched shut not with thread but with stems and roots that had now sprouted new life. She wore a garment I did not understand—I couldn't even be sure it *was* a garment and not simply an outgrowth of her body—a covering of tree bark and netting and animal hides, all sewn together into sleeves and trousers and a tunic that hugged the reedy lines of her body like a second skin. She held a long black staff, and an array of knives hung from a leather belt at her hips.

With a sickening lurch in my gut, I saw that one of the knives gleamed with blood.

She caught me staring and cocked her head, birdlike, looking vaguely irritated. "You are not what I expected," she remarked, her voice incongruously smooth and rich, and then she grabbed my arm and yanked me out into the bathing room.

I went wild, screaming and clawing at her, but her grip was iron, her long strides unfaltering. She dragged me through the cottage and out into the foggy morning, where three other women waited, all of them similar in appearance to my captor. I searched the trees for Talan, shouted for him, but I couldn't find him. I searched within myself for whatever thing I'd done to banish the demon from the ballroom at Ivyhill; I would find that power, turn these women to dust, and wear their ash on my skin for the rest of my days.

But fear rendered me useless, my thoughts a scattered mess. Where was Talan? One of the women wiped blood from her lips, her skin gray and rough as the trunk of a tree. A pit of despair opened inside me. They'd killed him; they'd *eaten* him.

I thrashed and screamed, the woman who held me hissing at me to be quiet, but I wouldn't, I *couldn't*. I would scream my throat bloody and wake up everyone in the house, which was partially obscured in the fog and so far away that there might as well have been an ocean keeping me from it.

The woman with the bloody mouth swore in a language unfamiliar to me and marched over wearing a mean grin. She slapped me hard across the face; the explosion of pain blinded me, shocked me silent.

"Your man killed two of us," she said, her voice much harsher than the other woman's. "Rennora will not be happy."

Then she ripped a thorny flower from her shoulder, the petals an ominous bright red, and stabbed my neck with it. I choked out a scream that went nowhere, my body flooding with a sharp tingling sensation as if I were going numb, and the last thing I saw before I faded was the cottage door, standing ajar and splattered with blood. I tried to say Talan's name, but my mouth was useless, my voice gone. The woman who'd found me in the closet heaved me over her shoulder. Darkness crept across my vision: death, I thought, and I had no choice but to let it come.

Dull booms of pain brought me back to life.

I was not dead; I was alive, and every inch of my body throbbed as if I'd been punched all over. When I tried to sit up, a knife of pain pierced the aching place behind my eyes, and my arms buckled under my weight. My head hit the ground, and I lay there, panting a little, the grit of dirt in my mouth, and tried to force my sluggish thoughts into order.

I was in a dark wood of whispering pines. It was much cooler here than it had been at the Farrow estate. With a sinking feeling, I realized that I was now very far away from home.

My mouth tasted vile, as if I'd not cleaned my teeth in days. I blinked a few times, trying to clear the fuzz from my eyes, and realized I was not alone; the strange women who'd attacked the cottage were all around me. I counted at least twelve as I lay there stricken with fear. Some were pale like the one who'd found me in the closet; others had skin in shades of gray and brown, and some were even tinged with a sickly green, but all their colors were faded, muted, like dried flowers. Echoes of things that had once been alive. They were all hard at work—one was skinning a rabbit, one cleaned a set of knives, another chopped wood. Lopsided tents made of animal hide stood among the trees, and as I stared at them, I realized they had all been constructed beside a great wall of rock and moss and scrubby brush. I looked up and up until my sore neck protested and discovered that the great wall was in fact part of a towering mountain, the peak of which I could not see. The sky was dark, pricked with bright stars.

A sudden rush of air to my right, crisp and biting, prompted me to lift my head and find the source. When I did, my body ignited with fear; I shrieked, choking on my own breath, and scrambled back from the edge of a cliff, beyond which was a great drop into darkness.

Senseless, my palms clammy with sweat, I crawled backward until I hit something solid. I looked up and saw a woman standing over me with a long staff in one hand. Her eyes were black pools and her skin a scaly brown, faded and sickly, scattered with jagged lines of blooms and woven reeds. She wore her tangled black hair in a thick plait and had on a plain brown dress that hung loosely over a bony frame. The stench of her was terrible—musky and sour, fecal, and beneath that a note of sickly sweetness that reminded me of overripe fruit.

I gagged and jerked back from her, which made her bark with laughter, and as I looked around at the trees, I realized all the others had stopped to watch us—some grinning, some laughing, some simply watching with intense curiosity.

"I am Rennora," the woman said, bending down to look at me. "And you are Imogen."

"Where's Talan?" I said, my voice shredded and my throat aching.

"He ran away," Rennora replied, her voice rich with age and absent of any kindness. "He killed two of us, and the rest of us frightened him off. He ran without looking back, as a child would. Your choice of mates is poor. A pity that you will not have the chance to try again."

"You're lying. He wouldn't leave me."

"And yet he did."

"He went to find help, then."

"And he did a fine job of it, I would say."

A ripple of laughter moved through the trees. The horror of what was happening settled in my bones, leaving me feeling sick and fevered. A little flicker of movement drew my attention to Rennora's throat, where a clump of tiny yellow flowers had been woven into the puckered, faded skin of a bulbous old scar. A small gray spider crawled among them.

Rennora's smile was horrible, dispassionate. She pointed at the scar; the rotten black end of her finger sank into the flowers.

"They keep me fresh," she said. "Soon you will have them too, same as me. Fine ornaments for that shiny skin of yours."

At the thought of these women sewing flowers into my skin for a purpose I could not imagine, my growing terror split open, and my arms buckled under me once more. I couldn't help but think of the grotesque story my father had told—my infant self choking on a throat full of flowers. Was I in fact one of these women? Would they usher me through some vile rite of transfiguration into my true form?

"Please let me go," I whispered, reduced to begging in the dirt. "My father will pay whatever you ask. You'll want for nothing ever again."

"That offer comes many years too late to be of use to me," said Rennora. I'd dribbled spit onto her foot as I wept, and when she wiped her toes clean against the ground, she shed dry patches of cracked brown flesh like molting feathers. "Phaidra!"

A pale woman hurried out of the trees—the same one who had pulled me from the closet. Instead of her strange armor of bark and hide, she now wore a simple gray dress much like Rennora's, though hers bore a line of crude embroidered flowers near the collar.

"Yes, Mother?" Phaidra said with a clipped bow.

"Feed Imogen. Give her shoes. Build her strength. Watch her like a hawk. I hope I will not regret trusting you with this."

Phaidra kept her head low. "I will not disappoint you, Mother."

Rennora nodded briskly. "Ensure she is ready when they come."

"When who comes?" I demanded. I couldn't quite steady my voice. "What do you want with me?"

Rennora did not answer. Instead her irritated gaze slid down my body, assessing me. Her brow creased slightly as if something she saw confused her, and then she turned on her heel and stalked away.

The woman called Phaidra lifted me roughly to my feet. Reminded of her easy strength, I abandoned all my half-formed thoughts of escape. Her grip was hard on my arm; I would not be able to fight her, not unless I could somehow summon the strength I'd found in the ballroom, and to do that I would need to think, and in order to think I needed to do something, *anything*, to quiet my fear.

As Phaidra led me through the trees, I focused on my breathing, on the clumsy fall of my bare feet on the rocky ground. I was Lady Imogen Ashbourne. I was alive, and I had spent my whole life charming strangers. Why should these beastly mountain women be any different?

I swallowed a burst of frightened laughter as Phaidra led me to a patch of flat grass in front of one of the tents. I watched her as she started a fire and prepared a stew of roots and potatoes and bloody chunks of meat that I avoided looking at too closely. She was deft with her knife; she fetched mismatched jars of herbs and spices from inside the tent and began sprinkling pinches of things into the pot. Every now and then, she dipped one gnarled finger into the brew and licked it before returning to the jars for more seasoning.

I watched her, fascinated despite myself, and after pulling on the soft leather boots she'd given me, I decided to attempt a conversation.

"Rennora is your mother?" I asked.

Phaidra glanced over at me, the slide of her black eyes like a knife. "She was the first," she answered simply.

"She was the first of all of you who live here?"

Phaidra didn't answer. She dropped a chunk of meat into the steaming pot.

I tried again. "Who are you exactly? I've never seen women like you before."

"We are the Vilia," she replied flatly, "and soon you will know everything there is to know about us, so sit and be silent now."

I hesitated for only a moment. "The flowers in your skin are beautiful," I said, letting a note of awe creep into my voice. "What do they mean?"

She whipped her head around to glare at me. "Do you know what it means to be silent?"

My mouth went dry with fear. I nodded mutely.

"Then be silent or I will sew your lips shut."

That exchange drained me of what meager courage I'd scraped together. I cowered in the dirt as Phaidra finished cooking our meal, then meekly accepted the bowl she gave me. She started to eat at once, a fine silver spoon clutched in her hand like a hammer, and it was then that I realized the bowls we ate out of were glazed porcelain painted with a delicate pattern of pink and blue flowers.

They felt heavy, well made. My own spoon was silver too, with an elaborate scrolled handle.

Curious at the incongruity of seeing finery in such a place, I carefully tasted a spoonful, mindful of my tortured stomach and doubtful about the stew's contents, but I was shocked to discover it was delicious—hearty and aromatic, the warm spice of it an unexpected comfort. I ate for a few moments in silence, then looked up and froze. Phaidra had stopped eating to stare, and before she could hide it from me, I saw on her face an expression of naked longing—not for me, but for something I couldn't name, something beyond me, more than me. She was staring not at my face but at my hand, with which I held the silver spoon.

A beat of taut silence, and then her eyes flew up to meet mine. Her expression flattened, becoming guarded and unfriendly once more. She huddled over her meal, still squatting as if tending the fire, and scooped noisy spoonfuls of stew into her mouth with ferocious energy.

I resumed eating, my heart pounding so hard I could barely swallow. After a few tense moments, I sensed Phaidra looking up at me again, considering me. I watched sidelong as she awkwardly folded herself onto the ground to sit with her legs crossed, as I did. She fumbled with the spoon until, instead of clutching it like a bludgeon, she held it delicately, as if she sat at a table. After that she ate more quietly, her movements deliberate and careful, and the incredible thought occurred to me that Phaidra was imitating me, making an attempt at gentility.

I didn't know what that meant, but I thought of it later as I tried to sleep, Phaidra a watchful sentry just outside the tent. The ground was hard and cold, and my only protection from the night's chill was a stinking blanket sewn of animal pelts, but remembering Phaidra's curious, childlike expression brought me a strange sort of comfort and distracted me from the wretched hope that Talan *had* in fact run away, fear driving him to abandon me. That at least would mean he was still alive.

CHAPTER 28

Under Phaidra's rudimentary care, I spent both my waking and sleeping hours at her little tent, bound by no ropes or chains but simply by the hard blackness of her watchful glare.

My body ached from sleeping on the ground and from the nearness of magic. Phaidra didn't appear to use any in her daily tasks, but she was clearly magic-touched; the air changed when she moved through it, as if stirred awake by her presence. I grew accustomed to the ripples of pain that buffeted me whenever she did so much as shift her weight. The pain was different from anything I'd experienced before—deeper, sharper, and it left a sour taste on my tongue, like I'd bitten down on something metallic—which made me think that the magic causing the pain was different too.

Phaidra was maddeningly silent; I decided I would be as well, too frightened and defeated to voice any of the questions whirling through my mind. She often whittled by the fire, carving wooden creatures out of logs—foxes, swallows, wolves. Her blade was deft, her fingers quick. The little creatures charmed me against my will. They were exquisitely detailed, truly fine.

I watched Phaidra work while pretending to sleep; there was something mesmerizing about the flash of her knife.

—◆—

On the second night of my strange, quiet captivity, when our fire had burned down to embers and Phaidra's eyelids had at last drooped shut, I waited, shivering under my stinking blanket, and counted to five hundred. Convinced that she was asleep, I tried to run.

I slid out from under the blanket, my heart racing so wildly I was sure it would give me away, and bolted. I tore through the trees with no sense of where I would go or how far I was from any sort of civilized country. The mountain loomed, and beyond it was a vast land of darkness. The faint line of the horizon illuminated by the half-moon was meaningless to me. I saw no cities, no roads, only forested mountains with naked gray peaks.

I jumped over a fallen tree coated with bright green moss and tumbled through a clutch of wet ferns, and then Phaidra caught me. I had been running for perhaps ten seconds, if that. She was fast, agile, nearly silent. She darted past me and came back around to tackle me to the ground. She straddled me, pinned me flat, and stared down at me dispassionately while I struggled and then subsided, crying with frustration more than anything. I'd thought myself so clever to run, and where had it gotten me?

Exhausted and humiliated, I worked hard to regain my composure as Phaidra led me back to the hut. She shoved me down onto the ground and snapped, "Running will only tire you. You can try every day until they come, and every time I will catch you. So sleep and do not be a fool."

"Who are *they*?" I asked, just as I had Rennora. "Who's coming?"

Phaidra did not answer. She stoked the fire and said nothing for a long while. I lay down in the dirt, pulled my stinking blanket of pelts up to my nose, and tried to sleep.

Just as my eyes grew heavy, Phaidra quietly began to speak. "We Vilia are not free women," she said, "nor are we alive. We once were, and during that life, great wrongs were done to us."

Fully awake now, I watched her and listened. She worked a piece of wood with her knife as she spoke.

"Some of us were killed by our lovers," she said, "or betrayed, tricked into our deaths. At the moment our last breaths left us, at the place between this world and the next, the Brethaeus found us. They gave us a choice: die, or live again as revenants and seek revenge against those who had hurt us. They did not tell us our new lives would be only half made or that we would be bound to them forever, so we agreed."

She fell silent. I could only bear the awful quiet for so long.

"Who are the Brethaeus?" I whispered.

"Necromancers," she replied. "An ancient family of them. Many Vilia serve them. We are far from the only ones."

A horrible cold fell over me. "Necromancers. Masters of the dead."

She glanced my way. "So you are not as ignorant as you look. What else do you know about them?"

"Not much."

Her mouth thinned. "Well, soon you will know all there is to know. They are coming, and when they do, we will give you to them."

My mouth went dry. I sat up quickly. "What? Why?"

"Because Rennora says we must, and she is right to," Phaidra replied. "We bring them people. We keep them fed. The interesting, the grotesque, the strong, the pathetic. Their appetites vary. Some souls they consume. Some they resurrect and give back to us to strengthen our numbers."

Her eyes flickered up to mine and then back to her work. "I do not know what they will do with you. If they decide to consume you, perhaps you will satisfy their appetites for a short time. If they choose instead to make you a Vilia, you will be like us, a servant to the masters of the dead, and we will be stronger with another to help us hunt and feed them. It is an endless hunt. That is the price we paid to be brought back from death and born again: they are our masters, and their hunger for souls can never truly be sated." Her expression darkened as the fire crackled on. "We were fools. No revenge is worth what we have become."

The story she told was unthinkable. My mind screamed at me to flee, no matter how futile that flight would be, but I stayed right where I was, rooted by hopeless terror.

"Why did you capture *me*?" I asked. I pressed my fingers into the dirt, searching in vain for strength. "I've heard of your people. You've been abducting civilians in the Mistlands, and yet now you're here. You came all this way for me?"

Phaidra fixed her heartless black eyes on me. "We felt it the night you fought the demon. It was a shock to the earth and was felt for miles and miles, not only by the Vilia. You are a strange thing, and powerful, though you do not look it. It is intriguing, and it will please the Brethaeus. That is what we do. We please the Brethaeus."

My thoughts spun wildly with panic. I felt as if I'd stepped outside myself, outside the world I knew, and was hanging on to my sanity by a mere thread.

"How is it possible for the Brethaeus to come here?" I asked frantically. "They're necromancers. They're Olden. The Mist—"

"The Middlemist is a barrier, and no barrier remains without holes forever." Phaidra looked at me keenly. "I think you know that. I think your sister the Rose knows it too."

I quickly shook away thoughts of Mara. They were too dear, too dangerous. They would unravel me, and I was already finding it difficult to breathe.

"You don't have to do this," I whispered. "My family is extraordinarily powerful, favored by the high queen. If you help me escape—"

"There is no escape from this," Phaidra said. Her voice was brusque, her expression stony. "Sleep. If you are weak and ill when they come, we will all suffer for it, you most of all. You are meant to impress them. If you fall short, Rennora will gut you and ensure that you feel every dig of her knife."

She turned away from me, making it clear that our conversation had ended. I wept quietly, miserable, holding my aching body and trying not to imagine what it would feel like to be eaten. I cried until I felt too sick and tired for it and then lay shivering in the dirt. As I finally succumbed to my exhaustion, I thought I saw Phaidra glance over at me uncomfortably, as if she were ashamed of her part in my impending doom—but I immediately disabused myself of that fanciful notion. I was desperate for any kind of comfort, that was all.

I closed my burning eyes and listened to the fire. It was stupid of me to do it, but I nevertheless imagined I was back in Illaria's cottage, safe in bed and warm in Talan's arms. His skin gliding against mine, his lips in my hair, the scent of him—the piney spice of his cologne, the salty tang of his sweat. His voice murmuring my name. Each memory was a torment, but I held them close all the same. I prayed to Zelphenia that Talan would search for me, that he wouldn't rest until he'd found me, that he was nearing our camp even now. I fell into an uneasy sleep.

—◆—

Another week passed, and then another. The forest tempted me, but I never again tried to run. There seemed to be no point. I slept, I plodded along listlessly at Phaidra's heels as she saw to her daily tasks, I slept again.

When she went to the clearing where I'd first awoken, which seemed to be her people's central gathering place, I accompanied her. She refreshed her food stores, traded for supplies, picked over heaps of what must have been stolen goods—jewelry, fine linens with lace trim, heavy woolen coats, flatware and cutlery. Crude wooden cages hidden in the trees housed huddled figures: two women, three men, an adolescent child, all of them dead-eyed and dressed in tattered clothes.

I swallowed my revulsion as Phaidra piled my arms with her loot. "Who are they?" I asked quietly.

"Food," she replied.

"For you, or for the Brethaeus?"

She glared at me. "Vilia do not eat people. Have you lost your head?"

This struck me as ludicrously funny. I barely stifled a burst of hysterical laughter. *Had* I lost my head? I hoped so. That would mean I was simply lost in a horrific dream.

"Why are they caged while I walk free?" I managed to ask.

"They are fodder. You are something else. And you are hardly free."

I couldn't very well argue with that. I lowered my eyes to the ground and shrank away from her as she spoke with the other Vilia. All together I counted twenty-five. Their language was a strange blend of the common tongue and something else, perhaps two other languages, neither of which I recognized. Familiar words rose to the top of their conversations like bubbles in rushing water and then popped and were gone. I was keenly aware of the other Vilia watching me as we moved through the trees, their black eyes inscrutable. It was a relief to return to the safety of Phaidra's tent.

My sleep was fitful. I flickered in and out of dreams, sometimes jolted awake by the fear that Phaidra would leave me in the night, that the other Vilia would kill her for talking too candidly with me and take me to my own cage. Seeing her sitting across the fire, surly and watchful, flooded me with relief. I scooted closer to her each night until I started falling asleep beside her, my head mere inches from her bony knee and its pale cap of cracked skin. I pretended her body was Talan's, or Farrin's, or Mara's. I pretended she was Father, that I lay at his knee on the hearthrug and had fallen asleep to the sound of him reading some awful dry book about military strategy or intercontinental relations, a long-gone mainstay of my childhood. He had always tried unsuccessfully to tempt me away from my novels.

I wondered if he was looking for me, or if he was glad that I had disappeared, relieved he would never again have to look me in the eye.

When Phaidra bathed in the nearby stream—a grotesque sight, what with her gnarled, rotten skin, and clearly painful for her, since she gritted her teeth through the whole ordeal—I bathed as well. More than once, I caught her staring longingly at my naked body, but there was nothing predatory about it, and I was strangely not afraid. She seemed more fascinated than anything, and wistful.

After we bathed together for the third time, she snatched away my filthy nightgown and gave me a new dress of faded pink linen, plain but clean. It was far too big—I had to wrap the sash twice around my middle—and I was loath to put it on, this relic of some robbed girl, most likely either dead or a revenant now herself. But I couldn't very well remain naked, and Phaidra had already begun tearing my nightgown into strips, perhaps for cleaning or treating wounds. I refused to watch her do it; that garment was all that remained of the world I'd been taken from.

I waited until she'd finished and then looked right at her and said, "Thank you for the dress," and I meant it too. After the bath and the gift of clean clothing, I felt renewed, even as a resigned numbness fell over me. This was my new life, but at least I was no longer covered in filth.

Phaidra blinked at me, clearly caught off guard. For an instant her expression softened, and I thought she would say something kind in return. But then she grunted and looked away and began cooking our supper. She did not look at me again that night. I slept the sleep of the dead, and part of me hoped I wouldn't wake up.

One day, Phaidra brought me with her when she ventured into the woods to hunt and forage.

We had to roam far from the tent in order to find any prey—it seemed no animals dared come near the Vilia's territory—and by the time Phaidra actually started hunting, spear in hand and a quiver of arrows hanging from her back, I was exhausted, faint, and prone to tripping over the rocky terrain. I scrambled to keep up with her, crashing clumsily through the trees, which lost us our quarry at least half a dozen times before Phaidra finally threw up her hands and rounded on me.

"Are you a newborn colt?" she snapped. "Or some tottering child? Do you not understand how to use your legs?"

"I'm sorry," I whispered, too tired to feel ashamed. "I can sit here and wait for you. I won't run away, I promise."

Phaidra watched me for a moment, and when I looked up, her expression had gentled, and she didn't try to hide it.

"Here," she said, quieter now. "Look. Watch me."

She demonstrated with a new patience how she moved through the forest—what kinds of plants to avoid, because they housed a certain kind of beetle or bird that would erupt noisily when the plant was disturbed, or because the fronds would leave an acrid scent on your body that would scare animals away; where to step, *how* to step, how to use the wind as an ally, how to read the signs of the forest.

It was too much information for me to hold all at once, and I felt too shy to ask questions, but I listened hard, and the mere fact that Phaidra was trying to teach me imbued me with a certain amount of determination. She slowed her pace, and I shadowed her with dogged, awkward ferocity. We caught two rabbits and a single quail—a pathetic reward for our efforts, I thought, until I saw Phaidra beaming at me. Despite my determination not to care, the sight of her grotesque smiling face filled me with pride.

By the time we made the long trek back to the village to contribute our catch, and then to Phaidra's tent to eat and sleep, I felt delirious with exhaustion, my vision shimmering, every muscle aching. At least the pain was from activity more than magic and therefore felt strange and pure, a bizarre treat. I devoured the meal Phaidra prepared for me—roasted rabbit, a salad of sour black berries and tough brown roots and bitter greens—and then curled up in the dirt beside her.

"You are strong, Imogen," she said quietly, as my heavy eyelids drifted shut, "and every day you become stronger. Do not fear it. It could save you." She paused. "It could change everything."

A curious thing to say, and more than a little frightening, but my exhaustion was immense, insistent. I did not fight it.

Three nights later, I burst out of a nightmare I didn't remember, tears in my eyes and my whole body drenched with sweat.

Phaidra was there, lying beside me in the dirt, her eyes grave. She stroked my hair. The firelit shadows deepened her cracked skin into canyons, painted the tiny pink flowers sewn into her shoulder and throat a flickering orange.

"You dreamed of your love," she said quietly. "The man we fought. You said his name. You were in pain. We do not wake each other from dreams, good or bad. If they are not allowed to complete themselves, they live on inside us and fester."

"Talan," I whispered, remembering. "We were in bed. We were..." I trailed off, bashful. It felt strange to speak of such things around my undead captor.

"You were taking him as your mate," Phaidra guessed.

I nodded. "And then something changed, something went wrong. He was suddenly still, so heavy on top of me that I couldn't breathe. I was drenched, and I looked up and saw his eyes were frozen, open wide. He was dead. His blood was all over me."

Phaidra nodded. "You grieve his absence. Your dreams do too."

For a moment I was gripped by such pain that I couldn't speak. My stomach was tight with it, my chest aching. I curled in on myself and prayed to Caiathos, god of the earth, that the ground would open up and swallow me. Talan was dead, I was alone, and necromancers were coming for me. After they were through with me, would they find they had a taste for Ashbournes and go to Ivyhill? Was this the Basks' final plot, designed to ruin my family once and for all?

I could imagine it vividly: Alastrina and Ryder in the lair of the

Man with the Three-Eyed Crown along with their parents, Lord Alaster and Lady Enid. I'd never met them; they were reclusive and seemed content to let their children fight their war for them. They looked like their progeny, I assumed, all of them dark-haired and pale with fierce blue eyes, all of them beautiful, horrible. In this imagined scenario, they were all laughing, and the demon was too, the five of them huddling together in conspiracy like wolves tearing at a kill. In their midst lay Talan's corpse, which they would no doubt use for some foul purpose. Perhaps the demon would feast on him, digesting him slowly over many years.

My spiraling thoughts plunged into darkness; my skin crawled with the familiar itch of panic. I wrenched myself away from Phaidra and began clawing at my skin, determined to scratch out the images my mind refused to let go. I felt so sick I could hardly speak, but I managed it, turning frantically to Phaidra.

"Kill me," I whispered to her. "Please, Phaidra. You've shown me kindness, and I don't think you had to do that or were even supposed to. I don't think you hate me. You might even be fond of me. Please, then, do this last thing for me."

She sat up and stared at me, clearly baffled. "You want me to kill you."

"I do."

"I cannot do that. Rennora would kill me if I did. Or the Brethaeus would. They've been promised a great treasure."

"All right, then. We'll have to make it look like I did it myself so you won't be blamed. Or maybe I *can* do it myself, I just... my body won't want to die, so I'm not sure if I'll be able to finish it. Is there a poison you can feed me, something it's conceivable I could have foraged on my own? I think a poison would be less frightening than—"

Phaidra slapped me, shocking me into silence.

"Stop this," she said fiercely. "You are not going to die, not by your hand and not by my own. How dare you wish for death in my presence? How could you—" She stopped herself, visibly struggling for restraint. When she spoke again, her anger was more measured. "Why do you act this way? Because your love is gone?"

Her voice dripped with scorn. I shook my head miserably.

"It's not only that," I whispered. "I'm *tired*, Phaidra. I'm tired of this, all of this." I gestured weakly at my body. My glass-dusted arm caught the firelight and glittered. And then I told Phaidra everything, the words spilling out of me in a quiet, desperate cascade—the pain I'd lived with for as long as I could remember; the panic that took over my thoughts and my body without warning; the horrible violence my parents had done to me; the horrible violence I had done to them, and to myself, when I was small and unwitting.

I told her of the plans Talan and I had concocted to degrade the Basks and seek out the demon that had pitted my family against them, what Talan and I had done to Madam Baines. Phaidra's eyes narrowed at that, but she listened with remarkable patience as I finished my story—the bargain I'd made with the demon, his attack on Farrin, my attack on *him*. Talan, Talan, Talan. How my pain faded when I was near him, even when he was not using his power to help me. How he saw strength in me that no one else ever had. How he loved me, and how I loved him, as I'd never loved anyone before.

When I finished, a silence fell, broken only by the crackling fire. After telling my story, the desire to be done with it all settled in my mind like the final leaf of autumn. I felt scraped clean, hollowed out, deadly tired. If Phaidra had in that moment held out a handful of poisonous berries, I would have eaten them all in one go.

"You are not going to die," she said slowly, her gaze distant. "Not by my hand, and not by your own. The Brethaeus will try, but..." A pause, and then she looked up at me fiercely. "I have not lied to you. You *are* strong, perhaps strong enough to fight them as we cannot do on our own."

It was such an unexpected thing for her to say that for a moment I simply stared at her. "You wish to *fight* the Brethaeus?"

Phaidra's mouth tightened into a thin line. She glanced around, then shook her head. "Tomorrow when we hunt, I will tell you everything."

CHAPTER 29

The next morning, I followed Phaidra through the forest until midday, when she finally stopped and allowed me to rest. The sun was hot on my neck, even high in the mountains as we were and with the pines all around us.

I sat on a fallen tree, wiped my sweating face with my sleeve, and took a long drink from Phaidra's waterskin. Phaidra abstained, somehow not thirsty at all. With her long staff tied to her back, she climbed nimbly atop a huge stump—twice as tall as she was, draped in thick moss, and surrounded by the serpentine mass of its own roots. Her hunting clothes were those she had worn when the Vilia attacked the cottage—a skintight garment of animal hide, coarse netting, and tree bark sewn together like plates of armor. She perched there on the edge of the stump's jagged top like some forest cat and surveyed the surrounding trees, perfectly still except for small cocks of her head.

Clothed as she was, with her mottled skin and her flowered scars, she looked a true creature of the forest. I half expected her to snatch right out of the air one of the small black birds that flitted by unawares—an image that reminded me of that horrible mad dash through the Middlemist, the bird I had chased, the persistent wriggling of my insides thereafter that had sent me stumbling into the washroom at the high queen's ball, convinced that something lived inside me, plotting and wicked. I supposed something *did* live inside me: the work of the artificer my parents had hired to remake me, his magic of years ago perhaps stirred by the power of the Mist. Maybe that was what I had felt that night at the Citadel—the smothering beast the artificer had created turning in its sleep.

What a world away—a *lifetime* away—all of that seemed. How strange it felt, and distant, as if I were reading the events of my life in a book toward which I was largely indifferent.

As I sat there musing, a prickling chill crept over me. At first I ignored it; what did I care if there was a chill? What did I care about anything?

But then the chill grew teeth, and my stomach roiled with sudden nausea. There was an immense magic nearby.

I turned to search my surroundings, following the feeling, but the wood was just a wood: ferns and trees and then more of the same. I had almost given up, convinced I was imagining things, when my vision caught on a dip in the forest floor—an unremarkable ravine padded with moss. But the air was different around it, close and dark. The woods were still and quiet; only pale sunlight managed to push through the thick green canopy. But this place, this ravine, had a different kind of stillness, not of emptiness but of waiting.

Curious, I rose and began walking toward it, even though each step sent a fresh jolt of pain shooting up my legs. By the time I reached the ravine, black spots dotted my vision. My ears had closed up, muffling the sound of my footsteps, and my throat tightened around every breath; the air pressed hard against me, as if it was full to bursting and would soon erupt and take me with it.

I knelt, breathing hard, and peered down the ravine's winding path toward the woods beyond, where the trees grew crooked and thicker than ever, a jet-black tangle soaking up every scrap of pale sunlight. I stared at that dark place, horrified by the sight of it even though it was only a shadowed thicket of trees. A vile taste built in my mouth; pain pulsed tightly in my temples. Something was there in those trees, something with magic strong enough to shatter me.

But the ravine was dry, its moss a cheerful bright green. It looked like an inviting path, and I very nearly crawled down into it. My arms and legs were no longer my own; magic gathered in my chest like a fist and pulled.

Then a hand grabbed my shoulder and yanked me back from the ravine.

I fell hard onto my back and lay there, stunned, as Phaidra and two other Vilia came into view, looking down at me.

One of the new Vilia was short and thin with matted gray hair worn in two sloppy knots. An alarming expanse of her green-tinged skin was covered in weeping sores and gangrenous black rot. Her expression was placid, her movements stilted. The other Vilia was tall, muscular, fearsome, her skin rough and gray like the bark of a tree. With a lurch of fear, I recognized her as one of the Vilia I'd seen at the cottage—the one who'd stabbed me with the poisonous flower.

"Phaidra?" I whispered. For all my fatalistic bluster the day before, I suddenly felt terribly afraid. "What is this?"

She ignored my question and instead gestured at the ravine and the dark trees beyond. "Do not ever go near this place again," she said. "Do not even look at it. Not the ravine, not the trees.

Hold your breath as you pass by. It is a terrible place. Something foul and Olden lives there. We have watched animals lured toward it, docile and unafraid, as if they are being led by a beloved voice. They do not return. We call it the Mouth, and it is a good place for secret meetings. None of the others will come here. They are too afraid. We can speak freely."

Phaidra dug around in one of her pockets and thrust something at me—a carved wooden hare on a thin leather cord.

"Here," she said, "wear this. A talisman. It will ground you in your own world and help you resist the Olden's call."

Stunned by the gift, I hesitated. "But that's yours. I don't want to take it from you."

"I have many." To prove it, she took several more from her pockets and showed me the one she wore under her tunic—a wolf with a fearsome stare. It was perfectly suited to her; I found myself strangely moved by the sight of its delicate paws.

I slipped the necklace over my head and immediately felt more at ease with the hare's slight weight against my sternum.

"If the talismans are meant to help you resist the Olden's call," I said, "shouldn't they help you break free of the Brethaeus?"

The taller Vilia, watching me with her arms crossed, gave me an appraising glance.

"They haven't yet," Phaidra replied, tucking the wolf away, "but maybe someday they will, if I make enough of them."

"Phaidra," the taller Vilia said, not unkindly, "insists on hoping for things."

Phaidra looked defiant. "Hoping hurts no one but my own self." Then she held out her hand to help me up.

The taller Vilia watched me stagger to my feet, clearly unimpressed. "That she was so easily lured by the Mouth does not inspire confidence, Phaidra. I thought she was supposed to be strong. A demon slayer. To my eyes she is merely a pretty rich girl with pretty glass skin."

"Not every kind of strength in this world looks like yours, Nesset," said the shorter Vilia, whose voice was kind but rough, as if it were having trouble holding itself together.

"Imogen, this is Nesset," said Phaidra, pointing to the taller Vilia, "and Lulath." She helped the shorter Vilia, who moved haltingly, sit on the tree I had abandoned. "They are my friends. I would trust them with my life," she said with a wry smile, which made Nesset bark with laughter.

"We must be mindful of the time," Lulath murmured, gazing absently at the sky. Her eyes were rheumy and gray. A huge boil rimmed with blackened skin had overtaken one corner of her mouth. "We cannot return home without food."

"Yes, of course." Phaidra turned to me, hands on her hips. "There is much to say, Imogen. Listen and listen well. I have told you that we felt your fight with the demon even from far away. You possess power we do not, and with that power you faced one of the strongest Olden beings and survived."

"The first demons were born of Zelphenia's tears," Lulath murmured. "Children of sorrow cursed to ache with the woe of their goddess."

The eerie lilt of her voice left me feeling deeply uneasy. I barely resisted glancing over my shoulder at the Mouth and its shadows.

Nesset placed a gentle hand on Lulath's shoulder and looked grimly at me. "Lulath enjoys rambling on and on about Olden lore. Just ignore her when she does that."

Lulath shook her head. "When I do that," she countered serenely, "you should listen to me more closely than ever. There is truth in the lore, truth that might save your life, or someone else's."

"It is not a common thing," Phaidra continued, "for a human to fight a being as powerful as a demon and win. Not even an Anointed human. We have waited a long time to find someone like you."

"It was like a storm up here in the Little Grays," Lulath said happily. "When you fought him, it shook the mountain as thunder does."

My heart sank as a map of Gallinor rose in my mind. I had known we were far away from Ivyhill, but I hadn't let myself believe the Vilia had taken me as far away as the Little Grays, a long range of mountains on the continent's western coast nearly one hundred miles from my home.

"Something inside you is strong enough to drive away a demon," Phaidra said, "and after what you told me last night, I believe even more that this is so. The things you did as a child were mighty indeed. They were wild and horrible. They were unique. Your parents knew that. You frightened them as your sisters did not."

"What things?" Nesset asked, suddenly eager. "What did she do? Did she kill anyone?"

Phaidra held up a hand, silencing her.

"But Father said the artificer they hired completely remade my insides," I said weakly, "burying my magic underneath gods know what. Whatever is there, whatever I was born with, it's long dead, warped, mutilated."

"Perhaps that was once true," Phaidra conceded, "but it seems, Imogen, that it is no longer. This power you carry still lives, never mind what the artificer did to it. It seems that something is waking it up. You could have grown weaker during your days of captivity, but in fact you have gotten stronger, and braver." She cocked her head, considering me. "How much stronger could you become, and your power with it?"

Suddenly I remembered my question from the previous night, and the reason for this secret conference became clear to me.

"You want me to fight the Brethaeus for you," I said quietly. "You want me to free you."

Phaidra came to me and held my arms in her rough hands. There was an eager light in her eyes that I'd never seen before.

"Nesset and Lulath and I no longer wish to serve the Brethaeus," she confirmed. "Others, too, think as we do, but Rennora has no wish to fight our masters. She is content with her life of servitude. She has done it for so many years that she remembers little else. We who long to fight tire of enslavement and would undo our choices if we could. But we cannot, so instead we wish to break free of the curse that binds us to the Brethaeus. And we want you to help us do it."

The conversation made me feel helpless and a little crazed. "Phaidra, not once in my life have I broken a curse or even read about doing so. I wouldn't know where to begin."

"We will help you. The answer no doubt lies in the power you hold."

"No doubt? Phaidra, I have many doubts, and so should you. When the demon attacked my sister, I acted without thinking, and I haven't been able to do it again since. And nothing about that night had anything to do with cursebreaking."

Phaidra's resolve was unshakable. "We will help you learn how to use your power with intention. That will be the first thing."

"And how exactly will you do that?"

"I have been watching you these past days, learning of your determination, what your mind and heart are made of. I have heard the story you told me. We will begin there."

I sat back down on the tree and held my head in my hands. "That is not a real answer. This thing you ask of me is half-formed at best."

"You see?" Nesset said sharply to Phaidra. "I told you this was folly."

I looked up at Nesset. "Do *you* know anything about cursebreaking?"

She shook her head, looking disgusted with all of us. "Only that this curse is a triad, crafted in three parts to give it great strength."

"I have seen it done many times," Phaidra said. "I watched them bind Nesset."

"And I watched them bind Phaidra," Lulath added fondly. "Such a wee thing she was then. Newly reborn."

"Phaidra," I said, struggling to sound reasonable though I felt anything but. "The Brethaeus brought you back from death and gave you life. If you tried to break free of them, couldn't they snuff you out again just as easily, this time for good?"

Nesset let out a burst of hard laughter. "There is nothing *easy* about life and death."

"We could not *try* to break free of them," Phaidra said. "We would have to succeed."

"And then?" I persisted. "Once you're free of them, how will you escape their wrath? Surely they would pursue you, or bind you again before you could properly get away? Would you ever truly be safe anywhere? And without the curse holding you together, would you be able to keep living at all?"

"She asks good questions," Nesset muttered. "Questions I have asked myself."

Phaidra's patience snapped. She threw such a glare at Nesset that even Lulath looked startled.

"I would rather die a free woman," she snapped, "or know freedom for even a moment before losing it again, than live another day as I do now. Whatever we do is worth the risk. We decided this."

Abashed, Nesset said nothing.

Then Phaidra turned to me. "And you, Imogen," she said firmly. "If you do not help us, if you do not try to strengthen your power and use it against the Brethaeus, then the day they come will mark the end of your life. You will either be killed, your soul consumed, or you will become one of us. Not a woman, not dead, but a revenant. Trapped forever in an in-between life. Is that what you wish to happen?"

I looked at her in silence for a moment, searching her strange, gnarled, flower-woven face. A bird dipped through the trees overhead, casting its tiny shadow over us.

"No," I said quietly. "It isn't what I want."

"What do you want?" Lulath asked, looking at me pleasantly. A sickly brown liquid dripped out of her mouth and down her chin.

I wasn't certain how to answer her and said so.

Lulath's smile was one of sheer delight. "I do not know either, not past the moment we find our freedom. What fun, that we will learn together."

I was still wary; this *plan* hardly deserved the word. But the alternative was surrender, sitting and waiting to die, or waiting for something close enough to death, and I suddenly found that I wanted neither of these things.

I wanted to live.

The feeling was tenuous, fragile. I held on to it for a moment before I dared to move, then rose from my seat and held out my hand to Phaidra. "Do Vilia shake hands?"

Phaidra smiled. "We were not sculpted from nothing, Imogen. We were once women just as you are."

Then she wrapped her hand around mine and shook it once, firmly, and with that, the deal was done. A chill of foreboding shook me, but I blamed the Mouth, looming dark and strange at the end of the ravine. I refused to look back at it, though I desperately wanted to; I placed my hand over the little carved hare under my dress and followed Phaidra through the trees, leaving the Mouth to its shadows.

◆◇◆

Whatever my power was, wherever it lived inside me, the Vilia and I soon discovered that it did not want to wake up.

Phaidra and I began working quietly at her tent, my head bent over a pile of knives and rags. We hardly spoke. She stood glaring down at me with her hands on her hips and a fearsome scowl on her face. If Rennora or any of the other Vilia tramped through the forest to visit us, they would see only Phaidra putting her captive to work with endless chores.

"Try this one next," she muttered, stalking around me with visible impatience. I hoped it was all for show, part of our act, but I suspected it wasn't, that she was flummoxed by my lack of progress.

"*Firintala foratalem talembora talabirin,*" Phaidra whispered.

I listened hard and focused on the nearby fern we'd chosen for experimentation. The flowers in my throat as a child, the tree I'd grown and trapped myself in—Phaidra pointed to these as evidence that I had inherited from my mother some strain of elemental magic.

"*Firintala foratalem,*" I repeated, the words strange and clumsy on my tongue, "*talembora talabirin.*"

It was a small spell, one of many that Phaidra, Lulath, and Nesset had collected in the long years since their rebirth. They couldn't perform such spells themselves; whatever magic they may have possessed in their first true lives had been lost upon their deaths, as had their memories of it. They knew only what they had collected during years of half-alive thievery and soul-hunting for the Brethaeus, and this collection was considerable. Gareth would have been beside himself if he'd gotten the chance to talk to them: three actual revenants with a vast library of ill-gotten magical knowledge.

My throat clenched up to think of him, of home and Una, and Farrin watching over me as I slept. The chair in my bedroom where Jessyl had always sat. Talan's arms around me in that little cottage, his ardent whispers in my hair.

"Think hard, Imogen," Phaidra said quietly. "Not of then, not of next, but of now."

It was a frequent admonishment; too often my thoughts strayed to despair, worry, anger, memory. I was exhausted, utterly discouraged. Thus far I had achieved nothing. I had managed not even one minor work of magic. The old familiar panic bubbled in my gut, held at bay only by sheer force of will. If I let it rise, it would ruin yet another spell. The incantation would lodge in my mind, fraught and sour and intractable.

I nodded at Phaidra, blew out a sharp breath, and fixed my eyes on a single frond of the hapless fern. If I succeeded in crafting the spell, this one stem would sprout thorns so poisonous that a single prick could knock a big man flat for a solid hour, a smaller man for even longer. A useful spell, I supposed, and certainly a subtle enough one to practice covertly, but I hated the idea of working magic with words, and this spell felt particularly ungainly on my tongue, as if I were trying to bend my body into a painful shape.

"*Firintala foratalem,*" I said again, "*talembora talabirin.*"

Phaidra and I waited, staring. I held my breath.

Nothing happened. I thought I saw the fern shiver a little as if jostled, but that could have been merely the wind.

I slumped, worn out and defeated. That was the sixth spell I'd attempted that day, and the sixth failure.

"I don't think I'm suited to working magic with words," I said, too ashamed to look at Phaidra. "I'd like to try silent workings next."

If Phaidra was disappointed, she hid it remarkably well. She sat and resumed patching a tattered pinstriped tunic. "We will rest, then," she said, "and try again tomorrow."

Tomorrow, I thought. After that, according to Phraidra, only six days would remain before the Brethaeus arrived. My fear and frustration made me petulant. I jerked my head at the tunic in her hands.

"Do Vilia kill the people they steal from?" I asked.

"Some do," Phaidra replied, her voice much calmer than mine. "I do not."

Ashamed, I said not a word for the rest of the day.

The next morning, Phaidra shoved me out of sleep and hissed at me to run.

A jolt of fear sent me scrambling to my feet. I did as she said, tearing after her through the forest. Once, I looked back over my shoulder to see what was chasing us, but I saw nothing, and that was somehow worse than if I'd seen some beast barreling after us, or maybe Rennora in a rage, having discovered our secret plot.

We ran until I no longer could. I collapsed against a tree, sucking in painful breaths, my vision full of dark spots.

Phaidra, not at all winded, came back to me with a smug smile. "Good. You see? You may be terrible at spells, but you have grown much stronger in body. A few weeks ago, you would have tired far more quickly."

I stared at her, stupefied and dripping. "You mean there was nothing to run from? We were just *running?*"

She shrugged. "After you fell the necromancers, you will need to run, and run far. They will not stay felled forever. Now"—she jerked her head at a nearby sapling—"make it grow."

I hated her faith in me, how unwavering it was. I stared sullenly at the sapling. "We tried that one already."

"Try it again."

I blew out a sharp breath and glared at the sapling, so tired and angry that I wanted to sit down and scream.

"*Gorenbula garamberen,*" I snapped.

A narrow channel of air stretching between the sapling and me rippled sharply, as if an invisible arrow had shot through it. There was a high, brief whine, and then the sapling snapped in half. Its top half tipped over forlornly and dropped to the ground, emitting the sour, smoky scent of a burnt dinner.

Phaidra clapped me on the shoulder. "Well worked, Imogen!"

I laughed shakily, more than a little terrified of what I'd done. "But that was a spell designed for *growing* a plant, not for stabbing one."

"Then we will try again until we get it right. But you are learning the workings of your power, and that is no small thing. When the Brethaeus come, you will be ready."

"Phaidra." Her confidence made me despair. "Breaking a sapling is not the same thing as breaking a curse."

"I think one is not so far from the other for an Anointed demon slayer."

"But I'm not a beguiler! I have no knowledge of how spellworking should feel, or if I'm even capable of doing it."

Phaidra dismissed my concerns with a slight wave. "Come. We will catch our lunch."

She marched off with her staff in hand, grinning and triumphant, but I lingered by the sapling, spooked by the sight of it and strangely saddened. Hastily, I covered it with leaves so I wouldn't have to look at it and then hurried after Phaidra, sick with the certainty that I would fail her.

→◆→

Four more days of this—half-made spells, surprise runs through the forest with Phaidra, Nesset teaching me an assortment of basic defensive combat moves—and I was truly beginning to panic. In two days, the Brethaeus would arrive, and besides the decapitated sapling, the most impressive bit of magic I'd worked was a sky-blue streak glamoured into my own hair, which had faded within five minutes.

"I do not understand," Nesset growled, pacing ferociously through the woods. "How could such a creature as this fight a demon and *win*?"

Phaidra, for the first time since we'd made our bargain, did not jump to my defense. While Nesset paced and Lulath sat in the dirt, absently braiding a crown of flowers, Phaidra stood with her arms wrapped protectively around herself, looking lost and small.

We were far from our tents in the quiet part of the forest near the Mouth, which had become our secret place to meet and train. I looked away from Phaidra's miserable face and allowed myself one sidelong glance at the Mouth, which loomed to my left, a distant jagged slash of darkness. Disheartened as I was, the Mouth had never seemed more appealing. Perhaps the animals lured down into the ravine had passed through that darkness into oblivion and been glad for it. Oblivion was quiet, neither good nor evil; it demanded nothing.

"She says she conjured up flowers and trees as a child," Nesset ranted, still pacing, "but when she tries it now, she gets only a handful of smoke or a snapped twig. She says she changed the appearance of her mother to that of a monster, and yet all she can change now is the color of her *hair*."

"I'm trying my best," I began, but Nesset silenced me with a glare.

"What are you, rich girl? Elemental or stylist? Child of Caiathos or child of Kerezen? Do you want to know what I think?"

"No, none of us do," said Phaidra wearily.

"I think she is what she told us at the start. I think she is mutilated. I think she is dead inside. I think whatever she was is warped beyond repair."

My eyes filled with furious tears. "None of that was my doing. I have been trying every waking hour since we made our bargain to fulfill my end of it. Spoken magic and silent magic, spells and curses and glamours. I have done everything you asked of me and more."

Nesset stopped to look at me, her stare hard and flat. "I will not argue with that. But we were mistaken to pin our hopes of freedom on you."

Silence fell among us, horrible, hopeless. Nesset stormed off into the trees and Phaidra hurried after her. Lulath rose, her flower crown in hand, and lurched over with her gruesome blistered smile. She gestured for me to bend down so she could place the crown on my head, and I obeyed, bewildered by the bizarre act of kindness but grateful for it nonetheless. Perhaps it wouldn't be so awful to be a dead woman sewn together with pretty blooms.

"The crown will keep you safe while I fetch the others," Lulath said in her raspy voice. "Nesset does not mean the cruel things she says to you. She is simply afraid."

I attempted a smile. "I know the feeling."

I watched Lulath totter away through the trees. In her absence, with the others gone, the quiet was deafening. The forest seemed to grow around me, the trees stretching ever taller, the thick carpet of ferns inching slowly closer. The damp air was oppressive. I stared at my feet and focused on my breathing, determined to look at nothing but the boots Phaidra had given me. The crown of flowers would protect me. I sat rigidly with my palms flat on my thighs. I had no reason to move from this spot.

And yet the Mouth was right there, not so very far from me, its turbulent magic roiling quietly at my fingertips. My curiosity was too great, my desolation too complete. I had failed my friends; I had failed myself.

Maybe, I thought, the Mouth held all the answers. Oblivion or, less likely, a salvation I could not imagine.

I searched the trees to make sure the others weren't already coming back and then stood on shaky legs. I took a deep breath and closed my eyes, then turned to face the ravine, keeping my palm against the hare under my tunic. I hoped Phaidra was right and the carving would tether me to what was real and good and natural. The ravine wound through the woods perhaps two hundred feet away, cloaked by trees, its path a bright-green mossy tongue. I climbed down into it, using the roots of trees as footholds. The soft ground gave slightly under my feet, welcoming me. When I looked down the ravine toward the Mouth, my body pulsed with pain. My eyes burned as if I were staring at something far too bright. I sighed, relieved. The agony of the Mouth's nearby magic was reassuring, familiar. I was on the right path.

I followed the ravine for ages, pushing past tangled ferns and boughs heavy with moss. The endless trudging lulled me into such an exhausted reverie that I didn't notice when the forest changed, when a new silence fell, until the stillness became so complete and stifling that it slapped me awake.

I looked up sharply and froze. The shadows were thick as veils against my skin. The only illumination was sickly pale, and I could not determine the source of it. I looked over my shoulder to search for the ravine and saw it a great distance away, a vivid green pinprick in a black landscape. I heard a muffled sound—someone calling for me from a great distance. A flicker of movement across the green. Phaidra running after me?

I turned back to the shadows before me, my heart pounding.

I had entered the Mouth—and as I searched the vast reach of its gloom, I realized, my stomach dropping, that I had been there before.

Dense and still, no wind, no animals, no sky. The trees were not the plain pines of the Little Grays; they were ancient, more formidable. Bulbous mossy branches grew from trunks thick as the Citadel towers. A slope thick with rotten undergrowth led down to a clearing sunk into the ground, surrounded by thin white trees. Old and terrible magic was near; a greenway, one I'd traveled through before.

Suddenly I couldn't breathe. I knew those trees. I knew these shadows.

This was the demon's lair.

Movement behind me made me turn with a scream in my throat, but it was only Phaidra, Nesset, Lulath. They'd come after me; they'd run into the Mouth and come after me. I reached for Phaidra in a blind panic. Her steady hand caught mine and she tried to pull me back toward the distant ravine, but I refused to budge. My wild fear gave me wild strength. Though I couldn't understand it, a horrible instinct urged me to stay right where I was.

"I know this place," I whispered to her. "I've been here before."

Phaidra's eyes widened. Nesset, breathing hard, growled a question in a language I did not know. Lulath wrung her hands, her eyes squeezed shut. She was murmuring something, perhaps a prayer. I caught only one word: *Zelphenia*.

The air in the clearing below us was shifting, pulling tight around an immense new weight. My heart pounded in the back of my throat. I put a trembling finger to my lips, pleading with the Vilia to be silent. White stars of pain burst open in my every joint; some mighty act of magic was unfolding, and the sensible thing would have been to run. But I had to see it, whatever it was. My desperation was more than curiosity, more than a wish for death. It was a ravenous, animal need.

Suddenly a terrible presence dropped into the clearing: heavy, swift, a boulder of magic crashing through water. I reeled, gasping for air. Phaidra kept me standing, but only just. I forced open my eyes to see a thick tangle of shadows unfurling within the circle of white trees—black to gray to vivid white, then black again, the whole great mass of it juddering sharply as if yanked back and forth between two warring armies. Out of the shadows came a furred flank, a thick curled horn, a long white belly. I caught a quick flash of yellow—three eyes floating in blackness.

Then the air shifted once more, violent and horrible, as if all the wind in the world had changed direction in one fitful moment. My ears popped; my head exploded with pain.

The shadows in the clearing below tore away from each other. Some scattered into the trees like roaches; others rose up into the air and joined together, a jagged knot of smoke, and formed a familiar shape: a man, crouched in the dirt, eyes closed as if in prayer. He was tall, pale, his dark hair damp and curling. He rose, his eyes closed, as the last lingering shadows curled lovingly around his naked white body and clothed him—plain trousers and a mud-spattered coat. His feet and chest remained bare. He breathed deeply, and he opened his eyes. Dark, framed with thick lashes. He strode across the clearing toward a gaping hollow in the base of a massive tree, his every movement assured and familiar.

I dug my fingers into the ruined flesh of Phaidra's arm, fighting against total collapse. The man in the clearing was no captive, afraid of the awful forest he'd found himself in; his was the fluid confidence of someone secure in his home. Rapt, horrified, I watched him kneel by a small pool, cup his hands in the water, splash his face and neck clean. He raised his head, eyes closed, and let the droplets run down his torso.

Please, Zelphenia, I prayed, *have mercy on me. Show me the truth.*

But the goddess of the unknowable was long dead, and the man in the clearing below me was no trick, no illusion.

He was Talan.

The Man with the Three-Eyed Crown was Talan.

CHAPTER 30

At first I couldn't move. The horror of what was happening nailed me to the earth. I couldn't swallow. I couldn't feel my fingers. The world dragged on around me, and I was no longer a part of it.

"Gemma?" Phaidra asked tensely. "What is happening here? Who is that?"

The thought of answering her, admitting how utterly I'd been betrayed, lit the kindling of my rage. I wrenched away from her and tore into the clearing. Talan whirled around to stare at me, stunned. He couldn't believe it, he couldn't understand how I was there, and he didn't have the chance to ask. He opened his mouth, and I flew at him with a terrible, furious scream. Suddenly everything was clear to me. There were thick roots all around us, each as thick as a man's torso; I reached for them and pulled them out of the ground and flung them right at Talan's chest. I tore branches from their trunks and launched them like spears. I ripped vines from the ground, sending up stinging sprays of soil, and lashed them at him, turning them into whips.

He dodged some of my weapons but couldn't evade them all.

One huge root swung through the air with a great creaking groan and struck him across the chest. A speared branch grazed his neck. In no time at all I had him on the ground, his wrists and ankles bound with vines and another winding slowly around his throat. I straddled him, roaring all over, my skin hot and crawling, and I sat there on top of him sobbing, furious, and watched him choke.

"Gemma, wait," he gasped, arching up against his bindings in desperation. "I'm sorry, I...Gemma..." Tears slid down his cheeks. His body went slack and his eyes fluttered closed. "I'm so sorry. I didn't...I never meant..."

The strangled sound of his voice was horrible. I couldn't bear it. I rolled off of him, ripped the vines free of him, and stamped them flat, terrified by how savagely they'd responded to my wishes.

Phaidra joined me, silent and grave, Nesset and Lulath wide-eyed behind her. Phaidra knelt beside Talan and inspected him. I feared the worst; his eyes were closed, he was hardly moving.

She looked at me. "He lives. Shall I kill him?"

Lulath shook her head mournfully.

"No," I said. "Leave him."

Nesset blew out an astonished breath. "Gods remade, what was *that*?"

In the wake of my outburst, I was cold, and everything ached. "I don't understand this. He lied to me. He was lying all this time. He was inside me, he was *inside me*, and he—"

He loved me, and I loved him. The words were right there between my teeth. I refused to say them.

Phaidra's expression was troubled. "You have not been truthful with me, Imogen. Your father is a sentinel and your mother an elemental with a talent for plants and flowers? No, I think they are more than that. That magic you did just now, it was wild. It was Olden. Look. Look at what you did."

I did, and what I saw confounded me: the clearing was in ruins, every thin white tree reduced to splinters, every stump smashed flat except for the enormous one Talan lay beside. Amid piles of shredded vines, severed tree roots tumbled everywhere like a nest of upset snakes. Some were charred, smoking; others flickered strangely, their bark turning to scales and then back again, as if they were trying right before my eyes to become the serpents I'd imagined them to be. Insects and worms lay scattered in the dirt, unearthed by the chaos, some dead, others wriggling about in confusion. The ground shivered with their numbers, agleam with fluttering wings.

A stretch of thick moss and huge ferns on the far slope flickered in and out of being—the moss torn, the ferns trampled, and a familiar yawning blackness churning fitfully beyond them. It was the greenway I'd taken the night I'd followed Father and Farrin, the same greenway that had brought me here to bargain with a demon made of shadows, and it seemed I had broken it.

Astonished, revolted, I didn't know what to say. I looked at my dirty, glittering hands. "I don't understand," I said once more. "I didn't try to do all of that. I was angry at—" My voice caught on his name. "I was angry."

Phaidra was quiet, watching me. Then she said, "Do you know of the fae?"

I nodded blearily. The fae, beautiful and strange, long-lived and cunning, were the subjects of many children's stories. "The god Caiathos and the goddess Kerezen were lovers for a time," I whispered, reciting the familiar tale, "and their union gave Kerezen twins, each possessing the powers of both their parents— the senses, the earth—and these were the first fae."

"Their powers are vast and unpredictable," Phaidra added, "as they straddle the realms of two gods. Tell me more about your mother."

I laughed in disbelief. I was unthinkably tired; I wanted to lie down in the dirt and never rise again. "You think Philippa Ashbourne was a fae?"

"I think she could have been."

"It would explain much of..." Nesset waved her hand at me. "*This.*"

"My mother was a human woman with an elemental talent for botanicals," I said, "and her low-magic family is also human, like mine. Not once have I ever seen evidence to the contrary."

"The fae are masters of deception," Lulath said quietly, "equaled only by the demons."

"Perhaps your mother was taken when she was an infant and a fae child was put in her place," Nesset suggested. "She may not have known she was a fae until much later in life. I have heard of such legends. Changelings, these children are called."

Phaidra nodded, pensive. "Perhaps that is why she left. She was beginning to understand her true nature."

"Yes, I've read all of those stories too," I snapped, quickly growing impatient and terribly frightened. "I've also read stories about how the gods feared the fae, their own creations, and laid traps for them everywhere, in addition to the Middlemist and other such defenses, so they could never enter Edyn."

"Did they not take the same measures to defend Edyn against demons?" Nesset pointed out.

Phaidra nodded. "Demons and fae—two of the most powerful beings in the Old Country. So many traps laid to protect you from them. And yet here before us is a demon." Phaidra glanced at Talan. "I do not think we can say that no fae could ever find their way into this world."

I thought of the Mistfires, Mara's caverns full of silvered corpses and perverse art, and felt suddenly very cold. If something was wrong with the Middlemist—and Mara certainly thought there was—then would Edyn someday be flooded with such creatures? Demons and fae and gods knew what else. The idea seemed impossible, too horrible to consider.

"And what about my sisters?" I demanded. "Farrin is a savant, Mara a sentinel. Their abilities have always been clear to everyone. If our mother was a fae, would they not have the same blood as me?"

Phaidra seemed unmoved by my growing desperation. "I am no scholar of the arcana. I know only the scraps I have shared with you. I cannot answer that question."

"I can, at least in part."

Talan's voice was in shreds, and he could hardly sit up, his face and bare torso streaked with blood—but his dark eyes were clear, familiar, and fixed steadily on me.

Phaidra jumped back from him, fist raised to strike. With a growl, Nesset readied her staff, and Lulath reached for me as if to pull me out of harm's way.

"Wait," I commanded. The desire to touch Talan was terrible, overwhelming. My heart ached to see him, even now, even after everything.

"Speak quickly," I told him, cold as ice.

My voice clearly rattled him. When he spoke, his words were soft, heavy with pain. "I cannot speak to Mara and her power, since I haven't met her—"

"And you never will," I snapped.

He flinched, but he didn't look away from me. "I *can* tell you this. While it's true that Farrin's power is clearer than yours, both in feeling and in manifestation—which I assume means her body was not modified by an artificer, as yours was—there is a mystery at the heart of her, just as there is in you. What we have seen of her power is incomplete. I don't think she has been hiding that truth from everyone; I think she is unaware of it."

I hated the sound of his voice, how ragged it was, how he labored to breathe. I had done that to him, and it was what he deserved, but I hated it all the same. I found myself unsure what to pray for: that my love for him would fade quickly and permanently; that I would wake up and find that he and I were still asleep in the cottage with rain pattering on the windows and his arms around me, heavy with sleep.

"Then you think we have fae blood, as Phaidra suggests?" I managed thickly.

"I don't know what I think. I know only that you and your sister are full of things I cannot see. When I reach for you, I can feel the surface of what you feel—passion, fear, rage. But there is an underneath, a vast one, that is beyond what my power can read. And I have never encountered that in anyone else, not ever."

He smiled faintly; it was the saddest smile I'd ever seen. "That's one of the many reasons why I fell in love with you. The mystery of you—the challenge, and the peace. It was a relief not to know the whole of you all at once. I'd found someone I didn't entirely understand, and to me that was a blessing. Meeting you felt like finally finding a place I could someday call home."

I rose and moved away from him, arms rigid at my sides. I would not cry, I would not scream, I would simply stand there and wait until I found my voice again.

"Oh, please, rich girl, let me kill him," Nesset said. "Spear to the throat, pin him to that stump, and let him hang there rotting while creatures come to pick the meat off him. Say the word and I will do it."

I ignored her and turned back to look at Talan. He had not moved, still lying ashen in the dirt.

"How can I trust anything you say?" I demanded.

"I don't know," he said quietly. "I wouldn't trust me either, Gemma. All I can tell you is that I'm sorry, that every day I deceived you was torment, one of the most terrible things I've ever lived through, and that I never would have done it if I'd had a choice in the matter. I would never have deceived you, would never have hurt you. *Never.*"

Nesset scoffed. Phaidra said nothing, but her silence was full of fury. She glanced up at me, her expression clear: *Be careful.*

And I would be. But I deserved answers, and I would have them, even if I couldn't entirely trust them.

"What is your true name?" I asked.

"Talan," he said, the word leaving him on a tired breath. "I am Talan of the Far Sea."

"Not Talan d'Astier?"

"The name d'Astier is a fiction."

I laughed darkly. "What of you *isn't* a fiction?"

"My family was not named d'Astier," he said. "Our family name is sacred, and I will not say it here in this foul place. But we lived near the water, by a sea called Farther, in a remote house, huge and splendid and cold and dark, and so I am Talan of the Far Sea."

"And you are a demon."

He responded without hesitation. "Yes. I am a demon."

I thought of his shadowed form, the shuddering, awful darkness of it, the flashes of haunch and bone and horn, and my mouth filled with bile.

"You kept your true nature from me, hid yourself in a beautiful human shell, and you charmed me, and you kissed me, and you *fucked* me," I said, spitting the words.

He gestured at his body. "This is no shell. This is *me*. The beast you saw, the creature, is a form I take when my master tells me to—one of many—and I despise it as much as you do." He struggled to sit up, his battered torso a map of blooming bruises. "I wanted so many times to confess everything to you, but whenever I started to, the words froze on my tongue. I'm not even certain I can tell you now."

His face changed as he spoke, twisting, anguished, and then he bent over and retched into the dirt, a putrid yellow-green bile. Phaidra and Nesset backed away in horror; Lulath simply stared, fascinated.

"No, please…" Talan gestured at them. "Please, I beg you, come closer. The magic of the Brethaeus is Olden and clear and sharp, and it runs deep in all of you. It will muddle his reach for a while." He looked up at me, reached across the dirt for me, and when I knelt beside him, ignoring all the good sense I possessed, he fumbled to take hold of my hand and pressed his thumb into my palm, gentle, careful, his expression crumpling.

"There you are," he whispered, smiling weakly up at me. "There you are."

Phaidra shifted uneasily. "Imogen…"

I glanced at her, then at Nesset and Lulath, imploring. "Please do as he asks, and if he tries anything, if you sense even a flicker of trouble, kill him."

This seemed to satisfy Nesset. She marched over and crouched beside him, staff at the ready. Phaidra and Lulath did the same.

I hoped I hadn't just sentenced them to their deaths.

I took a deep breath and looked back at Talan. "This is you," I prompted him. "The beast is not."

He shook his head. "My master likes to toy with me. He loves games, and he loves dealing pain. When he can combine those things, he is at his happiest. This is my true body." He put a shaking hand to his chest. "Demons are like any other intelligent creatures that walk this new world or the Olden one. Some of us are good, some of us are wicked, most are somewhere in between, and all of us are messy and complicated and full of weaknesses and passions, just as humans are. We simply have more power than you do, so our goodness and our wickedness are likewise more extreme. Our lore tells us that we were born from the tears of the goddess Zelphenia, though our lore is as fanciful as yours and no one can say with authority what is truth and what is embellishment. We are long-lived and difficult to kill, but it's not impossible to do so. We are flesh and blood and bone and sinew, like you, but we have many gifts, and one of those is deception, hence why I can take many forms besides this, my true one."

He spoke quickly, each quiet word clearly an undertaking. He was so pale it frightened me; his skin glistened with a sickly sheen of sweat.

"There are greater demons," he whispered, "and lesser demons; my family is the former. This means that in my ancestry boils both the blood of Zelphenia, as is true for all demons, and of Jaetris— goddess of the unknowable, god of the mind. I wonder if they knew what monstrous things their union would create and chose to mate anyway. I wonder if Caiathos and Kerezen knew that their passion would bring forth the wild and deadly fae."

He let out a rueful laugh and shook his head. "Having the power of both gods in my lineage is an honor—a terrifying one, something to be treated with care. But my parents abused this blessing. They were cruel, and that is too pale a word. Think of the worst things your stories have told you about what demons are, and you will begin to understand. They were mighty, and their many appetites were voracious and depraved. They adopted whatever forms their victims found most terrifying and were loath to assume their true bodies—too similar to humans, which they considered an insult from the gods. Hot-tempered, sadistic, they loved pranks and lies and power more than anything. More than their children—my sisters, who are now all dead, and me."

Talan closed his eyes. His hand shook around mine as he tried to catch his breath. I touched his slick brow, brushed back a wet lock of dark hair.

Nesset hissed a warning, but all Talan did was open his eyes, smile at me, and rub his thumb softly across my knuckles. My heart ached, burning with anger and pity and a terrible, insistent tenderness. I did not allow myself to return his smile.

"Keep going," I said, my voice carefully flat.

"As you can imagine, my parents' exploits made us many ene- mies. There was no being they would not torment, no creature, however mighty, that they would hesitate to seduce, confuse, mutilate. They liked most of all when they could simply sit there and give commands and watch their victims commit the violence themselves—against their own bodies, against their loved ones. They didn't like filth. Our house was immaculate, the servants worked to the bone and happy to do it because they adored my parents, because they were told to love them and had no choice but to obey. Jaetris's powers of the mind and Zelphenia's powers of deception were bound together in them—not only demons, not simply empaths or telepaths, but all of those things and more. It should never have happened. When Zelphenia birthed the first greater demon, she should have seen the horror that was to come and killed the thing before it could draw breath to cry. But she didn't, and so, ages later, here I am."

Talan inhaled, steadying himself. "One night when I was much younger—fourteen, I would say, in your years—I awoke to the sounds of battle. Our house was under attack. Titans had risen up from the ocean to drown us in our sleep. They didn't like what my parents were doing to their sailors, you see. There are more humans in the Old Country than you would think—offspring of slaves and captives, or fools who ventured too far into the Middlemist and were seduced away from Edyn. They were easy prey for my parents, who had no regard for the territory and property of others. And so a clan of sea titans came to ruin us with fists of foam and great sucking whirlpools for mouths. But of course my parents fought back—or, I should say, they made my sisters fight back. Their three daughters, all of them cruel and cunning and eager to win our parents' love. Mother especially always favored them, which meant I was left to my own devices most days, for which I was grateful.

"The house shook with the tides, water pouring through every crack and window, flooding every corridor. Of course our parents wouldn't fight. Cowards. For a while it seemed to work—my sisters were fast, clever, and tricked the titans into pounding on each other. But the titans kept coming and *coming*, an endless charge of them, and my sisters couldn't hold them back. The house began to collapse. A fallen beam trapped me, smashed my legs, and I was able to free myself only when the house shifted once more under the onslaught and the beam rolled off me. I limped out of the house to the sounds of my sisters being torn to pieces. I ran, and I didn't look back. The pain was unimaginable. If I'd been a human, I couldn't have moved. I heard the titans pull our house into the sea. The waves chased me all the way to the woods, which is where I found him."

The hatred in Talan's voice, the naked fear, sent chills rushing down my body. I glanced at the Vilia; all of them were held rapt by his story, just as I was.

"Him?" I asked.

"His name is Kilraith," Talan said. "I don't know what he is. He wears many faces, and I don't know which is true and which is a lie, or if they are all lies."

"He is a demon too?" Phaidra asked tensely.

"No. Not a demon or a fae. Not a titan or a Wind or a vampyr. I cannot name him." Talan looked up at me, and in his wide, dark eyes I could see the story he told—the young boy, drenched and terrified, and a grand house devoured by an angry sea. "He found me in the woods. He'd been searching for a new servant, and the titans' attack on our house must have drawn his attention. Sometimes I think he was always there, that he'd been there since the time of the gods. Sometimes I think he is in all places at once."

Talan gripped my hand harder. "I don't remember everything about that night, about him. But I do remember a tall creature, pale, with bare arms and warm hands. He appeared out of nowhere. The woods were empty, and then they weren't. He knelt and opened his arms to me. 'Your parents are furious,' he said, and he sounded so sorry about it. 'Poor dear child. What did you do? Why did you run away? They will kill you if they find you. They will kill you and wear your skin.' I couldn't stop sobbing. I was wild with pain from my shattered legs, and I was shaking all over, exhausted, terrified. I couldn't hold myself up any longer. I fell, and he scooped me up and held me. 'Will you be mine, then?' he asked. 'If you say yes, I will keep you safe. They will never find you. You will never have to go home, not ever again.'"

Talan's voice changed when he spoke as this entity, this Kilraith. It became soothingly kind, mellifluous. He closed his eyes. "I said yes," he whispered. "I said *please*. I didn't know what else to do. I was cold, and he was warm. He touched me, and suddenly I felt no pain. I didn't even ask him for his name, and he didn't tell me, not for years. My guesses amused him."

Lulath nodded, her expression solemn and knowing. "You are bound to him."

"I am. In my desperation that night, I agreed to my own doom. I am not me anymore, not entirely. Whatever binds me to him is far fouler, far more complex, than any workaday curse. He *lives* in me—only a piece of him, and most of the time he is far away, but I can't predict when he will surface and speak through me, or order me to do something terrible. I am part of Kilraith's will, his eyes and ears and hands. I torment as he instructs. For years I went where he told me, committed crimes I was helpless to refuse. I am one of many, far from the only instrument of terror he controls. Long ago I gave up fighting him. I tried and failed to escape too many times and had resigned myself to this fate, to never again holding the reins of my own life, until..."

He opened his eyes, his expression soft with love as he beheld me. "Until I met you, Gemma."

Somehow I found my voice. "It's him, isn't it? Kilraith. He's the one who turned my family and the Basks against each other."

"Yes, and I am merely the latest in a long string of puppets he's engineered to torment you." His expression flickered with memory. "The one who held the position before me was a lesser demon. When Kilraith became bored of him, he flayed him and put me in his place. I became the Man with the Three-Eyed Crown. The name is old, but the servant bearing the curse and its title is never the same for long."

"But *why*? Why does he do all this? And why not do any it himself?"

"I don't know. Perhaps because he doesn't have to. Why exert himself unless he chooses to? But I can't say for certain. Despite all the years I've spent in his chains, I know very little about his true nature. What I have learned—because he loves to talk when he's bored, when he's angry with me, when he's happy with me—is that he is the force behind many dark workings in both Edyn and the Old Country. I am only one of his tools, and your family and the Basks are only two of his victims. What these workings are, what they do for him, or if he simply finds them diverting amusements, I don't know."

Overwhelmed by the horror of his words, I could only keep asking my quiet questions. "Why did you come to Ivyhill?"

"Because with a new demon to fill the role of the Man with the Three-Eyed Crown, Kilraith wanted to try a new strategy as well," Talan replied. "A more intimate one. I was to insinuate myself into your family's good graces, make you think I was helping you, and then kill one of you—draw it out for ages—and pin the blame on the Basks. You hadn't struck at each other for some time, and he was growing impatient for blood. He bores easily."

The way he said this, matter-of-fact and tired, sickened me—for my sake and for his.

"At first I did as I was told. But then I met you, Gemma, and after that..." He shook his head, smiling sadly. "Everything changed. The thing he had asked me to do—infiltrate your family's house in my own skin, charm all of you with my own face—was the very thing that led me to you, and to the first stirrings of rebellion I'd felt in years."

"And the visits to Ravenswood?" I said, so disgusted and angry and horribly, utterly sad that I felt numb. "Our schemes to humiliate Alastrina and Ryder?"

"I thought if I entertained him well enough in other ways, he would be satisfied for a time. And I thought..." He brought a shaking hand to my face. "I thought that the more time I spent with you, the closer I could keep you, the stronger I would become. And maybe then I could fight him, truly fight him, as I'd never dared to before. Maybe, with you by my side, I would find my courage."

I cupped his hand with my own, pressed my cheek into his palm. "And the wardstone. You were the one who stole it, weren't you? You left it in the Mist to be destroyed."

He nodded miserably. "The wardstone was spelled to recognize any demon bound to Kilraith. If Gareth had dismantled it, he would have learned what I was. I couldn't allow that."

"You knew where I hid it. You followed me to my safe room."

He closed his eyes, overcome with shame I desperately hoped was real.

"Were you really in the capital with Gareth?" I said.

"I was, looking for answers about Madam Baines, and Ryder, and demonic possession. That much was true."

"Yet you came to Ivyhill to attack Farrin and then went back to the city so quickly. Then you came to Illaria's to find me. How did you achieve this?"

"I can travel very swiftly when I want to," he replied, "and my time serving Kilraith has acquainted me with old greenways, even older and more well-hidden than your father's."

I felt weary with questions but could not allow myself to rest until I'd asked them all. "Did you tell Madam Baines to kill Jessyl?"

Grief took hold of Talan's face. "No, I didn't. But I think I was responsible for her death—for both their deaths—all the same. I was rash that night we pried information out of Madam Baines. Something of Kilraith must have gotten into her, either an intentional piece of him or a mere stray thought. Whichever it was, I think it got inside her and slowly drove her mad."

I had to shut my eyes for a moment. I let the guilt of my part in all of that fully sink into me, teeth and all.

"And why did you run from me?" I whispered at last, flush with shame at the memory. "That night in the gardens?"

"I was terrified. I didn't know what had happened to you, but

I knew your transformation was interesting enough to draw his attention. He would sense it through me. He would sense *you* and maybe come for you himself. I had to run. I couldn't let him see you. And besides that..."

He squeezed his eyes shut, looked away from me. "Gods, Gemma. I was afraid that being around me was corrupting you. You were bewildered by what had happened to you; it seemed you had no control over it. And there I was, kissing you, holding you—a demon, bound to something even worse than that, more powerful than that, infecting you with my own foulness. I had to run. I should have never come back to Ivyhill, but he ordered me to do so. He could sense that I had fallen in love with you and thought it highly amusing. A doomed romance. I would destroy your family and break my own heart in the process."

"And when I met you that night, when you were..." I swallowed hard, revolted at the memory. "When I was here, and you were not yourself. Why did you tell me to bring that eye back to Ivyhill to spy on Farrin?"

"Kilraith loves her music," he said simply. "After her performance at the tournament, he wanted to go to Ivyhill and take her himself as a trophy. The eye was a compromise. I fought for it tooth and nail, convinced him it would be a grand game. I thought it would give you time to save her, time to fight me. When I came back here, licking my wounds, I told him your father had attacked me. I'm sure he didn't believe me, and he certainly let me have it for daring to return without Farrin, but my lies were entertainment enough, I suppose. I'm unsure of the extent of his power—he keeps it hidden, even more of an enigma than yours, Gemma—but I think he could enter my mind and take hold of my thoughts whenever he likes, unravel all my lies and excuses, learn how loving you has given me the will to fight him, even in small ways. But where would the fun be in that? He prefers to play with his food, keep it guessing."

Talan's voice was hoarse and thin. He blew out a breath and settled back against the mossy earth. Beads of sweat stood on his brow; his lips had lost their color. I tried not to feel guilty for giving him such a sound thrashing.

Nesset dropped her staff and scrubbed her hands through her tangled black hair, shedding flakes of dirt and skin and crusty old leaves.

"Shit of the gods," she swore. "Never since being reborn in this piss pot of a body have I wished more passionately that I could still get drunk."

Lulath let out a faint trill of nervous laughter. She retrieved my tattered flower crown and placed it back on my head, uncertain, then picked it up once more and plopped it onto Talan's head instead. She stood there, considering him, while I tried to find the right words to say. Phaidra watched me, unblinking, staff still held at the ready. If I told her to, she would attack. That brought me much-needed comfort.

"Talan," I said at last, "do you know anything about cursebreaking?"

He smiled faintly, his eyes still closed. "A fine thought, but whatever Kilraith bound me with, as I said, it is no simple curse. It runs too deep to touch. When I was in the capital with Gareth, I did my own research as he slept. I could find no mention in any volume of a being like Kilraith, a binding like mine. I've tried to trick him, run from him, and all I've ever managed is a few moments here and there. A day at most, when some nearby act of magic is powerful enough to muddle my bindings." He reached for me, held my hand with heartbreaking tenderness. "After you attacked me in the ballroom, I enjoyed the quietest two days of my life. Even knowing all my hiding spots, it took him some time for him to find me. Your magic fogged his senses."

"I wasn't thinking of breaking *your* curse," I told him, glancing up at Phaidra. "Not yet."

Wide-eyed, Phaidra lowered her staff.

Talan propped himself up on his elbows and looked curiously at me. "You're feeling hopeful quite abruptly. What are you thinking?"

My heart was indeed racing with a sudden burst of inspiration. "Phaidra, Nesset, and Lulath wish to break the curse that binds them to the Brethaeus. If we can manage that, might it be a strong enough bit of magic to confuse Kilraith for quite some time? Time enough for you to run?"

Talan stared hard at me. "You're serious."

"Isn't it possible?"

"Gemma." His expression softened into something horribly sad. "Where would I run? He would find me someday, whether in three days or five or ten."

"In those three days or five or ten, we would find a way to break his hold on you for good." I waved him silent before he could protest. "Just humor me for a moment, all of you, and answer my questions."

Talan looked unhappily up at Phaidra. "What is your curse's nature? Blood? Bone?"

"And teeth," Phaidra replied.

Talan grimaced. "A triad. I've seen such curses before. Breaking them is not impossible, but it's certainly difficult. I've never tried it myself."

"But do you know the theory of it?" I persisted.

"Yes, but—"

"Then explain it to me from beginning to end."

He shook his head. "You need to run away from here, Gemma. Take the greenway back to Ivyhill." He jerked his head at the clearing's far slope, where shadows churned fitfully in a mess of uprooted ferns. "The Vilia will move on from these woods eventually, and when they do, Kilraith will sense that something strange has happened. He'll wonder why revenant magic was muddling his senses for so long and come investigate. I don't want you anywhere near me when that happens."

"I'm not going home," I said flatly. "Not right now. Not yet."

"*Gemma*—"

"I don't care if it's a difficult thing to do," I interrupted fiercely. "I want to free the Vilia, and when that's done, I want you to run away with me, and nothing you can say will change my mind. We'll leave these woods and hide somewhere safe, then send for Gareth. If there's a way to free you from Kilraith, he'll know how to find it, or at least where to start looking."

Talan's expression was so dear, so pitying, that looking at him left me hardly able to breathe. His love was too obvious, his color too pale. He didn't think I could do this impossible thing I was proposing.

I turned away from him and met Phaidra's eyes, then Nesset's, and Lulath's last of all. She had her hands clasped under her chin, beaming up at me. I felt only a twinge of doubt upon seeing her excitement; hopefully I wouldn't disappoint them.

"Phaidra, you and Lulath said you've watched the Brethaeus work their binding magic," I said. "Can you remember the entire sequence of it from start to finish?"

Phaidra nodded. "I believe so."

"Good. And how many of the Vilia are like you, ready to fight?"

"Nine, including us three," Nesset answered, her eyes flashing eagerly. "The rest are loyal to Rennora."

I winced; those numbers were not ideal.

"What are you proposing, Imogen?" Phaidra asked, watching me closely. I knew her well enough now to see that she was trying desperately to stay calm and fight the pull of hope.

I took a deep breath for courage. I was used to planning parties, not battles. But the only other choice was unthinkable: the Vilia still prisoners, Talan bound forever to Kilraith, myself a revenant or dead, or home and heartbroken, waiting for Kilraith to murder Talan in a fit of rage and send another demon to destroy my family.

No, those were possibilities I could not abide.

"Tomorrow night," I said, "we'll return from a hunt with Talan in tow. A prisoner." I nodded at Phaidra. "You hunt people to present to your masters. Well, I will present Talan to Rennora, a tribute for the Brethaeus, to prove my worth to her."

Nesset lifted her eyebrows in surprise, but Phaidra simply smiled, stretching the flower-sewn scar on her cheek.

"A cunning plan, Imogen," she said. "That will please Rennora."

Encouraged by her obvious pride, I continued. "She'll suppose that my time with you has warmed me to your people, that I yearn for death so I can become one of you. She'll be happy with you as well. She'll sleep easily, suspecting nothing. Talan will use his power to make sure of that. And the next day the Brethaeus will come, not knowing what awaits them. I will attack them, Talan will break the curse, and you, Nesset, Lulath, and your allies will hold off Rennora and the others until our work is done. The act of breaking the curse will be strong enough to confuse Kilraith for a time. Talan and I will run. Phaidra, you and the others will be free to go your own way."

Phaidra straightened and lifted her chin. "I will go with you, Imogen. If we are successful, I will accompany you and protect you for as long as I can."

"As will we," Nesset added, jostling Lulath with her elbow.

Lulath, her cheek pressed lovingly against her staff as if already imagining the carnage to come, nodded in agreement.

Deeply moved by their offer, I squeezed Phaidra's hand and then turned to Talan. He was sitting dejectedly in the dirt, shaking his head.

"No, Gemma," he said hoarsely. "You can't do this. It's too dangerous. Do you know what will happen if you die? He'll keep me alive for as long as he can. I'll have to live with the knowledge of your death for centuries. I can't bear that. Please don't ask me to."

I knelt beside him, caught his face in my hands, and made him look at me. "You said that meeting me felt like finding a place you could someday call home," I said. "Do you think you're the only one who felt that way?" I smiled sadly. "I should hate you. I should be disgusted by you, no matter your tragic past, but even now I don't, and I'm not. You make me stronger than I was. Around you, I don't care quite so much about how deeply it hurts to live inside my body. When you look at me, I feel beautiful not because of my looks or my family's name or all my fine things, but because I'm *worth* something."

Remembering that night in the queen's gardens before everything went wrong, I whispered, "That night when you saw what I'd done to myself, you didn't shrink from me or scold me. You cared for me. You dressed my wounds and told me I was exquisite. You were so gentle with me."

He shook his head helplessly. "Gemma, love…"

I kept on. I wouldn't allow him to dissuade me. "Since our first dance together," I whispered, "you've said that there's a fire burning inside me, which no one else had ever said about me, not *ever*—and for the first time in my life, I'm starting to believe it could be true." I caressed his cheeks with my thumbs. "I refuse to let you give up. We're going to free the Vilia, and then you're going to run away with me, and we'll find a way to free you. I swear it, Talan. We'll find a way to free us both."

I kissed him hard and quick, then pressed my brow to his.

"I'd be a fool to argue with you after that," he said quietly, tears in his eyes. "Tell me then, wildcat, where will we run to?"

An idea came to me, so perfect and tidy that I had to smile. "I don't think you should know until we're there. For now, tell me everything you know about curses made in threes."

"There is..." Talan struggled to find his voice, brushed the backs of his fingers against my jaw. "Gemma, there is so much to say."

I captured his hand and pressed it to my cheek. "I know."

"I've hurt you, even though I didn't want to. Gods, I didn't want to."

I kissed his fingers, silencing him. Remembering all he had done, all he had kept from me, left me uneasy. I shoved the feeling aside. Later there would be time to sort out how I felt about all of this—at least I hoped there would be. I hoped I wasn't making a terrible mistake.

"We'll talk through it all later, when we're safe," I told him briskly. "Now, look at me and focus. The curse: tell me how we're going to break it."

He nodded, squeezed my hand, and began to speak.

CHAPTER 31

A s Rennora had said they would, the Brethaeus came two days later—five of them, trickling out of the dawn like rivulets of dark water. They wore black all over, from their tall boots to the tips of their fingers to the sharp lines of their jaws. They even wore black hoods, tight against their scalps, and their long tunics fluttered like black moth wings, and they hid their faces with matching white masks—featureless, smooth except for four little slits. Eyes, nose, mouth.

Wearing a fine gown of blue silk that Phaidra had selected from her stash of stolen goods, I watched the Brethaeus come, a slick of fear in my stomach. Behind me, gagged and bound to a tree with thick black rope beside all the other captives marked for consumption, was Talan. I kept my back to him, terrified of what I would do, what I might give away, if I turned and saw his face, bloodied and bruised from Phaidra's fists. Ruse or not, it was an awful picture, and though this plan was mine, though things between Talan and me were new and strange, I didn't trust myself not to go to him and ruin everything.

The Vilia knelt in tribute behind Rennora, who stood to greet the Brethaeus with bowed head and a fist held against her chest. The Brethaeus said nothing; all five of them came to Rennora and placed their hands on her shoulders, making their fluid movements in eerie unison. If they were speaking with her somehow, I couldn't hear it, but her arm lifting to point in my direction was clear enough.

As one, the Brethaeus turned to look at me. If I'd been standing on my own two legs, they would have buckled. The Brethaeus glided toward me, their steps smooth and silent. The Vilia scrambled to get out of the way, staying as low to the ground as they could, their heads still bowed. I didn't dare look for Phaidra, Nesset, or Lulath. I was an eager recruit. I held my head high.

"My name is Imogen," I said, remembering Phaidra's instructions, "and I stand before you with death in my heart. Here is a man who has wronged me, and I offer his blood to you in tribute."

Then I went to Rennora, my stomach in knots. She grinned, no doubt delighted at the favor all of this would bring her, and held out a staff—new, freshly carved and painted, meant for me. I took it and walked slowly to Talan, past the watching, waiting Brethaeus, my heart pounding harder with every step. Talan, bound to his tree, began to struggle, twisting against the ropes that held him, and I could no longer delay the inevitable. I looked up at him.

Our eyes met—mine cold, his wide with horror. He screamed, his voice muffled by the gag stuffed in his mouth. The sound tore into me; he was too good at pretending terror. A thousand frantic thoughts raced through my mind: What memories was Talan drawing upon to create those desperate, anguished screams? Was he sending out feelings of fear, as he'd said he would, to convince Rennora and the Vilia and the Brethaeus that the story we'd woven was true? He had said he would work carefully. He had said he would touch their minds only enough to convince them that all was well and nothing more. He had said it would not be enough to alert Kilraith that something was happening, that his puppet was straining against his strings.

He had said all of this, but in that moment, as I raised my staff and prepared to strike, I felt a treacherous flicker of doubt. Maybe this was folly. Maybe the Vilia loyal to Rennora would overwhelm us in an instant, or Kilraith would come and flay us all.

I paused, staff in the air, stricken with terror—until a faint caress of feeling pushed against me. A feeling of reassurance as tender as any kiss.

Talan.

He was there, he was not hurt, and the sense of his belief in me swelled against my mind like a wave.

I closed my eyes and allowed myself an instant to breathe, to think through what I must do, just as Talan and I had practiced.

I thought of Farrin being dragged across the ballroom floor, and how I had been so furious that I'd crashed through the doors and flown across the room without thought, without fear. My sister was in my mind, and Talan too—the rage I'd felt upon realizing who he truly was; the euphoric pleasure of kissing him in the palace gardens.

In each of those three instances, I'd worked magic. I hadn't meant to do it; I'd been afraid, angry, charged hot with pleasure, and the magic had come. It had *erupted.* Wild and Olden, as Phaidra had described it. My magic was wild.

Think of how you felt each time, Talan had told me as we'd planned our attack in the ruins of his lair. *Think of the passion, the fury. Remember it. Live it all over again. Terror, lust, rage—they are weapons. Use them.*

Terror. Lust. Rage. Over the past two days, I'd practiced sinking into those memories and learning their texture, their shape, their color. The explosion of furious heat in my chest when I'd seen the shadows unfold to reveal Talan's face, how I had run at him and torn through the trees like they were paper and lashed him to the ground. The cold waves of terror that had crashed through me when I'd seen the demon dragging my sister across the floor. The ecstasy of Talan's body beneath mine as I had ground against him on the garden wall—our skin slick with sweat, my silken skirts hiked up around my hips, his hands cupping my bottom as I'd moved on him, faster, harder, wanting him, *needing* him.

I imagined the Brethaeus in my mind's eye, the picture of them stark and terrible. They wore thin leather straps tied around their hips and torsos, each strap heavy with hundreds of tiny velvet pouches. I knew what those pouches held: teeth, bones, vials of blood. I didn't know which belonged to my Vilia, and I didn't care. We would burn them all.

My eyes snapped open, my mind clear and sharp as the glass I now wore on my skin. Terror, lust, rage—my weapons. They roared in my blood, and I grabbed on to their blades with both hands.

Breathing hard, I whirled around and let my staff fly.

My magic was a beast unleashed. A dozen roots erupted from the earth, thick and coiling and groaning, following the arc of my staff. I threw them at the Brethaeus, all twelve of them at once. They smashed into the necromancers from all directions, and the air exploded with sickening cracks—snapped ribs, skulls knocked against skulls. The Brethaeus fell.

Nesset hurried over and with a great slash of her knife cut through all the ropes that held Talan. Rennora howled in fury and drew a dagger from her belt, but Phaidra was already running for her. She barreled into her, sending them both crashing to the ground and Rennora's blade flying off into the trees.

Bedlam spread quickly. Those Vilia loyal to Rennora launched themselves at Phaidra, but she was not alone. Four others rushed to defend her, including Lulath, her staff flying fast and her grim blistered face ferocious with battle fury.

I dropped to the ground, trying to shake off the pain crowding my vision and cursing the artificer who'd scarred my insides. The magic careening through the chaos clawed at me from head to toe. Nesset ran back into the fray as Talan hurried to me, limping slightly. He helped me stand, his hands on my arms and his mind touching my own.

"Talan," I whispered just once, a small stolen breath of thanks, and then hurried with him to the Brethaeus, tugging along with me a seething nest of vines and brush and fallen branches. As I wove a pyre of forest scraps around the necromancers, binding their bodies together with thick thorny vines and praying to all the gods that my crude facility with my power wouldn't falter, I risked a glance at Talan.

He looked awful, his color wan, his hair plastered to his neck. I didn't know if this was due to Phaidra's blows or if Kilraith had begun to sense Talan's rebellion and was already punishing him. My stomach turned over. Talan had assured me no less than twenty times that the cursebreaking would hide him from Kilraith—but for how long?

Talan held out his hand. "Don't be afraid for me, Gemma," he said, his dark gaze steadying me. "It's past time to fight him. I want this. I want to be with you, whatever comes next."

I swallowed my protests, my throat aching with love, and put my hand in his. He withdrew a small knife from his coat's inner pocket, and I tried not to wince as he cut into the tender flesh of my forearm. My blood was neither dead nor demonic; Talan had therefore deemed it the safest to use as a cursebreaker. He guided my arm over the Brethaeus, letting my blood drip onto their bound, battered bodies.

"What was made is now broken," Talan intoned quietly. "What was bound is now free."

It was a spell we had written, pieced together from Talan's memories of other curses he had encountered. I prayed desperately that it would hold; neither of us was a beguiler, practiced at such works. We had to hope that his demonic power and my unnamed one would be enough to give the spell teeth.

Lulath crept close to us with a flaming torch in hand and looked up at me questioningly. I nodded, woozy with pain. She gave me a small smile, the mottled ruin of her face stretching grotesquely. Then she tossed her torch onto the trapped Brethaeus.

With a thunderous rush of hot air, the fire ignited the pyre I'd made and spread swiftly, reducing the torch itself to ash in an instant. The necromancers' bodies twitched, but they did not burn. With each jerk of their bodies popped a faint shriek of sound, like wood creaking in a blazing hearth.

Talan winced, and I stumbled against him, feeling each shriek as if it were a blade piercing my skin. He guided my bleeding arm over the Brethaeus once more. The blood sizzled where it fell, and with each drop the flames grew. My eyes watered from the climbing heat, and my body was a throbbing pillar of pain.

"What was made is now broken," Talan repeated, his voice louder now, his arm shaking as he held up mine. "What was bound is now free."

The Brethaeus convulsed, writhing, their bodies straining at the thick layers of vines and roots that bolted them to the earth. They might have been awake, or maybe they were still knocked out cold, furious even in their oblivion; with the smooth white masks hiding their faces, it was impossible to tell.

The shrieking became a chorus, shrill and enraged, its climbing pitch winding tighter and tighter, as if soon the sound would snap open and release something terrible. Even so close to the awful heat of the fire, even with sweat rolling down my body, I felt horribly cold. My teeth chattered, and I shivered all over, and suddenly it seemed entirely sensible to thrust my arm into the lovely warm fire.

Talan yanked me back against his body before I could do it. He couldn't speak—doing so would confuse the incantation—but his grip was urgent, even painful, and it snapped me back to my senses.

Fear dropped over me like an icy curtain as I realized what I'd almost done. *Curses are cunning, especially ones that bind,* Talan had told me as we'd practiced. *It won't want to die. It will do anything it can to stop us.* His expression had been dark and bitter, and I'd wondered how many times he'd muttered spells over himself, desperate and alone; how they had hurt him when they'd failed; if Kilraith had been watching all the while, delighted by Talan's futile efforts.

I drew in a shaky breath. The growing flames licked at our fingers, and my head pounded so violently that it was torment not to reach up and press my palms against my temples. A threefold curse. Once more, and it would be done.

Talan held my bleeding arm firmly and guided it out over the fire. He squeezed more blood out of the wound; a sharp pain bloomed through my whole body. The flames roared higher, climbing closer and closer to our skin. The air was black with smoke, and the Brethaeus thrashed, their bodies snapping into awful, unnatural shapes. They howled in fury, and their bestial cries chilled me to the bone.

Talan's body sagged against mine, both of us shaking with the effort of staying upright. Every inch of my skin crawled, horribly hot and itchy, but I couldn't scratch, I couldn't let the curse persuade me to surrender. I let out a single gasping sob and thought, *Hurry, Talan*.

"What was made is now broken," Talan shouted over the din. "What was bound is now free."

All at once, the hundreds of tiny pouches strapped to the Brethaeus burst into flame. The forest erupted into piercing, agonized screams—the broken curse, Talan had said, would be a terrible thing to hear. Lulath, wide-eyed, clapped her hands over her ears and crouched low to the ground.

A boom shook the world, knocking us all off our feet. My ears ringing, my head a roaring storm of pain, I groped blindly for Talan and let out a relieved cry when his slick hand found mine. We helped each other rise, clinging to each other, and looked at what we had done—the bound Brethaeus, now still and silent, their bodies wreathed in hundreds of spitting black flames as the shuddering pouches of blood, bone, and teeth burned to ash.

Phaidra ran to us, followed by Nesset. They looked clumsy, frantic, unmoored by their new freedom.

"Are there any others?" I asked, coughing on smoke.

Phaidra shook her head. Her eyes were fierce and sad. "We killed nine," she said. "The rest of them ran once the curse was broken."

"Rennora?"

Nesset, dripping all over with black liquid I thought must be Vilia blood, shot us a mean grin. "Not even a revenant can weather a knife to the head."

Lulath stared in awe at the ruin we had wrought. "They're not burning," she said, the firelight casting sinister shapes across her face. "Everything else is, but not them."

"And they won't," Talan rasped, holding me tight against him, "but this will hold them for weeks, I hope, and muddle every trace of magic for miles."

A thrill of fear shook me as I heard the words he didn't say. Kilraith's name hung in the air, unuttered and terrible. I wouldn't let myself imagine that Talan was wrong—or worse, that he was lying for some purpose I could not see. I would be able to imagine all of those horrible things once we were safe and not a moment before. Already I could feel the panic brewing in me, somewhere deep and meaty, kept at bay only by exhaustion and the need to run.

"From your lips to the ears of the gods," Phaidra whispered. "I hope you are right, demon."

"Those who have mastered the art of death will not easily let it defeat them," Lulath added softly, looking grave. "They will rise and rise again."

"And I do not wish to be here when they do," Nesset snapped. "Come. It's a long walk to where we're going." Then she strode off, staff in one hand and a knife in the other, Lulath tottering eagerly at her heels.

Talan looked down at me tiredly. "Where *are* we going?"

"North," I said. I met Phaidra's eyes, and she nodded at me, grim and ready. "We're going north."

When I knocked on the front doors of Rosewarren, I was exhausted to the point of delirium, far too tired to be intimidated by the pair of stone falcons staring down at me in disdain.

The doors opened, revealing a child perhaps ten years of age. She was pale and fair, wearing a plain brown dress over plain brown trousers, her feet were bare, and she was gawking at me. I couldn't very well blame her for that. I was filthy and stinking, my arm crudely bandaged, my blue silk gown tattered and singed, and the bits of my skin that weren't caked over with mud and sweat glittered softly in the twilight.

"I'm Lady Gemma Ashbourne," I announced, "and I'm here to see my sister Mara. Fetch her, please, or you may bring Cira instead, or Brigid. But don't tell the Warden or anyone else besides those three that I'm here. Can you do that?"

By the time I'd finished speaking, the girl was looking up at me with shrewd narrowed eyes. She said nothing, clearly waiting for something.

I sighed. "The Warden gives you a small monthly stipend, yes? And you can spend it on whatever you like when you go to town?"

The girl nodded warily.

"Well, I'll give you ten times that amount if you do as I ask. I'll have it sent here straight from Lord Gideon Ashbourne himself. Mara will vouch for me and for him. Has my sister ever given you reason to distrust her?"

After a moment, the girl relaxed and shook her head.

"Very well, then. Your name?"

"Vash," she said shortly.

"Thank you, Vash. You can expect your payment by the end of the month. Off with you now, and hurry."

The girl hurried away into the priory's shadows, letting the door swing shut behind her, and not five minutes later, Mara ran around the corner of the house to greet me, sweaty and flushed, her clothes and boots smeared with mud. The air surrounding her was ripe with stinging sentinel magic; she had been training. I leaned hard against the priory's stone wall, fighting the urge to collapse.

"Gemma," Mara breathed. "Your *skin*."

I waved her off before she could embrace me. "I need you to gather food and clothes," I said quietly, "and basic medical supplies—bandages, tonics for pain, enough for five people—and two of the priory's horses, if you can manage all that without drawing undue attention. And then I need you to come with me, right now, and I'll explain everything as we ride. Oh, and there's a stolen horse tied up in those trees over there who needs a good rubdown, water, food, and a home in your stables until I can return him to his owner."

Gods bless my sister—life in the Order of the Rose had taught her to recover from shock quickly. She nodded at a clutch of trees not far from the house. "Wait over there," she said. "I'll return in fifteen minutes."

I obeyed her, crouching watchfully in the trees even though all I wanted was to lie down in the clover and weeds and sleep for a year. When Mara returned, I could have cried with relief. She had bags of supplies and two fresh horses, reedy little mares who looked eager to run. Mara helped me mount the one with the muddy-brown coat and took the dark dapple gray for herself.

"Where are we going?" she asked, following me as I set off through the trees. Her voice was tight with worry. "Who are we meeting? And Gemma, please, *what* happened to your skin?"

Behind us, the Mist loomed over the priory's turrets and the trees beyond, its great silver canvas bleeding into the sky. Even thinking about it made me prickle all over, as if the Mist *knew* I was thinking about it and wanted me to *know* that it knew, that it would watch me for as long as it could.

To distract myself, I told Mara everything from the horrible night at the masquerade ball to my journey north over the past two days. Talan and the Vilia and I had walked for miles through the Little Grays until we'd finally reached the narrow old greenway that would take us north. Phaidra had discovered it months prior while out hunting, and since then the Vilia had used it several times to steal bits of finery and food from towns in the Mistlands. The greenway was prickly and cantankerous, its magic clearly affronted by our presence, but it dropped us near the small village of Fenwood just as Phaidra had said it would.

Fenwood was south of the priory by a good ten miles, but at least we were out of the Little Grays. With Talan's help, I'd coaxed a horse out of its paddock at a nearby farm, too exhausted to feel guilty about it. I would return it later, I had told myself, or send the farmer money for it, including interest, but with my ruined clothes and shimmering skin, I couldn't very well march into Fenwood and buy a horse without causing a scene. I'd ridden hard after that, alone and exhausted and looking constantly back over my shoulder, but nothing had pursued me. I didn't want Talan anywhere near the Mist, and the Vilia had stayed behind to guard him, all of them huddled in a mean thicket full of briars. As for me, I had kept to the trees and watched the northern sky for the Mist. Not once in my life had I been happy to see that awful churning silver until that moment.

"And now here I am," I finished, worn out from the telling. "I haven't told Talan that we're going to the capital. I don't want to frighten him. But if anyone can help us, it's Gareth, and we'll need every book and scrap of paper he has access to."

Mara was quiet, her face wearing its familiar thoughtful expression. "You want me to hide the Vilia in the caverns while you're gone," she guessed.

"Only while Talan and I are in the city. They'll hate being left behind, but I don't know how being so newly freed will affect them, and I want them out of the way while they recover. They certainly can't come to the capital. The caverns were the safest place I could think of."

"And the more people know of them, the less safe they become."

"I wouldn't ask unless it was important, Mara," I said quietly.

"I know," she replied, her voice gentling. We rode in quiet for a time, and then she said, "This Kilraith—I'm curious about him. I've never heard of such an entity. I'll have to ask the Warden—"

"No. Don't tell anyone about him, not yet. Until Talan is safely freed, the fewer people know about Kilraith, the better."

"If he *can* be freed."

"He can be." I gripped the reins tighter, refusing to look at her. "I won't accept that an unbreakable curse is possible. Everything can be broken."

More silence, all of it weighted with Mara's concern. I flushed all over, suddenly embarrassed and uncertain; after only a few minutes in my sister's company, the doubts I'd so ruthlessly shoved aside were beginning to crawl back toward the light.

"Can you trust him?" she asked. There was no judgment in her voice.

"I don't know," I answered. "I want to. I can't abandon him after what he's told me. If even some of it is true, it's to our family's advantage to keep him close."

"Keep him close even with this Kilraith supposedly embedded somewhere inside him?"

"The alternative is to kill him," I snapped, bristling, "and I'm not prepared to do that, and I'm not even sure we *could* kill him. Kilraith could rise up through him and kill *us* for trying. This is the safest course of action, Mara. I've been thinking on it all the way here and can come up with no bearable alternative."

After a time, Mara said slowly, "I think you're right, at least for now. But you love him, Gemma, and love can't be trusted. I have to ask these questions. My eyes are clear, and yours are not."

My throat was painfully tight. I struggled to find my voice. "I know, and you're right to ask them."

After that I could no longer speak. I urged my horse into a faster gait. We rode on in silence.

A dream woke me, but I couldn't remember it. My eyes shot open, and I lay in fuzzy silence as I recovered my bearings.

The caverns were quiet. Mara was on watch, and Phaidra, Nesset, and Lulath slept. They didn't need to, Phaidra had told me, but it was a joy of the living that they sorely missed, and so when they could manage it—when they were as tired as we all were now—they went through the ritual of it anyway. In the morning, Mara would distract them while Talan and I took the horses back to Rosewarren, where we would use the greenway that led to Ivyhill. We would collect Farrin, travel with her to the queen's city, and bring the problem of Kilraith to Gareth.

My stomach knotted up as I thought about seeing Farrin again after everything that had happened. I was not proud of how I'd left her so soon after Talan's attack in the ballroom, with blood still fresh on her face and her whole body trembling with rage from Father's confession. I closed my eyes for a moment, ashamed at the thought of her weathering that particular storm without me, all on her own, with Father a wreck and the whole staff gossiping.

I turned over, desperate for the oblivion of sleep but not confident I could find it again. My body ached all over from sleeping on the damp rock, and the rough dress and stockings Mara had taken from the priory made my skin itch. Then I saw Talan. He lay very near me, sleeping on a pallet of stolen blankets, but something was wrong. He was sweating, his brow furrowed and his whole body shivering. A nightmare, or worse.

It was foolish to go to him. For all I knew, the nightmare was Kilraith whispering to Talan to wake up and strangle me. But I couldn't see him in such obvious torment and do nothing.

I scooted closer to him, my stiff body protesting, and lay down beside him. He had his arms crossed and was curled protectively around his middle. I brushed damp locks of hair back from his forehead. He looked so young and vulnerable shaking there in the dark.

Finally he opened his eyes. They were bloodshot and terrified. His face crumpled when he saw me, and he wrapped his arms around me and drew me hard against him. He buried his face in my hair and sucked in a shuddering breath.

"He's angry," he whispered. "I can feel it, though he's far away. Like a dull ache you can at first ignore. He doesn't know where I am—he's lost my scent—but he's looking for me, and someday not long from now, the necromancers will wake up and collect themselves, go home to lick their wounds, and the cloud of our cursebreaking will vanish. He'll find me then. He'll come for me. I want him gone, Gemma." He choked out a sob against my neck and cupped my head with one shaking hand and clung to me. "I hate him." His voice was ragged, desperate. "I won't let him hurt you. I won't hurt you. I *won't*. Not you, love."

My heart pounded with fear—for me, for him, for all of us—but I didn't move away. One of his hands was clutching my back; I unfolded the desperate fingers of the other and brought it up to wedge between us. Gently I laid his palm against my chest and covered it with my own. I looked up at him; I would not let him see that I was afraid.

"Listen to me," I told him. "Look at me, Talan. I'm here. I'm right here, and he's not. You're safe right now. We're all safe. I'm here with you, and I'm not going anywhere."

He pressed his brow to mine, his eyes so near that I felt I could sink into them and float forever inside them, a warm dark sea.

"There you are," I said, smiling, "and here I am. I've got you."

After a time, his eyes fluttered closed. His body relaxed; his shivering ceased. He slid his arm back around me, tucked me tenderly against his chest, and kissed me.

"Thank you," he said quietly into my hair. "My brave Gemma."

Wrapped up in each other atop that awful, cold rock, we slept until Mara woke us gently at dawn.

CHAPTER 32

When I knocked on the door to Farrin's bedroom, I braced myself, expecting the worst: she would be furious, cutting, her eyes like iron and her spine made of steel. I had left her, I had run away without explanation, and she would never forgive me for it. Perhaps she would bolt me to the wall with chains and stand guard over me with no weapons but her vicious tongue.

I stood in the long, broad hallway that housed our family's bedrooms, jumpy and furtive after sneaking into the house through our network of secret passages, looking over my shoulder every two seconds to make certain no one had seen me. The house was quiet and felt unsettlingly huge. My body ached from Talan's and my passage south through the greenway, and each moment that crept by drove me closer to panic. I had left Talan outside in the hedge maze, a decision that seemed suddenly foolish. Better to have brought him inside and risked him being seen by someone, no matter the questions that might have arisen given his weakened state, than to leave him hiding on the grounds, alone and vulnerable.

I couldn't bear it any longer. I reached for Farrin's door just as it swung open. She stood on the other side, shocked and bleary-eyed, wearing one of her modest, high-collared gray nightgowns with ribbons tied tightly at her wrists and neck. Her golden-brown hair fell over one shoulder in a loose braid, and her face was drawn, as if she hadn't been sleeping well. When she saw that it was me standing there, she grabbed my hand and led me inside at once. She closed the door quietly, then pulled me into her arms with a small, anguished sound.

"I thought you were dead," she whispered. "Illaria and Gareth heard gunshots. They found the cottage empty, blood all over the door. Gemma..."

Farrin drew back to look at me and cupped my face in her hands, tenderly, astonished, as if she couldn't quite believe I was truly there. "How are you? Are you hurt? What's happened? Does Father know you're here?"

I caught her hands and held them still between us. "No, he doesn't, and I don't want him to. Farrin, we have to talk, and quickly."

Farrin's eyes narrowed, but she said nothing. We sat on her bed—white all over, and cleanly made, as if she hadn't touched it all night—and I told her everything. When I explained who—*what*—Talan really was, Farrin grew frighteningly still, her face pale and furious. When I told her about Kilraith and the story of Talan's family, she rose abruptly and went to stand at the window, her back to me. She stayed that way until I was finished.

Weary, utterly worn out, I waited for her to speak.

"And now you want me to go with you to the capital," she said flatly, "and help you find a way to free this *demon* from his keeper. This demon, mind you, who attacked me. An attack you made possible, thanks to your misguided attempt to...what? End all of this on your own? Go behind Father's back with some half-formed plan and possibly enrage the demon holding all of our lives in his hands?"

Her voice was so thin and quiet with fury that it shocked me, even prepared for it as I was. "Yes," I replied simply, "I want you to go with me to the capital. I tried to fix all of this alone, and it didn't work. I need you and Mara with me, both of you. She's done her part and will do more if I ask her. Now I need you to do yours."

Farrin whirled around to glare at me. "How can you trust him? He hurt me, Gemma. He attacked me in my own home."

"He didn't want to."

She scoffed. "If he really didn't want to, he could have stopped himself."

"Just as you could have looked Father in the eye when he told you to run the estate because he couldn't be bothered, to bear his secrets, to let him take over your life and someday take over his war, and said *no*?"

If I'd slapped Farrin, she wouldn't have looked more stunned.

"Think of all the lectures on the arcana Gareth has spewed at us over the years," I said gently. "Do you really think, given everything he's told us—and imagining everything he *hasn't*—that it's impossible for a creature such as Kilraith to exist? A creature who could possess another and bend that victim to his will, as he has done to Talan?"

Farrin took two quick steps toward me, her eyes glittering. "Talan is a *demon*. He's the demon who has consumed our father's every waking thought for years. The demon who turned the Basks against us, and us against them, and—gods—think of poor Madam Baines, and your Jessyl! He's the cause of everything terrible that's ever happened to our family."

Hearing Jessyl's name was a horrible blow, but I lifted my chin, defiant. "He is only one of many Kilraith has possessed and forced to bear the title of the Man with the Three-Eyed Crown. And *he* isn't the cause of anything terrible. None of them were. Kilraith is."

Farrin threw up her hands and stormed across the room. "These distinctions don't matter to me, and they shouldn't to you. I'll allow for a moment the idea that Talan's will hasn't been his own for some time, that he's never wanted to hurt so much as a fly. Is that supposed to comfort me? Is such a trapped creature, whose loyalties cannot be safely determined, deserving of your trust? Your love?"

I opened my mouth to argue with her, but she pushed on, permitting me not a word. "Were it not for Kilraith," she said, "or Talan, or some other demon—it seems to me they are all one and the same—maybe we never would have begun fighting with the Basks. Maybe Mother and Father wouldn't have been so terribly afraid of you and your strange magic falling into the wrong hands. They might never have hired that artificer, and you might have grown up to become a normal woman."

Struck speechless, I could only stare at her. A look of horror fell over her face. I felt grimly satisfied to see it.

"I'm sorry, Gemma," she whispered. "Gods unmade, I'm so sorry. I didn't mean to say it like that. I meant that you wouldn't have to live with the pain you do, that you'd be able to use magic like the rest of us—"

"I know what you meant." And I did, and I felt too tired to be angry with her. "Please, Farrin. Do this for me. For *us*, for our family. This could be the answer. If we free Talan, maybe it's possible to ensure Kilraith binds no one—no demon, and no human—ever again. This could end our subjugation, this endless war I know you hate, and save us all. Can you imagine?" I blew out a bitter laugh. "Living a *normal* life?"

"No," she answered quietly. "I can't imagine that."

Something gave way on her face as she spoke, some plate of armor that cracked open to show the weariness underneath. This was a part of her I rarely saw, and I couldn't bear the sight of it, how she looked faded and stretched thin and desperately unhappy. I rose from the bed and went to her and took her hand gently in mine.

"Consider this," I said. "We'll be in the capital, and if Talan turns out to be a liar and betrays us, we can send for Queen Yvaine, and she'll come roaring down from the Citadel to save you."

Farrin lifted an eyebrow. "Roaring? She's not a tiger."

"You probably wouldn't even need to send for her. She'd sense that you were in danger and just appear there before any of us could draw our next breath."

Farrin looked at me fondly for a moment, and then she leaned in and kissed my cheek so sweetly that I wanted to cry. She fetched a cloak and boots from her closet, slipped them on over her nightgown.

"We'll bring Talan inside for a bath," she said as she briskly wove her hair into a neater braid. "I know a passage that leads from the hedge maze to the guest quarters on the second floor. No one will see us bring him inside. And you'll need a bath too. A *thorough* one. We can't show up at the university with the two of you looking like you've just crawled out of a mud pit. And I'm sure you want to make this journey as quickly as possible, so we'll take one of Father's greenways to the capital instead of traveling by carriage. But you absolutely cannot ever tell him that I showed you where it is, and you also can't use it by yourself, not without me."

I ran over and crashed into her with a huge clumsy embrace, cutting her off.

"Thank you," I whispered against the hood of her cloak. "Thank you, *thank you.*"

"Stop blubbering," she muttered, "you're *crushing* me." But I glanced at the mirror and caught her little smile before she could hide it, and that small glimpse felt like being warmed by the sun.

I hoped she would have no need, not ever, to regret the marvelous gesture of trusting me.

The queen's city of Fairhaven sat atop pale cliffs high above the Bay of the Gods, on Gallinor's southwestern coast. A cascading labyrinth of tidy streets brought it all the way down to the dazzling white shore on one side and sent it sprawling across clifftops on the other. The queen's palace—the Citadel—marked the center of it all, a towering construction of white stone capped with a landscape of gleaming domes and spiraled turrets.

I had always liked going to the capital despite the bustle of magic that permeated the air—or perhaps because of it, as I'd always known that would set Father on edge, and the moments when he was irritated with me or worried about me were the only times he paid me any attention at all.

If only I'd known, during all those years of longing for my father's love, that he deserved none of mine.

I thought of that as Talan, Farrin, and I hurried through the grand entrance hall of the university's largest library, which housed Gareth's private office. Truly, I thought of a hundred different things; my mind had been a hive of buzzing thoughts since we'd left Ivyhill. Our footsteps echoed like gunshots against the gold-veined marble floor. I hated how open that massive room felt, how many eyes could fall upon us from the mezzanines above, the reading rooms flanking the hall, the professors and students we passed on the stairs to the third floor. And my skin was no help; to casual passersby, the glass could easily pass for shimmering powder meant to offset the severe gray taffeta of my gown, but I felt as though it was a beacon calling Kilraith right to us. My thoughts whirled to terrible, dark places. I would need to teach myself to craft dependable glamours, and quickly, if my power would allow such a thing. I had to hope that it would, that the handful of occasions when I had changed my appearance—either by accident or design—meant *something*.

Talan caught my left hand and squeezed it gently, pulling me out of my inner turmoil. I glanced over at him and felt a horrible pang of fear in my chest. Every moment he strayed farther from his lair, every moment Kilraith looked for him and couldn't find him, left him more exhausted, as if he were constantly pulling hard at a chain. He looked awful—pallid and sweaty, dark circles under his eyes. We would have to mop him down when we reached Gareth's office. People would think he had a fever or that he wore a cheap glamour. Farrin had stolen a dark suit with a vest of crisp brocaded silver from Father's closet, and I wished we'd dressed him in something shabbier. In such finery, his sickly color was even more obvious.

"I'm all right, Gemma," he said quietly, with a faint smile. "It's not as bad as it looks."

But I knew he was lying. I knew it the way I knew that Gareth would light up like fireworks when he learned we'd brought him such a mystery.

"Not much longer," I whispered. "Just hold on to me."

I pressed as close to Talan's side as I could without tripping us both. I longed to turn off into a quiet dark room and draw him to me, as if merely the shield of my body could protect him from the monster who hunted him. I saw a door standing ajar just down the corridor and nearly bolted for it, Talan's hand in mine, to lock us away in the shadows for a while, only a little while. I could soothe him to sleep just as I had done in the cavern. I could kiss away his fear, and mine too.

But then Farrin was rapping sharply on the door of Gareth's office, and his assistant, a rather severe young woman named Heldine who had a habit of glaring with withering suspicion at anyone who dared request a moment of Gareth's time, ushered us inside.

Gareth's office was a small suite of rooms overrun with books, sloppy stacks of them teetering on every surface and in every corner. His private study was the messiest of them all, much of it occupied by an impractically mammoth desk carved all over with Olden beasts—griffins, merfolk, chimaera. Gareth sat there, head propped on one hand, eyeglasses pushed up into his messy blond hair, staring forlornly at a mess of scattered papers. His sleeves were rolled up to his elbows, his shirt was stained with ink and coffee, and he plucked nervously at one of his suspenders. When Heldine announced our presence with a prim little cough, he glanced up, sat there frozen in shock for a moment, and then jumped to his feet.

"Gemma, oh, thank the gods," he said, the relief plain on his face. He hurried around the desk, knocking over the unfortunate stacks of books that stood in his way. Heldine glanced at the ceiling as if pleading silently with the gods for patience and shut the door behind her.

Gareth pulled me into one of his typical bone-crushing hugs. "We thought you'd been killed. Oh, darling, I've been out of my mind with worry, missing classes, not eating…and Talan, my friend, I'm delighted to see you alive and—"

Gareth reached out to shake Talan's hand and then stopped,

aghast. His arm dropped. "Well. Sorry to say this, but you look terrible. What's happened?" He looked around at all of us, his expression turning grave. "Something's wrong. Tell me."

"I'm sorry we didn't write you," Farrin began, "but we didn't want to risk the message being intercepted—"

"We need your help," I said, stepping away from Gareth to hold Talan's hand, and then the whole story burst out of me.

When I'd finished, Gareth sat on the edge of his desk, his eyes full of stars. I could practically *feel* the wheels of his mind spinning madly.

"Kilraith," he whispered. "I've not heard the name, but that means nothing. The arcana is vast." He thought for a moment, then clapped his hands together and strode across the room to consider one of his bookshelves, which burst at the seams like all the others. "Whatever binds you, Talan, is obviously some kind of curse, but for Kilraith to overpower a demon, it would take magic of extraordinary strength. We can start with curses of the upper arcana, perhaps fae curses, which are notoriously slippery...or maybe curses written during the Fourth Age of the Gods, although..." He clucked his tongue. "Bah. The literature from that era that we've managed to excavate and restore with at least moderate accuracy is woefully incomplete. If only there were five of me. Sleep, you know, really interferes with my productivity. This will take some time."

I had never loved Gareth more fiercely than I did in that moment. He had neither cast aspersions on Talan's demonic heritage nor doubted the veracity of his story. Gareth's friends needed a mystery solved, and he would be the one to solve it.

But time was something we did not have in abundance. Talan sank into a chair, his eyes falling shut, and my throat knotted with worry. He was tired, and there was precious little time to rest, and

I couldn't trust that anywhere would be safe for him—except for one place, if only I could get us there.

"We need information quickly," I said. "Could you perhaps take us to the royal archives? The university libraries are expansive, I know, but—"

Gareth spun around and cut me off with an incredulous laugh. "Oh, you're a funny one, Gemmy-Gem. The royal archives? Do you know how long it takes to get a permit for entry? I've had an application pending for *three months* just so I can spend five minutes in *one collection* to verify *a single quote* said by some boring old scholar fifty years ago. *Three months.* And I'm a seated professor. *Seated!*"

"All right, Gareth, calm down," Farrin said, pinching the bridge of her nose.

"But you're right to think the royal archives are your best bet when it comes to searching for obscure information. No one knows how vast they actually are, but they are *vast.* I mean, *big.* I don't think even Queen Yvaine knows everything that's in there. Some people believe—and I'm one of them—that upon the Unmaking, the gods not only did whatever they did to make the high queen the high queen and turn her white as bone and give her a long life and so forth, but they *also* created the archives, a whole sea of ciphered texts we haven't even made a dent in. And there's a gigantic team of scholars practically living in the place, transcribing from dawn till dusk, trying to break these godly ciphers and learn what they can from—"

"*Gareth.*" Farrin looked up, exasperated. "Please, get to the point."

"Right, of course. The point is, the royal archives are both your best bet and your worst. I would wager my life on the fact that the information we need is in there—but finding it? It might very well take a lifetime."

"Unless we ask the queen to help us," I said, the idea occurring to me just at that moment. "She may not know everything about the archives, but surely she knows more than anyone else, isn't that right?"

"Conceivably," Gareth agreed. "Who's to say all those indecipherable texts in the archives aren't copies of whatever knowledge the gods crammed into her mind before they died?"

I looked to Farrin eagerly. "Farrin?"

She sat straight as a board in her chair, her expression stern. "Absolutely not."

"But Farrin—"

"I will not take advantage of my friendship with Yvaine to wheedle our way into the archives out of turn."

"Dearest Farrin," Gareth said gently, "your lifelong preoccupation with following rules is most troubling. You could learn something from your little sister, you know. And besides, why do you care about cheating our way past a bunch of stuffy professors who also just happen to be my competitors for university funding?" He put a hand to his heart. "Darling, you wound me."

"And we wouldn't be taking advantage of your friendship," I added quickly. "We would simply tell the queen what's happened and ask for her guidance. She might very well suggest bringing us to the archives without us even needing to ask."

Gareth snapped his fingers. "There. You see? An excellent suggestion."

"And don't you think she'd *want* to know about a being like Kilraith, if she doesn't already? I'd want to, if I were the high queen."

Farrin raised an eyebrow. "Gods, there's a horrific prospect."

A sharp groan from Talan stopped me from saying anything else. With a terrifying suddenness, he lurched over in his chair, chest to thighs, as if he were going to be sick on the floor. He drew in great ragged breaths.

"Gods help me," he gasped, clutching at his chest.

I ran over to kneel beside him. "Talan? What is it?" Fear painted my insides black and cold. "Is it Kilraith?"

He shook his head, squeezed his eyes shut. "No. Not yet. Not fully. But he's getting closer. The cursebreaking magic must be beginning to fade in earnest. I can't..." He reached for me, his hand trembling. "Gemma," he choked out, his voice snagging on a sob.

"I'm here. Talan, I'm here." I drew his head down onto my shoulder, holding him as he shook.

"It feels like...something inside me is..." He clung to me, his fingers digging desperately into my back. "*Moving*. Scraping through me. Like a..." He pressed his face hard against my neck. "Like a beast turning deep on the ocean floor. Stirring...bubbles rising thick to the top...a great heat, boiling..."

His words devolved into gibberish. Trying not to cry, I looked at Farrin, desperate. "*Please*, Farrin? Besides access to the archives, being near the queen might give him some relief. If the cursebreaking magic could muddle Kilraith's senses, then surely the magic of the queen could do so even more effectively."

"All right." Farrin rose from her chair, her face pale as she watched Talan shudder. I found some small comfort in knowing that surely now, in the face of his suffering, she could no longer doubt that what he said was true. "Gareth, send for your carriage. We'll go straight from here to the palace as soon as it arrives."

CHAPTER 33

I had spent many visits to the capital at the palace, but only ever in the wing meant for guests. The rest of the Citadel was a mystery to me, and as two of the silent, gold-armored queensguard led us to the queen's rooms—their expressions inscrutable, their faces hard as rocks—I felt a little thrill of fear, as if I were entering another realm entirely, one not meant for me.

The queen's wing was enormous. I couldn't imagine uses for all the rooms we passed, their closed doors carved with scenes from beloved folktales. The Shepherd Who Heard the Song of the Skies standing on a hilltop with his arms outstretched and his flock milling around him, forgotten. The Robin and the Raven, one circling the sun, the other the moon, doomed to love but never meet. Valtaine, the little hearth-sweeper, crouching in the ashes with her broom, eyes wide, for she had just discovered messages written in the unreadable tongue of the gods—messages she could miraculously understand.

The queensguard took us through that last door into a small anteroom, lavishly appointed: thick blue carpets with golden stars woven throughout—*arranged just as they are in the night sky at midsummer*, Gareth whispered, beside himself. There was the Great Bear, there the Seer. Gorgeous tapestries hung along the dark, wood-paneled walls, and the ceiling was white stone carved with a swirling pattern of stars trailing tails of light.

"Gemma," Talan whispered, leaning heavily on me. He looked around, dazed, his eyes cloudy. "Is there somewhere I can lie down?"

The queensguard nearest me cut a sharp look at Talan, clearly unhappy about this sweating, possibly sick man coming anywhere near the queen. But they didn't dare protest; the queen wanted to see Farrin and her friends, and the queen would be obeyed.

I helped Talan settle on a small divan in the corner of the room, the fabric a supple rust-colored velvet. He sank onto it with a small groan of relief. I wedged a tufted pillow under his head and knelt beside him. Farrin found a stack of folded linen napkins beside a spread of tea and cakes; she brought me one, and a pitcher of water. I took them both gratefully and set to work cooling Talan's fevered brow.

"Has the pain faded at all since entering the Citadel?" I asked quietly.

He nodded against the pillow. "It's quieter here, inside and out. I feel...settled. Exhausted, but settled, or at least *settling*. Like I've walked a hundred miles and am finally able to sit down and rest my ruined feet. They're burning with blisters, but at least I'm no longer walking." He looked up at me with a tired smile and brought my wrist to his mouth. He closed his eyes and kissed me—wrist, palm, fingers. He sighed against my skin.

"Gods, this is a very fine couch," he mumbled, "and you are a very fine nurse."

My heart swelled with tenderness. He looked so tired lying there, his long body curled up in a position that couldn't have been comfortable, and yet his face was soft, peaceful at last. I brushed my lips across his forehead. I wanted him in my arms, but that small kiss would have to do.

"Rest, darling," I whispered. "I'll be here when you wake."

There was a damask curtain hanging from the ceiling nearby, tied back against the wall with a golden tasseled sash. I tugged it loose and let it fall, hiding Talan from view, then joined Farrin and Gareth at the tea table. None of us touched a crumb of the food.

"If he can sleep even for a few minutes..." I said quietly.

Farrin nodded and took my hand. "It would be a blessing."

Quiet fell. It stretched on for so long that I grew restless and started to pace, my footsteps muffled by the thick carpet. Gareth heaved a huge red book off a nearby shelf, quickly flipped through it, then held it open, staring at it, not turning a single page, his leg bouncing in agitation. Farrin sat with her hands folded tightly on the tabletop, saying nothing, her mouth thin.

I stopped my pacing for a moment in front of the closed door. The two implacable queensguard stood on either side of it, but I ignored them and instead studied the door's carving. It was the same as on the other side, a mirror image—Valtaine, dressed in rags and on her knees in the ashes, staring at messages only she could see.

Suddenly the queensguard stiffened, straightening to even stricter attention, and from behind me came a soft rustling of cloth and a gentle voice: "And whatever secrets the ashes held, Valtaine told them to no one. Instead she built with her own hands the Falkeron Cloisters, the first and greatest temple devoted to the worship of the goddess Zelphenia, and once that was done, she took her own life so the secret knowledge she had gleaned from the ashes would die with her."

Startled, I turned to find Queen Yvaine standing at Farrin's side, a hand on my sister's shoulder. Whether she had entered the room through a concealed door or simply appeared there through some obscure spell known only to her, I could not say. The not knowing didn't sit well inside me.

"Your Majesty," I murmured, sinking into a deep curtsy.

The queen was, as ever, resplendent, her gown a soft cascade of peach chiffon with billowing sheer sleeves that gathered at her wrists with satin ribbons. Her skin glowed in the dim lamplight, and she wore her white hair pinned up in a diamond headpiece studded with tiny burgundy roses. Her gaze flicked over me— she was seemingly unperturbed by the glitter of glass coating my skin—and as I met her eyes, one violet, one gold, I wondered if in her long life, she had ever seen anything like me.

"You're struck by the art," the queen said with a smile, joining me near the door. "Is the story of Valtaine a favorite of yours?"

Surprised by the question, I answered bluntly. "Not particularly, Your Majesty. In fact, I find it terribly sad."

The queen appraised the door thoughtfully, as if she'd never before considered that a story about a woman killing herself might be sad.

"Yes," she said quietly after a moment. "Yes, I suppose it is." I thought I saw something pass over her face, the barest hint of a shadow, but then it was gone. Perhaps it was merely my own unsettled fancy.

She turned her back to the door and gave us a serene smile. "Well, perhaps during your next visit, I can show you all the story doors and tell you about the artisans who crafted them. But for now we should speak of other things." She glanced at the queensguard. "You may leave us, please."

Two brisk bows, a clank of armor as they passed through Valtaine's door, and the queensguard were gone. We were alone.

Queen Yvaine softened—her face, the lines of her body, her voice. She took my hand and led me back to the table. Her touch was smooth and cool, her fingers frighteningly slight in mine. I worried I might snap them in two.

She sat beside Farrin and looked at me gently. "Now. First I must apologize for my tardiness. It has been a strange sort of day here at the palace. I've been distracted and irritable, and I can't seem to get my head on straight." There it was again—that slight ripple of disquiet on her face, as if she were trying to remember a dream that continued to elude her. "But I'm here now, and I'm ready to listen. Farrin tells me you are distressed, Gemma, that someone you love is in grave danger. Please tell me what's happened, and I'll do my utmost to help you."

In the absence of her guards, Queen Yvaine was even more splendid—warmer, more present, as though she had been merely a cold echo of a woman and now she was truly here with us, flesh and blood and infinite kindness, her presence a beacon of light, her beauty astonishing.

I swallowed hard, suddenly nervous, and began once more to tell the story of everything that had happened. Farrin and Gareth, bless them, helped me get through it. When I spoke of what my parents had done, my voice cracked all the way open. It felt like the hundredth time I'd said the horrible words, and still my heart couldn't bear the weight of them. Farrin took my hand and held on tight; her unwavering grip pulled me through.

But as I began to tell Talan's story—the titans attacking his ancestral home, his flight into the woods—something changed. The queen's attention wandered; though her eyes were still on me, I could see something distant moving behind them. She was there with us, and yet she was somewhere else too. I continued to speak despite the flutter of nerves in my throat. The queen's brow furrowed, a single delicate line just below her pink, star-shaped scar. And then I first uttered Kilraith's name, and she went very still, her whole body stiffening. I stopped talking at once, a little chill slipping down my arms, and looked to Farrin for help.

She touched the queen's hand, which shocked me. Even though their friendship was no surprise, I always felt a bit unnerved when I saw the evidence of it: surely touching the royal arm was a privilege given to no other guest.

"Yvaine?" Farrin said softly. "What's wrong? Are you all right?"

"Yes, I..." The queen frowned, looking just as bewildered as we were. "I'm not certain what...strange." She gave herself another little shake and nodded at me. "Please continue."

I did, with some hesitation, but as I began to explain how we'd come to the capital in search of knowledge that would help us break Kilraith's curse, the queen flinched as if something had bitten her and rose swiftly to her feet.

"I think I'm beginning to understand," she said quietly. She grabbed the back of the chair she'd abandoned, released it, backed away from it. Then she looked right at me, her eyes bright as jewels. "Where is he? Talan of the Far Sea." She looked around the room, quietly frantic, a child realizing she'd lost her mother in a crowd, until she found the curtain and stared at it. "I must see him. I must see him with my own eyes."

She hurried across the room and ripped back the curtain, revealing Talan's sleeping form. He was dead to the world, his face slack with exhaustion. I would have been pleased to see the slight color that had returned to his cheeks if I hadn't been so terrified. Something was horribly wrong.

"Farrin?" I whispered, but she had no answers for me. Gareth clutched the book he'd been reading in both hands, as if preparing to wield it as a weapon.

The queen sank to her knees at Talan's side. She reached for his face, then shrank back. Her hands hovered in the air, trembling. "Who are you?" she breathed. "Who is that calling for me?"

Talan's eyes opened at last. Sleep lay heavily on him. He blinked at the queen in confusion, then startled fully awake. "Your Majesty," he said, trying to push himself up. "My apologies—"

"Whatever made you," she said, staring at him, "is ancient and furious. Not you. The thing inside you. Still." She touched his face. "Stay still."

Talan obeyed, looking uneasy. I could hardly breathe as I watched the queen feather her fingers across his cheeks, his chin, his brow. She closed her eyes, straining against something. Talan's dark eyes found mine, boyish with fear.

"This is what I've been feeling," the queen whispered. "Something...in here. I've felt this all day. I've felt it coming. I've heard...voices. Familiar. Distant."

Farrin sat on the edge of the divan and watched the queen's face closely. If she was afraid, she hid it well. "What voices, Yvaine? What are they saying?"

The queen shook her head and went very still. Then, with excruciating care, she cupped Talan's face in her slender white hands. "A curse. Terrible, cruel. It feeds on you, and so does he. It hungers for blood. It craves, and you are its keeper, one of many. It needs violence to survive, it gulps down lies and despair like a starving child, and you have been neglectful in your duties, Talan of the Far Sea. Why do you run from me?"

Her eyes snapped open. She gripped his head hard, her face crumpling. "*Why do you run from me?*"

A low boom rippled through the room like a rushing pulse of blood. Queen Yvaine fell back from Talan and scrambled away from him. She crawled to the center of the room, panting, then rose unsteadily to her feet, her back to us.

"Whatever you have done over the years in his service," she said, her voice low and ragged, "whatever all of you have done—you and the others before you—it has fed him, made him stronger. He has his claws in so many."

She looked back over her shoulder at Talan, breathing quickly, her eyes bright, terrified. "I cannot be near him, not ever again. Not while this thing lives inside him. It is quiet, confused, but every day it grows closer. It is hungry, mad with craving, and what it hungers for more than anything is me."

Farrin looked stricken. "Yvaine, I'm sorry, we didn't know."

"Of course you didn't. Even I don't know how to make sense of everything I just saw. You may stay the night—I'll send for someone to escort you to your rooms—but you must leave in the morning, and you will not see me again while you are here. I regret that I cannot allow you into the archives." Her gaze flitted to the book Gareth held in his hands, then once more to Talan. "Do not bring this man back here, not even to the city itself. Talan of the Far Sea…" She shook her head, her expression heavy with sadness. "I am truly sorry."

Then she hurried out through the door of Valtaine and left us.

Our rooms for the night were a lavish suite on the Citadel's western face. A wall of wide windows opened onto a sweeping terrace that gave us a gorgeous view of the bay far below, its waves kissed red by the setting sun. Each of us had our own bed, piled with massive clouds of pillows and blankets and crowned with gauzy curtains that fluttered in the salty breeze coming in off the water. There was an enormous bathing room, immaculate and gleaming, with tiles of cream and coral and gold fixtures polished to a perfect shine.

But I couldn't relax, and I could barely eat. I nibbled at the supper sent up to us—a light summer meal of chilled green pea soup topped with fresh herbs and crispy onion curls; a platter of freshly cut fruit; nutty sliced cheese; and thin crackers dusted with rosemary—but even the few bites I ate sat like heavy stones in my stomach.

Everyone was uneasy in the wake of the queen's distress, Talan most of all. I persuaded him to eat a few mouthfuls of food, and then he disappeared into the room farthest from the suite's entrance. I gave him perhaps five minutes to himself and then couldn't bear to be away from him any longer. I left Gareth poring over the book he'd taken from the anteroom, Farrin peering in confusion over his shoulder, and I slipped into the back bedroom and closed the door gently behind me.

Talan sat on the edge of the bed, facing the window and the sea beyond. His hands were in fists on his thighs, and when he turned to look at me, his face was streaked with tears.

"I hate him, Gemma," he said. "The way the queen looked at me like I was a monster, something unnatural and vile. You don't know how many times I've thought of just being done with it all..." He shook his head, his expression tight with disgust. "But I don't even know if I could do *that*. Most likely I would get close, and then he'd pull me back from death at the last moment. Yes, I think that's exactly what would happen. He'll keep me alive forever. A prisoner, forever."

He fell silent, his jaw working. His eyes were ferociously sad and shadowed anew, as if the queen's horrible whispered words had drained him of something essential and fine.

I came around to stand before him and lifted his chin. The

sadness on his face wrenched my heart and left me aching—to touch him, to protect him, to be the thing that put light back into his eyes.

"I've thought of death too," I confessed quietly. "You know I have. More often than I would like to admit, I've thought of it."

He gathered my hands and lifted them to his mouth and kissed them, his eyes squeezed shut as if I'd dealt him a horrible blow.

"For a long time," I continued quietly, "I couldn't see past the next day, maybe two. I tried to tell myself I liked being me, rich and beautiful, everything I could ever want at my fingertips. But that was a lie, and what I really wanted—to live without pain or panic, to feel loved, *truly* loved, neither resented nor forgotten, to belong in the world and not feel as though I lived outside it—all of that felt like an impossible dream. So I thought about death. Sometimes I prayed for it. I understand, I think, at least a little of what you're feeling. I wish I could take those thoughts away from you, lock them away where they can never find you. Oh, Talan."

I smiled at him. "Remember that night in the garden, before everything went wrong? No," I said, putting a finger to his lips, "no, that wasn't your fault, and I won't hear you say it was. You were right to leave me. You were trying to protect me. Now, remember: You saw what I'd done, how I'd hurt myself, and you told me you weren't afraid of it. You told me you understood. Well, I understand you. I don't care what scars you bear, because I have them too. I'm not afraid of your grief. I'll help you carry it, Talan, and you'll help carry mine. We'll never have to bear it alone, not ever again."

He let out a soft sound, a hoarse little cry. "Gemma," he said, shaking his head, overcome. "Do you mean it? Can you truly look at me now, knowing what I am, and love me even so?"

In answer, I bent down and kissed him, slow and soft, and held his face gently, a treasure between my palms. When he responded with a groan, opening my mouth to deepen the kiss, I tried to pull away, knowing even as I burned for him that he needed to rest— but he kept me close, his hands gentle on my hips, and pressed his cheek against me.

"Stay with me," he said, his voice rough and velvet, his breath hot on the swell of my breasts. "Please, Gemma. I need you." He looked up at me with those sad eyes, twin black moons, frightened and lonesome, and my breath caught in my throat. He had always been beautiful, but in that moment, with his face washed clean of anything but desperate, anguished need, he was something close to divine.

"I understand if you don't want to," he whispered, "and if you don't, please tell me, but I…gods, I could listen to you speak forever, I could do nothing but touch you and be happy. You're the only thing that makes any sense to me." He nuzzled the embroidered flowers lining my bodice, let out a shaky breath. "Gemma, Gemma. Stay with me, darling."

And I did, because I could think of nothing I wanted more in the world than to be with him, to wrap him up in my arms and keep him as close to me as possible. No Kilraith, no strange muttering queens. The room was full of sunset, tangerine and rose, everything soft, everything dim and gold, the gentlest light I'd ever seen. I bent once more to kiss him.

"I'm right here," I whispered against his mouth. "I'm here, and this is everything, right now. This is all. You and me."

I sank onto his lap as I spoke, and the sound he made as my hips touched his was unbearably tender. Relief, and delight, and his hands coming around me like the slow slip of honey. Our kisses were languorous, assured, and when I circled my hips, I felt him hard against me, and I gasped, letting out a soft laugh. I would never tire of feeling him press against me, his desire obvious and exhilarating. My happiness inspired him; he drew me back down to him, my name falling roughly from his lips, and he held me tight against him as we moved, our hips locked together as if we were already joined. Another moment of that, and my head was spinning with want. I needed more of him; I needed *all* of him.

We fumbled to help each other out of our clothes, and I didn't understand how we managed it, with our trembling fingers and the hum of our bodies and the blush of sunset painting us impossibly soft, impossibly lovely. But then he was drawing me back to him, and the press of skin to skin was everything—smooth and soft all the way down, his body hot and hard against mine. He sat on the bed and pulled me atop him, and I sank down onto him with a sob in my throat, my legs already shaking. He helped me settle against him, his hands gentle on my hips, and then he thrust up into me, and I gasped out a sharp cry of pleasure that he trapped with a kiss.

I wrapped my arms around him, wove my fingers into his hair, and bent my head over his as I began to move slowly, murmuring what I wanted against his ear. He found my breasts and kissed them all over, nuzzled between them with a ragged sigh, and then his arms came fast around me, desperate, and he held me to him, his movements growing rougher, erratic. I clung to him, said his name over and over, told him I was his, that he was mine, that what he was doing felt so good I would scream if he wasn't careful. I said that with a smile, and he heard it in my voice and looked up and smiled back at me, dazed and flushed, before lifting me, turning me, laying me back across the bed.

The separation was awful, but then he was kneeling, gently parting my legs. "There you are," he whispered, dropping kisses onto my quivering belly, the crease of my thigh. "Gods, you're beautiful, Gemma. You're lovelier than the stars." He pressed his face between my legs, nuzzled my thatch of blond curls, and then he looked up at me, his expression earnest and grave, as if he had something to tell me, something I needed to know immediately.

"I love you, Gemma," he said, wonderingly, like he could hardly believe his luck, his voice soft and clean as the dimming sunlight. Then he put his mouth on me, and I arched up against him with a silent cry, pleasure licking up my body like white fire. I wound my fingers through the black silk of his hair, and when I looked down the glittering expanse of my body, my skin painted a shimmering sunset gold, the sight of him unraveled me—his head buried between my legs, his hands pressing into the flesh of my thighs, holding me open for him. He groaned against me, his tongue light as a bird's wing, and I came suddenly, the taut bow of my body humming gold as midday. I sank back against the bed with a muted cry, reached for him through my haze of bliss, pulled him onto me.

"Inside me," I whispered, still shaking. I kissed him, hooked my legs around him, and clutched his nape, scrabbling, artless. "Please, Talan."

He didn't hesitate; he held himself over me, and I reached down and found him, the heat of him scorching my palm, and guided him into me. He gasped out my name and brought my hands over my head, laced our fingers together, and pinned me there as he moved, slick and hot and fast. I turned and kissed his arm, pressed my heels into his hips to pull him deeper into me. I was sure Farrin and Gareth could hear us in the other room, if they hadn't already run out of the suite with their hands clapped over their ears, an image that made me arch up against Talan's body with a laugh.

He moaned and kissed me. "I love the sound of your laugh,"

he breathed, and then he pressed his forehead to mine, and I wrapped myself around him, clung to him. When he finished, it was with a muffled sob, his whole body shuddering as he drove into me. He tried to move off of me, but I didn't let him, kept my legs firmly wrapped around his. I would be sore tomorrow, and I shivered with delight to think of it, how I would move through the world with the memory of Talan's passion burned into my thighs.

I held him and stroked his hair. The room began to cool, the sun nearly gone. Talan dropped a kiss into my hair, settled beside me, and drew me into the warm curve of his body. I tucked my head against his neck as he pulled the quilt up around us, a cocoon of sweat and sex and soft skin. He slid his hand up into the damp mess of my hair. There were words to be said, fears to assuage, but at the moment that felt far from us, dim and unimportant. He cradled my face next to his, nuzzled his cheek against mine, heartbreakingly soft, and then he kissed me—my lips and throat and hair, the tip of my nose, the tender spots behind my ears— until I fell happily into sleep.

CHAPTER 34

We awoke in the darkness to what sounded like someone trying to bash down the bedroom door. Talan's arms tightened around me, his body suddenly tense and alert.

"Everyone in there had better be wearing clothes," came Gareth's muffled voice, "or at least wrapped up in something that covers all your bits, or else everyone out *here* will be very upset."

Talan fell back against the bed and threw his arm over his eyes. "Can this not wait until morning, Gareth?"

"Afraid not, no." A beat. "Well? Are you decent?"

Giggling, I scooted up to sit against the headboard and pulled on Talan's arm. "Come on, then, make yourself appropriate."

Talan obeyed with a grumble, and once we'd tucked ourselves securely into the bed linens, I called out with unruffled dignity, "You may enter."

The door swung open and Gareth strode in, the book from Queen Yvaine's receiving room in his hand. Farrin was just behind him and studiously avoided looking at me as she lit the room's lamps. I swallowed a smile. I knew Farrin had overheard at least some of my previous romantic liaisons, but perhaps none of them had been quite so shockingly enthusiastic.

Gareth came around to sit in a bedside chair. "I am going to pretend I don't see this mess of clothes on the floor," he said, "and tell you what we've discovered."

He dropped his book onto the bed and pointed at pages of what looked to me like utter nonsense, indecipherable and obviously arcane—but before he could begin to explain, a rumble shook the room. Not loud or violent; if Talan and I had still been asleep, I'm not sure we would have felt it.

As it was, the feeling terrified me. I grabbed Talan's hand, suddenly wishing we'd taken the time to dress.

"What was that?" I asked. "An earthquake?"

We all looked at each other for a moment, unsettled, listening hard. Then it happened again—a tremor, louder than the first, then a pause, and then another tremor, louder still, and another after that, like the crashes of monstrous waves.

"Something's here," Talan said quietly, frowning. He held up his hands and turned them over, inspecting his fingers and palms.

Dread fell through me like cold rain. "Is it Kilraith?"

When he looked up at me, his face was ashen. "No, I don't think so. But something's here that shouldn't be. We need to leave *now*."

All at once a furious clamor of bells rang out, both inside and outside the palace walls. Talan scrambled out of bed, and I followed him, my heart pounding at the back of my throat. We tugged on our clothes and shoes; Farrin helped me fasten my bodice as quickly as she could, her fingers shaking. Gareth ran to each bedroom, gathering the pokers and long iron tongs from every hearth. He gave each of us a weapon, then tucked his book under one arm and hurried to the door, cracked it open, stood there listening. The tremors continued, a new one rumbling every few breaths.

"What's in that book, Gareth?" I whispered.

He shot me a grave look. "Something too important to leave behind."

Farrin gripped her poker with both hands. "Do you see anything?"

"No, but I hear something. It sounds like—"

A roar interrupted Gareth—distant, beastly. From somewhere below us came the explosive crash of shattering glass. My entire body gave an involuntary shudder as I recalled the night of Talan's ballroom attack. My skin prickled, as if each tiny, embedded shard of glass had bristled to attention.

Talan stared at the floor, his gaze far away. "They're coming closer."

"*What* is coming?" I asked.

Another roar, and another, and then a chorus of panic—soldiers shouting commands, guests screaming in fear.

"Something's come for Yvaine," Farrin whispered. "Oh, gods. What if we've led Kilraith right to her?"

"The queen is the safest person in this palace," Gareth said. "If something's coming after her, they'll have to get through a thousand guards and innumerable traps."

Talan gathered himself and looked sharply at Gareth. "The greenway that brought us here from Ivyhill—is there something closer?"

Gareth's face was grim. "Not that I know of. Farrin?"

She shook her head. "I'm sure there is, but not one I have access to."

My stomach turned as I remembered the long carriage ride that had brought us up to the palace from the university and its forested parks.

A piercing scream from downstairs sent me hurrying to the nearest window to peer outside. A dark stream of ants swarmed through the palace courtyards far below.

"People are running downcity to the shore," I told the others.

"And then what?" Gareth said. "They'll be trapped between the bay and whatever chaos is unfolding up here."

Talan looked increasingly agitated, a fresh sheen of sweat on his brow. "We have to leave, *now*. We'll head in the opposite direction of all the noise and go as fast as we can toward the university, and we won't look back."

"I'm not leaving Yvaine," Farrin said quietly.

Gareth blew out a sharp breath. "*Farrin—*"

"No. I'm not doing it." She stood stiff and tall, knuckles white around her makeshift weapon, brown eyes flashing. "I'm not going to abandon my queen and, more importantly, my *friend* while her home is under attack. What if she needs our help?"

Another tremor, this one violent enough to upset my balance. I stumbled and caught myself on the doorframe, but my head and one of my feet and part of my arm pushed out into the corridor, and as soon as they did, it was like I'd dipped those parts of my body into hot oil. A current of magic surging up the hallway raked over my skin, scalding me. The pain was so abrupt and immense that for a moment I could neither breathe nor speak. In a daze, I looked down, expecting to see ruined skin, shining blisters, but my arms looked just as they had before.

"She has many soldiers to help her, Farrin," Gareth was saying, his voice nearly drowned out by the pain roaring in my ears. "We would only get in their way."

"Gemma?" Talan held my waist, steadying me. "What happened?"

"It hurts," I croaked, and then I pushed away from him and threw my whole body out into the corridor. The magic rushing along the carpet knocked me to my hands and knees. I huddled there, gasping in shock. We were going to have to run, and I hoped acclimating myself to this new blinding pain would be akin to venturing into the first waves of summer before the ocean had warmed—better to plunge in all at once than to creep in toe by toe.

Talan crouched beside me, and Farrin too, with Gareth standing watch over us. They were all speaking to me, but their voices were distorted, incomprehensible. I dug my fingers into the carpet, braced my arms against the floor, and breathed through the hot pulses of pain—in and out, slow, measured, until at last I could lift my head again. I reached under my collar for Phaidra's talisman and realized that in my haste I had forgotten to put it back on. But there was no time to spare. We needed to move.

"I'm all right," I said faintly. My tongue felt fat, my words slow, but with Talan and Farrin on either side of me, I managed to stand. I leaned against Talan as we all crept down the corridor, staying flat against the wall until we came out into an atrium: elaborate stained glass ceiling, stately coastal trees standing tall in each corner, the central space bounded by six rectangular mezzanines that stood open to the floor below. Horrible noises floated up to us—gurgling screams, spitting gunfire, the crunch of bone, the meaty chop of swords.

A roar burst into the air, a rattling throaty sound, furious and hungry, and then the roar became a shriek, its tones splitting into a wretched chord. Someone below us in the atrium screamed— "No, *no*, wait!"—and then fell abruptly silent.

Gareth crouched low, crept to the polished wooden railing, and peered over it. He went very still. Then a sickening snap from below made him jerk away and hurry back to us.

"Chimaera," he spat, his expression dark with fury.

I clutched Talan's arm in terror. Suddenly the sounds of violence from below us made horrible sense. My mind filled with images of every nightmare from my childhood storybooks: fat scuttling serpents with six furred legs; tawny feline monsters with crowns of antlers and scaly hindquarters ending in cloven hooves; leather-winged beasts with three heads—raptor, bat, stag—all of them furious, all of them horrific, malformed shadows of their counterparts in Edyn. Olden lore told us that Neave, goddess of the beasts, had, in an ancient act of vengeance, scoured the Old Country for every creature who had ever betrayed her and transformed them into chimaera as punishment. Other tales insisted that Neave had created the chimaera not out of vengeance but out of a restless desire to achieve the perfect bestial entity.

Whatever the reason for their existence, the chimaera were Olden and should not have been able to set a single foot in Edyn, much less in the Citadel—and yet they had, and my faith in Gareth's knowledge was too complete to doubt his assessment.

Farrin, however, stared at him, aghast. "Chimaera? But that doesn't make any sense!"

"I agree, and yet here we are," Gareth replied darkly.

"You're telling me that not only have... How many are there?"

"That I could see? Five."

"You're telling me, then, that not only have *five* chimaera somehow breached the Middlemist, but they have traversed the entire southern reach of Gallinor and managed to invade the Citadel with no one stopping them? No one sending a message of warning to Yvaine? Impossible."

Talan put his head in his hands and moaned quietly. I braced myself against him, trying to hold him up as best I could even as my own body throbbed with pain. But at least I wasn't burdened with a curse that bound me to some entity no one could understand. I gritted my teeth and pushed through the agony lashing at my muscles.

"Mara thinks something is wrong with the Mist," I said quickly. "Fires have been erupting without warning, killing everything they touch. And the Brethaeus managed to bind human revenants to them here in Edyn." I felt sick as my thoughts traveled to all sorts of terrible places, panic tingling at the tips of my fingers. "I think it is in fact quite possible, Farrin."

Gareth's eyes were wide. "Wait, fires? In the Mist? What do you mean, fires?"

"Later, Gareth," Farrin snapped, glaring at me. "And I do mean that, Gemma. It seems you haven't told us everything there is to tell."

Once I would have blanched at the furious look on her face. But I knew that her anger masked something deeper, an awful fear I felt myself. If the Middlemist was damaged, perhaps irreparably, life for Mara would become even more dangerous than it already was.

I tightened my arm around Talan and said shortly, "Fine. Later we'll talk. But now we need to run."

"You cannot outrun them," Talan murmured, his cheek pressed against my brow. "They will keep coming and coming until they have what they want. He will make certain of that."

Gareth ducked to meet Talan's eyes. "Who are *they*, Talan? The chimaera? Or something else? Is Kilraith controlling them?"

I jerked my head toward the atrium. "Farrin, what's the quickest route out of here that keeps us away from the fighting?"

Farrin nodded grimly. "This way."

We followed her through the palace, a path of servants' stairwells and twisting hallways that felt maddeningly circuitous, as if we would never escape the Citadel and would be doomed to navigate its labyrinths forever. Panic swept past us on all sides—palace staff screaming at each other to hurry, guests from every continent racing for the doors in their nightshirts and dressing gowns. Bestial howls followed us all the way down to the ground floor, every one of them different—yowling, shrieking, thunderous groans—and I realized with a shock of fear that the five chimaera Gareth had counted could not have been alone.

When at last we emerged into the Pearl of the Sea Ballroom, a sobbing laugh of relief burst out of me. The gleaming floor was vast, but on the other side of it stood doors leading out into the gardens, and from there, the city with its fresh air and broad streets, and beyond that, the coastal plains and roads that led north to safety.

"Remind me to write Queen Yvaine and thank her for hosting you so many times over the years," I whispered to Farrin. "Well done, my darling."

She shot me a little smile, and though she said nothing, I could see the worry for Yvaine in her eyes. As we hurried across the ballroom floor, Talan's weight and my own pain making me stumble, I thought of the queen and uttered a quick prayer to Zelphenia—*Oh, Goddess unknowable, that you could lure Death to your bed; oh, Goddess divine, that you could for one night draw away his heartless gaze.*

We had nearly made it to the doors when something enormous slammed into the floor just behind us, throwing us all off our feet. My hearth tongs went flying off into the shadows. On my hands and knees, I scrambled for Talan—and then froze, shrinking back in fear from the creature towering over us not ten paces away.

Its head was reptilian, slender and clever, framed with a ruff of matted fur that glistened with blood. Its massive body was lupine; its tail lashed restlessly through the air like a whip, thick and naked, ratlike. It looked down at us with eight yellow eyes, cocked its head, purred deep in its throat as if it were amused at the sight of us cowering before it. Each of the serrated talons on its front paws had to be at least five inches long. My mouth went dry. I couldn't move, couldn't even turn my head to find Talan.

Then, out of the corner of my left eye, I saw Farrin push herself up from where she had fallen, shake herself a little, try to stand. She staggered; she had hit her head. She hadn't yet seen the chimaera. I tried to scream her name but couldn't find my voice. The chimaera crouched, ready to pounce. From behind me, Gareth shouted a desperate warning, but it was too late. Farrin turned, eyes wide, just as the creature lunged for her, talons out, fangs bared.

Something zipped through the air—there was a thick, fast sound like the crack of a whip and then a hard meaty thunk. The chimaera's body jerked, then crashed to the ground, giving Farrin time to scramble away. The beast wasn't dead, but a huge black arrow had pierced its side, and it staggered for a moment, stunned, chirruping like a bird.

I whirled to find the archer who had saved my sister and saw Ryder Bask, dressed in plain garments: a gray tunic, brown trousers, brown boots. He was filthy, splattered with blood, and thinner than when I'd last seen him, but he was still a beast of a man, swift despite his size, and handsome, with that slash of dark beard across his pale skin and his movements sinuous, feline. He threw himself between the chimaera and Farrin, raised a gigantic crossbow that bore the royal crest, and loosed three more arrows into the stunned chimaera's chest.

The chimaera shrieked in fury and reared up with a terrible gurgling roar. It was a gigantic creature, and even four arrows weren't enough to fell it. Ryder backed away slowly, his last arrow nocked and raised. He was murmuring in some arcane language I didn't know.

Gareth crawled toward me, his face sallow with pain. He cradled one of his arms against his chest; it was clearly broken.

"He's speaking Ekkari," Gareth grunted. "An arcane bestial language. *Go home*," he translated. "*Go below. This woman is poison. These people are poison.*"

"Below?" I whispered.

The chimaera shook its head, agitated. It slammed one set of talons into the floor and clawed five jagged ruts into the ruined parquet.

Then another voice joined Ryder's. "*Go home*," Gareth continued to translate through gritted teeth. "*Go home and never come back.*"

Alastrina Bask moved slowly out of the shadows, one arm outstretched, the blue eyes that matched her brother's fixed hard upon the chimaera. Her garments were identical to Ryder's, her black hair falling greasy and loose to her shoulders, and as I watched her approach, my astonishment gave way to understanding: the Bask siblings both wore the garb of prisoners. They had been in the Citadel for weeks, detained by the queen since the night of the ball.

A ferocious gladness curled around my heart as I imagined them huddled in whatever miserable accommodations Queen Yvaine had provided for them—but then something miraculous happened. The chimaera shrank down, belly to the floor, and curled its naked tail around its legs. It waited for Alastrina, placid as a kitten, and when she touched its scaly head, it whimpered, cowering.

Alastrina stared down at it, her face cold with revulsion, and uttered one last sentence—"*Go home*," Gareth translated, his voice strained, "*and climb the highest mountain, and find a cliff on its slopes, and throw yourself off of it.*"

The chimaera did not hesitate for even a moment. It slunk away through the shadows, hunched as if expecting a blow. My bile rose as I watched it leave; it was a vile creature, to be sure, but as I imagined it obeying Alastrina's commands, her cold voice lodged in its head until the moment of its death, I felt a surge of pity. It was not a death I would have chosen for anyone.

Once the chimaera had gone, Alastrina swayed, her face deathly pale, and collapsed. Ryder was there beside her at once, holding her head up, helping her stand.

Somehow I found my voice. "What was that all about?" I demanded. "What did you do?"

"We wilded the beast away for you," Alastrina croaked. "It was *not* easy." Her blue eyes fluttered open and glared at me, glittering with hatred. "You're welcome."

"But why?" The currents of the Basks' wilding magic had left me weak, my knees wobbly, but I struggled to my feet anyway and met Alastrina's glare with my own. "You saved Farrin. You saved all of us. But you hate our family. You could have let that chimaera kill us all, and that would have..." I stopped before I could say anything else, keenly aware of Talan shivering at my feet. "Why did you help us instead?"

"I didn't want to," Alastrina said, her words slurred. "I wanted to go back and help the Citadel guards kill the rest of them. But Ryder...well, he saw that one attack you and couldn't resist playing the hero. Especially—"

"Shut up, Trina," Ryder snapped. His eyes found mine, then flicked up and down my body. His brow furrowed with confusion, and I realized this was the first time he had seen my glassy skin. "If you're fleeing to Ivyhill, take us with you," he said gruffly. "The journey north is long and taxing, and both my sister and I are too weak for it. We'll tell you what we've seen, how the chimaera breached the Citadel. And you...you know what this is all about, don't you?" His eyes narrowed. "Or else your sister does. The Rose up at the Mist. You'll tell us what you know. An exchange of information."

I kept my face flat, determined to give nothing away. Standing beyond Ryder, Farrin shook her head at me, her expression furious.

Ryder blew out an impatient breath and dragged a hand through his unkempt hair. "Look, Ashbourne, I don't want to help you any more than you want to help me, but none of that will matter if the Old Country tears us all to pieces. What if this chimaera attack is only the first of many? Who will stand in their way and protect the people of Gallinor? Isn't that why our ancestors were Anointed, why we were given our power in the first place? To protect and defend our people after the gods no longer could?" He gave me a sharp, unhappy smile. "You know I'm right, though we all wish I wasn't."

I couldn't argue with him, as dearly as I wanted to. Even Farrin wore an expression of grudging acceptance. I knelt beside Talan and tenderly lifted his chin so I could meet his eyes.

"He's telling the truth," Talan whispered. "I sense nothing but honesty from him, and exhaustion."

"And disgust, and hatred," I added quietly, smoothing his damp hair back from his face.

Talan smiled weakly. "I was trying to be tactful."

My heart twisted as I looked at him. His eyes brimmed with pain.

"He's getting closer, isn't he?" I whispered. "Kilraith."

Talan shuddered, turned his cheek into my palm. He said nothing, but that was all the answer I needed.

It went against everything I had ever known to ally even temporarily with the Basks. My every sinew screamed in protest. But chimaera had breached the Citadel, and the Middlemist was on fire, and Ryder was right—the gods had chosen our families for a reason, and together we would be stronger than we were apart.

I had to believe that.

I had to believe, as I gestured irritably at the Bask siblings to follow us, that I wasn't making a terrible mistake, and that they wouldn't kill us as soon as we lost our usefulness.

CHAPTER 35

I didn't dare bring our strange little group to Ivyhill. Father would have taken one look at the Basks and flown into a murderous rage, and I was in no mood to face him just yet myself. I hadn't seen him since the night of his terrible confession, and I realized with a faint jolt of alarm that I hadn't missed him in the weeks that had passed since then. I hadn't missed him even once.

I stewed on that particularly ugly thought as Illaria—gods bless her—bustled around the room she'd brought us to with food, tea, blankets, bandages. Her housekeeper assisted her, as well as a housemaid I recognized as having been employed at the Farrow estate for years. Their faces were grim; they worked quietly. The only sounds in the room were the fire crackling in the hearth and their murmured words—*have a bite, lift your arm, would you like another pillow?*

When they had finished, Illaria led both women to the door, embraced them briefly in thanks, and ushered them out. Then she turned back to us, her ordinarily warm brown eyes gone brittle and sharp. She took a small padded stool from a writing desk near the door, brought it toward our pathetic little circle, plopped herself down on it, and clasped her hands in her lap.

"So," she said briskly, "Gemma has told me some of what happened, but not in enough detail to satisfy me. Is someone going to tell me the rest? Or are we just going to sit here in awkward silence?"

Her voice was strained. She looked around at all of us, but her gaze passed quickly over me. I stared at the cup of tea in my hands, ashamed. I would never forget the strangled noise of relief Illaria had made when she saw me—alive and well, returned to her at last after weeks of her thinking me dead—and instead of reassuring her, instead of allowing her time alone with me to work through the shreds of her grief, I had burdened her with yet another wild story and immediately asked her to house not just Farrin and Gareth and me but Ryder and Alastrina, whom she despised on my behalf, and Talan, whom she despised on her own.

I glanced at Talan, who slept restlessly on the divan beside me. He frowned, dream movements flickering across his face in the firelight. I had mopped his brow only moments before with a clean cloth, but already his skin was soaked with sweat. My heart ached to see him like that, his body shivering with silent pain.

I dreaded the moment when that pain would become too much to bear. Would that be when Kilraith came for him, when all his defenses had been eaten away and there was nothing left between him and his master but the power of the curse that bound them together?

Remembering Talan's words from the Citadel made me feel sick and shaky. He had said Kilraith had never let him hurt himself, *would* never let him hurt himself, but that was before, and now everything was different. Talan was attempting escape; he was fighting Kilraith with every ounce of strength he had. Neither of us could predict what Kilraith might do next, spurred on by wrath and vengeance.

My panic-riddled mind had always excelled at conjuring up awful scenarios to frighten myself with, and this time it showed me a truly terrible one: Talan, smiling and content, his mind clouded over with Kilraith's will, bringing a knife to his own throat.

I set down my cup to avoid dropping it.

"Well?" Illaria asked again. "Someone speak, or I'll toss all of you out into the woods."

"It's simple," Alastrina answered from a velvet chaise near the hearth. Her eyes were closed, her breathing shallow. The chimaera that had attacked us wasn't the only beast she had wilded in the Citadel, and even with Ryder helping her, the effort had left her utterly sapped. "Chimaera breached the Citadel. The guards let me and Ryder out of our cells to help fight them because they knew we possess the magic of the goddess Neave. We did help them, but then we saw your friend and her sister, and Ryder insisted on using the remainder of our energy to help *them*, of all people—"

"You said you knew how they did it," I said to Ryder, interrupting Alastrina before her voice could get any more vicious. "The chimaera, how they got into the palace."

Ryder sat at his sister's side, perched on a footstool that was far too small for him. He looked rather like a vulture brooding on a branch that could barely support its weight. He nodded, glowering at the floor.

"The chimaera didn't come from outside the Citadel," he said quietly. "They came from within it."

A horrible silence followed his words. Gareth, sitting near the window with his arm in a sling, stared at Ryder in disbelief.

"You're joking," he said.

"I wish I was," Ryder replied.

"But the Citadel is a fortress," Gareth continued. "The gods themselves constructed it before the Unmaking!"

Ryder lifted his weary eyes to glare at Gareth. "What's your name again?"

Gareth sat up straight and pushed his glasses up his nose with one long finger. "I'm Gareth Fontaine, a seated professor and librarian at the—"

"Excellent. Are you Anointed?"

Gareth blinked at him. "I am. I'm an Anointed sage."

Ryder nodded. "Even more excellent. We'll need someone like you if we're to figure out what's really going on here. In the meantime, all I can tell you is what the guards told us as they released us from our cells: 'Something has collapsed in the Citadel's foundations. There's a sinkhole. A sinkhole of light and shadow. And the chimaera crawled out of it.' That's what they told us. I don't know what it means, but maybe you do, Professor."

Ryder's voice made the word a mockery, but Gareth seemed untroubled. He sat back in his chair, rubbing his forehead. "A *sinkhole*," he murmured. "Now, that's interesting."

Farrin, standing alone by the fire with her arms crossed, said quietly, "That must be what we heard up in our rooms. That thunderous booming sound."

Gareth nodded. "I wonder...you don't suppose...but it's a possibility..."

"Speak out loud, Gareth," I reminded him gently.

"Right. Sorry. Right, so, here it is: Even the gods couldn't craft a whole world without a few seams showing. There's the Knotwood in Aidurra, and the Crescent of Storms in Vauzanne. On each continent there's a rift. Some are smaller than others, and the Middlemist cloaks the largest rift of all, which is why the gods built the Citadel here in Gallinor. And in the Citadel lives the high queen, whom the gods chose to be our world's greatest defender."

"Librarians are all the same," Alastrina muttered from her chaise, her eyes still closed. "We don't need a history lesson. We know all of this."

Illaria's mouth quirked into a smile, which she quickly hid. "What are you getting at, Gareth?"

"I'm wondering," said Gareth, "if it's possible that another rift exists, or has *formed*, beneath the Citadel. Gemma mentioned violent fires breaking out inside the Mist, which is something I've never heard of, and I've heard of a lot of things. I'm wondering if something similar is happening in the Knotwood or in the Crescent. I'm wondering if the seams, to extend the metaphor, are starting to rip open."

Another silence, this one chillier than the last. In his sleep, Talan murmured something too quiet for me to hear. I tucked his blanket more firmly around him, desperate for something to do.

Farrin turned around, looking spooked. "That's a wild theory, Gareth."

"Of course it is, and I'd be laughed out of every lecture hall at the university for saying it, but think of everything that's happened." Gareth rose to his feet and started to pace, his broken arm seemingly forgotten. "Fires in the Middlemist. People in the Mistlands suffering grotesque visions. Necromancers who managed to create revenants here in Edyn—"

"You southerners are like babes in the woods," Alastrina interrupted, chuckling dryly.

"You think your Brethaeus were the first necromancers to set foot in Edyn?" Ryder added. "Those bastards straddle the line between life and death and therefore find it easier than you'd think to cross the line between Olden and Edyn. Come live up north for a while and see for yourself. See what we've been doing, what we've been fighting against, while you've been frittering away your days at sunlit parties, wasting the magic the gods gave you. And *gods unmade*, Farrin, will you please step away from there before your skirts catch fire?"

Ryder glanced up at Farrin and then looked away, his hands clenching and unclenching. Alastrina, her eyes open at last, glared at her brother but said nothing.

Farrin, looking as bewildered as I felt, glanced down at her skirts, then at the fire, and after a moment's hesitation slowly stepped away from the hearth.

"Gods, what I wouldn't *give* to spend a term studying up north," Gareth said eagerly, oblivious to the strangeness of what had just happened. "I haven't yet been able to convince the board to send me, but after all *this*, perhaps they'll be more amenable to the idea."

"You were *saying*, Gareth," Illaria prompted, frowning thoughtfully at Ryder.

"Right. So all of that has happened, and then there's Talan." He stopped pacing to glance at Talan, his expression solemn. "A demon bound to something even more powerful than a demon, an entity not even he can name. An entity that terrified the high queen herself. Even simply *learning* of it through another person's mind was enough to scare the wits out of her. And on that very night, chimaera from the Old Country invaded the Citadel. I cannot accept that these are all simply coincidences."

None of us could argue with that. We sat in an uneasy silence.

Then Talan stirred beside me. The pillow beneath him was soaked. I tossed it aside with an apologetic glance at Illaria and helped him settle his head on my lap. He mumbled something, turning onto his back so I could fully see his face. It was remarkable how beautiful he was even then, skin slick with sweat, lips chapped, shadows in the hollows under his eyes. He was still there beneath that mask of pain—his fine cheekbones, the smooth, sharp line of his jaw. I ached to lean down and kiss him but contented myself with touching the damp waves of his hair.

"What is it, Talan?" I whispered. "Say that again, my darling."

"The book, Gareth," he rasped. "What's in the book? Too important to leave behind, you said."

Gareth snapped his fingers. "Ah! Yes. Now, *this* might be the most interesting thing that's happened tonight, and that's saying something." He retrieved the book he'd taken from the queen's receiving room, pulled a chair up to our little circle, and laid the book open on his lap.

"When we were waiting for the queen earlier this evening, I grabbed this book and thumbed through it just for something to do, but it was nothing compelling—eight hundred pages about the different kinds of shells one can find on the southern coast of Gallinor. Which, all right, I'm sure someone finds that fascinating, but I certainly don't. When we were brought to our rooms, I didn't realize I'd tucked the book under my arm until we were already upstairs. I suppose I'm just used to carrying books around, you know, so it was only natural to hold on to this one. And then the two of you"—he looked at Talan and me with a roguish wink—"went tumbling off to bed, *ahem*, and Farrin and I looked through this book and found…well, something exceptionally strange."

Talan struggled to sit up, squinting at the book. I helped him rise, and my heart fluttered when he gently wrapped his hand around mine.

"It's written in Neskatesh," Talan observed, confusion plain in his voice.

"Indeed it is," Gareth agreed. "One of the holy tongues, a language once spoken by the gods. They left it embedded in artifacts and stones around the world. It took scholars years to compile and understand it."

Alastrina looked skeptical. "You're telling me the high queen leaves holy books just lying around her palace for any visitor to find?"

"Gareth, you said the book you took off the shelf was eight hundred pages long," I said quietly. I pointed at the book in his lap. "That book is *not* eight hundred pages long."

"Right you are, Gem." Gareth lifted the book for everyone to see—a slim volume bound in stained black leather. I was absolutely certain I remembered seeing Gareth browse a huge red book as we awaited the queen's arrival.

Cold prickled the back of my neck.

"In the few minutes between when we left the receiving room and arrived at our rooms upstairs," Gareth said quietly, "not only did this book somehow shorten itself *and* change the color of its cover, it also changed its contents entirely. This book, when I first saw it, was written in the common tongue. Not so anymore."

Ryder's expression was solemn. "What does that mean?"

"It could mean any number of things. A spell, a glamour, some crafty librarian's idea of a joke—take the book out of its proper room and it'll change faces on you." Gareth sighed wistfully. "I'll have to look into commissioning a beguiler to spell my own collection with such safeguards."

"Gareth," Farrin said tightly.

"Right, sorry. This is the truly extraordinary thing: I'm one of maybe ten people in Gallinor who is truly fluent in Neskatesh. It's one of the lesser holy tongues, very plain and straightforward. Therefore few scholars are interested in it. It's fallen out of fashion. The other holy languages are much *shinier*, to put it simply."

"And yet this book is written in Neskatesh," Illaria said slowly, "and somehow found its way to you."

"Indeed. And this book?" Gareth glanced at Talan. "It has a singular focus: curses. The whole thing, front to back. And not just any curses—obscure ones, including ones I've never heard of, not in all my years of working with the arcana. One of them, a binding curse, is particularly interesting." He bent his head over the book and pointed at a particular passage. "The gods called it *ytheliad*, or so the book says, and they feared it, for when crafted by a formidable enough being, its power could be carried by another and 'cross the great rivers.'"

"The great rivers," I murmured. "Like the Mist."

Gareth nodded. "Maybe. And like the Knotwood, and the Crescent, and perhaps whatever now sits below the Citadel. Talan was bound to Kilraith in the Old Country, and yet the curse is still effective here in Edyn. 'Across the great river.' Which makes me think that this, Talan, is the curse that binds you. The gods destroyed all knowledge of the *ytheliad* before the Unmaking for fear that someone, either in our world or theirs, would manage to create it on their own and abuse it if the boundary separating the realms ever began to weaken."

"Like it is now," Ryder said darkly.

Farrin glared at him. "We don't know that."

"Of course we don't. But we can guess, and I bet if we asked your sister up at the Mist what she thought, she'd agree with me."

"Don't you dare talk about my sister," Farrin said, her voice tight with anger. "You've done it twice now, and you won't do it again."

Ryder raised one dark eyebrow, his blue eyes gleaming with amusement. "Who's going to stop me? You? What will you do, little sparrow? Sing me into submission?"

Alastrina grinned. "No, Brother, she wouldn't do that even if she could. She's a songbird, pretty but useless, and terrified to leave her cage."

My whole body flushed red hot with anger, but Talan's hand around mine kept me pinned to the divan. Farrin, however, stormed across the room toward the Basks, fists clenched at her sides. Alastrina let out a bark of laughter; mortified, I had to agree that Farrin looked utterly foolish charging at them, like a puppy baring its teeth against wolves. Ryder rose to his feet and waited with his hands behind his back, as if he *wanted* Farrin to take a swing at him. I was struck by the expression that flickered across his face—not one of anger or of hatred, but instead something guarded and terribly sad, which made no sense to me at all.

"Enough!" Illaria snapped angrily. Her voice stopped Farrin in her tracks. I watched with a lump of embarrassment in my throat as Farrin turned away from Ryder and hid her face, her shoulders square and furious. Ryder sank back onto the stool at his sister's feet and stared sullenly at his shoes.

"If any of you come to blows in my house," Illaria said evenly, "that will mark the end of my hospitality. You are guests here and will behave accordingly. Now." She turned to Gareth. "Explain to me how the knowledge of this curse, this *ytheliad*, all of which was supposedly destroyed by the gods themselves, could have made its way into this book, and why it came to *you*."

"I think the high queen is a walking library," Gareth said plainly, shocked into brevity by the sheer force of Illaria's glare. "I think the gods created the royal archives as a sort of failsafe. All those books and scrolls being constantly deciphered and translated and copied by the world's brightest scholars—I think those are mere echoes of the knowledge that exists in the queen's mind. I think that mind is fathomless and that not even she knows everything it contains. And I think she left us in that receiving room thinking hard about Talan and Kilraith and the curse that binds them. She told us how sorry she was, and that she couldn't allow us into the archives, and perhaps the fear she felt left her unguarded, her thoughts pliable and open—"

"You think she sent us this book," I whispered, awestruck.

Gareth nodded. "Possibly without even knowing it."

Even Alastrina looked shaken. "That's...Professor, that's extraordinary."

"As is the queen."

The silence in the room felt suddenly reverent, as if by speaking of Queen Yvaine in this way, we had trod upon something sacred.

"Does it..." Talan licked his cracked lips. I could hardly bear to see the hopeful expression on his face. "Does it say anything about how to break the *ytheliad*?"

Gareth turned a few pages, then ran his finger across a line of text. "The *ytheliad* requires an anchor to function, an object of some kind that keeps the curse grounded in the physical, the real. Otherwise the curse's power is too weak to 'cross the river.'"

He looked at Talan eagerly. "Do you remember seeing such an object? It would have been present at the time of your binding, and it could have been anything—an artifact, a piece of the land itself. If we can find it and bring it back to Edyn, we can hire a team of beguilers to destroy it." Gareth glanced at me. "It'll cost a pretty bit of coin. I doubt it would take fewer than a dozen curse-breakers to unravel something this strong."

Talan shook his head. "I don't..." He touched his temple, staring at something far beyond anything in this room. "It's difficult to remember. I remember...I remember the woods. I remember the angry sea."

I kissed his clammy knuckles. "Think hard, Talan. I know you don't want to remember that night, but—"

Talan pressed our hands to his heart and closed his eyes. "There was a light. A terrible pressure. Hands on me, and a mouth in my stomach. Gaping open. Drawing me in. Eyes...eyes in my bones..."

With a suddenness that terrified me, Talan wrenched himself away from me and staggered to his feet. He turned away from all of us, hands on either side of his head, and drew in great ragged breaths. When I went to him, he shoved me away.

"Don't touch me!" he cried. "If you touch me, he'll find you!"

I fought against the pull of fear and steadied my voice. "Listen to me, Talan. I'm right here, and I'm not going anywhere, and he can't find us. He will *never* find us. Do you hear me?"

"No, no, you don't understand. He feeds on me. He hungers for blood. He craves, and he hungers, and I have fed him, I've made him stronger. He has his claws in many."

Those were Queen Yvaine's words, the ones she'd uttered in terror as she'd knelt by Talan's side with her hands on his face. A horrible fear raced through my body, trailing cold in its wake.

"Talan, look at me—" I began.

He whirled around, anguish plain on his face. "He has his claws in many!" he cried, and then stumbled away from me, hands outstretched as if to fend me off. He crashed into a chair, sent it toppling over, then crouched beside it, hands in his hair, his every breath catching on sobs.

My heart beat wildly with fear, but I ignored it. Farrin and Illaria warned me to stay back, but I refused to listen. I went to Talan, braced myself, and knelt at his side. I touched his arm.

"Talan," I said. "Look at me."

He shook his head, his mouth screwed up tight.

I tried again, keeping my voice gentle. "Look at me, darling. Look at me and see how much I love you. He can't take that away from you. No matter what happens, that is something he'll never be able to touch."

I waited, heart in my throat, until Talan finally lifted his head from his hands and looked at me. His beautiful dark eyes were swollen, red-rimmed, as if he hadn't slept in days.

"Gemma," he said, his voice breaking on my name, and then he drew me hard against his chest. He clung to me like a dying man, his hands in my hair, his face pressed to mine.

"I'm here, Talan," I whispered, struggling to speak for the fear in my heart. "I'm here. You're safe."

Alastrina hissed out an impatient breath, breaking the awful silence that followed Talan's outburst.

"Why are we wasting time on this?" she snapped. "May I remind all of you that this is a *demon* blubbering here before us? One of the very same who has been part of our families' long torment?" She turned furious eyes on Talan, her mouth curling in disgust. "I've been patient until now, but no longer. I say we throw him into the Mist and let his master do with him what he will."

"Trina," Ryder said tiredly, still staring at the floor.

"You can't possibly tell me that you pity this creature," Alastrina spat at him.

"You're a fool," Farrin said, glaring daggers at Alastrina. "Haven't you been listening at all? Talan is a part of this. He's been *feeding* a creature that terrifies even the high queen, and he's been powerless to resist doing so. Breaking the curse that binds him can only help us—all of us, even you."

Illaria nodded grimly. "If this Kilraith is part of what's happening to the Mist—and I agree with Gareth that this confluence of events can't be a coincidence—then depriving Kilraith of one of his servants could delay whatever he's trying to accomplish."

My love for both of them swept through me so fiercely that I had to look away from them or else lose my composure. I couldn't do that, not with Talan falling apart before my very eyes.

Gareth watched us thoughtfully. "Talan," he said, "do you think you could remember *where* Kilraith bound you? Even if you can't recall what artifact he used as an anchor, it seems to me that the location of your binding would be the most logical place to begin searching for it."

Talan took a deep breath and nodded. "I remember those woods," he said roughly. "I've never been able to forget them."

"But those woods are in the Old Country," I pointed out.

Gareth blinked at me. "Of course they are."

Farrin shot him an exasperated expression. "Gareth, we can't go to the Old Country."

"We *can*," Gareth said. "We shouldn't, but we absolutely can. Even before these latest incidents began, things wriggled out of the Mist every now and then. If that weren't the case, there would be no Order of the Rose. There would be no need for them. So..."

He trailed off, looking first at Farrin and then at me.

"No," Farrin said sharply.

"Farrin, I think she would do it," I said quietly.

She threw me an incredulous look. "I'm not going to ask our sister to break every rule she has sworn to uphold and sneak us into the very place she risks her life *every day* to protect us from. I can't believe you would ask that of her."

"Mara has already broken the rules of the Order," I shot back. "She's done it ten times over. The Warden doesn't want her scavenging around Mistfire sites and harvesting corpses, but she's doing it anyway because she knows something's wrong, and no one else is moving quickly enough to stop whatever it is from getting worse."

Gareth sighed, looking unhappily at the book in his lap. "We could actually be helping her in the long run, Farrin. If Kilraith is behind all of this, even in part, and freeing Talan weakens him even temporarily—"

"Then the Mist could become less dangerous," Farrin finished, all the angry fire gone out of her. She hugged herself again, gazing miserably at the fire. "I see your point."

I watched my sister's eyes glisten with unshed tears, and my heart ached with too much feeling. I wished desperately for the blessed nothingness of sleep.

"I don't like it either," I said quietly, "but none of our other options are particularly palatable to me."

"We can't abandon the demon," Alastrina admitted grudgingly. "He knows too much now. He's been all over the Citadel."

"His name is Talan," I said, bristling.

Alastrina glared at me. "*Talan*, then."

"Could this be a trap?" Ryder asked, glancing up. It was the most he'd said in a long time, and the sound of his deep voice startled me. "The chimaera, the book…could all of it have been designed so we would do this very thing? Venture into the Old Country and walk right into an ambush of Kilraith's making?"

None of us answered him, though as I looked around the room at the grim faces gathered by the fire, I knew each of our answers would be the same.

Yes, everything that had happened could very well be part of a trap—but that hardly mattered. We would do it anyway and hope that if some monstrous doom awaited us at the end of this path, we would be smart enough to escape it.

CHAPTER 36

The next day at the fall of dusk, I stood at the doors to Rosewarren, once again refusing to cower before the glaring stone falcons. This time, at least, I was not alone: Farrin was beside me, clutching her gray cloak tightly at her throat as if baring even a sliver of skin would subject her to some unknown horror lurking in the trees.

I couldn't rightly blame her for that.

I knocked once more on the doors. The sound was awful, a resounding boom that echoed loudly in the twilit silence and made Farrin flinch. The journey north through the greenways—first from the capital to Ivyhill, and then from Ivyhill to Rosewarren—had left my joints wracked with such twisting, burning pain that my vision shimmered red and black. It took every bit of strength I possessed to remain standing. The panic was beginning to bubble in my stomach, and if someone didn't open the doors soon, it would rise up and drown me from the inside.

Each moment that passed was another moment I was separated from Talan, whom I'd left in Mara's caverns along with everyone else—including Phaidra, Nesset, and Lulath, who had nearly crushed my ribs with the threefold force of their embrace. Phaidra in particular had been mightily unhappy to be left behind yet again, but it felt too risky to bring anyone else with me to Rosewarren. The priory was too close to the Mist; even the caverns were too close for my liking.

And as much as I hated to admit it—and I never would have to her face—Farrin would be the least able to help defend Talan if it came to that.

Besides, I was glad for the company.

The doors began to creak open. Without thinking, I grabbed Farrin's gloved hand, jolted with some primal fear left over from childhood. I was tired and frightened, and my sister would protect me.

Then I saw who had opened the priory doors, and my heart sank.

The Warden stood there, prim and pale, dressed in her customary black gown—long tight sleeves; a stiff, high collar that covered every inch of her throat; frightful square shoulders. The combination of those shoulders and her stern black eyebrows made her look truly formidable. I was reminded once more of an owl watching patiently from the trees, searching the darkening forest for its breakfast.

She made a little sound in her throat, a soft hum of astonishment. "Farrin and Imogen Ashbourne." She clucked her tongue. "I would remind you of our family visitation rules here at the priory, but I fear that would seem like an insult to your intelligence."

Unperturbed, I flashed her a sweet smile. "Apologies, Warden, for the intrusion, but we are here to see Mara, and it's a matter of utmost urgency. I'm afraid we can't be detained any longer."

Then I swept past her and strode serenely through the entrance hall, tugging Farrin after me. The Warden didn't follow us. She stood at the doors and watched us go, so eerily still that I knew the shadow of her unmoving silhouette would darken my dreams.

"Gods remade," Farrin whispered once we were out of ear-shot. She let out a nervous laugh as we started up a set of wide, winding stairs. "That was incredible, Gemma."

I let myself bask for a moment in the warmth of her praise. "What can she do? Escort us off the grounds like common crimi-nals?" I whispered back. "Father would throw a fit when he heard, and no one wants to deal with that, not even the Warden."

The comment slipped out before I could stop it, and I imme-diately wished it unsaid. Mentioning our father left me with an awful knot of sadness in my throat, and an ache in my chest that I feared would come and go for the rest of my life, as constant a companion as the panic. Farrin said nothing, but she squeezed my hand and held on tight—a better comfort than any words she might have offered.

As I led her through the house, following the path Cira had shown me when I'd visited Rosewarren weeks ago, pale shapes flickered in the shadows—Roses watching us, perhaps trailing us up the stairs and down each winding corridor on orders of the Warden. But they didn't interfere, not even in the enormous room outside the dormitories where they huddled in the gigantic tree's roots and watched us pass with wide eyes, whispering to each other. I thought I saw Danesh watching from the shadows with a fearsome glower on her face, but I didn't dare look again to confirm it.

When we reached Mara's room, the door stood ajar, the light inside warm and golden. Before we could push it open, Mara did it herself. She glared at us for a moment, but she couldn't hold that anger for long. Her face softened, and she ushered us inside. Once the door was closed, she embraced us both—her strong arms warm as a furnace around me—and then she stepped back, looking stern once more.

"What in the name of the gods are you doing here?" she said, quietly furious. "*Again*, Gemma? Do you understand what happens every time you come here out of turn? It breaks the others' hearts. The young ones aren't used to life here yet. They cry every night, just as I did when I first arrived. And some of the older Roses' families stopped visiting them long ago. It kills them whenever someone visits because they hope, every time, that it'll be someone come to see them, and it never is. And my family always visits—now *more* than they ought to. It isn't fair to them. You're not being fair."

She turned away, collecting herself. When she looked back, her face was flushed but her eyes were dry. "Why are you here?"

I was so overcome that I could hardly speak. "Will the Warden be angry with you?"

Mara waved dismissively. "I don't care about her. I care about the girls under my care and the women who have lived here longer than I have. Their lonely hearts, all the hurts they try to hide."

"We didn't realize—" Farrin began.

"Of course you didn't. For you the world is vast, full of possibilities. It's very easy, I would think, to forget about us up here. Our world is small, contained. Easily pushed aside." Mara scoffed, looked up at the ceiling. "I don't want to be saying these things to you. I want to wrap you both up in my arms and tuck you into bed with me, like we did when we were small, and never let either of you go. But you had to march in here like damned spoiled brats with no regard for other people's feelings and ruin everything."

I was, quite frankly, speechless in the face of her obvious passion. I wasn't used to seeing Mara in such a state. She was the steadiest of all of us and always had been. I was a creature of constant brimming panic, and Farrin bristled with some deeply held anger even I didn't understand. But Mara was even-tempered, fearless. She had cried the day the Warden had taken her from us, but only quietly, politely. I had wailed myself sick, and Farrin had raged at everyone who would listen, but Mara had simply let herself be led away and told us not to worry for her. She would be fine. Everything, she had promised us, her brave, brown eyes full of tears, would be fine.

"I'm sorry," Mara muttered, face still turned to the ceiling. She closed her eyes. "I really *don't* want to be saying these things to you. I know you wouldn't have come unless it was something important." She took a deep breath and looked at us, gently took our hands, and led us to her rumpled bed, its plain gray linens splattered here and there with paint that matched the walls: Ivyhill green, Ivyhill blue.

"What is it, then?" Mara asked. "What's happened?"

We told her, Farrin and I, back and forth like the girls we had once been—three sisters whispering secrets when we should have been sleeping. When we'd finished, I held my breath, bracing myself. Mara would hate everything about this. She would think we had lost our senses, perhaps have us confined in quiet rooms at Rosewarren until we'd regained our wits.

But instead she simply nodded, her brow serious and thoughtful, and said, "The first thing we'll need to do is convince the Warden that I've sent you away. Then we'll wait a day, maybe two, to ensure her attentions are elsewhere. Then we'll enter the Mist. I'll tell you where to meet me. Crossing over to the Old Country is easier in some places than others."

She paused, glanced at each of us with a slightly furrowed brow. "You realize that crossing over will be painful. Especially for you, Gemma. I've not done it yet myself, but I've heard all manner of awful stories from the older Roses. They chased some creature back into the Old Country and accidentally took a few steps too far. They were on patrol in the Deep Mist and were called to the Oldenside by what they thought were their mother's voices. The lucky ones found their way home—the Mist allowed them to. Some have never returned."

She shivered a little, drew her knees up to her chest as a child would. "The Mist protects us, yes, and divides the worlds, but these days it is also cunning and curious. Unpredictable. The places where Mistfires have scarred the earth are our best bet. I'll begin my search there, but I can't promise I'll be able to find an opening. I also can't promise that if we do cross over, we'll be able to come back."

I drew in a slow breath, my belly full of nerves. "I understand."

Beside me, her knee pressed against mine, Farrin nodded. "As do I. The risk is terrible, but…"

"But after everything you've told me, we have to take it," Mara said. She unfolded herself from the bed and pulled aside a curtain strung across the other end of the room. Behind it hung a huge map of the Mist. A thick silver sea with mere slivers of land above and below it hinting at the rest of the continent: the smaller, rugged north and the larger, more verdant south.

As I looked at the map, a memory surfaced: Ryder, just before he'd snapped at Farrin to step away from the fire, had said something strange: *Come live up north for a while and see for yourself. See what we've been doing, what we've been fighting against.*

Ominous words, and I realized with a sinking, exhausted feeling that I hadn't asked him what they meant.

There were too many questions to ask, too many things about the world I didn't understand. And I sensed that what I'd come to realize I didn't know merely scratched the surface of my true ignorance.

I resisted the urge to collapse into Mara's pillows and pull her blankets over my head. Instead I put my shoulders back and fought against the pull of panic simmering under my skin. I was Lady Imogen Ashbourne, I reminded myself, and what I didn't know, I would learn. What I couldn't see, I would find.

And what I couldn't fight...

My fingers tingled as I recalled running at Talan in the ballroom, bringing his forest lair to ruin, trapping the Brethaeus in a snare of roots and thorns. *Terror, lust, rage*, the memory of Talan's voice murmured in my mind. *They are weapons. Use them.*

Perhaps the number of things I couldn't fight was no longer as staggering as it had once been.

"I'll scout here on the eastern coast first, and then here on the western one," Mara was saying, pointing to the map. "It's quite possible we could visit the Old Country a hundred times and never find Talan's Far Sea—it's that enormous a place, and only small sections of it have been mapped—but setting out from our own seas seems sensible for a start. It's possible that—" Mara paused, gazing at the map with a haunted expression on her face, then shook her head.

"Whatever it is, say it," Farrin suggested. "I don't think we can afford to dismiss anything, no matter how ludicrous."

Mara turned to look at us. "It's possible," she said slowly, "that the Mist will take us where we need to go."

A puff of nervous laughter burst out of me. "What, as long as we ask nicely?"

"Essentially, yes. The Warden discourages this line of thinking, but some of us Roses believe the Mist is less a *thing* and more of a...well, an entity."

I was no longer laughing.

Farrin stared at her. "You mean the Mist could be *alive*?"

"Some of us think so," Mara mused, turning back to consider

the map. "The Warden thinks those theories are merely hysterical. We learned long ago not to voice them around her. She treats mad girls like infections. You have to cut them out lest you lose the whole leg."

The matter-of-fact flatness of her voice frightened me even more than the idea of the Mist as a living being with a will of its own.

"Mara..." Farrin said quietly.

Mara ignored our obvious horror. "If the Mist is alive, even only halfway, even if its *version* of life is different from ours...then perhaps we can intrigue it, pique its interest. If," she added, with a wry glance at me, "we ask nicely enough."

A horrible thought occurred to me. "If the Mist is alive," I said, "then what do the Mistfires mean? Is it...ill?"

"Or someone is trying to kill it," Farrin added faintly.

None of us spoke for a long time after that. Mara was the first to break the silence with three brisk taps on the map—a location at the Mist's southern reach, about ten miles west of Rosewarren.

"Here's where we'll meet," she said, "the day after tomorrow at midday. There's a greenway near this wood, one of the most reliable known to the Order. And at midday the Mist will be quiet, less likely to bother us. That will give us time to make the journey to whichever coast my scouting trips show to be most promising. We'll arrive there by nightfall, when the Mist will be most active, thereby giving us the greatest chance of a successful crossover." She glanced at me. "We'll be traveling through several Order greenways, Gemma, beyond just this first one. Otherwise, to reach either of the coasts on foot would take us—"

"Weeks, I know." I flashed her a smile that even I didn't believe. "Not to worry. After what I've been through..." I trailed off, gesturing at my body and its faintly shimmering coat of glass.

Mara smiled, but it didn't reach her eyes. "Of course."

As she told us what would happen next—how she would march us out of the priory, pretending indignant fury at our constant flouting of the visitation rules; what path we would take from the caverns to our meeting point on the Mist's southern border—I listened dutifully, though half my thoughts were elsewhere, with the woman I had been not so long ago. That woman had beaten bruises across her arms, struck her face until it went numb, scratched her skin bloody. That woman had been willing to make a bargain with a demon for the chance to be remade, to have magic as her family did, to be whole and healthy.

The realization burst open quietly inside me, a bright flower blooming: I *did* possess magic now, or at least some vicious, half-alive version of magic, and with it I could make terrifying workings. I could fight demons, break curses spun by necromancers.

And yet I'd nevertheless been felled by whatever foul power the chimaera had brought with them into the Citadel. That magic had scalded me, rendered me weak for far too long. The hungry, sucking power of greenways still left me breathless, battered, faint. What would happen to me after traveling through greenways painted strange and silver by the Mist? What state would I be in by the time we managed to cross over to the Old Country, if indeed we did at all? Would I be able to help my friends, my family, the man I loved? Or would I be reduced to a helpless heap in the dirt, mute and limp with pain?

I imagined Kilraith as Talan had described him—a pale, tall creature with bare arms and warm hands, a kind smile. He would find me inert on the ground and toe at me with one foot and cluck his tongue, pitying me. He would destroy everyone I loved while I watched, helpless to stop him. He would consider me too small a threat to bother with and leave me weeping alone in a ruin of bone and blood.

The panic came swiftly and without warning, a hot rushing wave that twisted up my insides and lit up every inch of my skin with a stifling, tingling heat. My lungs shrank; my breathing became pinched, pathetic. Suddenly I couldn't bear to be in Mara's room any longer. I stood up fast, startling both of my sisters.

"Is there a bathing room nearby?" I asked, pleased that my voice sounded steady even though my insides were chaos, rapidly devouring all reason, all courage.

"Of course," Mara replied. "Turn right out of my room and follow the corridor to its end. You won't miss it." She paused, looking more closely at me. Her expression gentled. I couldn't bear it. Her pity would break me.

Farrin looked sharply between us. "What is it, Gemma? Are you ill?"

"I simply want a moment to refresh myself," I said, and left them before Mara could explain to Farrin that what she was seeing was the panic, yet another one of her youngest sister's many oddities. I would scream if I had to listen to her say that; I would die if I had to watch Farrin's expression change from confusion to abject pity.

I stumbled into the bathing room and found a private basin to collapse beside. Of course I couldn't make myself sick and find some relief for my knotted stomach that way; of course the cool stone beneath me did nothing to soothe my overheated skin. I sat there on the floor and shook, fighting the urge to scratch my legs red and raw, and tried to breathe, and tried to breathe, and tried to breathe.

I blinked back tears as I fought hard against the terrible thoughts beating their wings against my skull: Maybe the panic had nothing to do with the artificer's work. Maybe it was something inherent to my existence, a part of me that I could never tear out no matter how hard I tried, no matter how passionately I wished to be rid of it, no matter how fearsome my magic might become. There I was, nascent power brimming at my fingertips and skin painted with glass—and if Phaidra's suspicions were to be believed, veins boiling with wild fae blood. And yet clearly I was no closer to being free of the panic than I had been when Talan was simply a beautiful man I longed to bed, when I knew nothing of the great evil my parents had done.

Maybe, I thought, crying quietly in the soft lamplight, their true evil was not hiring the artificer to stifle my magic but was instead a lack of ambition. Clearly the artificer's knives had not cut deep enough. Mother and Father should have insisted he keep digging, keep splicing open and sewing shut, until I was no longer Imogen Ashbourne, sickly, panic-riddled freak, but someone else entirely. Carved open and magicked clean.

I searched my mind for prayers. That's what a good woman of Edyn was *meant* to do: pray to the gods for peace, for clarity, for comfort. But I couldn't be sure which of the gods was responsible for what I was. Kerezen, who ruled the senses? Zelphenia, goddess of the unknowable? Or maybe I was a child of no god and should pray instead to something else—the Mist itself, the stars in the sky. Ryndar, the realm beyond life and death, beyond Edyn and Old Country alike. Maybe *pain* was my god, and I should send my prayers right back to my tormentor.

Finally my thoughts took me to where they should have from the beginning—not a god but a demon. Talan's gentle hands cleaning my wounds, bandaging my thighs, kissing all the places that hurt. Understanding me. Hearing me. Unafraid of my strange, glittering reflection in the mirror.

I closed my eyes and chased the memory, clinging to the basin, fist pressed against my mouth.

Talan, I prayed until the panic slowly began to subside. I breathed his name and followed every breath to the next, and the next. In older times, when the presence of the dead gods still lay heavily upon the world, praying to anything else would have been considered blasphemous. But I felt the rightness of it all the same.

These were my gods—Talan's mind and body, how we were learning each other's hearts; my beloved sisters, who were as surely a part of me as my own blood and bone, no matter the miles between us; my friends, old and new, who would soon follow me into the unknown.

I said each of their names: *Farrin. Mara. Phaidra. Nesset. Lulath. Gareth. Illaria.*

Talan.

I hesitated. If they were going to come with us, it would be foolish not to pray to them as well. So I said their names last of all: *Ryder. Alastrina.*

I whispered this humble litany until they'd worn a soft path in my mind. Brave people, brilliant minds, power and purpose. With them I was as safe as I would ever be.

Farrin.

I was not terrible.

Mara.

I was not a burden.

Talan.

And I was not alone.

I finished my prayer with a tired sigh and then, with shaking fingers, pulled up my skirts to inspect my thighs. I had done it; I had resisted tearing them to pieces. They were scarred but whole, the fading marks of past angry fingers mere pink slivers.

I slumped back against the wall and smiled in the dim light. The cool air felt sublime on my bare legs. Even in my relief, I knew the panic would not always be vanquished so easily; I was too familiar with its many tricks to believe such a lie. But I had done it at least once, and perhaps, if I was lucky, I could do it again. Perhaps it would be easier to do it every time I tried.

I stood on wobbly legs and returned to my sisters, the names of my strange new prayer held like jewels in my heart.

CHAPTER 37

The next day, we all gathered in Mara's caverns to rest, eat, and prepare. Gareth remained at the Farrow estate with Illaria; his broken arm would be a liability on such a journey, though Gareth had passionately fought that decision until he'd realized he was outnumbered. He then proceeded to scribble out no less than one hundred and two pages of information about Olden arcana for us to take in his stead.

I sat in a quiet corner of the caverns keeping a nervous eye on Talan, who slept near me, and binding Gareth's notes into a leather packet Mara had taken from Rosewarren. My nerves jangled hopelessly. It was a mad thing we were going to do, and there we were, nearly ready to do it. I had tried for hours to think of alternatives, but all that had done was leave me feeling tired, with an aching, too-full head. It was no use. The mad thing was our path.

As I worked, I silently recited my prayer, seeking a calm that remained elusive: *Farrin. Mara. Talan. Illaria. Gareth. Phaidra. Nesset. Lulath. Ryder. Alastrina.*

I am not terrible.

I am not a burden.

I am not alone.

Then Phaidra found me. As she settled beside me on the hard ground, I caught a smell of wood about her and the faint perfume of the tiny flowers sewn into her body.

She watched me work for a moment, then said bluntly, "I heard you lost the talisman I gave you, and Farrin told me you have a dog." She thrust out her hand, looking more nervous and awkward than I'd ever seen her. Tiny wood shavings coated her gray fingers. "Do you like it? Will it satisfy? I have never met her, of course, but Farrin described her thoroughly. I carved a cat for her. Her cat at home. I carved something for everyone, to ground us in Edyn even while we travel to the Olden lands."

Tears pricked my eyes as I beheld the little wooden carving in Phaidra's palm. It was my Una—long snout, long legs, the proud fan of her tail, even the wavy tufts of hair along her body. It was remarkably accurate; looking at it, I could almost smell the warm musk of Una's fur, feel the quiet weight of her pressing against my leg.

"It's perfect," I whispered. I lightly drew one finger down the length of this tiny Una's spine. "It's a piece of home."

Phaidra beamed at me with that awful, wonderful Vilia smile, gnarled from corner to corner. Tenderly I touched Una's tiny paws, then placed the necklace over my head and tucked the talisman under my collar.

"That is the kindest thing anyone has ever given me," I told her. "You could make these and sell them for a fine price. Maybe when we return you should consider it."

Phaidra fell quiet for a long time. I started to wonder if I had upset her when she said quietly, "Lulath is dying."

My shock left me numb for a moment. Then I blurted, "No, she isn't."

"She is. It is as you suggested in the forest: without the curse holding together her remade body, she can no longer do it herself. She is very old. She was made so long ago."

"Where is she?" I shoved everything off my lap and stood. Gareth's papers went flying.

Phaidra caught my wrist, her grip firm. "Sit down. She doesn't want to see anyone just now. It is not a pretty sight. Nesset is with her."

I obeyed, sitting miserably in the pile of papers. I began to cry, furious and quiet. "This is my fault."

"*We* decided to fight the Brethaeus. We decided it long ago, not you. Do not take that victory from us, Imogen."

Abashed, I nodded and looked down at my hands. Tears fell onto my fingers. "I'm so sorry, Phaidra."

I very nearly asked her the horrible questions flooding my mind: Would she die too? And when would it happen? And was it possible to forestall it somehow or prevent it altogether? Was there a spell that could replace the curse's structure, but kindly?

Instead I began gathering Gareth's papers and fumbling to put them back in order. It didn't seem like the right time to ask such questions. It seemed disrespectful to Lulath, and besides that, I wasn't sure I could bear the answers. I certainly didn't want to take that knowledge with me to the Old Country. I needed to hold on to every scrap of hope I could.

Phaidra began to help me. "Too quick you are to hate yourself," she said quietly. "I wish you would not do that."

I didn't know how to reply to such a kind statement. My prayer felt too new, too private. I couldn't share it with anyone just yet.

Instead I thought of how I had felt in the bathing room at Rosewarren, the quiet triumph of my unhurt legs, and said truthfully, carefully, "It's getting easier not to hate. A little bit, anyway."

"A little bit," Phaidra repeated, nodding. "That is not such a very bad thing."

—◆—

The next day, as the strange gray skies of the Mistlands darkened to nightfall, I lurched out of the last of the five greenways we had used to travel to Gallinor's western coast and fell at once to my hands and knees, my stomach heaving and my vision swirling. I could hardly keep my eyes open; my whole body felt weighed down by something terrible and endless, stretched out past my bones and nailed ruthlessly to the earth.

Distantly I sensed movement around me and heard the murmur of voices, but after passing through the vicious mouths of five greenways—*five*, the whole wretched Mist was studded with them—I couldn't speak, couldn't move. I let whoever it was lift me from the dirt, leaned blindly into a pillar of solid warmth.

When I found the strength to fully open my eyes, I saw a scrubby woodland, charred earth scattered with pebbles, patches of black sky. I heard the crash of distant waves, but the water itself was hidden by the shimmering silver sea threading through the trees: the Middlemist, thick and clinging. Its inner light was the only illumination besides the spellcrafted flat lanterns affixed to each of our belts—tools used by the Roses when they ventured into the Deep Mist, where the sky was opaque and silver, thick as mud. But the lanterns seemed weaker now, their light pale and flickering, as if the Mist itself was determined to douse them.

"Now, think of the Far Sea," a voice above me murmured. "All of us must do this, not only Talan. Remember Talan's description and draw the image clearly in your minds."

I shifted a bit to look up at whoever held me, and my tired heart swelled with love to see Mara there, fierce and strong, her dark brown hair tied back in a tight braid, the old scars on her neck glimmering in the Mist's eerie light.

She glanced down at me and smiled tightly. "Can you stand, Gemma?"

I nodded, grateful for her arm around my waist, and surveyed what little of our surroundings I could see. "A Mistfire erupted here?"

Mara nodded grimly. "A few days ago. Do you feel how thin the air is here? More pliable than where we've been? It's easier to move."

I stood quietly for a moment, letting the Mist wind around me. Mara was right: Even though we were deeper in the Mist than we'd yet been, it was easier to breathe, to *think*, than it had been near any of the other greenways we'd taken. I stepped away from Mara and felt no resistance in the air, no sucking weight trying to pull me down to the earth. The Mist's touch was light and cool. When I walked, my wobbly knees found it easier to function.

I leaned down and touched the scorched earth. Ashes, black and silver, came away on my fingers. Quickly I brushed my hand clean on my trousers. I hated the sight of this place, the wrongness of it, the still black sky, the muffled sound of an ocean I could not see.

To calm my racing heart, I searched for the others, let my eyes land on each of them for a moment before moving on. Ryder and Alastrina wore the plain traveling clothes Illaria had given us before leaving her estate. Ryder held the huge crossbow he had taken from the Citadel, a thick arrow nocked and ready. He glared at the Mist with those piercing blue eyes as if daring it to try anything. Alastrina stood not far from him, sulking, with her arms crossed and a belt of knives at her waist. I tried to ignore the unease that twinged in my chest as I looked at her. Since fleeing the Citadel, none of us had spoken of the feud between our families; there had been more important things to consider. But animosity lingered in the air like fumes from a fire.

Alastrina's gaze cut to mine, jolting me; she had caught me staring.

I looked away, finding Phaidra instead. Crouched a few paces from me, hands empty and bared, she sniffed the air like a hound. Her weedy brown hair framed her pale face like a wild mane. She had woven bright new wildflowers into the scars of her gnarled body, and she had sewn additional layers of animal hide onto the strange woodland garment she wore, which covered her from ankle to throat. She held her staff at the ready, and her knife belt was heavy with blades.

Our eyes met, and Phaidra nodded grimly, ready to fight. Her cracked lips formed a gruesome smile, which comforted me. Ryder and Alastrina may have been unhappy to be fighting alongside me, but Phaidra was eager for it, her Vilia instincts honed and ready. I loved her for that, and I focused on that love, not on Lulath dying back in the caverns, or Nesset having to watch, or whether she and Phaidra would meet the same sad end.

Then I found Farrin and Talan, and all my resolve vanished in an instant.

They were on the ground; Talan was shivering, curled up like a child, his face tight with pain. He had gotten much worse since leaving the Farrow estate, as if Kilraith, wherever he was, knew exactly what we were planning and was determined to make the attempt as painful as possible.

Farrin knelt beside Talan, trying valiantly to help him sit up, but when he finally did, he could only lean heavily against her, his eyes closed, his face as deathly pale as Phaidra's.

"Let's try to stand, Talan," she whispered, hooking her arm

through his, but when she started to rise, he merely sat there, looking up at her with glazed eyes.

Farrin glanced over at me, true fear on her face.

My unease blossomed into the beginnings of outright panic. Had I made a terrible mistake by bringing everyone here?

I turned and took a few steps away from everyone, into the trees. I grabbed on to a slim trunk, and the whole thing crumbled at my touch—a tree burned by Mistfire, its glittering ashes floating slowly to the ground. I stared at the ruin of it in horror, my blood pounding in my ears. I closed my eyes and tried to breathe past the great pressure clamping down all over me—shoulders, chest, temples. Frantically I reached for my prayer—*I am not terrible, I am not a burden, I am not alone*—but the words wriggled away from me like minnows.

Then I heard movement behind me, and I whirled around, expecting any number of faceless monsters. Ryder stood there instead. A monster, perhaps, but at least one I'd brought with me. He had slung his crossbow over his shoulder and held his palms up in a gesture of peace.

"What do you want?" I snapped.

He smiled unkindly, gave me a sardonic bow. "I'm not looking for a fight, Ashbourne. I want to talk. One of your sisters is busy scouting the area, and the other one is busy trying to keep your lover from collapsing in on himself, so I suppose it's up to me to talk you down from your panic."

I flinched hearing that word fall from his lips. Was I that obvious? My mind whirled, thinking of how Ryder Bask might use knowledge of the panic against me.

Desperate, I could think of only one thing to say. "Have I made a mistake?"

"Perhaps," he said at once. Not angry or scornful, simply honest.

I glared at him. "I thought you wanted to help me."

"I didn't say help you. I said talk you down from your panic. As ludicrous as it might sound, you're our leader, and leaders can't hide themselves away in the trees."

"I'm not hiding," I bit out, ashamed. "I'm thinking."

"All right." Ryder gestured at me with one hand. "Then do it out loud. Talk to me."

I gave him a withering look. "Talk to *you*."

"This is not the time to carry on about how our families hate each other, and I think you know that. So talk to me. If you don't talk to someone, you'll never leave these trees. Your fear will eat you alive."

His measured tone caught me by surprise. This was not the Ryder Bask I knew, the Ryder Bask who had beaten my father at the queen's masquerade and crowed defiant northern chants as the royal guard hauled him away to his cell.

"There aren't enough of us here," I said bluntly. "We should have brought more help. Roses, maybe, and soldiers from the Upper Army who know how to fight Olden creatures."

"The Warden would have never allowed Roses to join us, and if a whole group of them had disappeared, she'd have chased us down and brought us back." Ryder gave me another small, hard smile. "You don't steal the Warden's chicks, Ashbourne. Come, now, even southerners know that. And the Upper Army?" He hissed lightly through his teeth. "Armies mean rules and regulations and petitions and schedules. Kilraith would come for us all and they'd still be sorting through their transfer papers."

He was right. I knew he was right, and hearing him speak so plainly was a strange, shocking comfort. But I couldn't let go of my fear that easily.

"We moved too quickly," I insisted. "Our plan is rash and depends on too many *ifs*."

"We had to move quickly," Ryder countered, unperturbed. "Talan can't evade Kilraith for much longer. He's *dying*, Ashbourne. That's clear even to me, and I'm not the one who's been fucking him for months. Once he buckles, we don't know what Kilraith could do—not only to Talan but to Gallinor and the larger world. The queen is terrified of Kilraith. You saw that with your own eyes. She said Talan has been feeding him, making him stronger. Strong enough to do what? Feeding him for what purpose? These are the most important questions— remember that. They mean something, and they don't mean anything good."

Desperate to ignore the casual gut punch of what he'd said about Talan, some prim, indignant part of me fixated instead on his crude language. "Talan and I haven't been *fucking*."

"Whatever you want to call it," he said dryly. "Go on, then. Next problem."

I stared at him, hating him with the force of a clear white fire—and yet my mind felt more settled, my fear smaller, quieter.

"I'm worried that Gareth and Illaria won't be safe without us," I said. "We shouldn't have left them down south."

"They're far safer than we are. Kilraith's attention will be on us, not them. Let them enjoy their peace while they can. And the Vilia too," he added, anticipating the next item on my list.

"Nesset and Lulath," I interrupted. "Those are their names."

"No one will find them. The caverns are hard to find, and that Rose your sister brought to protect them is a fine fighter. She'll guard them well."

"*Brigid.* Can you not remember anyone's names?"

"I remember the important things."

I scoffed and looked away. "You're a brute. You have rocks for brains and an appalling lack of manners, like all northerners." The words embarrassed me even as I said them—petty, childish, and simply not true; northerners were fine people on the whole, albeit gruff and solemn—but I couldn't help myself. If I had to work with a Bask, I would let him know very plainly that we were not friends and never would be.

But Ryder only grinned at me. "Excellent. Keep going."

"Gareth," I said quietly after a moment. It was a worry I couldn't shake.

Ryder frowned. "We've already addressed that one."

I shook my head. "We should have brought him with us."

"His arm is broken. He can't fight. He would have slowed us down."

"But he knows more about the Old Country than any of us. Without him—"

"We have his notes. And have you forgotten, Ashbourne? Your lover boy is a *demon*. He's Olden inside and out."

"But he's not a scholar or a sage," I said desperately, "and he's been in captivity for years, learning only what Kilraith wants him to learn plus whatever scraps he can pick up on his own. And he can hardly stand!"

Ryder shook his head. "You're creating problems for yourself. That's a waste of time. The fact is that Gareth's arm is broken. He'd be a danger to himself and to us. We couldn't bring him. Next problem."

I stood there in silence for a moment, searching my mind for another worry to present—but the truth was that Ryder was right: Talan, my Talan, was dying, and the queen was terrified of the creature who hunted him. The Mist was full of fires, and chimaera had invaded the Citadel.

Those were the things that mattered. I couldn't let my fear distract me from that truth.

Instead I had to use it.

The panic was a force, a great beastly thing that lived inside me and maybe always would. I could let it consume me, I could believe its lies, I could run from it in vain—or I could somehow learn to understand it and look it straight in the eye, to feel the power of it and know when to dodge it, when to let it rage, when to pray it quiet, and when to strike back.

Bewildered, stunned by my own thoughts, I took a breath, and then another. My tense shoulders relaxed ever so slightly.

Ryder searched my face, then nodded and clapped a huge hand onto my shoulder. "Good. You're ready. Let's go."

But as I followed him back to the group and emerged from the trees, something caught my ear—a tone, an unearthly voice, soft and distant, high and clear. It rose and fell like an echo of the unseen waves.

I slowed, listening, my heart lurching into a gallop. It was the same song I'd heard weeks before, the one I'd followed wildly into the Mist. This song, though, was more urgent. There was a desperate quality to it, as if something were singing for its life.

As I stood there on the ruined black ground, I looked up to find Farrin and saw the truth in her glistening eyes:

She heard the song too.

"What is that?" she whispered.

"Think of the Far Sea," Alastrina was saying, full of mockery. It was obvious she heard nothing but her own voice. "We're supposed to think of it," she went on, "and then the Mist will take us there? Is that right?"

She stood with her hands on her hips, glaring at us when we didn't respond. "Well, is that right or isn't it?"

"Hush," I spat at her.

Indignant, she opened her mouth to protest, but Ryder silenced her with a look.

Phaidra raised her staff, her narrowed eyes darting around the trees. "I do not like this," she muttered. "You say you hear a song, and now the sound of the sea is growing louder, as if it is crawling toward us."

"Do you hear it, Talan?" I asked quietly.

"Hear what?" he rasped, shivering on the ground beside Farrin. He looked up at me, pale and gaunt, as if the journey through the greenways had sucked meat off his bones. I felt a terrible chill and went to him, tenderly pushing the wet hair back from his brow.

"The song," I said. "You don't hear it?"

He smiled tiredly, held my hand against his chest. "I hear only you," he whispered. Then a shadow moved across his face, and his smile widened. "I hear only him."

Farrin knelt beside us, her eyes bright, her cheeks flushed. I recognized the look of terror and wonder on her face; I'd felt it too, that day in the Mist.

"Is it Kilraith?" she whispered. "Some kind of trick?"

"Maybe," I said, doubtful, "but I don't think so." I felt a tug at the heart of my deepest self, something unseen embedded in me, pulling at me, insistent, and my mind cleared of everything but the certainty that this song was meant for me, for us, and that we needed to follow it.

Mara emerged from the Mist and hurried straight toward us, breathing hard, her eyes a bit wild.

"You hear it too," she said, glancing quickly at each of them. "I can see it on your faces. I thought I was mad, that the Mist had gotten inside me."

A chill raced down my arms. *Both* my sisters heard the song. Huddled as we were around Talan's shivering form, I felt the import of the moment, as if some sacred rite were beginning. I didn't understand the feeling, the rightness of it, and yet my bones rang with it, and my mind was clear.

"I've heard this before," I said quietly, "when I visited Rosewarren before the queen's masquerade ball. Remember?"

Mara's expression turned grave. "Of course. Brigid found you. You'd climbed a tree."

"And this is what you heard that day?" Farrin asked sharply.

I nodded, my body humming with a strange, cold thrill of feeling that I couldn't name. Excitement? Terror?

"What are you all whispering about?" Alastrina demanded. "How long are we going to stand here waiting for some door to open? Hours? Days?"

"Shut up, woman," Phaidra growled. "You're trying my patience."

Ryder took a few steps toward us. "Describe what you're hearing."

We paused for a moment, letting the song wash over us. I was beginning to hear cycles in the melody, a distinct pattern, and with each new cycle the voice grew louder, its tone more urgent.

A lure? Or a plea?

"A woman's voice, perhaps," Mara said. "Or a child's?"

"No melody I recognize," I added, "and no words. Just..."

"Sadness," Mara whispered, her expression distant, guarded.

Farrin's mouth twisted. "And *anger*. Desperate, ageless anger."

"Strange." I looked up at both of them. "To me it sounds... terrified."

And all at once, I knew what we had to do. It was a ridiculous idea, but that didn't matter. Something could be ridiculous and right at the same time.

I leaned over Talan and kissed his fevered brow. "I'm not

leaving you," I whispered. "Don't be afraid, darling. You're coming with me. I'm *not* leaving you."

He looked up at me, bewildered, his bloodshot eyes full of pain. "Gemma?"

My heart broke in half to see the fear written so plainly on his face. If I kept looking at him, I would lose my courage. I glanced up at my sisters instead.

"We have to follow the song," I told them. "Mara, you said the Mist could be alive in some way, that it might take us where we want to go."

Mara smiled a little. "If we ask nicely."

"It would seem that we did," Farrin said with a shaky laugh. "It is possible that this voice could belong to the Mist itself?"

A wild, chilling question that none of us knew how to answer.

I looked up at the others. "Alastrina, help Talan walk. Ryder, Phaidra, don't let anything happen to him. All of you, follow us."

Alastrina laughed, gaping at me. "Have you lost your senses?" When I didn't answer, she glared at her brother and threw out a hand at me. "Has she lost her senses? Are you going to let her lead us toward some figment of her imagination?"

"I am," Ryder answered simply, then gestured at Talan. "Help the demon walk." At a look from Phaidra, he sighed and amended nastily, "My apologies. Help *Talan* walk."

Satisfied, and taking no small delight in the blazing fury of Alastrina's expression, I closed my eyes, focused on the sound of the voice, and started walking toward it, my sisters at my heels. With each step, the lingering bite of the greenway's magic lessened, leaving my joints supple and loose, my limbs sure and strong. The acrid air grew sweet; I smelled Ivyhill in springtime, new buds on the trees and fresh damp earth everywhere and hothouses bursting with blooms.

Behind me, Farrin drew in a sharp breath, and Mara let out a muted cry of longing; I wondered if they had caught the same scents, or if for them the aroma was different. I opened my eyes.

The charred ground had turned into a velvet carpet, ash and pebbles giving way to moss and tiny white flowers. The scrubby trees leaned toward us, their branches elongating. Charred bark peeled away in gleaming flakes, and fresh green buds sprouted from the mottled new bark beneath—white and brown, healthy, tender. I turned up my face to the gray sky and drank my fill of the air. It was cold and sharp and clean as an autumn morning.

"What in the name of the gods..." Alastrina said somewhere behind us, her voice shaky and awestruck.

I reached back, and my sisters grabbed hold of me—Farrin my left hand, Mara my right. We began to run, and it shouldn't have worked, all of us linked like that; we should have tripped and fallen, tumbled down on top of each other. But instead we ran through the trees, easy and eager, a silver river at our backs and the song roaring in our ears. Sadness, anger, terror—yes, the voice held all those things, all of that and more, and I needed to understand the rest of it that I couldn't yet hear.

The ground was sloping upward, a gentle climb. We raced across tufts of shining green grass, boulders flat and sun-warmed, Farrin laughing behind me as I hadn't heard her laugh for years, Mara's long strides gliding past me, a she-wolf on the hunt. As we reached the slope's crest, a gentle rise spilling over with clover, I thought I heard someone yelling at me to stop. A voice behind me, familiar and dear. A man, terrified, my name harsh on his lips.

I turned and called out over my shoulder, "Hurry! You *must* follow us now, before the tide changes!"

I didn't know why I said it, only that the words were there

on my tongue and needed to get out. I wasn't bothered by them. They were of the song, and the song would show me the way.

A name floated to the front of my mind: *Talan.*

The man's voice belonged to him. He was shouting for me, warning me to stop, but the song was growing louder, raucous, exultant, and quickly drowned him out—a great chorus of voices, hundreds of them, a storm of sound in my ears.

Then all at once, the ground fell away under my feet. A cold blast of wind hit me in the face, knocked me away from my sisters and shocked me breathless. When I at last managed to gulp for air, I tasted nothing but salt. I reached blindly for Farrin and Mara, felt the cold, frantic grope of their hands on either side of me. I grabbed on to them, heard the heartless crash of waves closing over my head, and went tumbling into inky blackness.

CHAPTER 38

Wherever I was, the air smelled different—fuller, richer, every scent amplified. Salt, loam, damp wood, and a slight sour smell that reminded me of our childhood summer holidays at the southern shore: the picked-over remains of crabs rotting in the sun, a beach strewn with seaweed after a storm.

I took a slight breath, testing the cool air, and it was as if a crystalline spring had rushed through me, over me, washing me clean inside and out.

I tested my arms and legs; they did not hurt. *Nothing* hurt. I ran my tongue over my teeth; they were all intact. Astonishing. I had landed hard; I could still feel the vibration in my bones. But no pain accompanied it. My joints and muscles were quiet, content.

When I looked around, the sharp vibrancy of the world stunned me. I was in a woodland, thick and dark. The branches glittered black—obsidian, onyx, a silvered charcoal that reminded me of the Mistfire's ruin—but their cascades of thin leaves were a startling bright green. The sandy soil beneath me glimmered with an iridescent sheen, and beyond the woodland was a vast plain carpeted with golden grass and white reeds.

A cool, salty wind whispered across the plain, making the grasses sway and ripple, and in the distance surged true waves—a rolling ocean under a darkening sky. Even from such a distance, the crash of those waves rattled my bones. They roared thunderously, like mountains splitting open. A storm was coming; far out over the water, fat clouds spat tendrils of lightning.

And right at the shore, nestled on the rocky cliffs between grass and sea, stood an enormous dark house, square and severe, with a crown of fearsome parapets and golden windows like a dozen unblinking eyes.

My stomach tightened with fear. I hated the sight of that house. It looked evil sitting out there, and terribly lonesome.

"A sea called Farther," Farrin whispered. She had come to stand beside me, Mara just behind her. "Did we actually do it? Is this the Old Country?"

I turned to face my sisters, and the sight of them struck me speechless.

They were resplendent—their skin glowed with inner light just as the Mist had, just as *I* had when my body had changed on that awful night in the queen's gardens. Their hair was lustrous; even with Mara's dark locks bound in a braid and Farrin's in a tight golden-brown knot at her nape, the new sheen of it was obvious, as if someone had combed their tresses with fingers dipped in stars. Their brown eyes sparkled with golden flecks, and the air around them trembled. They looked, quite simply, rejuvenated, as if their old selves had peeled away to reveal secret treasure.

"Gemma…" Farrin whispered, hand at her mouth.

Mara's brow knotted with worry. "What's happened to you?" She glanced at Farrin. "To *us*?"

I looked down at my arms. Their gleaming coat of glass shone brilliantly, as if I were caught in full midday sunlight. Until now, the shimmer of my skin had been easily enough explained away as a style choice, but this was different. This was obvious and radiant and dangerous, a beacon that would make it impossible to hide and draw straight toward us whatever lurked nearby. Olden beasts, Olden beings. Fae, demons, vampyrs, anything eager to collect a glittering human oddity—perhaps even Kilraith himself.

I knew immediately what had to be done. I knew it with an instinct certain as breathing. Just as I had on the long-ago night of my party, sitting at my dressing table mirror with no understanding of why I'd gone there or what I was doing, I lifted my hands and imagined what I wanted to create: a glamour to cloak my whole body. It was swift work; my hands were light as feathers on my skin, and my thoughts were diamond-sharp. And unlike that night at my dressing table, when I'd felt as if I were being steered by something, my movements not quite my own, standing in those black woods, I felt utterly in control. The power cascading down my body was mine and mine alone; it would work as I commanded.

When I finished, my eyes were stinging with tears. Thinking about the night of my party had reminded me of Jessyl, and just as everything else in those woods felt like a greater, brighter version of itself, so too did my grief. I didn't turn away from it; I held on to it as I would a weapon, and I opened my eyes to look at my sisters.

"Did it work?" I asked them.

"It did," came a voice from the nearby trees—Ryder, a bit unsteady on his feet, his grim face bearing fresh scratches. Alastrina and Phaidra were behind him, helping Talan walk.

"A solid glamour, Ashbourne," Ryder added. "Maybe now we stand a chance of not getting picked off by some Olden magpie once we leave the shelter of these trees."

His voice was wry and unflappable as usual, but I saw a new

guardedness in his eyes, and when I went to Talan, Alastrina left him to Phaidra and warily stepped away, her eyes wide and frightened as she gaped at me.

Phaidra, though, merely nodded at me, unafraid. "Fae blood, Imogen. I told you it was so."

"Fae blood?" Mara said. "Not possible. Neither Mother nor Father—"

"Perhaps not them, but somewhere in your bloodline," Phaidra interrupted. She nodded at me, her eyes full of pride. "See how easily she crafted that glamour? See the way the trees lean toward you, all of you, as if in prayer? The blood of both Kerezen and Caiathos burns in your veins just as it did in the veins of the first fae."

It was true: Every one of the black trees within sight had shifted. Their branches now arched toward Farrin and Mara and me, very like the trees that lined the long pebbled drive at Ivyhill. Under the hiss of the sea, the wind carried a chatter of whispers, and the same instinct that had told me how to craft the glamour told me that those whispers belonged to the trees. They were talking amongst themselves. They were talking about *us*.

"Gods unmade," Alastrina breathed. She was starting to look furious. "It's all a trick. They *lured* us here. They brought us to be some sort of sacrifice to their unholy fae clan—"

"We aren't fae," Farrin snapped, her eyes flashing. At her feet, a cluster of spindly weeds shivered and stretched up toward her shins.

"Then what are you?" Alastrina demanded. "Ryder and I look the same as we did before crossing over, and so does the Vilia, and your demon lover too."

She wasn't wrong. I ignored the unease roiling in my stomach and went to Talan, took his face in my hands. His cheeks were cold and clammy; he could barely open his eyes. His face was an echo of itself, thin and wan, his cheekbones eerily prominent, his jaw the edge of a knife.

"Can you hear me, Talan?" I whispered. "Is this the right place? Is that the sea called Farther?"

"Gemma," he said. He turned his face into my palm with a soft broken sound. "Gemma, he's coming."

I stroked Talan's cheek with my thumb, trying not to show him how afraid I was. "Kilraith? He's near?"

"He's here, he's there, he's everywhere." He laughed a little. The shape of his mouth was unfamiliar, hooked at the corners, and my bile rose at once, all the hair on my arms standing on end.

That smile did not belong to him.

I swallowed my fear. "Talan," I said firmly. "Talan of the Far Sea. Look at me. Hear my voice and know me. Listen to me, not to him. I'm here, and I love you. We need you to help us search for the anchor of the *ytheliad*. The anchor of the curse that binds you to Kilraith. Remember? We need to take it back to Edyn so we can destroy it."

Talan stared at me, his breathing quickening. Then he squeezed his eyes shut, shook his head, stepped away from me. His legs gave out, and he crashed to his knees.

I knelt beside him, made myself touch him. I would not be afraid. I was Lady Imogen Ashbourne, and I would not be afraid.

"Talan, you need to focus, you need to think," I told him. "Look around you. Is that the sea called Farther? Did the Mist bring us to the right place?"

When he didn't answer, instead holding his head in his hands and hiding his face from me, I braced myself and tried again. "Are these the woods you ran into? Is that the Far Sea, Talan, where the titans live? Is that your house out there on the rocks? Is that where you lived as a child? Where your parents lived?"

Slowly he lifted his head and looked at me, astonished. "The house?" he whispered.

I hated to do it. I wished I could have hidden his face against me and taken us far away from that horrid place. But instead I pointed at the distant black house with its staring golden windows.

"Is that your house, Talan?" I repeated.

The silence was terrible; even the trees seemed to be holding their breath.

"It is," Talan said at last, gazing in wonderment across the plain. "That's our house. It's so very old. Generations of us have lived there. We call it Brimgard."

Farrin came to me and placed a warm hand on my shoulder. I reached up and squeezed her fingers gratefully. Her touch grounded me; I could breathe more easily with her near.

"But that isn't possible," Talan said. He rose unsteadily, waving me off when I tried to help him. "The house fell into the sea. The titans claimed it."

"That was a long time ago," I said gently. "Maybe your memory—"

"The house fell into the sea!" he said again, frantically now. His eyes were wild, desperate. He tore away from me, hurried through the trees until his foot caught on a root and he fell. He huddled there, hands over his ears. "It's not possible, not possible..."

I started to run after him, but Mara caught my wrist, held me fast.

"Gemma," she said, her voice full of warning.

I followed her gaze through the trees, and what I saw made my heart stop: Five figures clad in black from head to toe. Tight hoods, long fluttering tunics, smooth white masks singed with ash.

The Brethaeus.

And they were not alone.

Lurching figures peeled away from the trees, flanking the necromancers, darting ahead of them, weaving between them: gray and pale and brown, all of them with gnarled skin and scars woven shut with wilting flowers. Vilia, nine of them, using their staffs to pull themselves fast across the ground. And like the masks the Brethaeus wore, these Vilia were smudged with ash. Burns glistened on their skin; fresh wounds leaked black blood.

One of the Vilia, scurrying ahead of the rest, was familiar—skin a scaly brown, eyes furious and black. The plain brown dress that hung off her bony frame was threadbare.

My mouth went dry.

It was Rennora. The other eight, then, I thought frantically, were the ones who had been loyal to her, all of whom Phaidra, Nesset, and Lulath had killed that day in the Vilia's woods.

Phaidra let out a strangled cry and stumbled back, her staff hanging uselessly at her side.

"But they died," she whispered. She looked at me, her eyes full of grief. "We fought them and killed them. They were *free*."

"The Brethaeus remade them," I said faintly. I noted the leather straps tied around the necromancers' torsos. Once they had held hundreds of tiny velvet pouches full of teeth and bones and blood, binding their revenants to them. Now those straps were bare except for a few fresh pouches sewn of crimson velvet that dangled from their makers like hunks of raw meat. Nine pouches for each necromancer.

Suddenly the burns and fresh wounds on the Vilia made a terrible, sickening sense. No doubt the Brethaeus, upon resurrecting the Vilia's corpses to serve them yet again, had decided to punish them—with fire, with blades, with their own dark magic.

"Necromancers," Ryder growled in disgust, then raised his crossbow and fired a single shot, one thick black arrow that lodged in Rennora's chest and knocked her flat.

It was the match that set the rest of them on fire. The Vilia lunged for us, screeching, their rotten teeth bared. The world slowed around me as I watched them come, but my thoughts raced like mad animals: we should have brought Nesset and Brigid, we should never have come, we were dead, we were finished.

Ryder launched arrow after arrow, fierce and fearless, but each Vilia he felled wrenched herself back to her feet not long after. Alastrina shrank back and hid behind a tree; Phaidra ran at Rennora, her staff flying, a horrible scream tearing out of her throat, and I hated it, I hated that once more she had to fight her own kind for my sake.

Then Mara was there, snapping me out of my terrified stupor. She shoved Farrin and me behind her and leapt into battle so swiftly, so effortlessly, that in my shock I could only sit there in the weeds and watch her. She was a sentinel; she fought in the Order of the Rose. These things I knew. And yet in the Old Country she became something else entirely.

She didn't transform as she had that day so long ago; the ancient magic, seeded by the gods, that bound her to serve at the Mist and allowed her to assume a beastly aspect when on duty did not, apparently, extend to Olden lands.

But even fully human, fully woman, she was a sight to behold. She flew through the air and kicked one of the Vilia in the chest with a sickening crack, breaking all her ribs at once. That one fell, screaming, and Mara spun around to strike another one in the throat. The Vilia staggered and fell, hands clutching her neck, choking.

Three other Vilia leapt at Mara, grabbed on and clung to her like burrs, gnashing and clawing, but Mara let out a harsh cry and jumped up into the trees, shaking off the Vilia like flies. They dropped hard to the ground—it was a terrible fall—but when Mara landed among them, it was with the lightness of a bird.

A soft touch at my ankle drew my attention to the cluster of weeds at my feet—brown and green and yellow leaves, fuzzy purple flowers, winding, glossy vines studded with thorns. I loved them with a sudden absurd tenderness. I didn't know what it meant that the whole great knot of them was curling softly against my legs, reaching up to me with their little leaves pursed like mouths.

But I knew all at once that I could use them.

I grabbed Farrin, who was huddled beside me, and dragged her back into the trees. Alastrina was not far from us, crouched behind her own tree, her hands flat against its bark. She was muttering in what sounded like Ekkari, the bestial language Gareth had mentioned at the Citadel. I couldn't translate the words but hoped to the gods they would help.

I held the back of Farrin's head, keeping her still, forcing her to look at me.

"Listen," I said quickly. "I need you to sing."

Farrin's eyes widened. She glanced past me at the chaos—Vilia falling, Vilia rising once more; Ryder's arrows, Phaidra's staff, the mountainous, tireless force that was Mara; the slow, inexorable approach of the Brethaeus. I looked back only once, and a horrible shock of fear tore through me as I saw the Brethaeus silently, as one, raise their right arms. The ground beneath us began to tremble.

I turned back to Farrin, desperate. "Look at Mara. She's stronger here than she's ever been at home. I think we are too. Whether it's fae blood or something else, that doesn't matter now. We have to use it."

Farrin shook her head. "No, I can't. Not here. I don't know what it will do."

"You won't be alone. I have my own magic to work." I made

myself smile at her, even though my insides were a mess of fear. "I'm going to tear these woods to pieces, Farrin. I'm going to wrap up whatever baddies I can find in tree roots as thick as their torsos. And you're going to sing and bring the rest of them to their knees. Understand?"

"Gemma, *no*. Please don't ask this of me."

"Do you want us to die, Farrin?"

"The others can, *you* can—"

I wanted to shake her. "What are you afraid of?"

Her eyes were hard, furious, but I saw beyond that. I saw the frightened fourteen-year-old girl who had sat down to play her beloved piano, only to be mobbed a few moments later by two hundred people screaming her name, sobbing for her to touch them.

"You've seen what my magic does to people back home," Farrin said harshly. "How am I to know what it will do here?"

A scream sounded behind me; I didn't know who it belonged to, and I whirled around with my heart in my throat, fearing the worst. Mara, Phaidra, *Mara*—

But it was neither of them. It was the Brethaeus: first one, then two, then all five of them shrieking a shrill note in grotesque chorus. They held their right arms in the air and began to raise their left. Their shrieks climbed higher and higher, such a deafening, evil sound that my ears boomed with pain.

It was an incantation. My new, stronger body—buoyed by whatever Olden power this land possessed—did not ache or crumple as it would have at home, but I nevertheless felt the presence of the foul magic they were working. A great pressure fell upon me, crushing and scorching hot, and just as I started panting for breath, the trembling ground burst open.

Specters tore out of the dirt—spirits of the dead raised by the Brethaeus's spell. The woods suddenly teemed with serpentine shadows, taller and spindlier than the trees, too swift to fix my eyes on. I had never encountered specters outside of children's stories and books about the arcana, but I nevertheless immediately knew them for what they were. They did not keep the same shape for longer than an instant: one moment a dark pillar, wide as a door; the next a thin line, blinding white. I felt hands on me, heard voices whispering so close to my ears that they seemed to be coming from inside me. They said only one word: my name. *Gemma. Gemma. Gemma.*

They clogged the woods like smoke. I could catch only brief glimpses of the others—Mara's fists, Ryder's arrows, Phaidra's staff, the five expressionless white masks of the Brethaeus.

I ran without knowing where I was going, unable to see more than a few steps in front of me, but I could still feel the trees: the net of their roots beneath me, the canopy of their branches above. Where I ran, they followed, limbs groaning and creaking.

I muttered the little prayer Talan had taught me that day we'd trapped the Brethaeus: *Terror. Lust. Rage.*

My power answered at once, easy and eager. White lightning blazed up my body and back down into the earth. I ripped roots from the soil, flung them straight at the necromancers' slitted masks. This time, though, they knew what to expect from me. Three Vilia leapt in front of them, protecting their masters; the roots lashed through them like whips, and the Vilia collapsed, severed body parts dropping into the dirt. I tried again—reached for a nearby tree with an apology on my lips, tore the whole length of it from the earth, sent it flying at the Brethaeus like a battering ram—but the Vilia I'd massacred had already reassembled, gruesome patchwork dolls sewn back together in an instant. The tree slammed into their stomachs—one, two, three—and sent them flying back into the brush.

The Brethaeus watched, motionless, unflinching. Though I couldn't see their faces behind their masks—I couldn't be sure if they even *had* faces—I could feel their amusement, their delight, and knew that they would keep toying with us for as long as they could, simply for the joy of it.

I tried again and again, sending snarls of vines hissing fast across the ground like snakes, but always, always, the Vilia were faster than me, snarling and dauntless, taking every blow meant for their masters.

Something hard flew into my right side and I fell, hit my head against the ground. I looked up, dazed, tasting blood, and saw Rennora crouched not far from me, hands braced in the dirt, ready to pounce again.

Phaidra leapt between us just as Rennora jumped. Their bodies crashed together, and they dropped to the ground, entwined, snarling, and I screamed Phaidra's name, reached for her—but then darkness fell before me, smothering my voice for a moment before flittering away. A long gray shadow curled around me so tight I couldn't breathe, then released me; a white bolt of heat, jagged as lightning, tore across my vision and then was gone.

Specters: they were swarming me. They couldn't stay in one place for long—they rushed at me, wound around me, pasted themselves over my mouth and nose, and then were gone again—but there were so many of them, and they kept coming, their awful whispers slithering into my ears and between my teeth: *Gemma. Gemma. Gemma.*

I wrenched away from them long enough to howl my sister's name. "Farrin, *please!*"

More specters spun around me, whipping at me like a howling wind, cutting off all other sounds—until I heard, ever so faintly, like a single pinprick of light fighting to shine in a sky dark with storms, the sweet, crystal tone of my eldest sister's voice.

The song was unfamiliar, but her voice was like coming home—to Ivyhill as it should have been, all of us together and whole. Mother had never left us, and Mara had never gone to the Middlemist. No artificer had ever touched me; no fire had ever burned our house; Farrin had never known the taste of smoke. And when Father looked at me, it was warm and lovely and kind—no anger, no weariness, no guilt or fear.

It was a melody full of longing, far more beautiful than the eerie voice that had helped us cross over. There was no deception in Farrin's voice, no guile or agenda. The glide from each note to the next was a kiss that left me aching. If the stars could sing, they would have voices like hers: pure and clean, rich and easy and ageless.

As Farrin's song flooded the woods, the specters began peeling away from me. They darted away, then flittered back, shadows in the corners of my eyes. They collided with each other in rapturous confusion, slammed into the ground. They crashed up into the trees, flinging branches left and right.

I pushed myself to my feet, my knees like jelly and my breath coming in sharp, painful bursts. Rennora had hit me hard; my whole side felt bruised. I searched for Farrin, saw her standing beside the tree where I'd left her—flushed pink and golden from the joy of her song. Her eyes were open and clear, the lines of her body relaxed, assured. An Upper Army soldier facing a chimaera would not have looked more formidable. Absurd, that I'd ever thought Farrin incapable of combat; her armor was song, and her weapons were her voice, the strength of her nimble fingers, the precision of her ear.

Ryder stood in front of her protectively, his crossbow aimed and ready. On his bearded face was an expression so passionate, so ferocious, that I felt I had intruded on something intensely private. One look at him, and it was clear to me that if anyone or anything came for Farrin, he would die before he let them touch her.

Reassured that at least one of my sisters was safe, I whirled around, ready to keep fighting with whatever strength I had left, though each breath was painful and I wondered if I'd broken a rib. Rennora and Phaidra were still locked in combat, and Mara fought the remaining Vilia all at once. She was marvelous, breathtaking; when they rose, she kicked them flat. When they flew at her, she knocked them from the air with one swift jab of her arm.

Then one lowered her head at Mara, a bull ready to charge, and ran at her, drove hard into her stomach.

I watched in horror as my sister went flying. She skidded across the ground until her back slammed into a tree. After that, she did not move.

"Ryder!" I screamed, pointing frantically, but he was already firing, his arrows whipping through the air and thunking into their targets. One Vilia fell, then another—but I knew, flushed all over with a wretched chill of fear, that they would rise again, and again, as long as the Brethaeus willed it to be so.

Then a hand on my arm: Alastrina tugging me back to hide with her in the trees.

"No!" I screamed, hitting uselessly at her arm. She was surprisingly strong, her grip like iron. "Let me go! Mara needs help!"

"Shut up and stay out of the way," Alastrina hissed. Then she jerked her head at the woods and grinned. "Watch this."

I was so out of my mind with worry for Mara that for a wild moment I considered ripping up the tree we stood behind and using it to slam Alastrina to the ground. But then I heard it—a low rumble, like thunder rolling near. First quiet, and then louder, nearer, deafening. I looked up at the sky, expecting to see storm clouds, but instead I saw a great billowing blackness—distant, but rapidly growing closer.

Beside me, Alastrina had resumed her Ekkari muttering, and I understood all at once what was happening in a flash of relief so immense I had to lean hard against the tree to stay upright.

Birds. The black cloud was *birds*.

They descended on the woods, hundreds of them: feathered black wings, furry round bodies like bats, forked fleshy tails, sharp brown beaks as long as my middle finger. I stared, horrified and entranced. They weren't birds after all; they were Olden creatures, vaguely avian in aspect but monstrous otherwise. Chimaeras, maybe, or something even stranger.

I glanced at Alastrina, wondering if she realized what exactly she'd been summoning as she wilded in the shadows, but she seemed perfectly content. There was something feral about her as she stood there muttering, her blue eyes glittering.

The birds thundered through the trees, an awful cacophony. The Brethaeus shrank back, masks raised to the skies. They tried to run, but for all their power over the dead, they could not outrun this. The birds swarmed them, an unstoppable black wave. They latched on to the Brethaeus with their wicked talons, stabbed them with their beaks. The shrieking, fluttering weight of them must have been terrible; the necromancers collapsed almost at once, and when they began to scream, all of them buried in that writhing black cloud, the sounds were horrible to hear, ragged and wordless. No power, no intelligence—simply pure animal agony.

With the Brethaeus trapped, the Vilia scattered, as confused as the specters had been. Ryder shot two of them in the back as they fled, then lowered his crossbow, glaring after the rest of them. He had run out of arrows and began muttering the same Ekkari words as his sister.

I ran to Mara, terrified of what I would find, but she had already started to rise, looking as strong and whole as ever. With a sob I crashed into her, held her so tight against me that it hurt, but I didn't care. If I could have, I would have held her for the rest of my life.

"I'm all right, Gemma," she murmured, and then gently detached herself from me to look around at the ravaged woods— fallen trees everywhere, great ruts in the ground from where I'd uprooted them.

Farrin let her song end at last. Once the final note had faded, she swayed a little, clearly about to fall. Ryder abruptly stopped wilding the birds, dropped his crossbow, and caught Farrin before she could collapse, but she took one look up at him and put an end to that right away. Her face darkened with anger and she shoved him back.

"Don't touch me, Bask," she hissed, stumbling away. "We're allies, not friends. If I need your help, I'll ask for it."

"Fine," he said shortly, his expression inscrutable. "Next time I'll let you fall."

Alastrina strode forward out of the trees, looking smug. Hands on her hips, she surveyed her work, utterly unmoved by the fading, gurgling screams of the Brethaeus.

"What did you tell them to do?" I asked her.

"I sent out a call to whatever was nearby and hungry," she said matter-of-factly, "and I told them to come eat the people wearing masks, to pick them clean right down to their bones. It seems wilding works just as well here as it does in Edyn. You're welcome." She looked to Ryder and gave him a satisfied nod. "And good work, Brother. I wouldn't have been able to finish without your help."

Then she glanced past me and her smile fell. I thought I saw a flicker of something soft and sad move across her face before she jerked her head and said tersely, "Your Vilia friend, Ashbourne."

Phaidra.

I turned around, cold all over, and saw what Alastrina had seen—two Vilia lying sprawled across the ground, unmoving. One had been stabbed through the throat with one of Ryder's arrows and lay gaping up at the sky: Rennora, her fist clenched around a knife, her black eyes frozen with death—*true* death, now that the Brethaeus were no longer there to resurrect her.

And the other...

"No, no, no," I whispered, sinking to my knees at Phaidra's side. I touched her cheek; a scarred ridge of flowers pressed against my palm. Her eyes were glazed over, drifting aimlessly. She couldn't find my face.

I refused to cry. Phaidra deserved my utmost courage. "Phaidra," I whispered. "Can you hear me?"

She was alive, but only just—a terrible stomach wound gleamed black with blood. Wilted flowers spilled from the gash of it. Her chest rose and fell quickly, her breathing erratic, and her eyes at last rolled up to meet mine.

"Do not grieve, Imogen," she rasped. "Far better than dying in a cave."

I leaned down and held her face in my hands so she could look nowhere else but right at me.

"My friend," I whispered, "we didn't know each other for long enough. Not nearly long enough. I wish we could have had years."

I thought I saw Phaidra's mouth twitch. "Free."

I smiled down at her, no longer able to hold back my tears. "Yes. You're free, Phaidra. Rest, now."

Gently I pressed my lips to the knotted skin of her brow, right at the tip of a flowered scar. I lingered there for a moment, gathering myself, and by the time I sat back on my heels, Phaidra was gone. I fumbled under my coat for the little carving of Una on its leather cord and pressed it hard against my heart.

Mara knelt beside me. "She died a good death," she told me quietly. The steady warmth of her voice was a comfort; Mara knew better than anyone what it was to lose a friend in combat.

"She died in a battle that she chose to fight," Mara added, gently squeezing my hand. "She died a free creature. You helped her achieve that."

I nodded, unable to speak. I wanted to pray over Phaidra's body, beg the dead gods to send her to Ryndar at last, to the Realm of the Far Light, where she would finally be at peace and where no necromancers could find her. And then after that, there was so much left to do: the whole woods to search, the anchor of Kilraith's curse to find—

Terror came fast as lightning. I scrambled to my feet and frantically searched the trees.

"Talan?" I cried. "Talan!"

I tore into the woods, ducked under branches, swatted tearfully at the vines that curled up to greet me. But when I reached the spot where I'd last seen Talan—hands over his ears, huddled among the roots of a tree—it was empty. He wasn't there. He wasn't *anywhere*.

Panic blurred the world. I spun back to the others.

"Where is he?" I demanded, as if they were keeping some secret knowledge from me. I found Alastrina; she was far too calm. My friend had just died, and my love had vanished while we had all fought for our lives, and I needed this implacable daughter of the House of Bask to feel the same terror I was feeling.

"What did you do with him?" I demanded.

Alastrina stared at me in disbelief. "Have you gone mad? I didn't do anything to him. I was here the whole time, wilding—and saving our lives in the process, I'll remind you."

Farrin touched my elbow before I could say anything else.

"Gemma, look," she said quietly, looking toward the sea.

I did, and my heart sank at the sight. I heard Ryder mutter a low curse behind me.

A dark figure was cutting a swift path across the field beyond the woods—Talan, heading fast for the shore and for the house perched above it like a beast, golden-eyed and waiting.

CHAPTER 39

As soon as we stepped through the doors of Talan's ancestral home—Brimgard, he'd called it—I knew we were not alone.

The house was dark and preposterously huge. Every wall was papered with intricate patterns in deep crimson, forest green, muted gold. Lamps glowed warmly in elaborate iron brackets. A grand staircase of immaculate dark wood greeted us as Ryder pushed open the front doors, which had ominously been left open.

Frantic with hope, I immediately began to search for Talan—on the stairs, at the mouths of corridors branching off the entrance hall, in every shadow, every golden pool of light. But he was nowhere. What I could see of the house was empty.

And yet a feeling of nearness, of someone breathing on the back of my neck.

No, we were not alone.

Oh, Talan, I thought. *Be safe, wherever you are. Come back to me.*

I ached to scream his name, to go tearing through the house in search of him, but instead I tried to calm myself and search more deliberately. The parquet floor of the entryway was spotless, scattered with plush carpets. Alcoves set into the walls housed statuary: blue-veined marble beasts, grinning and horned; proud bronze steeds with a mottled green patina; naked humans made of stone, some contorted in obvious agony, their mouths agape in silent screams, others splayed open and smiling, welcoming paramours only they could see.

I approached the grand staircase, at the bottom of which stood two great white urns spilling over with greenery. There was a funny look to the leaves, a velveteen fuzz, and the same power that had helped me rip trees from the earth pulled me closer to investigate.

Each leaf was huge, easily the size of my face, with curly fringed edges. Bursting up from the leaves was a spiky bouquet of red flowers, but it was the leaves themselves that interested me. Once I got close enough, I saw that the fuzz I'd noticed from afar was in fact a fine gray coating of something that looked like ash.

I reached for the leaves, then hesitated. I tore a small button from my jacket and dropped it onto the nearest leaf.

The button sank into the ash and crumbled right before my eyes, its brass finish slowly flaking away until all that remained was a thin wisp of smoke.

The leaves curled slightly, shivering. Satisfied.

Now that I was looking for it, I saw the same faint sheen of ash covering every object: the statuary, the lamps, the oil paintings hanging on the walls in gilded frames. They made me uneasy, those paintings. The figures they depicted seemed to change when I wasn't looking—one of them shifted from a staid landscape to writhing lovers and then to a proud, stuffy-looking man in a soldier's coat heavy with golden chains. His eyes were blue, then black, his face pale, then furred, leering, then once again pale and bored and still. The walls were heavy with paintings, the light dim; was I imagining it all?

Shaking, I thrust my hand under my coat to find Phaidra's carving of Una. I clutched it tightly, pressing the edges into my fingers.

"Don't touch anything," I told the others. "Something's in here with us. Ash, or mold, or...I don't know what it is, but it will burn you if you touch it. Look." I went to the plant that stood on the other side of the stairs, tore another button from my coat, and dropped it onto a leaf. We all watched as the button dissolved into smoke with a faint hiss.

Alastrina stared at the smoke in horror.

Farrin looked ill. "What does that mean?"

"It means this place is a death trap," Ryder muttered, glaring down the nearest hallway with his crossbow loaded and ready. The quiver strapped to his back was full once more; he'd scoured the woods for every arrow he could find.

Mara, terribly pale even for her, said, "Another Rose once told me about something like this. She didn't know what it was: mold or ash or poison of some kind. She was one of the ones who crossed over accidentally years ago. I was quite young. When she came back to Edyn, she wasn't the same. She kept talking about breathing the whole world into your lungs, and how once it was in there, it changed all your senses, the way you saw things. I thought—all of us thought—she'd made it up. She was always making things up to scare us little ones. Part of our training, she said."

"Is this Rose still alive?" Alastrina asked.

"No." Mara's voice was steely, but I saw pain in her eyes that she couldn't quite hide. "She took her own life."

"Oh, excellent. If we stop breathing, we'll die, and if we keep breathing, we'll fill our bodies with Old Country toxins, lose our minds, and kill ourselves."

"That isn't helping, Trina," Ryder said tensely.

"Keep Phaidra's carvings near," Mara said to us all. "Touch them when you can. Anchoring ourselves to home however we can will help keep our minds clear."

She spoke with authority, but I knew she was only guessing at what might help us. Nevertheless, I curled my sweating fingers around Una and held her hard and thought of Phaidra, how nervous and dear she had looked when presenting the talisman to me. The thought was as horrible as it was wonderful; it was hard to breathe around my sudden grief.

Then Farrin came up beside me, rigid with tension. "Speaking of anchors," she said quietly, "if the curse's anchor is in this house somewhere, it too could be coated with this poison. We could find it only to be unable to touch it."

"Or by the time we find it," I said, "we'll have breathed in so much of it that our eyes will start playing tricks on us and we'll *think* it's safe to touch when in fact it isn't."

"And we'll burn our own hands off," Farrin said faintly. "If we even get that far. Is the floor poison too?"

I couldn't answer her. All I knew was that, so far, my feet were unharmed, which meant something—or someone—wanted me to keep going, at least for now. And keep going I would, no matter how completely it terrified me.

I swallowed hard, slipped the leather cord attached to my talisman over my head, and pressed Una gently into my coat pocket. I needed her where I could more easily touch her. The weight of her in my pocket was a comfort.

I moved past the staircase and into a set of three grand rooms connected by wide curtained doorways, a space clearly meant for hosting opulent parties. Chandeliers hung from the ceilings, dripping with diamonds. Huge mirrors adorned the dark red walls. I glanced only once at my reflection, then quickly looked away. The glass was warped, perhaps spellcrafted; my reflection was tall and shuddering and unfamiliar, as if I were looking at myself through the misshapen spyglass of a nightmare.

"We can't think of how many things could go wrong," I whispered to Farrin, though in fact I was doing precisely that. "We have to find Talan. He'll know how to navigate safely through all of this."

"Will he?" Farrin sounded doubtful. "He said his house fell into the sea, and I believe that's what he saw, what he thinks to be true. So either what he saw was an illusion, or something—some*one*— retrieved the house from the sea and reassembled it, or—"

"Or they built an entirely new house. An echo of what once was."

Neither of us dared to say the word *Kilraith*, and I was glad. Uttering his name in that awful house felt like the most extraordinarily foolish thing we could do.

Suddenly the air in the room shifted, pulled tight. The weight of it burned my shoulders. Beside me, Farrin stiffened. She felt it too.

Something was here with us in this room.

I spun around. In the corner of my eye, my reflection flickered darkly across the mirror.

But the thing that stood at the room's entrance was no monster, at least not the Olden kind.

It was our father.

He smiled at me, his face warm and soft. "Hello, Imogen. Thank the gods you're alive. I've been out of my mind with worry."

My relief was immediate and left me lightheaded. I nearly ran to him. Never mind everything that had happened; never mind the artificer and all those years of lies. Father would save me. He would wrap me in his arms and usher me safely out of this terrible house. He would tear down any creature who tried to hurt me. He was Lord Gideon Ashbourne, an Anointed sentinel.

But when I took a step forward, the slight weight of Una in my pocket bumped against my thigh.

I stopped at once, my skin prickling. The man standing before me certainly looked like my father—golden-brown hair like Farrin's, brown eyes, neatly trimmed beard. Tall and lean, a soldier in nobleman's clothing: a fine, gray summer suit with a pressed white collar and a brocaded green vest. His voice was his own, rich and familiar, the same voice I'd heard all my life, and yet I couldn't make myself go to him.

Father's brow furrowed gently. "What is it, my sweet girl? You look so frightened." He held out his hand. "Come with me. Let's go home."

It was awful to tear myself away from him, but somehow I managed it.

"Farrin?" I said, turning, expecting to see my sister just behind me—but she was far away, at the other end of the three enormous ballrooms. She stood rigidly, fists at her sides, facing an empty doorway that opened into another corridor.

"What do you want?" she said harshly. "Leave me. Leave me or I'll kill you."

With that Farrin turned away from the door, flushed with fury, and stood there for a moment as if listening to something I couldn't hear. A sick feeling filled my throat as I hurried toward her. Her expression crumpled, her posture sagged with defeat. She hid her face behind her fingers.

"Leave me, *please*," she whispered. "You did it once, now do it again. I beg you."

I grabbed her shoulders. "Farrin? Farrin, look at me."

But she didn't, even when I braced myself and slapped her. She simply wept into her hands. I strode past her toward the empty doorway, looked out into the corridor beyond. The whole great span of it was empty: dark green wallpaper, cheery golden lamps, the gleaming texture of the oil paintings that hung every few feet.

I stumbled back from the doorway, thrust my hand into my pocket to grab Una, ran across the room past the thing claiming it was my father, and returned to the entrance hall. At the foot of the grand staircase, I stopped short, my blood turning cold.

Ryder huddled in one of the far corners, his face stricken with anguish. His crossbow lay forgotten on the floor. Above him in an alcove set into the wall, a grinning statue stood frozen in the act of tearing off his own clothes.

As I watched, Ryder sat up straight, suddenly alert, and turned to the wall beside him. He placed his palms against it, pressed his ear to it. Listened, breathless.

"Gods help me, she's in the walls," he whispered.

Then he turned and saw me. His face lit up with hope. "Hurry, come help me! She's in the walls, and she can't breathe!"

He began to claw at the wallpaper, first with his fingernails, then with an arrow he yanked from his quiver. He gouged the wall with it, letting out horrible cries of despair as he worked. Ragged strips of paper peeled away, but Ryder was inconsolable, frenzied. He tossed the arrow aside, tore the heavy statue from its alcove, and began ramming its smiling head into the wall.

I nearly cried out for him to stop, that he would burn his hands, but he seemed to be unhurt, his skin whole and pale, and I couldn't decide whether to be relieved or even more frightened. Could the house—or whatever had made the house—choose how and when to poison us? Would Ryder's hands dissolve into ash once this unknown architect had its fill of watching him struggle?

"Why won't you help me?" Ryder called to me furiously, but I left him there in his clouds of dust and crossed the entrance hall in a daze. I stopped short when I saw Alastrina slowly climbing the stairs. She was gazing up at the landing on the second floor.

As I watched, Alastrina let out a muted cry and sank to her knees. She tried to hide behind the elaborate wooden banister and turned to the empty stair beneath her.

"Just be very quiet," she said, "and they won't be able to find us. Not here. Not ever."

I whirled around, desperate. Mara. Where was Mara?

The thing that was my father had come out into the entrance hall to watch me, his hands clasped behind his back.

"Imogen, you're worrying me," he said. "I really think you should come with me now. This place isn't good for you. Now, come, let me help you out of here. I know the way."

I hurried in the other direction, past the grand staircase, into a corridor I'd not yet seen.

"Imogen, stop this," he said sternly. Frustration thinned his voice.

I ignored him and searched the shadows, my heart pounding fast, my hand sweating around Una's wooden belly. Halfway down the corridor, two wide doors stood open, emitting a golden light. I raced inside, Mara's name on my lips, and found her standing in a gleaming kitchen—copper pots hanging from the ceiling, four huge stone ovens set into the walls, a gigantic mouth of a hearth with a fire crackling merrily inside.

And Mara, standing near a broad window that looked out over the sea. She held a shining silver cleaver.

"If you think it's best," she said, her voice hoarse from crying, "I suppose you must be right."

She raised the cleaver to her throat. It showed no sign of the mold, or ash, but its blade was dangerous enough—silver and sharp, winking at me in the firelight.

I tore across the room and crashed into her. The cleaver dropped, went spinning across the floor. I grabbed Mara's arm with one hand and with the other thrust Una at her.

"Mara, look at this," I choked out. "Remember? Phaidra made these for us. They're made of wood from Edyn. From *home*. She made them for everyone. Mine is Una. You remember her. You were there when we brought her home, when she was a puppy, only three months old. She's waiting for me back at Ivyhill. Where's your carving, Mara? What did Phaidra give you?"

Mara stared at the little wooden Una for so long that I began to despair. I had lost her; I was too late. Whatever foul magic lived in this house had claimed her for its own.

But then, slowly, she reached under her tunic and withdrew a pale wooden carving hanging from a leather cord: a curling sprig of ivy. Not a rose for the Order; not something belonging to the priory or the Mistlands.

Ivy. A piece of the home she'd lost.

I curled my hand around hers, pressed our fingers and Phaidra's talismans into a hard knot, and held them against her breastbone.

"That's right, Mara," I whispered. "That's where we're from. And that's where we'll go once this is done. We're going to go home."

Life seeped back into Mara's face. She rubbed at her cheeks and shook herself, tucked the ivy necklace back under her tunic, pressed her palm against it. Then she embraced me quick and hard and whispered, "Thank you." When she released me, she was herself again. Brown eyes, scarred neck, fierce and beautiful and strong. Her skin still glowed as it had since we'd arrived.

"Oh, thank the gods, you've found each other," said our father from the doorway. He leaned against the frame, his smile welcoming and easy. "Now we can find Farrin and go. We can leave this place and never come back."

Mara stiffened with shock. I turned her face to mine, held her firmly. "That isn't Father," I told her. "I don't know what it is, but it's not him. Don't listen to it, and don't be alarmed when you see the others. They're not themselves."

"The poison?" Mara asked.

"Maybe."

Or something worse. The words hung between us unsaid.

Mara glanced at our father, then looked back at me. "We have to get out of here quickly, with or without the *ytheliad*'s anchor, before whatever poison this is grabs hold of us for good."

"I won't leave Talan," I said at once.

"Gemma—"

"*No.* I won't do it. We'll find him and then we'll go, head back to the woods. The Mist will find us there and lead us back home."

Mara's expression flickered with doubt. My heart sank. She thought we should leave him. She thought we should run. Everything inside me reared up in protest; I wanted to scream at her that I loved him, that I would never be able to live with myself if I abandoned him, that I would hate her forever if she took me from him when he needed me most.

Instead I tried a calmer tack, one she would understand. "He's connected to Kilraith," I said quickly, "and Kilraith is dangerous. So says the queen. We should keep Talan close, then, so we can observe him, maybe draw Kilraith to us back in Edyn, where we might be better able to fight him. If we leave Talan here…"

"Better an enemy we can see than one we can't," Mara agreed, then nodded. "Let's find him, then."

Weak with relief, I hurried after her out of the kitchen, past the horrible thing waiting for us at the door.

"Fascinating," it said quietly, watching us go.

My skin crawled as I heard it follow us—slow, measured steps, my father's polished boots on the floor. There was no fear in that tread, no haste. And why would it hurry? This was its house, and it knew every corner.

We stopped at the bottom of the staircase. Ryder still clawed and beat at the wall, cursing, yelling in despair, his fingers bloody. Alastrina huddled halfway up the stairs, soothing the air beside her. "Don't be afraid," she crooned. "I'll take care of you."

I spun around, looking helplessly at all the corridors, the flights of stairs above us. The weight of the house pressed down on me; it was massive, endless. We could search for hours and never find him.

"Where do we go?" I whispered. "Talan, where are you?"

"You came and found me," Mara said slowly, watching Ryder rage. Then she looked at me, curious. "That...*thing*—it rendered the rest of us useless. It took us right out of our minds. But you fought that somehow. You shook it off and brought me back to myself. How did you do it?"

I shook my head, trying to think through what I'd done, but I couldn't recall anything clever—no tricks, no guile. I touched my pocket.

"I held on to Una," I said. "I felt her in my coat and held on to her, and then I knew that wasn't Father. I could see it so clearly."

Mara's gaze was keen. "I think it's more than that. There's a reason why the Warden keeps all of us Roses at the priory, why we come to her at an early age and grow up together and learn and train side by side. To fight the Mist effectively, to defend ourselves against whatever escapes the barrier between worlds, we have to forge bonds with each other, and quickly. We have to become a family. I don't like all of my sisters in the Order, but I do love them. I would die for them if I had to. We belong to each other."

The taste of my sudden jealousy was bitter and cut me to the quick; there was a part of Mara that I would never know or see, a part of her heart that belonged to the Order and not to the family she'd been ripped away from, and I hated that horrible truth.

I pushed the feeling aside. "What are you getting at?"

Mara glanced behind me. The footsteps had stopped. The father-thing was standing not far from us, waiting, watching.

"What I mean is that I think your love for Talan is protecting you," Mara said quickly. "It's the same love that protects the other Roses and me. It gives us purpose, it brings us focus when our minds are scattered with fear. None of us here loves Talan besides you. Therefore, even with our pieces of home helping us, we weren't prepared to fight the house."

The house. *Kilraith*.

I swallowed hard. Was that him, standing in the thing behind us? Was he staring out of my false father's eyes?

Mara gripped my shoulders, squeezed hard. She ducked down to meet my eyes. "Hold on to that love, let it guide you, and go find him. I'll wake the others before they do anything irreversibly stupid. Then we'll come straight to you, all of us."

"Farrin's in the ballroom," I said faintly, my thoughts racing. Then a jolt of fear: the cleaver's shining blade flashed through my mind. I caught Mara's arm. "Wait! If we split up, how will you stay safe?"

"I'll think of you," Mara said, smiling. "And I'll tell Farrin to do the same, and then we'll help the Basks. Now go, and hurry."

She turned and left me, and I didn't wait another moment, not with that thing staring at me, watching curiously from the shadows. I hurried up the stairs, past the muttering Alastrina, and kept going. My side ached insistently, reminding me that I was still wounded from our fight in the woods. My breath came in sharp bursts. Panting, I reached for the banister to pull myself along, but then I remembered the poison—or the mold, or whatever awful thing it was—and drew my hand back with a hiss. I trudged onward, upward, thinking of Talan.

The second floor stood open, a dark mezzanine looking down over the stairs. I turned left and ran down its broad main corridor, crashing into every room I found. There was no sense in being quiet about it; the house knew we were there.

"Talan, I'm here!" I cried as I ran. Bedroom, bedroom, a small study lined with books, a bathing room, a room painted black from floor to ceiling—no windows, no furniture, its only adornment two flickering lamps on the wall and a single round mirror.

I slammed that door closed, quickly left the room behind; the air in it had painted a sour tang across my tongue. I ran on, my eyes watering. I couldn't smell any smoke or strange fumes, but I felt something moving through the air: a weight, a wrongness. This house was poison, and we couldn't help but breathe it in.

"I love you, Talan," I said. I spoke the words aloud as I searched, fighting to keep my voice steady. The house would hear me; I wouldn't let my terror of it silence me. "Talan, I'm not going to leave you here. We're going to free you, and then we're going to go home. Home to Ivyhill. You'll live there with me. We'll walk through the meadow in the mornings, toss seeds to the birds so the skies fill with song."

The second floor was empty. I hurried up to the third, where the air was colder and the walls were bisected by elaborate molding: scarlet wallpaper above, wood paneling below. I ran from room to room—bedroom, bedroom, a parlor with a wall of glass. Beyond it, below us, the sea raged.

"We'll attend all the good parties and none of the boring ones," I continued. My hurried gait became a limp as pain shot up my side. I gritted my teeth and kept going. "We'll make love under the stars as often as we can. I'll read you my favorite books, and I'll do all the voices, even the ones that make me look foolish."

I pushed through a set of doors that led to an empty room with another door at the far end. I hurried across the space and pushed open the second door.

It opened into another room identical to the first: empty, bare wooden floor, a door standing open at the far end. I looked back at the first door, which still stood open to the corridor, then turned back, hesitated, stuck my arm through the second doorway—and watched, horrified, as my disembodied arm thrust itself out of the third door at the other end of the room, a perverse reflection. I waved my arm; my arm waved back to me.

I stumbled out into the corridor and slammed the door shut. Echoes followed just after—the distant slams of the other two doors I'd seen slamming closed just like the cousin I now stood beside.

Back flat against the wall, breathing hard, I fought against my climbing terror. I heard a soft rustling to my right: the father-thing making his unhurried way up the stairs to join me?

I hobbled as fast as I could in the other direction, struggling to find my voice, squeezing Una in one hand. "I love how peaceful you look when you sleep. I love how you make my body come alive so beautifully, even without the use of your power, that I don't notice my pain. I love how easily you love me," I added, my voice breaking. "Everything strange about me, everything difficult and frightening, things that would drive any reasonable person far away—none of them stop you from loving me."

Then I stopped, looked back over my shoulder. I'd almost missed it: a door set into the wall, no knob or latch, its edges barely visible. It was hidden in the shadows, the nearest lamp a good twenty feet away. Desperately hoping I wasn't wrong, that what I saw wasn't simply some imperfection in the wallpaper, I leaned against the wall with my shoulder and shoved hard.

It swung open, blessedly silent. I grabbed Una from my pocket, slipped the cord over my neck, shoved the carving down my shirt so she would press against my skin, and quickly shrugged off my coat, the sleeve of which was rapidly turning black. Clearly, the house, or its creator, was growing angry with me. I couldn't be sure for how much longer I would be allowed to walk these halls unscathed.

Past the door rose a narrow flight of stairs. At the top, another door stood ajar; this one was made of plain wooden planks with an iron knob and a knocker to match. Beyond it, a dimly lit room. A line of pale yellow light, barely visible, stretched down the stairs.

I climbed quickly through the dark, refusing to look behind me, and trying not to panic as I felt heat building beneath my boot's soles. Would even the floor soon be unsafe to touch? As I neared the door at the top of the stairs, I saw that the bottom of each plank was jagged, pocked with scratches and clusters of indentations. Teeth marks.

"I tried to chew my way out, once or twice," said a quiet voice from inside the room.

My heart leapt: *Talan.*

CHAPTER 40

I stepped inside and found him at the room's heart, slumped in a dark wingback chair.

Two lamps glowed in sconces on either side of the door. The ceiling was high and peaked; near the top of the wall across from me, far too high for anyone to reach, was a single round window, small as a dinner plate. Beneath it the wooden wall was scuffed terribly, gouged open. Planks had been torn away, revealing a span of gray brick. About ten feet above the floor, the marks stopped.

"They never put anything in here tall enough for me to stand on and reach the window," Talan said, his words slurred, heavy. He laughed quietly. "But oh, how I tried."

I hurried to him and knelt at his feet. The room was full of abandoned toys, all of them black with poison. Looking at them made me feel sick. Instead I fixed my eyes on Talan—his pale face, his glazed eyes. He wore the clothes he'd had on the night we'd first met: a vest of dark brocade beneath a red velvet coat, dark trousers, dark boots. Everything crisp and fine.

"This is the playroom," he said, staring at the floor. "The game was to try and get out before I ran out of time. My parents loved games." His eyes lifted to meet mine. Something like awareness flitted over his features. His brow furrowed. "I think I told you that. I think I know you."

"You *do* know me," I said, fighting back a sob. If I cried, I would lose him. I felt that with a horrible certainty. I needed him to keep looking at me, *really* looking at me, and hearing my voice. "I'm Gemma. I'm your wildcat. Remember?"

I lifted one of his cold hands and pressed it to my cheek. "I love you, and I want to be with you always. That's why I've come for you, to bring you back home with me."

He frowned, bewildered. "I am home."

"No, this isn't your home—not this copy, and not the original house. This is and always was an evil place. The sea came for it that night. Remember? And you ran away."

Talan's eyes glistened, darting about the room. "I would beat on the door until my fists bled. My sisters sat on the stairs and laughed at me. They were the favorites. They would do anything to win our parents' games."

I caught his face in my hands, brought him back to me. "Don't think about that, not anymore. It's done. That time is over, and those people are dead. Look at *me*, Talan. You know me, don't you?" I stroked his brow, let my fingers kiss his hair. "You remember me, and you remember what we came here to do."

He stared at me for a moment, unseeing. Then his breathing quickened, and his eyes sharpened, clearing. He found my hands and held them tight.

"Gemma," he said hoarsely, "you've got to leave. Run and don't look back. Run and leave me here."

"We'll *both* run, darling, that's what I'm trying to tell you."

He kissed my forehead, hot and fierce. There was a feeling of finality to it, a sense of goodbye, and my stomach twisted with sudden fear.

"No, no," he murmured against my skin, "Gemma, you don't understand—"

"We'll go home and rest, get your strength back, and we'll keep searching for the curse's anchor there, all right? The *ytheliad* is no match for us." I found a brave smile for him, kept my voice light. "Now, get up. We'll go find the others and return to the woods."

"*No*, Gemma."

He shoved me away. I fell back hard and stared up at him, stunned with pain. He held his head in his hands, shuddering. His fingers dug into his brow, pressed hard.

"It's *in* me—" he began, and then I heard a soft shuffle on the stairs, and Talan choked on his own voice. I whirled to look, scrambled away from the door on my hands and knees, but no one was there. The air shifted against me, cold and quick.

Then Talan began to laugh.

I turned back to him, my blood roaring in my ears. The change in him was obvious—he was still, relaxed, no longer wracked with torment. When he looked up at me again, he was smiling. His eyes were even darker, and his voice, when he spoke, was split: it was him, and it was the thing pretending to be my father.

"You are a most interesting creature," he said. He sat back and steepled his fingers, considering me. "I've never encountered anything like you."

I was shaking; I pressed my palm against Una and used the other hand to push myself to my feet. The floor burned my fingertips, leaving them red and tender, and I hissed in pain, blinking back tears.

"Talan," I said, my voice trembling, "I need you to come with me now. We're going home. Get up and follow me down the stairs."

Talan laughed. "Marvelous. Such brazen stupidity. As if it would be that easy."

I stood tall on shaky legs and made myself stare right at him, right at the mean black eyes that were such a cruel mockery of the man I loved.

"Who are you?" I demanded.

He blinked up at me, all innocence. "Why, I'm your Talan, little wildcat."

"No, you're not. You're in Talan, but you're not him, you're nothing like him. You aren't worthy of a single scrap of him. What are you? What is your name?"

"Why, Gemma." He put his hand to his heart. "That you could forget your own father. I am truly affronted."

Hatred boiled in me. I took a step closer to him. "What are you? What is your name?"

"I am Talan d'Astier of Vauzanne. I am Talan of the Far Sea. I am the Man with the Three-Eyed Crown. I am the heir to Brimgard, to the House of Farther." He looked up at me, guileless, and started laughing. "My, you are quite the sight when you're furious. I suppose you're used to people telling you how beautiful you are." He leaned closer, leering. "I know Talan has told you time and time again. He's besotted."

I would not rise to the bait. I thought of Farrin and Mara— their steel spines, the grief that bound us together, the memory of their hands holding mine. Farrin in front, Mara behind me, our fingers locked as we ran through the grounds of Ivyhill toward the stream that bordered the sunflower fields. Mrs. Rathmont had stuffed our pockets with pastries, and we would eat them on the little stone footbridge, all of us giddy with summer. I was six,

Mara eight, Farrin ten. No fire yet, no Warden. The artificer had come and gone, but I didn't know that. The memory was buried somewhere in the artificer's clever Olden magic. I knew only the safe, warm world of my sisters—and wrapped up in that moment of peace, clarity came to me, a soft burst of understanding.

It's in *me*, Talan had cried, fingers pressed hard to his brow just before he had disappeared behind that horrible, horrible laughing mask.

I am Talan d'Astier of Vauzanne, the mask had told me, mocking me, delighting in my helplessness.

I am Talan of the Far Sea.

I am the Man with the Three-Eyed Crown.

The Man with the Three-Eyed Crown.

My family's demon, bound to something far worse.

Olden instinct rushed through me, hot and sharp, eager. My eyes flitted to Talan's pale forehead. Something was there, buried and hidden. He'd tried to tell me before the monster wearing my father's face had taken away his voice.

Out in the woods, I'd glamoured away the glass fused with my flesh, disguising my true skin under a mask of my own making. But beneath that mask, the glass still shone; a glamour was merely a cloak, a lie. And I knew with a certainty clear as the sky what I had to do.

I prayed quickly for courage: *Terror. Lust. Rage.*

Mara. Farrin. Talan. Illaria. Gareth. Phaidra. Nesset. Lulath. Ryder. Alastrina.

"You lie," I said coldly, glaring down at not-Talan. "Your name is Kilraith, and you are not welcome here."

The smile fell from his face.

Just as I had in the Olden woods, in the Vilia's mountain home, in the ballroom at Ivyhill, and at my dressing table—alone and bewildered in my rooms all those long weeks ago—I let my power rise and take me where I needed to go.

I lunged for Talan, slammed my left palm against his forehead. Fire shot up my body, nailing my hand to his brow.

He screamed, a horrible sound, all agony and rage, and lurched up out of the chair, his body convulsing. He tried to run, but my power held him fast, digging beneath the mask to whatever lay beneath. There was indeed a glamour on him; I knew the feeling of them, had been around them all my life. Every party, every shopping trip to the capital. When Kerrish came to style me, I could smell them on her skin. One had fallen over me that night in the gardens, my passion for Talan overflowing in a confused burst of power. One covered me now, hiding my skin of glass.

And one was on Talan—a shell, a prison, hard and ancient, woven through his skull and sewn into his scalp and vibrating with anger as my power tore at it. The anchor of the *ytheliad*. A cursed crown, hidden and vile.

The Man with the Three-Eyed Crown: Kilraith had hidden the answer right there in Talan's title. It had been meant as a mockery, no doubt, a reminder of what bound Talan to his master and had bound every other demon before him. And now that mockery was the thing that would save him.

"You beast!" he howled, clawing at me. "Let me go, you foul creature!"

His blows were terrible, sharp lashes that sent pain zipping up my arms, but I held fast. Brilliant light burst from the place where my hand met his brow, spitting into the shadows of the playroom like white flames.

"Don't be afraid, Talan," I said, fixing my eyes on him. I wouldn't let this awful creature turn me away from the face I loved: dark waves framing a serious brow, grave eyes, lips I had kissed a hundred times and wanted to kiss a hundred thousand times more.

Tears streamed down his cheeks as he looked up at me, the light of my power painting his skin a garish white-blue. His eyes locked onto me; I saw him surface, the Talan I knew, his face tight with pain.

"Keep going," he pleaded, his voice in shreds. "Gemma, don't let go, no matter what he says, no matter what *I*—"

Then his face shifted, a shadow darkening him. His eyes flashed, and he surged up at me with a furious roar, knocking me to the floor. He fell with me; the light of my power bound us, snapping up my arm and down his spine.

"You can't do this forever, *wildcat*," Kilraith hissed mockingly. It was Kilraith, I told myself frantically—it was *Kilraith*, not my Talan. He pinned me to the floor, drove his knee hard into my stomach.

I gasped for air, my vision pulsing black. I gritted my teeth and grabbed my left arm with my right hand, bracing it, pushing it up against him. A horrible heat scorched my palm. My fingers were digging into the skin of his brow; blood dripped down his face, trickled down my wrist.

He leaned down, grinning. A thin shield of light and my burning hand were the only things separating us.

"I am the Destroyer," he rasped. "In my veins rages a cataclysm you cannot imagine. When it comes, even your dead gods will weep. And you think you can defeat me?" His voice rippled with the sound of my father's laughter—scornful, dripping with disgust. "Fool girl. You're nothing. You're broken all the way down to your pathetic patchwork insides."

I couldn't ignore him; he was right there, pressing down on me, blowing his sour breath on me.

But I could speak. I could use what voice I had left.

"Talan, it's all right," I gasped out. "I'm here, and I'm not letting go. I love you, I love you. I won't leave you."

"*Love,*" Kilraith spat at me. He looked away, squeezed his eyes shut, let out a wordless roar of pain. When his eyes shot back open, they were horrible, bloodshot, bestial, slitted. "And what would you do with him if you took him back to Edyn? A demon, scarred inside and out? He will bear the mark of me after this. You would not be able to hide it. People would fear him. They would *hate* him, and you too. They would hunt him."

Sweat rolled down my fevered body. My hand had disappeared into a spitting cloud of white fire, but I could still feel my fingers, each of them buried up to the second knuckle in Talan's flesh and muscle and bone.

I shook my head against the floor. "I'll protect him, and so will my family."

"He would tire of you. All your terrible fear, all that panic buzzing inside you like a kicked hive."

At my silence, he grinned. He knew he'd gotten to me.

"What would a demon prince, who could sit on a throne forever at my side, want with a pathetic half-made creature like you? A woman who isn't loved even by her own father? A woman who hides in corners and pounds bruises onto her skin? Ah"—his eyes fluttered; his grin widened—"I can feel your fear even now, even with all this power you're thrusting at me, as if it will do any good."

"It *is* doing good," I snarled, breathless, the world beginning to spin. "All *your* power, and you can't tear yourself away from me. And you're wrong: I'm not terrible. I'm not a burden. I'm not alone."

Kilraith laughed in the face of my prayer. He sucked blood into his mouth, sprayed my face with it.

"You would die long before he would," he said, smiling nastily, "and then who would keep poor dear Talan safe?"

The world was growing dark; my whole body was catching on fire, kindled by the inferno of my hand. I couldn't bear it any longer, couldn't keep sniping at this vile creature. With whatever strength I had left, I would tell Talan what I knew to be true.

"I don't care what scars you bear, inside or out," I told him, my breath thin, my voice strained. I forced myself to meet the enraged black eyes glaring down at me. "I have them too. I'm not afraid of your grief. I'll help you carry it, Talan, and you'll help carry mine. We'll never have to bear it alone, not ever again."

Some of the anger on Talan's face cracked open, contorting with pain. Fresh tears streamed down his cheeks, even as his hands closed hard around my neck.

"Gemma, I'm sorry," he cried, his voice his own again. "I love you, my darling, I—I'm trying to fight him, but—"

His body jerked against mine. "But he *can't*," Kilraith said, taking over once more. His face was red with blood, his eyes cold and full of hatred. He was clearly in agony—the veins stood out on his neck, and his arms trembled as he strangled me—but soon he would beat me nevertheless. I felt my strength waning, felt my fingers losing their grip on Talan's skull.

Kilraith's smile spread wide. "Yes, that's it. Go to sleep, Lady Gemma. Your dreams are calling you home."

And I nearly did. My eyelids were heavy, my lungs burning—but then a song pierced the air, high and clear as a bell.

Kilraith, startled, relaxed his hold just enough for me to give one last kick against the current of death lapping at my toes.

"What is that?" he muttered.

I smiled, my breathing ragged. "It's my sister," I rasped.

His eyes widened and his face fell slack. He sagged against me, but there was no force behind it. He was stunned; Farrin's voice had stunned him.

With a desperate cry, I shoved myself up against him and slammed him back to the floor. Now I was atop him, straddling his chest, digging my hand deeper into his flesh. Skin and blood wedged under my fingernails; I gagged, my stomach heaving as I fought desperately for air. Beneath me, Kilraith convulsed, threw himself up against me, clawed at my chest. His body contorted with a sickening crack. He would break all Talan's bones.

Then something beneath my fingers gave way: a series of snaps like a taut net bursting open. My fingers touched something hard and metal.

The crown.

Farrin's song grew closer. I glanced to my left and saw her kneel down beside me, unafraid, her face lit up by the storm of my power. Her song was the most beautiful thing I'd ever heard: lilting and sweet, full of longing, and growing in power with every note.

On my right was Mara, her expression grimly determined. She knelt behind me and used her unthinkable strength to pin Kilraith to the floor. No matter how hard he bucked, trying to throw us off of him, he couldn't break Mara's grip—but I didn't know how long that would last.

"Listen to me," I said to Talan, my voice stronger now. Having my sisters on either side of me, helping me, fighting for me and for Talan, renewed my strength. "I'm going deeper, Talan. I don't want to hurt you. You know that, don't you? I never want to hurt you, not ever." Tears blinded me, blurring the light of my fire. "It's killing me to hurt you."

Somehow, even trapped in the frenzy of Kilraith's agonized fury, Talan found a way to reach me. For an instant his body stilled: he looked up at me, his face more blood than skin. He sucked in a huge breath of air and gave me a small, shaky smile.

"Do it, Gemma," he whispered.

And with Farrin's music in my ears and Mara's solid warm weight beside me, I did: I pushed all my strength at him, all my power, and I thrust my fingers into the meat of him, gripped the crown's thick hot band, and pulled.

It was impossible, it was utter madness—but the Old Country was indefinable, as Gareth had always said, and here was proof of that right before my eyes, right under my fingers. It was like tugging a mountain out of the earth, and Talan's body arched up violently against me with an earsplitting cry of pain. I couldn't look at his head; it flickered between whole, unhurt, and utterly maimed, split open right across his brow. And the sight of this *thing* coming out of his skull, bloody and jagged, tongues of light whipping around it, made me want to give up right then and there, and I might have—I might have retched and collapsed and let Kilraith kill me over what remained of Talan's body—had it not been for the Basks.

Hands gripped my shoulders, huge and strong. I knew at once that they belonged to Ryder. I heard him bellow something to Alastrina—the only word I understood was her name—and suddenly the weight of two Anointed humans was pulling at me, helping me tug the crown out of Talan and fight through my own despair.

I had a good grip on the crown; the smooth round face of a jewel pressed into my incandescent palm. One more pull and I would have it, it would be free of him. Farrin's voice rang in my ears. Talan's body bucked and writhed, Kilraith spitting foul words at us, curses in some dark Olden language, but Mara held him fast, breathing hard with the effort.

Talan screamed, and I did too, as if the sound of his voice was pulling at my own. I let out such a harsh, terrible cry that I feared it would split me open. Something snapped loose under my fingers. A great power flung me back, knocking me past Ryder and Alastrina. I slammed into the wall, and my vision went black for a moment, then flickered back to life—and I saw it, the horrible, bloody thing. Clutched in my hand, a thick metal crown studded with three milky yellow jewels, one for each beastly eye.

I cried out, my voice ruined. I was making sounds, saying words, but I was insensate. I didn't understand my own movements or even my own thoughts—except for one.

Talan.

I tried to crawl toward him, tried to search the room for him, but my vision was a shifting blur of color, my arms and legs useless. I collapsed, shaking, and felt the floor tremble underneath me. A strange flash of light caught my eye; I gazed in stupefied wonder at my hand that held the crown.

It was scarred all over, a net of smoking white lines.

Voices moved above me. Someone was lifting me, and the whole world was shaking.

"The house is collapsing!" someone cried—Mara, I thought.

"Keep singing, Farrin," Ryder shouted. "That might slow it down!"

They were running, they were carrying me down a tunnel of shadows and smoke, and there was soft music in my ears—familiar, sweeter than birdsong, brighter than the stars. It reminded me of my sister Farrin, and it occurred to me that it was the last thing I would ever hear.

CHAPTER 41

I awoke expecting to find myself in Ryndar. I had died, and my soul, crafted by the magic of the gods, had found its way to the Realm of the Far Light, the Infinite Dominion, where I could rest at last.

But instead I saw Farrin's face, and beyond her a window framed with roses, pushed open to admit a sweet afternoon breeze.

"Farrin," I croaked, and then choked a little, wincing. My ravaged throat was on fire. Still, I had to know: "Am I dead? Is Talan dead? Are *you* dead? Is Mara? Where is the crown?"

My sister smiled down at me, her eyes soft and bright. "No, Gemma, you're alive, and so am I, and so is everyone else. Including Talan," she added gently. "The crown is in storage here at the priory, behind at least a dozen layers of protection, according to Mara. It's safe. You're safe."

The shock of her words, the pure brilliant relief of them, left me breathless. I gasped, a hitching sob startled out of me. When I'd found my voice again, poor abused rag that it was, I said quietly, "Tell me."

"Once you broke the curse, the house began to collapse,"

Farrin said. The sun was gentle, golden. It touched her hair, and her thumb rubbed mine. "I sang to slow it down—Ryder's idea, and it worked—but we still barely made it out before the whole thing crumbled to ash and the cliff it was sitting on dropped away into the sea. None of it was real. The whole house was a deception, spellcrafted and poisonous. The stench of it chased us all the way back to the woods, and that's where we found the Warden."

Alarmed, I tried to sit up, my arms shaking. "The Warden? How did she find us? How did she know?"

Farrin helped prop me up against the nest of pillows at my back and gave me a grim smile that didn't reach her eyes. "She's the Warden of the Order of the Rose, guardian of the Middlemist. She knows every inch of the Mist and feels it every time someone enters it or leaves it without her permission. So she explained it to us—rather haughtily, I might add. I suppose we were foolish to think we could cross into the Old Country and back again without the Warden realizing it."

I felt a pang of guilt. "Mara must have known that would happen, and yet she helped us do it anyway," I said. "Is the Warden angry with her?"

"I couldn't say. The Warden's had her hands full, thanks to us. The priory's healers have been working day and night tending our injuries, yours and Talan's especially."

I blew out a long breath, lifted my arms, tried stretching out my legs beneath the quilt. Astonished, I realized that aside from feeling weaker than I ever had, I was unhurt. My only pain was the familiar dull throb in my muscles and joints, which I recognized with a sinking feeling of disappointment.

Farrin frowned. "What is it? Is there pain?"

"Yes, but not anything out of the ordinary." I looked up at her and tried to smile, but in fact I felt numb and embarrassed and terribly sad. "I suppose I thought, what with everything that happened, and how strong and powerful I felt while we were in the Old Country, that if we made it home, things would be... different. I thought I would be better."

The sadness on Farrin's face was unbearable; her silence was worse. I shook my head and laughed a little, trying to brush off the whole thing, looking anywhere but at my sister. An embroidered white flower on the quilt tucked around me caught my eye, its fine thread gleaming softly in the sunlight, and the sight of it reminded me, horribly, of Phaidra.

I turned toward the window and squeezed my eyes shut. Shame was thick in my throat; there I was, alive and well, complaining about a pain I was quite used to, a pain I had lived with well enough for years, and Phaidra was dead.

"You're allowed to be disappointed," Farrin said softly. I knew she meant it as a kindness, but I didn't want to hear it, and I was glad when the door opened, admitting Mara.

She wore the plain garb of the Order, her boots soft and brown, her hair tied back from her face with a long leather cord. The cord at her neck matched it; I saw the slight lump of the wooden ivy underneath her tunic.

I tried to smile at her. It occurred to me that smiling should have been easier. We were alive; we were safe.

"How is everyone else?" I said. "Nesset? Brigid?" I paused. "Lulath?"

"Brigid is the same as she has ever been, which is to say that I'm not sure what she's feeling about all of this. Lulath..." Mara looked softly at me. "She has died, Gemma, but it's not a thing to be sad about. She was happy when she went. She was glad to rest. Nesset told me."

For a moment I hid my face in my hands, trying not to think

just yet about how long it would be before Nesset also died in a cave, or was stabbed by some creature I wouldn't be able to protect her from. At least she was the youngest of them, the newest Vilia of my three. Maybe there was time yet to find a spell that would keep her remade body from slowly falling apart. I added that to the long list of things left to do and lifted my head to smile bravely at Mara.

"How is Nesset?" I asked.

"Alive and well, and quite the center of attention, actually. She has set up shop in the Tree Room and is carving talismans for everyone in memory of Phaidra. I'm not sure what the Warden made of hers. She held it by two fingers and stared at it, baffled, like she'd inexplicably found herself holding a slug."

"Did Nesset give her an owl?" I asked.

Mara looked curiously at me. "Yes. How did you know?"

"Those eyebrows of hers," I replied, and then I scowled and pushed my own eyebrows into a poor copy of the Warden's fearsome, brooding glare.

I was glad to see my sisters laugh. If Mara was laughing, then whatever trouble our trip to the Old Country had landed her in couldn't have been *too* dreadful. Perhaps that particular guilt was one I didn't need to carry, at least for now.

"And where is Illaria? And Gareth?"

"One's camped out down the hall, teaching a thoroughly charmed passel of young Roses about scented oils and champing at the bit to see you the moment I allow it. One's been called back to the capital to help with the aftermath of the chimaera attack. I can't imagine you'll be able to guess which is which."

I smiled to think of them, but my happiness was fleeting. "Nesset knows what happened to Phaidra?"

"She does," Farrin said gently, "and while she mourns, she's glad Phaidra has found peace. She's told me at least a dozen times to reassure you that she doesn't blame you for Phaidra's death, or Lulath's, and that if you insist on blaming yourself, she'll...what did she say? 'I'll wait until she's well and then knock her flat on her ass.'"

Mara raised her hand with a small smile. "She's told me that at least *twenty* times."

Farrin made a face at her. "Show-off."

Their playfulness warmed me. I hadn't seen them like this—we hadn't been *together* like this, unguarded, intimate—in far too many years. The staggering rarity made it feel precious, a treasure I refused to relinquish now that I had it in my grasp.

"And Ryder and Alastrina?" I asked.

Mara glanced at Farrin, sobering. "They've gone home to Ravenswood for now. But they want to travel to Ivyhill next month and confer with you on several matters: unrest in the north, the Citadel attack, Kilraith. What it all means."

"Father will be positively beside himself," Farrin muttered. "Basks staying at Ivyhill? Not just as party guests but as *allies*?" She shook her head, her expression suddenly sullen and tired. "It would be better to meet with them at a neutral location. Maybe here at Rosewarren."

"The Warden isn't keen on the idea of the priory becoming a place of conference."

"Well, Father won't be keen on the idea of Basks sleeping in his house."

"He will adapt," Mara said quietly.

"Yes, and who will be the one holding his hand in the meantime and soothing all his tantrums?" Farrin snapped.

Silence fell between us, the warmth of a few moments ago fading fast.

Mara gently touched my arm, breaking the awful quiet. "How does your hand feel? Has the pain receded?"

Puzzled, I looked down at my hands, and it was only then that I noticed how the skin of my left one had changed, marked front and back with a gleaming net of pale scars. They were delicate but barbed, like lines of frost, with knotted lesions here and there that reminded me of snowflakes. Three marked my knuckles. A much larger one shimmered faintly in the cradle of my palm, a starburst of ice. But it was warm to the touch, indistinguishable from the rest of my skin—which, I was astonished to discover, no longer glittered with glass.

Mara spoke gently. "Talan thinks that when you tore through his glamour and broke the curse, the shock of power undid whatever magic had fused the glass with your skin."

"But I still have this," I said lightly, holding up my glimmering hand, "which I'm glad of, quite frankly. Much easier to hide a single hand than a whole body."

None of us laughed. I knew we were all thinking the same thing.

Farrin was the one to say it. "What does all of this mean?" she asked quietly. "The things we did there, the power we had? Ryder and Alastrina are Anointed, just as we are, and yet the Old Country didn't change their magic or their appearances." She looked at me, then at Mara. "Is it fae blood, like Phaidra said? Or..."

"Or something else," Mara finished. Her expression was grave, thoughtful. "Father might have some insight, if you can get him to talk about anything other than the fact that he no longer has a war to fight, now that Talan is freed and Kilraith—presumably, hopefully—quite severely wounded."

"Father will be unbearable," Farrin said miserably. "Every

party he attended, every merchant he patronized, every governor he visited was all in service of ruining the Basks. He's been planning something terrible in recent weeks, and I doubt Talan's freedom will be enough to stop him from carrying it out."

The thought chilled me, but my head was thick, fuzzing up with exhaustion, and I could only think about so many things at once. "If we can't learn what we need to know from Father or the family archives..." I braced myself. "We'll have to look for Mother."

Farrin blew out an incredulous breath. "Mother's dead, Gemma."

"We don't know that," Mara pointed out.

"She's *dead*. If she wasn't, she would have come back to us. She would have written. When the cursed forest around Ravenswood crumbled and the Basks were free again, she would have been worried about us. She would have wanted to assure herself that we were all safe."

Mara tried again. "Farrin—"

"Don't tell me she's alive," Farrin spat, rounding on her. "Don't you dare try to convince me she's alive."

Then Farrin pushed herself off the bed and stalked to the open window. She stood with her back to us; her arms were flat and rigid at her sides.

I let her seethe for a moment and then awkwardly climbed out of bed with Mara's help.

"We have to find out what we are, Farrin," I said at last. "Father kept part of that secret from me for too long. I won't let anyone or anything deny me the rest of the truth, and you shouldn't either— for all our sakes, and I don't mean just the three of us. What did Gareth and Illaria say? 'This confluence of events can't be a coincidence.' I agree with them. I think something is unfolding and that we're a part of it. And I think we have to find out what it is, whether we want to or not."

Weary, my head a muddle of exhausted questions, I leaned against Mara. "I want to see Talan," I told her, and let her lead me to him.

━◆━

He was sleeping when I entered his room, washed golden by the afternoon sunlight. His face was soft in sleep, his torso bare.

Despising the idea of waking him but unable to resist his nearness, I crawled into the bed as quietly as I could and nestled against his right side. With a lump in my throat, I looked him over: his sharp jaw, the fine straight line of his nose, his dark hair on the sunlit pillow, a spill of ink and gold. His chest rose and fell; I held a finger an inch from his lips. When I felt the soft puff of his breath and finally let myself believe that he was alive—that we were here, both of us, that we had escaped that horrid house by the sea—I dared to look up at his brow.

The scars there echoed mine: a web of faintly gleaming lines that crisscrossed his forehead and curled down his temples and into his hair, an echo of the three-eyed crown. Three lesions marked his brow, faint thumbprint scars that matched the one in my palm.

I feathered my fingers across them, and then I leaned up and pressed my mouth to them, three chaste kisses against their smooth shining warmth. When I pulled back, Talan was awake, his smile heavy with sleep.

"There you are," he said to me, his voice hoarse and quiet, as ruined as my own. He reached up to pull me back to him and kissed me—slowly, carefully, cradling my face in his palms as if I might break, as if he feared his own strength.

I felt it the moment the memory came to him: his hands around my neck, Kilraith's will pushing him to kill me. I lifted my face to look at him and saw the tears in his eyes.

"It was torment," he said, "to look down and see my hands hurting you, to try to tear myself away and fail. He laughed at me for trying. The things he said using my mouth, the pain he dealt you through me…I fought him, but it wasn't enough. My wildcat. My Gemma." He shook his head, his mouth trembling. "My love, I'm so sorry."

"I know you are," I whispered. "I know you. I know your face, and when I looked up at the man trying to kill me, I saw not your eyes but his."

He shook his head, his expression full of self-loathing, but I put my fingers to his mouth and silenced his protests.

"You fought, and so did I," I told him quietly. "We fought for each other. We fought together."

I kissed away his tears and let him kiss away mine. We said very little; there was nothing to be said, not right then, not in that quiet, sunlit bedroom. We were whole and breathing, miraculously alive. I tugged off my shift; I needed the warmth of his skin against mine. He held me against him, brought my scarred hand to his mouth, and kissed my palm. My face pressed tightly against his neck, his hand soft in my hair, we clung to each other and slept.

A week later, we were strong enough to make the journey home to Ivyhill, and the moment I stepped through the greenway into our hedge maze, I tore away from everyone and ran from them as fast as I could. Talan, Farrin, our escorts from the priory—I couldn't bear to be near them for another second.

Farrin called after me; I ignored her, breathing hard, pushing my weakened legs faster. The greenway's magic lingered painfully in my wrists and heels, tearing at me like teeth, but the panic was far worse: a rising storm sucking away all my air, crawling like lightning across my skin.

I stumbled to a stop somewhere near the maze's heart, a small clearing that held a stone bench, a pebbled path, a willow tree with shimmering white leaves. I hid beside an immaculately trimmed box hedge and sobbed, despising myself for it. There were things to be done, goodbyes to be said, and instead of cherishing every moment I could, I'd run off into the maze like a bawling child.

I sank to the grass, hugging my knees to my chest. It took every bit of my willpower not to tear away my skirts and scratch my thighs to pieces. I was itching everywhere, I couldn't breathe, I couldn't *think*, and Talan was going to…Talan was going to…

Then he was there, kneeling before me, quiet and beautiful in the dark traveling clothes the Warden had bought for him in Fenwood. Tenderly he turned my chin up, and when I saw the grief on his face, the regret, the terrible sorrow, my heart broke in two.

I wrenched myself away from him and hurried past the bench, into the willow's shadows.

"Please don't look at me," I told him. In my desperation, my voice turned harsh. "Please, go to the house. I'll meet you there. I just need a moment."

He rose quietly to his feet. "I don't want to be apart from you, not even for that moment. Not until I have to. Please don't send me away."

I went around the tree and pressed my back against its trunk, hiding my face from him. I looked up at the willow's branches, the starry sky beyond, and clutched my stomach, fisted my hands in my skirts. I searched for my prayer and couldn't find it. My sadness was too great for prayers. I didn't know what to do, what to scratch or tear out or pound on, what screams to let loose, but I needed to do *something* to relieve the pressure of the panic building in me, and I didn't want Talan anywhere near me when I did it.

I laughed once, choking a little on my own wretched sadness. Tomorrow, Talan would leave me. What I'd done at the Far Sea had stunned Kilraith, perhaps even wounded him, but none of us believed he was dead. He was out there somewhere, either in this world or the Olden lands, and until we knew more about him, until we understood what we were facing, Talan would need to go into hiding far from any of us, far from everyone.

I knew it was the right thing, the safest thing, but it was awful to think of him alone somewhere, without a home yet again, with none of us to talk to, to hold, to love. I didn't know where he would go. None of us did. For our own protection, he would say nothing of it.

Talan ducked under the branches of the willow and found me just as I gave up, with a sinking feeling of shame, and started to ferociously scratch my arms. He caught my hands, his dark gaze steady on me, and then he pressed my right hand to his chest and my left hand to his forehead, scar to scar, palm to brow.

"Feel me," he said quietly. "I'm right here, and I see you, and I don't want to look away from you. Not now, not ever." He breathed slowly in and out, over and over. The lilting rhythm soothed my crawling skin. He was warm under my palms.

"Please know that you don't deserve your pain," he said, quietly echoing what he had told me in the queen's gardens. "Hear me tell you that and believe it. You promised me you'd try." He kissed my fingers. "You'll go see the healer Gareth found, won't you? The one I told you about?"

This healer, Talan had informed me, was also a scholar of the mind, and she had heard of panic like mine. Supposedly, she could help me understand it. I nodded. Yes, I would go to this healer, if only because it would be something to occupy me when missing Talan became too painful to bear.

"Tell me with words, love," Talan said gently. "Promise me you'll go, that you'll hear what she has to say."

"I promise," I whispered, and then I looked up at him through a hot fall of tears. "I thought everything would be different now, that you would live here with me and we would be together always. I thought what we did in the Old Country would burn the panic and every bit of pain out of me. I thought I would come home to a life with you, feeling as strong as I did there under Olden skies." I shook my head. "What a fool I was."

"You're no fool. In fact, you're remarkable." He brought my hand down from his brow and kissed my palm. "You're clever and you're passionate, and your courage staggers me. And that life you dream of, our life together—I dream of it too. I pray for it. I *fight* for it." His eyes blazed with conviction, a fierce steady light that called me back to myself, to him, to the shore of his body.

I leaned into him, pressed my face into his chest.

"Keep talking," I said, my voice muffled. "You're saying lovely things."

He laughed quietly. I felt the soft rumble of it against my cheek. "When this is all over, I'll come back to you, and we won't leave your bedroom for a solid month. I'll love you day and night, and we'll sleep tangled up in each other, safe in your bed, and then I'll wake you with my mouth and we'll do it all over again." He kissed one of my temples, then the other, making me shiver. "And then," he added, practically purring, "I'll ask Mrs. Rathmont to teach me how to bake all your favorite things. And you'll eat every one of them and gush at me about how good they are, no matter what they taste like."

That made me laugh. "Damn you," I said, smiling tearfully up at him. "I don't want to laugh right now."

He looked entirely pleased with himself. "Oh, but I want you to laugh. The way your face lights up…" His expression melted into one of heartbreaking tenderness. He shook his head, marveling at me. "I want to do that forever. I want to be the one to make you laugh, to make you sob with pleasure, to make you feel safe when you're afraid and make you feel seen when you're ashamed to show your face to the world. That face of yours—my beautiful, brave Gemma."

He glanced at my left hand. I saw his jaw work, his mouth twist. When he looked back up at me, his eyes shone.

"I don't care what scars you bear," he said quietly. "I have them too."

My breath caught in my throat. I knew those words; I would never forget them. I would never forget how it felt to say them, and now I would never forget how it felt to hear them said back to me in my beloved's voice.

"I'm not afraid of your grief," he went on. "I'll help you carry it, Gemma, and you'll help carry mine. We'll never have to bear it alone, not ever again."

His voice broke on the last word. He pulled me to him fiercely, buried his face in my hair, and I clung to him there under the white willow and breathed him in—his warmth, his skin, the salt and sweat of him.

"It won't be forever, Gemma," he said hoarsely. "I'll come back to you."

A horrible thing to say when we both knew he might not. Alone, forced into hiding, without Mara or Farrin or the Basks or me to protect him, what would happen? If Kilraith found him, how would he possibly defend himself?

And yet I loved him for saying it. It was a beautiful dream, one worth fighting for—and I *would* fight for it, with my every breath. I would fight to bring him back to me.

"Promise me you'll try," I whispered.

"With everything in me, everything I am, I promise you that." He pulled back and looked at me, his face so full of love I could hardly bear to look at him. "And you must promise me to look after yourself," he said, "to treasure your body and your mind and your heart the way I treasure them."

Talan smiled softly, and then, eyes sparkling, gave me a slightly stern little frown. "This is the woman I love we're talking about. I don't say such things lightly. Take care of her. Love her in my stead."

In answer, I put my arms around him and stretched up on my toes and kissed him. He returned it with a passion that made my knees weak, his arms fierce around me, his hand in my hair. I broke the kiss only long enough to draw him down onto the thick summer grass. I lay back against the fresh moonlit cushion of it and pulled him on top of me, my chest aching with love.

It was the last time we would do this for gods knew how long, and it was happening too quickly; I knew it even as I helped him tear off his jacket, even as his hands slid up my thighs and his tongue found my aching heat, but I couldn't stop this, I couldn't possibly tame the fire blazing between us—not now, not on this night. We would have a lifetime to savor each other's touch, to make love so slowly that we'd shatter simply from the promise of completion. I had to believe that. I was Lady Imogen Ashbourne, and I would fight for the life I wanted, the *love* I wanted, until it was truly, safely mine.

My legs were beginning to tremble, my toes to curl. I tugged at Talan's hair until he came back up to me, his eyes glittering with passion, his smile soft. I kissed him, drunk on the taste of myself, and when he entered me, I gasped against his mouth, held him tight, arched my body up into his.

He breathed my name reverently against my neck, and I held on to him, clung to him as if I could press him right into my skin. I kissed his temple, his cheek, his delectable bottom lip. I whispered his name and smiled when he groaned mine back to me, and as we moved together under the night sky, the world around us—the willow, the air, our fevered skin—seemed full of endless stars.

When I woke up later, it was early morning, and Talan was gone. He had tucked his jacket around me, the foolish man. He would have to find another one wherever he went next. What if he went to the Unmade Lands in the far north, or to the Aidurran desert, where I'd heard the nights were ruthlessly cold? What if safely obtaining the proper garments for such places proved too risky? The more he used his power to assume a different visage, the more easily Kilraith would be able to track him.

The swirl of my horrible thoughts was quickly becoming an avalanche. I sat up and pulled the jacket tightly around me, comforting myself with the thought that Talan could have easily replaced this jacket with one from Ivyhill before his departure. And besides that, he was clever and resourceful, his spirit resilient, ferocious. I turned my face into the sleeve; the fabric smelled of him, of us, and I inhaled the scent as if it were my last chance at life.

Then I discovered in the left breast pocket a folded piece of paper bearing Talan's exquisite script. He'd written a simple note:

Take care of her for me. Love her as she deserves.

I pressed the note against my chest and closed my eyes for a long time, listening to the wind in the willow above me, the early morning birdsong, a distant horse's neigh. Ivyhill was waking up.

I rose to my feet and moved quietly out of the hedge maze, Talan's note clutched in my hand. The house waited for me at the top of the gently sloping grounds—gorgeous and grand, its white walls tinged violet in the rising sun, its thick curtains of ivy shining with dew.

I thought of Mara's ivy talisman sitting safely against her heart and smiled. We were set to visit her in two weeks. Such a short time to wait. Soon Farrin and I would see our sister again.

I took a deep breath, felt the cool morning air rushing into my lungs. I looked east and said a prayer to the goddess Kerezen, and then another to the god Caiathos. Strength for my Talan. Calm seas and clear skies on whatever roads he traveled—roads that would someday bring him back to me.

And until then, I would learn. I would work. I would fight.

I turned back to Ivyhill and started up the path toward home.

READ ON FOR A SNEAK PEEK AT
THE SECOND BOOK IN
THE MIDDLEMIST TRILOGY

A Song of Ash and Moonlight

PROLOGUE

F arrin opened her eyes to a strange world full of smoke.

She didn't recognize the walls around her, or the ceiling above her, and she didn't understand why the air was so dark, so choked and acrid. For a moment, she lay there frozen in her cocoon of quilts—yes, these were quilts around her, the ones from her bed; one white with tiny green leaves, one a soft gray like morning in winter, both sewn with her mother's embroidery— and she thought to herself, as she often did when waking from a nightmare, *My name is Farrin Ashbourne. I am eleven years old. I am safe at home, at Ivyhill. My sisters are Mara and Gemma. My parents are Gideon and Philippa.*

She pressed a finger to her thigh with each name: *Farrin. Mara. Gemma. Gideon. Philippa.* Five names, five fingers, and the familiar recitation cleared her mind. Rooted once again in the waking world, she was finally able to understand that she was not in her bedroom but in her music room on the second floor, lying underneath the piano in a nest of pillows.

The room had been hers since she could remember, and she loved it with every ounce of her being. It wasn't large, not from wall to wall, anyway, but it boasted soaring ceilings, and little stone birds among the ivied rafters, and huge windows of rippled glass. She liked to push those open on pleasant days and imagine her music drifting across the grounds to greet the earth, the flowers, the tenant farmers in their tidy fields. There were long curtains at each window—creamy, delicate, fluttery in breezes—and all along the far side of the room, organized neatly on gleaming mahogany shelves, was her collection of sheet music and composer biographies and treatises on bowing technique, and near the windows, on a fancy little pedestal, there was a tasseled velvet bed for her kitten, Osmund.

In the middle of the night, Farrin often left her bedroom to creep up to the second floor and make a nest under the piano, which felt secretive and wonderful, as if under the piano were a whole other cozy world, to which only she had the key. In a safe, pretty house, in her own safe, private room, in the safe, hidden world under the piano—this was Farrin's favorite place in the whole grand sprawl of Ivyhill.

And it was on fire.

That was the reason for the smoke, and the orange glow at the windows, and the feeling, everywhere, of terrible, encroaching heat.

Ivyhill was on fire.

Panic tore away the lingering fog of sleep, panic like nothing Farrin had ever known. Her heart hammering, horrible coughs seizing her all at once, she scooped up Osmund, who was cowering beside her in the pillows, his black hair standing on end, hissing at something—perhaps at the smoke, at the fire itself—and with Osmund cradled to her chest, Farrin ran for the door in bare feet, her braid swinging, and threw it open.

The hallway beyond was black, and seething, and the smell

of the smoke was terrible, nothing like the sweet, piney scent of wood crackling in the hearth, nothing like the warm breadiness of Miss Rathmont's ovens downstairs. It *stung*, lashing at Farrin's throat and nostrils with every breath she sucked into her lungs. She threw an arm over her mouth, eyes watering, Osmund clawing frantically at her nightgown. She could hardly breathe; the smoke was vile, unstoppable, and it was laced with something *else*, something other than fire and smoke, something biting and brittle, like the charge of a coming storm.

A chill swept through Farrin, even as she stood there, sweating, in the sweltering heat. She knew that smell. It was the smell of magic, searing and furious. A spell, she suspected; a spell crafted with wicked intent.

Ivyhill hadn't simply caught fire. No, someone had set fire to it. And Farrin knew only one family equal to such a task: a family with enough power and resources to rival her own, a family that hated the Ashbournes as much as the Ashbournes hated them.

The House of Bask.

Something crashed downstairs, something huge and groaning that made the floor shake under Farrin's feet. She staggered back into her music room, quaking with fear, coughing so hard it hurt. Tears streamed down her face as she peered right down the hallway, then left. The left, she thought, looked a bit dimmer than the right, which meant less fire, fewer flames. She hoped. She prayed, to Caiathos, god of the earth, though something in her heart told her the prayer was useless.

If the Basks had indeed set this fire—if they had found spellcrafters clever enough to break through Ivyhill's protective wards—then the long-dead gods couldn't help her. They were all going to burn. All of them. Mama and Papa. Mara. Gemma. Gilroy. Miss Rathmont. Madame Baines. Every maid, every cook.

The Basks wanted only one thing. Farrin had learned this at her father's knee.

The Basks wanted to destroy her family.

She tucked Osmund under her nightgown and pressed his tiny head against her breastbone, hoping somehow, miraculously, that the thin fabric would protect him from the smoke. Then she ran left down the hallway, hardly noticing when Osmund lodged his claws in her. At the hallway's end stood two staircases. One led upstairs; the other would take her down to the first floor.

Farrin paused, smeared the tears from her eyes. Her hand came away wet and black with smoke. Was the fire upstairs or downstairs? Which way to go?

She sucked in a breath and tried to yell for her parents, for her sisters, but she couldn't get out a word, only a sort of rasping sound, desperate and frightening. Had the smoke taken away her voice? Would she ever get it back? What if she chose the wrong stairs to travel? Having no voice would then, perhaps, be the least of her problems.

Farrin let out a sob. Her chest drew tight with a primal despair. Was she going to die? She was. Her house was going to kill her.

Osmund had gone still under her nightgown, though Farrin could still feel the frantic beat of his heart under her palm. She gave him a tender squeeze—*it will be all right, precious*—and decided, no, she was *not* going to die. She needed to get Osmund out. He was small and helpless, an innocent, grumpy little fluff-goblin, and she was his only chance for salvation.

She glared upstairs. The air was strange and shimmery with heat. Yes. That way, upstairs. It had to be. The stairs going down to the first floor looked brighter to her blurry eyes, and the air felt hotter. So, the fire had begun downstairs.

Racing up to the third floor, she began to feel a little twist of hope. If the fire was downstairs, then that meant upstairs could still be safe. Maybe the flames hadn't yet reached that part of the house. She could scuttle through one of the windows in the long hallway that led to the art gallery, and then crawl out onto the roof and use the glossy, crisscrossed carpet of her mother's vines to shimmy down to safety.

But when Farrin emerged from the stairs, she stopped short and froze.

The long corridor stretching out before her ended in flames. That was the art gallery, there past that roaring mouth of fire. All her parents' sculptures and paintings, all the dimly lit nooks where Mara would sit with her sketch papers to study the play of light on stone faces, the texture of brushstrokes on canvas.

All that beauty, turned to ashes.

Dazed, sick, reeling, Farrin turned to run back downstairs, but just then the whole staircase buckled with a horrible groan, like the house itself had given up. She lurched back with a scream, barely kept herself from teetering over the edge into that pit of singed carpet and splintered wood. Below, down the same set of stairs she'd run up only moments before, fresh flames licked up the walls, showing her their tongues.

There was nowhere else to go; Farrin turned left, away from the art gallery and the stairs-that-weren't, and hurried down another hallway, so thick with smoke she could barely see her feet. Down this corridor was a series of little parlors and studies meant for guests, and each one had windows, and windows meant fresh air. That was all Farrin could think of as she ran: air, windows, *out*. Those windows looked out over not the grounds but an inner courtyard, which wasn't ideal, but if she could only stick her head out some window, any window, and *breathe* for a few moments, she would be able to think more clearly and come up with a better plan.

Farrin loved plans. Music was full of them, and once you understood what the composer's plan was—how all the notes fit together and why—the whole of the music became clear to you, laid out in tidy little lines and phrases, like brickwork set piece by piece until a house was made, and then it was up to you, the musician, to expand upon that plan laid out before you and make it your own. Fill it with furniture, adorn it with color.

The notes of Merrida Jan-Tokka's *Sonata for an Autumn Morning* raced through Farrin's head—the third movement, joyous and urgent, leaves spiraling on a brisk breeze, whirlwinds of orange, torrents of gold.

Farrin held onto the notes with her mind and her heart. She had learned that piece when she was five, and she'd performed it for the household staff—her first performance, euphoric, terrifically nerve-wracking. A celebration, a perfect night. The house done up in shades of amber and tangerine, gilded scarlet, the windows thrown open to a black chilly sky, stars like snow flurries. Mara, three years old and overcome by the music, hiding her bashful face in Mama's sleeve. Baby Gemma, cooing with delight; gold curls and bright blue eyes, already a beauty, waving her socked feet from her perch in Papa's arms. Papa, beaming with pride, so handsome with his broad smile and strong jaw, his golden-brown hair that looked just like Farrin's.

And Mama—Gemma's blue eyes, Mara's brown hair, skin pale as the moon. She had pulled Farrin into her arms afterward, with the house all a-clamor, Gilroy wiping his eyes on his sleeve, Miss Rathmont—tearful, ruddy-cheeked—passing around iced petit-fours. Everyone elated, everyone's head full of Farrin's music.

Mama had folded Farrin into her arms, pressed her cool cheek to Farrin's hot one, and said quietly, in her clear, clean voice, "Your music, little bird, will give the gods new life."

Stumbling down the smoky hallway, pawing at the walls for a doorknob, Jan-Tokka's sonata ringing in her memory, Farrin finally found one of the guest parlors and shoved hard at the door. It barely gave way, swollen and sweating, damp with heat and a crackling, sour magic, and when she tumbled inside, she fell forward to her hands and knees, and she did not get up.

She *could* not get up. She could only crawl across the rug, and did so, one-handed, holding poor Osmund to her chest. He was frighteningly still, his heartbeat faint. Could she even still feel it at all? *Yes, he's alive,* she told herself, staring ahead at the far wall, stubbornly clawing her way forward, *he's alive, we're alive, I'm alive.*

Her head hit something solid. The wall. She'd made it. The wall held three windows, and the closest one was maybe only two feet above her head.

Gasping, blinking hard, she reached for it. She would push it open. She would pound it to pieces, if she had to.

Her hand shook, her arm buckled. She collapsed on the floor and stared at the red-and-blue floral wallpaper. It was peeling away from the wall in jagged strips. Each strip screamed a little as it unfurled, like the voice of a tiny log creaking in a fire. Woozy, coughing so hard she felt like her chest might burst open, Farrin laid her spinning head on the carpet and cried. Her sobs were weak, her lungs black, each breath harder than the last.

A single charred ivy leaf drifted down from the rafters and fell before her nose, and Farrin grabbed onto it and held it to her lips. It was a piece of her mother, and it was the last thing she would ever see. She tried to breathe, desperate to find some lingering scent of her mother's perfume, or the woodsy tang of her mother's botanical magic, but breathing only made the blackness come faster. Farrin closed her eyes.

Then—a light, flickering and white. It shone even through

her closed eyelids, and it was so strange, so clean and bright, that Farrin, teetering on the knife's edge of her young life, found the strength to open her eyes.

A figure knelt beside her. Right there, impossibly, next to the screaming wallpaper. Gangly, graceless, all awkward elbows and long legs. Half-boy, half almost-man.

And he was *shining*, a glow radiating from him as if some Anointed artisan had devised a way to paint a living being with starlight, and here was the being. Luminous, a beacon. A shining boy.

Stranger even than the light of him was the mask he wore— made of cloth, Farrin thought, with his nose and mouth covered and the eyes blacked out. The mask covered his face entirely, even hiding most of his hair, though Farrin could see damp, dark strands escaping the mask at his nape.

He reached for her. Pale hand, sweaty, soot-blackened.

"Don't be afraid," he told her. His voice was neither deep nor high, crackling somewhere in between. It was rough, but kind, and his dirty hand was steady.

"I know the way out," he said.

Farrin hesitated. The shining boy was bright and lovely, but the world around him was hot, shimmering, terrible. The house was furious; everything shook. The sound of shattering glass exploded— close, far too close; a great sucking noise like all the air in the room being gulped away. Right at the same moment, the boy lurched forward, knocked Farrin back to the ground, and threw his body over hers, and held her there, still, tucked safely against the wall. Both of them shaking, both of them breathing hard.

When Farrin opened her eyes, she saw a floor glittering with glass. A terrible hopelessness flooded through her. The house was falling apart around them; they would never find a way out.

The boy was lying; the boy wasn't even real. She was dying; she was dead.

Just then, Osmund poked his head out of her nightgown and glared up at the shining boy—angry yellow slits for eyes—and then he mewed, the plaintive cry he used to announce to the world that he was hungry. The squished, indignant sound gave Farrin strength.

She grabbed onto the shining boy's hand and nodded against his chest.

He squeezed her hand tight, then pressed something to her mouth—a thick cloth, cool and damp, the most incredible thing Farrin had ever known.

"This will help you breathe," the boy shouted, but Farrin was already gulping down whatever air she could find, leaning hard against the boy as he put his arm around her and hurried with her out of the parlor, down the hallway. Which hallway? Which stairs? Farrin didn't know, couldn't follow the path they were taking. The house was a shifting labyrinth, the throat of a beast, and the blessed cloth against her mouth was drying up. Her lungs were choking her again. Two black fists, twisting smaller and smaller in her chest. One hand cradling Osmund, the other held tight in the shining boy's hand.

Something crashed overhead. The boy spit out a word, something Farrin didn't know, a nasty curse, his hand so hard around hers that it hurt. He darted away, pulling her with him, just as a huge shadow fell out of the sky. A piece of ceiling, black and glowing, an ember crowned with seared ivy.

"This way!" the boy shouted, as if Farrin had some choice in the matter. The boy's grip was iron, his strength unending. Flames roared around them, spitting smoke and sparks. Collapsing walls chased them down hallways that seemed to never end.

And through it all, not once did the shining boy flinch. He was like some great eagle, Farrin thought dreamily, colors spinning in her eyes. Orange, gold, throbbing red, blots of black. A great eagle, with her held safely under his wing, flying her all the way out to the ocean. No wind could stop him, no storms, no shadows. His eyes were bright and clear, and he knew the way home.

"Farrin!" he screamed, from very far away. "Farrin, come on! Keep walking!"

But she couldn't keep walking. Her feet were made of stone, and besides, feet needed lungs, and lungs needed air, and there was no longer air to be had.

The world spun around her, lifting her, jostling her. She was running; no, the world was ending, quaking, splitting open.

No. The shining boy was running, and she was in his arms.

Her eyes fluttered open, and she saw a cloudy sky split in half. White light, cool and soft; the waxing moon. Then orange, shuddering, a whip of rage, heat bleeding into blackness.

Suddenly Farrin was lying flat on her back. Smoke behind her eyes, smoke down her throat. The shining boy, above her, smoothed the wet hair back from her face. Then he went very still, held his hand above her mouth for a moment, and let out a breath.

"You're breathing," he said. "You're going to be all right." He sat back, made a strange sound. Maybe he was laughing? "You're going to be all right," he said again, his crackling, not-quite-a-man voice gone rough from the smoke.

Farrin reached for him—confused, half-blind, seeing only the faint glow of him, the twin shadows of his strange, blacked-out eyes.

He found her hand and held it. Against the fire, his silhouette was a bewilderment: half shadows, half shine. "Star of my life," he said, pressing a quick kiss to her knuckles. The kiss sent a shock through her tired body. *Star of my life*, she thought. What a pretty thing to say, and odd, since he was the one who shone.

Then the boy's body went rigid beside hers. He released her and stood.

"I have to go," he said. He sounded bitterly, horribly angry.

Farrin reached for him, tried to protest. He was leaving her? But he couldn't! Where was she? Where was her family? Where was her house? And her piano, and all her music, all the things she loved... If he left her, the fire would come. If he disappeared, so would she.

"I'm so sorry," the boy said, quiet now, gentle, and he touched her face, his hot hand on her hot cheek. "They're coming, now. You'll be all right."

And then he was gone. Farrin turned to find his hand, the warm strength of him, and found only wet grass, cold earth. She managed to crack open her eyes, and through the crust of soot and tears, she saw the distant shape of Ivyhill. Her home, afire. Black and misshapen, outlined by a wicked molten pen.

She tucked Osmund under her chin and wept, and then her father was there, frantic, sobbing, pulling her up into his arms so fiercely that she dropped Osmund to the ground. And Gemma was bawling at their father's knee, limp golden curls hanging in ruined ribbons, and there was Mara, ashen but dry-eyed, crouching to catch a disoriented, truly vexed Osmund before he scampered off into the night.

And Mama?

Farrin twisted in her father's arms, heart in her throat, and found her at last—Philippa Ashbourne, her beloved mama, on her knees in the grass not far from them. She cried silent tears as she watched Ivyhill burn, her arms rigid at her sides.

Gemma clung to their father's leg while Mara tried in vain to comfort her. Osmund yowled restlessly in Mara's arms. A few of the servants had found them and were in frantic conference with their father and the head groundskeeper, Mr. Carbreigh, who was an Anointed elemental. All of them gestured wildly at the distant fire, and, thus distracted, no one else present noticed the change that came over Philippa Ashbourne that night.

But Farrin noticed. Farrin saw the moment when her mother became someone else—*something* else. Farrin saw when Philippa stood and wiped her cheeks, her expression hard and mean and unfamiliar. The fire lit up her whole face, turning her eyes to twin flickering suns. She was incandescent with fury. Farrin could feel it, even half-alive as she was. She knew the dips and curves of her mother's body even more intimately than she knew her own, and as the flames roared on, Philippa Ashbourne's body changed right before her eyes.

Every line of wrist and shin and rib became a weapon, every softness hardened to stone. The very air around her seemed to snap to attention, as if suddenly shot through with deadly magic, and even though what had happened was a catastrophe, something so big and terrible Farrin's mind couldn't wrap completely around it—nevertheless, Philippa Ashbourne gazed upon the fire and smiled. She smiled as if her husband had just whispered a naughty joke in her ear. She smiled as if she'd learned a most delicious secret.

And in that moment—so baffled and smoke-poisoned that, later, she would forget the whole thing entirely—Farrin, for the first time in her life, felt truly, unspeakably afraid of her mother.

ACKNOWLEDGMENTS

I began writing this series during a particularly challenging part of my life, and from the beginning, I was determined to write something that brought me joy. Sometimes, for me, joy takes the form of, as my friend Alison calls them, "romantic extravaganzas." Sometimes, joy is scenes featuring demonic possession and dark magic. And sometimes, joy is a scene during which a character manages to work through a panic attack and emerge on the other side feeling a little stronger, even a little triumphant. I hope these scenes—and all the rest—brought you joy, too, dear reader.

I'd like to thank, first of all, my editor, Annie Berger, and my agent, Victoria Marini, who have always been the most wonderful champions of me and my books. Warm thanks and affection to both of you for your support and enthusiasm.

I'd also like to thank everyone at Sourcebooks for working so hard to bring these books into the world and help them find their readers. Special thanks and admiration must go to Rebecca Atkinson, Shannon Barr, Stephanie Gafron, Alyssa Garcia, Heather Hall, Ashley Holstrom, Pamela Jaffee, Ashlyn Keil,

Madison Nankervis, Katie Stutz, Jocelyn Travis, and Dominique Raccah. I am also grateful to the artist Nekro, who created this book's stunning cover image.

Thank you to my friends and loved ones who cheered me on throughout this (and every) writing process, especially Alison Cherry, who was, in this case, both dear friend and brilliant copy editor.

And thank you most of all to my partner, Ken, who brightens every day and never, not ever, not once stops believing in me.

ABOUT THE AUTHOR

Claire Legrand used to be a musician until she realized she couldn't stop thinking about the stories in her head. Now she is the *New York Times* bestselling author of several novels for children and teens, including the Empirium Trilogy, the Edgar Award–nominated *Some Kind of Happiness*, the Bram Stoker Award–nominated *Sawkill Girls*, and *The Cavendish Home for Boys and Girls*. *A Crown of Ivy and Glass* is her debut adult novel.